THE GOV[illegible]
AND
PRIME SUSPECT

Also by Lynda La Plante in Pan Books

The Legacy
Bella Mafia
Entwined
Seekers
Cold Shoulder
She's Out
The Governor II
Cold Blood
Trial and Retribution
Cold Heart
Trial and Retribution II
The Talisman
Trial and Retribution III
Trial and Retribution IV
Sleeping Cruelty
Trial and Retribution V
Trial and Retribution VI
Royal Flush

Lynda La Plante was born in Liverpool. She trained for the stage at RADA, and work with the National Theatre and the RSC led to a career as a television actress. She turned to writing – and made her breakthrough with the phenomenally successful TV series *Widows*.

She has written eight subsequent best-selling novels, *The Legacy*, *The Talisman*, *Bella Mafia*, *Entwined*, *Cold Shoulder*, *Cold Blood*, *Cold Heart* and *Sleeping Cruelty*, and her original script for the much-acclaimed *Prime Suspect* won a BAFTA award, British Broadcasting award, Royal Television Society Writers award and the 1993 Edgar Allan Poe Writers award.

Lynda La Plante also received the Contribution to the Media award by Women in Film, a BAFTA award and an Emmy for the drama serial *Prime Suspect 3*. She has been made an honorary fellow of the British Film Institute and most recently was awarded the BAFTA Dennis Potter Writer's Award 2000.

THE GOVERNOR AND PRIME SUSPECT

LYNDA LA PLANTE

PAN BOOKS

The Governor first published 1995 by Pan Books
Prime Suspect first published 1991 by Pan Books

This omnibus edition published 2003 by Pan Books
an imprint of Pan Macmillan Ltd
Pan Macmillan, 20 New Wharf Road, London N1 9RR
Basingstoke and Oxford
Associated companies throughout the world
www.panmacmillan.com

ISBN 0 330 43676 7

1 3 5 7 9 8 6 4 2

A CIP catalogue record for this book is available from
the British Library.

Printed and bound in Great Britain by
Mackays of Chatham plc, Chatham, Kent

THE GOVERNOR

ACKNOWLEDGEMENTS

I sincerely thank: Governors Alison Gomme, Mitch Egan, Janet King, Sarah Fielder, Marjorie Gorman, Sue Lewis, John Galloway, Kevin Rogers, Gareth Davis, Peter Buxton, Paul Checkley, in England, and Governors Vincent McPherson, John Lanergan in Ireland. Derek Lewis, Audrey Nelson, Stuart Reed, Patrick Harrison, Deborah Hermer and all at the Prison Services and their press office. Roy Webster for his unending assistance and introductions. The Linholme Control & Restraint Centre, near Doncaster. John Dooley, P. J. Malloy and all prison officers in the UK and Ireland. My executive producer Steve Lanning, my three directors, Alan Dossor, Rob Knights and Bob Mahoney, the wonderful designer Keith Wilson, the post-production supervisor Howard Lanning, and the editors Terry Warwick and Phil Cook. My deepest respect and thanks to Gerry Toomey, to my cowboy Billy Westley, Gemma Fallon, all at the Dublin production office, and the entire crew of *The Governor* series for their professionalism, encouragement and dedication. David Collins and all at Samson Films, Ireland. I also give my sincere thanks to a wonderful cast of actors and to my superb leading lady, Janet McTeer, who plays the title role in *The Governor*, Helen Hewitt. A special thanks for the enthusiasm of the extras throughout the entire making of the series. Stan, Lol and all the unit drivers. Ann Fielden and colleagues for finding such talented actors. Clare Forbes, Susy Tullett and all at JAC. Keith Richardson, David Holgate and all at Yorkshire

Television, who had so much to do with getting the series made. The Irish Government for their co-operation. Marcus Plantin, Vernon Lawrence and Jenny Sheridan at the ITV Network Centre for making it all possible. David Neville, also Paul Killick and Annie Dalton. Linda Strudwick QC and Luke Blackburn. Marc Berners and all at the Essex Police TV Unit and Air Support Unit. My own team, Liz Thorburn, production liaison, Alice Asquith, researcher, and Betina Soto Acebal, my editor. Last, but by no means least, I thank all the inmates who gave me their time and their stories. I wish each and every one of them peace and, above all, a future.

THE GOVERNOR
is dedicated to
JUSTICE

I would like to acknowledge the talent of the writer
Trevor Hoyle, without whom the book of the series
could never have been published.

Part One

The Riot

CHAPTER 1

NONCE PERVURT
CHILD KILLER

WRITTEN IN blood, the scrawled words of hatred trickled redly down the pale green wall. On a plywood shelf above the bed with its neatly tucked-in blankets, the illuminated display of a practically brand-new Sony CD player was registering track 14. From the twin speakers the soaring voice of Pavarotti singing 'Nessun Dorma' blasted out at maximum volume, making the metal light-fitting vibrate in sympathy.

A half-finished letter lay on the small wooden table, written on blue-lined, double sheets of prison notepaper, stamped in the top right-hand corner 'HMP Barfield'. The letter, which began 'Dear Mum and Dad', would never be finished, because Michael Winchwood, barefoot, trousers undone, his shirt half ripped from his body, was lying in a reservoir of blood that was broadening and deepening as his heart pumped it out from both wrists and the gash that ran diagonally from his right ear to below his throat. His chest and abdomen had received a battering, and under the tatters of his shirt were reddish patches bearing the imprints of knuckles. In his agony, turning and twisting, he had bathed himself fully so that now a thick curtain of blood covered his forehead and coated his eyelids, nose and mouth, making his face a gleaming red mask that bubbled and frothed as he tried to suck in feeble gulps of air.

A slow-motion sledgehammer pounded in his brain. It jarred his skull with each sluggish heartbeat . . . pumping, pumping, pumping out his lifeblood onto the floor. Gradually the world began to recede, floating away to a rushing, roaring nothingness.

But then distantly, through all the rushing and roaring, a whole new cacophony of sounds penetrated Michael Winchwood's dwindling consciousness.

First, like a single giant heartbeat, the muffled boom of an explosion. He felt the floor tremble, and the vivid red pool in which he was lying shivered as if disturbed by a breeze. Seconds later, an alarm bell clanged down the wing. Then the grinding wail of a siren rising to screeching pitch. Shouts and screams as panic spread, the deafening racket of cell doors being flung open, smashing back on their hinges. Footsteps thudding along the landing and clattering down the metal stairways. Above it all, the raucous blare of the Tannoy: *Emergency! Emergency! All officers required to evacuate the VP wing. FIRE! FIRE!*

The mad whirl of sound dimmed and faded inside his head. Slowly the shouts and screams and the drilling alarm bell became fainter and fainter, and even the rushing and roaring ceased until there was nothing left except a wall of blackness and silence.

A dozen officers charged onto the wing and raced up the spiral stairway to the upper landing, rubber-soled boots thudding, key-chains jangling. Not breaking his stride, one whipped out his baton and smashed the glass plate of a fire alarm. Senior Officer Russell Morgan was throwing open cell doors and screaming at the prisoners to get the hell out. Already, dark smoke was spiralling up to the V-shaped glass roof that extended the whole length of the VP Wing. This housed the vulnerable prisoners, most of them convicted of sexual abuse against children, placed here on Rule 43 for their own protection. 'On the numbers', as the regular cons called it, with disgust, hatred and contempt. Catch a nonce – a child sex abuser – and they'd make the evil bastard pervert wish he'd never been born.

Tom Doughen ran past Morgan, both their radios squawking the general alert from the Central Control Room to the other five wings of Barfield Prison: '*MS2D to all outstations. All prisoners to remain in their house spurs.* LOCK DOWN. *LOCK DOWN. MS2D out.*'

This last instruction was the prison's first response to any incident or emergency: all inmates, without exception, to return immediately to their cells, and all cells to be locked. Gates connecting the wings to the main administration building to be shut and electronically secured. All perimeter exits closed off, with dogs and handlers patrolling the sterile areas between the outer wall and the eighteen-foot-high inner chain-link fence topped with razor wire.

Lock Down meant that Her Majesty's Prison Barfield was sealed tighter than a duck's arse.

But the VP Wing had to be evacuated, and fast, as the fire started to spread. The men stumbled from their cells, eyes glazed with panic, faces more ashen than their usual prison pallor. From the landing Doughen could see the flicker of flame down below, and was shocked to realize it had already taken hold on the ground floor as well. Thick smoke was billowing up through the metal mesh that stretched across the open central area, installed to prevent the prisoners getting injured should they fall, or more likely be pushed, from the upper landing.

Above the tumult of bells and sirens, the radio message crackled and buzzed from every single officer as the warnings went out: 'Attention, attention, all officers. We have second blaze in the lecture hall. All officers give wire warning alarm.'

Doughen dragged a petrified Vernon Black from his cell and shoved him along the landing to the stairway. Then he caught sight of O'Keefe standing at Winchwood's cell door. The officer was rooted to the spot. What was the stupid bastard playing at? He was about to scream at him, *Get the bugger out, don't just stand there!* when O'Keefe turned his head, his throat working in his broad neck, and Doughen heard him yell out, 'It's Winchwood . . . Get somebody in here. *Get somebody here!*'

Doughen pushed his way through. He drew back, wincing when he saw the bloodbath. Jesus Christ, he was swimming in it. Then he saw the words scrawled on the pale green wall. NONCE. PERVURT. (The stupid prats couldn't even spell.) CHILD KILLER. It was a horrible scene to behold, but even more horrible was the thought in Doughen's mind. He couldn't shake it off, no matter how hard he tried. *Winchwood deserved all he got*. After what the bastard had said, the evil notions he'd planted in Tom Doughen's mind, the officer could only feel that a kind of sick justice had been perpetrated, and he couldn't find within himself the tiniest morsel of sympathy or regret.

Shortly after midnight there were three more explosions. By now half the prison was alight. The windows of B Wing were blasted out, tongues of flame streaking into the night. The VP Wing, now evacuated, was ablaze on both floors, fire tenders drawn up in the exercise yard, playing their hoses over the roof where black smoke writhed through the slates. But with the Lock Down still effective, the inmates throughout the other four wings were trapped as the fire raced towards them. Hammering on their cell doors, screaming in terror, they could do nothing except wait with impotent fury, seeing through their windows the orange glow as the fire devoured the adjacent VP Wing.

Officers with fire extinguishers were fighting a rearguard action. Having abandoned the VP Wing, they retreated through B Wing, releasing prisoners from their cells and herding them towards the relative safety of D Wing. Senior Officer Russell Morgan, nominated as Bronze Commander in charge of operations at the scene, knew full well that they were storing up trouble. Inmates of all categories – from the most highly dangerous right down to the vulnerable prisoners – were being thrown together in a volatile mix. Already fights were breaking out. Morgan himself, with the combined help of three of his officers, had had to wrestle Tony Murphy to the ground. The big six-foot-two Scouser, built like a brick shithouse, a known trouble-maker, had gone berserk and attacked a frightened group of VPs as they were being taken down to the main yard.

And now Morgan was involved in another scrum, this time one of sheer mindless panic as thick black smoke came billowing in. Some of the inmates had managed to get out, but that left thirty men stuck in a log-jam, fighting, scratching, kicking, as they tried to funnel through the two sets of barred gates that led to the security corridor. This was the main thoroughfare connecting all five wings to the admin block, and was normally a sterile area – no cons allowed there except under escort. Officers on the other side of the gates were hauling bodies through, like prising sardines out of a tin.

When the blockage had cleared, Morgan ran back through the central association area which divided the two landings. This contained a couple of snooker tables, card tables and a stack of folding chairs, where the prisoners congregated during their free time away from the workshops and exercise yard. Here the smoke was thicker, but as Bronze Commander, in charge on the ground, he had to be sure that no one remained on the wing. He could actually hear the crackle of flames as he raced up the spiral stairway to the upper landing, but the landing was deserted, thank Christ, all the cell doors standing open. He turned to descend, and a full pane of mesh-reinforced glass came hurtling down and shattered on the handrail, missing him by inches. Looking up through the smoke, Morgan saw figures clambering high above, scaling the iron reinforcement struts and smashing their way through the glass panels. The veins on his neck stood out as he cursed them.

Those bastards weren't escaping from the path of the fire, they were rioting. Using the disaster as a chance to cause as much havoc and destruction as they could. As if the fire wouldn't do damage enough, they wanted to vent their hatred by smashing the place to smithereens.

Morgan dodged aside, shielding his head, more glass tumbling down around him. He thumbed the talk button on the radio attached to his belt. 'Hello Victor 1 from Bronze Commander. They're breaking through onto the roof of Bravo Wing! Bravo Wing!'

As if an oven door had been opened, a blast of heat and smoke struck him solidly in the face, and Morgan dived for the stairway, handkerchief clamped to his mouth, and stumbled blindly down.

The first grey light of dawn over the misty fields of Leicestershire revealed the full extent of the devastation suffered during the night by HMP Barfield. And it wasn't over yet.

At least fifteen prisoners had broken through onto the roof of B Wing, and were now hurling blazing mattresses, toilet rolls soaked in lighter fuel, slates, timber joists, and full-throated abuse down into the prison yard. Some wore improvised hoods made from the torn linings of their jackets, from their T-shirts with eye-holes ripped in them. Forced to retreat to one end of the smouldering ruin, the fire now under control, they balanced precariously on the steeply tiled roof, slipping and clinging to each other, yelling, screaming and laughing with the hysteria of illusory freedom that being out in the open air, under the wide grey sky, had given them.

Beyond reach of the missiles and burning debris, lines of officers were trying to organize the evacuation of nearly four hundred inmates. With a prison population of this size a total of almost three hundred staff were required, two-thirds of whom were uniformed officers, including dog handlers, PE instructors, health-care and workshop staff. All off-duty officers had been called in to contain the situation and maintain perimeter security. As if this in itself wasn't a tough enough task, they also had to keep order amongst the shambling ranks of men. Old scores were being settled. Property was being nicked. Many welcomed this golden opportunity to create as much mayhem as their crooked minds could devise. Fights broke out, and the air was thick with abuse, both amongst inmates and directed at the screws. The atmosphere in the crowded shambolic prison yard teetered on a knife-edge between a mad holiday spree and a dangerous confrontation with authority that could easily slide into a mass riot of frustration and fury – uncontainable, anarchic, bloody.

It was a simmering cauldron, and the race was on to disperse and isolate these potent ingredients before Barfield blew its top.

A convoy of white prison vans – sweat-boxes to the cons – was drawn up near the gate lodge. Each van was partitioned into fourteen separate cubicles, seven each side, with a central walkway for up to three officers. Into these went the Cat. A prisoners, for whom the maximum conditions of security were necessary, and, to quote the regulations, 'whose escape would be highly dangerous to the public or police or the security of the State'.

Getting them inside was a nightmare battle. These were the hard men, career criminals on long stretches for armed robbery, aggravated burglary, drug-dealing, GBH, and firearms offences. Many had to be handcuffed and, once shut inside their cubicles, they set up a horrendous racket, pounding the metal walls so that the sides of the vans seemed physically to bulge and buckle from the onslaught.

Behind the white sweat-boxes, green vans and coaches were moving into position, ready to take the inmates in the lower security categories, B and C. Prisoners in all three categories were being relocated to other prisons the length and breadth of the country, from Swaleside in Kent to Full

Sutton in Yorkshire, from Garth near Preston to Coldingley in Surrey. And some would end up in local nicks: three and four to a cell designed to provide overnight accommodation for the odd belligerent drunk or the vagrant who might otherwise have frozen to death on the streets.

Senior Officer Russell Morgan, eyes still smarting from the smoke and heat, had been asked by the Deputy Governor to supervise a detachment of about eighty inmates, who were to remain at Barfield in the undamaged C Wing. They were a mixed bunch, and he knew nearly all of their faces and could put names to them. Along with his officers, he was moving them from the central area behind the gate lodge into the exercise yard serving C Wing. They were going all right, but they weren't going quietly. Fists pumping the air, they were giving encouragement to the men on the roof. A chant started and was taken up, in time to the stamping of feet.

'JUSTICE ... JUSTICE ... JUSTICE ... JUSTICE ...'

The men on the roof whooped and yelled, swaying from side to side with arms raised, like fans behind a goal mouth.

A cheer went up when one, his head shrouded with a torn sweatshirt, shouted, 'Winchwood was a perverted child molester – he deserved all he got!'

This brought on a storm of noise from the hundreds in the yard below, like the baying of animals. Encouraged, the man on the roof screamed at the top of his lungs, 'Sex offenders should be hanged! Justice . . . justice!'

And the cry was taken up with a vengeance by the hundreds below.

'JUSTICE ... JUSTICE ... JUSTICE ... JUSTICE ...'

Barfield's outer perimeter wall was constructed of stained concrete slabs, twenty-two feet high, with a curved plastic overhang painted red – the 'gander' – to foil grappling hooks, and so smoothly rounded that it was impossible to gain a handhold.

Beyond this lay the visitors' car park, where the media were now gathered in force. Reports of the fire, and the subsequent riot, had been carried by UP and Reuters, and five television crews had arrived even before first light. Cameramen stood on the roofs of their vans, panning the wall and the end elevation of the VP and B Wings, though from this vantage point they didn't have clear sight of the prisoners on the roof.

Standing on a grass verge so that she was framed by the gate lodge, the reporter from Central TV was taping her intro to the early-morning bulletin, due in less than an hour's time. With little hard news, except for what she herself had witnessed, she could only hedge around the situation, filling out her report with a few facts hastily cribbed from the cuttings file.

'The fire at Barfield Prison, one of the top category B prisons, is now under control. The damage has already been estimated to be in the millions, three of the main security wings and recreational areas completely destroyed or made uninhabitable. Described as a "five-star nick" by some inmates when it was opened in nineteen seventy-seven, Barfield has recently been under review, as there have been accusations of drug-dealing, intimidation and bullying being rampant.'

She glanced over her shoulder towards the gate lodge. Luck was on her side, because at that precise moment a white prison van emerged through the gates and sped away. Quickly she took up the cue.

'The removal of inmates has been in operation since the early hours of this morning, and still continues. This will aggravate and create more overcrowding in the allocated prisons rehousing these inmates. The riot here comes shortly after the recent media coverage of the chaos at the new, privately managed prison in Doncaster, and the attempted escape of IRA prisoners at Whitemoor.' Her lips thinned, her voice taking on a suitably moralistic tone for the wind-up. 'It will not be just the Home Office demanding explanations about our prison system, but the general public . . .'

Not brilliant, she thought, but not bad either, given that she was making bricks without straw. Anyway, it was early days. The riot at Strangeways in Manchester had captured the headlines for months, even after the rioters had been captured and the prison made safe. There was no rush. Barfield wasn't going anywhere. Given the public's obsessional paranoia about law and order, this was a story that was going to run and run.

CHAPTER 2

HELEN HEWITT had prepared very carefully for the interview. She had not only rehearsed what she would say, but had also squeezed in a hairdressing appointment; she would have liked a facial and a manicure as she could not recall the last time she had had either. All she was sure about was that, like it or not, appearances were of great importance. She wondered if she'd gone a little over the top with the boxy jacket and tailored skirt, the plain white blouse buttoned to the neck, but she wanted at all costs to be taken as a one hundred per cent professional applicant rather than any *femme fatale* or ardent feminist. She hoped she'd found a happy medium but still wondered if the large bun at the nape of her neck might make her look like something out of *The Prime of Miss Jean Brodie*. Helen usually wore her hair in a long plait down her back. She was a tall, and not skinny woman: in her stockinged feet, she was five feet eleven, in the low-heeled brown court shoes at least six feet. It was always tough for someone as tall as Helen – and not a *Vogue* model type – to buy decent modern clothes: they were either too short in the arms or the skirt, and the new suit had taken an entire morning of hurtling round every major department store.

Helen surmised it was too late now to change her 'costume'. She parked her car, fed the meter, checked she was in perfect time, had a quick glance at herself in the wing mirror of her car, straightened her jacket, and headed into the main Headquarters of the Prison Services. One failed marriage, no kids, not even a close relative, Helen was on her own. She quite liked it: having only a fat cat and its litter tray to worry about meant she could give everything she had to her career.

Helen waited in a comfortable room with an array of newspapers. Every one of them screamed out with headlines about the Barfield Prison riot. She was half-way through the stack when she was told the board were ready for her. She straightened her jacket again. It was a habit that emerged whenever she wore one because she rarely did. She then picked up her briefcase, checked that the Miss Brodie was still in place and that no wisps of her hair were loose before she followed the neat secretary in the pleated skirt up the wide staircase to the main boardroom. The secretary knocked and inched open the door. 'Miss Helen Hewitt.'

She stepped back to allow Helen to pass and looked up with a brief nod to indicate that she could go in. Helen dwarfed her and she waited a moment before closing the door behind the Amazon. She had been surprised by how pretty Helen was. Odd, because you didn't really notice it straight away. She had rather a girlish face and large friendly blue eyes. She'd given a small nervous smile as she'd passed into the boardroom – that, too, had been unexpected. There was more to Helen Hewitt than the quick appraisal could possibly give credit to, a lot more – some of which Helen was not even aware of herself. She was a woman with a vocation. Right now, she was just feeling very nervous.

Given the choice, Helen would rather have been playing poker on the large green-baize-topped table in front of her. Instead she was enduring the Spanish Inquisition of a promotions board. But promotion was what she was after, to Governor 3, and what she felt she deserved. *Knew* she deserved. With her qualifications, background and experience in the Prison Service, Helen had no doubts about her own ability.

'We are obviously failing, and under the new sentence guidelines for magistrates, many more offenders will face immediate imprisonment.'

Give it to them straight. They weren't looking for a speak-your-weight machine. They wanted somebody with an agenda, plus the grit and guts to go through with it – even if privately they had doubts and didn't agree entirely with the solution she was proposing.

That's what Helen had chosen to give them, like it or lump it.

She had prepared herself, with clear, single-minded discipline and determination – of which she was capable when she wanted something – had honed her views and opinions to simple, direct statements. All she needed now was the chance to present them. And get through the whole bloody rigmarole without breaking into a sweat of fluffing her lines. In short, making a cock-up.

They were listening, quite intently, it seemed, the three people opposite her. But she was concentrating on Royston Andrews. As Operational Director based here at Prison Service HQ in the Millbank complex of Westminster, he had overall charge of fifteen areas, with several prisons per area. When it came to clout, he had enough of it to knock Sean Duncan, the Home Office man, and Mrs Donald, Mrs Tory Middle England Blue Rinse, into a cocked hat.

'A rapid rise in prison population can only lead to severe overcrowding,' Helen went on, hands reposing comfortably in her lap, 'which ultimately will lead to more crimes inside the prison itself. Or, as has just occurred, riots. To counteract the situation I would advocate . . .'

The red phone rang to Sean Duncan's right, cutting her off in her prime. He picked it up, murmuring in his fruity, cultured tones.

Helen held tight to her irritation. Promotion boards were never interrupted. The bloody exception to the rule had to be just when she was working up a head of steam. She battled on, trying to hold their attention, though she could see Royston Andrews's centre of gravity had shifted as he tried to listen in to what Sean Duncan was saying. 'Yes, understood. Is the Home Secretary there? Right, understood.'

'I would advocate that low-security offenders not be given prison terms,' Helen stated firmly, pressing on regardless as Duncan put down the phone. 'I believe the entire prison structure must be radically changed. It is imperative that every convicted criminal understands that the custodial sentence is the punishment – the loss of freedom.'

Andrews was nodding. Was she really getting through? Then she saw his eyes, behind the horn-rimmed glasses, roam to the note that the Home Office man was scribbling. It was passed along, Royston Andrews brushing back his elegant quiff of wavy grey hair and swearing under his breath. Mrs Donald craned over to read it.

Helen straightened her shoulders. She ploughed on. 'What must be given priority is professional medical and psychological therapy, for the well-being both mentally and physically of the inmate, which hopefully will result in his or her desire for education to create career opportunities on release.' It came out without a pause for breath, but she was making damned sure it got said, with or without those blasted interruptions. Again Royston Andrews was nodding, and her spirits rose – he was the one that mattered, and she was really getting through.

Her nails dug into her palms as the red phone rang.

'You read psychology, graduating with a thesis on the American penal system and specializing in Category A prisoners.'

Mrs Donald looked up from the dossier. Helen nodded. She knew that, at the very least, Mrs Donald was a Governor 2 because members of the promotion board had to be two ranks above the applicants they were interviewing.

'However, Miss Hewitt, you are lacking in actual practical experience of Category A prisoners . . .'

The dossier said as much, so there was no point in replying.

Royston Andrews looked up at yet another interruption. This time in the round-shouldered, balding, agitated shape of John Bunny who, being an area manager in the Central East area, was responsible for HMP Barfield amongst several other prisons. Andrews, as his immediate superior, got up to confer with him, leaving Helen to the tender mercies of Mrs Donald.

'. . . and you are, let me see, thirty-three years old.'

Helen blinked. 'I see no reason why my age should count against me in applying for Governor Three rank.'

John Bunny had placed his briefcase on a chair and was wiping his forehead with a spotted handkerchief. Even though he kept his voice to a low, urgent murmur, it was perfectly audible. 'They've got the fire under control. The media are swarming around like flies.' Royston Andrews waited, stony-faced, as Bunny delved into his briefcase and produced a sheet of paper. 'Three unaccounted for, possibly absconded, and half a dozen still on the roof of B Wing.'

'You're not married?' Mrs Donald said, eyebrows raised.

'No,' Helen said. 'I'm divorced.'

Bunny said out of the side of his mouth, 'Michael Winchwood died on his way to hospital.'

'Jesus Christ!'

Andrews turned away. He stared out of the window for a moment at the dark redbrick façade of Westminster Hospital, directly across Page Street. He turned back to the green-baize table, noticing Helen as if she had just that instant materialized out of thin air, rubbing his hands with the abstracted motion of a man with twenty things on his mind, all of them more important than this.

'Do we have any further questions for Miss Hewitt?' he asked impatiently.

It was a lost cause, and Helen knew it. Trust her to be

up for the promotions board on the morning of a riot. From the early newscasts on TV it hadn't seemed that the disturbance was on the same scale as the one at Strangeways back in 1990, but a riot was still a riot. If the board remembered her at all, she thought gloomily, it would be as a minor, irritating distraction to a major traumatic incident that would bring in its wake all the inevitable consequences: Home Office inquiry, questions in Parliament, tabloid outrage, public condemnation. And almost certainly the chopping block to set heads rolling about like skittles.

Already Royston Andrews had turned his back, listening to John Bunny. Sean Duncan had joined them. Helen waited politely for the board to dismiss her officially. Mrs Donald gave her an icy smile, so she got to her feet, tucking her slim leather briefcase under her arm, and waited, still uncertain.

'Any estimation of the damage?' she heard Andrews say.

'Bloody catastrophic. Three of the five accommodation wings virtually demolished. They've systematically smashed every bathroom, plumbing ripped from the walls, water dripping down, gas cylinders ignited to fuel the fires . . .' John Bunny gave a small helpless shrug. 'It's bloody tragic.'

Mrs Donald came round the table. She was a short, dumpy woman with a large bust that had no discernible shape to it. Helen towered above her. She could even see where the blue rinse had faded to white at the roots.

'Thank you very much, Miss Hewitt.'

The same icy smile, no offer to shake hands. This was her dismissal, Helen knew. Nothing further to be said. She went out.

And that was that.

Cattering Hall was a women's remand centre and closed prison, situated on the Northamptonshire border, seven miles west of the A1. Helen made good time on the drive back from London, even allowing for a Little Chef all-day American breakfast, which she preferred in place of the lunch menu. For once the Mini Metro didn't act up. Always promising herself she'd part-exchange it for a newer, more powerful car, she had a fondness for the old heap, knowing full well that sentiment and mechanical reliability were mutually incompatible. Still, it hadn't let her down for at least a fortnight, so the omens were good.

The windscreen wipers squealed, clearing a smeared track of squashed bugs and the spattering of large raindrops. It had been threatening since Stevenage, and now down it came, a steady and monotonous grey curtain.

She drove past the visitors' car park and slotted into the space stencilled Deputy Governor in yellow paint. She didn't have her mac, and was running for the entrance, briefcase shielding her head, when she spotted Beryl Allington getting into her car. Helen swerved and loped across through the puddles, her face already cold from the stinging drops.

'Beryl – can I have a second?' Beryl had started the car, and Helen had to rap on the window with frozen knuckles. 'Beryl!'

Beryl wound down the window. An outreach worker with the local Department of Social Services, she was a year or two younger than Helen, dark-haired, with strong cheekbones and intelligent brown eyes. Helen liked her and, more importantly, trusted her. She was about to say, 'Tina James,' but Beryl was one jump ahead.

'We've found a foster home,' she said, shying back to keep dry. 'So we can't delay it any longer.'

'Shit.' Helen half crouched, peering in. 'Have you told her?'

'What do you think?' Beryl gave her a pained look which said, 'It had to be done, so I did it.' 'Look, she's known it was coming, and the longer the delay, the worse it'll be.'

'Okay.' The shoulders of Helen's jacket were getting a soaking, though she didn't seem to notice. She bit her lip. 'But I wanted to be with her when she was told.'

Beryl raised one hand, fingers spread. 'I waited, Helen.' She put the car in gear. 'She'll need supervision for a while, a lot of it.'

As Beryl drove off, Helen stepped back, right into a puddle. She didn't notice that either.

Like a model young mum, Tina James had everything to hand and neatly laid out, just as she'd been taught: tissues, cream, talcum powder, plastic disposal bag.

Standing with Clare, the officer in charge, inside the door of the mother and baby unit, Helen felt a pang, watching the girl so patiently and studiously changing her baby daughter. Still only a skinny kid herself. A few weeks past her seventeenth birthday, she could have passed for fourteen. Like watching a child change her doll. Oh, Christ, Helen thought, I love the job but I hate this part of it. Facing up to a Cat. A lifer was infinitely preferable.

Helen went over, finding a smile. She'd swapped her suit jacket for a loose cardigan with a thick roll collar, but her shoulders still felt chilly. 'Hi, how you doing?'

Tina wouldn't look at her at first, and when she did her eyes were hooded, her thin face sullen. Helen went down on one knee, putting her arm around the girl's shoulders. 'Hello, sweetheart.' She tickled the baby's dimpled chin. 'Who's a good girl, eh? Eh?'

Tina smoothed the nappy tabs flat and pulled down the little vest over the smooth belly, lightly dusted with powder. Her fingers were trembling. She said huskily, close to tears, 'Don't let them take her, please.'

'Come on, Tina, we've been preparing for it. You knew it would happen and . . . Tina!'

Helen sat back on her haunches as Tina snatched up the

baby, wrapping her protectively inside a blanket, and stood up, holding her close. 'She only knows me, she's mine.'

'Of course she is, but you knew it would have to happen.' Helen felt wretched. With a sigh she got to her feet. 'Tina . . .'

'I know, I know!' Tina half turned away, gathering the tiny bundle in a tight embrace. 'But not yet, you can't take Karen yet, I won't let her go.'

She moved off across the nursery with a swaying motion, rocking the baby to and fro. Helen looked to Clare, standing placidly by, the short sleeves of her uniform shirt straining to contain her pale fatty arms, folded high across her chest, thumbs hooked in her elbows. She was a big-boned, ruddy-faced young woman who carried her weight well, with a calm, sympathetic disposition, who Helen had never seen wear a lick of make-up.

On her way to the door Helen had a quiet word. 'Keep your eye on her.'

'She's a good mother,' murmured Clare.

Helen turned. 'She's also a prisoner, so don't you get sentimental on me. It's going to be tough all round.'

Parting Tina from her baby was bad enough, but it was the aftermath that concerned Helen. Many young mothers, understandably, couldn't take it. Resources were stretched thin as it was at Cattering Hall, without the extra burden of twenty-four-hour surveillance to prevent an inmate topping herself.

Helen waited until after the evening meal, served between six and seven, before she sent for Mona Cafferty. A teenage mum herself, Mona was not an attractive sight, with her shorn head, acned complexion and bad teeth. Scrawny arms covered in purple and green tattoos protruded like sticks from her baggy, oversize T-shirt. She lolled in the chair in front of Helen's desk rolling a cigarette, fingernails bitten to the quick.

'Because you've been through it, Mona, that's why,'

Helen said for the second, if not the third time. It amazed her how calm and reasonable she sounded.

Mona stuck the fag in the corner of her mouth, looking bored and a bit resentful. 'What do I say to her?'

'What it was like for you, how you came to terms with it . . .'

'Oh, I did, did I?' Mona looked at the ceiling and snorted. 'Well, that's nice to know, a real comfort.'

Helen leaned forward, trying to appeal to the girl's better nature. That's if she had a better nature. 'Which is why I am asking you to bunk up with Tina, just for a few weeks.'

'Don't want to. Why should I?'

'Because I am asking you.'

'Fine, I'm refusing,' Mona said. She picked a shred of tobacco off her lip and flicked it away. 'I don't wanna do it, I don't wanna have her howling her eyes out day and night, I don't want that, I don't want her screaming. I don't want it,' she said flatly. She stared Helen out.

'Is that what you did?'

'No, this . . .' Mona thrust the inside of her pathetic little arm across the desk, showing the hard puckered scars of puncture marks. She pulled her arm back and took a deep drag so that the paper scorched and curled. 'They took away the only thing that ever loved me.'

Helen said gently, 'You put your son up for adoption, Mona. That was your choice.'

'Bullshit! I never done that.'

'You signed the papers, Mona.'

Mona twisted her face like a deformed pixie's and gave Helen a savage glare. 'I was so screwed up I'd have signed for a fuckin' lobotomy!'

Helen wondered idly whether anyone would have noticed the difference.

The boardroom on the fourth floor of HM Prison Service HQ in the Millbank complex was not a happy place to be at eight thirty that evening, particularly for Brian Langham, Governor 1 of Barfield Prison. He'd been awake for twenty hours straight, and was functioning on coffee, cigarettes, and what was left of his nervous energy. At forty-nine, this was the worst moment of his nineteen-year career in the service. There had been deaths before under his command, usually suicides – throughout the prison system over two hundred suicides in the past four years. In his nick there had been fires, minor disturbances, of course, and several serious incidents. Nothing unusual about that, considering that in one year alone, 1993, there were 2540 assaults on prison officers and staff nationally, and nearly two thousand assaults on inmates. He'd had his share, along with every other governor. Par for the course. Now he had a death, a fire, a riot, and a wrecked prison, all in the space of a single night.

Most of it was there on the TV screen in the corner, caught on closed-circuit cameras and the videos that had been shot by his officers. Hooded men wielding chair legs, wooden planks and lead piping, smashing up everything in sight. Some of them laying about their fellow inmates, and going after the officers with a savagery and viciousness that chilled the blood. Fires being started in the cells and flaming debris hurled from the windows into the main yard. Scenes of panic and confusion as the fire spread through the VP Wing, then more explosions as gas cylinders went off, blowing out the windows and sending fireballs curling across the landings.

It was too painful to watch. Brian Langham had to shield his eyes, while Royston Andrews, the Operational Director, Sean Duncan of the Home Office, and several other of the top brass watched in grim silence. Head down, Langham spoke into the carpet, pausing now and then to take in a lungful of smoke. 'When we began to move the inmates from their cells, that's when the trouble started. That was about nine forty-five. More fires were started, some inside the cells, and prisoners went on the rampage.

By five o'clock it was estimated that four hundred prisoners were involved. By five thirty the ambulances had finished taking all casualties to the hospital, under guard. At ten – shortly after – the riot was under control.'

'Under control?' Sean Duncan said. His drawl and pompous delivery weighted the words with scepticism. 'According to an interview you gave to a reporter at the scene of the riot you stated that there was a disturbingly high level of drug abuse at Barfield. Was it drugs that instigated the riot?'

Langham turned weary eyes upon him. With five thousand seizures of drugs in Britain's prisons in the past year, everything from cannabis to heroin, crack cocaine to LSD, where had this cretin been living? He said bitterly, 'Right now my prisoners are displaying all the symptoms of an endemic drug culture.'

'You discussed this with a journalist,' Duncan said, waving about a copy of the *Evening Standard*, 'but had you reported it?'

'Yes!' Langham was on his feet. Duncan took a step back. 'I've repeatedly asked for more officers to deal *specifically* with the inflood of drugs.'

'But you yourself instigated this personal lock-up method,' Duncan persisted, pointing the finger. 'And the prisoners have keys?'

'Yes, only to their cell, they couldn't leave the spur.'

Duncan gave a thin, superior smile. 'Obviously doesn't work.'

Brian Langham could have smashed him in his smug face. He might have done, had he the strength left.

Royston Andrews tapped a newspaper on the boardroom table. 'Press are assuming your employees not only shopped for groceries for the inmates, but could have brought in drugs as well. You read the *Independent* this morning?'

Langham shook his head, but he had to smile. He hadn't had time to take a crap, let alone read the papers.

'It's a bloody fiasco,' Andrews told Duncan as they walked along the corridor to the Operational Director's office. 'Langham's virtually admitting that the prisoners control his prison, or control it within the spurs. Maybe he was the wrong man for Barfield.'

'Wherever we direct the blame,' Duncan said, thinking aloud, 'we've created something that's hard to imagine, a totally corrupt environment. What a place to put anyone, never mind an offender.' Suddenly his lean, ascetic frame shuddered. 'God Almighty, what a mess. Semtex at Whitemoor, guns at Durham . . .' He followed Andrews inside and closed the door. 'It's like the entire prison structure is falling down around our ears.'

Royston Andrews was at the drinks cabinet, pouring two healthy Scotches. 'Yes,' he mused, 'and we need someone who's going to get the press off our backs . . . and fast!'

Helen was relaxing, or trying to, in the officers' rest room at Cattering Hall. It had been a lousy day, and she was in a foul mood, tense, on edge. The interview had been a fiasco. She'd done her best, but under the circumstances it had been hopeless, a lost cause. She sat tapping her foot, watching *Newsnight* from an overstuffed armchair, sipping tea from a cracked mug. She preferred coffee, but not the cheap instant muck that the kitchen provided. Clare lounged companionably nearby in an easy chair, her meaty calves in their regulation black hose propped up on the plastic coffee table. Jeremy Paxman was interviewing a motley assortment of politicians, Home Office suits and prison officials in the studio about the Barfield riot. There were some shots of the rooftop protest, taken from outside the wall, and then a vox pop segment in which shoppers on a High Street somewhere were asked their views. A smart, middle-aged woman with piercing eyes was giving vent.

'I have had my car vandalized, I've had my home burgled,

I have lost my nerve to go out at night. I don't want to hear that if and when they catch the criminal – I don't want to hear that he is living in luxury. I think there have to be stricter regimes in all the prisons.' She was quivering. 'I mean, forty million pounds' worth of damage!'

Footsteps echoed in the corridor, and the tall, angular figure of Maureen Redwood appeared in the doorway, a raincoat over her arm, carrying a briefcase. Clare slid her feet down.

'You off then, Gov?' Helen said.

'We've had to segregate Tina, she's causing problems,' Mrs Redwood informed her. 'Pity Mona wouldn't help out.'

Helen sat up. 'Well, I don't think it would have been a good idea, anyway.' Probably not. Mona would have inducted young Tina into the finer points of shop-lifting, kiting, and fleecing the punters. She nodded to the TV. 'That riot's causing a storm.'

'. . . I think those men that destroyed Barfield Prison should be made to pay for the damage, not the public,' the woman was saying.

Mrs Redwood stood watching, the handle of her bulging briefcase clasped in both hands, as another woman, fortyish, working class, came on, speaking in a drab, defeated voice with a nasal Brummie accent.

'My daughter was raped and left for dead. When I read in the papers that these prisoners are living in the lap of luxury, I feel that justice was not done. My daughter has a life sentence. No one cares for the victims in this country.'

'Can I have a word?' Mrs Redwood said.

Helen heaved herself up and went to the door. She liked the Governor, got on well with her, but she sensed this was a ticking-off.

'Wasn't very convenient you taking the morning off, especially with the Tina situation,' Mrs Redwood said. 'In future give me more warning. Keep your eye on her.'

Helen smarted at the rebuke, but bit her tongue.

'See you tomorrow, g'night.' Mrs Redwood leaned in. 'Night, Clare.'

Sighing, Helen slumped back into the armchair. 'She knew I was going. I told her days ago.'

Clare shrugged in sympathy. Out of the blue she said brightly, 'We got all the balloons. You want to see what we got?'

Helen was mystified. 'What you talking about?'

'For Beryl – she's getting hitched on Saturday, it's the hen party Thursday night.' A wicked grin spread across her rosy cheeks. 'Hey! We're gonna get a bloke, Tarzan, you know, one of the kissograms. That's why I stayed late, get it organized.'

'Great,' said Helen, her attention on the TV. They were interviewing an ex-con. 'So what did you get her?'

'A dinner service. You got to sign the card—'

She broke off as Helen put a finger to her lips and pointed at the screen.

'It's not right that men should be treated like animals,' the ex-con was complaining bitterly. 'I spent three years in Stanhope. I was fed disgusting food, locked up eighteen hours a day . . .'

Puffing on his pipe, Royston Andrews sifted through the documents spread across his desk. Under the halo of the lamp his elegant grey hair gleamed like a silvery cap. 'She's got an honours degree in psychology. Played a substantial part in suicide-awareness support, and also—'

Sean Duncan stood at the darkened window, sipping his whisky. 'We'll all be needing more than support,' he said gloomily.

'Excellent results from the field.' Andrews beat a tattoo with his knuckles on the mahogany desktop. 'She's very accomplished. She's not married, very dedicated.'

'She's still very young.'

'But she's had two years in the US studying their penal

system.' Andrews flipped the dossier shut and leaned back, puffing out a billowing blue cloud. 'I think she's a very good candidate to put on the investigation team.'

Seeing that the Operational Director had made up his mind, Sean Duncan gave a nod. 'Mmm, good to have one woman.' He nodded again, more for his own benefit. At least keep the politically correct mob happy.

Helen tossed down her bag and stood for a minute, yawning hugely, in the middle of her tiny living room, massaging her temples. She'd no real notion of the time, but it must be gone midnight. She said tiredly, 'Give me a second to get my breath.' Her black cat with the white patches was mewing and rubbing itself against her ankles, demanding food and affection. Helen stroked its back, which arched under her hand. 'Been a long day, kitty.'

The breakfast dishes were stacked in the sink. She took a tin of Whiskas, half full, from the fridge, prised off the plastic top, and used the special fork to empty it into the dish.

'Here you go.'

On her way to the bedroom she took a passing glance at the answerphone, not expecting anything. But the light was winking. She pressed the button, stifling another yawn, and the yawn went in a trice.

'Helen, it's Maureen Redwood. The Prison Service Operational Director, Royston Andrews, would like you to call him first thing in the morning. I believe congratulations are in order. You've been promoted.'

Helen ran it back and played it over. By now she was wide awake, eyes bright, grinning from ear to ear. Governor 3. By George she'd done it. *Governor 3!*

CHAPTER 3

'MISS HEWITT to see you, Mr Andrews.'

The secretary stood aside and ushered Helen in. Royston Andrews came round the desk, smiling. He held out his hand. 'Thank you for coming at such short notice. And may I congratulate you on your promotion to Governor Three.'

'Thank you,' Helen said, shaking hands. She felt a little breathless. It had happened so fast, and against her expectations, that it took a bit of getting used to. And Royston Andrews seemed genuinely pleased for her. Away from the stiff formality of the promotions board, he gave the impression of being far more human and relaxed, and certainly more attractive. She felt that he liked her, and this made her warm to him.

His secretary brought in coffee, and they exchanged pleasantries while she poured and served. Royston Andrews tasted a mouthful and put down his cup.

'You must obviously be aware of the recent riots that took place at Barfield Prison,' he began briskly, getting down to it.

Helen nodded, rather taken aback. What had Barfield got to do with her? 'Yes, of course I was aware of it. I think everybody in the Prison Service must have been more than aware of it when it happened. It was headlines for days.'

He cleared his throat.

'I might as well come straight to the point. There's to be a full-scale investigation into the riot and subsequent death of the prisoner Michael Winchwood. As part of your studies, you are, I note from your records,' tapping a dossier on the blotter, 'familiar with prison suicide awareness.'

Not certain how to respond, Helen merely nodded. He had her on the hop. What was this?

Andrews took a sip of coffee. He put the cup down and favoured her with another of his direct gazes. 'I would therefore like you to agree to be part of the investigation team, Miss Hewitt.'

Going down in the lift, ten minutes later, Helen was still attempting to get her thoughts into some sensible order. Her promotion and now this, part of a major investigation into a riot-torn Category B high security jail, one on top of the other. She couldn't believe her luck. What was she thinking of? She'd paid her dues, it was all down to merit, luck didn't come into it. She didn't believe in luck anyway.

Which was just as well, because the Metro decided to knock her down a peg or two by refusing to start. Sitting behind the wheel, the Three Tenors blasting from the stereo, Helen tried again, holding her breath. The engine coughed and died, and so did the Three Tenors. They did three more faltering encores before finally, praise God, the little beast relented and rumbled into life.

Gingerly, she put the car in gear, and just then her portable phone beeped. It was Clare from Cattering Hall. Helen listened, eyes closed, a large pebble, hard and cold as ice, way down in the pit of her stomach. 'Okay, look, try and keep her calm. I'll be right there. Yes, now!' She banged the handset into its slot. 'Bugger it!'

It was late afternoon when she got back. Enid, the duty officer in charge of the hospital unit, panted along in Helen's wake as they ran down the corridor, giving her a breathless update.

'We sedated her, she'd cut both wrists.' She fumbled for

her keys. 'She seemed to accept it, then the next minute she went into association, and we . . .'

Enid ran out of breath, puffing hard. She couldn't see what all the panic was about. The girl had been saved, hadn't she? But Miss Bleeding-Hearts Hewitt, of course, had to charge around, demonstrating her care and compassion, which in Enid's opinion was wasted on these young girls, slags rather, who had no one but themselves to blame.

She slammed the big brass key in the lock. 'She did it with Doreen Rigby's glasses,' Enid whispered.

The heavy door swung open.

'Wait outside,' Helen said. She was pale and tight-lipped with anger. She went in. Enid watched her, rolling her eyes behind Helen's back, and shut the door. She turned and mouthed to another officer, further along the corridor, 'You heard? She's just been promoted to Governor Three.'

Helen sat on the edge of the thin, hard mattress. Tina was curled away from her, bandages and tape on both her wrists. Her eyes were open, staring at the wall.

'I'm sorry I wasn't here, Tina.' Helen touched her shoulder, small and bony, little more than a child's. 'Did you hear what I said?'

'Yeah.' It was the hoarse croak of someone who'd cried themselves to the point of exhaustion. Tina let go a long, sighing breath. 'I got it all worked out. I said to myself, if they take her, really take her, then I'll kill myself. Soon as I'd made up my mind, I could sleep, like I'd made the right decision.' Her thin face was rigid, though her chin was trembling. 'I knew she'd gone, the way everyone was lookin' at me, all nervous, everybody lookin' at me, waitin' for me to do somethin'. So I did.'

The hard cold pebble was still lodged in Helen's gut. She said helplessly, 'I'm sorry I wasn't here, Tina.'

'That's all right, Miss Hewitt,' Tina said forgivingly, and Helen had to swallow, blinking rapidly.

Staring at the wall, Tina laughed softly to herself. 'It was funny. I got that fat girl's glasses, you know her? Doreen?

Yeah, Doreen Rigby, in for kiting. Anyway, I nicked her glasses. I planned it. They took my baby, so I'd nobody else—'

Her voice choked off. 'Oh, Tina, Tina,' Helen said, reaching for her limp hand and squeezing it.

'The bloody things wouldn't break. They're not glass, but plastic, they wouldn't break. I trod on them but just the frames cracked and I could hardly break me skin, never mind kill myself.' Her shoulder was shaking, her chest juddering. 'It was ridiculous, and I started laughing.'

Her mouth opened and an almost soundless, wheezing laugh came out. Her shoulders, her entire body, were shaking, and the laughter became shrill, getting louder, her face at full stretch. The laughter went on and on, the girl's face twisting grotesquely, until up from the depths of her came terrible racking sobs, broken and ragged.

Helen gathered her up and rocked her. Slowly, over time, the sobs subsided to a wailing dirge, and then faded to whimpering. Helen rocked her gently to and fro, tears squeezing out from under her eyelids and streaming down her own cheeks, the pain inside the shuddering young body too much for her to bear.

Helen didn't care that Mrs Redwood would know she'd been weeping. They were dealing here with human beings with harrowing lives, zero futures, the world stacked against them; they weren't operatives on a production line, assembling cars and trucks. To have ignored, or been unmoved by, Tina's tragic plight would have been far worse – the worse for herself – in Helen's estimation.

She'd splashed her face with cold water, which had soothed her eyes but not cooled her anger. She stood in Mrs Redwood's office, letting it pour out, not giving a damn.

'I just want to know why, after I left specific instructions, why nobody took the time to sit with her and *stay* with her.' Helen sniffed and dabbed her nose. 'Do you know what she did? She tried to gouge out the veins in her arms with a bloody pair of glasses!'

'We had three new admissions today,' Mrs Redwood said quietly, which inflamed Helen even more.

'That's no excuse. What about the probation officer, one of the officers?'

'I am short-staffed as it is, and the last thing I needed was my deputy disappearing—'

'So it's my fault?'

'Nobody is directing blame at anybody, Helen.'

'But I am.' She could see the girl's face, hear her pitiful sobs. Helen thumped her chest with the balled-up handkerchief. 'I am saying that we are to blame.'

'And I am saying that with three new admissions we did not have anyone available.'

'We should have made them available.'

Mrs Redwood gave her a look. 'You should not have taken time out without consulting me.'

Helen stood silently fuming, getting nowhere, wanting to smash something or somebody hard, not knowing what or who. Not Mrs Redwood, she just happened to be in the line of fire. She was straight and fair-minded, and Helen trusted and admired her.

Helen went to the door. She'd said her piece, for what little good it had done her. As she grasped the handle, Mrs Redwood said, 'I understand you've been asked to be part of the investigation team looking into the riots at Barfield Prison.' Helen turned round. Mrs Redwood was standing, hands in the pockets of the long, rather shapeless cardigan that almost reached her knees. 'I think it will be very good for you, but a word of advice.' She gave Helen that look again. Not unkind, but very direct.

'Just look and listen, don't run before you can walk, or you'll fall down right on top of your ambition.'

Helen stared at the carpet, biting her lip. She sniffed. 'Thank you for your advice, Mrs Redwood.'

Mrs Redwood was smiling. 'Congratulations.'

Helen nodded. She had stormed into the office filled with righteous wrath, and she was leaving it in chastened mood, feeling her insides had been scoured out.

Shit and corruption. The first day of the investigation, keen to make a good impression, and she was bloody well late. Late on the first pigging day.

Helen has risen early, showered, taken care over choosing a conservative dark grey two-piece suit and a V-necked russet-coloured blouse. She'd taken time with her make-up too, though her eyebrows could have done with some pruning. Fruit juice, coffee and toast and out into a mild September morning. She was keyed-up and confident. She'd been given the chance and she was determined to prove she could handle it.

She set off in good spirits. Less than forty miles as the crow flies from Cattering Hall, Barfield Category B Dispersal Prison was situated in the green belt south-east of Leicester, a rural area of villages and small working farms. Even allowing for traffic – and there wasn't much – the journey should have taken an hour at most. It actually took nearly twice as long, thanks to the Mini Metro, which conked out on the A14, south of Market Harborough. The AA arrived promptly to her call, but it took an agonizing half-hour to sort out the problem with the distributor. Helen drove the final few miles in frantic haste, feeling like the White Rabbit racing against time, threading her way through the narrow country lanes until at last the high walls of Barfield came into view. Was this an omen? She hated to think so. And just when she'd started to believe that someone up there liked her.

In the staff car park she took a few precious minutes to compose herself, tucking in her blouse and smoothing the creases in her jacket. She made a grimacing inspection of her face in the mirror, and used her fingers to comb back her shoulder-length hair. The officer behind the screen in the gate lodge checked her ID, taking his own sweet time about it, and finally she passed through the 'airlock' system of electronically operated sliding doors into a small waiting area. More delay while an officer was summoned to escort her across the yard to the administration block. Helen followed him up an open stairway and along a maze of corridors. He tapped on a door and in she went, slightly breathless, hoping she didn't look as flustered as she felt. She had a smile ready to go with the apology, which was a great way to start.

'I'm sorry, I'm very late . . .'

She had expected several people, but there was only a portly man with a set of jowls and a sour expression, fortyish or thereabouts, who rose heavily from behind the desk and came round to greet her. 'I'm the Deputy Governor, Gary Marshall. Would you like some coffee?'

He was a Londoner by the sound of him, making no pretence as he looked at his watch that the offer wasn't for real. Subtle type, Helen thought.

'No, I think I'd better join the others. Is everyone here?'

'Yes,' Marshall said, the obvious answer to a stupid question. He pinched his fleshy nostrils, a definite lack of enthusiasm in his washed-out brown eyes with the lined pouches. 'I've been instructed to give you a tour, hopefully catch them up later. As you said, you're very late.' He stuck up his hand in an abrupt gesture, indicating a large wall map. 'Let me show you the prison layout.'

Perhaps his bluntness was understandable, Helen realized charitably. Outsiders coming into his prison, poking around, lifting the stones to see what was squirming underneath. Of course, as Deputy Governor, he would resent that. With his prison under investigation, Marshall's arse was in the blender.

Standing by his shoulder, she dwarfed him as he showed her the map.

Although she had never worked in a high security prison,

Helen had visited several, so she wasn't surprised at the size of the place. And it was big. The site covered forty-seven acres. In addition to the five accommodation wings there were extensive outbuildings for workshops, the education section, laundry, catering, a hospital unit, chapel, assembly halls, gymnasium, and a sports field with a full-size soccer pitch. Each wing had its own separate exercise yard. There were two visitors' rooms, one for 'open', the other for 'closed' visits, in which inmates were sealed off from their family and friends. The admin block, in which they were standing, housed the support and ancillary services, including probation officers, psychologists, and a drug rehabilitation unit. Out of a total staff of 540, half were prison officers, from basic grades through senior officers to principal officers.

Built in 1977, Barfield operated at a cost per prisoner of £21,223 per annum. Not the cheapest in the country, but still below the national average of £23,000 for each prisoner place.

Marshall's hand moved in a general arc. 'Before the riot every one of these wings was full, four hundred and thirty-two prisoners.'

'How many do you have resident now?' Helen asked.

'Eighty-eight. The worst offenders, basically because no other prison would have them. But due to security problems, Mr Langham is shipping as many of them out as possible.' He glanced at her quickly, jumping in first to ward off any criticism. 'The Governor, Mr Langham, is a great man, we all respect him. Everybody likes him.'

'Did the inmates like him?'

'I've never heard one complaint against him,' Marshall said stiffly, 'and I've worked with him for five years.'

'Where were you before?'

'Strangeways.' He went to the door. 'Moved the wife and kids some time ago when I got the job.' He opened the door. 'After you, Miss Hewitt.'

Helen hesitated, but the Deputy Governor, technically her superior, wafted his hand. It was a feeble courtesy, about all he could manage. Helen went through, marvelling at how short a time it took for you to dislike a person.

Helen was wearing a new pair of black Firenze ankle boots, which she soon came to regret. They were soft and supple, extremely comfortable, and in no time at all covered in mud and water and brick dust from the piles of rubble she had to stumble through. The rampaging prisoners had done a thorough job. B Wing, which Marshall showed her first, was a total write-off. Chairs and tables smashed, sinks ripped out, bedding strewn everywhere and set alight. The safety mesh across the landings torn down. The observation 'bubble' – the sealed room where the officers kept watch – broken into and ransacked. Impossible to estimate what this would cost to replace and make good. Helen gave up when an endless series of noughts trailed before her mind's eye.

Marshall must have looked at his watch twenty times. 'I don't want to rush you,' he kept saying, which of course was precisely what he was doing, as well as reminding her that her lateness had made this privately guided tour necessary in the first place.

From B Wing they went across the yard, strewn with clumps of concrete and twisted iron bars (her boots!) to the officers' canteen. Same story here. Blackened walls, floors littered with smashed crockery, a tangled wreckage of tables and chairs heaped in a corner, every window put through. Helen crunched through the debris while Gary Marshall stood with his arms folded, shaking his head in a sad, resigned fashion. 'Nothing salvageable in here.'

'Is this where it started?'

'No, that was over in the VP Wing kitchen, according to the fire team. But there was more than one fire. They mushroomed up all over the prison. They were here for days, the fire team, plus there has been a full-scale police inquiry.'

'Are they also aware of our investigation?' Helen asked, stepping over a mound of charred plastic that might once have been a cash register. She glared down. There was a deep scar right across the toe of her left boot.

Marshall gave her a sideways glance. 'The police? Yes, Miss Hewitt, they are aware. Mind how you walk here.' He gestured her ahead. 'After you.'

'Are these inmates?' Helen asked, her nod indicating five men in brown overalls who were sweeping up broken ceramic tiles and shovelling them into large plastic sacks. They were in the shower recess on the upper landing of C Wing. Water dripped from severed pipes, and there was a pong of blocked drains.

Marshall shook his head. 'No, contractors. There are about twenty men allocated to clear the place out as fast as possible.'

Helen moved along the landing to the first cell. A cool breeze sighed through the windows, not a pane of glass left intact. She looked down to the grassed area below, criss-crossed with cinder paths. The gate in the chain-link fence stood open, men in overalls pushing loaded wheelbarrows to a waiting lorry.

'One of the exercise yards,' Marshall said at her shoulder. 'They're using the yards to remove the rubble.'

'So the men held here now have no exercise area?'

Marshall didn't bother to reply. Turning away with a shrug, he stood waiting for her at the door, checking his watch and humming impatiently to himself. Helen took the hint and ignored it. Let him stew awhile; she had her own job to do. She craned through the window as a group of dark-suited men came in sight, heading towards the gate lodge. She recognized Brian Langham, Governor 1 of Barfield, leading the way, in conversation with Judge Simms, white-haired and rather stooped though sprightly enough at the age of seventy-one. He had been appointed to lead the investigation team. Two of the others she knew personally: Matthew Ettinger and Norman Littlejohn, both governors of senior rank to Helen.

She turned away, batting the front of her suit where it was covered with dust and grime from the window-sill. There was a gritty taste on her lips and a dark smear on her elbow – oil or grease or something. Damnation.

'From what I've gathered there were major drug problems,' she said as they descended the metal stairway to the ground floor.

'No more than any other prison of this size,' Marshall replied gruffly. He paused, head bent over, as his belt radio emitted a squawk. 'Hello Victor 2 from Sierra, over,' said a distorted voice, and Helen walked on as he acknowledged it. She heard him say, 'Miss Hewitt, yep. Over.'

'Victor 2 from Sierra. Judge Simms suggests you continue with Miss Hewitt. They've gone to the golf club for lunch. Out.'

Marshall switched off. 'Did you hear that?'

Helen gave a wry smile. 'Well, I guess I've missed lunch,' she said, walking on. Marshall, shoulders hunched, stared at her back, and stumped after her. Not the only one to have missed their bloody lunch.

Half an hour later, under a fitful sun casting pale shadows, they stood in the main prison yard, watching a work party of trusties, supervised by officers. Trusties, or 'Red Bands' as they were known, were not a breed favoured by the other cons, who usually referred to them as 'toe-rags' or worse. By now Helen had seen all she wanted to. She gazed down at her suit and ruined Firenze boots, and it was her turn to look at her watch.

'Any chance of something to eat?'

'You want to eat here?'

'Well, whatever is convenient . . .' She turned as the work party went by, Marshall nodding to the escorting officers. 'How many women are working here?'

The question seemed to throw him off-balance for a second. Then he actually grinned, shaking his head. 'Not many.' The grin became sardonic. 'This is a men's prison. You got male officers at Cattering Hall now, have you?'

Helen smiled. 'As a matter of fact, yes. We also have gardeners, therapists, instructors . . . same as Holloway, they have a number of male staff now.' His grin had gone all watery. Helen beamed at him. 'You're behind the times, Gary.' She set off purposefully, leading the way. 'I'll skip lunch.'

Marshall stared after her, jaw clenched, breathing heavily. She was getting right under his skin, this bint, and he didn't care who knew it, her included.

But the bint already knew that.

CHAPTER 4

GARY MARSHALL was leaning against the wall outside the officers' rest room, arms folded, staring moodily at his shoes, when Tom Doughen appeared along the corridor.

'The Gov's in your office. I said you were still showing her around . . .'

He took a peek through the door's glass panel. Inside, Helen sat chatting with the afternoon shift, just coming on, and sipping coffee from a styrofoam cup. Nearly everyone except her was smoking, the room wreathed in a thick grey fug. Officers were strapping on their radio transceivers, slipping the ten-inch wooden batons into their trouser pockets. One or two were in shirtsleeves, though most wore the thick ribbed dark-blue sweaters with 'HM Prison Service' embroidered on the cloth epaulettes.

Listening and nodding, asking a question now and then, Helen seemed completely at ease surrounded by a dozen or so hulking men.

Marshall didn't spare her a glance. 'When she's through here, buzz me and I'll collect her and wheel her out. Where are the others?'

'Not back from lunch.' Doughen had his beefy face with its black moustache pressed close to the glass. 'Bit young, isn't she?' Not the only surprise. Slim and attractive too, with lively open features, dark-blonde hair swept casually back from a centre parting. And – as near as he could judge under the smartly tailored suit – well stacked in all the right places.

'Yeah, and a know-all,' Marshall growled. 'She's a bloody university high flyer. Four years I waited for Governor 3. I just heard she's been promoted to it first time.' He scuffed the carpet. 'Bloody stupid.'

Doughen said, 'Arnie Franks is creating a bit. The usual, only he's getting very het up.'

Marshall released a long-suffering sigh. This wasn't his day. Helen was still chatting, and some of the officers were smiling, even laughing with her. He jerked his thumb. 'Just keep her busy,' he muttered, and ambled off down the corridor.

Nothing Doughen would have liked more than to keep that tasty piece busy. Fully occupied, in fact. He went in and joined the group. Damon O'Keefe was giving her a rundown on some of the more notorious prisoners held at Barfield, pointing them out on the notice board. Names, photographs, offences, sentences.

Helen flicked a stray wisp of hair from her forehead. 'Heavens! I didn't know you had him here.'

'Yeah,' O'Keefe said, who despite his name had a Cockney accent. 'And he's not a happy man. We got a formal complaint after Winchwood, says he doesn't feel safe with a murderer on the loose. Considering he's a mass killer, he's got a bloody nerve.'

'What?' Helen said, staring at him. 'Does he reckon Winchwood was murdered?'

O'Keefe brushed it aside. 'No. Winchwood was just the spark that caused the riot.' He took a quick swig of coffee.

'Do you know the ring-leaders, then?'

'Yeah, we know 'em.' Helen turned to Russell Morgan, a senior officer in charge of a wing. An ex-Para with fourteen years' service under his belt, including the Falklands, he was a big, broad-chested man with a neck like a tree trunk. He weighed over sixteen stone, and if he didn't keep on top of it with workouts three times a week would scale eighteen plus. The smell of Lynx shower gel and aftershave nearly knocked Helen over. 'In fact, they were the problem,' Morgan told her. 'We tried to get 'em out without a row and all hell broke loose.'

'That's not our problem any more,' Doughen chipped in. 'They've been shipped out.'

O'Keefe was studying her with narrowed eyes. 'So . . . is Mr Langham going to be shafted?' he asked softly.

'I wouldn't know,' Helen answered truthfully. Something about the burly, bearded O'Keefe niggled her, though she couldn't say what. Thought himself smart, maybe smarter than he actually was. 'Tell me more about Winchwood. I presume with his record he'd be a vulnerable prisoner, so was he segregated to the VP Wing?'

Not a flicker from any of them. Helen let it go. She crushed the styrofoam cup and tossed it into the bin. O'Keefe was working some grit from under his thumbnail. 'Will Gary Marshall be taking over if Langham retires?'

'It'll be up to headquarters,' Helen said. She squared her shoulders and pulled her jacket straight. 'Could you take me to Mr Marshall, please?'

Doughen looked none too happy about it, but he had little choice. You didn't argue with a Governor 3.

There was a hell of a lot of banging and cursing going on in the VP Wing. About a third of the cells had sustained damage of some kind, but most of the upper landing was still functional. Doughen unlocked the gates and led her up the spiral stairway, which was enclosed in a circular cage of iron bars. Above the racket, magnified and echoing down the length of the hollow, rectangular wing, Helen could hear Marshall's exasperated voice.

'Arnie? Listen to me, Arnie. I won't come in and talk to you unless you calm down. Arnie . . . you going to listen to me? Show your face now at the hole.'

Feet planted apart, an officer either side of him, Marshall

started thumping the iron door. Helen came onto the landing, but he was too preoccupied to notice her. 'Come on, Arnie, show yourself.'

The metal swivel flap to the spy-hole was already pushed aside. This was known to the cons as the 'wank flap', because they covered it over on the inside for privacy when masturbating. More than ever necessary now with the introduction of female officers. Marshall put his face into the concave bevel of the door, peering through. Arnie Franks got up scowling and pushed his head forward belligerently. A tall man in his forties, with staring blue eyes, he had a long string of convictions for sexual offences against juveniles of both sexes.

'Arnie, I can't take you up to the visits room if you don't have a visitor,' Marshall explained reasonably.

'I got a visitor, you know I got a visitor.' There was white mucus on his red lips, a dribble of saliva on his chin from shouting and screaming. 'I asked for a visiting order and it was agreed,' Franks insisted hoarsely, 'an' now they're saying I got no VO.'

Marshall stepped back wearily as the door was pummelled and kicked. His jaw tightened then, when he saw Helen for the first time, with Doughen lurking sheepishly in the background.

'Take her to the office area,' Marshall said tersely. He turned back to the door, feeling in the mood to give it a damn good bashing himself.

Brian Langham, the Governor, had returned from lunch and was on the phone when Helen walked into his office. 'Oh, excuse me,' she said, as he held up his hand.

'See if you can calm him down. If not, get back to me.' He dropped the phone down with a clatter.

'I'm waiting for Mr Marshall,' Helen said.

'I'm Brian Langham.'

'Helen Hewitt . . . with the investigation team.' She held out her hand, but Langham had turned away, a fatigued expression on his face as he stared bleakly out of the window.

'I have to uproot my wife, my kids from their school. I think I'm still in shock. The riot was bad enough, but they really pulled the rug from under me. Enforced retirement!' He gave an empty laugh. 'Well, I suppose somebody had to be the scapegoat.'

'I'm sorry,' Helen said. She fidgeted for a moment, and then plunged in. 'Can I ask you something? Michael Winchwood.'

Brian Langham looked at her, lips pursed, but said nothing. The silence prolonged itself.

'It's been put out it was suicide,' Helen said quietly.

Langham wouldn't be drawn on that one. 'We won't get verification until the post-mortem reports are finalized.'

Helen had another question, but was stalled by the phone. Langham snatched it up, looking harrowed and relieved at the same time. 'I'll be right down.' He bustled past her, fluttering his hand. 'I'm sorry, I have to go to the VP Wing.'

'You mind if I come along?' Helen said, only a pace behind, matching his stride.

Some of the inmates had gathered on the landing, lounging against the guardrails, and there was a knot of them down below in the central association area, all taking an interest, any diversion more than welcome, especially if it was that nutter Arnie Franks.

'I wanna speak to Mr Langham!' The dull thump was Franks's head beating against the door. 'I wanna speak to the Governor.' *Thump*. 'He knows. He knows about my situation.' *Thump*.

'Arnie, will you just listen?' Marshall pleaded with him. 'Just listen to me.'

Franks howled. *Thump, thump, thump*.

Langham bounded up the stairway. One of the officers passed him a pair of white rubber gloves, and he pulled them on.

'Hey, Arnie, what d'you think you're doing, mate?' Langham signalled for the door to be unlocked. 'You got the whole corridor up out here.'

'It's about my visiting order,' Franks howled. 'I want my VO.'

'You'll go to the visits room at—' Langham looked at the circle of officers, shrugging his shoulders '—ten minutes to two, okay? Arnie?'

At his nod the door was pushed open and he slipped through, three officers crowding in behind him. While they were busy inside, the prison doctor, Lorcan Thomas, arrived at the run, his bag under his arm. Helen wasn't averse to a bit of erotic fantasy, and Dr Thomas would have fitted the bill quite nicely. He didn't notice her, however, too preoccupied with what Arnie Franks was up to. 'Does he need to be sedated?'

Langham pushed through, red-faced and perspiring. 'Five minutes. Give me a little time.'

Helen was perplexed. Wearing a faint frown, she murmured to Doughen, 'This is all a bit over the top, isn't it?'

The officer shot her a glare, eyes hooded. 'He's not had a visitor for five years. This just starts to grow out of all proportion until he's completely out of control – and because he's got full-blown Aids he's very dangerous. He's also mentally subnormal and as strong as an ox.' Franks was howling again. 'And very active,' Doughen said with a leering grin, 'sexually.'

Helen was looking past him to the opposite landing. One of the cells was staked off with black and yellow tape: POLICE – NO ADMITTANCE.

'Is that Winchwood's cell?'

But right then there was a flurry of movement, bodies colliding to get out of Franks's way as he head-butted the wall. Dr Thomas reversed rapidly onto the landing. 'Back off, he's bleeding all over the place!'

Seeing Helen there, observing all this, Gary Marshall nearly blew his top. He looked sharply at Langham. The Governor saw his point. Fists clenched, his voice under tight control, he said, 'Doughen, take Miss Hewitt up, will you? Get her out!'

Helen smiled at him, and without waiting went on ahead to the stairway. Behind her, Doughen did a double-take at the barred gates below, the investigation team passing through led by Judge Simms. He frantically semaphored to Marshall.

'They're coming up here now! They want to look over Winchwood's cell.'

At Langham's signal, the officers moved along the landing, bellowing out, 'Back in your cells, get back in your cells,' to the lounging watchers, who slowly and reluctantly trailed off. 'Get behind the door. Come on, back in!'

'Judge Simms, Miss Hewitt has arrived.'

It wouldn't go down as the warmest greeting Helen had ever received. Judge Simms, his pinstriped suit hanging loosely on his gaunt frame, the gold chain of a fob watch looped in his waistcoat pocket, merely raised an eyebrow as Gary Marshall came up, Helen a step behind, and made the introductions.

'Not just,' Helen said with a smile, wanting to set the record straight. 'I've been catching you up, been on a guided tour and—'

Judge Simms cut her off, gesturing to the group. Maybe he didn't like her personally, or women in general, or her arriving late. Or maybe a combination of all three. His voice was dry and somewhat difficult to hear, his delivery pedantically precise. 'Miss Hewitt, these are Governors Ettinger, Swallow, Hartingdon, Littlejohn, and er . . .' He looked round at no one in particular. 'Are we to wait for Mr Langham?'

Helen was shaking hands. As well as the governors there were two male assistants to the team, a clinical psychologist, and an anonymous little man from the Home Office. Knowing a couple of them helped ease her in. 'Hello, Matthew . . . Norman.'

Matthew Ettinger had been at Risley Remand Centre in Cheshire, Helen's first posting in the Prison Service as a uniformed officer, straight down from Reading University. He'd risen through the ranks to Governor 1, attached to the Director General's department in Millbank. Norman Littlejohn, a Governor 2, she had met several times at various conferences over the years. Helen said in his ear, 'Have you been taking notes?'

'He mumbles to the secretaries,' Littlejohn said, indicating the assistants, 'but I've made my own.'

'Right, gentlemen.' The judge called them to order. 'I have asked to see Winchwood's cell. If we can cut the chit-chat . . . ah!'

A slightly flustered Brian Langham had joined them, thinning hair clinging damply to his head. He led the way up.

'Which one is the psychologist?' Helen asked Ettinger from the side of her mouth.

'Nervous one with a twitch,' he said, straight-faced, and Helen couldn't hold back a warm, rich peal of laughter, which she had to smother quickly as Judge Simms gave her a look that was straight out of the freezer.

Langham removed the black and yellow tape, allowing the party to cluster around the narrow doorway. 'The police have asked us not to touch anything inside the cell,' he cautioned. 'Do you want to go inside?' he asked Judge Simms.

The judge nodded and peered inside. 'I doubt if it will be necessary for all of us—' He went stock still then, as if his stooped body was locked in rigor mortis. 'My God!'

Though she was near the back, Helen had a clear view over Norman Littlejohn's head. The floor of the cell had a dull red patina. The washbasin was splashed with dark stains. More stains on the small writing table, the bed-clothes, and half-way up the cheap timber door of the single corner wardrobe. On the wall opposite, a large smudge of dried blood, smeared across for no purpose, it seemed, unless it was to obscure something.

'Suicide!' Helen murmured to herself, the very word having the hollow ring of a sick joke.

Relaxing at the bar in the lounge of the Olde Bear Hotel, where the investigation team were staying the night, Matthew Ettinger and Norman Littlejohn were on their third pint when Helen came down. She'd had a long delicious soak, washed the smoke and dust out of her hair, and changed into a long, dark-green dress and matching suede high heels. She swung onto a bar stool next to Ettinger, swirling her hair back, eyes bright and smiling; knowing she looked good made her feel better than she had all day. 'Can I get a round?'

'Nope. Hawk-eye has almost finished his dinner.' A reference to the crusty old judge, mopping up his gravy in the dining room. 'Congratulations, by the way,' Ettinger said. 'Hear you've been promoted.'

Helen nodded. 'Large Scotch and soda, no ice, and crisps or nuts,' she said to the barman.

Littlejohn didn't mean her to hear his muttered, 'What rank is she now?' And when Ettinger showed three fingers, Littlejohn mumbled, 'Bloody hell!' into his pint glass.

'You sure you won't have another?' Helen asked, trying to quell the laughter bubbling in her chest. The Prison Service was a real bastion of male supremacy, and it amused her to observe old fart dinosaurs like Norman Littlejohn lumbering baffled and bemused into a world that had indoor plumbing, flying machines, and women making careers for themselves.

'Half, then,' Ettinger said. 'What do you make of it?'

'I don't know. I'd like to read the statements.' Helen took the first swallow, a good deep one. 'Have you got them?'

Littlejohn was burbling something about it's not what you know, it's who you know . . .

'Didn't you have a folder in your room?' Ettinger asked.

'No.' She looked round the bar. 'Your room okay?'

'Yeah, yours?'

'Next to the car park, the lifts, and if there's a disco I suppose I'm on top of it.'

Ettinger laughed. He liked Helen, had seen her as potential rising-star material even back in the Risley days. Norman Littlejohn drained his pint hurriedly, thumb jabbing towards the conference room at the rear. 'He's just gone in. Better knock these back.'

He got down from the stool, giving Helen a heavy wink. 'Don't pay, it's all on the slate. And congrats, you're certainly flying up through the ranks.'

Oh, yeah, Helen thought. She could see Stormin' Norman was dead chuffed about it. With any luck it might give him a sleepless night.

They adjourned to the conference room, Helen taking along the rest of her Scotch and soda: Judge Simms, fussing over a pile of documents at the head of the table, waved imperiously as the team came in. 'Get yourselves a coffee and then grab a chair.' His gaze roamed round, in that vague manner affected by High Court judges, and attached itself to Helen.

'Miss Hewitt, have you had a moment to study the file?'

'No, I've only just been given it,' Helen said, showing the blue folder Ettinger had passed to her.

Judge Simms tapped his fingertips together. Then his hands flew apart, like birds escaping. 'I want to open the discussion straight away.' A model of Barfield Prison, as it had been prior to the fire and the riot, had been placed in the centre of the table around which they were gathered. He stared at it for a long moment, finally raising his head.

'Mr Ettinger, do you feel that the governor in charge, Mr Langham, is liable for any disciplinary action? Please keep your answers short and to the point.'

'Well, to be quite honest—'

'That is the point,' said the judge drily. 'Yes?'

'I do think there is a time discrepancy in the statements from several officers.' Ettinger referred to his notes. 'In particular, O'Keefe, Doughen, Jenson, Fuller, Macaulay and Senior Officer Morgan.'

Judge Simms pointed to the model. 'All these stated, I believe, that B Wing was, at the time of the first fire, locked. Yes, continue.'

'But taking into consideration the victim's injuries, he could have been attacked.' Ettinger used his pen to point out the position of Winchwood's cell in the VP Wing.

Judge Simms frowned. 'But it has not been verified by the police that Michael Winchwood *was* attacked. To the contrary. We must accept that the wounds were self-inflicted to his—'

Ettinger tried to interject, but the judge ignored him. Helen was trying to keep up with this. Having only moments ago got hold of the file, she was speed-reading the pages of documentation to extract the key points. Even without detailed knowledge, however, she couldn't believe Judge Simms was seriously suggesting that Winchwood's wounds were self-inflicted, solely on police conjecture. The state of his cell raised serious doubts, never mind the state of the body.

The judge was reading from the medical report. '... injuries to right and left wrist, artery. Throat, frontal and two chest wounds.' He scratched his chin. 'Excessive, I'll agree.'

Merely a slight understatement, Helen thought. What was Michael Winchwood trying to do – kill himself five times over?

'According to the reports, Winchwood also had extensive bruising,' Ettinger pointed out.

'But this has not been proved to have been inflicted on the same night. It was in fact . . .' Judge Simms looked to his assistant. 'Do we have the medical report from his previous prison?'

Norman Littlejohn said, 'Winchwood arrived at Barfield from Hull two weeks prior to the riot with bruising to his abdomen, back and buttocks.'

This more than satisfied the judge. He riffled quickly through the pages. 'I think we must move on from the Winchwood injuries, as I said, until we have verification that it was suicide and not, for want of a better word, murder.' A dismissive, rather mocking glance in Ettinger's direction, for having the temerity to raise such a ludicrous prospect. It was perfectly obvious to Helen that Judge Simms was attempting to bulldoze the investigation, pushing aside unpalatable facts that might get in the way of his own prejudices and cast-iron opinions.

The judge continued: 'I am uppermost interested in finding out how and why the riot occurred, and where the blame is to be directed.'

He paused, distracted by Helen, who was whispering in Ettinger's ear. His irritation showed. 'Miss Hewitt, I would appreciate it if you read the files in your own time. Please pay attention to the discussion.'

Helen felt herself flush. She sat upright, facing front and centre, like a good little girl in class.

With one eye on the minibus parked at the entrance, Helen was on the phone in the hotel foyer. Members of the investigation team were standing on the gravel forecourt, enjoying a brief glimpse of late September sunshine before being ferried to Barfield. Judge Simms was stumping about, demanding to know when his car would be brought round.

Helen tried to hurry up, but Officer Shaw at Cattering Hall was being particularly dense, not to say difficult, this morning.

'Can you get the Social Services to make a set of photographs of Tina's baby?' Helen sighed, nodding to Matthew Ettinger, who was giving her the time-to-leave signal. 'Because I am asking, Enid, that's why. If need be I'll pay for them.'

The others were climbing aboard. Making a show of consulting his pocket watch, Judge Simms frowned sternly at Helen. She slammed down the phone, picked up her bag, and hurried out.

'Previous injuries determined as severe bruising, scar tissue to lower abdomen and buttocks.' Speaking into the pocket tape recorder, the green-gowned senior pathologist moved along the row of large-scale X-rays pinned up on the frosted screen of the light box. Behind him, on the stainless-steel sluice table, lay the naked body of Michael Winchwood. The dried lacerations and dark bruises stood out starkly against the white, flaccid flesh.

'Injuries sustained on the night of the riot: both wrists cut, right wound deeper than the left, severing the main artery. The throat wound, a jagged-edged cut, ten and a half centimetres from just below the left ear . . .'

His assistant entered, waving a clipboard. 'Results from Winchwood's stomach contents. His last meal was flavoured with traces of glass.'

'About bloody time. Let me see.' The pathologist slid his glasses from his head onto his nose. 'Well, not enough ground glass to kill him.' He sucked his lower lip. 'Would have been painful if he'd lived.'

He handed back the clipboard and carried on his running commentary.

The dry, droning voice made it hard to concentrate on what Judge Simms was saying, though Helen was giving it her best shot. The judge was at the front, set a little apart from the rest of the team. Directly facing him across the table, Royston Andrews had Sean Duncan on one side of him, Mrs Donald on the other. The model of Barfield Prison was on a small table over by the window; maps and aerial photographs were pinned to the walls of the Millbank HQ boardroom.

In the second row, behind the more senior governors, Helen leaned forward, crossed arms resting on her knees, frowning hard at the toes of her shoes. The voice droned on, finally, and thank God, reaching its conclusion.

'The known ringleaders of the riot have been named and are being dispersed. However, as over a hundred and fifty of the prisoners admitted to taking part in the riot, it will be a time-consuming and financially punitive undertaking to review each man's sentence. That said, I think in time the ringleaders must be publicly named and their sentences adjusted accordingly.'

Royston Andrews was nodding agreement. 'Governor Langham has agreed to take early retirement. No disciplinary action will be taken against any of Barfield's officers.'

Helen's frown deepened. She slowly straightened up, brushing her hair back from her shoulders. Everybody seemed happy; everybody seemed agreeable. A job well done.

Andrews's secretary came in and handed an envelope to Sean Duncan. A satisfied smile settled over his face as he read the contents. The hum of conversation died away as he held up his hand.

'The Home Office pathology report is being sent over

by courier. It is determined that Michael Winchwood committed suicide.'

More nods of agreement, and even more satisfaction. Judge Simms began packing away his files. A smiling Sean Duncan was passing the note to Royston Andrews. In the front row, Ettinger and Littlejohn appeared to be sharing a joke.

Behind them, leaning back in her chair, arms folded, Helen was shaking her head in total disbelief.

CHAPTER 5

HELEN STRODE into the Governor's office at Cattering Hall, a pile of that morning's papers in her arms, and dumped them on the corner of the desk.

'Suicide! It's now been made public. It's a complete whitewash.'

Maureen Redwood slid the top one off the pile to scan the headlines. 'Not entirely,' she said calmly. 'Brian Langham's lost his job.'

Helen pulled a face, mouth turned down sceptically. 'Only one report adds . . .' She rooted through and pounced on it. 'Here it is. "Detectives conducting the inquiry said that they had previously believed it impossible for a man to sustain the injuries that—"'

Mrs Redwood cut her off. 'If you had anything to say about it, you've missed your opportunity.'

Helen leaned over the desk. 'I took your advice. I looked, listened, and said nothing. But I wish I had.' She swung away and paced up and down, fist smacking her palm. 'If Michael Winchwood killed himself he was a bloody contortionist.' Muttering angrily to herself, she headed for the door.

'A moment,' Mrs Redwood said. 'Mr Bunny, Barfield's Area Manager, you've met him?'

'Yes.' Helen recalled the round-shouldered, balding little

man who had appeared at her promotions board, agitated over the news of the riot.

'He just called to offer me Barfield Prison.'

It took a moment for Helen to recover. She moved slowly back to the desk. 'Are you going to take it? Would that mean I'd run Cattering—'

'I turned it down,' Mrs Redwood said. She gave a tiny shrug, leaning back in her chair, perfectly composed. For a moment she toyed with her pen, her gaze coming up to meet Helen's. 'He asked me about your operational experience in male prisons . . .'

Helen goggled. 'Me? As Governor?' A surge of wonderful excitement welled up inside. She felt breathless all of a sudden. 'Are you serious? Me?'

'It'll take a considerable time before the main wings will be habitable, and obviously it's not up to me, but—'

'Did he say there was a possibility?' She could hardly believe this, it was too incredible. *Governor of HMP Barfield?*

The door opened and Joyce, Mrs Redwood's secretary, came in. 'Sorry to interrupt.' She said to Helen, 'The photos of Tina's baby have arrived. Enid said you were going to pay for them.'

'What?' Helen frowned. 'Oh, yes, I did.'

'Apparently you said it was urgent,' Joyce insisted, giving her a look, and laying two folders in front of the Governor.

'Right, right.' Helen suddenly threw up her hands in an agony of frustration. 'Right, I'll see to it.'

'You have two adjudications, Mrs Redwood.'

'Thank you, Joyce.'

Helen had halted at the door, in a daze. Then she took a huge breath and marched out.

Watching her go, Joyce said in an undertone, 'You don't think they'll offer her Barfield, do you?'

'I have a nasty feeling they might,' Mrs Redwood said pensively.

'God help her.'

'My sentiments exactly.' She flipped open the top report. 'Right, let's get these sorted.'

Later that afternoon, John Bunny was in conference with Royston Andrews and Sean Duncan at Prison Service HQ. The problem hadn't been resolved, and for the sake of smooth relations with the press, if for no other reason, it had to be, and quick.

'Mrs Redwood felt that her priority should be to remain at Cattering Hall,' John Bunny explained. He fidgeted in his chair, anxious to get the whole business out of the way.

Royston Andrews wore a grin. 'I thought as much. She's a wily old cow, good governor. Right, let's have a look at the short list.' He puffed on his pipe, muttering round the stem, 'Strong contender is Gary Marshall, the present deputy of Barfield. Then there's Matthew Ettinger, Norman Littlejohn . . .'

'Have we put Helen Hewitt down on the list?' Sean Duncan asked.

John Bunny blinked at him. 'She's only just been promoted.'

Sean Duncan flicked a glance to Royston Andrews. 'I am aware of that, Mr Bunny,' he drawled.

Two drunken men were murdering the Everlys' 'Cathy's Clown' when Helen arrived, pushing her way through the crowd to the hen party, which had commandeered four tables slap bang in front of the karaoke stand. Clare and Enid were there, along with eight of the other officers, two social workers, and three women from the canteen. Plates of sandwiches and bowls of crisps were being passed round, and the small tables were crammed with bottles and glasses.

Helen leaned over to give Beryl Allington a kiss. 'Sorry I'm late.' She covered her ears, wincing at the noise. 'I said – sorry I'm late.'

'*Sit down*,' Beryl yelled back. She beckoned for the wine bottle. 'Drink for Helen, down here.'

She filled a wine glass to the brim and Helen raised it and took a gulp. 'Good luck, Beryl.' She took another. 'Cheers, Beryl.'

The Everlys were straining everything they'd got, receiving whistles, boos and catcalls from the tables below. Helen drained her glass, which was refilled immediately. She drank, licking wine from her lips, and burped. 'God, I hate this,' she told Beryl, grimacing up at the two guys swaying in the pink spotlight. 'I don't know how any sane person can get up and make themselves look so ridiculous.' She gave a pitying shake of the head. 'You'd never get me near one of those things.'

Enid nudged her. 'You got a lot of catching up to do, Helen. We've been here since seven.'

'Cathy's Clown' was mercifully put to death to a storm of applause, boos and jeers. Helen looked round as another commotion started, and pressed both hands to her face.

A big strapping bloke with gleaming muscles, naked except for a loincloth, was climbing over chairs and people. Somebody pointed out their table. He swaggered up and planted himself, legs apart, beating his chest, and with head thrown back let rip with a jungle cry.

'*Me Tarzan . . . Jane! . . . Jane!*'

Clare jabbed her finger, pointing at Beryl, who started screeching as the kissogram guy presented himself to her, swaying his oiled torso and thrusting out his pelvis.

'Oh, Beryl, Beryl, my idea of heaven . . . to lose you to another man . . .'

Beryl bounced up and down, screaming, as he opened his arms imploringly and reached out for her.

Laughing so hard that she nearly spilled her drink, Helen knocked it back in one, feeling the lovely warm alcoholic glow spreading through her.

'I want the new Governor settled and primed before we announce it to the field, and in particular the press,' Royston Andrews said. It was late and he was tired, but he felt happier now, the decision made.

John Bunny had departed over an hour ago. The Area Manager had made his recommendation, then left it to the Operational Director and the Home Office, whose ultimate responsibility it was.

'We're taking a big chance,' Sean Duncan said. 'Risk more like it.'

'I don't think so.' Andrews had his game-plan already worked out. 'The risk is minimal. She'll have two hundred prison officers looking after eighty-eight men. She's strong academically, with practical experience. I can actually see no risks, given the ratio of prison officers to inmates. If she works out, she can stay on. If not, it's a possibility that the prison will be recategorized and somebody of a higher rank will automatically take over.'

Duncan at once saw the beauty of it; he was filled with admiration. The plan was fail-safe. Helen Hewitt's present rank as Governor 3 was senior enough for her to be in charge. But when Barfield was re-established and possibly upgraded to a Category A maximum security prison, it would require, at the very least, a Governor 2, possibly even an Assistant Director. Helen Hewitt wouldn't qualify and could be moved on, quietly and without fuss.

'You're right,' Duncan nodded, 'it's a good choice. And she fitted in very well on the investigation team, and knows how to keep her mouth shut.'

'Press will love her,' Andrews said confidently. 'So it's agreed. Helen Hewitt will be the new Governor of Barfield.'

Clutching the microphone, face contorted in the pink spotlight, Helen was delivering a terrible strangled rendition of the Gloria Gaynor hit song to the swaying crowd below. Her two backing singers, both prison officers and equally piddled, were belting out the chorus.

'My God,' Beryl mumbled to Clare, 'I hope she's not driving herself home.'

Helen was really with it, whipping up the action to loud cheers, head thrown back, shaking and swinging her hips as she finished on a wail. '*I will survive, ohhhh yes, I will survive.*'

If HQ had had a glimpse of the proposed new Governor of Barfield in action, so to speak, they would have had more than a few doubts. Their choice, right at this moment, seemed highly questionable.

It had all been done in a rush. Helen had walked into an estate agent's in Market Harborough and fifteen minutes later walked out with the lease on a flat. It was on the second floor of a Victorian house on the edge of town, two rooms that had been knocked into a decent-sized living room overlooking a small park, bedroom, kitchen, and a tiny bathroom with a grumbling heating system. The wallpaper was insipid, the carpet stained, the paintwork grubby, but it would have to do for the time being; she had far more pressing concerns, and redecorating was at the bottom of the list.

At ten minutes past eight, dressed and ready for work, she stood in the hallway, anxiously watching as the removal men ferried in her things. She hoped they knew what they were doing. At the moment her Habitat sofa was half in, half out of the bedroom, her TV and stereo system festooned with wires on top of the small sideboard she used as a drinks cabinet.

Two men came up the stairs carrying a tea-chest apiece. Helen looked at her watch. Better get a move on.

'I've marked the items, which room and what goes where, so can I leave it with you?'

The foreman squeezed past, and with a grunt plonked the tea-chest in the doorway of the living room.

'You do all the unpacking?'

'Yes, ma'am, but you'll have to sign receipt of delivery.'

'Ah, well, I can't wait.' Helen shrugged into her raincoat, picked up her briefcase and shoulder bag. 'Will you send it to my office? I'll check it all later.'

'Sure, where you want it sent?'

'Barfield Prison.'

'Inmate, are you?' The foreman grinned.

'No, the Governor,' Helen said, half-way down the stairs, leaving him with his jaw hanging open.

A quarter of an hour later she drove past the visitors' car park and stopped the Mini Metro at the striped barrier, the outer gate entry to the staff compound. Closed-circuit cameras on high aluminium poles surveyed the area, feeding images back to the central control room above the gate lodge. The gate guard, buttons winking on his black tunic, peaked cap pulled low over his eyes, came out of the glass-walled cubicle, clipboard under his arm. He raised his hand, shaking his head in reprimand.

'This is a restricted area.'

'I know,' Helen said. The guard stared at her. 'Did nobody forewarn you of my arrival?'

'No.' He frowned down at the clipboard, then stared some more. 'Who have you come to see?'

Helen held up her ID. 'I am the new Governor of Barfield.'

From inside the gatehouse he watched her drive through, lowered the barrier and then flicked on the intercom. Mouth close to the mike, he alerted the officers monitoring the screens in the main control room. 'She's the new Governor of Barfield . . .'

Gary Marshall was not a happy man, but that was none of her doing. She'd been given a job to do, and her only concern was to do it, and see that it got done, to the best of her ability.

From his own office, two doors along, he took her into the Governor's office and stood by the desk, shifting his weight around, while Helen dumped her things. It was a corner room, light and airy, two large windows looking out onto the main prison yard, comfortably furnished, with two deep armchairs and a sofa grouped round a coffee table as an informal discussion area.

'Congratulations,' Marshall said, without much warmth. 'I presumed I'd be taking over. They at least had the decency to let me know.'

'I'm sorry.' Helen draped her raincoat over one of the armchairs and turned to him, chin up. 'But from you as my deputy, Gary, I'm going to need all the back-up I can get.'

He met her gaze. 'You'll have it.'

The door to the adjoining office opened and a plump, matronly woman with frizzy hair poked her head in.

Helen turned. 'Yes?'

'Er, do you want coffee?' she asked, addressing Marshall.

'I'm sorry, I don't know your name,' Helen said.

'Mavis O'Connell. I'm—'

'Secretary? Good, nice to know I'm not alone.' Helen beckoned her forward, holding out her hand.

Marshall said, 'This is Miss Helen Hewitt, Mavis, the new Governor.'

Mavis's faltering look passed from Marshall to Helen, her features sagging into a weak smile. From her bag Helen took a foil bag of vacuum-packed ground coffee and two china mugs.

'I like my coffee black, no sugar, and in a china mug. Do you have a percolator?'

Mavis was in a whirl, large brown eyes goggling. 'Er, yes . . . I think so.'

'Good,' Helen said brightly, passing them over. 'It's Amaretto coffee. I got used to it in the States.'

Marshall was hiding a faint derisive smile. Naturally, Asda's own brand wouldn't be nearly good enough, would it? Had to be some poncy foreign crap.

'Are we computerized here?' Helen asked as Mavis fumbled at the door.

The woman jumped, nearly dropping the mugs. 'Pardon?'

'Are the staff files on computer?'

'Er, no, not all of them.'

'Ah! Well, we'll have to get that sorted out.' Helen gave her an encouraging smile. 'Thank you, Mavis.'

Helen went round the desk. She picked up a note from the blotter. 'What's this?'

Marshall waited until the door had closed. He said quietly, 'Michael Winchwood's family is unhappy with the findings of the investigation results.'

'What?'

'I've referred them to the prison authorities.'

'Did you?' Helen said, studying him closely. She let the note fall to the desk. 'You want my honest opinion?'

Marshall raised an eyebrow. 'You're entitled to your opinion,' he said blandly.

'I don't think it was suicide,' Helen said, staring at him hard.

Tom Doughen and Damon O'Keefe were strapping on their radios, preparing for the morning rounds, when Gary Marshall walked in. He jerked his head. The two men sidled over to the corner. Marshall kept his voice down, even though the rest room was noisy with banter and the clashing of locker doors.

'You have a problem. New Governor doesn't believe Winchwood committed suicide.'

O'Keefe slammed his fist into a locker door. Marshall gripped his wrist, gave a warning shake of the head. 'You stick to the same stories. Okay? Agreed?' He looked into the eyes of each man. 'It'll be all right.'

'She can't prove anything, can she?' Doughen said, hooded eyes sullen.

'Not if we make sure of it.'

A general message came over the radio net from the control room, calling all outstations.

'Governor Hewitt would like all staff and personnel available to go to the cinema in thirty minutes, ten hundred hours. All stations from MS2D standing by.'

The three men exchanged glances, and then Marshall was gone, the door banging shut behind him.

Mavis came out of her office and stopped short, seeing Helen standing there, apparently for no purpose. Helen pointed to a door marked 'Toilet' at the end of the corridor.

'Is that the ladies' loo?'

'No.' Mavis turned to indicate the opposite way. 'You go to the end, first right, past the lifts, and it's at the bottom of the stairs at the end of the second corridor. You'll need a key.'

Helen strode off. 'Well, I haven't got time to walk half a mile if I need the loo. We'll make this one the Ladies'.' She pushed open the door of the Gents' and disappeared inside.

Mavis looked three ways at once, fluttering her hands. Helen had got her in such a spin she didn't know whether she was coming or going. She had worked at Barfield for nearly six years, ever since the kids were off her hands at school, the last three as Governor Langham's secretary. Up until now everything had been calm and orderly in her little world; one day much like the last, nothing to disturb the daily routine. Mr Langham had let her get on with things in her own way, and at her own pace. Mavis liked that. What she didn't like was to be rushed, and most of all she didn't like change. Why couldn't things stay the same? In less than two hours her safe little world had begun to tilt. Not only talk of computerizing the files, and having to brew fancy coffee, but now the most major disruption of all: turning the Gents' into the Ladies'.

She was at her desk, writing LADIES in black felt-tip on an A4 sheet of paper, when Gary Marshall came in.

'Got you working hard, has she?'

'You can say that again.' Mavis wore a look of silent suffering. 'You know that toilet, one at the end. Can you ask Maintenance to fix a proper "Ladies Only" notice on the door?'

Marshall pursed his lips in a sigh, dropped the files he was holding into a tray and started to leave.

'Oh, yes,' Mavis said. 'Michael Winchwood's family will need visiting orders for tomorrow. Will you sort them?'

Marshall looked at her over his shoulder. 'They coming here?'

'To collect his belongings, I presume.' Mavis was nodding and then started shaking her head. She threw up her hands. 'I haven't a clue, I don't know what I'm doing. She's got me running round like a scalded hen.'

'Tomorrow?' Marshall said. 'They're coming here?'

He barged out, making Mavis jump. She jumped again when Helen swept in.

'I want that replumbed and a shower unit put in.' Mavis hastily scribbled a note. She raised her head, pen poised.

'Right,' Helen said, checking the time. 'Where's the cinema?'

Tom Doughen was at the door, keeping look-out. He ducked back, mouthing, 'Here she comes', and nipped smartly into the second row, next to Damon O'Keefe.

Helen strode in, followed by Marshall. The assembled officers, forty or more, made a feeble effort at rising, some of them even managing a 'Morning, ma'am', before settling down again. As usual, given any opportunity, a majority of them were smoking; it was strictly forbidden to smoke in front of the inmates, and some governors frowned on lunchtime drinking because getting a whiff of an officer's breath sometimes riled the prisoners.

Helen stood before them with her arms folded. She was deliberately taking her time. Let them get a good look at her while she did the same with them. All men, of course, as she expected, not a female officer in sight. And the usual mix of ages, shapes and sizes. Big strapping blokes, like Russell Morgan in the front row, who kept in good shape with regular workouts. More the exception than the rule, though, the rest of average height and build, and some of the older officers a couple of stone overweight, with double chins and pot bellies. Plus one or two, Helen noted, really tough, mean-looking bastards, who but for their uniforms you might have mistaken for cons, not officers.

The NEPOs – Newly Enlisted Prison Officers – mostly at the younger end, were not long out of their nine-week training course at one of the two Prison Service colleges, Wakefield or Newbold Revel. The insiders' joke was that Newbold Revel turned out officers, while Wakefield turned out 'screws'. With a starting salary of £17,000, there was never a shortage of recruits, always a waiting list.

The older officers, many of whom had joined the Prison Service after a spell in the forces, were a hardened and, in many ways, a cynical bunch. Not without good reason. Over the years they had watched the law and order debate swing from 'hard' right to 'soft' left, hovering for a while in the liberal centre before swinging left or right and back again. Most of them were wearily resigned to the weather-vane of political chopping and changing, and also to the public's abysmal ignorance of penal institutions. Led by the nose by any tabloid editor who needed a quick, cheap, easy news fix, the poor deluded public simply didn't have a clue as to the realities that lay behind the screaming headlines.

Not that any of this really mattered. Not in strictly practical, operational terms anyway. Whichever particular reform was in vogue – lock 'em up and throw away the key, or use the resources for education and rehabilitation – it always came down to one simple truth. It was them that got the shitty end of the stick. They had to handle the situation, right there and then, at the sharp end. It was they who had to deal day in day out with the murderers, rapists, terrorists, professional criminals and gang bosses, the pimps and drug-dealeers, the socially inadequate and mentally subnormal, right down to the scrapings at the bottom of the barrel who were just plain evil little turds.

Helen was well aware of their attitude. But she had her own agenda too, and she was quietly, steadfastly determined to implement it, even if it meant upsetting a few fond, treasured traditions.

'First of all, can I say how pleased I am to be here as the new Governor of Barfield. There are three issues that are probably worrying you about my appointment.' Veiled looks along the rows, a few snide grins. 'One, that I am a woman. Two, my age. And three, am I going to stay? The first two I can do nothing about. But with regard to the third, let me tell you – I'm staying.'

She became aware that several of the officers were not looking at her, but at Gary Marshall behind her, probably studying his face for a reaction. She wouldn't have minded studying his face herself.

'As you must all be aware, the rebuilding of Barfield will continue, so our priority will be security during this period. But we are in the enviable situation of having only eighty-eight inmates and enough officers to control four hundred.' Many of them were nodding; in for a cushy ride, no doubt. Long tea-breaks. Fill in the pools.

Helen's eyes raked over them. 'I want this prison cleared of drugs.' She had been expecting a response of some kind. What she got was total silence and stillness, as if everyone in the smoke-filled room had suddenly mummified. 'I am fully aware that the main ringleaders of the riot have already been transferred, but the Home Office investigation implied that over one hundred and fifty men were involved in the peripheral skirmishes fuelling the riot. I intend to take a harsh line with any inmate attempting to create further disturbances whilst Barfield undergoes refurbishment. I will put my intentions in writing on the bulletin board, and I ask each and every one of you to give me every assistance in establishing the new regime.'

Nobody was watching Marshall now.

'My first order, as from today,' Helen said, 'is to withdraw all inmates' personal cell keys.' She glanced at her watch and clasped her hands together. 'I look forward to working with you all and getting to know each of you on a personal basis. If any of you now have any complaints or queries, please feel free to voice them.'

The rows of men were silent. The only sign of movement, as they dragged deeply on their cigarettes, was smoke rising in clouds.

'Thank you very much,' Helen said. And with a brief nod to Marshall she left the room.

Mavis scowled, almost getting elbowed out of the way as she pinned up notices on the bulletin board. The ruck of men crowded around her, Tom Doughen in the thick of it, his finger tracing the lines as he read out loud: '"If it is discovered that any man employed here has assisted or passed on any narcotic substances . . ."'

'What?' Damon O'Keefe said, thrusting forward.

'". . . as from now, every man coming into this prison must be willing to be searched, which includes all staff. My intention and priority is to clear Barfield Prison of drugs."'

A chorus of angry grumbles and scornful abuse from the officers at the back, trying to get a look-in. The woman needed her head examined.

'She wants every cell and inmate strip-searched as from eleven thirty tomorrow morning,' Marshall said, turning away from the board with a weary shake of the head.

'She's shipped in dog-handlers from Frankland to assist the search,' Russell Morgan said. His sandy eyebrows came together in a thick bristling bar. 'What's this?'

'Rate she's going,' Marshall jeered, 'be more bloody canines than inmates.'

'Bloody hell, look at this one,' Doughen said, reading over Mavis's head. 'She wants the prisoners in the yard to see the dogs and see we are searching their wings.'

'There is no exercise yard in use,' Morgan said.

'Wrong.' Marshall was shaking his head. 'Yard 2 is to be cleared by prison staff.'

O'Keefe pushed his way out, his face tight and livid. 'She's nuts, they'll go ape-shit when we take their keys off them.' His voice went up. 'She's going to start another fuckin' riot!'

'From us or the inmates?' Morgan wondered aloud.

Helen trudged up the stairs and let herself into her new flat. She was dying for two things: a hot shower and a hard drink. Well, three things would have been OK, if she could have raised the energy, but there was no likelihood of that at the moment.

It took a little time, fumbling on the strange wall to find the light switch, and then the bare bulb in the hallway came on. Helen stared around and sagged against the doorframe.

Piled high, one on top of the other, the hallway was filled with tea-chests and boxes, some of them half unpacked, most of them not. She poked her head into the kitchen. Boxes on the floor, on the work surfaces, even on the cooker.

'Shit!'

It was some small achievement that they'd put the bed in the bedroom, leaning on its end against the wall. In the centre of the room, her dressing table and wardrobe formed a cosy group, along with a large cardboard box of pillows and sheets half unpacked.

Helen closed her eyes and sighed, then she tossed off her coat and heaved the unmade bed down, flopping across it in total exhaustion. She lay there, too tired to move, too frazzled even to contemplate how she was going to get through the next day. But get through it she would. She just wished for someone to talk to but there was no one.

Meanwhile the return of all prisoners' keys was in progress, each prisoner listed, each key tagged and checked, and the brewing unease was felt by every officer. It was only the beginning of the new regime, just the beginning.

Chapter 6

THE GANG of workmen lounged against the lorry at the perimeter gate, sneaking a quick fag while their foreman had a long chin-wag with the guard. Finally he returned, shaking his head. 'Okay, fellas, new ruling. Every man's gotta be searched before we enter the gate and when we leave.'

'But, gov,' one of them protested, 'I'm just workin' here. You sure they're gonna bleedin' let us out?'

A green prison van drew up. Three officers went round and opened the rear doors, and much to the amusement of the workmen led out two muzzled cocker spaniels.

'Oi!' one of the workmen shouted. 'Can't you lot run to a German shepherd, then?'

Laughing and pointing, he spun round and nearly leapt out of his skin as four huge German shepherds, snarling and barking, went past at a trot, straining at their handlers' leashes.

'Bloody hell!' he gulped.

Senior Officer Russell Morgan, in charge of C Wing, had them all out on the landings, standing there in vests and underpants, as his officers conducted a 'spin' – the thorough cell search that all inmates hated, seeing it as an invasion of their home and private space, an intrusive mauling of their personal belongings.

'Come on, move it!' Damon O'Keefe shouted to a couple of laggards. 'Governor's orders!'

'You tell that new bastard he'll be sorry,' Tony Murphy said, spitting out the words in a strong Liverpool accent. On the outside he was known as 'Mad Eyes' Murphy, for the perverse reason that his eyes never showed any emotion whatsoever. His brown-eyed stare under bristling dark eyebrows remained flat and dead, his thin mouth half hidden under a straggling Zapata-style moustache. But no one ever called him 'Mad Eyes' to his face. He was the wing 'boss', serving nine years for armed robbery, respected and feared by the other cons on Charlie Wing. Each wing had its boss, its top man, which the prison authorities knew about and tacitly went along with.

'You can tell Miss Hewitt yourself, Murphy,' O'Keefe said, grinning. The news that the new Governor was female hadn't filtered down yet. He barked out, 'Vernon, move it!'

Vernon Black was leaning indolently against the wall, his eyes heavy-lidded. He'd been on the waccy-baccy since nine that morning, and it was a rude surprise when the screws suddenly appeared, hauling him off his fluffy pink cloud. Nearly six feet tall, long in the face with an angular jaw, the gold stud in his ear and spiky blond hair gave him a punkish appearance. As if he had all the time in the world, he ambled across the landing to the rail, carrying a CD player in the crook of his arm.

'Better put that on your possessions list, Vernon,' Tom Doughen warned him. All inmates' possessions were supposed to be listed, to prevent pilfering amongst them. It was a serious breach of regulations to omit anything.

Officers moved along the line, giving each inmate a rub-down – a quick body search. Tony Murphy stood with bunched fists, staring straight ahead, a muscle twitching in his neck as he endured this humiliation. Next to him, Dougie Jellings, not quite as tall as Murphy but with massive shoulders and brawny, tattooed arms, uttered a low stream of abuse as he watched the cell spin in progress. Everything came out – was tossed out onto the landing. His bedding, clothing, all his personal gear, pictures stripped off the walls, books dumped on the floor, not a stick of furniture or the smallest item overlooked.

'Come on, get back in,' Doughen shouted when it was over. 'Get yourselves in order.'

Each man had to replace all the furniture, collect his own belongings and make his cell ship-shape. They hated this almost as much as the spin itself.

Gary Marshall came up, nodding to O'Keefe. 'Governor's doing a round.' He lowered his voice. 'Let's show we're doing her order to the letter.'

At the far end of the landing, Russell Morgan raised an arm.

'We're clear, ready for inspection.'

He patrolled slowly along past the open cell doors. 'New Governor's coming round. One of you put one foot out of line and you go down the Block.'

A voice behind him, belonging to an officer, muttered, 'You talking about us?' He didn't sound to be joking.

Royston Andrews had only just banged the phone down when Sean Duncan entered his office. He looked up, tight-lipped. 'Just hold the press circus off Barfield and Helen Hewitt.'

'Now what?'

'Her deputy's just called and said she is using, and I quote, "Gestapo methods".' Andrews picked up his empty pipe from the ashtray and blew through it. 'She's brought in extra sniffer dogs and handlers from Frankland, Durham, Whitemoor—'

'Yes, I know.' Duncan dropped into a chair and crossed his legs, plucking at the crease in his trousers. 'I gave my approval. She also wants to implement random urine tests. Again, with my approval.'

Andrews felt a spasm of irritation. He said curtly, 'I'll have to speak to the Area Manager, John Bunny, tell him to advise her to slow down. Sounds like she's staging an advert for Pedigree dog food.'

Sean Duncan was unperturbed. His allegiances were political. 'The Home Office would be very pleased to know that steps are being taken to solve the drug problems at Barfield.'

'Well, there's another problem,' Andrews said, hoping at least to dent that smirk. 'Michael Winchwood's family are unhappy with the investigation into their son's death. They have asked for a meeting with the new Governor.'

'Well, good.' Sean Duncan spread his hands. 'She was on the investigation team, she can put their minds at rest.' He inclined his head, a ghost of a smile hovering. 'Perhaps you should make sure that she does.'

'Staff are getting very edgy about the landings being searched,' Gary Marshall told Helen as they passed through the double set of gates into C Wing.

Helen waited while he relocked the inner gate. Being within earshot of the prisoners, she kept her voice down. 'If there are drugs in this prison, then I am going to find them, and I am going to find out who is bringing them in.'

'You ever think that maybe, just maybe,' Marshall said with faint sarcasm, 'it could be the prisoners?'

They were walking along the ground floor, the inmates sitting at their small tables or on their beds, watching them pass by through the open doors. Officers were stationed on both landings, observing but keeping a discreet distance.

'The prisoners?' Helen frowned at him. 'What are you telling me? They're leaving here, going out and scoring and bringing it back in?' He wasn't the only one who could be sarcastic.

'I meant their visitors,' Marshall said testily.

'Ah, visiting rights.' Helen peered inside a cell and moved on. 'They will be reinstated, as from tomorrow.'

Marshall had promised himself he would remain cool, but she was pushing and pushing, and his cool was running out. 'That's going to weigh very heavy with security,' he told her, trying to keep his voice even.

'And as from now,' Helen went on, 'we need to get back to the basics of security.' She stopped and confronted him, eye to eye. 'Any visitor discovered passing or bringing drugs in will have their visits curtailed, and further visits reviewed, possibly facing criminal charges.'

Marshall bridled. 'I am warning you—'

'And I am warning you, Gary.' Her eyes didn't waver. 'Because I have not finished. I've only just started.'

She turned away, quickly scanning the details on the card of the nearest cell, and leaned in. 'Good morning, it's Mr Leighton, isn't it?'

A rather meek-looking, middle-aged man shuffled forward in carpet slippers, smiling hesitantly.

'This is the new Governor, Helen Hewitt,' Marshall said stiffly.

'Nice to meet you, Miss,' said Leighton, taking Helen's proffered hand.

Helen smiled and moved on. She passed from cell to cell, nodding, smiling, shaking hands, having the odd friendly word. Marshall traipsed behind, swallowing his boiling anger. Just look at her. Lady Bountiful. Like the bloody Queen Mother.

Marshall's heavy tread followed Helen into Mavis's office. 'I'd like to tour the VP Wing after lunch,' she told him, looking round for the absent Mavis, who at that moment appeared behind them from the corridor. She looked uncertainly at Helen, and then at Marshall.

'Yes?' Helen said. She didn't mean to sound sharp, but she was getting sick of Mavis deferring to Marshall all the time.

'Mr and Mrs Winchwood have arrived, plus a Norman Sewell.' Mavis used her thumb to indicate the visitors' waiting room. 'And I have two girls from the temp agency waiting to be interviewed . . . oh, and the furniture removal firm have called twice.'

Helen held up a hand. 'Hold the Winchwoods, send in one girl at a time, give them five minutes each, Mavis.' She went to the adjoining door to her office. 'And, Mavis, arrange for someone to clean out my flat, will you? Ring an agency, anything, but it's a mess. Tell the removal company I'm missing two crates.'

She opened the door. 'I'm sorry, Gary, you'll have to excuse me.'

Already following behind, Marshall checked his stride. 'Don't you want me in on the Winchwood meeting?'

'No.'

The door closed. Marshall swung round, brows beetling. 'Has HQ called her about the Winchwoods' visit?'

Mavis shook her head. 'I don't think so.'

What the hell was going on around here? Marshall brooded, heading back to his office. He'd spoken twice to HQ. It was his understanding they were going to call Miss Fragrant Drawers, knock it on the head.

He put a call through to Royston Andrews, but it didn't get him very far. In fact it didn't get him anywhere; apparently the visit had been rubber-stamped by the Home Office. Andrews said testily, 'Just find out what the Winchwoods want and get back to me as soon as you can, or ask Miss Hewitt to contact me.'

Fat lot of use that was, Marshall brooded, putting the phone down. How could he find out when he wasn't even in the damn meeting? Things were getting out of hand. Spinning out of control. But definitely.

Moira Levitt was tall, black, with a mass of black, tightly curled hair that seemed to hover around her dark elliptical eyes and slanting brows and, as if that weren't enough, a wonderful figure. Quite a stunner.

Her long tapering fingers tapped expertly at the computer keyboard in Mavis's office while Helen stood watching, arms folded, more impressed by the minute. Certainly better than the first girl, by a mile.

'It's WordPerfect program,' Moira said, 'good.' She called up the main menu, nodding to herself. 'Mind you, probably with the amount of staff references you'd be best to have the Windows program on hard disk as well.'

'Does it worry you about working in a prison, even just temporarily?'

'No, why should it?' Against the smooth dark complexion her smile was dazzling. 'They're not running the offices, are they?'

This made Helen chuckle. 'I don't know about that.' She glanced at her watch and held out her hand. 'Okay, thanks for coming in. We'll call your agency.'

Moira collected her bag and coat. 'Thank you for seeing me.'

Helen ushered her out.

'Show in Mr and Mrs Winchwood.' Helen paused at the door. 'Who is the man with them?'

Mavis was stumped. 'Er, I dunno.'

'Ask, Mavis, and all will be divulged. And the last girl, if her details are okay and she checks out with Security, give her the job.'

'That one?' Mavis said, pointing to the door which had closed but a moment ago.

Helen nodded patiently; she didn't even sigh. 'There were only two, Mavis. Oh, did you get someone to clean my place?'

Mavis bit her lip. Helen did sigh. She made a 'be gone' motion of her hand and went back inside, and did a swift refurbishment job: flicked a comb through her hair, freshened her lipstick, and gave herself a squirt of Chanel.

Seated at her desk, she spread her arms helplessly at the

mess in front of her. Letters, memos and official documents with the Prison Service logo were piled high. Two huge stacks of prisoner dossiers and progress reports she was supposed to be working her way through threatened to topple over. Duty rosters and catering menus for the coming week waiting to be authorized. She needed help, urgently, and organization, before she was engulfed. She had cleared most of it to a side cupboard, the rest on the window ledge, when Mavis entered and stood aside, holding the door open.

'Mr and Mrs Winchwood and their legal adviser, Mr Norman Sewell.'

'Do come in.' Helen rose with a smile. 'I apologize for the state of my office.' She called out as the door was closing, 'Coffee, Mavis,' and indicated the semi-circle of leather-backed chairs. 'Please do sit down.'

'Thank you,' Mrs Winchwood said. She perched uneasily on the edge of the chair, clasping her handbag in both hands. A thin woman with greying hair, recently permed, and anxious, restless eyes, she was smartly dressed in a tweed topcoat and pleated skirt.

Helen hadn't formed any preconceptions about the Winchwoods; nevertheless she was slightly taken aback that they were eminently respectable, middle class and fairly well-to-do. But, then, what had she been expecting? The tragedy of having a son commit such crimes against children was not restricted by class, wealth, or respectability.

Mr Winchwood cleared his throat. 'We wished to see you with regard to the police investigation into our son's death,' he began quietly, and then hesitated, looking towards Norman Sewell, who had no such reservations.

'We are very disappointed,' Sewell said at once, in an unpleasant nasal voice, one that could cut through saloon-bar chatter and get him served first. 'No arrest has been made and yet everyone concerned in this tragic affair knows that Michael died in what can only be described as a horrific, violent and disgusting manner.' He pronounced it 'vio-lent'.

'I am sorry,' Helen replied, 'but Michael's death was determined as suicide by the Home Office pathologist.'

Mr Winchwood pressed his palms together. 'You must understand, Miss Hoolitt—'

'Hewitt.'

'I'm sorry . . . Miss Hewitt.' He coughed. 'We know the crimes my son was charged with, and no matter what we feel, what shame we shared with him, he was still our son.' His face was wretchedly bleak, his eyes full of pain.

'I do understand,' Helen said gently.

'He was prepared to do his sentence,' Mr Winchwood went on, 'serve his punishment. He should have been protected from the other inmates, from himself.'

'Michael was – as you must have been aware due to the type of crimes he had committed – segregated from the main prison wings.'

'In his letters he said he was frightened ever to leave his cell,' Mrs Winchwood said tearfully. 'He was even scared to eat the food he was given . . .'

Mr Winchwood leaned forward. 'When they moved him here, he said it was even worse than the other prison, that he'd be better off dead.'

Evidently, in Sewell's opinion, it was time to get down to cases. He fixed Helen with piercing eyes. 'Mr and Mrs Winchwood have asked me to undertake a private civil action against Barfield Prison, citing gross negligence to blame for the death of their son, Michael.'

Helen drew a lined pad towards her. She unscrewed her pen. 'Did Michael ever mention any particular prisoner who made threats? Not from his first prison, but here, Barfield?'

'No, but he had lost so much weight,' Mrs Winchwood said, the tears welling, 'and when we last saw him his nerves were very bad—'

She choked up, shaking her head, lips tightly compressed.

Her husband added, 'We even warned the previous governor, Mr Langham, that Michael was suicidal, and yet no action was taken.'

Helen nodded. She let a moment or two pass, and then said, 'You must understand that, well, even though every precaution is taken to protect sex offenders, particularly child sex offenders, and in Michael's case a brutal child murder—'

Sewell's elbow was on the corner of her desk, his head thrust towards her. 'There is no need for this, Miss Hewitt.'

Helen stayed calm. 'I am just stating facts, Mr Sewell, and the problems we have with men on Rule 43 within a prison of this size.' She looked to the Winchwoods. 'They are not all sex offenders. Some are in debt and scared to be on the main wings. Some are mentally vulnerable . . .'

There was a short interruption while Mavis brought in a tray and placed it on the coffee table. She seemed to be lingering, setting out the cups and saucers, as Helen went on, putting the record straight: 'There was a full-scale police inquiry and an investigation by the prison authorities into Michael's death.'

Sewell had a nasty grin. 'Investigation or cover-up? Have you seen the medical reports?'

He swivelled round in his chair as Helen got up and crossed to the coffee table. 'There was, to my knowledge, no cover-up, Mr Sewell,' Helen assured him. 'None whatsoever.'

Watching Mavis as she straightened up, Helen said, 'Black or white, Mrs Winchwood?' She gave an icy smile. 'Thank you, Mavis.'

Mavis swiftly departed, pulling the door shut behind her with exaggerated care. She let go the handle and looked over her shoulder.

'What's going on?' Marshall said.

'She said there was no cover-up, none whatsoever,' Mavis hissed, her eyes wide and round.

Inside the office, Helen screwed the cap on her fountain pen and sat back, folding her arms.

'Would you drop the civil action if I personally undertake an investigation into your son's death?'

'All I want is justice.'

Helen nodded slowly. She breathed out. 'I'll see that you get it, Mr Winchwood.'

Chapter 7

MAVIS SHOWED Moira Levitt to her desk. She was in two minds about the temporary as she herself had coped perfectly well with everything for Governor Langham, and even if she was a bit frazzled at times, she usually got everything done . . . eventually. Moira was quiet, methodical and seemed to have her desk organized within minutes. She then set up her word processor, asking Mavis a stream of questions. She wanted to know where everything was kept, from print paper to discs. At the same time out came a neat collection of pens, pencils, jotting pads, yellow stickers, and she clocked on fast that Mavis, although able to use the computers, was limited to the fundamentals and seemed obsessed with 'save', repeating over and over to Moira that she must be careful to ensure that she save all the files as she had on numerous occasions lost half a day's work. She passed over Helen's thick leatherbound diary.

'Did Miss Hewitt say how long she would be requiring you?'

Moira shrugged. 'Oh, the agency said I would probably become full time. Do you mind if I suggest that we should use the Windows program to formulate Miss Hewitt's diary so we can see at a glance what her schedule is, where she is right now?'

Mavis pursed her lips, unsure how you got into the Windows program. She busied herself with her In and Out trays. 'Yes, you can begin that, dear. I've got a lot to be getting on with. I think she's gone over to the VP Wing.'

Moira's hands flew over the keys and rattled the irritated Mavis, who took herself off to brew some coffee. Full time! It would have been nice if Helen had mentioned that to her.

Accompanied by Curtis 'Jumbo' Jackson, Helen was on her way from the admin block to the VP Wing. There were many hulking great men on the officers' roster, but Jackson outdid the lot of them, in height, weight and girth. An ex-regular, after serving eleven years and leaving the Forces as a drill sergeant, he'd joined the Prison Service five years ago, starting out at Wakefield, or 'Monster Mansion' as it was known due to the large number of sex offenders incarcerated there. Barrel-chested and as solid as a tank, he had a full dark beard, a nose like a squashed potato, and a Black Country accent you could cut with a knife. In his army days he'd been the regimental karate champion, and was no mean practitioner at judo and Thai boxing.

As they crossed the yard, Helen was gratified to see that the sniffer dogs had been brought out into the exercise yard. They trotted, noses down, tails wagging, in and out of the circling line of inmates. She stopped and watched as one dog dashed over to the corner and started pawing the cindery earth. Found a hidden stash, no doubt. It wouldn't be the last. A burst of cheering went up, the laughing inmates giving the slow handclap.

Seeing Helen pass by made Damon O'Keefe jittery. He strolled over to Tom Doughen, the pair of them overseeing the exercise period. 'Where's she off this morning?'

'VP Wing. Stop panicking.'

'Just as long as she's not talking to those two bastards,' O'Keefe said, jerking his head to where 'Mad Eyes' Murphy and his constant companion, Dougie Jellings, stood watching the dog's antics.

They were just finishing breakfast on the VP Wing. Men carried their own trays down to the trolleys on the ground floor, then hung around whiling away a few extra minutes before the unbroken boredom of the day got a grip.

Arnie Franks was sitting on his unmade bed, picking morosely at a scab on his mouth. His breakfast tray was beside him, untouched.

Helen went in, Jackson filling the doorway behind her.

'I'm the new Governor,' Helen said, giving the cell the once-over. Slopping out was still necessary on some of the wings, but thankfully not here; even though it measured only thirteen feet by six feet six, this cell had its own toilet bowl, minus seat, and tiny stainless-steel washbasin. The small high window could be opened from the inside by reaching through the yellow-glossed bars. A pair of 'greys' – dark grey trousers worn for visits – hung over the bedrail. There were a few bent and tattered paperbacks on the small table, a chess set, a greasy pack of cards, and not much else, unless you counted a faint yet pervasive odour, unpleasantly rancid, as if something was slowly decaying. 'I'm afraid Mr Langham isn't here any more.'

Franks didn't look up. 'They told me he's gone,' he said, hardly audible. He inspected a smear of blood on his thumbnail.

'You've requested a visiting order, haven't you?' Franks nodded at the floor. 'There you are,' Helen said, holding out an applications slip. 'All you have to do is fill this in.' She placed the 'app' beside him.

Franks looked at it and squirmed away, his face breaking down, fists clenching at his temples.

'It's what you want, isn't it?' Helen asked kindly.

He was nodding and weeping, pushing his fists into his eyes, shoulders hunched and shaking.

Helen came out. Wearing a frown she consulted her clipboard, asking Jackson his first name. 'Curtis.'

She was tall, but next to him she felt like a pygmy. 'How long has Arnie Franks been on all this medication?'

'I don't know. He's just been brought back on the wing from the hospital. He should be in Broadmoor, not here,' he said sourly, and gave an indifferent shrug. 'I don't know what gets him going.'

'You had better try to find out.' He didn't much like the sharp look, she could tell. 'These men are in your care. It does help if you know or are aware of what upsets them. I'll speak to Dr Thomas.'

'Hey!' Grinning, Jackson looked over her head. 'He's just eaten that form you gave him.'

'Perhaps it's preferable to that congealed mess we call breakfast,' Helen retorted, walking off. 'See if you can get him some exercise today.'

He lumbered after her. 'If you say so.'

'You were not on duty the night Michael Winchwood died?'

'No, I was called in for the riot. We all were.'

'How did you get on with Winchwood?'

'I didn't.' He was answering her questions sullenly now, the bare minimum that courtesy would allow.

Helen stopped and looked up at him. 'Curtis, I worked hard to get the title "Governor". Please use it.'

He reddened, following her down the wing. These ball-busters got on his tits.

Some of the cells were empty, having sustained damage during the riot, rubble on the floor and pools of water from leaking pipes. Helen checked her clipboard, moving on to the next occupied cell.

'Nonces, nonces! Dirty perverts . . .'

The enraged shouts were coming from the exercise yard, directly below the windows of the VP Wing.

'I screwed your mother, dirty fuckin' nonces!'

'We could have trouble,' Jackson said, nodding towards the shouts, getting louder by the minute. Helen ignored the comment, pointed to the cell door. With a sigh he couldn't be bothered to hide, Jackson turned the key and pushed open the door with a hand the size of a shovel. 'Prisoner 653, Gregory Colly, Governor.'

Surprised and charmed, Helen's mouth curved into a smile as she gazed inside. The cell was filled with models intricately made out of matchsticks. They were beautiful – galleon, windmill, farmhouse, castle, the Eiffel Tower, and dozens more, including a vast model of Big Ben still under construction. Gregory Colly got to his feet, a small, bald-headed pixie of a man, knocking on for sixty, with twinkling brown eyes and a ready smile that revealed missing front teeth. He shuffled forward, thin veined hands clasped at the chest of his blue workshirt.

'Good morning, Miss, welcome to my billet. Did they tell you about my glue sit-iation?' Cockney born and bred. 'Mr Langham always saw to it personally.' He gently touched one of the models. 'I never cheat, never stick a few together, always one at a time. Perfectionist, me,' he added proudly.

'Very impressive,' Helen said, bending to inspect the galleon. 'You were on the same landing as—'

'Michael Winchwood? Yers, that is correct, Miss, I was, but . . .' He leaned close, as if to confide in her. 'It's imperative I get me glue,' he whispered hoarsely. 'Now I know the problems, Miss, I know. But I have never, swear on the Bible, ever bin under the influence.' He leaned even closer. 'It's too precious a substance to me, you understand, Miss?'

'I know about your request, Gregory. I will see you get your glue.'

'Oh, Gawd bless you,' Colly whined, wringing his hands. 'I've not bin able to sleep—'

'Where were you the night Winchwood attempted suicide?'

Colly was shaking his head, eyes wide and so sincere it hurt. 'Out for the count, heavy sleeper, Miss.'

Not bad for an insomniac, Helen thought.

'You ever hear any threats against Winchwood? Talk to him?' She was aware of Jackson's breathing behind her; though perhaps with his bulk he always breathed heavily.

'Me? Who, me?' Colly said, pointing to himself, as if astonished. 'I'm a special.' He gave a guarded look towards Jackson, his voice dropping to its hoarse whisper. 'I used to be segregated for me own safety. I still don't ever see nobody. I miss the music, though,' he muttered reminiscently. 'Winchwood played nice music, hopera.'

'Nice little bloke, no trouble,' Jackson said, locking up. 'That's why we moved him from the seg unit, but we still exercise him solo.' Hooking the chained bunch of keys onto his belt, he looked down at Helen. 'Know what he's in for?'

Muffled by the iron door, a strangulated rendition in ripe Cockney of 'O Sole Mio' escaped onto the landing.

'Yes.' Gregory Colly had thirteen convictions for child sexual abuse going back over twenty-five years. Arrested yet again, he had confessed to the murder of three small children, disposing of their bodies on the same waste tip in Stoke Newington.

'Ah, well, he's got his hobby,' Jackson said.

'Did Michael Winchwood have a hobby?'

'Yeah, making our life difficult.' His radio crackled. 'Hello Tango 3 from MS2D. DCI Dunes is here to see the Governor.'

Jumbo Jackson acknowledged the message, sounding as relieved as if his piles had just healed.

Mavis had the percolator on simmer in the small open kitchen area when Marshall appeared along the corridor. She pulled a face at him. 'She only has it in china mugs.'

'Make it two.' Marshall waggled his thumb to indicate a rather gaunt-faced man in his late thirties ambling along behind him, hands in raincoat pockets. He had watchful, deep-set dark eyes and a thin cap of hair brushed forward to offset his receding hairline.

'Detective Chief Inspector Francis Dunes for Miss Hewitt,' he said with a smile, and tapped his watch. 'Bit early.'

Marshall followed the pair of them along to Mavis's office. Watching out for Dunes to show had paid off: he wanted to keep tabs on this situation.

A minute later Helen arrived, slightly out of breath, a faint bloom of colour in her cheeks. Dunes shook her hand, a smile on his lips, his dark gaze a damn sight too appreciative for Marshall's liking. 'Nice to meet you. I'm Detective Chief Inspector—'

'Dunes, unusual name,' Helen said, returning his smile. 'Well, I suppose you know who I am. Helen Hewitt.'

He nodded and smiled again. Marshall stood on the sidelines rubbing his double chin, getting a mite pissed off with this mutual smiling contest.

'How are the sniffer dogs doing?' asked Dunes.

'From what I've heard, reeling!' Helen said with a laugh. 'And not just from drugs. Inmates somehow got their hands on mustard powder and pepper. Our dogs are sneezing, never mind the handlers.'

She held out her hand, ushering him towards her office.

Marshall became alert. 'Do you want me in with you, Governor?'

'No, thank you.' At the door Helen turned. 'Mavis, could you see if Dr Thomas can see me at some point today? Just for a general chat.'

She went in, leaving Marshall glowering at the closed door. He stood there, rubbing his knuckles, shoulders up round his neck.

'Michael Winchwood,' Helen said as Francis Dunes removed his raincoat and settled himself. 'You think it was suicide?' She nodded thanks to Mavis, who placed the tray on the corner of the desk and departed. At least her desk didn't look as if a whirlwind had passed over it, Helen thought gratefully, now that Moira Levitt had come on board. She decided to employ her full time.

'We have statements from Officers Phillips, O'Keefe, Morgan, Jenson, Fuller, Macaulay, plus further statements from two auxiliary officers.' He reeled them off lightly, on top of the case, no need for notes, which impressed Helen. 'He was alone in his cell,' Dunes concluded, dark eyes fixed upon her.

'Obviously, if eight officers say he was,' Helen murmured, with a half-smile, and leaned over to pour the coffee.

'Consensus is, he deserved what he got,' Dunes said. 'White.' Helen added milk. 'But if you unearth any further evidence, the inquiry will swing back into my lap.' He accepted the coffee and took a sip. 'Until it does, we accept the suicide as read.'

Helen looked up, irritated, as Marshall tapped on the door and put his head round. 'Yes?'

'Sorry, Governor. One of the cooks, he's just been held at the gate, big commotion.'

'Thank you, Gary, I'll be right down.'

Marshall hung on a moment, until it became apparent that she meant in her own good time. Then he reluctantly withdrew.

Helen's irritation was still on her face when Dunes said, right out of the blue, 'You mind if I ask, are you married?'

'No, no, I'm not.'

'Maybe we could have dinner one night – I mean when you're not so busy . . .' Dunes smiled, but was left alone with his hopeful smile as Helen swept out.

The cook causing the commotion at the gate lodge was a young black guy wearing jeans and a black leather jacket, dreadlocks pinned to his head under a woollen ski cap. He was backing away, palms raised, surrounded by two gate officers and a sniffer dog that was straining at the handler's leash.

'You know me, man, what you think I am, one of them?' He jabbed towards the wings through the barred gates. 'No way. Get away from me. I soddin' work here, man – no way – you are not gonna do this to me, what you think I am?'

The gate officers were attempting to placate him, but he had his eyes on the dog, dancing out of the way as it sniffed at his trainers.

'No way! GET BACK FROM ME!'

'Everybody has to be subjected to it, Jonah, we've all had it done. It's a new regulation,' the gate guard soothed him, edging forward. 'Now just ease up . . .'

'I've worked here for four years!'

The cook's indignation sounded genuine enough, but it didn't convince the dog, emitting loud yelps now, dragging its handler forward. Helen glanced at Marshall, his face like a thundercloud.

Mentally she chalked one up for herself.

A dozen or more small plastic bags, sealed and tagged, were lined up on the table in the officers' rest room. Helen was in the process of checking them out, holding them up for inspection, shaking the contents. Quite a selection. Dried-leaf cannabis, Algerian Red by the look of it, and small cubes of cannabis resin. Some whitish-grey rocks that looked like crack, and two or three bags containing white tablets, possibly Ecstasy mixed with amphetamine sulphate, 'sulph' as it was known.

Helen checked them out, but didn't break the seal; all prison staff were trained not to touch raw substances with their fingers.

'Now, we know where some of the gear's coming from, but is this all we got out of their cells?'

'They're tossin' it,' said Marshall with a shrug.

'So they're all just flinging it out of the cell window, are they?' Helen sighed, shaking her head. She looked round searchingly at the group of officers, expecting, or at least hoping for, some input.

Damon O'Keefe shifted his seventeen-stone bulk onto

the other foot. The marked redness of his face above the scrubby gingerish beard was a permanent fixture, Helen had decided, more to do with blood pressure than undue exertion or the sunbed.

He delivered his usual caustic opinion. 'No matter how decent the cell, own toilet, all that, etcetera, they still have to chuck their shit out the window. And not just the type you smoke,' he added, labouring the point.

Helen raised her hand. 'Thank you, Mr O'Keefe,' she said wearily, and pointed to a plastic bucket on the floor.

'Home brew in their slop-out buckets,' Russell Morgan said. 'Disgustin' home-made hooch – it's lethal. They put the lid half-way, fill it with yeast, sugar, fruit. That's the fourth bucketful we got.' He favoured Helen with a snide grin. 'Get the same problem in Cattering Hall? You want to try it?'

Helen wrinkled her nose in distaste. The officers exchanged grins. She ain't seen nothing yet.

'I'd say this is about all we're likely to get,' Marshall told her.

'Is there any way any prisoner from C Wing can transfer goods from their division to another?' She looked from face to face, waiting for a response. 'Apart from throwing it out of their cell window?'

It was like pulling teeth, getting information out of this lot. Talk about a closed shop. Her stare rested on Doughen, who finally cleared his throat.

'Yeah. They tie it with a bit of dental floss and swallow it. I mean, you want us to get X-ray units in here next?' He tried to stare her down, an insolent twist to his mouth. 'They shove it in their ears, shove it up their noses, shove it up their arse—'

Helen got the picture. 'Thank you,' she said curtly. 'I still want another search.' This didn't go down at all well. Mumbles, grumbles, head-shaking, some muttered obscenities. 'This time we'll go in at night, when they're not expecting it,' she ground on, cutting through their objections. 'I want every prisoner out of his cell. That's *all* non-VP prisoners.'

'What? No way,' Marshall objected. 'Right now, tension is already getting out of hand. After the strip-searches this'll—'

Quiet and clipped, Helen addressed the room. 'So, we give them something to take their minds off the tension.'

She gave a quick nod and went to the door, touching Marshall's sleeve as she passed. 'In my office, please, Gary.'

'Hey, you hear she asked Colly if he'd talked to Winchwood?' O'Keefe said when Helen and Marshall had gone. He affected a prissy posh accent: '"I am familiarizing myself with all the cons' records."' He blew a fat raspberry.

'She's commandeered that toilet near the offices,' Morgan put in. 'Means if Gary needs to take a leak he's got half a mile to walk. New toilet, shower, tiles . . .'

Doughen guffawed. 'Hey, you hear about her with Arnie Franks? Jumbo Jackson told us – said she must have remembered what the old Gov did, you know, sayin' he got a visitor, right? She only gives him a bleedin' VO app to fill out. Dun't even know he can't bleedin' read or write! Jackson said, "Excuse me, Arnie's just eaten it . . . "' He choked with laughter. 'Eh? I wish I'd seen her face!'

Moira Levitt tried to catch the Governor's attention the moment she entered the office, but Marshall was a stride behind, banging the door shut, already in full flow. Moira waited patiently by the computer, looking like a stunning model about to step onto the catwalk, even managing to hold her notepad gracefully.

'I'm sorry, but you can't have eighty-odd men cooped together,' Marshall said, his breathing audible. 'We'd never control them.'

Helen went round the desk, her lips a thin straight line. 'Really? I'm beginning to wonder who runs this place. What is it, Moira?'

'You wanted to speak to Dr Thomas.' She pointed to a memo sheet on the blotter. 'These are his surgery and home numbers.'

'Thank you. See if he's free for lunch.'

Marshall stood silent, except for his breathing, while Moira made an exit. He stumped up to the desk.

'You ever heard of caution? You've only dealt with women. Let me tell you, these men are ready to blow. They're already uptight over losing their cell-key privileges, and you can't keep pushing prisoners like Murphy and Jellings.'

Facing him squarely across the desk, Helen said crisply, 'When did these men last have a movie?'

This completely took the wind out of Marshall's sails. He squeezed his forehead and stared into space. 'Before the riot.'

'Right, so we'll have a movie night.' As far as she was concerned, the subject was closed – with one important addendum. 'And, Gary, in future please remember I am the Governor here, not you.'

Marshall had plenty more he wanted to say, several volumes, but he bit his tongue. They were sitting on a powder-keg here and she was talking about movies. Give him strength. 'What do you want, *Aladdin*?'

Helen didn't rise to the bait. 'I want the inmates to see the movie voluntarily, Gary.'

'Oh, right. Will Sharon Stone do?' Marshall asked, laying the sarcasm on with a trowel.

'That'll do fine.'

Marshall could do nothing but gape at her. The damn woman was even smiling at him. Then, very calmly, she picked up a sheet of paper, resuming her work. 'And could you tell Officer O'Keefe I'd like to talk to him this morning? I'll be in the gymnasium in ten minutes.'

Marshall went out. Fetch me, carry me. What was he – bloody messenger boy now?

*

Tom Doughen was brewing up at the hotplate, pouring water into the teapot, when Damon O'Keefe slammed into the rest room, his boxer's mug more choleric than usual. Following behind, Russell Morgan nearly got the door in his face. Other officers were at their lockers, kitting up, stowing their personal effects ready for duty.

'She wants *me* now,' O'Keefe said, aggrieved, to no one in particular. 'What does she want me for?'

Doughen looked up sharply, suspending the pouring operation. 'Has she asked to see me?' he said, squinting through the rising steam.

'You'd think she'd have better things to do than harp on about that fuckin' pervert.' O'Keefe kicked a chair away from the table and slumped into it, staring past his boozer's gut at his black shoes.

Morgan gave each of them a look. 'Get your stories right, boys,' he warned, his Scottish accent putting barbs on the words. 'She's sniffin' about like one of her dogs.'

Doughen stirred the pot and plonked the lid on.

'Just so long as she doesn't piss on my leg, I don't care what she does.'

But he was watching the scowling O'Keefe as he said it, scratching at his beard with stubby fingers.

Helen freshened her make-up, standing before the mirror in the ladies' loo. She was running a comb through her hair when the door clattered open and one of the young male clerks from admin skidded to a halt. Helen glared at him in the mirror.

He gulped – 'Sorry, I forgot' – and dived out.

Helen checked her appearance, tucked in her blouse and fastened her jacket. She took a breath. 'Mavis!' And a bigger chest-swelling breath. '*Mavis!*'

The door clattered open again, this time to reveal a palpitating Mavis, plump cheeks flushed.

'Get a proper notice put on the door, "Ladies Only". Please.'

'Oh. Sorry. Yes.'

'Is DCI Dunes married?' Helen asked.

'Er, yes, two kids.'

Helen nodded to herself. 'Mmm, thought so.'

Moira pushed open the door and leaned in. 'Dr Thomas has got an appointment all day in town but he'd be happy to meet for a drink and a sandwich at lunchtime at the Bear, if that's okay.'

'Fine.'

Helen strode out. Mavis nudged Moira, giving her a look from under her brows. 'Well, *he*'s not married, just trouble . . . with a big T!'

CHAPTER 8

THE GYMNASIUM was on the ground floor, on the opposite side of the main yard to the accommodation wings. Helen stood looking out through one of the tall narrow windows reinforced with steel mesh, barred on the outside. A medley of sounds filtered in: barking dogs, shouts of prisoners in the exercise yard, the scrape of shovels as the workmen cleared the last of the debris. Prisons were rarely silent, day or night. In addition to the usual activity, there were always a few inmates making a nuisance of themselves, constantly 'on the bell': attracting the officers' attention by means of the red emergency light next to each cell door, often for no purpose other than wilful bloody-mindedness.

'Can you tell me about the night of the riot? Exactly where you were and what interaction you had with the prisoners?' Helen turned to face O'Keefe, standing a few yards away, feet planted apart on the sprung pine floor, hands clasped behind his back. Why he'd chosen to adopt this formal stance she didn't know, unless it was to make some sort of silent protest. Maintain an 'Us and Them' distance.

She consulted the clipboard in the crook of her arm. 'According to the roster you came on at seven thirty p.m.'

'Yes, I was on evening duty with—'

'I know who you were with,' Helen interrupted. 'Just tell me in your own words exactly what you personally did.'

'We've all given statements to the police, to the investigation team,' O'Keefe said stolidly, as if that settled the matter.

'Yes, I know, so it shouldn't be too difficult to recall your movements that night.' Helen tilted her head, raising an eyebrow.

'I did the lock-up checks on B Wing and then checked all the open areas' – a twitch of the neck – 'that's in here, the cinema, and the laundry. I went up to the canteen—'

'Alone?'

'No, I was with Tom Doughen, Russell Morgan, and . . . I think Andy was with me, PT instructor, Andy Gordon. Jenson, Fuller, Macaulay.'

'The canteen? Yes, go on.'

'I had a cup of coffee, a sandwich.' O'Keefe suppressed a sigh. 'Then at about, oh, maybe half eight, I went to do the VP Wing.'

Helen flipped over a couple of pages to a map of the prison layout, the wings marked in different colours. 'Where Michael Winchwood was held?'

'Yes.'

'Alone?'

'Yes, he was segregated.'

'No, were you alone?'

O'Keefe frowned as if this required great mental effort. 'No, er . . . Tom Doughen was with me.' He blinked rapidly, chin jutting out. 'This is all in the report book, you know.'

'Yes, I know.' Helen kept her temperature cool even as O'Keefe's was climbing up and up. 'Do go on.'

'We checked Winchwood. We'd had a few threats against him, so we were keeping him under supervision.'

'A few threats?' Cooler yet. 'Do you want to elaborate?'

'Well, we always get 'em with a child molester, sex offenders, part of the norm,' O'Keefe said, as if explaining something childishly simple to somebody basically stupid.

'I am aware of that,' Helen said evenly. 'But which

prisoners did you know had made threats to Michael Winchwood?'

'Most of them at some time or other.' O'Keefe sounded indifferent. 'They all get 'em, all the VPs.'

'But on the night in question,' Helen said, studying her fingernails, 'two prisoners, Murphy and Jellings, according to the report book, were excessively violent.'

'Yes, they were,' O'Keefe conceded.

Helen let a moment lapse before raising her eyes. 'Do you think they had anything to do with Winchwood's death?'

O'Keefe stared back. A slow, deliberate shake of the head. 'No, I don't.'

'Did these two men openly threaten Michael Winchwood?'

'Not to my knowledge.'

Helen referred back to her notes. 'And you discovered Michael Winchwood at . . .?'

'At approximately nine fifteen, possibly a little earlier.' O'Keefe unclasped his hands, flexing his fingers. He started cracking his knuckles.

'You said it was eight thirty in your report.'

'I'm sorry, that night was a bit of a frightener. Anyway, I was the first person to find Winchwood.'

'Blood over the walls, wrists cut, his throat cut, but still alive, correct?'

'Yes. I immediately rang the alarm, at the same time the fire alarms began. But you must know all this, you were on the investigation—'

'Yes, I was,' Helen said crisply, 'but now I'm doing my own investigation.' He was really squirming now, shifting his weight about, the anger almost spilling out of him. 'You and Officer Doughen were instigating lock-up when the fire broke out.'

'Yes.' Lips barely moving.

'Were all prisoners locked in their cells?'

'Yes.'

'Could you ask Officer Doughen to be in my office, say, in ten minutes?'

'Yes, Governor,' O'Keefe said.

Helen looked at her watch and checked it against the wall clock in her office. Running late, as per bloody usual. She'd landed herself with two full-time jobs, governing the prison and conducting her own investigation. Having Moira full time had made a big difference in sorting out the daily routine, which was one huge blessing. She'd got the E-mail system functioning, so that Helen was able to deal with the bulk of her correspondence electronically. But on top of that there was an avalanche of circulars from HQ, covering all the changes in rules and working practices throughout the prison system. Then to be dealt with were prisoners on report adjudications, applications for visiting orders, medical and probation reports, plus regular meetings with heads of departments: inmate activities, health care, management services, catering, education, and once a month, an exchange of views with the Prison Officers Association.

In twenty minutes she had a lunch date with Lorcan Thomas, so she'd have to speed through the interview with Doughen, as and when he deigned to honour her with his presence.

Helen flicked the intercom. 'Mavis, if Officer Doughen is out there, could you send him in?'

She drew a file towards her and was studying it intently when Doughen came in. She spared him a quick glance, enough to see that he was picking his fingernails, and went back to the sheaf of statements in front of her.

'On the night of the riots you have stated that all prisoners on the VP Wing were locked up when the fire started.'

'Yes, that's right.' The broad Yorkshire voice was slow

and phlegmatic; it would have made asking the time sound like a veiled threat.

'On that night, Vernon Black was on the VP Wing.' It wasn't a question, though Helen raised her eyebrows, seeking confirmation.

'Yes,' Doughen nodded, 'but he's subsequently been transferred to C Wing.'

'After the fire,' Helen said, checking the report.

'Yes.'

'So he's not a vulnerable prisoner?'

'Not any more.' Doughen gave a half shrug. 'I think he owed money. They're not all sex offenders on—'

'I know that, Mr Doughen.' Helen sat up straight. 'I am simply making sure that Vernon Black was, on the night of the fire, locked in his cell.' She flipped the file shut. 'The reason must be obvious.'

'I'm sorry . . .'

Was this an act? Helen wondered. If he really couldn't make the connection between a known 'sparky' and the events on that night, he must have been playing the bluff pedantic Yorkshireman for real. She spelt it out, just in case he was.

'Vernon Black is an arsonist. And according to the fire team's findings the first fire began in the kitchen area of the VP Wing.'

'Well . . . he must have been questioned,' was all Doughen could offer.

'Yes, he was.' Helen stood up, her smile fleeting and polite. 'Thank you, Mr Doughen.'

It was a blessed relief to get outside Barfield's walls, if only for an hour.

Helen sat at the bar in the lounge of the Olde Bear, sipping a half of lager and debating whether to wait for Lorcan Thomas before starting on the round of wholemeal sandwiches with a scattering of lettuce leaves and half a tomato that the barman had placed before her. Hunger decided. She set to, and was munching away when there was the roar of an exhaust, and a red MG flashed past the leaded window. A minute later he came in, stooping under the slanting lintel, a long, unbuttoned black trenchcoat swirling behind him. Under it he wore a vivid green polo shirt and dark grey twill trousers. Helen got the impression that he would have preferred to wear a sweatshirt and jeans to work, if only it wouldn't have frightened his patients half to death.

He slid onto the barstool, giving her a warm smile. 'Sorry I'm late. Can I get you another?'

Helen's mouth was full. She shook her head, chewing and swallowing. 'No, I'm fine.'

Lorcan Thomas raised a finger. 'Usual for me, Don.' He looked round. 'There's a table free. I sit at the bar,' he told Helen cheerfully, 'and it's open surgery.'

Without waiting he picked up her drink and led her to the table. He did wait, however, while she seated herself, and then nodded thanks to the waitress who placed his glass of Michelob on the dimpled copper. He shrugged off his coat and draped it over a stool.

'So, Miss Hewitt, or do I call you Governor?'

'Helen. You want a sandwich?'

'Thanks.' He took a large bite, jaw moving rhythmically, making appreciative noises. 'Mmm, lovely, thank you.' He raised his glass, 'Cheers', and drank, licking the fringe of foam off his upper lip.

Helen watched him furtively, like a schoolgirl. It was ages since she'd had lunch with such an attractive man. Ages since she'd done anything at all with one. Not only tall and good-looking, with long dark hair loosely brushed back and growing thickly over his collar, Dr Lorcan Thomas passed the voice test too. And the eyes test. Probably every other test if she got near enough to find out.

Seductive as the daydream was, she stirred herself, aware that time was passing, and that this was supposed to be a professional meeting, not a romantic liaison.

'Tell me, in your opinion, was Michael Winchwood suicidal?'

Lorcan Thomas chewed for a moment, shaking his head. 'I don't know. I've looked over his records, obviously. My predecessor didn't appear to think so or he would have made a note of it.' He examined the remaining wedge of sandwich before popping it into his mouth. 'Is this tuna?'

'Quite possibly. You've never worked in any other prison?'

'No.'

'But you must be aware of the present problems we have with narcotics?'

'Of course I'm aware.' His look was direct, even a bit challenging. 'But until the Government or the Home Office admit that it's a problem, as far as I can ascertain, I turn a blind eye if it keeps them quiet.'

Helen wasn't shocked, or even surprised, by this attitude. She knew of many people in the Prison Service, officers in particular, who actually endorsed the smoking of cannabis and the taking of soft drugs by inmates because it made them more docile, and as a consequence less of a hassle to deal with.

She said, 'You have prescribed heavy sedatives for Arnie Franks.'

'Yes, but no more than necessary.' When he drank she noticed that his hand gripped the glass tightly, the long fingernails pale under the pressure. He put the glass down. 'And don't, Miss Hewitt, think for one moment I condone the misuse of drugs, or am in the habit of over-prescribing sedatives.'

'I'm sorry.' Helen's rather weak smile was intended to be placatory. 'I didn't mean to sound offensive, but I have made it a priority to clean up the drug situation inside Barfield, and . . .'

She lifted both hands.
'And?'
'I just wanted a perspective from someone who . . .' She was struggling again; this was harder to admit than she'd realized. And it had nothing to do with his attractiveness – at least she didn't think so. She tried again. 'You've only been at the prison since the riot, and . . . I don't know who I can . . .'
Lorcan Thomas waited. She found the courage to look him straight in the eye.
'I need someone I can trust,' Helen said.
'I've passed the test, have I?' Far from smiling, his eyes were quite cool, his face stern. 'Is that what this is about? Look, Miss Hew– Helen. I'm a doctor, I don't know anything about running a prison. I don't take any sides, I just do my job when I'm called out.'
She had no quarrel with that. 'And I intend to do my job and clear Barfield of drugs,' Helen said firmly.
He nodded, and then reached out for his coat, which was emitting tiny bleeps, patting the pockets until he found the pager. He stood up. 'I'll give you every assistance because you'll need it.' He read the message and turned off the pager.
'Thank you,' Helen said, also rising. 'Maybe we could meet again? Discuss drug rehabilitation and—'
Dr Thomas was already on the move, heading for the bar. 'Sure – you know where I am, all you have to do is call.' He signalled to the barman. 'Okay if I use your phone?'
He was punching numbers when Helen came up, and said to her half over his shoulder, 'I can arrange for you to meet the local rehab centre's administrator.'
Helen smiled and replied quickly, before the call went through, 'Perhaps we could also instigate sessions within the prison, and if perhaps you're free for dinner we might . . .'
'I'm on your side, Miss Hewitt.' Even though he flashed

her a smile she could see he had other things on his mind, and a dinner invitation was not amongst them. 'Dr Thomas here.'

She watched him, both elbows on the bar, a strand of hair hanging over his forehead, all his concentration on the phone, and none left to spare.

The 'evening' shower was between five and six o'clock, after the workshops shut down for the day, and before supper was wheeled through from the kitchens in the big stainless-steel trolleys.

As boss of Charlie Wing, Mad Eyes Murphy was at the head of the queue, along with his close mate Dougie Jellings. From the Cheetham Hill district of Manchester, Jellings was on a six-year stretch for drug-dealing, aggravated by the use of firearms in resisting arrest. He'd served fourteen months in Strangeways, six of them on remand, before being transferred to Barfield for the remainder of his sentence. With an automatic two-year period of remission, and having served a total of eighteen months, his EDR (earliest date of release) was two years and six months away. However, he had yet to be given a date when he would become eligible for parole. And once given it, his case would have to come up before the local review committee for a final decision. If they decided he wasn't ready, and Jellings received a 'knockback', he would have to wait a further ten months before reapplying for parole. There was no appeal against a knockback and no reason required to be given.

Doughen and O'Keefe were amongst the officers on shower duty, attempting the impossible, which was to keep the noise down. The rule was 'no talking, no smoking, no eating'. It might have been 'no breathing' for all the use it was. Bursts of singing and shouting echoed from the tiled cubicles. There was some horseplay, wet towels stinging naked buttocks. Occasionally this would erupt into something more serious. Like children released into the playground, all the cooped-up energy and frustration spilled out, and the officers were always on edge, expecting an argument that could turn into a fight, or an old score being settled under cover of the hissing showers and billowing steam.

'They bring those fuckin' dogs inside our pads again, I'll have her,' Mad Eyes Murphy shouted, his long black hair plastered down the back of his neck. He soaped his hairy chest and tattooed arms. 'You hear me?'

From the next cubicle Jellings yelled back, 'We got every man on our side, Tony. They try and put anything on us and we'll have another bloody riot for that stiff-drawered bitch.'

'Anybody havin' her and it's me!' He sluiced himself down, face turned up into the spray, and pushed open the cubicle door. 'Piss off, Vernon!'

Vernon Black stood waiting his turn, his streaked punkish haircut hidden under a shower cap, his long angular face twitching, always a sign he was coming down from some stratospheric high.

'Hey,' he mumbled, head jerking for no reason, 'you heard we got a film show? It's that one with Sharon Stone showin' her cunt – '

'Piss off, Vernon,' Mad Eyes Murphy snarled. 'Go on, get out of it and gimme me towel.'

Black passed it over, head nodding like a marionette's.

'Honest! Doughen just told us – it's on the board.'

There was a minor altercation in the end cubicle. Somebody's nose connected with the tiled wall and he fell down, groaning, belly streaming with blood. No one had seen it happen, of course. Neither had they seen the person responsible glide off through the steam. Two officers rushed forward, hauling out the injured man. He stood, naked, between them, holding his nose, whimpering apologetically, 'Slipped on the soap, gov. I slipped on the soap.'

Towelling his hair, Mad Eyes Murphy moved to the slatted bench seat. 'Oi! Mr O'Keefe. Is he havin' us on?'

'On the level, Murphy,' Damon O'Keefe told him.

'Sharon Stone? You lying bastard.'

'Not in person, Murphy.' O'Keefe gave him the thumb. 'Come on, you bin in here over your time.'

Mad Eyes Murphy wrapped the towel round his waist. He moved close to O'Keefe, sticking his chest out, slitted eyes dead as a moray eel's. 'You got a problem with that?' The voice was flat, one-note Liverpudlian. 'Or you shittin' yourself because Winchwood's parents came here?'

Standing at the door, a constant stream of prisoners passing in front of him so that he had to peer round them, Doughen saw Murphy jabbing his finger, and O'Keefe backing away. Dougie Jellings was lurking close at hand, taking it all in, a real nasty expression on his pale, ravaged face.

Doughen had to raise his voice above the babble, laughter and shouts booming out from the cubicles.

'She wants to see Murphy and Jellings before association.'

O'Keefe turned. 'What about Vernon Black?'

'Him, too.'

Murphy and Jellings swapped glances. Then Murphy slowly backed away from O'Keefe, gently wagging a finger. He scooped up his clothes and padded out.

He was stretched out on his bed, hair still damp, one brawny arm tucked behind his head, when Helen entered the cell. Senior Officer Russell Morgan stood just outside, the harsh fluorescent lighting bouncing off his domed head through the rapidly thinning sandy hair.

Murphy made a token gesture of politeness, but didn't alter his indolent posture. He wore a black T-shirt that read 'No Turning Back', stretched taut across his chest, grey tracksuit bottoms fastened with a drawstring, and trainers on his bare feet.

Helen pulled out the single hardback wooden chair and sat down, facing the wall behind Murphy's head. The gloss green wall with its high window also happened to display his collection of porn: mostly of the mild Readers' Wives variety, with one or two stills from hard-core German videos. Murphy got a charge from seeing her register it, but he was disappointed when her expression didn't change, and she made no attempt to realign her chair.

Helen looked round. On the cork board above the table he had pinned up photographs of his wife and family, holiday snaps, school photos of a son and daughter. Some of them had been cropped to exclude Murphy himself; inmates were not permitted to possess photographs of themselves, even as one of a group.

'What do you think of the food here?'

'S'okay.'

'You work out, though, don't you? You think you get enough protein?'

'Yeah, I get in extra.'

'You get it brought in for you?'

'Yeah, we all do – well, them that can afford it.' He levered himself up onto one elbow and started making a roll-up from a battered tin of Golden Virginia. 'Not telling tales – it was even in the papers. You smoke?'

'No,' Helen said, and saw, directly in line with the toe of her shoe, a small ragged circle of squashed cardboard, the remnants of a used roach.

Murphy licked the paper with a lascivious roll of the tongue, loving every minute of it, a lewd smile hovering under the straggling moustache. He took his time. Helen sat there and stared him out.

'So,' Murphy said, lighting up, 'you're the new Governor. My, my, my. Whose face did you sit on?'

Helen turned aside. 'I didn't hear that. What other perks do you get?' She waited. 'None?'

Murphy smoked, propped on an elbow, totally at ease. This was his patch, his piece of turf, his private territory. He didn't give a fart in a high wind who or what she was, or thought she was.

'The night of the riot, Mr Murphy, would you tell me what happened?'

'You a bull dyke, then?'

'What did you say?' Though she knew perfectly well.

'You a dyke?'

'Am I a what?' Ice in her voice.

'Lesbian.' He let the smoke trickle lazily up from his mouth past his eyes. 'You one, are you? That why you got the job? Act like a man? You a dyke?'

Helen folded her arms, sitting very straight.

'The night of the riot, Mr Murphy. Answer the question.'

His gaze roamed up to the ceiling. 'Banged up as usual, then the fire started and they unlocked our spurs, held us over in the quad.' He looked at her, eyes flat, expressionless. 'That's it. This movie, Sharon whatsit, for real, is it?'

'What time were you taken out of lock-up?'

'Dunno, my watch stopped.'

Helen took the clipboard from her lap. '"Prisoner 493, Anthony Murphy, became violent and abusive,"' she read. 'This was at eight thirty, Mr Murphy, correct?'

'I dunno,' he said, lying propped up, squinting through the smoke. 'Me watch stopped.'

'Did you know Michael Winchwood?'

'No.'

'But you knew who he was?'

'Yeah, we knew he was here.'

'What did you think about him?'

Murphy sat up, arms resting on his knees, head pushed towards her. 'He raped and tortured two little girls, aged nine and seven, and he buggered an eight-year-old boy, then buried him.' His eyes flicked to the photographs on the cork board and came back to rest on her, hard. 'Why don't you tell me what you think about him?'

'Did you ever threaten him?'

'Personally? No.'

'You didn't?' Helen's lips tightened. 'You must be the only man here who didn't.'

Murphy slowly swung his legs down. There was less than two feet of space between the bed and the chair, and he seemed to be almost on top of her. She could smell soap on him, and a whiff of aftershave. Under the thick dark eyebrows his eyes bored into her.

'Par for the course, isn't it? Perverted, twisted animal. All nonces should be castrated—'

'So you did threaten him?'

'You're puttin' words into my mouth, luv,' Murphy sneered, with obscure sexual innuendo.

Helen resisted with all her strength the temptation to shy away from him; in the confined space his powerful frame and latent hostility amounted to blatant intimidation.

'I never said I did and I never said I didn't, eh? He topped himself, saves a lot of aggravation and saves the Government a lot of dosh. Costs one grand a week to keep filth like him segregated.'

'Costs almost as much to keep you too, Mr Murphy,' Helen said coldly.

He grinned without warmth, shaking his head contemptuously. 'You're new at this, then, are you? Otherwise you wouldn't bother wastin' your time with shits like Winchwood. What time's the movie start then?'

He lay down flat on the bed, legs apart, one hand rubbing the bulge in his tracksuit pants.

Helen stood up. There was no movement in her face, but her eyes were sharp as needles. She tucked the clipboard under her arm, fingers laced together at her waist.

'Mr Murphy, I will treat you with respect as long as you apply the same rules to me. When I interview you again, one – just one – sexual innuendo, and I will take it personally. I am the Governor of this prison. You stand up when I enter your cell, and when I leave, is that clear?'

Making a great show of grunting and groaning, Murphy got laboriously to his feet. He stooped, making an ironic bow, and then straightened up because she was close, very close, almost touching. And because she had been sitting down throughout the interview he had not really sussed her size; now she stared face to face, eye to eye. She held his dark expressionless eyes and didn't waver, as if waiting, and it paid off because it was Murphy who broke the contact. He was well and truly fazed by the fact that she seemed completely unafraid of him.

'Thank you, Mr Morgan.' Helen nodded as she walked out confidently. No one could have detected that her stomach was churning. She had never felt such deep loathing from anyone in her entire life.

Russell Morgan pulled the cell door shut, casting a glance at Murphy and failing to hide his amusement. She was definitely no pushover, not if she could cut Mad Eyes Murphy's balls off with one stroke.

Murphy listened to the key turning in the lock, stroking his moustache with his fingertips. His lip curled. 'Suck on it, sweetheart,' he muttered under his breath.

CHAPTER 9

DOUGHEN, JINGLING his key-chain nervously, stepped forward to intercept Helen as she approached along the upper landing of C Wing.

'It's almost association, Miss Hewitt. I don't think it's wise to keep them banged up—'

Helen continued on her way. 'I want to see Douglas Jellings and Vernon Black, then you can start unlocking the cells.'

'They won't like it.'

'I'm not exactly having a ball myself,' Helen responded tartly. She pointed to Black's cell door. With a weary sigh Doughen inserted the key in the brass plate, mumbling to himself, 'Squeezing a few through, aren't you?'

'I heard that,' Helen said, giving him a look as she went inside.

'She knows this is a waste of time?' Doughen said, turning as Russell Morgan ambled up.

'Don't get over-confident,' Morgan said. He jerked his head, grinning. 'I just saw her handle Murphy.'

Black was hunched up, arms wrapped round his knees, chin sunk on his chest. He raised his head as she came in, blond hair gelled to spiky points, the gold ear-stud winking. He was quite extraordinary-looking, Helen thought. Apart from the hair and long narrow face with the prominent jaw, his eyes under the fair brows were of the most intense green.

On the shelf above him, his stereo CD was playing a track by Fruit Tumor, which to Helen sounded like somebody having his teeth extracted to a background of industrial machinery. He reached up to switch it off.

'It's Vernon Black, isn't it?' At his nod she said, 'You are here for five years, and you've been here . . .' She consulted her notes.

'Eighteen months,' Black said. 'I was transferred from Leeds.'

'Did you prefer it in Leeds?'

'It was easier for me mother to see me there.' He came originally from Scunthorpe, had worked as a chef in Newcastle; his father had died when he was sixteen, ten years before.

'Why were you on the VP Wing, Mr Black?' Helen asked.

'I owed Tony – Murphy – a few quid for phone cards. I had to wait for a visit to pay him off.'

Phone cards had taken the place of tobacco as prison currency. Inmates were allowed to purchase two £4 cards a week, but with their earnings from workshops and the £6 a week of private money from outside, it was possible to amass a considerable amount. A wing boss like Murphy might have two or three hundred pounds' worth to use as barter.

'And you've paid him back?'

'Yes, ma'am.'

'Thank you, Mr Black.'

'That's okay.'

The security floodlighting wasn't yet on, though daylight was fading fast as Helen returned to the admin block along the covered walkway which bordered the exercise yard. Arnie Franks stood all alone in the centre of the grassy patch, staring around him with frightened and bewildered eyes. Two officers, one of them unmistakably Jumbo Jackson from his height and girth, were chatting together, sneaking a quick smoke.

Catching sight of Helen, Jackson nodded in Franks's direction and touched his finger to his cap in a mock salute. 'Orders carried out, ma'am,' was the rather ironic message.

Through the chain-link fence Helen saw Franks make a sudden dash towards the brick wall of C Wing. He ran smack into it, rebounded, scrambled up, and banged his head against the bricks.

Jackson looked towards Helen, eyebrows raised, and went back to his fag and conversation.

Helen turned sharply away and walked on.

'Murphy knows Winchwood's family were here,' Damon O'Keefe said, eyes bulging in his red face. He and Doughen were standing in the doorway to the rest room, just out of earshot of the officers milling about inside. 'Christ knows how they get to know everything that's bloody going on.'

Doughen shrugged. 'As long as we stick to what we've said throughout, nothing can happen. And the rate Wonder Woman's going on she'll not last out the week,' he added, a malicious glint in his hooded eyes as he looked towards Helen's office, situated at the far end of the corridor.

They fell silent as the door opposite them, marked 'Deputy Governor', opened and Gary Marshall and Senior Officer Russell Morgan came out. They were deep in conversation, working out the strategy for the extra cell search ordered by the Governor. Not one of the officers was keen. The general feeling was that using the movie to get the men out of their cells was a big mistake. The aftermath of tension following the riot was still palpable, the whole place in a volatile state, and now was not the time to push the inmates ever nearer to the brink.

'First we get all the VPs locked up, straight away,' Marshall was saying. 'Choose a small number of officers to do the cell search – as few as possible because we'll need all the other officers in the cinema. C Wing is the priority, then D Wing.'

He pushed past O'Keefe and Doughen and entered the rest room. 'We've got to keep them in the cinema as long as possible. It'll take a good two hours to complete the pad spin.'

'I don't think she has any idea what she's bloody doing,' Doughen said, following him in. 'What if they don't want to see the movie?'

Marshall's eyebrows shot up. 'Sharon Stone? You kidding?'

He went over to check the rosters on the big notice board. A moment later he was joined by Russell Morgan. The two men studied the board for a while, until the sandy-haired Scot said in a speculative tone, 'Maybe she's not the pushover we thought.' Marshall glanced sideways at him. Casting an eye at O'Keefe and Doughen, Morgan uttered in a low voice, 'There's such a thing as being over loyal.'

Marshall frowned at him. 'What's that supposed to mean?'

'I'm not involved in this and you don't have to be either.' Morgan stared at the board, his lips hardly moving as he said, 'You'd better tell her before she finds out.'

Marshall took a deep breath, but said nothing, his face grim as a stone mask.

Helen strode along the corridor and entered the crowded rest room. It was a few minutes after seven, the movie scheduled to start in half an hour. She felt tired, frayed at the edges, and knew that she looked it. She didn't need the glances of the men to tell her that. Days into the new job, and the pressure was beginning to tell. If only she had some back-up, felt that she had their trust and support, it would have made all the difference. But she felt the opposite: that she was battling against the officers and inmates combined, and it was wearing her down.

There was a general bustle as officers kitted up at the lockers, a dozen or so standing round drinking coffee while they waited. Helen stood at the board, looking at her watch.

'How are we doing for time? How many more still scheduled to arrive?'

Jumbo Jackson was collating the reports from the various wings, head bent to his radio. 'Waiting on another fifteen, gov.'

Gary Marshall pushed through, holding up a list, which he passed to her. 'You've almost got a full house. These are the no-shows.'

'Well, let's hope Sharon simmers them down,' Helen said with feeling.

'I wouldn't bank on it,' Marshall said drily.

Mavis was at the door, craning her neck and waving to catch Helen's attention. 'There's a Mr Andrews from the Prison Service.' Helen turned to pick up the nearest phone, and Mavis called out, 'No, he's here.'

'Oh, boy!' Helen exclaimed, running a hand through her hair. 'That's what I call timing.'

Marshall watched her leave; he looked like a cat that had been promised a double helping of cream. He pushed through after her, and was just in time to see Helen disappearing into the toilet, a large sign now tacked to the door saying 'Ladies Only'.

Hoping for a pre-emptive strike, Marshall kept a sharp look-out for the Operational Director, and he wasn't disappointed, because a moment later the tall, elegant figure of Royston Andrews appeared round the corner, a tweed overcoat draped over his arm.

One eye on the toilet door, Marshall worked fast, keeping his greeting brief. Andrews listened impassively as the Deputy Governor poured it out: the strip-searches, the cell spins, the drug busts, the rumours running rife that Miss Hewitt was digging up the dirt on the Winchwood death.

Marshall leaned in, thumb jerking over his shoulder. 'We've got eighty-odd men down there, all of them, after this business, very edgy. We've got every officer to spare on duty, that's day and night staff, and—'

'Do you think she's just out of her depth?' Royston Andrews asked pensively, stroking his chin.

'I'd say she's drowning.' Marshall's hand snapped up. 'Joke, just a joke,' he said with a smile that was nearer a grimace.

He froze a little as Helen emerged from the toilet, and stood back while they shook hands.

'Has Gary given you an update?' Helen asked, and the very innocence of her smile told Marshall that he'd been rumbled. She was nobody's fool, for dead certain, and it made him consider again what Russell Morgan had mentioned in the rest room. Loyalty was a fine attribute, he thought, providing it wasn't misdirected.

Helen was leading Royston Andrews to her office. 'Soon as you've got the men in the cinema, let me know.'

Marshall nodded, a lot on his mind, and watched them disappear inside.

The inmates of C Wing had been separated into two groups, of sixteen and nineteen, the first group already filing out through the double gates into the main corridor. Four officers escorted them, two at the front, two at the rear. Doughen stood just inside the wing spur, speaking into his radio. 'Hello MS2D from India 2, Charlie Wing. First batch on its way over now. Out.'

The message would be relayed via the central control room to the officers in the cinema. When MS2D received confirmation, the second batch would be sent on its way.

Sooner the better, Doughen reckoned. The men lined up behind him were keyed-up, jumping about and barging into one another. The prospect of the movie had them giddy with excitement. Even the older guys, a couple of them over sixty, were grinning like loons. Some of the younger, harder men were using this as an opportunity to bait the officers. It always happened, whenever there was a crowd of them bunched together, and unless it was directly personal the best policy was to ignore it.

Six of this batch were black, and as usual they stuck together. Wherever they went – exercise yard, workshops, chapel – the West Indians formed their own exclusive group, laughing and joking and speaking a patois only they could understand. After a long time listening to them, Doughen still didn't have a clue what they were saying. They might have been insulting him to his face, and calling his mother a whore, and he'd never know it.

He listened with half an ear to a joke somebody was telling – an Irish joke told by an Irishman. About the bloke who goes into a builders' yard and orders 25,000 bricks. What for? asks the gaffer. To build a barbecue with, says the Irishman. You don't need 25,000 bricks to build a barbecue, laughs the gaffer scornfully. You do if you live on the nineteenth floor of a tower block, says the Irishman.

Doughen gave a wry smile and thumbed the button on his radio. 'Hello MS2D from India 2, Charlie Wing. Second group ready to come over. Murphy is in this bunch, so keep your eye on him. Jellings also in the last section. Out.'

He unlocked the gates and led them through. As they marched along the main tunnel, Doughen at the rear, they passed three officers led by Russell Morgan heading in the opposite direction. None of the men paid them any attention, which was just as well, Doughen was thinking. Because if they got an inkling their cells were yet again about to be done over, there'd be no holding them. And with the inmates outside the secure accommodation areas, he for one didn't want to be in the middle of another riot when the shit hit the fan.

Helen's shrewd guess about Royston Andrews's unheralded visit proved spot on. He didn't waste any time in getting to the point.

'Mr and Mrs Winchwood have informed me that you are instigating a new investigation into the death of their son. Is that correct, Miss Hewitt?'

She was in the hot seat. Although as Governor of Barfield she had jurisdiction over the prison's internal affairs, in a matter of this gravity she should first have cleared it with her area manager, John Bunny, or referred it right to the top, to Royston Andrews himself at HQ.

'I do not believe Michael Winchwood committed suicide, but that he was physically attacked,' Helen stated firmly. 'I am not sure which of the officers were involved, but I think they were prepared to turn a blind eye if Winchwood just got a severe beating . . . and it got out of hand.'

Royston Andrews eyed her levelly. 'Do you have any evidence to substantiate what you have just said, or is it all supposition?'

Helen chewed her lip. She was floundering, and she knew that he knew it. She was trying to formulate some sort of a reply when the door was rapped and Marshall put his head round. He was breathing quite heavily. 'I suggest you come to the cinema immediately.'

Five minutes later, Helen leading the way, they entered the single-storey building which housed the workshops, the canteen – as the prison shop was called – and the chapel-cum-cinema. Dull booming sounds like the beating of waves reverberated down the corridors. As they turned a corner, these resolved themselves into the stamping of feet and the chanting of 'SHARON, SHARON, SHARON, SHARON', accompanied by orgasmic groans and cries of longing.

Helen's appearance through the double doors, flanked by Andrews and Marshall, made no impression. Stamping and chanting, fists punching the air, the men were seated on swivel chairs which could be turned to face either end of the hall but which were presently facing an arrangement of aluminium poles supporting a screen, behind which a thick curtain masked off the chapel area. Six officers were in a line at the door, radios in their hands, and the room was ringed with twenty more, their eyes never still as they sought out potential trouble-makers.

'SHARON, SHARON, SHARON, SHARON . . .'

'Settle down, quiet!' Jumbo Jackson's voice was nearly lost in the racket. He stepped forward, both arms raised. 'Settle down. The Governor wants to talk to you all.'

The stamping died away as Marshall led Helen to the small platform at the front, but then the chanting turned into boos, yells and catcalls, and a deafening chorus of shrill whistles went up as he helped her up the two steps.

'Siddown, keep your seats!' Jackson bellowed. 'Any prisoner causing trouble will be down the Block.'

Hands clasped at her waist, chin up, Helen faced the room. Her expression impassive and her eyes calm, she waited for the noise to die down. She was aware that Royston Andrews was watching her intently from the doorway, arms folded, fingers stroking his jaw.

At the side of the platform Marshall held up one hand.

'All right, quiet. Shut up. Quiet for the Governor, Helen Hewitt.'

There was a restless shifting as the men subsided. Helen waited a few moments more, then straightened her shoulders and took a breath.

'Show us your knickers, get 'em off,' a voice called out, which got a huge laugh.

'Suppose a fuck's out of the question,' shouted somebody else, to another eruption of raucous laughter.

Jackson loomed forward threateningly and the laughter died away to silence. Helen took another, deeper, steadying breath.

Everything movable had been stripped out of the cells on C Wing. It was piled in heaps on the landings, teams of officers rummaging through it, riffling paperbacks, opening cassette tapes, removing the batteries from radios and CD players, checking personal letters and papers; a meticulous and painstaking search of each and every item from pillows and mattresses down to the last tube of toothpaste.

Senior Officer Russell Morgan moved slowly along, collecting the haul in a large black plastic bag, each stash already sealed and tagged with the cell number and its occupant's name and number. By the time he reached the kitchen area at the end of the landing the bag was nearly a quarter full.

He frowned, seeing that some stupid berk had left a kettle steaming on a low light. The kettle rattled as he removed it and turned off the gas. 'Shit!' Morgan muttered as he lifted the lid and peered inside. At the bottom lay three hypodermic needles being boiled clean.

It was a battle of wills, and Helen wasn't all that certain she was winning it.

They'd quietened down, the jeers and rude remarks had ceased, yet there was a terrible undercurrent of tension, as if a potent nerve gas had been siphoned into the room, infecting everyone.

She struggled on through the whispering and sniggering, the lurking smiles of derision, the muffled snorts of laughter.

'. . . and for long-term prisoners and lifers I want to introduce new and better educational programmes, which I'm sure—'

A slow handclap started, led by Mad Eyes Murphy. It was taken up by the rest of them, who then raised their voices in time to the steady beat of the handclap.

'WHY ARE WE WAITING . . . OH WHY ARE WE WAITING . . . WHY ARE WE WAITING . . . OH WHY WHY WHY . . .'

Helen shied away as a toilet roll flew towards her, uncurling itself in a long white ribbon. Cigarette packets were flung, socks, trainers, and Helen shielded herself with both hands as coins rained down. With the barrage of missiles came the relentless thump-thump-thump of stamping feet. Helen tried to stand her ground, raising her voice in order to be heard.

'You want to talk to me, I will listen, I promise that.' She ducked as an empty tobacco tin whistled past her head. 'Any grievances, let me know . . . about food, exercise, association. You have a complaint, let me hear it. *I will listen!*'

Murphy leapt to his feet, both hands cupped to his mouth. 'Yeah, I got a complaint. Why don't you fuckin' shut up and let us see the movie?'

By now half the room was on the third chorus of 'Why are we waiting' while the rest of them had again taken up the chant of 'SHARON, SHARON, SHARON'.

From then on it disintegrated fast. Benches were kicked over, fights broke out, and the noise swelled to a roar of yelling and stamping feet. Officers moved in, drawing their wooden staves, attempting to maintain order. But it was reaching the point of wholesale pandemonium. Three officers had closed in a protective circle around Helen. Jackson grabbed her by the elbow. 'You'd better get out of here!' he shouted, and without waiting for an answer propelled her from the platform, his massive six-foot-four and man-mountain bulk forming a barrier between her and the seething crowd.

In seconds she was whisked away, passed from hand to hand, with Royston Andrews finally dragging her outside.

'Start the bloody film!' Marshall ordered, mounting the platform. 'Somebody start the video, get the bloody film on!'

Only one thing could prevent another riot, it seemed, and that was the promise of a glimpse of the movie-star's pussy.

*

Helen gripped the sides of the washbasin and leaned over, heaving. Nothing came except a thin, watery stream of bile that burned her throat. Head slumped forward, hair unravelled and covering her eyes, she stood there gasping, her whole body shaking.

The long table in the officers' rest room contained a more varied pick 'n' mix than you could get at Woolworth's.

Russell Morgan held up a clear plastic bag containing green capsules for Royston Andrews to see, who looked questioningly at Doughen, writing up the haul in the reports ledger.

'Temazepam sleeping tablets,' Doughen informed him. 'The prisoners on prescribed tabs store them up – especially them – cut 'em open and mainline 'em.'

Andrews gazed thoughtfully along the row upon row of plastic bags, and then blinked when he saw the kettle. Morgan removed the lid to show him.

'Using their own kettle to clean the needles. We've found three so far.'

Still looking thoughtful, the Operational Director nodded and left the room.

With his fingertips Morgan was kneading two grams of white powder through the clear plastic, holding it an inch or so from his eyes.

'Maybe she's not as dumb as she looks,' he mumbled softly to himself. He glanced from under his brows at Doughen and tossed down the bag. 'I'd swear this is bloody pure heroin.'

Hands in the pockets of his tweed overcoat, Royston Andrews's expression hovered between sympathy and concern. 'Would you like me to get someone to take you home?' he asked kindly.

Helen shook her head. She was sitting on the edge of

Mavis's desk, her face very pale, eyes still watery. 'No, I'm fine. I'll be fine.'

In the light from the desk lamp Andrews could plainly see that she wasn't, but said nothing. He liked Helen, respected her ability, and didn't want to see her fail.

After a moment she raised her eyes and gave him a sort of bitter half smile. 'Well, I made a real fool of myself.'

'Everyone has at one time,' Andrews replied. 'Made a fool of themselves.' He inclined his body towards her. 'The discovery of drugs was very good, but when the film finishes there is going to be trouble. Fortunately we have enough prison officers to handle it, so . . .' He leaned further, speaking quietly. 'Go home, Helen. We're all at your disposal whenever you need us.'

Helen stood up, smoothing down the shoulders of her jacket, tugging the sleeves straight. 'Thank you.'

She moved slowly to the door of her office, feeling so drained and weary she could have curled up and slept for a week. And Andrews's obvious concern and genuine kindness did nothing to boost her morale, which at this moment in time was lower than a snake's belly.

He had one parting piece of advice. 'Just drop this Winchwood business and put tonight behind you.'

Helen looked at him over her shoulder. Then she turned the door handle and went out.

CHAPTER 10

NO, SHE couldn't face it, not right now. Despite her tiredness and the lateness of the hour, the prospect of going back to that bloody dreary, dreadful flat depressed her even more.

She drove over to Cattering Hall, without any real plan or idea of why she was going there. She dragged herself up the main staircase to the offices, and gave a smile of joy as she encountered the first friendly face in a long while. It belonged to her cat, Helen's moggy, which she'd bequeathed to them when she'd left for Barfield. She felt that with her new job and the pressure it would be better off at Cattering Hall. She had been right about the pressure, but she had never anticipated that it would break her and, right at this moment, she wished she had never left.

Helen sat down on the stair, stroking the cat as it purred and rubbed against her ankles. The place was quiet at this hour, peaceful, and footsteps on the landing above sounded unnaturally loud.

'She's settled in fine,' Mrs Redwood said, leaning over the banister.

Helen looked up. 'I didn't expect to see you here.'

'Catching up with paperwork. My youngest has been ill. She's better now.'

'I just came to see Tina,' Helen said, thinking that some explanation was required. 'Driving past, so . . .'

Mrs Redwood nodded. 'How's everything at Barfield?'

Helen dropped her head and stared at a hole in the worn carpet. 'Out of control.'

Mrs Redwood said nothing. She stood in her sensible low-heeled shoes, hands in the pockets of her long shapeless cardigan, waiting as Helen came up to the landing. The look on the young woman's face troubled her. In all the time they had worked together she had never seen her so despondent. Helen was a resilient and resourceful creature, had always tackled every problem and situation with energy and resolve, plus a healthy leavening of common sense and good humour.

'I made a big fool of myself tonight,' Helen confessed with a soft laugh as they walked together along the deserted corridor. 'And in front of the Operational Director.'

'I'm sorry.'

'Oh, he was very nice about it.' Helen's tone of resignation matched her expression. 'There's a lot of resentment about my appointment.'

'Well, that was expected, wasn't it?' Mrs Redwood remarked sagely.

'Since my divorce my work has been . . . well, everything,' Helen said, engrossed in her own train of thought. 'Barfield was the ultimate prize.'

'It isn't a prize, Helen, it's a tough and thankless job. I could have warned you but you wouldn't have listened.' She touched Helen's shoulder to show she was being honest, not critical or unkind. But this only made Helen feel all the more miserable and nakedly vulnerable.

She followed Mrs Redwood inside. Her emotions, so tightly bottled up, were having their revenge.

'I didn't think it would be so lonely,' she forced herself to admit. She gnawed her lip. 'I've lost my confidence and I don't think I can finish what I started.'

'Then use me, Helen, don't take it all on your shoulders.'

It was too much to cope with, this sympathy and understanding, and Helen's face crumpled. Mrs Redwood opened her arms and Helen stumbled into them, tears spilling down her cheeks. She clung on tightly, her heart shuddering like mad in her chest.

After a moment she said huskily, 'I'm sorry to do this, but I had nobody else to talk to.' She pulled away, sniffing, wiping both cheeks with the back of her hand. 'When I was a kid I used to run always to my dad. He'd be somewhere on the farm and he'd open his arms, swing me round – "Come on, gel, spit it out." He was a very big man. I don't just mean . . .' Not only in physique, her gesture indicated. 'His heart.'

Pain creased her forehead as she struggled to stem even more tears evoked by this childhood memory.

'I wanted my husband to be like my big dad, but he wasn't.' Helen sniffed, dabbing her face with her handkerchief. 'I don't know why I'm telling you all this crap.'

Mrs Redwood's look was direct and searching. 'You're not going to quit, are you?'

'I feel like it,' Helen said, in a small voice ragged with tiredness. 'Michael Winchwood was murdered. He didn't commit suicide. And then I hear what the men say about him, that he was a disgusting piece of humanity, and I think, why should I care about what the hell happened to him? He got what he deserved.' She gazed with bright, moist eyes at Mrs Redwood, shoulders slumped, helpless and defeated.

'If you believe there has been any injustice, any cover-up at Barfield Prison,' Mrs Redwood told her gravely, finger raised, 'prove it. Let them be resentful, hostile, whatever. You be angry and get to the truth.'

Mrs Redwood's fierce expression softened into a tiny smile. She led Helen to the leather settee, then went over to the small cupboard next to the filing cabinet. A minute later she placed a large gin and tonic in front of Helen, and sat down beside her with a glass of orange juice. Helen put her handkerchief away and took a sip, then a deeper one. She leaned slowly back against the cushion, staring into her glass.

'Do you know why they gave me Barfield?'

Mrs Redwood hesitated. She sipped her own drink first, her expression thoughtful, and then looked at Helen straight. 'I think when the prison is refurbished the category will possibly be changed. Which would mean you are not of a high enough rank and . . .' She paused.

'I'd be replaced?'

'It's just a supposition. I may be wrong, but it's going to cost millions to put that prison back in order, and, well . . .' She gave a small shrug.

Helen stared again into her glass. She looked ashen. 'The bastards.' Her voice was barely a whisper. 'And Marshall, my bloody deputy, you think he knows it?'

'I think it's common knowledge, Helen.' Mrs Redwood sighed, shaking her head. 'That's why I turned it down.'

Helen straightened up abruptly. She knocked the rest of her drink back in one. An angry glint appeared in her eyes.

'Just a caretaker, am I? Well, I'm going to prove that I'm a hell of a lot more than that.' She banged the glass down. 'Barfield is my prison. It's mine.'

She got to her feet and snatched up her coat. Mrs Redwood was smiling. She was witnessing the rebirth of the Helen Hewitt she well knew, the one that just for a short while had taken a back seat. Now the born-again Helen Hewitt, Governor of HMP Barfield, was back in the driving seat.

'I'll see this through and then just let them try and shift me!'

Helen's raging eye caught sight of Mrs Redwood's smile. She herself began to smile, the smile turned into a chuckle, and then she threw back her head in a lovely loud bellow of laughter.

'Bastards, bastards! You bastards! FUCKIN' BASTARDS!'

Mad Eyes Murphy gripped the gantry rail and leaned

over, the veins swelling in his neck. Scattered at his feet was the debris of the cell spin – mattress, bedding, his books and records, all his personal belongings.

Lining the rails of both landings, the prisoners screamed abuse at the officers outside the barred entrance gates. Returning from the cinema, they had been smartly herded inside, and that's when the roof of C Wing had been nearly blown off with uncontrollable, explosive anger.

'You tell O'Keefe I wanna see him,' Murphy yelled, in a red-mad rage. He jabbed his finger as if poking it through solid iron. 'You think you had a blaze before, well, you ain't seen nothin' yet, mate!'

Outside the barred gate to the wing, four officers clustered round Doughen, batons drawn, uncertain what to do. So was Doughen. They had to go in there, before serious trouble started, but he was buggered if he was going to lead a suicide mission with just the five of them.

He put through an emergency call to central control: 'We have trouble on Charlie Wing, need some back-up urgent, over—'

It was nearly impossible to make himself heard above the echoing din. Murphy's voice alone was like the bellow of a raging bull.

'They conned us – they conned us! Watch their fuckin' movie and they done our pads over.'

Running footsteps boomed along the main tunnel. Russell Morgan, O'Keefe, and four extra officers arrived. Seeing that the inmates were out of their cells, Morgan bashed his fist against the bars.

'We're more of a prisoner than they bloody are. We goin' in? *I wanna go in there!*'

O'Keefe grabbed his arm. 'Stay back – don't go in. They're going fuckin' crazy!'

Morgan shook him off. He was sick to death of covering for the likes of O'Keefe and Doughen. He had his pride as an officer, and he hated having rotten apples in the same barrel as him.

He rattled his baton against the gates, trying to be heard above the relentless clamour.

'Listen to me. This is Senior Officer Morgan, and we're comin' in. ANY PRISONER NOT IN HIS CELL, DOOR CLOSED, WILL BE DOWN THE BLOCK!' He turned, and with almost a snarl said to O'Keefe: 'Right, we're gonna sort this, mate. You comin' in with us?'

Shaking his head, O'Keefe backed away. Doughen, too, eased himself away from the others. The assembled officers turned towards them in a silent row, faces hard and unyielding. It began to dawn on both men that they'd pushed things beyond the limit; this time they were out on their own.

A mile or so from her flat when she received the call on her car phone, Helen swung north and headed for Barfield, less than four miles away. She entered the admin block and raced up the stairs. The door to her office was open, and Gary Marshall's voice floated clearly down the corridor as she turned the corner.

'. . . I want every available officer standing by C Wing, is that understood?'

'They want to go in,' she heard Jumbo Jackson say.

Marshall exploded. '*Nobody* goes into that bloody wing until I say so!'

Helen stood in the doorway, panting. 'Don't you think it's until I say so?' Her eyes were dangerously bright, alight from within with a fire they'd never seen before. Marshall for one was confused; after the events in the cinema earlier that evening he'd mentally written her off as someone who'd suffered a public humiliation and lost all authority, had her spirit broken.

Now here she was back in the fray, and in fighting fettle.

*

Murphy was in fighting mood himself, urging the men to leave their cells. Seeing the officers massing at the gates, most of the prisoners had scurried back into their cells and pulled their doors shut. But no longer could they lock themselves in. Murphy was now wielding a broken chair leg. He moved along the landings, hammering on the doors, chanting, 'OUT-OUT-OUT!'

'Get them out here,' he called to Dougie Jellings. 'Come on, get 'em out. OUT-OUT-OUT!'

He punched Vernon Black on the shoulder, who backed off, holding up his hands. 'I can't get 'em out, they won't come out,' he said in a wheedling tone. 'They don't wanna know, Tony . . .'

Murphy picked up what was left of the chair and hurled it against the wall. He glared over the rail as the entrance gate clanged open.

Helen strode in, flanked by a dozen officers. She halted in the centre of the association area, looking up at Murphy. He stood with legs apart, tapping the chair leg against his thigh, watching her with slitted eyes as she mounted the iron stairway. Then with a contemptuous smirk he turned away.

Helen came onto the landing. One glare at Black and he immediately backed away. The intense green eyes blinked rapidly. 'I'm not doin' anything.'

Helen advanced. 'This the big riot?' She stuck out her finger at Murphy. 'You . . . back to your cell.' She swung her finger towards Jellings. 'And you. What are you doing?'

The broken chair leg Jellings was holding dropped to the floor.

'Nuthin'.'

Helen said to Morgan, 'Tell every man I want their cells back in order by the time I do my morning round. Lock up.'

She turned on her heel and Morgan watched her, a half smile on his face, as she went down the stairway and marched out of the wing. Whatever else you might think of her, the bloody woman had guts. The smile froze when his eyes alighted on Tom Doughen and Damon O'Keefe. The two men stared up at him. They looked scared.

Helen unlocked the door of the Mini Metro and tossed her briefcase onto the passenger seat. It was a few minutes after ten thirty, and this time she really *was* going back to the flat, and straight to bed.

'Night, ma'am.'

Shrouded in an anorak, Russell Morgan was wheeling his Honda motorcycle from the bike bay, a black crash helmet hooked on his arm. A thin drizzle had started, sweeping finely through the floodlights which bathed the car park in eerie daytime brightness. Helen went over, pulling up the collar of her raincoat.

'Thank you for calling me. Why did you?'

Morgan looked down at her in silence for a moment. 'This is not tales out of school, right? I don't think the cons should have been allowed such privileges. They could lock us out, they could do anything they wanted in there.' He pulled on his crash helmet and flipped up the visor. 'You were right to withdraw cell keys, that's all.'

'And that's why you tipped me off about tonight?'

Morgan zipped up his anorak. The shiny black helmet made him look like an alien monster. 'Ma'am,' he said in his Scottish burr, 'talk to Vernon Black.'

'I already have. He's an arsonist,' Helen said.

'He's also a junkie.' Morgan leaned forward. 'And with nothin' on the wing he'll be in need of a fix. He might just talk to you.'

'About what?'

'Michael Winchwood.'

He snapped the visor down and rode off. Helen returned to her car. She was too tired to feel excited, yet something very like elation was bubbling beneath the surface. Hopefully after a good night's sleep it would still be there, only stronger. She drove home with keen anticipation.

Michael Winchwood's cell in the VP Wing was still cordoned off, not because it was required by the investigation but because of the damage that had taken place inside it. The cell was earmarked to be redecorated and replumbed along with a number of others on the wing that had fire damage. The corridors had been washed and cleaned, but the empty, blackened cell felt ominous.

Helen picked through it, careful not to get any soot on her black skirt and russet-coloured single-breasted jacket. Daft thing to wear today, she thought, cursing her own lack of foresight.

Yellow chalk marked the position of the body. The blood that had flowed from it had congealed to a purplish matt red, like a sticky floor covering. Dark spots were randomly scattered everywhere. Beneath the window, a smear of dried blood extended across the wall. More blood in the wash-basin, with long hairs stuck in it.

Helen held up a smoke-blackened CD cover between finger and thumb. *Nessun Dorma* by Pavarotti. Another lay open on the table – *The Golden Greats of Opera* – with the disc still inside, a dark smear on the mirror surface. She looked through his collection of paperbacks. Michael Winchwood, the keen opera buff, went strictly for horror in his reading matter: Stephen King, James Herbert, Dean Koontz, and a compendium of classic Victorian ghost stories.

Wiping her fingers on a tissue, she stepped through the doorway and reared back a little as a shadow blocked the light.

'You gave me a shock. I was just checking Winchwood's belongings. His parents would like to have them. Did you want me?'

O'Keefe's ruddy, bearded face wore a truculent look.

'Officer Doughen said you wanted to see Vernon Black. He's in woodwork.' He moved aside, his eyes following her, raising his voice as Helen went along the landing. 'He's got the shakes, won't get any sense out of him.'

Doughen stood lone guard over Black in the woodwork shop. With a vastly depleted prison population, most of the craft and trade sections were not in use, just opened up on an *ad hoc* basis.

Doughen, about to follow Helen across the floor, didn't like it when she told him to wait at the door. He dithered, and Helen said sharply, 'Just wait outside, please.'

He backed away, hooded eyes watchful, and took up station near the glass-panelled double doors.

Helen, not wishing to be overheard, put more distance between them, and beckoned Black to her. He was shaking so badly he could hardly stand, let alone walk. His streaked, spiky hair wilted with the perspiration pouring off him. He leaned against a workbench and wiped his face with a shirtsleeve that was already saturated.

Helen went up close, keeping her voice low. 'On the night of the riots, Vernon, you told me you were on the VP Wing. And when the fire started you were already in your cell.'

A nervous spasm made Black's face one continuous, hideous twitch. Tremors shook his hands, as bad as an old wino's on the street.

'Y-yes . . .'

'You are serving a sentence for arson, aren't you?'

'Yes.'

'Did you begin one of the fires the night Michael Winchwood was killed?'

Black's trembling arms were crossed over his chest, hugging himself. He raised his head and looked over Helen's shoulder to Doughen, his bottom lip white where his teeth dug in.

Helen said, 'Would you wait outside the door, Mr Doughen?' She turned back. 'What's the matter, Vernon, are you sick? Are you running a temperature? What's the matter with you, Vernon?'

'I dunno anything' . . .' He croaked it out, Adam's apple jerking in the long pale throat. 'But I . . . I might . . .' The watery green eyes in the twitching face stared hard at Helen. 'I want to go back closer to where me mum can visit me. It'd help me remember.'

Helen tightened her lips. 'Don't you play games with me, Vernon. I'm not here to make deals with you. When was your last visit?'

He cleared his throat. 'Bin over a month.'

'So you lied to me.' Helen pointed the finger. 'You told me, Vernon, that you were on the VP Wing because you owed money – which you were able to pay after a visit. Now, I'm asking you again: on the night of the fire, were you locked in your cell?'

He looked away, blinking.

'On the night Winchwood died, did you see anything?'

He stared at the wall.

'Did you hear anything?'

He stared at the wall.

Helen sighed, shaking her head, and went over to the door. 'Take him back to his cell,' she said, and went out.

Very slowly Black turned round. He flinched when Doughen made an abrupt gesture to get moving. Eyes shifting away like a wary animal's, he headed crablike for the door, skirting round Doughen, and scuttled out.

'Michael Winchwood had a radio CD player listed on his prop sheet.' Helen glanced up from the file. 'It's not in his cell. Any idea where it is?'

When Marshall shrugged, she went on, 'He must have had one – there were two discs still in his cell. Could you check it out for me, Gary? Better still, get me the prisoners' property lists, C Wing.'

Marshall left the office and went down the corridor to

the officers' rest room. Doughen and O'Keefe were sitting with mugs of tea, both of them smoking like chimneys. As Marshall entered, Russell Morgan came in behind him, crash helmet under his arm.

'You know anything about Winchwood's CD player?' asked Marshall. 'Governor wants all the C Wing inmates' property lists.'

The two men shook their heads. O'Keefe waited until Marshall had turned his back, and then leaned over. 'Shit!' he murmured in Doughen's ear. 'Did Vernon put it on his bloody list?'

Doughen tugged at his moustache. 'Dunno.'

Morgan watched the pair of them from the doorway. He caught Marshall's sleeve as he was leaving, and said in a quiet aside, 'Don't back the wrong horse, Gary. She's getting closer.'

Helen was on the phone, making notes on a yellow scratch pad. She looked up as Marshall tapped and entered, then waved him to remain silent.

'Do you recall what make it was, Mr Winchwood? Yes . . . yes . . . and any of the CD discs you would know Michael had.' She scribbled, nodding her head. 'Ah, you sent them.'

Marshall said, 'I need to talk to you.'

Helen covered the phone. 'Not now, thank you.'

'When, then?'

Trying to concentrate, Helen said irritably, 'I don't know, Gary.' He rubbed his chin, agitated, and departed. Helen leaned forward, frowning. 'Sorry, what was that? Serial number LP20049D. Thank you very much, Mr Winchwood.'

Staring at the pad, Helen thoughtfully cradled the phone. An instant later she was on her feet and running for the door as the general alarm bell made an almighty clamour.

She might have guessed where the trouble was. She arrived to find O'Keefe and three other officers at the gates to C Wing. The alarm was sounding, and a voice boomed over the Tannoy: 'STAY IN YOUR CELLS, STAY IN YOUR CELLS.'

Helen pushed forward. 'It's not a fire, is it?'

Then through the barred gates she glimpsed Dr Thomas and Tom Doughen racing up the spiral stairway to the landing.

O'Keefe said, 'They're all accounted for. The others are in the visitors' area.' He put out an arm to restrain her. 'Don't go in.'

'What's happened in there?' Helen demanded. She knocked his arm aside and entered the wing.

'I wouldn't go in,' O'Keefe called behind her.

On the upper landing all the cells except one were closed. Doughen, stony-faced, stood to one side of the open door as Helen ran up. Dr Thomas was on his knees, bending over the sprawled figure of Vernon Black. His crossed hands pumped at the man's chest.

'Come on, Vernon. Come on, son.' The pinched mouth opened suddenly in a dry gasp, sucked in air. 'That's it, come on . . .'

Black coughed, his arms flailing about, and Dr Thomas straightened up. 'Get him to the ward fast as you can.'

Helen made way for the stretcher. 'Has he taken something?'

Two officers lifted him, and above the grey blanket Helen saw an angry red patch on Black's throat. 'Did somebody do this to him?'

Dr Thomas pushed past her. Black was carried out moaning, his narrow face covered in sweat. Dr Thomas hurried along the landing behind the stretcher, Doughen in front.

Exasperated, Helen looked round the cell for what might have been signs of a struggle. Her eye fell on the Sony CD player on the shelf above Vernon's bed. He'd been listening to some punk trash thing, she recalled, when she'd interviewed him in here, but she hadn't given it a thought. She reached forward and touched one of the buttons. A metal tray slid out, with a circular recess for CD discs.

Helen stared at it for a moment. The missing pieces were falling into place. One by one. She strode out onto the landing, the CD player under her arm.

CHAPTER 11

VERNON BLACK was propped up on pillows, his pyjama top unbuttoned. His eyes were shut, but he was breathing normally and seemed almost to have recovered.

Dr Thomas moved from the foot of the bed and reached over to push the pyjama top aside. 'He's got severe bruising to his neck' – he indicated the region – 'and also to back and buttocks. You can virtually see the imprint of a fist.'

Helen leaned forward, her shoulder almost touching his. She was taking a close interest, but was suddenly aware that the close interest had as much to do with Lorcan Thomas as with the patient. In profile his face had a leaner aspect, hollows curving under his cheekbones. Dark lashes slanted over his eyes, and that damn casually brushed-back hair curled at the nape of his neck. She inhaled a lemony fragrance, soap or aftershave.

She snapped back to what he was saying.

'. . . he insists that he fell down the stone steps, but he's obviously been used as a punch-bag.'

Helen took charge. 'Vernon, open your eyes and look at me. Look at me.'

His eyelids flickered. He blinked several times and then gazed dully into nowhere.

Helen said sternly, intending to shock him to attention, 'You had Michael Winchwood's CD stereo in your cell. Do you know what that means? Do you understand, Vernon?'

'Leave me alone,' he mumbled, hardly moving his lips.

Helen sat down on the bed. She stared him in the face. 'Oh, I will leave you alone, Vernon. Everybody's going to leave you alone because you could be charged with Michael Winchwood's murder.'

'No!' He huddled down, his thin pale hands clutched to his bony chest. 'I didn't touch him, I never touched him.' He began to cough dramatically. 'I'm sick, I'm sick . . .'

'Who did it, then, Vernon?' Helen asked quietly. 'Who was in Michael Winchwood's cell the night he died?'

The curtain surrounding the bed was whisked aside and Gary Marshall appeared. His bottom-heavy face was undecided between a frown and a scowl.

Helen sighed as Black turned away his head and began to weep in blubbing sobs, saliva dripping off his chin.

'What's happened?' Marshall said.

Helen stood up. 'We'll discuss it in my office.' Without looking at him she pushed past and went out.

Her anger was smouldering nicely by the time they reached her office. She paced up and down while Marshall stood fidgeting with something in the baggy pockets of his jacket.

'Come on, this is ridiculous, you know the rules.' Helen was consciously taking deep breaths, not allowing her frustration to blast off into orbit. She was close, she knew it, she wasn't going to lose it now.

'Every prisoner must list his personal possessions on the property sheet. It's a bloody CD player and it's not on Vernon Black's list. It was never on his list because you know – I know – it belonged to Michael Winchwood. You were part of the cell search, Gary, so who is covering up for who?'

'I am not covering up for anybody,' Marshall insisted stolidly.

'Somebody is. At least admit you know that.'

'No, I don't know that.'

Helen halted in front of him. 'But you are aware by now

that there could be a murder inquiry?' She let the silence gather, not in any hurry now. She was in control. 'This is your opportunity, Gary. You can come clean with me.'

Marshall slowly removed his hands from his pockets. 'I have nothing to hide.'

'Good.' Helen nodded, apparently satisfied. She went round the desk for her briefcase. 'In the meantime I want to know the name of every single officer on that cell search. I want the name of every officer near Vernon Black's cell before he was beaten.'

Marshall's eyes followed her as she came back with the briefcase and picked up her raincoat from a chair.

'Beaten?'

'He's also an arsonist,' Helen said, pausing to give him a meaningful look. 'And if I discover he was not in his cell the night of the riot, he will be a witness. Plot thickens – with me?'

She walked to the door. 'Goodnight,' she said without turning, and was gone.

Helen slowly pulled back the curtain. Vernon Black looked up from the comic he was reading. He didn't move a muscle as she came in, but the pages of the comic started to shake when he saw her place the Sony CD player on the bedside table.

Helen moved to the foot of the bed and swung round to face him, hands gripping the rail. There wasn't a sound on the small ward. The other beds were unoccupied, the two guards at the far end in their glass-walled cubicle playing three-card brag.

Black swallowed, the big Adam's apple jerking in his throat.

'I talk to you and they'll kill me.' There was more breath than solid sound. He hunched forward, his eyes terrified, imploring. 'Murphy and Jellings will kill me.'

'Who are you more afraid of, Vernon?' Helen said very quietly. 'Murphy and Jellings – or certain prison officers?' Her eyes narrowed. 'Who beat you?'

'I fell down the stairs.'

Helen shook her head. She leaned forward over the rail. 'Nobody's going to hurt you. Just tell me the truth, Vernon, and no one will hurt you.'

Black laid the comic on the bedclothes and stared down at the coloured images of Judge Dredd. Helen had to lean even further to catch the numbed whisper. 'I saw it . . .'

Smoothly and carefully, so as not to break the spell, Helen moved nearer until she was sitting on the edge of the bed. Now it was her turn not to move a muscle as she sat, hands folded in her lap, listening to Vernon Black.

Helen walked towards her car, stretching out her hand to deactivate the alarm. It was then that she saw the shadow move. Instinctively she drew back, half turned, ready to run. She looked round the staff car park which, although brightly lit, was deserted at this hour.

She tensed as the shadow moved again, and then Tom Doughen stepped into the light. 'It isn't the way you think,' he said in a low voice, shaking his head. Helen took a step backwards, and he held up his hand. 'Hey, I'm not going to hurt you. I just . . . we want to talk to you.' He looked towards a Ford Granada parked next to the fence, and then back at her. 'Please.'

It took a moment to decide. She tossed her briefcase into the Metro, locked the door, and went across with him to the Granada. Doughen opened the passenger door for her and climbed in the back seat. O'Keefe was sitting behind the wheel, smoking. He offered her a cigarette.

Helen said, 'No, thank you, I don't smoke,' and wound down the window.

Doughen lit up, a red glow in the darkened rear of the car, and as an afterthought wound down his window too.

She could hear the wheeziness in his voice when he said, 'Michael Winchwood used to taunt us, taunt the other prisoners. He's been made out to be some kind of victim, but in reality the man was a perverted, twisted bastard.'

'He wasn't like the other segregated nonces,' O'Keefe tried to explain. 'He was always sort of gloating, like he was somehow superior, playing his classical music, his opera . . .'

Helen stared through the windscreen. 'Get to the point.'

'Tom's got two kids,' O'Keefe said. 'Winchwood used to keep on about what he would do to them.'

The red glow brightened as Doughen took a deep, shaky drag. 'I was bathing my little boy and I drew the curtains 'cos I didn't want anyone to see me holding my own little boy.' His voice thickened with a bitter hatred. 'That's what Winchwood did to me.'

'We just wanted to shut him up, make him scared,' O'Keefe said. He sneaked a quick glance at her. 'We knew we couldn't do it.'

'So you used Murphy and Jellings?' Helen said.

O'Keefe leaned towards her, and there was beer on his breath. 'We wanted to talk to you, to tell you and ask if you'd—'

'I think I know what you're going to ask me,' Helen said, 'and the answer is no. There's been enough covering up.' She turned sideways in the seat to face them. 'If Murphy and Jellings killed Winchwood, he has the right to justice. Or his family does.'

'He deserved all he got,' Doughen said, not an ounce of remorse or repentance in his voice.

'We just wanted to teach him a lesson, nothing more,' O'Keefe said hoarsely.

'But it was more, a lot more.' Helen opened the door. 'Governor Langham covered for you, didn't he?' She stared at O'Keefe and at the red glow of Doughen's cigarette. 'No? What about Gary Marshall? Did he? Did he know?'

In the wash of light from the security floodlights

O'Keefe's face was void of expression, and she couldn't see Doughen's face at all. It didn't matter. She had all the pieces she needed. And neither did she feel any great tug of sympathy for them. They were prison officers, and in spite of the pressures of the job, the provocations (and there were many) and the daily crock of shit in having to deal with the worst that society could throw at them, above everything else they had a duty to obey the unwritten code; instead Doughen and O'Keefe had broken it, and allowed their emotions to get the upper hand.

It was a shitty, thankless job right enough, Helen thought, getting out of the car. But somebody had to have the guts to do it.

It was Saturday morning, and judging by the look on Royston Andrews's face he was giving up a round of golf to attend this hastily called meeting at the Millbank HQ. Sean Duncan's expression was harder to fathom. To Helen it didn't seem its usual smug self, but carried an air of *This had better be worth it or else*. There was little change in Mrs Donald: she had looked faintly disapproving on every occasion that Helen had met her.

From her briefcase Helen took out a small tape recorder and placed it on the green baize in front of her. She might have brought out a miniature time bomb, because a stiffening tension was at once perceptible in the board members sitting opposite. Their reaction was perhaps more instinctively accurate than they realized.

Helen looked up and smiled.

'Thank you for seeing me. I'm sorry to disrupt your weekend but I think you should hear this tape, and . . .' She took out several thick document files and laid them down. '. . . these are the statements of the officers involved, Officers O'Keefe and Doughen. But they didn't do it on their own. Also involved in the events of that night were Officers Jenson, Smith, Mallard. They are all named.

I leave you to make your own decision regarding Deputy Governor Gary Marshall, as he is not yet privy to this information.'

Andrews leaned back, one hand over his mouth. Duncan's expression had become confused, as if he was struggling, none too happily, to take this all in. But Helen hadn't finished.

From her briefcase came more files, which she placed alongside the others, all spread out before them on the green baize.

'Here are prisoners Anthony Murphy and Douglas Jellings's case histories, and lastly Vernon Black's tape recording. Could I play it now? It was actually recorded on Michael Winchwood's own cassette player.'

Helen inserted the tape and the soft, whispering voice of Vernon Black, speaking close to the microphone, filtered into the room.

'I was in the kitchen area . . . Murphy and Jellings was brought in. Officers O'Keefe and Doughen gave them the nod . . .'

He's very quick at it, practised, and not a bit nervous. The casual stroll along the landing to make a last brew before lock-up. No one pays him any attention. The wing is settling down for the night, the men loitering by their cell doors. 'Nessun Dorma' floats from Winchwood's cell, while the tall thin figure of Winchwood himself leans on the rail outside in languid repose, the mass of thick curly hair hanging to his shoulders.

Standing in front of the water heater, Black can't hold back the giggles. *This is one I prepared earlier*, he thinks, taking the box of Swan Vestas and length of thick twine from his shirt pocket. A quick glance over his shoulder. All quiet on the Western Front. He puts his mouth close to the aperture and blows out the pilot light. One end of the twine into the box of matches, the matches stuffed into the aperture. Quick as a wink. He winds down the trailing length of twine. Another sharp glance behind, the flare of a match in his cupped hand, and he breathes out a tremulous sigh of pleasure as the twine starts to smoulder.

Black strolls back along the landing, nods to Winchwood, and continues to his own cell next door.

Perfect timing, as the Tannoy booms out: 'Lock-up, lock-up. Everybody back to their cells. Lock-up.'

Standing with O'Keefe at the end of the wing, Doughen covers his mouth. 'They're coming up now.'

The two officers separate, taking opposite landings. Doughen looks over the rail to the officers below. They begin to ease away from the central area, making themselves scarce.

'Get in your cells,' O'Keefe shouts. 'Black, Winchwood, inside. Lock-up.'

From below, the clang of the entrance gates banging shut. Two officers walk off, pocketing their keys, and disappear. The figures of Murphy and Jellings emerge into the open area and begin a swift silent ascent to the upper landing.

At his cell door, an alarmed Black sees them run towards him. 'Stay out of this,' Murphy growls, and Black hurriedly backs inside, slamming the door shut, his eye appearing a moment later at the peep-hole.

Winchwood jumps up as the two men fill the doorway. In the tiny space between the bed and the table and the toilet bowl there is nowhere to go, nowhere to hide. Murphy advances, one fist clenched, in his other a chiv – a razor blade inserted into a toothbrush. Jellings comes in and heels the cell door shut. Murphy nods at Winchwood and smiles his dead smile.

Outside on the landing, O'Keefe moves along, checking each prisoner before he locks the door. He turns the key on Black and then stands at the door to Winchwood's cell, giving a 'five-minute' signal with his hand to Doughen on the landing opposite. From within the cell the voice of

Pavarotti suddenly swells as the volume is turned right up, drowning any other sound.

O'Keefe leans over the rail.

'Lock-up secure on landing,' he reports, and moves on.

Winchwood's long hair comes in handy, because Jellings uses it to hold him down while Murphy lays into him. A fist in the face and kicks to the body, thudding in very satisfactorily. Murphy is enjoying himself. He aims a kick into Winchwood's groin, thinking, That'll learn him, and grins as Winchwood squirms in agony on the floor, his screams lost in the deafening boom of Pavarotti from the stereo speakers.

The two men are really getting into it now. The more Winchwood screams and squirms, the more they like it. Jellings grips the curly hair and smashes Winchwood's head against the floor with a hollow clunk. Murphy leans over, lank black hair hanging over his ears. He isn't grinning any more. He's too far gone for that. He swings his arm and swipes the blade of the chiv across Winchwood's throat. Blood spurts like a fountain, bathing Winchwood's face in a glistening mask. Not done yet, Murphy slashes both wrists for good measure. He straightens up and steps back, blood dripping from the chiv, and watches with heaving chest as Jellings approaches the pale green wall with brimming hands and scrawls across it –

NONCE PERVURT
CHILD KILLER

Doughen reckons time's up; they'll have sorted that sick, twisted bastard out by now. From the opposite landing he signals to O'Keefe, who nods and moves quickly to Winchwood's cell and pushes the door open.

Before he can see inside, two things happen, one on top

of the other. In a headlong rush to get out, Murphy and Jellings pile into him, almost knocking him flat. And from the kitchen area further along the landing comes the crackling blast of an explosion, sending a tongue of flame streaking clear across the central area.

Acrid black smoke billows to the V-shaped skylight as O'Keefe stands in the doorway to the cell, staring in shocked disbelief at the blood-bath inside. He whirls round, screaming, 'It's Winchwood – get somebody in here. Get somebody here!'

Jellings is tearing along the landing, heading for the stairway. A few yards behind, Murphy trips and goes sprawling. Scrambling up, he runs straight into Doughen, and the two men lock together in a clawing, grappling struggle that bounces them from the wall to the rail and back again. Murphy swings a fist which never lands. Morgan's arm snakes round his neck, almost jerking his head from his body, and his shoulders are pinioned by two officers, twisting both elbows up to his shoulder blades.

Inside the cell, O'Keefe takes a long stride over Winchwood's body and the widening pool of blood. With his sleeve he smears out the scrawled words, and then backs away, almost slipping on the wet floor, and stumbles out onto the landing.

Above the clanging fire alarm and the wailing siren comes the blare of the Tannoy:

'Emergency! Emergency! All officers required to evacuate the VP Wing. FIRE! FIRE!'

'I didn't start no other fire but the one in the VP kitchen, 'cos I hate the animals in there. I never did nothin' to Michael Winchwood. Murphy and Officers O'Keefe and Doughen agreed not to say nothin' about it. They gave me his stereo – I never nicked it. Then they tried to take it off me and they beat me up . . .'

Helen leaned forward and switched it off. In the silence

that followed a spattering of raindrops hit the window pane. Royston Andrews would have had to abandon his game of golf anyway, it seemed.

He took a deep breath. 'Thank you, Miss Hewitt. I think we would now like to discuss these developments. You have been very tenacious.'

Helen rose and picked up her briefcase. As she reached for the tape recorder, Andrews held up his hand. 'Would you please leave the tape recording?'

Helen nodded, fastening her briefcase. She stood facing them and said quietly, 'There is a copy in the file, plus a written transcript.'

Sean Duncan and Mrs Donald exchanged guarded looks. Andrews gave Helen a single penetrating stare, which was fine by her. She knew that she had them by the short and curlies. And so did they.

Swaggering and full of bravado, Tony Murphy and Dougie Jellings, handcuffed to two officers, were led to the green prison van waiting in the main yard. Stepping onto the rear platform they raised clenched fists in a victory salute, acknowledging the cheers and the waving handkerchiefs from the wings. In the eyes of the inmates – and their own – they were heroes, and they would have plenty of leisure time during the next fifteen years in which to savour it.

Seated between the Operational Director and Sean Duncan, Helen smiled into the battery of cameras. Not only had the press turned out in force, there were also reporters and crews from ITN, the BBC, BSkyB, and a satellite team from Germany.

Helen had cut her hair, had even had it streaked – there was no bun at the nape of her neck, no attempt to make herself staid and unglamorous. She had treated herself to a manicure and facial. She was wearing make-up and glossy lipstick. This was, in some ways, a new armour, a new confidence, and she liked the feeling because that was just how she felt – confident. She had come a long way and it was hard to believe that it was only a short time ago that she had been sitting on the other side of that green baize table. Now she was the centre of attention and she liked it.

Helen smiled towards the forest of hands, picking out one with a slight inclination of her head.

'Miss Hewitt, can you tell me what it feels like to be taking on the notorious Barfield Prison?' asked the man from the *Mail*.

'It's a challenge – and I know it will be hard work.' That had to be the mother of all understatements, Helen thought with a flash of gallows humour. She went on, sounding sincere because her belief was real: 'The new investigation into the death of Michael Winchwood proves that, inside or outside prison, every man deserves and has a right to justice.'

Royston Andrews nodded agreement. Given the crisis in the Prison Service, that quote alone could do a power of good, and he noted with satisfaction that they were all scribbling away. He relaxed.

A blonde woman thrust a microphone forward. 'Is it true you're the youngest governor in England?'

'I believe so.'

'Is it true you are the youngest female governor in England?' someone called out.

'Yes,' Helen said, and that was the one, the smile they were waiting for, the flashlights popping off like crazy. 'That is correct.'

Part Two

The Escape

Chapter 12

Edward Maynard was a man of very little patience, compounded by a violent temper which he took pains to conceal. To the other inmates of Barfield, as to the world in general, he conveyed an impression of calm equanimity, perfectly at ease with himself. Most of the cons were taken in by the pose. After all, Maynard was a cut above them. Well educated, nicely spoken, every inch the wealthy professional gentleman, right down to his plump pink fingertips.

He also happened to be a Category B prisoner – 'for whom escape must be made very difficult' – a professional gentleman who over the years had defrauded the Stock Exchange, the international currency markets and several banks of well over three million sterling.

Wearing a pinstriped suit, crisp white shirt and grey silk tie, an overcoat draped across his shoulders, Maynard waited with a soft indulgent smile as Jumbo Jackson unlocked the gates of C Wing. A fit, trim man in his younger days, in the university rowing team, his figure was now more than adequately padded. His round smooth face had the slightly mottled look of someone who had indulged most of his appetites. Stepping through, Maynard again waited for the gate to be locked before proceeding at his own pace along the main corridor, slightly ahead of the two escorting officers as if he were a visiting dignitary with his own retinue.

Two Red Band orderlies were mopping the floor, and

they eased deferentially aside as Maynard passed by. One of them, eyes sheepishly on his shoes, managed a hushed, 'Morning, Mr Maynard.'

Maynard slowed. 'Your sister out of hospital, is she, Tommy?' he inquired, eyebrows raised, condescending to show an interest in those mortals less fortunate than himself.

'Yes, sir, thank you, sir.'

'Keep walking,' Jackson said, though he kept his voice down and made no attempt at physical contact.

Maynard gave a pained sigh and a careless wave of the hand. Stan Field, the other trusty, clutching his mop, dropped his head in a nod that was almost a bow. Passing on, Maynard favoured him with a quick, surreptitious wink.

'Good luck,' Field mouthed back.

Two officers were waiting at the external gate to the main yard. Both were well over six feet, and together with the guard on gate duty had a combined weight in excess of fifty stone. Maynard was patient once again as locking and unlocking went ahead; he had little option, because between his cell in C Wing and Reception this same procedure had to be got through nine times.

Jackson contacted MS2D Central Control, identifying himself as Tango 4. 'Prisoner walking, main yard to Reception. Exit clear, is it? We got him at Gate 2, over.'

Clearance came through. Before Maynard had the chance to move, however, one of the officers produced handcuffs.

Maynard was not well pleased. 'What's this?' he demanded with a frown.

'Governor's orders,' Jackson replied. Neither his eyes nor his voice showed the contempt the big, bearded officer felt for this arrogant, slippery weasel.

Maynard released another of his famous world-weary sighs, and indolently held out his right arm to be cuffed.

After a short stroll across the yard he was taken into Reception, a single-storey building adjoining the gate-lodge. Every prisoner, coming in or going out, was dealt with here. It was here that new inmates were received and processed, given a prison number, allocated a cell, and where their belongings and the effects they had brought with them were stored. And, in Maynard's case, where he collected them for his court hearing.

Above the long counter with high racks of shelves behind, a large noticed stated:

HMP BARFIELD ALL INMATES' PROPERTY COMING INTO BARFIELD WILL BE X-RAYED NO EXCEPTIONS

Maynard stood with arms outstretched as the metal detector played over the immaculate suit, past the knife-edge creases in his trousers to his gleaming black shoes.

'Hand-made for me, this.' Maynard smiled. 'You can always tell a good whistle. See? No pull when you hold out your arms.'

As Senior Officer, Russell Morgan was in charge of the operation. He exchanged looks with Jackson. They both knew Maynard was flaunting his wealth for their benefit: you poor saps in the Prison Service, on a few measly grand a year. Just look what I'm worth, suckers!

A large brown box was brought from storage and placed on the counter. The duty guard checked each item on a clipboard as it was taken out. Leather wallet. Credit cards. Business cards. Small onyx comb with gold clip. He took out a Rolex Oyster watch with a solid gold casing, and seemed rather reluctant to put it down.

An officer was checking Maynard's overcoat, running his

thumb along the seams. Maynard watched him, amusement in his dark shadowy eyes. 'Cashmere, second only to a young woman's skin,' he murmured silkily.

The duty guard took out the last item. A thick wedge of fifty-pound notes, solid as a brick; three grand or thereabouts, Morgan estimated. He was warm. The counterfoil Maynard had signed on arrival at Barfield stated £3,200.

'Governor's orders, he's to be cuffed at all times,' Morgan said quietly, taking one of the escorting officers aside. 'Officer Jackson to travel inside the wagon with him. You hand him over to Security.' With a brisk nod, he turned back to the counter, where Maynard was fussily arranging his precious cashmere coat over his shoulders.

Morgan weighed the Rolex in his palm. 'This a fake?'

Maynard's stare was taunting. 'You tell me.'

Morgan stared back. 'I'll tell you, Maynard, your kind make me sick to my stomach. It's easy to play big inside, but all you really are is a cheap thief. Your money stinks—'

'Like roses when you've got it,' said Maynard imperturbably.

The sandy-haired Scot didn't respond. He merely pointed to the onyx comb and instructed the duty guard, 'That's all he's allowed to take out with him.'

For one bare instant Maynard's dark eyes flashed. His mottled complexion turned a deeper hue. It was a glimpse of the dangerous jagged iceberg below the surface, the violent temper that was always there, threatening to erupt. Then it was gone, his air of languid repose back in place. And with a faint smile on his lips he took up the comb and combed his hair.

'Coming! I'm coming!' Helen yelled, as the doorbell rang. She ran through from the bedroom into the hallway, raincoat half on, half off. The plan was to be ready in plenty of time, and she had been, until she'd decided to catch up on the mountain of paperwork she'd brought home the previous evening. She lost herself in it, and the next thing she knew the six o'clock news was on Radio 4 and she wasn't even dressed.

She stood in the hallway, dithering. She pulled on her raincoat, grabbed her shoulder bag, stuffed her portable phone inside, and then stood, not coming or going, racking her brains for anything she might have forgotten. She winced when she caught sight of herself in the long mirror. She looked frazzled, and no bloody wonder. She ran a hand through her hair, flicking strands away from the centre parting. Her make-up looked okay, though she wasn't too sure about that shade of lipstick. Too pale for TV? Christ, what if she came over looking like Sandie Shaw on *Top of the Pops*, circa 1966?

Coming out into the daylight, Helen got quite a shock. A black stretch Mercedes with tinted windows stood at the kerb, the driver in a grey uniform with matching cap holding open the rear door.

Helen went forward with a lighter step, giving him a smile.

'They really meant it when they said they would send a car for me!' She tossed her head jauntily and stepped inside to the smell of leather and mahogany. 'Very impressive. Thank you,' she said, smiling delightedly, as the driver touched the peak of his cap and the door clicked shut.

At least the forty-minute drive to the studios on the outskirts of Birmingham gave her time to relax and get her thoughts in order. In the days following the press conference at Millbank HQ, Helen had been in constant demand by the media. She'd taken part in two radio phone-in programmes, given a dozen interviews to the press, had her photograph taken in front of Barfield's gate-lodge. She was doing it, she told herself, not for the personal publicity, but because she had a strong conviction that the public should be as informed as possible about the prison system. And informed by somebody who knew what they were talking about. It was all very well Tory politicians and tabloid editors – the 'lock-'em-up-and-throw-away-the-key' brigade – ranting on about how prisoners should be dealt with. It made for glib headlines and easy votes. What was actually needed was a dose of hard reality served cold. Caging men up in a strict, comfortless environment and denying them any privileges went down a storm at party conferences. What everyone forgot – politicians, media, and the public – was that the body of men and women who made up the Prison Service had dumped upon them the task of enforcing such a harsh regime. Keeping the prison population secure was difficult enough even with men allowed a few home comforts. Deny them that, treat them no better, or indeed worse, than you would animals in a zoo, and the prisons could only function as the gulags did during Stalin's reign of terror.

Perhaps, Helen reflected grimly, that was what the public really hankered after. Build one huge fortress-like prison in the Shetland or the Orkney Islands, ship the lot of them out there and leave them to rot. Problem was, you would still need governors, staff and prison officers to keep control, and she wasn't entirely sure she could adapt to the long winter nights.

Television studios always reminded Helen of a cross between the hushed atmosphere of a cathedral and the dry suffocating heat of a sauna. She could feel the bubbles of perspiration breaking out even before the programme went on air. This segment was being fed 'down the line' to the live breakfast show in the London studio, from where it would be transmitted on all national networks.

Helen had been lightly dusted with powder, her dark grey jacket checked on the monitor to make sure it wouldn't 'jazz', and seated on a long curved cream sofa. A technician attached a button mike to her lapel.

The interviewer, quite handsome in a florid way, with

wings of silvery-grey hair, was listening through his earpiece to the control gallery. He nodded rapidly.

'Okay, yep . . . yep. Get to her first, then . . . yeah, we got the slides set up? Good, okay.'

Helen hadn't been expecting there to be another guest on the show. The floor manager led her forward, or rather had to assist her, as she seemed to have trouble walking. She was a plain, dumpy woman in her forties with lines bitten deep around the eyes and a kind of permanent frown. She wore an old-fashioned print dress and clutched a shiny plastic handbag. Helen studied her closely as she was seated opposite on an identical sofa, and a sixth sense set off a tiny alarm bell. With the interviewer separating them, this looked suspiciously like an adversarial situation.

'Any minute now,' the interviewer said, giving each of them a brief professional smile. He straightened up, took a breath, and faced the camera. The floor manager spread his hand, fingers curling one by one as he silently counted them in. Five-four-three-two . . .

The camera's red light winked on.

'Last week it was announced by the prison authorities that the new governor of the riot-torn Barfield Prison was to be Helen Hewitt.'

Another camera moved in, framing Helen in close-up. The interviewer swivelled in her direction.

'Miss Hewitt, at thirty-three you are the youngest woman governor in charge of a Category B all-male prison.'

'Yes, that is correct.'

'If that weren't enough of a challenge, you will also be overseeing the Government's plans to refurbishing Barfield.'

Helen nodded. 'Yes, that is so.'

'The press have speculated that your appointment could have been a publicity stunt to overshadow the riot which—'

Helen hadn't been expecting this, but senses alert, she cut in quickly. 'I do not believe my appointment was in any way a publicity-seeking campaign by the Prison Service,' she said firmly.

The interviewer turned to the woman opposite. She was leaning forward nervously, knees pressed together, moistening her dry lips.

'Joining us this morning, Miss Sarah Smith. You feel very differently about criminals, don't you, Miss Smith?'

Helen stiffened as a series of colour slides flashed up on the studio monitor screen. What the hell was going on? They were police photographs, showing a barely recognizable Sarah Smith, her face marked with purple bruises, a gash down one cheek, her left eye nearly obliterated by an angry crimson swelling.

'Eight years ago I was mugged and raped only a few yards from my own home,' Sarah Smith was saying in a voice husky with nerves. 'I sustained injuries to my spine and have been unable to walk any distance since. My house was recently burgled, although the police doubted if the two crimes were connected. I was unable to deal with the terror that he had . . .' she tried to clear her throat '. . . that the man who raped me had come back.'

'But there was a reason for that, wasn't there?' the interviewer prompted her.

'Yes.' A spasm flickered across her face. 'He threatened me, he said he knew where I lived and would always be able to find me.'

Helen wasn't sure where this was leading, but she had a nasty idea. She tried to stay cool, retain her poise, though she was starting to fume inside that they'd got her here on a false pretext.

'And so you connected the burglary with the rapist?' the interviewer said, bringing her along.

'Yes, I did. You see, by that time he had already been released from prison.'

'And how does this make you feel?'

He was really milking it, Helen saw, as the poor woman's

face suddenly seemed to collapse, her eyes tightening with hidden pain, holding back the tears.

'Angry . . . very angry. I live with a life sentence, not him.' Her voice was a croak. 'All I want to know is that he is locked up and unable to hurt and abuse another woman.' She couldn't hold on, and tears leaked from her eyes. 'He ruined my life . . .'

The interviewer had the small decency to pause before, nodding in sympathy, he turned to Helen.

'Miss Hewitt, do you feel that more Government support is given to the criminal than to the victim?'

This was a minefield, and Helen trod carefully. 'Every victim has a right to justice, but my job is not to act as judge and jury. I do not sentence the men in my charge. My work is to rehabilitate so that when a prisoner is released he will no longer be a threat to society.'

'But it doesn't work!' Sarah Smith burst out, hands twisting in her lap. 'The man who raped me raped another woman six months after his release.'

'Considering the costs to keep a prisoner in today's luxury—' the interviewer went on, but Sarah Smith was determined to have her say, addressing her question to Helen: 'Why don't the Government spend more money on the victims rather than the criminals?'

Always the same hot potato, Helen thought. Up it came, regular as clockwork. She said evenly, 'The main costs are to ensure total security, that the prisoners do not escape. I do understand and feel for the victims, such as Miss Smith, but there are, at this present time, over fifty thousand men in prison.' From the corner of her eye she saw the floor manager giving the wind-up signal. 'We can't operate a "lock-'em-up-and-throw-away-the-key" regime. We must at all costs attempt to rehabilitate so they do not—'

'At all costs, Miss Hewitt?' asked the interviewer, eyebrows raised. He turned to Sarah Smith. 'Did you receive any compensation?'

'Ten thousand pounds.'

'Ten thousand pounds,' he repeated, shaking his head. 'A very small amount in comparison with the estimated forty million pounds' worth of damage which occurred during the riots at Barfield Prison.'

'Since Barfield was built in nineteen seventy-seven there have been many changes implemented by the prison authorities,' Helen said, and then made the mistake of pausing as he held up his hand.

'But it was a luxurious, modern and well-equipped prison.' His veiled accusation almost seemed to suggest she'd wrecked the damn place herself, Helen thought, getting really riled. 'Surely,' he went on, 'if the intention was to rehabilitate the men held there, it failed. The comfort or "softly softly" approach has shown itself—'

It was Helen's turn to interrupt. 'I have no intention of applying a "soft" approach during my term as Governor,' she made plain. She'd been wrong-footed right from the start of the interview; the whole thing had been rigged, pitting her against the wretched victim of a brutal assault and rape. And the interviewer still had an ace up his immaculate sleeve.

'In today's paper,' he said, holding it up, 'Barfield Prison has just been allocated sixty million pounds for the rebuild. Surely that is an *astronomical* amount of money, Miss Hewitt?'

Helen was thunderstruck. She was also flaming angry. Her reply, tight-lipped yet polite, drained every bit of patience and self-control she had left. 'I have not been informed of exactly what funds are to be allocated to Barfield.'

'It was in *The Times* this morning,' he said, giving her a rueful, rather pitying look. 'Perhaps this breakdown in communication is an indication of mismanagement,' he suggested, concluding the interview with his stern pundit's face turning to camera. 'Sadly, yet again, the victims of crime seem to be the losers.'

The floor manager's hand chopped down, indicating they were off air. Helen felt as though she had been chopped off at the knees.

Even as the black Mercedes was sweeping out of the studio gates, Helen was on the portable, trying to reach John Bunny. The car was moving slowly in city traffic when she finally got hold of him, and she stared through the tinted glass at the crowded pavements, her knuckles white from gripping the phone.

'Was anyone at Barfield informed? Well, why?' She pressed her lips together. 'How could it get leaked to the press without any consultation with me?' She shook her head angrily as he waffled on. This was a bloody fiasco. No wonder the Prison Service got a bad press.

Her patience all gone, she laid it on the bottom line. 'I would like to see the proposed plans for Barfield. I know, John, you're my area manager, but considering I am Governor in charge I may possibly have some suggestions.' Her sarcasm was only lightly sketched in, but John Bunny got the point. Helen looked at her watch. 'Fine, I'll be there.'

She gave the driver directions and leaned back into the soft leather, tapping her foot.

Richard Greenleaves was a senior partner in the firm of architects, and younger than Helen had expected. In his mid-thirties, he still had something of the gangling student about him, a thin bony face with a mop of unruly brown hair and gold wire-framed spectacles with tiny round lenses. His dress suited his name: a green corduroy suit with leather patches on the elbows, and a knitted tie casually pulled loose from the collar of his bottle-green shirt.

He spread out the plans and drawings on a large map

table and swung over a cowled lamp. The bright glare dazzled Helen's eyes for a moment.

'The prison authorities have not agreed to all these structural changes,' he told her. He sounded put out by something; probably at her turning up without a prior appointment, Helen reckoned. What the hell. 'Obviously nothing is set, well, not as yet.'

'I should hope not.' Helen stared at him. 'I mean, has anyone from Barfield been privy to these designs?'

'I really wouldn't know,' Greenleaves replied offhandedly. 'I'm just the architect.'

Helen was nettled. She said acidly, 'Well, it would make sense to ask people working there for their input.'

'I've only had meetings with the prison authorities,' he said, as if none of this concerned him. He showed her a small plywood model of one of the new cell units, like a room in a doll's house. 'The new plumbing is to be a priority, toilets and washbasins in every cell.'

Helen stood back and folded her arms. 'These men spend twelve hours a day inside their cells. They have to eat all their meals in there.' She was shaking her head. 'It's totally insanitary, never mind unhygienic.'

She leaned forward, frowning, pointing to what appeared to be a blank rectangle on the plans. 'What's this?'

'Proposed football pitch. Astro turf—'

'Astro turf? No wonder it's costing sixty million!' She pointed to another blank area, smack in the middle of the complex. 'This a swimming pool, is it?' Helen asked, giving him a sardonic look from under her eyelids.

Greenleaves certainly wasn't in any mood for facetious humour. 'This is proposed to be built inside the new, larger perimeter. It's a complete secure unit within the unit.'

'Is it SSU or a control unit?' It was important for her to know which. Special Secure Units housed maximum security Category A prisoners: IRA, international terrorists, the Mafia, the godfathers of the drugs trade. Control units were for any hardened criminal who caused trouble and wouldn't fit into the main prison. Once in the control unit, they had to earn their way out by good behaviour.

'A sort of prison within a prison,' the architect said.

'You mean a secure unit, Mr Greenleaves.' Helen's phone beeped and she reached inside her bag. 'In America it's nicknamed "the Cage" – but from your designs it resembles a four-star YMCA hostel.'

The call was from the security escort at the courthouse. Apparently Edward Maynard's solicitor was protesting that his client was being subjected, quite unnecessarily, to an excessive degree of restrictive supervision. Surely a man of Mr Maynard's standing ought to be allowed a certain freedom of movement inside a court of law.

Helen gave it short shrift. 'I don't care what his solicitor says. I want Maynard cuffed to an officer throughout the hearing.'

She zapped in the aerial and tossed the phone into her bag, aware that Greenleaves was watching her covertly. He was blinking behind his round spectacles, expression confused, as if belatedly realizing what clout this assertive young woman possessed. Secretly, Helen was enjoying it. In future he might give more thought to consulting her and taking her views seriously. As well as smartening up his act and getting rid of that tetchy manner of his.

There had been no joy from that bloody bitch, and Maynard was fuming. Locked in the cramped cubicle of the white prison van, bumping and jolting all the way from Barfield, with Jumbo Jackson's hairy mug peering at him through the tiny square grille in the door.

Sitting with his knees jammed up against the metal partition, Maynard could hear voices outside the van. A uniformed police officer was talking to the driver, wondering why they'd sent a sweat-box and three officers for one prisoner.

'What the hell you got in there? If it's a terrorist, we're bloody vulnerable.'

'Can you check out the courthouse before we open up?' the driver said. 'They reckon this bastard's got friends waiting.'

Maynard was growing impatient. 'What time is it?' he asked sharply, and Jackson held his watch to the grille. Maynard sighed. 'I'll need time with my accountant and business adviser. This has already been agreed. My solicitor will require—'

A fist banged the side of the van. At the signal, Jackson unlocked the rear doors. Two police officers stood waiting.

'Okay, bring him out. With the bracelets.'

Holding the cashmere coat to his shoulders, Maynard squirmed sideways to get from the cubicle into the narrow central walkway. Moments later he stepped down from the van, handcuffed between Jackson and another officer, and was led across the closed, paved courtyard into the rear entrance. One of the police officers went ahead, the other walking behind, speaking into his radio. 'Moving him in. Stand by.'

Maynard's solicitor and accountant were awaiting him in a holding cell in the basement. A metal-frame bed took up most of the space, and a small table and two chairs had been jammed in for them to sit and lay out their documents. Released from the accompanying officer, though still handcuffed to Jackson, Maynard sat on the bed, inspecting his fingernails. His hand was perfectly steady, which was the direct opposite of how he felt. Only a slight deepening of his mottled complexion gave a hint of the bottled-up frustration.

'Without more time we were unable to accommodate your requests,' his solicitor apologized weakly. Spread out on the table were what looked like plans of an office building. Jackson had glanced at them indifferently; it was foreign territory to him, all this high-powered financial stuff.

'What in Christ's name have I been paying you for?' Maynard asked with a heavy sigh. He looked up. 'They can't freeze those accounts, can they?'

The other two exchanged glances. They might have come out of the same pod as Maynard. Natty dark suits, gold watches and rings, hand-made shoes.

The accountant said, 'Mr Maynard, this has gone beyond that stage. You are being charged with—'

Maynard leaned forward, dragging Jackson's arm with him. 'I'm a discharged bankrupt so they can charge me with what the hell they like. How much? Come on, the pair of you, how much are they trying to get me for?'

The accountant tapped a sheet of paper, column upon column of figures. 'It's not just the Inland Revenue, Customs and Excise . . .' His eyes shifted to Maynard's, held them meaningfully for a long moment. 'Transporting anything is a very costly business.'

'There has to be a way to salvage the original plan. I don't care what the price is.' Maynard snapped his fingers for a pen. Jackson was drawn forward as Maynard leaned right over to study the plans and blueprints. Oddly enough they contained no written descriptions, only a series of ruled lines and dimensions.

'This building is under construction,' Maynard said, circling one area. 'This one too. Are you telling me neither one can be made accessible?'

The solicitor pursed his mouth. 'We might get round to it,' he said slowly, 'but it will cost.' A radio squawked in the corridor, and a uniformed officer appeared at the door. 'They ready for the hearing?'

Maynard stood up, and gave a dry chuckle. 'They're trying to clean me out,' he told Jackson, who couldn't have cared less, according to his expression. He wafted his hand for them to get moving.

Maynard jiggled the handcuffs. 'Any chance these can come off . . . just for the hearing?' The big, bearded officer gave him a stony stare. With a small shrug Maynard said, 'I mean, they know I've been nicked, no need to overplay it and lose the sympathy vote.'

He leaned closer, raising his own hand and Jackson's together, and murmured confidentially, 'Ten grand? No? Twenty? Come on.' He sniffed. 'Okay, final offer, thirty grand.' Then he reared back, eyebrows up, as he saw Jackson's nostrils flare. 'Just joking!'

He was led out, squeezing past the two men who had risen to stand pressed against the table. None of them spoke, but looks passed between them. With Jackson in front, two officers behind, Maynard went up the stairs.

Left alone, the two men waited several moments for the footsteps to fade away. 'Can you do it?' the solicitor asked softly.

The accountant rolled up the drawings and slotted them into his briefcase. He snapped the catches. 'I'm gonna have to find one hell of a pilot.' He sighed, frowning into space.

CHAPTER 13

'YOU MUST be the new lad from Pentonville. I'm the senior officer on C Wing, Russell Morgan.'

'James Malahide,' said the new lad. 'Jimmy.'

They were in Exercise Yard 2, the one ordered by Helen to be cleared of builders' rubble for use by the inmates. Thirty or more were using it now, though there wasn't much exercise going on. The men were huddled in small groups, chatting and smoking. One or two were doing desultory push-ups, while others ambled about aimlessly, or stood staring through the chain-link fence, eighteen feet high topped with razor wire, to the sterile area patrolled by German shepherds and their handlers.

From the nearby wings could be heard the clatter and clang of tools as the workmen stripped out the damaged cells. Tarpaulins covered some of the windows to keep out the weather. The smell of brick dust and old plaster hung on the breeze.

'So what made you sign up?' Morgan asked.

'I was in the services. Couldn't settle into civvies. Wife just had a baby and, well . . .'

He had a Yorkshire accent, with a burr to it that marked him out as from the Dales rather than the industrial towns. Blond and blue-eyed, he had an enormous round face, a neck like a tree trunk, and a six-feet-four frame to support it.

Morgan was nodding, remembering proudly his own time in the Forces. 'Fourteen years, 3 Para.' It pleased him that young Malahide had served: ex-members of the army had an instinctive rapport, were accustomed to getting on with the job and ignoring the bullshit.

They strolled round the yard, while Morgan genned him up with the routine. 'Exercise period is one hour every day, from nine thirty to ten thirty. We keep 'em comin',' he said, casting a glance at the sky. 'Unless it rains.'

He nodded to Stan Field who, now having finished his corridor swabbing detail, was moping about, biting his nails. Thin-faced, hair pulled back in a ponytail, he had sly slanting eyes and a shifty, nervous manner.

'Morning, Stanley. Your governor coming back, is he?'

'Why? Yours not?' Field had a snide grin. 'You see her on TV this mornin'? Not what you'd call *Baywatch* material, is she?' He turned away, sniggering, gnawing at his fingers.

'That's Edward Maynard's runner,' Morgan said. 'Carries all his messages backwards and forwards like a ferret.'

They strolled on. Malahide had dealt with some tough men at Pentonville, and this bunch seemed no different. The usual mix, in fact. Unlike some prison officers he didn't always mug up on the offences committed by the inmates. He felt that it gave him a more even-handed approach, treating all cons equally. If he knew why they were inside, and found the particular crime repugnant, he feared that his personal feelings might come through, that disgust would get the better of him. So he preferred not to know.

Morgan pointed out a very tall, thin, gangling black guy with dreadlocks. 'He's your drug dealer, the Rasta. Oswald Snooper – Snoopy to his mates. We had one inmate in here, paid off the local butcher.' He grinned as Malahide looked puzzled. 'Only bringing in a ton of grass up a carcass's arse!'

Field had sidled over to Harry Reynolds, a broad, well-built man in peak physical condition, fair hair cropped close to his scalp. 'Cigarette?' Field offered with an obsequious grin. It was not permitted to exchange anything in the yard, so he held it in his cupped hand. 'Ex-RAF, aren't you?' He ducked his head, the words sneaking out of the corner of his mouth. 'Mr Maynard needs some advice . . .'

Morgan nodded towards a trio of heavily muscled men who regularly worked out in the gym. 'Those mothers watch out for Maynard. Day off for them.' A roly-poly figure waddled by, a crescent of pale flabby belly hanging out of his blue work trousers. 'Chubby one is Roddy Marsh.' Morgan touched his temple with a twirling finger; not only a few slates missing, the entire bloody roof.

'Christ,' Malahide goggled. 'He ate his grandmother, didn't he?'

'Yeah, he's a vegetarian now.'

A curly-headed, sombre-looking young man, thin as a rake, was being admitted into the compound. He wore normal prison clothing, blue sweatshirt and dark blue trousers, with strips of yellow material sewn into them. The guard locked the gate and the young man wandered off disconsolately on his own.

'What's with this guy?' asked Jimmy Malahide.

'Oh, he's harmless, Howard Webster – just keeps on gettin' over the wall. They got those stripes in Pentonville, haven't they?'

'Yeah, just never saw them worn.'

'Nah, not used much nowadays. Bloody prison watch-dogs reckon they're too humiliatin'.'

Webster was an E-man, as an inmate who had tried to escape, or actually succeeded, was known. He was 'in patches', the strips of yellow marking him out as someone who had to be watched closely.

'Morning, Governor,' Morgan called out, as he spied Helen striding from the gate-lodge to the admin block. She acknowledged him with a brief smile and a wave. '*Big Breakfast* go all right, did it?'

Helen didn't rise to the bait. She knew she would receive some stick for her appearance on the TV show that morning, and the only thing was to ride over it, let them have their harmless fun.

Snoopy was really buzzin'. The tall Rasta had smoked some excellent shit after breakfast, and the world had been suddenly transformed into a much nicer place. At least his version of it had, his skinny torso bumping and grinding to a reggae beat only he could hear. Even Brian Samora couldn't spoil it, yakking away in his ear.

'But I was told there was no loss of me privileges,' he was complaining in a broad Scouse accent. 'Just twenty-one days' punishment . . .' This had been fretting Samora for days now. He had a problem getting his head round such matters, and the fact that he couldn't read or write didn't help. He crossed his arms over his torn green knitted sweater, rocking on his heels. Half Jamaican, half Irish with a dash of gypsy, he'd been a petty criminal since his early teens, and at twenty-nine he was doing a stretch for holding up a post office in the Walton district of Liverpool.

'Hang about, you doin' four years, right?' said Walter Brinkley, a young Londoner, staring at Samora through glasses that had Sellotape holding them together in place of hinges.

Samora nodded.

'You lost twenty-one days,' Brinkley said, 'so you tellin' me you're goin' out on your old release date?'

'Yeah, man.' He nodded vehemently.

Dancing with the clouds, Snoopy said hazily, 'But what about you doin' chokey for head-buttin' that screw, eh? You got twenty-one days, man.'

Even stoned out of his skull, Snoopy was light years ahead of Samora, who had trouble remembering his own birthday.

'They just said my time went on pause.'

'Well, if your time went on pause,' Brinkley said, running out of patience, 'when did it start again?'

'When I got back to me pad.'

'No way.' Brinkley was definite. He tapped his palm. 'If you got twenty-one days extra, they got to be done.'

Samora scratched his head, none the wiser.

Some pushing and shoving had developed into a scrap, and Morgan was quick to spot it. He went over, jabbing a finger. 'Break it up, you two. I mean it.'

Jack Bulmer, a black prisoner in his late fifties with two gold teeth and several missing ones, had finally, after much taunting, lost his rag and gone for Mark Lewis. Lewis was a real nasty piece of work, inside for armed robbery, who had a talent for riling everyone he came across, and more often than not went out of his way to come across them. He looked daggers at Bulmer before turning away with an arrogant shrug.

'Mr Morgan?'

Morgan knew the soft, empty voice right away. The tub of lard that was Roddy Marsh stood diffidently by his elbow, his white gut hanging obscenely out of his trousers. He gazed up with large vacant brown eyes.

'Bugger off, son,' Morgan said, not unkindly. He beckoned Bulmer to him. 'Jack, come here. Now, what's your problem?'

Bulmer was no trouble-maker. Up to now he'd been a model con, always quiet, dignified, keeping his own space. He was in jail for murdering his wife.

Bulmer stared after Lewis and came over. His goatee beard was a tangle of grey, and the brown dome of his head poked through a mop of frizzy hair that spread out to cover his ears.

'You've got a pad thief, Mr Morgan, on C Wing,' he said quietly, and then turned and walked off.

Morgan glanced at Malahide, and gave a weary shake of the head. This was a common problem in all prisons, an inmate who thieved from the cells when the occupants were in the workshops or association. It caused ill-temper and suspicion on the wing, and was bad for morale.

Webster, the E-man, was sitting with his back to the wall, hunched over and staring at the ground. His eyes flicked over to the two officers, and then very casually he moved the heel of his trainer through the cindery earth, bringing the bent rusted screw he had spotted within reach. He waited until their backs were turned, rammed the screw inside his mouth and clenched his teeth down hard. He spat out the screw and wiped the blood from his mouth, hiding a little smile. The plan was hazy as yet, but he'd work it out.

Stan Field and Harry Reynolds had moved nearer the fence to continue their quiet conversation away from the rest. Fat Roddy Marsh wandered by, scuffing his shoes in that idiot manner of his, but he didn't count.

'You sure about that?' Field asked, rubbing his cheek. His nails were bitten raw, down to the cuticles. 'How long would he have?'

Reynolds shrugged. 'I dunno.'

Field turned his head aside, speaking into Reynolds's ear. 'There's money in this for you, get it sent to your wife.' He wafted his hand irritably for Marsh to piss off. That summed up poor Marsh's story: excluded, derided, pushed to the back of life's queue.

'You sure it'd take twenty minutes before the scream went up?' Field said.

'Night the riot went down, it took forty minutes.' Reynolds glanced over his shoulder, nibbling his lip, uptight, as if battling against something inside himself. The battle raged within him day and night, never ceased, was never won. 'I'd go for it.'

Field nodded, gave a sly smile of thanks, and palmed him two packs of Dunhill King Size. The transaction was clocked by Marsh, rocking back and forth, head wobbling on his flabby shoulders.

A moan went up as the bell rang for the end of the exercise period. The men started to drift slowly to the gate.

Webster approached Morgan, tenderly holding his hand to his mouth. 'It's been throbbin' all night,' he said, in pain. 'Might be a wisdom tooth, but it's started bleedin'.'

'Lemme see.' Webster opened his mouth. 'Which tooth?'

Brinkley went by, still trying to sort out Samora's problem with his remission. 'If you're right and you say your sentence did not go on pause, and you say none of your privileges were taken away, you should be entitled to them.'

'Yes, man.' Samora nodded, lost in a thick fog. 'Yes, man.'

Brinkley drummed his fingers on Samora's shoulder as they moved into the line. 'But they usually put them at the end of your EDR. So if you got three months, where did they put them?'

EDR was the Earliest Date of Release.

Brinkley spun round furiously as Marsh's huge gut bumped into him. 'Don't fuckin' push me!'

'I dunno . . .' Brian was shaking his head, more lost than ever, and getting more frustrated. He took it out on Marsh, shoving him out of the line. 'Piss off!'

'What you gotta do is ask them to explain,' Brinkley said. 'Ask the SO.' The senior officer, or wing officer, was the first port of call for queries or complaints.

Marsh was pushed out again by the men behind, and was bounced down the line to the end. He shuffled along, head down, last as usual.

'So,' Morgan said to Malahide as they stood at the gate, watching the men go through. 'Now you've met some of the players, what d'ya think?'

'Okay.' Malahide nodded, quietly confident. 'I think I can handle them,' and Morgan believed he could.

Marsh shuffled past, last man out. 'Mr Morgan, there's somethin' goin' down . . . big.' He was mumbling it into his chest so that Morgan had to strain to catch it. 'I think it's a delivery.'

Morgan's eyes tightened. He looked at Malahide with a grim little smile. 'Welcome to Barfield.'

*

The arrival of Moira Levitt seemed to have done the trick. Mavis had really sharpened up her act, Helen thought, going through the morning's mail. Urgent items had been flagged, background notes were appended, and Moira had already dealt with the more routine stuff.

Helen buzzed for her to come in, having completed the duty roster for the coming week. Moira took it, and said, 'C Wing SO has arranged a dental appointment for prisoner Howard Webster. Four o'clock this afternoon.' Helen nodded and made a note.

At the door Moira paused, and said with a smile, 'I thought you were very good this morning.'

Helen rolled her eyes. 'I didn't. Oh, Mavis, did you get any kind of press release from HQ?'

'I'll check the fax machine.' Mavis went out, leaving the door open for Russell Morgan, who entered at Helen's gesture.

'Everything okay?' she asked him.

'You missed your rounds this morning. Mr Lyons isn't here but I've shown young Malahide the ropes.' Graham Lyons was governor of C Wing, many years in the Prison Service, a man of the old school, liked by everyone.

'He's the new officer,' Helen said, pointing to a chair.

'Yep. I think he'll settle in.' Morgan sat down, unfolding an official complaints app he took from his breast pocket. 'Bit of aggro going down. Inmate 435, Jack Bulmer, has complained that he lost phone cards, two one-ounce packs of tobacco . . .' He read on. 'A Gameboy, four games, plus a Sony Walkman and some tapes.'

Helen looked up from Howard Webster's F2050 dossier, frowning. So there was a pad thief on the prowl. Unless one of the officers was getting light-fingered.

Morgan said, 'I also got a good informant on the wing. He seems to think something is coming in.'

'Like what?' Helen asked, head bent over the file. 'Dixon's opening a branch here?'

'Anyway, I put it in my report. The lad sometimes makes

stuff up.' He laid it on the desk. 'Mr Marshall coming back, is he?'

Helen's voice had an edge to it. 'I have not been informed by HQ. But, then, I wasn't privy to the press release about the refurbishing costs.'

'Is it true? They're going to spend sixty million on this place?' The question was as subtle as a block of concrete.

'I really don't know,' Helen said, feeling her temper rise. If he was trying to needle her, he was succeeding.

'It was in *The Times*,' Morgan pointed out, meaning, of course, that Helen ought to have known all about it, and he was gleeful because she'd been totally clueless, caught with her knickers down. He got up and went to the door. 'We recorded the breakfast show in the club,' he said, a grin lurking.

'I bet you did, Mr Morgan,' Helen said, trading a glare for his grin. But it was lost on the closed door.

Later in the morning she carried out her rounds. Jack Bulmer was first on the list. Helen stood just inside his door, listening with folded arms while he poured out the tale. Russell Morgan and another officer watched from the corridor.

Bulmer was trying to remain his usual calm, dignified self, but it was obvious how agitated he was by the thefts. Part of the reason, Helen suspected, was that he felt there was a racist element at the bottom of this, not greed pure and simple.

'This is the situation, Miss. I had five phone cards, and Mark' – he jerked his head to the wall – 'next pad, he asks me if he can borrow one of my phone cards. I tell him no because I know he won't pay me for it, right?'

Helen nodded, listening closely. Five phone cards were worth a total of £20.

'I come back from association last night and my pad's bin cleaned out. And this morning on exercise I hear a rumour that somebody on D Wing has been offered one – and someone on this wing's bin offered one too.' He cupped a hand across his mouth, fingers digging into his greying beard, emotion threatening to overwhelm him. 'It's really got me down, Miss Hewitt. I mean, that Gameboy's worth at least fifteen phone cards.'

'I'll look into it,' Helen promised. She cocked her head, adding, 'But you know, Jack, its against prison regulations to do these trade-offs.'

She went out onto the landing, consulting her clipboard. 'Now, Howard Webster. You've arranged a four p.m. dental appointment. What time is Dr Thomas due?'

'Two o'clock,' Morgan replied. 'But Webster needs a dentist. And also, can I have a word about . . .' He hesitated. 'I think there should be some new arrangement. See, if an inmate wants a doctor's appointment, they got to wait until two.'

'Yes, and?'

'Well, it clashes with visiting times, so if you have to see the doc you miss your visit. And they won't miss their visit.'

'Okay, point taken.' Helen made a note. 'Thank you.'

By the time she'd finished her rounds and returned to her office it was gone two o'clock, and she was starving. She'd been up since six that morning for that damn TV fiasco. She was wishing now that she'd never done it. Next time she resolved not to be so bloody gullible and trusting.

Mavis brought up sandwiches and a packet of crisps from the officers' canteen, and percolated a full pot of coffee. Helen ate and drank while she tackled her paperwork. There were tons of it, but it had to be got through. She put a call in to Royston Andrews at Millbank HQ. Not there, dammit. She left a message, asking to see him in person at the earliest opportunity; if the Operational Director, or anyone else at HQ, thought they were sweetly going ahead and drawing up plans for Barfield's rebuilding without Helen's ten penn'orth, they were very sadly mistaken.

'Dr Thomas is here,' Mavis said, putting her head round.

'Ah, good. Show him in, Mavis.' Mavis vanished, only to reappear a second later as Helen called out, 'Oh, and was there anything from the press office?'

The look of guilt that passed over her face told its own story. Helen sighed, grabbed the phone and punched an internal number. So Mavis had sharpened up her act, had she? Perhaps a gentle reminder, like a boot up the backside, was required.

Helen got through to Reception. 'Can you get Security to use the inserts on the handcuffs for Webster. Prisoner Howard Webster, 355, a dental appointment has been arranged for him. He's absconded three times before, so . . .' She nodded. 'Good, thank you.'

In the outer office, Mavis interrupted her frantic search to jab her finger towards Helen's door. 'Dr Thomas, she's waiting.'

Reluctantly, Lorcan Thomas slid off the corner of Moira's desk. With the looks, hair and figure of a model, the tall, willowy girl seemed totally out of place in these humdrum surroundings. Mavis saw him wink at Moira, who was laughing at something he'd said, and then watched him saunter into the office. As the door closed, she wagged her finger. 'Don't get involved, he's got a shocking reputation.'

'As what?'

'Ladies' man,' Mavis said darkly. 'He belongs to the same golf club as my husband.' She lowered her voice. 'Different one every weekend, and they're not golfing partners.' Flushed and irritable, she started hunting again. 'Where's that press release that came in from HQ?'

Helen wiped away crumbs with a tissue, and swallowed. How was it that every time she met him she had a mouthful of sandwich?

Lorcan Thomas stood in front of the desk, hands stuffed in his pockets, thinking it over. 'Well, I do have quite a big practice, but there's four of us, so maybe I can.'

'It's just that if the men lose their visit because of a doctor's appointment they will either not get the required attention, or—'

He held up his hand. 'Leave it with me.'

A flushed and flustered Mavis tapped and hurried in, waving a shiny fax sheet. 'I'm sorry, I thought I'd put it on your desk. It's only the press release for the article in *The Times*.'

Helen didn't quite snatch it from her. She stared at it, biting her lip, and then said to Dr Thomas, 'Could you just give me two seconds?'

He hesitated, glancing at his watch. 'Actually, I'm sorry, I can't.' He gestured, half turned. 'I should go, I'm on duty.'

'Oh, well, don't let me detain you,' Helen said, meaning quite the opposite. Whenever she had the opportunity he always seemed to be dashing off somewhere. 'We can talk another time.' It sounded feeble, and that was how she felt.

Mavis waited nervously until he'd gone. 'It was faxed in late and you had the six o'clock TV call.' She gave a weak smile and fluttered her hands. 'I mean, you couldn't have seen it, anyway.'

'In future, Mavis, anything that comes in from HQ, you give it to me straight away.' Helen glared at her, then shook her head at the wall. 'I looked a total prat this morning.'

'I'm sorry,' Mavis mumbled, and trailed out.

Lorcan Thomas was busy, but not too busy to linger awhile with Moira before starting his rounds. Moira held up the phone as Mavis returned to her desk. 'It's headquarters, Mr Andrews's secretary.'

Mavis took the call on her own phone. Dr Thomas leaned over, arms outstretched, hands flat on the desk, as Moira, trying to be efficient and at the same time not to smile, got on with her work.

'You free for dinner?'

'No, I'm sorry.'

'But I didn't say which night.' He inclined his head to catch her eye. 'How about Tuesday . . . or Thursday?'

'No.' She swung away as the fax machine started to chatter. 'Now excuse me.'

'Saturday night, then?' Dr Thomas said, straightening up and following her with his eyes as she went over to the machine. Helen's sudden appearance made him whip round as if caught out by a stern Victorian headmistress.

Mavis put the phone down. 'Mr Andrews can see you this afternoon, Miss Hewitt, three o'clock.'

'Bugger it! I'll have to go all the way back in now.'

'I'm sorry, do you want me to change it?'

'No.'

The door banged shut. Dr Thomas looked after her with a naughty schoolboy grin. 'Got a temper, hasn't she?' He pointed his finger accusingly. 'Mavis, what have you been telling this sweet innocent girl about me?'

Mavis couldn't help a giggle. 'That if she wants to stay sweet and innocent she should stay well clear of you and the nineteenth hole!'

Lorcan Thomas laughed, flashed a wicked grin at the pair of them, and went off.

'You'd better give this to Miss Hewitt,' Moira said, tearing off the fax and bringing it over.

Mavis read it, head going back. 'Well, she's not going to like this! Gary Marshall's been reinstated.' And she thrust the fax into Moira's hand as if it was radioactive. 'You take it in.'

CHAPTER 14

STANDING NEAR the inner gate of C Wing, Russell Morgan and the new lad Malahide kept an eye on the men as they collected their metal trays and lined up at the lunch trolley. Two orderlies and a civilian cook dished it up: beef and onion pie with gravy, boiled potatoes and carrots, apple tart and custard, tea or coffee; there was also a serving of Quorn lasagne for the vegetarians, and special diets for those with a medical condition.

Brian shuffled along in the line, puzzling over a piece of paper. He could read the numbers but not the words. The fact that he'd been on the pipe for the past hour didn't exactly aid his concentration. He showed the paper to Walter Brinkley. 'They give me this with my dates on it.'

'And?'

'They say it explains it.'

'Does it?'

'No.'

A terrific clatter from the end of line made everyone jump. Any sudden noise made officers and inmates alike jittery. Morgan had been in a pub one time and when somebody on the TV blew a whistle he'd fallen off his bar stool. He looked round quickly: Jack Bulmer had smashed down his tray. As Morgan went up the man said angrily, 'Is somebody doin' somethin' about my stolen property?'

Morgan waved a hand to calm him. 'Get your lunch and back in your cell, Jack, there's a good lad.' From the look on Bulmer's face, he needed watching. The senior officer had never seen him so worked up.

'Start lock-up,' Morgan said to Malahide, while he himself waited by the food trolley until Bulmer, still seething, had collected his food and stumped off to his cell.

Morgan watched him go and then headed for the officers' annex, situated just inside the gates, observation panels on three sides giving an all-round view of both landings.

An announcement came over the Tannoy: 'Anyone with visiting orders please report to the SO on the wing. If you have a visit, please report to the SO on the wing.'

Morgan spoke on the phone. 'Mavis, is Miss Hewitt in?' He listened, and a huge grin spread across his face. 'Soon as he's here can you ask Mr Marshall to come to C Wing. I think we might have a problem.' He put down the phone and, still grinning, turned to the three officers clutching mugs of coffee and fagging it. 'Good news, Marshall's coming back!'

Come on, you bastard, start. At the third try it did, and Helen closed her eyes and gripped the wheel, offering up a prayer.

She was about to reverse out when a blue metallic Rover 216Si slid into the parking space marked DEPUTY GOVERNOR next to hers. He hadn't wasted any bloody time. Back here quick as a shithouse rat. She wound down the window.

'Afternoon, Governor,' Marshall said, lowering his passenger window. 'I was just coming in to see you.' His eyebrows went up. 'Saw you on TV this morning. Very good. You didn't see the article in *The Times*, then?'

The next person to mention that, Helen resolved, would get a smack in the teeth. 'We'll talk later,' she said stiffly. 'I'm just going to HQ.'

'Any problems?'

'Nothing I can't take care of, thank you, Gary.'

Thank God the engine was turning over because she was able to reverse out and shoot off without making an idiot of herself. But it didn't work out that way. The slip road leading from the staff car park was being used as an access road by the builders' lorries. And, of course, a lorry loaded with bags of cement was blocking the way. Helen banged on her horn, conscious that her plight was being observed by the security cameras dotted about everywhere.

And it was.

Passing through the reinforced-glass double air-lock doors in the gate-lodge, Marshall could see Helen on the monitor, now out of the Metro and marching forward to give the driver a mouthful.

'Hey, Gary, good to see you back,' one of the guards greeted him.

'I don't think her ladyship feels the same way.' Marshall grinned back, nodding towards the screen.

The gate guards were falling about laughing at Helen's pantomime performance. It got even funnier, as far as the guards were concerned: another lorry had pulled up behind her, the driver leaning out and gesticulating.

'Better give her a hand, she's wedged in!' one of the guards said, tears practically running down his cheeks.

If the cameras had been infra-red they would have shown steam coming out of Helen's ears.

'Get it out of here, *right now*! And as from today this entrance is *not to be used*. It's a security risk. No vehicle is to be parked across this entrance or exit.'

A smiling guard walked casually across from the gate-lodge and waved the lorry on. It rumbled off, sending waves of cement dust into the air. Wafting it aside, Helen got back in her car and turned the key. The engine whirred and died. She ground her teeth, which didn't do any good because the engine did it again.

The guard leaned in at the window. 'What was that about not blocking the exit, Miss Hewitt?'

Helen nearly jumped out of her skin as the irate driver behind blasted his horn. But once again the engine refused to start. In a real rage now she got out and thumped the Metro's bonnet with her fist. Then she remembered the cameras all around her, and turning to survey them she started to laugh out loud.

'Bet those bastards are taping this!'

On the monitor Marshall saw the white prison van escorted by two patrol cars enter through the huge gates into the prison yard.

'What's this?' he asked the gate guard.

'Maynard's back.'

Marshall nodded thoughtfully. Instead of going up to his office in the admin block, he cut across the yard to the main corridor leading to the wings. Having collected his keys at the gate-lodge, he let himself in through the iron door. The corridor stretched away into the distance, like an underground tunnel, evenly lit by strip lighting behind toughened glass, cameras angled down every ten metres from the curved roof.

A few minutes later he heard the grating of keys and Jumbo Jackson appeared from Reception. He unlocked the gate and held it open for Edward Maynard and two officers to pass through. Maynard swanned by like the King of Siam with his courtiers in attendance, but there was a cloudy look in his eye, like that of a man with a weight on his mind.

Marshall fell into step with Jackson, who had relocked the gate and was following behind.

'Good to see you, Mr Marshall.'

'He doesn't look a happy man.' Marshall kept his voice low; the tunnel magnified all sound. 'You have any problems?'

Jackson rubbed his wrist. 'I never left the bastard's side,' he muttered through his beard.

'How much they get off him?'

'I dunno – claimed two million back in VAT, listed about eighty different companies. I've never heard anythin' like it.' Jackson's mouth went close to Marshall's ear as they walked along. 'To be honest, I reckoned he might have set up somethin'. Governor did too – she was real edgy about him.'

Waiting while the next set of gates was unlocked, Maynard half turned to look back at them.

'Hear you might have your stay with us extended,' Marshall said as they came up.

Maynard's mouth smiled but his eyes were chips of ice. He said softly, 'Don't bet on it.'

Wearing his prison-issue blue sweatshirt and dark blue trousers with the yellow patches sewn in, Howard Webster stood quietly at the counter in Reception as Officer Longfell snapped the handcuff on his slender right wrist.

'Well, you can wiggle out of that, can't you? So . . . not takin' any chances.' Longfell took it off and slotted the metal inserts inside the cuff. He snapped it back on. 'How's that?'

'It's too tight,' Webster said through his swollen mouth. He was a morose young man, tall and painfully thin; a gentle face bordering on the effeminate, with soulful dark brown eyes fringed by thick lashes.

'That's the way we like it,' Nicholas Hobart told him with a grin. He and Longfell were on escort duty. Both were in their mid-fifties and weren't far off retirement, having worked a total of forty-seven years between them in the service.

The outer door opened and one of the security guards, nicknamed 'Burglars' by the inmates, gave the nod. They wore their caps with the peaks pulled low over their eyes, which gave them a sinister appearance in keeping with their reputation as hard men. As well as being responsible for perimeter security, they were also called in to sort out any prisoner who was being particularly troublesome, and the grapevine had it that they were none too fussy how they went about it.

'The cab here, is it?' Longfell clicked the other handcuff onto his wrist. 'Now, you're on trust, Webster, so don't mess us about.'

'Be tough unless we want to quickstep together,' Webster muttered, his wrist tight inside the cuffed insert.

The two officers sat either side of him in the taxi, an old Ford Granada with a dancing skeleton in the windscreen and purple furry seats that made Hobart's legs itch through his trousers. The officer gazed out at the fields and hedgerows, then glanced up at the banks of dark clouds rolling in from the fens and the Wash to the east. 'Looks like it might rain.'

'Oh, I dunno, forecast said it was gonna keep fine.' Longfell bent his neck to peer upwards. 'I hope so, plan to do a spot of fishin' this weekend.'

The driver's eyes flicked up to the mirror. 'What's he in for?'

Longfell met his inquisitive look with a stare. 'Shot a cab driver in the back for being nosy.'

That kept him quiet for the rest of the journey. In the dentist's surgery Longfell sat behind the leather chair toying with the handcuffs and listening to the hiss of the suction tube in Webster's mouth as the dentist and his female assistant went to work. There were long hours of inactivity in the prison routine, for inmates and officers alike, and Longfell had got used to coping with them. He could think about a stretch of river, real or imaginary, and how he might fish it. Or replay the highlights of Leicester City's last match – if there were any – in his head, and sometimes make the outcome different. Like last bloody Saturday, for instance, when Ormondroyd missed a sitter against Villa.

Longfell yawned and rubbed his chin. The time on his watch said three thirty, and he looked up at the wall clock to make sure. He went to the door and peered into the waiting room where Hobart sat reading *House and Garden*. 'Check the cab's still on standby, will you?'

He returned to his chair, folded his arms, and stared at the curly top of Webster's head, listening to the gurgle, hiss, gurgle. Longfell winced as he noticed the nasty red weal around the lad's right wrist. Well, that's what you got for being an E-man.

The big blond Yorkshire lad, Jimmy Malahide, was taking it all in. He saw Jumbo Jackson hesitate because for a moment he couldn't place Roddy Marsh. Malahide was about to say something but Morgan tapped his temple and said, 'Roddy, you know, he's a bit . . .'

Jackson nodded. Right, the retard who shambled round with his horrible white gut hanging out.

'Don't pay him any attention, he should be in a mental home. What the hell would he know about any delivery? He can't tie his own shoelaces.'

Gary Marshall came in, and his ears pricked up as he caught the tail-end. 'You think this tip-off's for real, a delivery?' he asked, frowning.

Morgan shrugged. 'Might be nothin', but Roddy Marsh reckons something's brewin'. And with all this rebuilding goin' on . . .'

'I'll have a word with Security,' Marshall said, and went off to his office.

'Don't know about you but I'm glad he's back,' Jackson told the others. 'Hey, you want to see her on TV?' he chortled, bearded face splitting in a delighted grin. 'We got it taped!'

The visits room resembled a cafeteria except that the plastic-topped tables were laid out in regimented rows, a wide space separating each one. Officers at the central desk and several more patrolling about kept watch on the proceedings. With adult visitors that wasn't too difficult: no interaction was allowed between them and the inmates, and it was forbidden for any object to change hands. Babies and toddlers presented the real problem. While the adults had been searched and anything they carried put through the X-ray device, children were exempt. As the men held and cuddled their infants, it was child's play to retrieve the plastic-wrapped packages from nappies and the pockets of ABC romper suits, then slip them away – inside the mouth, flies, socks, or some other conveniently accessible place.

Jack Bulmer had no interest in scoring; he was too het up, the frustration boiling inside. 'My stereo, my Gameboy, tapes, five phone cards. It's destroyed me, man,' he moaned to his younger brother, Terry. 'Five phone cards, my Gameboy and stereo. I told her, I told the new Governor, five phone cards, my stereo . . .'

Three tables away, Brian Samora was on the verge of tears. His wife watched him with an anguished expression, partly caused by the struggle to comprehend what the hell he was on about.

'See, I reckoned I'd be out, right? I mean, they never said nothin' to me about attachin' on an extra twenty-one days *plus* another twenty-one days. I don't understand it, 'cos if I done it, then why add it? See what I mean?'

'Yeh,' his wife said, shaking her head.

'Well, can you arrange it?' Maynard asked his solicitor, who was shuffling a stack of papers, and sliding out the ones that needed to be signed.

'Is there any other open area?'

'No, and there's not much time.' He stroked his lips. 'When you go out, take a good look,' he said behind his fingertips.

The solicitor nodded. He pushed the documents across the table, unscrewed his pen, and glanced round to the nearest officer, holding up the pen and seeking permission. Maynard scribbled his signature. 'You'd better not come in again. I'll call you.' He pushed the papers over and handed back the pen. His look was full of meaning precisely because it was so opaque. 'I'm flush with phone cards.'

The cab driver leaned out of the window, watching with more than passing concern as Howard Webster was helped down the steps to the street. Handcuffed to Longfell and supported by Hobart, the young chap looked pale and groggy, eyes half closed.

'He's not gonna be sick in my cab, is he?' he asked worriedly as the officers settled Webster in the back seat.

Hobart slammed the rear door and climbed in next to the driver, who was staring anxiously over his shoulder. Slumped sideways against the window, Webster was moaning, eyes closed in a face of pain.

'All right, son,' Longfell said gently. He had taken pity and removed the insert, the cuff dangling like a bracelet on the skinny wrist. 'You're not gonna be sick, are you?'

Webster shook his head. 'Thanks,' he mumbled.

'Okay, let's go.' Hobart waved his hand, and the driver scraped into first gear.

Fifteen minutes later they were on the outskirts of town and heading into the countryside. Crouched over, hugging his stomach, Webster had already wriggled his hand free, and was holding the cuff in a tight grip to maintain the tension on Longfell's wrist. He kept up the moaning a while longer, too, because it seemed to reassure the officers that he was in a bad way.

As soon as he saw the green fields, he got ready. The door catch wasn't locked, he saw, fingers creeping towards the handle. Better and better. And Longfell was leaning back in the centre of the seat, his other hand resting on the seat in front. The taxi slowed behind a tanker, and as the driver changed down, preparing to overtake, Webster had the door open. A split second later he was up and out, trainers blurring as they hit the road, running behind the car and veering off onto the grass verge.

'Oh, shit!' Longfell stared out through the rear window. The car had screeched to a stop in the middle of the road, its door hanging open. Hobart was first out, yelling at the top of his voice, 'Webster, you fucking idiot!' He pounded down the road, scattering loose change, fourteen stone and out of shape, chasing after the slim curly-headed figure leaping over a hedge, arms held high.

Longfell ran a few paces and then turned back in despair, the empty handcuff dangling from his wrist. He thumped the taxi roof.

'Oi!' came the driver's indignant voice. 'Has he been sick?'

Webster landed on his toes, light as a spring lamb, and ran fast and easy, elbows pumping, head up. The sun broke through and he felt its warmth. He sucked the air into his lungs, which tasted fresh and wonderful, miraculously different from prison air. He leapt the next hedge with ease, Hobart a distant blue smudge far behind, and raced through the green countryside, a smile on his face.

Late afternoon, the atmosphere on C Wing became more relaxed as association time approached. Lines of men were forming at the taps in recess, filling their metal pots with water and carrying them back to their cells. The officers stood by, watchful but swapping the odd joke, happy to keep everything all sweetness and light. Made life easier for everyone.

Russell Morgan came onto the wing, anything but sweetness and light. He moved past the knots of men in the central area and went up to the landing, face like thunder.

There was a loud click as the Tannoy came on. 'Evening classes have not yet recommenced. Those with passes for the gym please report to the SO. Return to cells. Showers and association will commence as usual at eighteen hundred hours. Please return to your cells.'

Morgan passed Brian Samora, bending some poor sod's ear. '. . . when they give you extra days, where do they put 'em? I mean, did you do them in here or did they move you?'

Snoopy was behind Jack Bulmer in the line for the taps. Taller by a mile, he leaned right over him, speaking tersely in his ear. 'Look, I don't want any trouble . . .'

'But that's my Gameboy Mark Lewis is sellin' you, Snoopy, it's mine. He stole it from my pad!'

'Aw, come on, man, I give it back to you and I'll get carved up!' Snoopy waved his long gangling arm. 'No way, oh, no way.'

His usual suave self, Edward Maynard strolled towards Officer Malahide, minders in attendance, ferret-faced Stan Field pushing aside any prisoner who was too slow in getting out of the way.

'Can I make a phone call?' Maynard asked.

'Wait your turn like everyone else,' Malahide said, nodding to the three men waiting at the phone.

'I was just being polite,' Maynard said with a tiny, indulgent smile. 'Prick,' he murmured, turning away.

Walter Brinkley stepped up, phone card at the ready, and was about to insert it when a muscular arm hauled him away. 'Hey, hey, you just gotta ask,' Walter said, cowering back. He blinked through his specs. 'I'm sorry, Mr Maynard, didn't know you needed to make a call.' He bowed his head and shuffled off, muttering under his breath, 'Bastard, mean bastard . . .'

A tight-lipped Morgan was standing at Malahide's side. He waited until there was no one who might overhear, and said very quietly, 'Webster's done a runner.'

The hour-long drive down the M1 to Millbank HQ had given Helen time to organize her thoughts. Two things she was certain of: she was going to have her say, whatever the cost, and she was determined not to be fobbed off. She knew Royston Andrews for the wily old devil he was, and she also knew that politics figured in all this somewhere. Her role as the token woman on the investigation team for one. And now using her status as the youngest female governor in the history of the Prison Service to present a new, improved, squeaky-clean image of Barfield's tarnished reputation purely for media and public consumption. One other thing Helen was dead sure of: she hadn't the slightest intention of being anyone's token woman ever again, and when push came to shove she could be as strong-minded as the best of them.

Andrews had the architects' plans of the new prison layout on his desk. They discussed these in general terms while they sipped their coffee, and then Helen got down to cases. She pointed to the Special Secure Unit. 'To make this area into a prison within a prison is, to my mind, a step backwards.'

'This type of unit has been proven a success in the United States. Your prison will be the first to—'

'My prison?' Helen interrupted sharply. 'And yet not one person from Barfield, including myself, has been asked for their opinion.'

'This is still under discussion, Miss Hewitt,' Andrews said, a touch pained, wafting a hand carelessly over the drawings.

Helen tapped her finger on the desk. 'My priority is rehabilitation.'

'Well, you made that reasonably clear this morning on television,' Andrews said with asperity. Not his style to get into a slanging match, but he had his moments.

'I'd have made it a damned sight clearer if I'd been privy to the fact that Barfield had already been allocated sixty million,' Helen shot back. She had her moments too, damn him.

He said, 'Barfield, on completion, will be the most secure prison in England.'

For that kind of money you could have built it on the moon, Helen thought, but held back from saying it.

Time was getting on, and there was a lot more on her mind. Here she was in the lion's den, and this was the moment to spit it out. Now or never.

'Phone-cards have become prison currency so I would withdraw them. The inmates could be planning a riot, an escape, anything. It's a blatant security risk.' She was on her feet now, pacing, letting the thoughts flow. 'I also believe we should do away with the privilege of the prisoners' own food store. Opening a shop inside prisons is yet again an admission that the food served has to be supplemented, when in reality we are already attempting to make nutritious meals, catering for ethnic diets as well as medical.'

Puffing on his pipe, Andrews said laconically, 'I thought you were, as I am, against the 'lock-'em-up-and-throw-away-the-key' regime, Miss Hewitt.'

'Oh, I am.' Helen was vehement. She faced him, her energy level jumping off the scale. 'I am advocating far *longer* out-of-the-cell periods – because if the prison is secure we would not require men banged up for fourteen hours, which allows the frustration to build and boil over into anger and violence.'

Andrews was shaking his head doubtfully. 'I would think withdrawing all currency would create a veritable time bomb.'

'Boredom is the bomb.'

'Some of these bored men have very short, dangerous fuses.'

'If that short fuse scares us into allowing a criminal's dominance, then all we are doing is creating a more dangerous' – her bleeper went – 'criminal, and each time they reoffend is proof that our present system is failing us and them.' She dived into her bag. 'Excuse me.'

Marshall gave her the glad tidings straight off.

'Howard Webster's absconded. You allowed a dental

appointment this afternoon. The police are on their way to Webster's family.'

She could tell from the fat, smug ring in his voice that he was leaning back in his chair, stirring the wooden spoon and loving every minute of it.

'Just keep me informed. As soon as I'm finished here I'll come straight back.' She banged in the aerial with her fist and tossed the radio into her bag.

'Everything okay?' Andrews asked.

'Fine.' Helen drained her cup of lukewarm coffee. 'One of the prisoners has a dental problem.'

Chapter 15

WORD HADN'T leaked out on C Wing that Webster had done a runner, and Russell Morgan wanted to keep it that way. It only made the cons excitable, planted fanciful notions in their heads, and not least made the prison staff look a right bunch of dickheads.

He stood outside the door of the officers' annex, watching the constant movement and bustle as they moved freely on the wing. Association was the one time of the day when it wasn't possible to keep the noise level down. Apart from the snooker and ping-pong games going on in the central area, there was the TV in the corner, turned up loud whatever programme was on. The kitchen was busy, men making their own fry-ups and brewing tea and coffee. Underneath it all, the rumble of conversation, punctuated by shouts of laughter and some fairly boisterous horseplay.

As senior officer, Morgan was on hand to talk over any problems any of them might have, offer advice if he could, and receive apps to be forwarded to the Governor. These were mostly applications for visits, but could also include requests for transfer to another wing, or to another prison if the man wanted to be nearer home. This was the moment to pick up on the usual grouses and grievances, and sort them out or nip them in the bud before they festered into serious resentment and frustration that could lead to a breach of good order and discipline; if that happened it meant a loss of privileges for the inmate, or he was sent 'down the Block' to the segregation unit, where he could cool off in a bare cell with a mattress and a toilet bowl for company.

In the corner, staring at the TV screen but not watching it, Jack Bulmer sat nursing a mug of hot tea and his boiling anger. One hand was in his pocket, curled round the handle of a toothbrush. The bristles had been removed, the end prised apart, and a razor blade inserted to make a chiv. Mechanically he turned his head. He blinked, focusing on the two men on the far side of the snooker table. He couldn't fucking believe it. They were arguing over it – his property – right in front of his eyes.

Mark Lewis's finger stabbed at Snoopy's face while his meaty fist jabbed into Snoopy's side.

'Look, Markie, back off me, man . . .' The tall black youth held up his palms. 'I need a bit more time. I got gear comin' in.'

Biting what was left of his nails, Stan Field hovered anxiously at Maynard's elbow. This was the first proper chance he'd got, since his confab with the ex-RAF bloke Reynolds in the exercise yard.

'Harry said when the riot went up it took forty minutes,' he confided.

Maynard gave him an icy sideways look. 'Who else have you opened that big yapping mouth to?'

'Just tryin' to help, Mr Maynard.'

'When I need it, Stanley, I'll fucking tell you.'

Field's slanting eyes gazed up, like a rodent's peering out from under a stone. 'Is it on, then?'

Outside the annex, Morgan turned as the small, balding figure of Graham Lyons came onto the wing. 'Evening, Gov.' Lyons gave a friendly nod. Morgan beckoned Malahide over and made the introductions. 'This is our wing governor, Mr Lyons. This is the new boy, Malahide, James.'

'Well,' Lyons smiled, 'you've had a blinder on your first day.' He made sure no one was within earshot. 'Bloody Webster. She should never have let him out.'

'Good evening, Mr Lyons. Had a day off, have you?'

Maynard called out to him. 'I don't suppose there's any chance of getting Channel 4 or BBC2 on the TV, is there?'

Then, as it always did, the violence erupted from nothing and out of nowhere. One second a relaxed, informal, jokey atmosphere, an instant later a sudden flurry of movement that brought a deathly hush as heads whipped round, laughter and conversation frozen in mid-air.

First, the mug of hot tea, full in Mark Lewis's face. Gasping and choking, he instinctively raised his hands as Jack Bulmer followed up with the chiv. A slash across the knuckles and another down the cheek. Completely taken off guard, Lewis staggered back, blood spraying everywhere. But as well as being a mean and evil bastard, he was a head taller, two stone heavier and twenty years younger than the grey-bearded man. Once he'd shaken off the shock of surprise and the hot tea from his eyes, he went for Bulmer with a vicious, snarling vengeance.

Whoops and shouts went up, everyone craning forward, some baying and jumping up and down as the two men grappled together. Bulmer shrieked and let go the chiv as Lewis bent his wrist outwards, at right angles to his arm.

Maynard stepped forward, his face livid. 'For God's sake, break it up.'

'Don't get involved, Mr Maynard,' Field said, grabbing his arm.

'I'm not,' Maynard snapped between his teeth. 'But you better get bloody involved, they could just stop exercise!' He waved an arm to his minders. 'Break it up. GET IT SORTED!'

'Shit!' Field gulped as the penny dropped. He waded in, along with Maynard's three heavies, and moments later there was a general free-for-all, everybody swinging punches, bodies colliding with the snooker table, men rolling on the floor.

It was less than twenty seconds since Lewis got the tea in his face. The alarm bell was clanging. Morgan and

Malahide went in, hauling bodies out of the way while four officers from the annex charged straight through the scrum to get at Lewis, who was beating the living shit out of Bulmer. He had him by the throat and was smashing his head against the wall. It took all four of them to drag him off, Lewis berserk with rage and half blinded by his own blood. Bulmer, too, was spattered with it, the front of his shirt covered with the blood pouring down from his nose and mouth.

The fun was over for today. The screws were back in charge. Most of the inmates started moving off, well out of harm's way, while the few who wanted to keep the trouble going were swiftly segregated.

The alarm continued to shrill as the Tannoy boomed out: 'Everybody back to your cells. Back to your cells. Lock-down! Lock-down!'

Slithering down the muddy bank, Howard Webster hit bottom and lay spreadeagled, chest heaving, completely knackered. In the darkness and the heavy rain he'd missed his footing.

He closed his eyes and counted to fifty. Hoped to Christ he hadn't sprained anything. He moved his ankle experimentally. Seemed okay. He'd been running for hours, never stopped once since he'd made the break. Flat, open countryside, field after field, jumping ditches, skipping across single-track lanes, avoiding any isolated cottage or farmhouse, and now it was pitch black and pissing down. No wonder he'd taken a tumble.

He clambered to his feet, wiped his face with his sodden T-shirt. His short denim jacket was hanging heavy with water and mud, his jeans were ripped at the knees, his trainers pulverized. He hadn't been so utterly weary and exhausted in a long while. It was brilliant.

Pushing through a thorn hedge, picking up some scratches and more rips to his clothing, Webster felt solid tarmacadam beneath his feet. He cocked his head. In the distance he could hear barking dogs, the bleat of a siren. He closed his eyes, nearly done in and he knew it. He sucked in three very deep breaths, gritted his teeth and set off along the darkened lane, dragging his legs as if they were filled with lead.

Not far to go now, he thought, grimacing into the darkness. Go with the burn. No sweat.

Helen came over the brow of the hill, the rain slanting down through the headlights, the hedgerows whipping by. She was gripping the wheel and concentrating because the conditions were so atrocious, but she wasn't ready for the figure that suddenly loomed up in the beams, running straight at her. He raised an arm, blinded by the headlights, and seemed to fall towards the car as Helen slammed on the brakes.

She flung open the door and almost fell out of the car. Oh God, no, had she hit him? The Metro had juddered, but that could have been the crap suspension. She ran forward, feeling inexpressible relief as he got slowly to his feet. His clothing was torn and saturated, his face smeared with mud, hair plastered down. He straightened up in the headlights and Helen's jaw sagged.

'Webster?'

He came towards her, hands reaching out, mouth gaping. Helen stiffened, took a pace back. But then he staggered and collapsed against the bonnet, sucking in great gulps of air, snorting and gritting his teeth. 'Sorry about this . . . Miss Hewitt . . .'

Helen moved back alongside the open door. 'Put your hands on the bonnet of the car, Webster. Just do as I tell you.'

She reached inside for her phone, eyes flicking down as she punched the numbers. 'Just stay facing forwards, Webster.' The call took an age to go through, her eyes never leaving him, and when finally it did the voice at the other end seemed to be coming from Mars. 'Hello?' she almost shouted. *'Hello?* This is Helen Hewitt, put me on to Security. *Now! Yes!'*

Again the waiting. It made her jittery.

'Just stay where you are – *hands on the bonnet!*' She spoke into the phone. 'I'm about five, six miles from the main lane on the north side of Barfield, just before the turn-off. Get somebody out to me as fast as you can. I've got Webster with me.'

The squawk sounded like a confirmation. She zapped the aerial in, took a pace forward. Head resting on the bonnet, arms splayed, Webster was gradually sliding down as his knees gave way.

'Stay on your feet,' Helen ordered. *'Stand up!'*

He kept going down, his hands slithering on the wet metal. 'Sorry, Miss. I'm sorry . . .'

She winced as she heard the bony thump of his knees on the road. His head banged against the grille, and he half lay against the front of the car, his head hanging down. Helen ran a hand through her hair, looking both ways into the darkness. Now what? She moved a fraction closer. His hands were shaking, and this transmitted itself to his entire body. His teeth were chattering, muscle spasms coursing through him. Drenched and cold, his face pressed against the car, eyes closed, he looked sad and lost and vulnerable.

Helen unfastened her belt. 'I'm going to pass you my coat. Don't lift your hands.'

She edged forward, tucked the coat round his shoulders, and stepped back. From the depths of it she heard a mumbled 'Thank you.'

Helen folded her hands beneath her armpits, feeling the rain soaking through her thin blouse. She looked again into the darkness, shivering, then back at him. 'Get in the car, Webster.'

She watched him carefully as he levered himself up and, using the car as support, managed to get to the passenger door. Helen removed the keys from the ignition and reached across to unlock the door. He fell into the seat, shoulders slumped inside the coat, head lolling forward. Helen remained standing by her open door, peering in. Her blouse was stuck to her, her fair hair, darkened by the rain, clinging like rats' tails to her neck.

He raised his head and gave her a long, slow look.

'Put your hands on the dashboard where I can see them.'

Webster put his hands on the dashboard, gazing into the darkness beyond the spray of headlights, breathing through his mouth.

'He looked sick as a dog and I thought he'd had an injection.'

Sitting in the officers' rest room, staring morosely into the tea leaves at the bottom of the mug, Longfell looked even sicker.

'So his toothache wasn't real?' Marshall said. The glee in his voice was unconcealed. Another black mark for Miss Snooty Drawers. She'd arrived with all guns blazing, going to revolutionize the system, show the boring old farts where they'd got it all wrong, and here she was sinking slowly in the west, holed below the waterline.

'Dentist said he'd got an infection of his gums.' Shaking his head, Longfell admitted, 'I didn't put the slips inside the cuffs. It's down to me, nobody else.' He sighed. 'I never lost one in twenty-five years.'

Marshall looked up brightly as Jumbo Jackson stuck his head round the door.

'Governor's contacted Security. Webster's with her, few miles from Barfield.'

'*What?!*'

Helen had the engine running so that the heater could feed him some warmth. He'd stopped shaking, sitting beside her huddled up in her coat, his curly hair plastered flat to his head. 'Done it again, haven't I?' In the greenish glow from the instrument panel she could see that he was smiling.

'I don't think what you did is anything to joke about. Bloody stupid.' Helen glared at him, which seemed to have no effect whatsoever. She burst out, 'How many more weeks, months are you intent on getting on your original sentence?'

That didn't seem to bother him either. He just shrugged.

'Why? Why did you do it?'

Webster turned his head away.

'Do you have marital problems?'

'No.' He stared off into the darkness. 'I wasn't running home.'

'Is it a girlfriend?'

'No. I don't want to talk about it.'

'Well, you're going to have to talk about it – to me, to the probation department, to the prison authorities.' Helen felt like grabbing hold and shaking some sense into him; instead she leaned across to grab his attention. 'Don't you understand what you did? You absconded, Howard, whilst in custody, for the fourth time.'

He turned his head to look at her. 'I was goin' back in, like I done before.' He added quietly, 'I wasn't stayin' out.'

Helen was so frustrated she could have thumped him one. She looked out at the road and then at her watch. 'It doesn't make sense. You abscond and then you run back to Barfield. Where do you run to? Who did you run to? Where were you going?'

Webster dropped his eyes. 'Nowhere.'

'Look at me, Howard. Do you think I'm stupid? You think I believe this crap? Running to nowhere . . .'

'Yeah, that's it, running,' he said defiantly. 'You wouldn't understand.'

'Understand what?'

He sank lower in the seat, then without warning he

twisted the handle and sprang out. Cursing under her breath, Helen snatched the keys from the ignition and went after him. 'Webster! Howard! Don't. Howard!'

He was moving in front of the car, head down in the rain slanting through the headlights. But he wasn't running, she saw, he was pacing up and down, still wrapped in her coat, staring at the ground.

'I can't run in the yard. Few paces, gotta stop, few paces, stop. Bumping into everyone, can't run in the yard. I was goin' crazy, and I . . . I couldn't stop myself.' He nodded fiercely at the ground. 'I had the chance so I took it! I wanted to run . . . to run . . . just to run.'

'You escape to run?' Helen's voice was thin with disbelief. 'Howard, are you serious?'

'Yeah, to run.' He gulped, near to tears. 'Nobody understands.'

Helen glanced down the lane. Hugging herself, she moved nearer, looking hard at him. 'Howard, they'll be here any minute. If you want to tell me . . . come on, Howard, talk to me.'

'My dad was my trainer, he was a great athlete.' Clearing his throat, he looked at her from under his eyebrows. 'He got sick and, anyway, used to just concentrate on me. He pushed and he pushed at me like I would be everything he couldn't be. He wouldn't leave me alone. I wasn't ready, I knew it, but he wouldn't listen. I was on the starting block one time, I heard the starting pistol, but I couldn't move . . .'

Beams of approaching headlights flashed in the distance; he didn't notice, though Helen did.

'I think I nicked the first motor to get at him,' Webster said gruffly, his throat working. 'Well, I got at him. He died when I was sent down. He . . . my dad reckoned I'd be a champion but he—' Tears ran down his face. 'He pushed me too hard. Now all I think about is—'

He saw the bright splash of headlights now, and heard the engine coming closer. He wiped his wet grimy face on the coat sleeve and then realized what he was doing. 'Oh, sorry, this is your coat. You'd better have it back, don't want any trouble for you.'

He handed the coat to her and went to stand in front of the car, arms spread on the bonnet, feet apart. Helen looked round, squinting into the headlights as the white prison van pulled up with a screech of brakes and the doors slammed back.

She said quickly, 'Would you give me your word not to abscond again if I arrange for you to have the yard clear so you can run, Howard?'

Webster was lifted off his feet by the three burly officers, cuffs slapped on, and he was bundled towards the van. The last sight she had of him was as he turned towards her, face mud-caked and streaked with tears. Then he was thrown in the back and the doors slammed shut.

Dimly lit at this hour of the night, C Wing was all quiet save for a few muffled coughs and a radio softly playing jazz as Webster, in T-shirt and boxer shorts, still soaking wet, was led back to his cell.

Governor Lyons watched one of the escorting officers push him through the door and follow him inside, while the other stayed on the landing, arms folded, eyes moving slowly along the closed doors of the landing. Lyons turned away.

From inside the cell came a dull thud. There was a strangled gasp, a low moan, and then silence.

A moment later the officer came out. He locked the door, checked the spy-hole, and strolled back with his colleague to the entrance gate. Strange mumblings and eerie murmurings came from behind the doors. Governor Lyons fretfully stroked his bald head, and stared off down the wing, the cavernous barn-like interior with its railed landings sounding like a whispering gallery.

'This is gonna create. I told her he should've been down the Block.'

Hushed voices could be heard calling out.

'What's goin' on? Is that Jacko back?'

'Is it you, Jack?'

'It's Webster. Webster's back.'

Governor Lyons vented his anger on the cell nearest. He shot back the metal flap of the spy-hole. 'Shut it!' Then he turned and bellowed down the wing, 'QUIET, ALL OF YOU!'

The mumbling and murmuring fell away but didn't cease altogether. Lyons stood with his two officers, listening, waiting for peace to resume. The officer who had been in Howard Webster's cell rubbed the knuckles of his right hand.

Chapter 16

MARSHALL QUICKENED his pace to keep up with Helen as she strode along the covered walkway bordering the exercise yard. The yard was empty at this hour, the inmates still eating breakfast.

Marshall wished he were still eating his, instead of trying to keep up with this manic energy flux who seemed to want the day over and done with by twelve o'clock so she could start the next one.

'Gary, you know I don't approve of you being reinstated back here, but there seems little I can do about it.'

Don't shilly-shally about, Miss Hewitt, Marshall thought. Come straight out with it. He said, 'My wife and kids are here, I was offered another position.'

'Were you? Well, Gary, this is my position. You *are* here so we make the best of it. We had a bad start but I am prepared to make it my job to get along with not just you but every man working here.'

Marshall was keeping up with her, but it was costing him. He wasn't all that fit, he was overweight, and he was nearing fifty. Approaching the heavy iron door leading to C Wing, mercifully the whirlwind at last slowed down, giving him the chance to catch up.

'Governor Lyons is not happy about putting Webster back on the wing, doesn't look good. It'll cause aggro.' He paused to get his breath. 'You know, there was a rumour something was going down. Somebody must have sussed it was Webster going again. We thought it was a delivery.'

Helen unlocked the door with the keys chained to her belt and returned them to her jacket pocket. She winked at him over her shoulder. 'I delivered him back, didn't I?' And off she went, laughing merrily at her own joke, leaving him simmering.

On the upper landing of C Wing she waited while an officer unlocked Snoopy's cell. Reggae pounded through the door.

'Did Mark Lewis have a Gameboy listed on his property?' Helen asked Jimmy Malahide, standing beside her.

He ran his finger down the list. 'Er, no, he didn't.'

Helen tapped her foot. 'Mr Malahide, it is very important that prisoners' cell belongings are checked on a regular basis.'

Already deafening, the thumping reggae beat became ear-splitting as the door was pushed open. Snoopy was sitting cross-legged on the bed, his mouth full of bacon and fried bread, baked beans on a fork about to join them.

'Good morning, Mr Snooper.' Helen reached into her pocket. 'What do you know of this?'

Snoopy's long body craned forward, the motion of his jaw becoming slow and mechanical as he studied the white plastic unit with its LCD screen in the palm of her hand.

'Did Mark Lewis offer you this Gameboy?' Helen made a pained face at the CD stereo. *'Can you turn that off?'*

He flicked the switch with his thumbnail and carried on eating.

'Nothin', never saw it before, Miss.'

'It's Jack Bulmer's Gameboy?'

'I don't know.'

'Is that his name printed on the side? See it? Now, were you offered this? Were you going to buy this, Mr Snooper?'

He chewed and swallowed, shaking his head. 'I've never seen it before.'

Helen looked round his cell, nodding to herself. She looked back at him. 'You know, Mr Snooper, you've only got – what? Another eighteen months?' Her eyes moved down to the Gameboy in her hand. 'But Jack Bulmer, he's got eleven years.'

'I know, he's a lifer,' Snoopy said. 'I know who he is.'

'Then you know with that amount of time you don't like trouble. You don't have a parole, you have to try and do your time and create as little problem for yourself as possible.'

He was silent for a moment, as if digesting this along with his food. Helen wondered if he really was. Snoopy was here for drug offences. Getting nicked was an occupational hazard, part of the job description. You accepted it and got on with it. Bulmer was in for murdering his wife. Whatever the circumstances of her death – and Helen wasn't particularly concerned to know of them – Jack Bulmer, at sixty-three, had very little to look forward to, never mind to live for. This was the only life he had.

It was as she thought. Snoopy's bony shoulders twitched in a shrug. 'I'm sorry for Jack but I don't know nothin' about that.' He nodded disinterestedly at the Gameboy.

'So Mark Lewis never approached you to buy it?'

'No. Can I ask you something, Miss?' He held up his plate. 'We get scrambled eggs every morning and—'

Helen didn't even bother. She walked out.

Edward Maynard was coming along the landing with his breakfast tray. He stepped graciously aside, oozing oily charm. 'Morning, Miss Hewitt. Bit early for your rounds, isn't it?' Helen nodded politely and carried on. 'Excuse me, Miss Hewitt, but because of what happened yesterday . . .'

Helen stopped and turned.

'That little fracas during association.' Maynard's florid face tried out an expression of innocent appeal. 'It won't mean we'll not have exercise, will it?'

Helen's look was measured. 'If you weren't involved in the "fracas", as you call it, you will have the usual exercise period.'

'Good!' Maynard broke into a relieved smile. 'Just that it's a lovely day, didn't want to miss it.'

Marshall was waiting for her at the top of the stairway. She wondered if he'd been born with a scowl, or had worked to perfect it. He was holding a pale green letterhead: directive from the Governor, HMP Barfield.

'Excuse me, can I have a word?'

'Yes, Gary?'

'Webster absconded, you put him back on the wing, you know my feelings about that. But now to give . . .' He waved the paper in her face. 'This is bloody stupid.'

'Why?'

The simple question seemed to infuriate Marshall. Or maybe it was her cool demeanour. He brought his face forward, voice low and rasping. 'It's like he's getting a perk for legging it, and when the rest of the inmates—'

Helen cut him off sharply. 'It's not a perk, Gary, it's a punishment. Now, if any other prisoner wishes to join Webster's punishment, then he's—'

'Why?' Marshall wanted to know. 'Why put yourself on the line like this?'

'I gave Webster my word, and in this place that's of utmost importance.'

Marshall's chest slowly filled with air. 'Fine. I'll tell the SO on the wing.'

'No, I will, Gary.' Helen started down the stairway. 'I want prisoner Mark Lewis transferred from Barfield. We do a trade-off if need be. I just want him out of here.'

On the upper landing Malahide was collecting the breakfast trays and locking the prisoners away for the half-hour until exercise. Leaning in the doorway, Maynard handed his over. 'Lovely day,' he said with a faint knowing smile. The next cell along, an agitated Stan Field stood with his tray ready, trying to catch Maynard's eye. He didn't get the chance as Malahide rattled his bunch of keys and waved the two men inside. The doors thumped shut.

Three cells down, Brian Samora was staring hard at his dog-eared bit of paper, muttering to himself, 'Well, somebody should tell me what it means.' He looked up pugnaciously as Malahide approached. 'I dunno if they're attachin' those twenty-one days to my release date or not.'

Malahide shoved him inside and locked the door.

Down on the ground floor, Senior Officer Morgan turned a key and rapped on the door with his knuckles. 'You decent, Webster?'

There was no reply. Helen pushed past. 'Has he had breakfast?'

Morgan shrugged. His hooded eyes connected with Marshall's; the Deputy Governor raised his eyebrows as he moved past him.

Helen raised her hand. 'Just wait one moment, thanks.'

Marshall stiffened. He stood glowering at Helen's back as she went in. Morgan had to turn away, hiding a smile. He didn't hold with having women in men's prisons but, Christ, when this one went into battle she didn't take any prisoners.

Lined up with twenty inmates at the gates of C Wing, waiting to be taken to the exercise yard, Maynard was tense enough already. The last thing he needed was that greasy toe-rag pawing at him with his bitten fingers.

'Stop grabbing at me, you're driving me nuts.' He yanked his elbow away, impatiently edging forward as the gates were opened and the officers waved them on.

Beneath the soft shuffling of feet in the main corridor, Stan Field's voice was a nagging whine. 'Is it goin' down? I done everythin' for you. I'm with you, aren't I?'

'Shut up!' Maynard said through gritted teeth, his eyes fixed directly ahead. There was the grating of keys, the clang of the big iron door opening, and glorious daylight poured in.

Maynard moved towards it, nerves jangling like piano wires. Stepping through to the outside, he took a deep breath of fresh air. It smelled of freedom.

Jack Bulmer didn't look distraught, as Helen might have expected; he looked catatonic. He sat bowed on the striped flock mattress on top of the concrete base in the punishment cell of the segregation unit. His hands rested limply at his sides, palms up, his soft brown eyes dulled and glazed. The cell contained nothing except a toilet bowl; not a scrap of personal identity, not a picture; nothing except graffiti and scrawled obscenities.

'I'm going to be moved, aren't I? I know.'

Helen stood with Marshall, two officers filling the doorway behind them. Further down the Block somebody was whimpering and snuffling.

Helen said, 'You accused Mark Lewis of stealing a list of items. Are these the belongings taken from your cell?' She held the sheet in front of his eyes.

After a moment he nodded listlessly. 'Yeah, he did it at six forty-five on Tuesday's association. I know because I went to make a phone call.'

'Nobody actually saw him entering the cell, so how can you be sure?'

'Because he wanted some Sellotape. I said he could get it. I saw him going in as I went down the landing. Later, when I came back, he was in his cell.' Bulmer might have been reading the ingredients on a packet of cornflakes. 'I said to him, you finished with my Sellotape? He said he hadn't needed it. On returning to my pad it was lock-up. Then I saw my gear was missing.'

'But you didn't see your belongings in Mark Lewis's cell?' Helen persisted.

'Next day at lunch I'm told by someone that Oswald Snooper has been offered a Gameboy by Mark Lewis. So it had to be him.'

'So you took the law into your own hands.'

Bulmer raised his head, blinking at her. 'I never touched one of the bosses, ma'am, I never touched one of them.'

Helen gave a curt nod. 'I am taking that into consideration.' Attacking a prison officer outweighed any other offence, short of killing another con. The penalties were the most severe the authorities could inflict, and they didn't stint themselves.

'Also your previous good behaviour and that you were provoked,' Helen continued. 'But I cannot condone such violence, so you will obviously be punished. But you will have your belongings returned to you. Eventually.'

She saw Marshall's jowls quiver, and heard behind her an indrawn breath from the two officers. She knew what punishment they would have prescribed: three months in chokey, embargo on visits and confiscation of all personal property.

Some feeling had returned to Bulmer's eyes. Naked fear.

'You put me back on the wing with him an' . . . he'll kill me.'

'Mark Lewis will be transferred from Barfield,' Helen said.

It was beautiful to see. Like the sun breaking through dark stormclouds, the realization dawned slowly over him that the sky wasn't about to fall in. He wasn't going to be moved. He wasn't going to spend months in solitary. He was even going to get his precious Gameboy back.

Helen turned and went out, leaving Marshall dithering for a second, still in shock. As he joined her, Bulmer's voice floated from the cell. 'I owe you, Miss Hewitt, and as I'm down here no one'll know it came from me. Rumour is there's gonna be a delivery. They're wrong – it's a collection.'

Helen looked at Marshall. He was frowning back at her with a baffled expression that perfectly matched her own.

*

There was a gentle mild breeze in the exercise yard; for so late in the year it was surprisingly warm. The sun was poking out now and then and, looking up to the patches of blue, Edward Maynard was smiling to himself, thinking, Perfect flying weather.

At his elbow, like an odorous shadow dogging his every move, Stan Field was gnawing his cuticles and working up a sweat. Maynard could almost smell him. He turned away in disgust, but then saw something that made him smile. Outside the wire-mesh fence a team of maintenance engineers was engaged in repairing the anti-landing wires which had been torn down during the riot. Strung with bright orange plastic ballcocks, the wires were fastened to poles and traversed the exercise yard twenty feet above the ground. Tomorrow, or the day after maybe, they would be reinstalled, Maynard guessed. What you might call cutting it fine.

Brian Samora still didn't get it. Clutching the scrap of paper he stared into Walter Brinkley's eyes. 'Now give it to me straight.'

Brinkley groaned. 'I told you yesterday. What it means is you get an extra three months, you prat.'

'Three months! Oh, man . . .'

Snoopy, head gone, was gazing blissfully upwards at a speck in the sky. The faint scything of blades permeated the air. 'Take me to your leader!' Snoopy grinned, arms open wide.

Other faces were turning up now. Russell Morgan broke off his conversation with Malahide, shielding his eyes. 'Is that the cops?'

No longer a speck, the helicopter was swooping lower, the beating of its rotors getting louder and louder. Then, as if the pilot had realized too late, it suddenly veered away and disappeared behind the buildings.

Somebody yelled gleefully, 'They're still out lookin' for that nutter Webster. Somebody should tell 'em he walked inside himself!'

Webster was in the yard, watched over by two officers. He didn't hear the shout, hadn't noticed the helicopter; he was too concentrated on limbering up, stretching his calf muscles ready for the run when the yard was cleared.

Brinkley spotted him and nudged another prisoner. 'I heard that Webster come back with the Gov. He got out to give her a fuck, that's what I was told.' He sniggered.

He turned his head in surprise as the noise suddenly swelled and the helicopter clattered in, lower than ever, skimming the roof where workmen were replacing the slates. They ducked down, and Brinkley yelped, 'He's runnin' a bit of a risk, ain't he?'

Marshall pulled the iron door open and Helen was first through, charging onto the walkway. The helicopter was turning in a wide arc over the gate-lodge and heading back.

'*Get the alarms on!*' Helen shouted.

'Jesus Christ!' Marshall stared up and then dived back in, hitting the alarm button. A bell clanged, and a moment later the general-alert siren wailed throughout the prison.

In the exercise yard, Morgan, Malahide and the other officers were as confused as any of the prisoners. Everyone was rooted to the spot, watching with a mixture of fascination and disbelief this incredible display of daredevil flying. Helicopter escapes were not unknown, but they were literally fantastic. They occupied the same place in the imagination as road accidents: they always happened to somebody else, never to you. Witnessing one was like living through some bizarrely impossible dream that, any second, would flip back to reassuringly normal reality.

But this was happening for real.

'Bloody hell,' Samora muttered, gawping. 'It's coming down!'

'Holy shit,' Brinkley gasped. 'It's the Mafia.'

Maynard and his ever faithful shadow Field had moved a little apart from the rest. Maynard buttoned up his jacket with trembling fingers. 'This is it. You think he's gonna make it?'

Crouching beside him, Field was like a sweating runner in the blocks, jerking forward in a series of false starts. Maynard swung out an arm, almost knocking him to the ground. 'Don't move yet. WAIT!'

The helicopter was manoeuvring directly above the exercise yard, about fifty feet up. The combined noise of beating blades and the shrill whine of the engine was an onslaught on the senses, forcing the men to back away, hands over their ears. Slowly descending in little shimmying movements, it sent a swirling back draught that flattened the square patch of grass and blew the criss-crossed pathways into clouds of cindery dust.

At the gate, Helen was trying to peer through the gritty murk. This was bloody hopeless! Difficult to see anything, almost impossible to be heard. More officers were arriving at the run from the gate-lodge and the main buildings, and she could only stand back, fists clenching impotently, as they swarmed through.

Marshall was yelling hoarsely, 'Get the men out of the yard! Get them out!' His voice was lost in the racket, but already Morgan was wading in, herding the prisoners towards the gate. 'Move! Everyone out of the yard! Out! Out!'

Malahide wasn't doing anything except stand in the middle of an excited crowd of prisoners with his mouth hanging open. All around him they were jumping up and down, infected by the noise and confusion and their own amazement, waving to the pilot and bellowing out, 'Over here, mate! Over here!'

Maynard got ready, his face contorted against the blast as the helicopter touched down. Field was on his marks, his nerves screwed up so tight he was practically pissing himself. Then he got a real shock as Maynard turned towards him, a strange glint in his eye, and grabbed two handfuls of his T-shirt.

'Not this time, my old son.'

Grunting, Maynard gave a heave, tried to send him

sprawling. Field struggled free. He backed away, white-faced with anger, his slanting eyes cloudy with disbelief. '*You bastard!*'

But Maynard didn't hang around. He was off and running, body bent over as he scuttled under the blur of spinning blades. Field went after him. With a sinking heart he knew he didn't have a prayer. He'd wasted precious seconds and never should have made it across the ten yards of grass in time – and wouldn't have if Maynard hadn't gone for the wrong door. Maynard yanked at the handle, and didn't seem to understand at first, even though the pilot was wildly gesticulating through the curved canopy and screaming at him to get to the other door. He ran round, got it open, and hauled himself in. Field was nearly sliced in half by the rear rotor as he ducked under the fuselage. He saw Maynard's legs disappear inside, and as the door slammed shut he dived for the handle and missed. Engine howling on full power, the helicopter lifted off. Field made a despairing lunge, grabbed hold of the landing strut, and lifted off with it. He hung on, legs dangling, the helicopter tilting forward and revolving slowly as it gained enough height to clear the fence and the surrounding buildings.

Fists punching the air, the men in the yard were cheering and whooping as if their side had scored the winning goal at Wembley.

Snoopy lay flat on his back, spreadeagled, gazing upwards with a wide ecstatic smile as the helicopter and the dangling Field rose high above him into a blue sky with white fluffy clouds bathed in sunshine. 'Oh, yes, man! This is lovely, this is so far out! This is worth it, man! *Oh, yes! Yessss!*'

Helen pushed her way past the officers at the gate. Catcalls and derisive laughter met her as she entered the yard. Ignoring them, she stood alone, staring after the rapidly speeding speck, heading south. 'Oh, my God . . .' She was still struggling, and failing, to take it in. The headlong rush of events had been crowded into four, maybe five minutes at the most. She felt numbed, a yawning black pit where her stomach should have been.

'They ran fucking past you!' She turned to see Marshall, eyes bulging, choleric, his finger thrust under the nose of young Malahide. 'Why didn't you stop them?'

It was too soon for recriminations, Helen thought bleakly. And besides, when they came, the buck wouldn't stop with Malahide. It would stop with her.

Morgan came up and stood beside her. 'I hope they remembered their passports!' Despite the Scotsman's feeble attempt at a joke she could tell he was totally gutted. The look was the same on the face of each and every officer, a mixture of seething anger, humiliation and helplessness. Even the Burglars – the tough squad of security officers – looked ashen and sick, as if they'd been kicked in the balls by a mule.

A cracked, cheerful voice started singing, and it was taken up by all the men in the yard. To the tune of 'I am sailing', they were bellowing out, 'I'm escaping . . . I'm escaping . . . cross the wide open sea . . . I'm escaping . . .'

Jogging alone round the perimeter of the yard, Howard Webster leapt into the air in sheer exhilaration. The thrilling sight of the two men being lifted into the sky had filled him with a sense of joyous freedom. Almost as if he was flying up there with them, free and light as air.

Marshall stood with a group of gate guards and security officers in the gate-lodge, watching the bank of monitor screens. The air was thick with cigarette smoke and heavy with a grim silence. On the screens, Helen was walking towards the car park, an officer either side and one in front. A swarm of jostling reporters and cameramen surrounded them, firing questions, elbowing in for a clear shot, cameras held high. Helen walked steadily on, straight-backed, as the officers tried to clear a path for her.

Marshall stared up at the screens. 'She's got a lot of bottle, I'll give her that,' he admitted grudgingly. 'I hope her ruddy car starts.'

'No comment,' Helen was saying, eyes front and centre.

'Can you tell us if there have been any further developments, Miss Hewitt?'

'No comment.'

The pack closed in around the car. The officer in front was pushing bodies out of the way, trying to reach the door. Two police officers moved in, forming a shield and allowing Helen to squirm through. She got the door open, offering up a silent prayer. Please, God, let it start first time. Just this once.

'Miss Hewitt, you have only recently been posted to Barfield, will this escape—'

'Miss Hewitt, Miss Hewitt – can you give us a further statement?'

'How many prisoners escaped, Miss Hewitt?'

The engine whirred, and coughed, and died. Helen closed her eyes. She turned the key and with immense relief heard the engine fire. She eased the car forward, flashlights going off, fingers rapping on the windows as the officers fanned out in front, waving her through, until finally, after ten seconds of eternity, she was clear and able to drive off.

Helen might have appeared cool or, as Marshall had said, that she'd got a lot of bottle, but her hands were clenched on the steering wheel. She knew this was going to create a major inquiry with HQ and the glossy, smart, confident Helen Hewitt would take a major knockback.

She sat alone in her flat watching the news. She'd made herself dinner but couldn't touch it. She felt physically sick because that escape was her responsibility. She had failed . . . and what a failure. Even if they put the blame partly on the rebuilding, it should have been down to her to ensure the security was even tighter. She wondered if she should call her old Governor and ask for some advice on how to handle the press, who would automatically give the helicopter escape front-page coverage – and, no doubt, use the photographs of her with the lip gloss, from the announcement of her being posted to Barfield.

She was still angry. Hours later, she lay in bed staring at the ceiling: even the thought of going in to work the following morning made her stomach lurch. They would certainly love this, all those snide bastards. They would love it and rub it in. She could just see Gary Marshall's glee. Helen didn't know, and wouldn't know for some time, that in fact the way she had handled the aftermath of the escape had impressed the officers. They were slowly coming round to their Amazon. As Gary Marshall had said, she'd got a lot of bottle, but right now she didn't feel as if she had any.

Yet again Helen had no one she could call for a heart-to-heart. She even contemplated calling Beryl; it was depressing, that feeling of solitude. She then remembered her old Governor's advice and by dawn she was angry, not just with herself that two men had escaped, but even more angry that it had been arranged, planned right under their noses, her officers' noses, *her* bloody nose. With the freedom allowed the prisoners, the prison watchdogs who were forever looking out for the men in her charge never considered the risk every single officer had to face. What might have happened was that helicopter could have killed her men, killed an inmate.

By morning Helen was calm and up early enough to have eggs and bacon, toast and coffee. She was hungry now and she was determined that she was going to go into Barfield with her head held high. If she'd been made a fool of, so what? Never mind that the stable door was open. What was important and uppermost was that she had to make certain she never allowed anyone to see that she could not handle the situation. She would tighten up the security and she would take a serious look at the privileges allowed the inmates. Almost without her knowing it, she was getting tougher, harder, and that she had got herself back on her feet without any help from anyone did not occur to her. She was responsible, full stop.

CHAPTER 17

THE CO-PILOT of the police helicopter leaned closer to the hooded screen, eyes glued to the infra-red image. He couldn't stop himself grinning. On the tiny screen the pitch-black moorland below resembled a somewhat muddy photographic negative: grainy grey background against which the fuzzy white shape of a human figure stood out in stark contrast. What a beautiful picture!

The ghostlike figure was running. Twenty yards behind, other blurred white shapes – men and dogs – were closing the distance. Down there they couldn't see a hand, or even a paw, in front of their faces, while from up here everything was as clear as day. Over his helmet mike, the co-pilot talked them in. Nearer now, less than ten yards away. The running figure stumbled as exhaustion overcame him. On the screen a dark vertical line marked what the co-pilot knew was a ditch. The figure tumbled into it and curled up, hiding from his pursuers. Unaided by the eye in the sky they could have passed by within ten feet and not detected him. But this was too easy. His fuzzy white blob was clearly outlined, cowering pathetically in the dark line of the ditch.

The helicopter hovered directly above, the beam of its searchlight stabbing through the night like a white probing finger. Looking down, the co-pilot saw the uniformed officers, the handlers and their dogs converging on the bright coin of light. Spotlighted, the man remained in his foetal crouch, too weary to move, the co-pilot guessed, or maybe just too shit-scared.

The pilot turned round, a grin from ear to ear, thumbs up. Like shooting fish in a barrel. Wasn't technology wonderful!

A monotonous steady drizzle was sweeping like a grey curtain over HMP Barfield as Helen hurried along the covered walkway towards the admin block. It was 7.25 a.m. She wasn't in the best of tempers; her arrival every morning was spoiled by the half-dozen reporters and photographers lurking at the main entrance. Even the foul weather didn't put them off.

'They got one of the escapees back,' the gate guard greeted her cheerfully, unlocking the inner perimeter fence. 'On the early news this morning. Stanley Field. Dartmoor – went to see his mother. Classic, isn't it?' he said with a laugh.

Helen was impatient to be on her way. 'I heard. Hopefully the press'll stop hanging around outside.'

'Good morning, Governor.' Marshall, clipboard under his arm, was heading for C Wing. He waved the clipboard. 'We've got two new admissions. Two escape, two take their place.'

As if I need reminding, Helen thought sourly.

'You know Stan Field's been picked up?' Marshall said. 'Only went to see his mother.'

'Yes, I know, Dartmoor. Classic, isn't it?' Helen responded drily. 'Thankfully they may keep him there and us out of the papers.'

She carried on to the admin block. The gate guard, mouth pulled down, looked at Marshall. In a bit of a mood this morning, wasn't she, Our Lady of the Cast-Iron Drawers?

On C Wing the men were lining up for breakfast.

Marshall heard the usual grumbles as he went past, moving on through the association area to the TV in the far corner where Governor Lyons and Jimmy Malahide were watching the BBC news.

'Stanley Field was arrested whilst attempting to visit his family.' A prison mugshot of Field flashed up, shifty eyes in the thin ferret face. 'Field was a partner in the daring escape from Barfield three weeks ago. There is still no sighting of the man believed to have instigated the escape, Edward Maynard. Barfield Prison, already the focus of media attention due to the massive riot that created millions of pounds' worth of damage, is now under reconstruction. The Governor of Barfield Prison is Miss Helen Hewitt, one of the youngest female governors . . .'

Malahide ground out his cigarette in a tinfoil ashtray. 'Well, they got one back.'

'Any money on it the other's sunning himself in Spain,' Lyons said with a grimace. He turned to Marshall. 'Thank Christ it didn't get out we lost another bloke the afternoon before. I dunno how she covered that, never even made the local press.'

'We got two coming in this morning, one a real hard bastard.' Marshall ran his finger down the clipboard. 'You got space, Graham, cell numbers . . .'

'Hey, come on.' Lyons's bald head nodded towards the upper landing from where hammering and sawing could be heard. 'We also got half the wing under construction.'

Marshall turned away, sighing. What a Mickey Mouse operation this was turning into. Worse than bleeding Whitemoor.

Malahide was standing at the head of the breakfast line, arms folded across his barrel chest. Walter Brinkley was peering at the food on his tray as if it contained a dog turd. 'Yuck, scrambled eggs and brick dust by the look of 'em.'

There was always one, Malahide thought. The Perpetual Moaner. Brinkley would have pulled a face at smoked salmon and caviar. Barry Simpkins, the guy behind him, was just the opposite. A mild, inoffensive man in his thirties with a pot belly and a timid smile, he seemed obsequiously grateful for everything he got. They were both in for kiting – buying goods and cashing cheques with stolen cheque books – which gave them a shared interest.

'Hey, Walter, I couldn't borrow your radio, could I?' Simpkins inquired. 'It's just I got a visit but I want to record a programme, educational, for me degree.'

'Okay,' Brinkley said promptly, stabbing his fork. 'I'll have your bacon.' He slid the two rashers on to his plate.

Malahide gestured for them to stop fannying around and get a move on.

'I'm goin',' Brinkley said in his whinnying Cockney. 'You wasn't in such a hurry to nab 'em before they took off in the helicopter, was yer?' He sniggered to himself as he moved off, singing, 'Oh, tie a yellow ribbon round a big prize dick . . .'

Malahide gave him a sharp look but said nothing. His attention fastened on Snoopy and Brian Samora, jostling each other and giggling like a couple of schoolgirls. The big blond Yorkshire lad shook his head. Not yet eight o'clock in the morning and they were stoned out of their skulls.

Marshall had the F2050 prison dossiers of the two new men ready to show Helen. She was deep into the thousand things she had to attend to: applications to the Governor, adjudications, complaints about meals, probation reports, and coming up later this morning (just to ensure idleness didn't lead her into mischief) a meeting with the head of management services, followed by a briefing of the wing governors and senior officers on the plans for Barfield's refurbishment and rebuilding programme.

Maybe if she started coming in at six thirty and leaving at ten she might have a chance of getting through it all.

'I dunno – where you want them? C Wing or D Wing?' Marshall pushed the dossiers across the desk. 'I've talked to Mr Lyons—'

'Well, we've got two spare pads in C Wing.' Helen shot him a look.

'We haven't.' Marshall was shaking his head. 'They're starting the plumbing, new fixtures, cell at a time. There's space in D Wing, one of the bigger cells – maybe put in another bunk?'

Helen looked over the F2050s, which contained mug-shots, detailed physical descriptions, medical records, sentences, and the inmates' prison history, if any.

Norman Jones, forty-four, had a criminal record as long as your arm, whereas nineteen-year-old Anthony John Kelly was a first-timer.

Helen glanced at her watch. 'Is Mavis in yet?'

'No, but Moira is.' Marshall pointed to the dossier. 'Maybe we should put the young bloke' – he craned his neck to read – 'Anthony Kelly, in D Wing, and the old lag, Jones, put him in C Wing where we can keep an eye on him.' He clicked his tongue. 'Right animal.'

Helen was impatient to get on, but she took the time to listen.

'Eight years, aggravated robbery, handling, firearms offences. Trouble. He's been shipped in and out of a lot of nicks.'

So why Barfield? Helen wondered. Unless he'd been ghosted, that would make sense. Troublesome inmates were shipped out late at night without any notice and transferred in secrecy to another prison – 'ghosted' – so that no one knew they were going or where they'd gone.

Just her luck to have one dumped on her.

Through the half-open door Malahide could see the cell was empty. Barry Simpkins was down on the ground floor somewhere, handing in his breakfast tray. There were Open

University textbooks on the table, a pile of green-backed exercise books, a plastic tumbler filled with pens and coloured pencils. Malahide went in. He looked round, idly leafed through an open textbook, and glanced at the radio-cassette player on the shelf.

Senior Officer Russell Morgan passed by on the landing. Malahide called out to him. 'This radio . . .' He pointed to it and then to the property list in his hand. 'According to Simpkins's list of personal belongings he doesn't have one – a radio.'

'Get it out, then, probably nicked it,' Morgan said, and carried on.

Malahide nodded, picked it up and left the cell.

The green prison van nosed up to the huge iron doors at the gate-lodge and waited, engine idling. The doors opened slowly, operated electronically from the control room, and the van drove into the main yard and pulled up outside Reception where three security officers, the peaks of their caps nearly covering their eyes, legs braced apart, stood ready to receive their charges.

From inside the van came a steady, rhythmic pounding as Norman Jones smashed his head against the metal side. One hand was cuffed to the central pole bar, which gave him just enough leverage. Handcuffed to the same bar, the only other occupant had squeezed himself into the furthermost corner, bony knees drawn up to his chest. Anthony Kelly's dark brown hair was plastered to his head, the sweat of fear reeking off him. Jones was like a caged, snarling animal, except that there seemed a kind of mindless purpose to this steady, relentless battering at the side of the van. And, even more frighteningly and bizarrely, a mad zest and enjoyment of it.

The driver reported back to base. 'Arrived at destination, Barfield Prison. Both transportees still aboard. Over.'

'Message received, X-ray Nine. Out.'

The hand-over was routine, and to any observer they might have been delivering a vanload of furniture. Greetings were exchanged, jokes swapped. None of them paid any attention to the banging and the howls echoing from inside. Most of these guys were head-bangers anyway. Stupid or puddled, made no difference.

Jones was taken out first, the three security men making it plain that they were more than happy to oblige him if he desired a little gentle exercise. Kelly followed meekly behind, head bowed, escorted by the driver and his colleague.

Senior Officer Andy Gordon was today's duty officer in charge of Reception. He enjoyed this part of the job because it gave him first chance to look over the new arrivals. Kelly was literally shaking in his shoes. Jones was harder to figure. In appearance he wasn't like your typical hairy-arsed villain. He was that dangerous combination of being both vicious and intelligent: alert brown eyes in a thin, handsome face, his long black hair brushed back, streaked with grey at the temples. His sole expression seemed to be a sultry glower, which he turned on any officer who dared look him in the face.

The two men were stripped of their travelling clothes, supervised while they took a shower, and then brought back, wearing just their shorts. Their clothing would be packed away in large cardboard boxes and they would be issued with prison clothing of blue T-shirts, blue shirts, denim trousers, socks, and rubber-soled shoes.

Gordon stood behind the long counter, facing the two semi-naked handcuffed men. Behind them were lined up six hulking security officers. Jones had been through this procedure many times before, but familiarity didn't make him like it any better. The humiliation of being paraded in front of the Burglars, of having six pairs of eyes appraising your nakedness, was almost more than he could take. On the counter were the prisoners' property boxes, which

Gordon was checking item by item. All these would be listed and signed for, and anything prohibited stored away until the prisoner was released or transferred.

'Shampoo, toothpaste, toothbrush. All right, all right.' Gordon ran his thumb through the bristles to make sure a blade wasn't concealed there. 'Shaver, soap. All right, all right. What's all this? You can't have this.' He pushed the carton of Kellogg's All Bran to one side, shaking his head. 'All right, all right, nope, can't have that, penknife. Book, yeah.' He shook it upside down and poked a pencil along the spine. 'Okay.'

Kelly didn't raise his head once as his possessions and personal clothing were minutely inspected. It was hard to tell if he knew where he was or what was happening to him.

With distaste Gordon started delving inside Jones's battered and stained old property box. The eyes of the six security officers swivelled downwards as he brought out a pile of hard porn magazines and calendars. Gordon flicked through them without much enthusiasm, and then finally nodded. 'Yeah, go on, why not?' Slowly and painstakingly he went through the lot. 'Yeah, all right, all right . . . what's this? Nope. No. Toothpaste, okay. Brush, comb . . . Ugh, dear God!' He dropped the greasy, hair-matted comb from his fingertips. 'You ever clean it?'

Underneath the glower, Gordon had the feeling that Jones was laughing at him. Well, he'd soon find out who had the last laugh.

Jumbo Jackson was in charge of a pad spin on D Wing. He had Harry Reynolds and Colin Foster out on the landing, stripped to their shorts, clothes piled beside them, while his officers conducted the cell search. Reynolds, the crop-haired ex-RAF man who was called Mr Angry behind his back by the other inmates, was living up to his reputation. His anger rarely spilled out, he just carried it around, bottled up, like a cylinder of inflammable gas that might at any moment explode.

'What's all this for? We was done last week. Why us again?'

'Harry, don't start,' Jackson warned him. 'You got a new pad mate comin' in. You know the rules.'

It was a standing order that a cell had to be searched before a new occupant could take up residence.

The officers came out, shaking their heads. It was clean. No weapons, no substances.

'Okay, that's it.' Jackson waved his hand. 'Pack your kit up again and get sorted.'

Reynolds started to gather his things together, cursing and muttering. 'This ain't a three-man cell, it's against the regulations.' He glared at Jackson. 'I want to see the Governor.'

'It's the biggest on the block and it'll be temporary, so quit bleatin'. Get in. Colin, you too.'

Foster jumped to it. He was a small, red-haired, spotty lad who was like one big twitch. On the wing he was regarded as a Joey, a weak inmate the other cons could boss around and get to do menial tasks for them.

Jackson turned to Steve Wolton, leaning in the doorway of the next cell, grinning as he watched the two men humping their gear inside. 'You want us to do yours next?'

The grin vanished. Wolton scuttled off down the landing. He jerked his thumb as Victor Braithwaite came by, carrying his water flask. 'They're puttin' another bloke in there.'

'Shit!' Braithwaite stared past him. 'We'll just have to put it off, then. But I'm havin' that nonth.' His missing front teeth prevented him from saying 'nonce'.

Braithwaite waited until Jackson had moved off, and then crept forward, making no sound. He came up behind Foster, who was bent over, collecting his things, and hissed viciously in his ear, 'I'm on to you, on to you, eh!' Foster jumped as if boiling water had been poured down his neck, dropping all his stuff.

'You!' Braithwaite said, putting his face close. '*I know about you* . . .'

Half crouching, Foster stared over his shoulder, terrified. But Braithwaite had turned away, done with him. For the time being.

Helen was on the phone when Moira entered bearing a china mug of steaming Amaretto coffee and a sheaf of neatly typed letters to be signed. Helen gave a small wink of thanks, nodding into the phone. 'I often double up new inmates, especially the younger ones without any experience or previous record—' She broke off as she was interrupted, rolling her eyes at the ceiling.

'Mr Bunny, I am simply informing you as per instructions from HQ.' She reached for her fountain pen, her attention already on the letters that Moira had placed on the blotter. 'Yes, yes, it can accommodate three. Well, for now. Yes, thank you, Mr Bunny.'

With a sigh she put down the phone.

'Moira, I might throttle our area manager. Because of the helicopter escape he's like a demented ferret.'

'Well, we certainly made the headlines.' Moira had a list of three timed phone messages on her pad. She tore off the sheet and laid it next to the letters.

'Princess Diana must have loved us,' Helen said, scribbling her signature. 'Is that model from the architect here?'

Moira nodded. Helen looked at her watch. 'Mavis arrived yet or is she planning on becoming part-time?'

There was a storm in a teacup on C Wing that was brewing into something more serious. Malahide was stirring it.

Walter Brinkley was finishing his breakfast when the officer pushed the door open, taking a sken inside. Of course, Brinkley took the opportunity for a grouse.

'Hey, boss, can't you do somethin' about the cook's obsession with boiled potatoes and scrambled eggs? I mean, every day . . . it's mon-ot-omus.'

'Where's your radio, Walter?' Malahide asked, checking the property list on his clipboard.

'I lent it to Barry Simpkins,' Brinkley said, unconcerned. 'He's doin' that Open University exam and—'

'You know that's against the rules and you'll be on punishment.'

Brinkley stared through his taped-up spectacles. 'Oh, piss off, you nerd. I lent it him.'

Malahide hadn't liked being called a prize dick by Brinkley, and being called a nerd compounded what he regarded as insulting behaviour. He was in a nicking mood, and the two of them were in the frame. He could stir it with the best of them.

Down in the officers' annex on the ground floor, he had Simpkins on the mat. 'Prisoner 590. Mr Simpkins, you will be placed on report for having unauthorized property in your possession.'

He tapped the radio-cassette with his ballpoint, then slid the pad of charge sheets towards him.

Simpkins stood in front of the desk, splay-footed, pot-bellied, and astonished. He never lost his temper, kept his head down, just got on quietly doing his bird, but the injustice of this made his blood boil. 'You're ruddy jokin'!' Incredibly he wasn't, Simpkins realized, seeing Malahide making out the nicking sheet. 'I was lent the radio. He *lent* me the radio.' Simpkins suddenly bridled. 'Did that prick Walter say I nicked it?'

'Shut it.' Malahide was bent over the desk, the neat parting in his blond hair a thin pink line of scalp. 'Your mate's on report for lending it you.'

Clenching his fists, Simpkins turned on his heel and left

the glass-walled office. He spun round, fuming. 'You're nuts – you mean, tight-arsed bastard! I wanted it to record a programme!' He checked himself, seeing Governor Lyons approaching, and stormed off.

Lyons came into the office, eyebrows raised inquisitively. 'What's that about? He doesn't usually get so het up.'

'I found Walter Brinkley's radio in his cell. He's on report for lending it.'

'Hey!' Lyons raised a cautioning hand. 'Take it easy. I mean—'

'It's against the regulations.' Malahide jerked his head up, his eyes sullen. 'When I checked out Simpkins's list of possessions a radio wasn't on his list.'

Lyons couldn't argue with that. The rules were quite clear, true, but weren't always enforced to the letter. There had to be leeway, just to make the system function. He said doubtfully, 'Mmm, okay, do what you have to.' He looked at his watch. 'Workshop's open.'

Malahide threw up his hands. 'I'm just doin' my bloody job!'

Lyons waved him down, as if calming a large and unruly child. He gave a tepid smile. If not peace on earth, at least peace on C Wing. Quickly changing the subject, he said, 'We got a new inmate coming on the wing. He's a tough bastard, so mark his card.' He scratched his neck. 'I got to go, governors' meeting. See you later. Get forty-eight ready for occupation.'

Fishing in his pocket, he went off towards the entrance gate, distractedly jangling his keys.

Malahide finished writing out the charge sheet and signed it. His hand was shaky. Give way on the rules and you got your arse busted, stick to the rules, ditto. Talk about a no-win situation. The officers were bringing the men down, ready to be taken across to the workshops. Two workshops had been reopened, painting and decorating, and woodwork. As they were lining up outside, Brinkley pushed his way through and stomped into the office. His face was flushed, his spectacles crooked. When he spoke his voice was creaky with suppressed outrage.

'I want my radio.' He pointed a trembling finger. '*That* is my radio. *You* took it out of Barry's pad.'

Malahide straightened up to his full six-feet-four. 'You can't have it.'

Brinkley raised both puny fists. Malahide could have snapped him in two between finger and thumb. It didn't seem to matter. Brinkley danced forward on the balls of his feet. 'You give me back my radio *now* or I'll smash your fuckin' face in.'

Malahide came round the desk, hands the size of shovels curling and uncurling, itching to take a crack at him. 'Get out! GET OUT OF THIS OFFICE!'

Brinkley backed off, spitting with rage. There were whoops and catcalls and shouts of encouragement from the men outside. Two officers strode forward and grabbed him by the elbows. Struggling and squirming between them, the little man was frogmarched away. He twisted his head right round, spectacles hanging off his nose, and screamed out, 'I screwed yer mother!'

'Yeah, go on, Walter, tell him,' the men yelled. 'Give it to him, Walter!'

Malahide filled the doorway. His baleful stare raked over the smirking faces, his ears burning with their muffled snorts of laughter.

CHAPTER 18

'I DON'T like it any more than you do,' Helen said. She was standing at the window, looking out at the grey drizzle sweeping over the main yard. 'Kelly is a first-time offender, but right now I don't have much alternative.' She turned to the desk, leaning her elbows on the back of her chair. 'The single cell on C Wing – I want Norman Jones in there.'

Phil Donner closed the dossier and tossed it down. 'From his records I don't think a Rottweiler would be happy sharing with him,' he remarked. Donner was head of management services, in charge of prison administration and financial matters.

There was a scuffling sound, and a moment later Mavis pushed open the door with her foot. It wasn't her day. Late arriving because her youngest had kept her up half the night with a hacking cough, she was trying to make amends, gallantly struggling in with the plywood and balsa model of the proposed new prison layout. 'Governors' meeting, Miss Hewitt.'

The model caught the edge of the door, and a green rectangular wooden block, meant to represent the workshops, tumbled to the carpet.

'No, Mavis, not in here.' With a sigh Helen crossed over and set the wooden block approximately back in place. 'Get that over to the boardroom.'

Round cheeks flushed, Mavis blew the curly fringe from her forehead. Helen held the door while she manoeuvred sideways to get out, making a command performance of it. Definitely not her day.

'Past experience, Gov,' Donner said, rising. 'Sometimes it's good for a new inmate to share until he's settled.'

Even if the advice was well meant, Helen was nettled. She said curtly, 'Just get the wing governor to keep an eye on him.' She nodded to Moira, who had appeared at the door, wrist held up, tapping her watch. The wing governors and senior officers were assembled for the briefing.

On his way out, Donner's foot kicked something which skittered across the carpet. Helen picked it up. A tiny plastic model of a prison officer. 'I hope that's not a bad omen!' she said ruefully.

Cigarettes were hurriedly stubbed out as Helen entered the boardroom. Somebody had opened a window, but the air still reeked of smoke. The model of Barfield Prison was in the centre of the walnut table. Moira had photocopied the plans and sheets of specifications, Helen saw, and placed copies around the table for the five wing governors and fifteen senior officers to peruse.

Russell Morgan, sipping a cup of tea, was standing with Governor Lyons. He half turned away as Helen moved to the head of the table, leaning closer to Lyons. 'Apparently Doughen and O'Keefe have been offered work,' Morgan confided. 'Almost double the wages from here and better hours. Private security company.' His eyes rounded meaningfully. 'Lots of the blokes are bein' dispersed – Detach Duty – from here, don't fancy comin' back. That'll mean we'll have a lot of new recruits, and if they're all like ruddy Malahide we'll be in trouble. Be over four hundred inmates with the new wings open – it's all a bloody mess . . .'

Helen was already into her spiel, the governors and uniformed officers crowding in as she pointed out the main features.

'The landings are as before, identical to C, D, and the

VP and segregation wings running at present. The same officers' unit, kitchen, association areas here.' She looked to Andy Gordon, the senior officer responsible for physical education. 'The gymnasium, as you can see, Andy, is in the same area but almost double the size, and this area here is the football pitch. Floodlit astro turf' – Helen gave a faint smile – 'and word has it to the tune of a hundred and twenty thousand pounds!'

There were a few low whistles. Morgan had his hand over his mouth. 'When the prisons go private they'll be head-huntin',' he muttered to Lyons. 'First that'll want out are those on Detach Duty.' His thumb and fingers went up as he listed them. 'Hawley, Nichols, Lithgow, Stubbs, Abbott . . .'

Helen's glance was sharp. 'Can you just hold the chit-chat?' She stretched out to indicate the Special Secure Unit, isolated from the main buildings in one corner of the layout. This was the 'prison within a prison' with its own twenty-two-feet-high mesh-link fence topped with rolls of razor wire. 'The SSU, maximum security unit, different from the segregation unit, as you can—'

'Play my cards right, you think I'll get a room?' Morgan chipped in, grinning round at the other amused faces.

Helen waited for the laughter to subside, and let the silence linger on. 'The men in SSU, Mr Morgan,' she said, icily quiet, 'never leave it.' Somebody started to laugh but quickly shut up when one of her looks shot his way. 'Roof is very tough Perspex: bullet, fire and bomb-proof,' Helen continued. 'Exercise yard all covered with protective metal meshing. The cells – fourteen, as you can see – are larger and wider apart for security reasons.'

'Well, it'll make our lives easier.' Marshall beamed.

'You mean you approve it?' Helen said.

Lyons also was nodding enthusiastically. 'Too damned right. Anyone working with the real animals would go for this.'

'Wrong,' Helen said. 'The control unit will still house

the violent prisoners.' She lifted the SSU from the model and held it up. 'I am against this due to the vast expense it takes to keep a handful of men segregated because the authorities believe they cannot be handled in the main prison.'

'A lot can't,' Lyons pointed out. He looked round, receiving nods and mumbled agreement. 'Our problems always come from the maniacs with no hope of release.' He was referring to the Red Flag prisoners, those highly dangerous men whose names (in the strictest confidence, known only to the prison authorities) had a red flag by them, meaning they would never again walk free.

Morgan added with feeling, 'The bastards that threaten our lives because they don't give a shit about their own.' He nodded brusquely at the model in Helen's hand. 'Best place for them.'

Helen replaced it with an irritable shake of the head. She folded her arms, gave him a piercing look. 'If you had been paying attention, Mr Morgan, you would have heard that it will not be used for restraining violent men. Everything inside this unit is built to contain not necessarily the most hardened criminals, but high-risk prisoners. Mafia, terrorists, drug barons—'

'Or rich enough to hire a helicopter!' Lyons said, with a chuckle.

'You may well laugh but it's close to the truth.' Helen looked at her watch, realizing she was running late. Her gaze swept over them. 'I have been asked to get feedback on your reactions to the new building. Any detail you believe should be incorporated into Barfield, now is the time to tell me. So have a think and . . .' Again she checked the time. 'We'll call it quits for today.'

She strode out, mentally ticking off another item dealt with on the day's packed agenda. Only another nine hundred and ninety-nine to go.

*

Malahide led the new prisoner up the stairway and along the landing to cell 48. Norman Jones carried his possessions in a black plastic bag slung over his shoulder, and under his arm a complete change of clothing plus gym kit, plimsolls, and a spare pair of shoes. Malahide pushed the door open and stood back.

'Right, Norman, get your kit sorted if you want any lunch.'

Lyons had tipped him the word that Jones was a real tough nut who needed watching. Jones didn't have that sort of look about him, but Malahide wasn't deceived by appearances. Some men looked hard and were soft as putty; men like Jones, who seemed quietly self-contained, even studious, could turn out to be the real vicious bastards.

The cell had been recently repainted, bright as a new pin, with toilet, washbasin, and a new metal-frame bed bolted to the floor.

'Little palace, isn't it?' Malahide said, framed in the doorway.

Jones dumped his stuff on the bed. He remained standing with his back to Malahide, as if he hadn't heard, or as if Malahide's opinion was of absolutely no interest to him, or as if Malahide didn't even exist. All he did was stand and wait, face expressionless, until he heard the door bang shut.

On D Wing, Anthony Kelly was going through the same process. Jumbo Jackson got him installed in cell 29, which he was to share with Harry Reynolds and Colin Foster. Kelly stood in the narrow space between the double bunks and the single bed, his bag of possessions and clothing heaped in his arms, a dithering mass of nerves.

'Right, lad, unpack, get your kit sorted, don't overlap anyone else's area.' Feeling sorry for him, Jackson added with a nod and a brief smile, 'Tea break comin' up.'

Kelly dropped his gear on the bed and turned, hand raised, like a kid with a question for the teacher, but Jackson had gone.

His hand went down as he gazed round slowly, taking in this strange, frightening environment. Originally from Edinburgh, he'd lived in England for most of his nineteen years; always a bit of a loner, he was a thin, gangling young man with defensive blue eyes, fine features and ears that seemed too large for his narrow skull. He wasn't sure he could take this. His heart was hammering like mad and he could feel tears pricking his eyes.

He jumped, blinking them back, as a sly, squint-eyed face popped out from the side of the doorway.

'You bunkin' in here, then?' Steve Wolton slithered in. He'd watched the new bloke being brought up, and one thing he never missed was an opportunity. 'What's your name?'

'Anthony.'

Wolton shook the thin, limp hand. His squinty eyes were everywhere, sizing him up, poring over Kelly's stuff on the bed.

'Got any burns? Smokes?'

'No, I haven't . . . sorry.'

'Any magazines? What you got with you, then?' He started pawing through Kelly's things. 'Any money? Phone cards? You got stuff to trade, then, have you?'

'You – out.' Jackson stood in the doorway. 'Move.'

Wolton slithered past him. Jackson raised a stern finger at Kelly. 'Keep your nose clean. We don't have cell association at Barfield.'

The cell door was pulled shut and the key grated in the lock. Kelly stared mutely at the door, at the lurid porn decorating the walls, at the tiny postage stamp of blue through the barred window. I'm not going to cry, he told himself. I'm not.

*

Helen had tried to shake off Mrs Ellis in the corridor, without success. She pursued Helen into her office. 'I need to know when the education department is to be reinstated. A lot of inmates are getting edgy – some are midway through studying for Open University degrees.'

'I am aware of that, but it must be obvious that the rebuilding is nowhere near completion yet.'

Helen's voice had a sarcastic edge to it, and Mrs Ellis bridled. 'Well, you did ask!'

Helen raised her hands, nodding. As head of the education department Mrs Ellis had every right to be concerned. It was just this damn business of trying to run a prison and at the same time get it rebuilt. 'Sorry I sounded off.'

'That's okay. You reckon it'll be a Cat. A prison, then?'

Helen frowned. 'I'm sorry?'

'Well, you'll have to play second fiddle. You wouldn't be of a high enough rank to run a Cat. A prison.' Helen guessed there had been talk of this amongst the staff, and now Mrs Ellis was spilling the beans. Behind the tortoiseshell spectacles her magnified eyes were wide and admonishing. 'Personal motives shouldn't be allowed to hold up expansion and progressiveness.'

The bloody nerve of the woman. Was she being taken to task?

Helen said testily, 'So you approve of the secure unit. Do you know how much it costs to run?'

'You don't query the costs of a floodlit astro-turf football pitch,' Mrs Ellis said, completely unfazed.

'I'd advocate anything that relieves boredom.' Helen could see she had to spell out her philosophy. 'Anything that can release pent-up frustration. An angry man isn't interested in taking further education.'

She believed that passionately, from the heart. But she was enough of a realist to know what Mrs Ellis, along with the rest of the staff, would suspect. That it had nothing to do with Helen Hewitt's personal philosophy and everything to do with her remaining as Governor of HMP Barfield. She hoped to God they were wrong.

Walter Brinkley was on the bell. He pressed his finger to the button next to the cell door and kept it there. The joke went that it was the prison officers' exercise bell: press it and see them run like hell. But this wasn't a joke. Brinkley was steaming mad. If the screws wanted to play head games with him, he'd beat them at their own fucking game.

'Open the door, you shithead!'

The slotted flap slid back and Malahide peered in. 'Just quieten down, Walter, I'm not opening up.'

Brinkley thrust his face to the spy hole. 'Well, I'll tell you what I'm gonna do, you *dickhead*. I'm going to heat up some cooking oil and throw it over that pig face of yours. *You hear me?*'

The flap slid shut and Malahide's heavy footfalls receded.

Brinkley beat on the door. 'I want my radio! *You hear me?*'

He listened, breathing hard, so mad with rage he was frothing at the mouth. All he could hear was silence and the blood pumping in his ears. Spinning round, he seized the first object to hand, the small wooden chair, raised it aloft and smashed it to the floor. He had a go at the table, but that was bolted down, so instead seized his mattress and bedding and flung it around the cell. 'That is my radio,' Brinkley panted, ripping up the sheets. 'I want my radio, you bastards, my radio, bastards . . .'

There was the thump of footsteps on the landing. Brinkley backed away as the door swung open to reveal six officers in line abreast. Russell Morgan curled his finger. 'Now, Walter, come out of your cell. Step out!'

'Piss off.' Brinkley glared through his broken specs. 'I'm not goin' anywhere!'

'Step out of the cell, Walter. *Now!* You want to be sent down the Block?'

'Piss off!'

Morgan nodded grimly. 'That's it, Walter. Walk out or you'll be dragged out. Now it's up to you.'

Teeth clenched, Brinkley did a slow stiff walk towards them, muttering under his breath, 'Bastards, bastards, bastards . . .'

Every man there was at least a head taller, yet they reared back as Brinkley suddenly let fly. But not at them. Berserk with rage and frustration he was tearing at his clothes, ripping off his T-shirt, then his trousers, and bending over, glasses dangling from one ear, pulling off his shoes and flinging them anywhere.

The commotion could be heard throughout the wing. Yet for Norman Jones, only four cells away, it seemed not to exist. Lying on his bed, flicking the ash off his cigarette with his little finger, he used that trick he had of blocking out any intrusion into the private world inside his head. The magazine he had taped across the window gave the cell an eerie half light. Humming softly to himself, he picked up his comb and from its greasy, congealed teeth extracted thin slivers of razor blades. One by one he lined them up on the grey blanket beside him, his lips barely moving as he softly sang the opening bars of a popular song over and over again.

'Then you tuck in the ends, real tight, just like in the army.'

Standing at the foot of his bed, Anthony Kelly watched as Colin Foster demonstrated. The small, red-haired man even did this with a twitch, shoulders jerking for no apparent reason.

'Were you in the army?' Kelly asked.

'No. Harry's ex-RAF.'

Kelly looked towards Reynolds in the top bunk, lying on his side facing the wall, one arm curled over his head. He was about to speak to him until Foster caught his arm. Mouthing it, Foster said, 'Leave him alone, he's got personal problems. His wife's givin' him the—' He stuck his elbow out.

Kelly sank down on his bed, hands clasped in his lap.

Foster did a little skip, again for no reason, and said, 'I'm doin' five for GBH.' He nodded to Reynolds. 'He's . . . a lifer,' he murmured out of the corner of his mouth. 'What you got up to, then?'

'Er, fraud.' Kelly gave a weak smile. 'Building society.'

'I hope it wasn't Abbey National. I'm in that.' Foster stared at him and suddenly let out a freakish high-pitched giggle.

Kelly's fingers dug into his knees. His eyes widened as he saw Reynolds sit up, holding a crumpled bunch of letters and snapshots which he started methodically to tear into tiny pieces.

Ignoring this, Foster eagerly craned forward. 'What books you got, then? Anythin' with a bit of . . .' He held his curled hand to his groin and mimed a super-fast masturbation. Then his mouth split wide and out came the screeching giggle. He twitched as a bell rang out on the landing. 'Tea's up. You all right, mate?' he asked Reynolds.

Eyes hooded, Reynolds flicked out a punch at him, which got Foster giggling again. Doors banged as the officers moved along, unlocking. Slumping down, Reynolds turned his face into the pillow. His muffled voice was tight with strain. 'Need some gear, Colin.'

The morning's drizzle had turned into a steady downpour. Wearing only his boxer shorts and socks, his arms wrapped round his thin bare chest, a shivering Walter Brinkley trotted along the covered walkway, on his way to the punishment block. Two officers flanked him, one carrying his bundled-up clothing and shoes.

Watched over by two officers, Arnie Franks stood alone in the exercise yard. He leered when he saw Brinkley and came over to the fence, wiggling his hips.

'Who you lookin' at, you dirty old nonce?' Brinkley snarled, hunching to keep out the rain.

'Come on, Arnie,' one of his escort called out. 'We're getting pissed through here!'

Franks pressed himself against the fence, rubbing himself up and down. Helen appeared from the main building, hurrying along behind Brinkley's semi-nude exhibition. 'What's that about?' she asked one of the officers with him.

The officer grinned towards the lewd pantomime at the fence. 'Arnie sees a bare arse, thinks it's his birthday!' Then he realized where her attention was directed. 'Oh, sorry. Brinkley, he's just refused to get dressed.'

Shaking her head, Helen went on her way. Behaviour like this was more suited to a kindergarten, she thought. Hardly surprising when some of the inmates had a mental age of five.

Through the glass panel she could see Russell Morgan standing at the notice board as she went by the officers' rest room. She put her head in. 'Can I talk to Anthony Kelly now.'

'He's gone for his medical. We got a bit behind with that ruddy Walter Brinkley.'

'What about Norman Jones?'

Morgan nodded. 'He's had his medical.' He picked up his clipboard and followed her out. On the way to C Wing he said, 'I wanted to have a word about young Malahide. Maybe try him out on the VP Wing. And I wouldn't mind having Jumbo Jackson back on C Wing.'

Helen said she'd consider it when the duty rosters came up for approval. Morgan unlocked the door of cell 48. 'Governor to see you, Norman.'

Jones was reclining on his bed, reading a paperback about the SAS in the eerie twilight that filtered in from the partially masked window. He didn't alter his position as Helen entered, and Morgan's face stiffened. 'This is the Governor, Norman, Miss Helen Hewitt. Stand up.'

'Everything all right?' Helen asked, looking round at the

neat cell, everything tidied away. The words that came into her mind were purpose and discipline. Not out of the kindergarten, this one.

Jones took his own sweet time in laying down the book and rising to his feet. He stood closer than he needed to, his face empty of expression, lips pressed firmly together.

If it was intended to be provocative, Helen betrayed no sign that it was having the slightest effect. She said calmly, 'I asked you a question, Mr Jones.'

Still no reply. In the army it would be termed dumb insolence; Helen let it ride, though she sensed that Morgan was getting worked up. Glancing at the clipboard in the crook of her arm, she said, 'You'll be having a meeting tomorrow with a prison probation officer. Any questions you would like to ask me?'

Nothing. The face was immobile, the mouth a straight hard line. He brought his hand up, and Morgan instinctively stepped forward, eyes wary, but it was only to lazily brush back the dark, grey-streaked hair that grew thickly over his ears. Yet even that gesture seemed like an insult.

Helen turned away. 'I won't hold up your tea break.' She nodded to Morgan, who followed her out and pulled the door shut.

Standing quite still, Jones stuck out his tongue. He swivelled his head to the stainless-steel mirror affixed to the wall, and very delicately, between finger and thumb, removed the sliver of razor blade from his tongue. He sucked in a long, slow, deep breath, and with the speed of a striking cobra slashed the blade through the air at eye level, right where Helen had been standing. That's how close to him she had been, and how close she had come to having her face sliced in two.

Two stacks of Mighty White sliced bread, a big plastic bowl of jam, a catering-size tub of margarine, and a plate of doughnuts were on the tea trolley. In the line-up, Colin Foster was trying to edge closer to Snoopy and further from Victor Braithwaite. He could see Braithwaite muttering to Steve Wolton behind him, and Foster knew, because Braithwaite's eyes never left him, what the muttering was about. The guy was nuts. Plus he was an evil bastard. But why take it out on him? Because he was nuts and an evil bastard, that's why.

Foster twitched and sneaked in behind Snoopy. He stared dejectedly over the ravages of the tea trolley. 'God, not one jam doughnut left.' He picked up two slices of bread. Holding them at waist height and craning forward, he cursed loudly while he slipped the three phone cards inside. 'Hey, mate, you got one wiv jam in it?' Snoopy had the very thing. 'Here,' Colin offered, 'have me bread.'

The exchange took place under the nose of Jumbo Jackson.

Reaching for the milk to pour in his tea, Snoopy gave Colin a quick wink. 'Good stuff, best yet, come in this afternoon.'

'I know he's a nonth, I know it.' Speaking to Wolton behind him, Braithwaite went on hoarsely, 'I don't care what he says he's in for, I know he's bent.'

He idled at the trolley, allowing Wolton to get in front of him. As Wolton collected his mug of tea, Braithwaite nudged his elbow, sending the lot down Foster's shirt and trousers. Braithwaite was in fast, full of apologies. 'Sorry! Here, lemme . . .'

Bending low to brush him down, he got Foster a swift vicious jab right in the balls, hissing under his breath, 'Nonth, nonth, thcumbag nonth.'

Foster winced. 'Ughhh, you piece of shit.' The red-haired lad was crouched over, his spotty face creased with pain.

'Come on, move it,' Jackson called out. 'Get your tea and stop yakking.'

Quite unperturbed, as if nothing had happened, Braithwaite poured himself a mug of tea from the big metal jug. 'Who's the new boy?' he wanted to know, nodding to Kelly, who was hanging back, too scared to go near the trolley.

'Tony. He's okay,' Wolton said.

'Good.' Braithwaite spooned in three heaped sugars. 'We're goin' to have some fun with that nonth.' His mouth widened in a gappy smile. 'How ya doin', Jumbo?'

'Better than you. Go on, move it, Victor.' He beckoned Kelly forward. 'You want tea, son, you'd better move it.'

Wolton looked back over his shoulder. 'Tea? More like gnats' piss.'

Braithwaite grinned, but not at that. He was watching with gloating satisfaction the trouble Foster had as he climbed the stairway, his eyes cloudy with pain.

'You probably need a new starter motor,' Malahide said, head cocked critically as the Metro whirred and whirred and finally stuttered into life.

'I probably need a lot more than that,' Helen said resignedly, keeping her foot on the pedal and revving the engine. Malahide detached the jump leads and slammed the bonnet down. She gave him a wave. 'Goodnight, thanks.'

He drove off in his old Volvo estate. There was a baby seat in the back and toys on the rear shelf, Helen saw. She gingerly put the car in gear, and was about to ease away when she saw the tall figure of Lorcan Thomas striding across the car park towards his red MG. He noticed her and came over.

'Hi!' Helen greeted him, her heart lifting.

'I wanted a word. You've got a Norman Jones, don't know his number off-hand. Arrived today.' He leaned in and she caught a whiff of musky violets.

'What about him?'

'He's very fit, physically. Mentally, diagnosed paranoid schizophrenic, from his records.' He raised an eyebrow. 'Did you know?' Helen nodded. 'Well, He's refused medication and I can't give it to him by force. Thought you should know. I've put it in my report.'

He gave a perfunctory smile and moved off.

'What about Anthony Kelly?'

Lorcan Thomas glanced back. 'Frightened.'

'I meant physically.'

'So did I. He's very frightened. Otherwise he's okay.'

'Goodnight,' Helen said, watching him stride away. She breathed deeply, trying to think of something else to say to him. She wondered if he'd detected that whenever she had a conversation with him, she flushed or felt that she was flushing. He was already starting up the engine of his MG, not even looking back in her direction. He obviously didn't fancy her, nor did he seem to have the slightest notion that she was interested in him. Helen watched his car moving out as she dumped her briefcase onto the back seat of the Metro. She tried to remember the last time she'd felt this way about a man: not for a long time. But she had made numerous hints about possible dinners and had even told him about needing to trust someone inside Barfield. He'd never referred to it or, for that matter, been anything but professional. Well, up to a point – he was, or appeared to be, moving through all the other female employees. She adjusted the driving mirror, to look at herself. Maybe he just didn't like tall women, maybe her being Governor put him off. She sighed, feeling inadequate because she really did have an almost schoolgirl crush on him. There was also, and she hated to admit it, an awful void in her life. She longed to be held in someone's arms, his arms . . . Hell! 'He's probably not worth even thinking about,' she muttered, as she banged the mirror back to its correct position. She started to back out of her allocated parking bay. As she headed for home, she wondered what was on TV, and then she remembered what Lorcan Thomas had said about Anthony Kelly; she made a mental note to make sure the wing governor, Mr Lyons, kept an eye on him, wishing she'd had time to interview him as was usual. She'd talk to the boy first thing in the morning. Her infatuation with the prison doctor already out of her mind, she started thinking about the frightened Anthony Kelly.

Wearing blue and white striped pyjamas Anthony Kelly leaned over the washbasin, brushing his teeth. The thick blue haze in the cell was making his eyes water. Harry Reynolds lay propped up on a couple of pillows, eyes closed, a thick joint between his fingers, half-way to Bliss-ville. On the lower bunk Colin Foster was rolling another huge spliff; the broken doughnut lay on the table, prised open to get at the stash in a sealed plastic wrap.

'Snoopy said it was good shit, come in today.' Colin twirled the end to keep the grass from spilling out and lit up. He sucked hungrily, holding the smoke in his lungs, and got a hit straight away. He exhaled slowly, his voice tight and high. 'Oh, yessss, he wasn't kiddin', eh.'

From the landings came the muted yet strangely echoing sounds of the prison settling down for the night. Mutter-ings and mumblings, a radio playing somewhere, distant yells and shrieks of laughter. Then the tramp of feet as the screws passed by, warning of lights out.

Kelly wiped the washbasin clean and folded his towel. He edged round to get into bed, and Foster held up the spliff.

'You want a hit?'

Kelly shook his head. He slid down, pulling the blanket up to his chin. The overhead light went out, and the cell was bathed in a murky twilight glow, seeping through the magazine taped over the window. Without it, the cell would have been bright as day from the blaze of the perimeter arc lamps.

Reynolds got down from his bunk and started pacing the five steps from door to window, window to door, door to window, the spliff glowing brightly as he took constant drags. He started to laugh softly and meaninglessly. Foster, hunched up against the wall, joined in the stoned empty giggling, mumbling dreamily, 'Oh, yes, it's good gear . . .'

Huddled down, Anthony Kelly stuffed the blanket in his mouth to stifle the sobs, trying not to make a sound. His whole body was shaking, the tears sliding down his cheeks.

Chapter 19

The young salesman gave Helen five minutes to look over the cars on the forecourt before he decided she was a real prospect and not just browsing. He finished his coffee and came out of the wooden cabin into the watery morning sunshine. 'Hi there. Can I be of any assistance?'

'I don't know. To be honest I was only just passing and . . .' She turned, brushing her hair back, looking from car to car. 'I've not given it much thought. Do you do part exchange?'

He nodded. She didn't trust second-hand car salesmen, and that counted double when they were young and good-looking with nice teeth.

'I was thinking about five thousand and whatever you'd give for my car.'

The salesman's eye passed over the Metro and didn't linger. It hadn't been washed in months and the interior was even filthier, if that was possible. He jerked his thumb. 'We've got more vehicles round the back. Do you do a lot of driving? Or do you just want a local runabout for the kids?'

What she really wanted, though didn't say so, was a car that started. She followed him round to the rear where row upon row were lined up, bumper to bumper, from basic Fiestas to top-of-the-range Saabs, BMWs and a couple of Mercedes. He could tell she hadn't a clue what she was seeking, though he remained patient for ten minutes while she sat in one car after another. When she slid behind the wheel of a silver BMW 700 series, however, he began to feel she was straying out of her league. Too powerful and too flash for doing the weekly shop at Safeways. He said, with a wry shake of the head, 'That's a lot more on what you said you wanted to—'

'I like the colour of the seats but I always get terrible static,' Helen said. She leaned back and gripped the wheel as if she were driving.

'You can test drive any of them,' the salesman said. 'Maybe have a think about it, come back tomorrow.'

'I need something a bit substantial, and then with good leg room.' She squinted forward. 'This has a big mileage.'

'If it hadn't it'd be more expensive.' Growing impatient now, he glanced at his watch. 'It's a lot more on your original price. I think you've sat in them all. Best would be to see how it handles. I can arrange a test drive.' He was looking beyond to a little VW Polo. Or maybe that Astra with the reconditioned engine.

'What's that one? See, right at the back.' Helen was out, threading her way to another BMW, dark green, with alloy wheels. With a sigh he trailed after her. Delusions of bloody grandeur, this one.

'How much for my car, did you say?' Helen asked, opening the door of the BMW. She was about to climb inside when her attention was caught by a low-slung Jaguar sports, navy with white interior, parked directly behind at right-angles to all the rest.

'The book is one thousand three hundred, but . . .' The salesman looked up from the guide in his hand, shaking his head rapidly as Helen moved towards the Jaguar. 'That one's not for sale.' She tried the handle. 'It's mine!' he yelled above the shriek of the alarm.

Gary Marshall was locking the door when there was the roar of a powerful engine and a sleek Jaguar sports car slid into the parking bay beside his Rover. His jaw dropped as Helen jumped out, greeted him with a cheery 'Good morning,' and flicked on the alarm as she moved off with her long-legged stride, briefcase swinging.

Malahide came over. 'Bloody hell,' he said, awed, taking in the graceful lines and gleaming chromework. He turned to Marshall. 'Jump leads would have been cheaper!'

There was always a trade-off, Helen realized. She was thrilled with her new car, but the time spent in purchasing it had put her thirty minutes behind. The routine she had established of doing her rounds at ten thirty every morning was getting a bit ragged; perhaps if she had a twin sister she might be able to get through the workload of a single day and have a minute to draw breath.

'I would prefer two of them to be female, and first priority to any local applicants,' she said into the phone, scribbling a note. 'A lot of the officers after the riot were put on Detach Duty. They're not keen on returning, so when we have a full quota of inmates . . .' She nodded, listening as the personnel director explained that they kept a list of job applicants on file. 'Are any of them black? Ethnic . . . yes. Wait a minute.'

Marshall had tapped and entered. He raised a finger – 'Two seconds' – and gestured to her in tray, which contained a pile of correspondence and documents five inches deep. 'You read the report from this morning, C Wing – prisoner Walter Brinkley 577. He's refusing to eat, he's down the Block.'

'What?' Helen said, trying to listen to two conversations at once. 'Could you just hold on a minute?' she said into the phone.

'Maybe keep him down there until he cools off, okay?' Marshall waited, eyebrows raised, and at her nod departed.

Helen tried to pick up where she'd left off. 'I'd like them to be female, and, if possible, I'd like a writer-in-residence.'

That floored him. What did he suppose she meant: find Jeffrey Archer a cell? 'Creative writing courses, yes!' Helen made clear. Mavis had crept in and slipped a phone memo onto the blotter. Helen read it, frowning, and caught her as she was creeping out. 'Mavis, did Mr Andrews give any reason for his visit?'

'No, just that he would be here this afternoon with the Area Manager. Oh, can you call Personnel, as they—'

'I'm on the phone to them, Mavis!' Helen said, waggling the receiver. Then she had to raise her voice above a thunderous racket of banging and drilling that had started up along the corridor. 'Oh, yes! Mavis, will you call all the insurance companies, see who gives the lowest estimate and check with my own?'

Mavis's round face dimpled in a smile. 'Oh, I heard you've got a new car! Jaguar . . . Mr Marshall's very envious. Third party or fully comprehensive?'

'The works.' Helen grimaced, waving her hand. 'And, Mavis, can you get them to stop hammering just for a minute?'

'But they're finishing off your shower room,' Mavis protested, making a token effort by shutting the door firmly behind her, which didn't make a scrap of difference.

Clapping a hand over one ear, Helen went back to her phone conversation. 'Hello? Hello?' She had been cut off.

It was cool in the main yard, and Helen felt a chill cut right through her jacket and crêpe-de-Chine blouse. She had sought out Jimmy Malahide and they were walking along the covered walkway that bordered the smaller of the two exercise yards. About a dozen vulnerable prisoners were inside, receiving the usual foul-mouthed abuse from the residents of C Wing who could see them from their windows.

'I just think it would be good experience for you to be on the VP Wing. All officers here work on a turnaround.'

Malahide was being stubborn, and she was trying to persuade him without being heavy-handed about it.

He said doggedly, 'But it's my experience that you can refuse to work with the VPs.'

'You don't have to if you don't want to,' Helen agreed, 'but in my experience all officers should be familiar with all the prison's inmates.'

'But I can refuse.'

He was hard work. 'You can but will you tell me why?'

'Dirty, filthy, arsehole nonces! Nonces, ponces, arsehole queers!'

Malahide looked to the windows where the shouts were coming from. Then to the men in the yard below who, in their T-shirts, windcheaters and blue trousers, appeared no different from any of the other prisoners. 'They just make my skin crawl.'

'I presume you are referring to the sex offenders?'

'The paedophiles, the rapists,' Malahide said, loathing in his voice, 'and the . . .' He stared broodingly into the yard.

'The homosexuals?' He nodded. 'How do you feel about the mentally retarded, the other vulnerable men?' Helen asked, trying to reason with him. 'They're in the VP Wing because they're in debt to other inmates. How do you feel about them? A VP Wing doesn't only contain sex offenders.'

'I just can't deal with them,' Malahide ground out. 'And the union says we don't have to. I also have a new baby. The HIV and the Aids lot are down there too, so—' He was shaking his head.

Helen's eyes narrowed as she spied Royston Andrews and John Bunny emerge from the admin block, accompanied by Gary Marshall. They hadn't seen her yet, and she didn't want them to. What was going on down here? Conspiracy? Or was she getting paranoid? Maybe so, but that didn't mean she didn't have good reason to be. She gave a quick nod. 'Thank you, Mr Malahide. I'll let you know my decision.'

Helen turned away. Marshall and the others were strolling on the far side of the small exercise yard, separated from her by two sides of wire-mesh fencing. Helen kept them carefully in view while she backtracked towards the admin block. Behind her, the VPs were crowding the wire, sending admiring wolf whistles at Malahide, and calling out, 'Hello, Blondie. Who's a pretty boy, then?'

The officer marched off as if he hadn't heard, but to their lewd delight his glowering expression told its own tale.

Royston Andrews had paused to inspect the work in progress at the end of C Wing. Huge green tarpaulins had been erected, and from behind them came the steady chuntering of a generator and the intermittent sound of drilling. 'I'd like to see round all the wings,' he told Marshall. 'Estimate how many more months we'll need. But we've got to be very diplomatic about it,' he added sagely, receiving nods from the other two.

Helen had almost made it. Keeping her head down, she breathed a sigh of relief as she neared the entrance to the admin block, and would have made it but for the lone figure of Howard Webster, the long-distance runner, on his third lap of the big exercise yard.

'Afternoon, Governor!'

Helen could have cheerfully rammed his boyishly good-natured greeting down his throat, but she forced a wooden smile before ducking inside.

Andrews raised his head, missing Helen but seeing Webster jogging round the perimeter, watched over by two officers. 'Lad in training for the marathon? What's going on?'

'Miss Hewitt's orders,' Marshall said, po-faced, yet smiling inside. Give her enough rope, he thought, and watch Miss High and Mighty hang herself.

*

'Malahide won't go to the VP Wing so I've moved him over to D Wing.' Helen was giving instructions over the phone to Governor Lyons.

'You've got Jackson as his replacement. Tip off – you'll probably be having the Area Manager and Operational Director wanting to look over the wings.'

She put the phone down and sat listening for a moment. From the adjoining office she could hear the animated murmur of voices. Moving quietly to the door, she raised one of the slats with her thumb and peered through. Christ, now she was acting paranoid. Maybe with good cause, given that Marshall, Andrews and Bunny were deep in discussion with the ever-faithful Mavis.

Helen returned to her desk and flicked the intercom.

'Mavis, as Mr Andrews and Mr Bunny are here, can you show them into my office?'

She flicked off, not waiting for an answer, and stood before the desk, tugging her jacket straight. Mavis appeared almost at once.

'Mr Andrews and Mr Bunny from Prison Service HQ.' She had a slip of paper in her hand, and almost as an afterthought she thrust it at Helen. 'Car insurance. Shocking prices, costs a fortune . . .'

The stupid woman made an outraged face and it was all Helen could manage not to bundle her from the room. Instead she waved her out, and from somewhere found a rather strained smile for her visitors.

'Good afternoon, Miss Hewitt, not interrupting anything?' Andrews said.

'No.'

Marshall was hovering, as if uncertain whether to stay or go. Andrews gave him the nod to stay, and he visibly relaxed. This only made Helen feel more edgy and uptight. Was this the old 'all boys together' act, ganging up on the ball-breaker? Stop it, she told herself, before they send for the men in the white coats.

'Please, sit down.' Helen indicated the chairs grouped round the coffee table.

'Miss Hewitt,' Andrews said, coming straight to the point, 'you at no time informed the authorities that on the same day two men escaped by helicopter there was also a third escapee, Howard Webster.'

'He came back voluntarily,' Helen said, perched uneasily on the edge of her seat. 'He's now due for release. He lost twenty-one days' remission, and both officers were placed on report, as was Webster.'

Andrews leaned back and folded his hands. 'We are obviously aware of how difficult it must be to run Barfield under the present conditions.'

Helen glanced sharply at Marshall, who seemed to have become suddenly fascinated by the colour of the carpet. Andrews went on imperturbably, 'And this in no way reflects on you. We have complete faith in your capabilities. But with two – correction, three – escapees within a period of—'

'One prisoner, Stanley Field, has been recaptured,' Helen interrupted him. 'And Webster is—'

Andrews held up his hand. 'You should, Miss Hewitt, have informed the authorities about Howard Webster. The reason I am here is to consider if Barfield should remain in operation.' He shook his head, and released a small sigh. 'It is now highly questionable.'

So that was the hammer blow. But it might have been worse, Helen realized. They could have chopped off her arms and legs and padlocked her torso in a trunk.

The cell door swung open and the light from the wide corridor in the punishment block fell upon Walter Brinkley, sitting bolt upright on his bed. He had consented to get dressed, and wore scuffed black shoes on his bare feet, a fresh strip of adhesive tape holding his glasses in one piece.

'Right, Walter, out. You're to take a shower and then eat your dinner.'

Brinkley didn't stir. 'No way. Until my radio is returned I'm on hunger strike.'

The officer stood with folded arms, debating whether to drag him out or let him stew.

'You tell that bitch Governor I'll starve to death unless I get my radio.'

That decided it. The door slammed shut and the key turned in the lock.

Russell Morgan was in the officers' annex on C Wing when the word came through. He listened, pushing his hand through what remained of his bristly fair hair, and hung up, reaching for a fag.

'You're not gonna believe this,' he said to Malahide, lounging in a chair with a cup of strong tea. 'That prat Walter Brinkley is on hunger strike unless he gets his fuckin' radio returned.'

'Shit!' Governor Lyons groaned, walking in to catch the tail-end of it. 'Right now we don't want any aggravation.' He jerked his head. 'Area Manager's in with the Governor, they might do an impromptu walkabout.'

Malahide finished his tea and stood up. He didn't like the way Morgan was glaring at him, and he liked it even less when Morgan started wagging his thick Scottish finger in the air.

'This is down to you, mate! Six months at Pentonville didn't teach you much, did it?'

Morgan was six feet tall, but Malahide towered over him, pushing his face forward. 'You told me to take the radio off Brinkley,' he snarled. 'It wasn't down to me!'

Lyons moved in fast to defuse the situation, the firm wing governor. 'Down to prison rules,' he told both men. 'If they can't obey them, they get what they get. So anyone starts even heavy breathing, come down on them. We got to look fuckin' tight as a nut. Word is they could be closing this place down – and I for one don't fancy being on Detach Duty in Christ knows where.' He nodded to the landings and gave Morgan a warning look. 'Let's open up for association, and keep your eyes on the new bastard.'

Morgan patted his tie down over his belly and went out.

'A second, Malahide,' Lyons said. 'If you've got any kit here, pack it up. You're going on D Wing.'

Malahide bristled. 'Why am I being moved?'

'Governor's orders. Come on, son.'

When the bell for association rang on D Wing, the occupants of cell 29 were floating on pink clouds in a sky so clear they could see tomorrow, and the vision was benign.

The doors along the landing were open, and Steve Wolton from next door had slipped in to fraternize, taking a puff of the six-inch spliff Colin Foster had rolled. He exhaled with a long whoosh of breath, shaking his head in gratitude and admiration. 'Oh, this is beautiful, beautiful.' He passed it up to Harry Reynolds in the top bunk, who was bent over, scribbling furiously. 'You on for a game of billiards?'

'Nah, going to get this bitch sorted out.' Harry took a hit, sniffed hard, and let the smoke dribble from his nostrils. 'Wow, this has got one helluva kick. You get it from Snoopy again?'

Foster didn't answer. He couldn't. His head was gone.

Reynolds held out the spliff. 'Here you are, Anthony. Try it.'

Kelly didn't smoke at all, so he was very hesitant. But he'd been observing the others taking long deep drags, so he did the same, and held it in his chest as they had. It came out in a rush, leaving him coughing and spluttering. Passing along the landing, Jackson toed the door open and glanced in.

'Smokin' them French fags again, are you, Colin?' he asked amiably, and passed on.

Kelly, holding the spliff in his shaking hand, stared out in fright. Wolton snaked to the door for a look-see and came weaving back, a smirk on his lips.

'Ah . . . s'okay, they ignore it, they all know we use it. Keeps us quiet, keeps us happy. Keeps us . . .' Then it didn't seem to matter what else it kept them.

Kelly tried again, dragging even harder. This time it lifted the back of his head off. His eyes were watering and he could have sworn there were ten men in the cell. He gave a strange little giggle. 'My God, I'm reeling.'

Reynolds had a go and handed it back. 'Have another drag, go on.' There was a very odd expression on his face; it was a smile. He clicked his fingers. 'Come on an' get happy, forget your troubles and . . . Get a good lungful – it's good an' it's cheap.'

Kelly leaned back, smoking. 'Are you going onto the landing?' he asked Wolton.

'Yeah. You play billiards, do you?'

'Er, no.'

'Chess?'

'No.'

'Rummy, poker, five-card stud?'

'No,' Kelly said. Eyelids fluttering rapidly, he tried to focus on the spliff in his hand. 'Bloody hell.'

'Well, I sincerely hope you wank or it's gonna be very boring in here for eighteen months, sunshine.' Wolton reached out. 'Hey, come on, pass it round.'

Grinning from ear to ear, Kelly passed it on.

Victor Braithwaite had it sussed. Leaning his heavily muscled arms on the rail, he watched Jumbo Jackson descend the spiral stairway. Men were already gathering below for association, brewing up in the kitchen, tossing coins for who had the first game of billiards, and the TV was blasting out in the far corner. This was as good a time as any, Braithwaite reckoned. He had a couple of reliable mates to stand guard and Charlie Brierley owed him one. He spread his fingers, indicating five minutes, and saw Brierley nod and start drifting across the open area towards the chairs grouped round the TV.

Outside the officers' annex, a perplexed Jackson had just been given his marching orders. 'Why am I being shifted to C Wing?' he demanded, confronting Tommy Nelson, the senior officer.

'Don't ask me. They just called through, Governor's orders. We got the eager beaver, Malahide.' Nelson lowered his voice. 'Plus the area manager's doin' an impromptu walkabout.'

Sighing wearily, Jackson went to collect his kit from the annex. A thought struck him, and he beckoned to Nelson. 'Oi! Get some fresh-air spray if they're coming down this landing, and check out cell twenty-nine. They've got waccy-baccy lit up in there.'

'Okay, I'll check them out now.' About to move to the stairway, Nelson spotted Malahide coming through the gates, a surly expression on his big square face. 'You're being shafted around, are you?' He grinned. 'Too tough for you on the other wing, is it?'

'Just lay off me,' Malahide said, not in the mood.

As trouble always did, it came out of nowhere. A chair clattered over in the TV area, and suddenly a row erupted, pushing and shoving, the men banging their chairs and yelling.

'Come on, my son, let's sort that out,' Nelson said, striding off. 'Only time they don't fight over channels is for *Baywatch*.'

Braithwaite grinned from the landing. Right on cue, Charlie boy. That'd keep the kangaroos occupied. His two henchmen following behind, he did a casual stroll to cell 29 and met Kelly in the doorway, about to go down with Wolton to association.

'Go back in, sonny.' The missing front teeth gave Braithwaite's smile a chilling, sinister quality. Kelly backed away, his eyes glazed, head still spinning from the weed. Foster blearily opened his eyes, and then jerked upright from his sprawling position as Braithwaite came in, leaving the two men posted outside.

'You know what this is about, don't you?' Braithwaite said softly, nodding at Foster.

'No, but you're gonna tell me, you cocksucker! What you want?'

'You know you're bunkin' up with a nonth?' Braithwaite said to Kelly. 'Do you know that?' He pointed at Foster. 'He's a nonth—'

'I'm bloody not. Eh! Come on,' he appealed to Harry Reynolds, who had laid aside his letter, leaning on one elbow, body slightly tensed. Foster looked round wildly. 'You know me, Steve, tell this piece of crap to shove off.'

'I seen it on reports, he was a VP, wasn't he?' Braithwaite flexed himself, broad chest straining his T-shirt, crude tattoos on his hairy arms. 'He's a nonth.'

'What proof you got?' Reynolds asked hazily, struggling to come down into the real world from his pink candy-cotton cloud.

'I'm not a ruddy nonce!' Foster protested again, his whole body one big twitch as the fear got to him.

'Okay, let's prove it.' Braithwaite looked round slowly. The cell went very quiet, blue fumes hanging in the still air. Kelly stood swaying next to his bed, trying to get a grip on what was happening. Wolton had his backside pressed up against the washbasin.

'We'll hold a kangaroo court right here. Harry, you can be judge. You' – to Wolton – 'defence counsel, and you . . . What's your name?'

'Kelly, Anthony,' Kelly said, petrified.

'Right, Anthony, you're his solicitor.' Braithwaite's hand shot out, pushing Foster flat in the chest as he tried to rise.

'Stay on your billet, shit-face!' He made a general calming gesture. 'Sit down . . . sit down.'

He glanced behind, getting a nod from one of the men at the door. The commotion was still going on down below. Braithwaite rubbed his chin, eyes flicking over them. 'Right. I'd say the court is now in session.'

'What are you, Victor?' Reynolds asked.

Braithwaite's smile came on like a lighthouse without a beam. 'I'm the hangman!'

CHAPTER 20

'IN VIEW of the time I'd like to tour the prison before association ends,' John Bunny proposed, leading the way from Helen's office.

It was a few minutes after five, according to Helen's watch, so he had almost half an hour. She nodded, and turned as Andrews said, 'Is there a good local restaurant?'

'I'll arrange a table,' Helen said. She ushered them to proceed, while she saw to it. 'Mr Marshall, will you . . .?'

With Marshall at his side, Andrews walked on, waiting until Helen had entered Mavis's office before he spoke. 'What's your reaction to the new plans for Barfield? Specifically, the proposed Special Secure Unit?'

'I think if we have criminals who require twenty-four-hour surveillance we need a more sophisticated method of housing and controlling them.'

'Staff approved of the plans too?' John Bunny inquired.

Marshall brimmed with zeal. 'Yes, without question, total approval. Apart from Miss Hewitt,' he added, as if it was a casual afterthought. 'She seems to be the only one against it.'

Andrews and Bunny exchanged looks. Marshall went on ahead, a smile glimmering.

Mavis had her handbag on the desk, preparing to leave, even though her clocking-off time was thirty minutes away. Rather under sufferance she was writing down Helen's instructions.

'Book a table and make sure it's the best. If not the best, the most expensive.' Helen looked round. 'Moira gone?'

'Period pains. I said she could go.'

'Can you relay that I've gone home to change? I'm sure Mr Marshall will take full advantage of my absence,' Helen said, smiling thinly, 'just as I feel sure you will inform him of it.'

Mavis coloured slightly, avoiding Helen's eyes. Helen leaned over the desk. 'Mavis, you are privy to a lot of personal information regarding myself and some inmates. You had better make the decision whose side you are on. If you can't keep yourself from gossiping – for want of a better word – I will consider you a security risk. Do you understand what I'm saying?'

Mavis gave a barely perceptible nod. She moistened her lips. 'So it'll be a table for three?'

'Exactly, Mavis.'

'Are you covered?'

'Yes, Mr Marshall can take over as night-duty governor.'

'I meant your car insurance.'

'Shit, I haven't seen it,' Helen exclaimed, scratching her head and grinning. 'Do I take out a bank loan?'

She moved to her office, while Mavis, appropriately chastened, stared after her. At the door she paused. 'Whatever, Mavis, please keep it to yourself.' Helen sailed out. 'Moira is very competent . . .'

Braithwaite looped the thick string round Foster's wrists and jerked it tight. The red-haired lad was shaking with fear, covered in sweat.

'Now, don't struggle, nonth! You'd be cuffed in court, right. Judge? Am I right?'

Lying on his bunk, Reynolds took a deep drag, passed the spliff Wolton had rolled on to Kelly, who was giggling like a schoolgirl. They were all stoned out of their tiny minds, even starting to enjoy this stupid game Braithwaite was playing.

The door was pushed open and one of the men on lookout beckoned urgently. Braithwaite darted over and stuck out his head. Marshall, Andrews and Bunny were coming up the stairway, led by Senior Officer Nelson. Braithwaite backtracked fast, and the two men at the door did a disappearing act.

'Some of the men prefer to remain in their cells during association,' Marshall was telling Andrews. 'This is good for inmates studying for exams. But doors must remain open at all times – Miss Hewitt's orders. She also withdrew all prisoners' cell keys.'

They approached cell 29, its door ajar. Reynolds looked up from the book he was reading. 'Good evening, Mr Marshall, sir!' He jumped down, smiling, and came to the door. 'Just give it a minute, he's on the toilet.' He wafted his hand. 'Safer out here – he stinks the place up.'

He watched them continue along the landing. 'I've asked to be moved. Unhygienic, three of us in a cell for two.'

He waited until they were at the far end of the wing. Kelly tried to push past him, and Reynolds blocked his way, shoving him down on the bed. A sock stuffed in his mouth, hands tightly bound, Foster was dragged from the lower bunk. Braithwaite stood over him, sucking deep long drags from what was left of the spliff.

'Right, now you're on trial for nonthing. That right, your honour?'

Reynolds picked up his book. 'If you say so.'

'What you on trial for, Colin?' Braithwaite whacked him over the head. 'Please answer the court. What you on trial for?' He removed the sock.

Foster cleared his throat. 'Nonceing.' He winced as Braithwaite kicked his shin. 'Your honour.'

'What you say to that, jury?'

Wolton had another joint going. He passed it up to

Reynolds, who took a grandiose puff as if smoking a fat cigar.

'As the judge I'd like to hear what evidence you've got. So far I am not satisfied. There is still reasonable doubt.' He took a hit and handed it down. 'Here, Ant, have a drag.'

Kelly was nearly out of it. He had a puff and lay back, eyelids drooping, the spliff smouldering between his fingers.

'Well, it's obvious, isn't it?' Braithwaite demanded. 'He's a nonth, and as such I sentence him to death. And I just happen to have handy . . .' From his trouser pocket he took a length of wire flex, shaped into a noose. Wolton giggled when he saw it. They were all so high that it seemed like a joke, especially because Foster looked so comical when Braithwaite rammed the sock back in his mouth.

'Come on, pass it on,' Reynolds said, clicking his fingers.

'Please leave me . . . I feel sick.' The spliff in Kelly's hand wavered to and fro. 'Just leave me . . .'

'So,' Braithwaite pronounced, fastening the wire flex round the horizontal lower frame of the window bars, 'sentence will now be carried out!'

He extended the noose and positioned the wooden chair beneath it.

'Get him on the chair, Steve. Come on! Kneel on the chair, Colin – Anthony, help him up.'

It was a pantomime performance in the narrow space between the toilet bowl and the bunks. The three of them pulled him forward and got him half kneeling on the chair, the sock stuck in his mouth. Braithwaite slipped the noose over his head. Foster was crying, his chest shuddering as he tried to draw breath. Braithwaite straightened up, or tried to, but he was so stoned that he staggered against the wall. His foot shot out and kicked the chair leg. The chair went over, the noose went taut, and there was a crack like a chicken bone snapping in two. Foster's head dropped and his hands went limp.

'All right, come on, Victor, joke's over,' Reynolds said. 'Cut him loose.'

The bell rang for the end of association. There was the hollow tramp of feet on the stairway, the banging of cell doors, and shouts of 'Lock-up, lock-up!'

Braithwaite slapped his face. 'Colin, stop messing about. *Colin*!'

Kelly reeled back, his face drained of all colour. Wolton's eyes were bulging out of his head. Braithwaite was about to slap Foster again but didn't, his hand in mid-air.

'Oi! Come on out, Vic, screws are coming.' One of the lookouts pushed open the door, and then his face sagged. 'Jesus Christ. What you done to him?'

He didn't wait for an answer but took off fast as heavy footsteps sounded on the landing. Doors were banging shut, keys grating in locks.

Reynolds knelt down, craning his neck to peer at the dangling head. Slowly he rose to his feet, and there was a dreadful shocking silence.

'He's dead, Victor.'

White to the lips, Braithwaite backed towards the open door. There was the rattling of a key chain, and the blond head of Malahide appeared outside.

Fists clenching and unclenching, Marshall stood next to the curtained-off area in the hospital wing. Seemingly in a daze, he blinked as the curtain swished back and the auxiliary nurse came out. She gave a slight shake of the head.

'I'm sorry. Has Dr Thomas been notified? I don't have the authority – Doc's got to say he's dead or not. He is, by the way.'

Marshall nodded, rubbing his heavy jowls, unaware he was leaving red marks. Malahide came in, a sheen of sweat gleaming on his broad neck. He glanced agitatedly towards the curtain. 'I found him.'

'We're trying to contact the Governor,' Marshall said, and turned away, sick to his stomach.

The Italian restaurant was better than Helen expected, even out here in the sticks. She indulged herself, as did John Bunny, though Andrews ate sparingly, she noticed. They didn't talk shop during the meal, but by the time the dessert trolley came round she was itching to broach the subject, and did so. Getting anything out of the pair of them, however, was like pulling teeth.

'But I need to know now exactly where I stand,' Helen said, hoping she didn't sound the nagging fishwife. 'It must be obvious that I've either been placed at Barfield to act as just a caretaker for the rebuilding process or . . .'

'I think that is a—' John Bunny began, but Helen jumped in.

'Correct assumption?' She'd drunk a gin and tonic and two glasses of red wine, but her head was clear. She tapped the tablecloth. 'If I've got almost eighteen months, I want to use that time to establish strong relations with my staff.' She sipped her wine. 'If it's closed down, you'll have eighty-eight men to rehouse.'

The waiter hovered at her elbow. Everything on the trolley looked delicious, and she didn't need to count the calories, but she had heaped on the pasta. She said, 'Just the fruit salad, no cream, and maybe' – oh, what the hell – 'a little slice of chocolate cake, very small taster.'

Andrews passed on dessert, though Bunny, no calorie counter either, had the gateau with a double helping of cream.

Helen dug in. The food and wine made her feel good, but it didn't blunt her purpose. 'Added to that, what do you intend to do with all the officers still employed at Barfield?' she asked, giving the both of them an interrogating stare.

John Bunny had his mouth full of gateau, and it was Andrews who answered with a languid wave of his hand. 'You must know, Helen, that the Home Office has the final say. All I can do is pass on my observations.'

Phooey to that, Helen thought. As Operational Director of the Prison Service he had the clout to make things happen – or not – within the strictures laid down by the Home Secretary.

Her bleeper went. Helen excused herself, and was directed to the phone by the maître d'. Three minutes later she was striding out to the car park, having made her apologies to Andrews and Bunny, who didn't appear heart-broken at seeing her go, and collected her coat.

She was opening the door of the Jaguar when a red MG turned in and roared to a halt. Helen raised her hand, intending to call to Lorcan Thomas as he climbed out, and then she saw he had a passenger. Looking like a million dollars, in a clinging sheath dress under a silk shawl, Moira Levitt was helped from the MG by her gallant escort. Inside the car, Helen watched through the wing mirror as they walked to the entrance, his arm around her slender waist.

Helen backed the Jaguar out and lowered the window. 'We have an emergency at Barfield.' They both turned. Ignoring Moira, Helen said to Dr Thomas, 'I'm sorry to interrupt your evening,' and drove off fast, gravel spinning under the wheels.

Period pains, eh? Helen nodded grimly to herself. I'll give her more than bleeding period pains.

Two officers had to carry Anthony Kelly through the double-barred gates into the punishment block. He was white as a ghost, having been violently ill, compounded by a numbed sense of shock and fear that left him incapable of standing. They locked him away, moved along, and took Harry Reynolds out, frogmarching him to the gates.

Protesting voices came from the cells.

'Oi, what's goin' on? Eh?'

'Shut it out there. Can't a man get some kip?'

'What the fuck's goin' on out there?'

'Harry?' Steve Wolton yelled, his ear pressed to the door. 'They taken you? Harry? *Harry? You still down here? Who's down here?*'

'I am.' Walter Brinkley's voice floated from the cell opposite. 'I'm on hunger strike. What's goin' on?'

The block officer moved along, banging the doors with his baton.

'No talking! Shut it!'

Brinkley pounded the door. 'I'll shut it, mate, *when I get me radio returned*!'

'He was dead when they got to the cell. They couldn't revive him.'

Marshall was distraught, and he was sweating, standing in front of the desk, gnawing his thumbnail.

Helen knew how he felt. She leaned back in the chair, rubbing her forehead. 'Well, I'd better inform his family.'

'They all say it was just a joke that backfired. They reckoned he was a nonce.' Marshall uttered a hollow laugh. 'Sick thing is, he wasn't.'

'How involved was Anthony Kelly?'

'Apparently he had a spliff in his hand. Joint.'

'Were they all using drugs? Do you know?' Marshall shifted his weight. 'Come on, Gary, you were on duty,' Helen said.

'Christ, it's not my fault.' Marshall jerked his thumb over his shoulder. 'I'd only just taken round Andrews and the bloody area manager! It happened like ten minutes after they walked off the wing.'

'Oh, did it?' Helen said, light dawning. 'And did they go to the cell where it happened?'

'Yeah, well, we passed it,' Marshall admitted uneasily.

'Oh, they passed the cell, did they?' Helen said wonderingly, storing up ammunition. An own goal for Andrews and Bunny. She folded her arms. 'You sure about that?'

Marshall couldn't bring himself to meet her steady gaze. 'Yes, I was with them.'

Helen stood up, suddenly brisk. 'Well, that's going to let me off the hook.' She turned away, looking back at him. 'I don't know about you.'

CHAPTER 21

IT WAS Officer Nelson's turn on breakfast duty in the punishment block, and just his shitty luck it had to be the morning that Walter Brinkley chose to create.

Tray in hand, Nelson opened up and pushed the door open. 'Here's your breakfast, Walter!'

'I'm not eatin', take it away.'

'If you say so. Get undressed, be ready for showers.'

'No fuckin' way. You want me to shower, you gotta undress me.'

Nelson marched out, red-faced, to be greeted with laughter by a couple of officers who'd just delivered their breakfasts. Nelson placed the tray on the floor, went straight back in, dragged Brinkley out and stood him up like a wooden dummy.

'Right, Brinkley, lift your arms.'

He wouldn't, which inflamed Nelson. He reached from behind, ripped open his shirt and yanked it off. The two officers had stopped laughing, and were edging in, scenting trouble. The other inmates, who just wanted a bit of peace and quiet, could hear the commotion; and Walter's muttered, monotonous cursing was driving them bats.

'Oh, shut up out there.'

'For God's sake shut it and eat your friggin' breakfast.'

'Oi, what was goin' on last night?'

'Anyone hear what happened last night?'

Nelson, redder in the face, stood panting behind Brinkley. 'Right, get your jeans off, Walter.'

Brinkley's arms hung at his sides. He flicked a glance towards the two officers who were closing in. When he saw the duty officer also heading his way, he unbuckled his belt. 'All right, all right. *I'm doin' it, okay?*'

Off came the jeans, vest, shoes and socks, as if he delighted in it, and lastly his underpants, which he flung to the ground, standing there brazen and bollock-naked. With a defiant look at them he strode haughtily into the cell, slamming the door shut behind him.

Standing in a circle around the discarded clothing, the officers looked at one another. Somebody's face cracked, and the next second they were all roaring with laughter.

Helen sensed it was going to be one of those days. But then, lately, every day seemed to be one of those days. The exceptions had become the norm.

She was in Mavis's office, sorting out Colin Foster's F2050 prison file, when Anthony Kelly's father came on the line. Helen took it on Mavis's phone. She explained why the visit scheduled for that afternoon would have to be postponed, endeavouring to strike the right balance between her duty as Governor and sympathy for the man's obvious distress.

'I'm very sorry, Mr Kelly, but I'm unable to discuss the incident or give you any further details. Anthony has been segregated and will require legal representation.' She listened, nodding. 'I'll tell him personally. Thank you.'

Mavis held up a visiting order as Helen finished the call. 'One of the other prisoners, 648, Reynolds, Harry – his wife is down for a visit. She's got to come from Leeds, but we've still not been able to trace the dead man's mother.'

'Is she his only relative?'

'Yes. Also Howard Webster's due for release, and you wanted to see him before he went.'

At least one small success in Howard Webster, Helen

thought. A good deed in a naughty world. She felt slightly cheered.

'Morning, Miss Hewitt,' Malahide said, coming in, rather subdued.

Helen's half-finished coffee had gone cold. She handed the china mug to Mavis and waved Malahide through to her office. 'Let's go over your report.'

Instead of putting the china mug out of harm's way, Mavis contrived to slop cold coffee over a pile of documents. 'Bugger it,' she muttered, reaching for a tissue.

Moira appeared with a beaming 'Good morning.'

'What's good about it?' Helen said. 'Sorry to interrupt your dinner last night,' she added sarcastically, and slammed through to her office, leaving Moira tight-lipped and Mavis holding up something limp and sodden.

'Here, type this again, will you?'

'Oh, shit, Mavis,' Moira groaned, taking the dripping document from her. 'This is the death certificate.'

Flanked by Senior Officer Gordon and the block officer, Walter Brinkley stood before Helen's desk, battered specs hooked over his ears and hanging skew-whiff on his face. Malahide stood to one side, his officer's report pad in his huge freckled hand.

'Do you understand the charges that have been brought against you?'

'Yes, ma'am. Charges are lending an item to an unauthorized person. My radio.' Brinkley wore the expression of a man badly done by. 'But as Barry was needin' it for his exam, I think – '

Helen's raised hand stopped him. 'Do you plead guilty to the charges?'

'Well, yes, I suppose so, but like I said, I mean he—'

'You plead guilty, Mr Brinkley?'

'Yes.' He sniffed. 'Guilty but with mitigations.'

'Would you explain your actions?'

'Well, yes, I bin tryin' to explain.' He thrust out his hands. 'You see, Barry Simpkins is doin' his Open University degree and he wanted to record a programme, so he asked if he could borrow my radio. So that's how it came about, and that is the entire truth.'

He was working up a head of steam now, oblivious to Helen's bored irritation as she sifted papers on her desk.

'Now I have created because I think I have been unjustly punished. But that said, I apologize and promise never to do such a terrible thing again.' He added, 'If I get my radio back – and I'll never lend it to nobody ever again', eyes burning with all the diligent fervour of a boy scout swearing an oath.

Helen said to Malahide, 'Would you read out the prisoner's wing report, please?'

'Brinkley is currently serving a seven-year sentence, and throughout his sentence he has made no attempt to conform to prison regime. He is constantly fighting with other inmates and is a subversive character, always intent on causing trouble for prison staff. He has been placed on report a previous two hundred and forty-five times spaced over six years.'

Brinkley looked hurt, as if his best intentions were always thwarted, and this was a travesty of the truth.

'For what reasons?' Helen asked, undeceived by the mild, apologetic demeanour of the little man in front of her.

'Mostly for fighting with other inmates.'

To this Brinkley had no answer, except a tepid half smile accompanied by a slight shrug.

Helen straightened up, hands clasped on the desk. 'I don't think being on report two hundred and forty-five times is anything to smile about, Mr Brinkley,' she told him sternly. 'Your punishment will be the confiscation of your radio for four months. You will also be fined three pounds and fifty pence, and you will be on CC for a period of–'

Walter Brinkley underwent a startling transformation. Cellular confinement. All privileges withdrawn. No tobacco, no radio. Mattress and bedding removed from cell between eight a.m. and eight p.m. No fraternization, segregated exercise.

'YOU FUCKIN' FASCIST BITCH.'

Andy Gordon and the block officer reacted fast, getting arm locks on this raging madman who had suddenly appeared in their midst, face contorted with black rage as he tried to lunge at Helen across the desk.

'Get him out,' she snapped. Her face was white, and she was trembling all over.

The struggling, kicking, spitting transformed mildman-into-madman was dragged from the room, screaming back at Helen, 'I'd rather die than let you bastards keep my radio,' as the officers, two giants wrestling with a berserk pygmy, got him through the door into the corridor. Brinkley's shouts never let up as he was borne along, feet hardly touching the floor, both arms twisted up his back.

'It's mine. *Mine!* That radio is *my personal property*!'

Helen stood up, wiping her damp palms with her handkerchief. She steadied herself for a moment before walking with Malahide to the adjoining door.

The big blond lad looked down at her. 'I'm very sorry, Miss Hewitt.'

Helen had regained her composure, at least outwardly. 'Sometimes, James, it's necessary to bend the rules, just slightly.'

'I meant about Colin Foster.'

'Ah, yes, well, we're all very sorry about that,' Helen said, walking into Mavis's office.

'What's going to happen?'

'There will be a trial, obviously, and a full-scale investigation by the Home Office.' All of a sudden she felt very tired, and bet that she looked it. 'Play it again, Sam.'

Malahide went out. Helen stood deflated by Mavis's

desk. Mavis raised her eyebrows with a little apologetic smile.

'Howard Webster's waiting.'

He started to rise from his bed as Helen walked in, and she motioned to him. 'No, no, don't get up, Howard. It's just that I know you're being released this afternoon. I wanted to wish you well.'

She held out her hand and he shook it timidly.

'And I hope I don't see you again, unless you're breaking a track record on TV.' It was hard work, but she found a smile. 'Is someone meeting you?'

'My mother and my wife are already waiting.'

'Well, I won't hold things up. Good luck, Howard.'

She was about to turn away when he reached out and took her hand in both of his. He held it, squeezing tightly for a moment, and then just as quickly, as if embarrassed, let it go.

His lips trembled. 'Thank you.'

Helen went out. Did this really make up for everything else? Howard Webster's soft shy touch to her hand seemed so little but meant so much. She doubted if he would reoffend and it meant a lot, but right now she needed and wanted some kind of assurance, because she was deeply affected by the boy Anthony Kelly.

Helen remembered holding the young frightened Tina in her arms, and knew how much she had changed since her days at Cattering Hall. Dealing with female prisoners had been so much easier. She could, and was allowed to be – or had allowed herself to be – far more tactile. But with the male prisoners she could not. The potential misrepresentation of any touch made professional distance a necessity. Helen had never been instructed to behave like this: it was instinctive. She was the Governor but she was also a woman, and she therefore had constantly to be aware of how the prisoners might misconstrue any familiarity. She could be kind, considerate and, in many instances, more understanding than her male counterpart, but most important was that she must at all costs command respect. Helen was learning this and sometimes, unfortunately, by her mistakes. Kelly was just one of the inmates. She had over eighty more, plus all the prison officers and prison clerical staff. She could only allocate a certain amount of her time to Kelly; there were other prisoners who had to be dealt with. Nothing could ever stop the day-to-day routine – if it did, the prison would grind to a standstill.

Whatever the reason – whether he possessed a sixth sense or not – Walter Brinkley got wind of Helen the moment she stepped through the gates of the punishment block.

'You tell that bull dyke I'm on hunger strike,' his voice yelled out from the cell. 'I'm not gonna eat or drink nuffink till I get my radio back. You hear me?'

'Shut him up,' Helen said sharply to Officer Legg.

'I'll kill her. I'll kill her mother, brothers, sisters. I'll burn her house down. I'll fix the brakes on her car.'

Andy Gordon thumped his fist on the door. 'Shut up, Walter.'

He moved on to Anthony Kelly's cell, giving Helen a look as he unlocked it. 'He is very upset, ma'am, he's not stopped crying.'

Kelly was lying face down on the thin mattress which rested on a low concrete base. The bare walls were filthy and stained with brown shit marks, graffiti hacked in the plaster and the usual crude sketches of female anatomy.

Helen stood inside the door, waiting rather wearily as, behind her, Andy Gordon yelled out, '*Shut it now, Walter, just shut up.*'

'Anthony, I spoke to your parents . . . Anthony, will you look at me?'

His gangling body didn't move, though his head turned towards her, eyes red and watery in a suffering face.

'They're going to get you a lawyer and they'll be visiting you tomorrow.'

'You told them?'

'Of course. They had a visit scheduled for this afternoon.'

'So my mother knows as well?' He controlled a spasm of emotion, his narrow chin wobbling. 'She's not been well and—' He swallowed. 'What did my dad say?'

'He was obviously upset.' Helen paused. 'They had to be informed, Anthony.'

'They tell Sandra? I suppose they'll have to tell Sandra. I don't want her upset.' He blinked up at Helen. 'She's my girlfriend, my fiancée. My poor, poor dad. He all right, was he?'

'They'll be here tomorrow.' Unlike the duplicitous Brinkley, here was a genuine, and rather pathetic, case of a young man utterly bewildered at his predicament and all at sea, Helen felt. She said, 'If you need anything . . . cigarettes?'

'No, no, I don't smoke, thank you.' He sat up, shoulders hunched, holding his knees.

'But you were smoking in the cell when Colin died.' Helen frowned as he hid his face from her, feeling suddenly uneasy. 'So you don't want anything?'

'I am so sorry. What's going to happen to me?'

'That will be for the court to decide.'

'But I didn't do anything.'

'Then you have nothing to worry about.'

Helen waited, rocking on her heels, as Andy Gordon locked up. She watched him open cell 12 and push the door slightly. 'Walter, do you want your dinner tonight?'

'No, I do not. Piss off!'

The door was kicked shut. Gordon shrugged and relocked it.

'Suit yourself, Walter, but you're makin' yourself ill.'

He joined Helen in the middle of the wide corridor. The kitchen boy came along, wheeling the big dinner trolley. The officers were gathering, ready to prepare the trays for delivery to the cells.

Helen watched this activity for a few moments, listening to the mumbling and whispering from behind the anonymous doors. It still gave her a weird feeling. Officers and prisoners existing together under the same roof, sharing the same space, yet separated by iron doors and bits of paper into Us and Them, Good and Bad. It struck her that it was like a barbaric charade, that they were all play-acting, that any second a hooter would go and they would congregate in the middle, officers and prisoners alike, and resume normal human intercourse, laughing and joking together, slapping each other's shoulders, the previous separation merely a silly childish game that hadn't fooled anyone.

'Is Kelly eating?' Helen asked, back to harsh reality, nodding behind her.

'No, nothing.'

Helen walked off, and Gordon called out, 'What you want to do about Walter?'

Helen stopped. 'I'm thinking about it.'

'Screw you, Nazi bitch! Gimme my radio back!'

Helen stared at his door, lips pursed. 'Tell him if he starts eating, and eating properly so he's no further problem to us, he can have his radio back.'

She turned on her heel and left the punishment block. Two good deeds in a naughty world. Would this make *The Guinness Book of Records*?

The next morning, shortly after ten o'clock, Helen walked John Bunny to his car. That he had arrived in person, instead of simply picking up the phone, told Helen two very important things. One, that the Area Manager thought it highly desirable their conversation should be strictly off the record; and two, that he was scared shitless.

'It is imperative you keep the lid on this,' Bunny said, eyes fixed on his brown brogues. 'I know you weren't on duty at the time of the hanging, and as both I and the

Operational Director were viewing the prison, the responsibility is equally shared.'

Ho-ho, Helen thought, how the mighty are fallen. Only two days ago Andrews and Bunny were quite prepared to drag her through red-hot coals over Howard Webster's absconding. With trouble she kept a straight face and allowed him to continue.

'But you do understand that as Governor in charge the overall responsibility is yours.'

Helen nodded dutifully. The straight face was killing her. 'Yes, I understand.'

'We cannot, at any cost, allow this unfortunate incident to be made public. All four prisoners will remain segregated at Barfield until the trial.'

They shook hands. Helen turned away, but it was too much to resist, and she turned back, stroking her chin.

'So, we will remain open, will we?'

The sight of his face did it, and she had to hurry away to hide the beaming grin of triumph spreading across hers.

Mavis waylaid her in the corridor as Helen strode towards her office.

'Walter Brinkley. He's now demanding kippers for his breakfast! He had chips last night.'

Helen raised both hands above her head and made them into claws. 'I will kill him. I will take his scrawny little neck between my hands and *strangle him*!'

Moira poked her head out of the office, a finger to her lips.

'What is it?'

Moira pointed to Helen's office. 'Colin Foster's mother.'

'Does she know he's dead?' Helen asked quietly as Marshall came out, inching the door shut. He nodded, and stood aside for Helen to enter.

Mrs Foster was a hunched, almost shrivelled figure, faded red hair scraped back from a pinched face.

'I am so very sorry, Mrs Foster,' Helen said, sinking down across the desk from her. 'There will be a full-scale inquiry into the tragedy, which sadly makes it very difficult for me to give you details.'

Head bowed, Mrs Foster turned a worn wedding ring round and round. 'I was at my sister's. It's such a long way to come each month so I break the journey.' She looked up, two deep lines creasing her forehead. 'Was it his asthma? He's always suffered with it since he was a toddler.'

Helen met her look squarely, shaking her head. 'No, Mrs Foster, it wasn't his asthma.'

Showered and spruced up, wearing clean clothes, Walter Brinkley was returning to his cell on the punishment block, escorted by two officers, when Senior Officer Gordon came up. 'Governor's here to see you, Brinkley.'

He glanced round eagerly. 'Has she got my radio?' His expression didn't falter, even though he saw Helen didn't have it. 'I've eaten me dinner last night and me breakfast this morning,' he said, beaming at her.

Helen's stare was frigid. 'Good. You will now be returned to C Wing, Brinkley, and I don't want to have any further trouble from you, do you understand?'

'Do I get my radio and cassette player returned?'

'They're holding it at the gate for you.' She felt like wringing that scrawny neck of his right this minute. 'I don't want to hear another word about that radio, is that understood?'

'Yes, Governor.' Brinkley was nodding and grinning fit to bust. 'Thank you very much for bein' fair and square with me.'

Helen made a sharp gesture for them to get him out of her sight, and Brinkley went off jubilantly.

With Andy Gordon following close behind she stopped at Anthony Kelly's cell and pushed the flap aside. He was sitting on the edge of the mattress, hands limp on his knees, gazing blankly at the shit-stained wall. 'Death to All Screws,' the graffiti read. 'I am Inosant.' 'JJ WAS HERE!' There were drawings of faces, daggers, a coffin, a crucifix, a hangman's noose.

Kelly slowly turned and looked to the small high window. Cheering and catcalls were coming from the other wings. A voice floated in from outside, 'Yes, yes, yes, yes!' Standing on tiptoe, Kelly tried to see what the fuss was about.

Carrying his radio clutched to his chest, fist punching the air as if he'd won the world heavyweight championship, Walter Brinkley was striding between two officers along the walkway. Acknowledging the whistles and cheers, the toilet rolls unfurling like streamers from the cell windows, Walter took his radio by the handle, swinging it high, broken specs set jauntily on his ecstatic face.

'I won! I beat 'em! I won, I won!'

Part Three

The Trial

CHAPTER 22

A HAZE OF brick dust filled the air, drifting from a jack-hammer that a gang of workmen were using on the reconstruction of B Wing. Piles of rubble lay about, and pools of stagnant water were filmed over with red dust. Christina Knatchbull couldn't have looked more out of place in a desolate moonscape. Tall and slim, with silvery-blonde hair swept back in a neat bun, she wore a full-length camel-hair coat over a grey suit and white blouse, and brown leather ankle boots with suede trim. If she was concerned about her immaculate grooming and expensive clothes amongst the rubble, the churning concrete mixers, the thudding machinery, she gave no sign of it.

Christina pointed her hand, sheathed in its grey kid glove. 'Get a good shot of that, few more in and around the most damaged area.'

The Pentax whirred and clicked as her young male clerk got a few angles on the large wooden sign, blue letters on a white ground:

NO PRISONERS ADMITTED
BEYOND THIS POINT

WARNING – ALL PERSONNEL
MUST CARRY IDENTIFICATION

NO ADMITTANCE

In the sterile area behind the chain-link fence, German shepherds and their handlers patrolled. Beyond that the outer wall rose sheer to the curved 'gander' nearly twenty feet off the ground.

'Thank you very much.' Christina smiled pleasantly at the officer accompanying her. 'Is there a quicker way to the visits room or do I have to go back to Security?'

There was no short-cut: he indicated the gate by which she had entered. Retracing her steps, Christina spoke in a quiet aside to her clerk. 'Get one of the dog handlers for good measure.' At the gate she showed her ID, which allowed her to pass into that part of the prison where the inmates were housed. 'Thank you.' She gestured behind her. 'I presume the men working here are not prison personnel?'

The officer didn't answer directly, merely nodded. Christina knew why. As the barrister representing Anthony Kelly she could expect their polite co-operation, but nothing more. The officers and staff didn't see why they should go out of their way to help the brief of someone involved in the murder of another inmate.

It was the same on D Wing when Governor Lyons showed her cell 29, clearly impatient to see the back of her. 'Can we hurry it up?' he asked, bustling along the landing. 'They're bringing the food trolleys up any minute.'

Christina nodded, but still took her time inspecting the cell, noting the usual array of porn pin-ups on the wall, the tattered paperbacks, the odds and ends scattered about.

'This was a two-man cell – the extra bunk was added, correct? Which bunk was allocated to Anthony Kelly?'

Lyons pointed to the left-hand bunk. 'We used one of the old-style double bunk beds. Kelly used the top one but as you can see it has been removed and the cell is now back to being a two-man cell.' His attention was distracted by the bangs and shouts coming from the restless inmates as they waited to be released. He glanced edgily at his watch, then stood rubbing his hands as she peered closely at the barred frame of the window, the wooden chair directly below it.

'The body was found hanging from here?' Christina checked her notes. 'The chair fallen to one side?'

'Yes. All four prisoners involved are in the segregation wing,' Lyons said. His mouth tightened as the banging got louder, the yells angrier. He couldn't let them out until she was off the wing. One or two might fancy themselves as Cary Grant, and they'd freak out if Grace Kelly suddenly materialized in their midst.

Andy Gordon shouted, 'Tray collection, stand at your pad door!'

He watched as the officers, two groups of three, moved either side down the punishment block. One officer unlocked, one took the trays, the third stood by, just in case. Harry Reynolds handed out his tray, next was Steve Wolton, then Victor Braithwaite appeared at his door, craning his head.

'You okay, Anthony? Eh, Anthony – you all right, son?'

'No talking, Braithwaite, get back from your door,' Gordon told him sharply. Braithwaite jerked back as the door was slammed in his face.

The last cell was unlocked. Gordon strode up, glancing down at his clipboard. He said to Officer Booth, 'Kelly to go down with us? Right?' The door swung open. Gordon beckoned. 'Give us your tray, son. Step out. Hands in front of you.'

Kelly shuffled out, looking like death warmed up. His tray was taken and handcuffs slapped on. He stood with head bowed.

'Right, Mr Kelly, let's go.'

'Anthony? Everything all right?' the hoarse voice shouted. 'Oi! Kelly, can you hear me?'

'Shut it, Victor,' Gordon called out, pushing the young man forward. 'No talkin'.'

Awaiting him in the visits room, an icily controlled Christina Knatchbull was beside herself with anger. 'I have never, ever, had to interview a client preparing for trial in this manner,' she told the nervous female officer. 'I would like my objections placed on record.'

'I'm sorry, Miss Knatchbull, but it's the Governor's orders. All the other counsels have been required to . . .'

Her voice trailed off because Christina wasn't around to listen. Camel-hair coat swirling behind her, briefcase swinging, the barrister stalked along the row of empty tables to one of the small cramped rooms where closed interviews took place. The room was divided off by a waist-high wall and a solid sheet of glass, the only contact between the inmate and his visitor via the intercom. She needed the few moments before her client arrived to compose herself. When Kelly was brought in and seated in the chair, still handcuffed, an officer sitting behind him, Christina was back in control, an elegant ice maiden with not a blonde hair out of place.

'Are you all right, Anthony? I'm sorry they put us in here for the last conference before the trial.'

'That's all right,' he mumbled, head down.

'No, it isn't, Anthony.' Christina leaned forward to engage his attention. 'The next time I see you will be in court. But I won't waste time on it now.'

Anthony looked up. 'Will my girlfriend Sandra be there?'

'Only if she's called as a witness. Because all the defendants are currently serving sentences, the trial will be held *in camera*.' She took a file from her briefcase and opened it. 'I believe you are innocent. Look at me, Anthony. You understand the charges. I know you have admitted to smoking illegal substances, but . . .' She tapped the glass emphatically with her pointed fingernails. 'You played no part in the murder of Colin Foster.'

'I didn't. I didn't. I swear before God I didn't.' His blue eyes were squarely upon her, large in his thin face. He swallowed, lips quivering. 'But I'm so s-scared.'

'I know, Anthony.' Her voice was calm and reassuring. 'That's why I have decided against making you testify. I believe I have enough evidence to prove you're innocent.'

'I am, Miss Knatchbull, I swear before God,' Kelly said fervently, and any lingering doubts she might have had evaporated.

'I've filled the meter,' Marshall said, 'just in case it's a long afternoon.'

Helen slammed the door of the Jaguar and activated the locking system. She gave him an uneasy sideways glance. 'You think it's going to be?'

'Yep. You all set?'

Helen straightened her shoulders. 'Yes, let's go.'

The two of them crossed the street to Cleland House, part of the Prison Service HQ in the Millbank complex. Under a silver-grey trenchcoat Helen was wearing a new double-breasted woollen suit in dark grey check, a wisp of blue chiffon scarf at her throat. She felt conspicuously smart, but that was the idea; anyway it was worth it for the confidence it gave her. Marshall, too, she was glad to see, had swapped his usual baggy jacket and distressed trousers for a natty gaberdine suit in slate blue which lost him a stone at a stroke.

As meetings went, this promised to be a tough one. Putting on an assured and united front might just give them the edge. That's if Gary really was on her team, Helen reflected, and not merely along for the ride.

They were processed through Reception, given ID lapel badges, and directed to the lifts. Helen pressed the button, stepped back, and as Marshall ambled up, fastening his badge, he pressed it too.

Helen said, 'Did you ever notice that when people are waiting for a lift and someone joins them, they always press for it as well? Strange, really.' Marshall blinked at her curiously, and Helen returned a weak smile. 'Just making conversation – it's nerves.'

She had hoped the meeting might be held in the more informal surroundings of Royston Andrews's office, but they assembled in the somewhat chilly atmosphere of the fourth-floor boardroom. The tall narrow windows admitted pale shafts of light, and the long mahogany table was like a gleaming runway that separated Helen and Marshall from the line-up which confronted them. Sean Duncan of the Home Office was there, of course, and John Bunny, and Andrews had wheeled in four others, including the chief press officer and senior members of the legal staff.

Andrews didn't mince his words. 'The Prison Services have taken enough hammering from the media. Officers' morale is at an all-time low. Public opinion is that we are *all* incompetent, corrupt idiots, incapable of running a nursery, never mind a prison. The forthcoming trial will be held *in camera*. No press.'

'Have you been informed that the trial will begin on Wednesday next?' Duncan inquired. He shuffled some papers around, and peered at Helen over his half-moon glasses.

'Yes. Feel a bit like I'm in the middle of one now.'

Her attempt at humour went down like a lead balloon. Duncan ignored it, and Andrews tugged at his lower lip in thoughtful fashion as he perused the file in front of him. He looked up. 'All four prisoners have their own legal representative, and have been awarded legal aid. However' – his mouth tightened – 'prisoner Anthony Kelly's family have chosen to hire the services of—'

'Christina Knatchbull.' Helen nodded curtly. 'I am aware of that.'

'She's a pretty formidable criminal barrister,' Andrews went on. 'Very well known for her manipulation of the media, the press in particular.'

Duncan leaned his pinstriped elbows on the table. 'Our main concern is with regard to the prisoner Anthony Kelly.'

They were building up to it nicely, Helen sensed. She got ready, hoping that Gary Marshall was picking up the same smoke signals.

Andrews's eyes were full upon her. 'Was it your decision to place Kelly with Foster and Reynolds?'

Out of the corner of her eye Helen saw that Marshall was deliberately looking away. As her deputy, she might at least have expected some token of support from him, but he was keeping his head well below the parapet.

'You never thought that it would be preferable to put the young and first-time offender Anthony Kelly into a cell by himself?' Duncan asked. The critical, even accusing, tone of his voice stung her.

'No, I did not.' Helen tossed her head back. 'In the past I have invariably discovered that with a first-time offender it is better to bunk them up with someone who can show them the ropes.'

Even as she said it she almost winced at her choice of expression, and Duncan wasn't slow to pounce.

'Well, he was most certainly shown them,' he commented drily. 'Colin Foster was hanged in his bloody cell.'

Thanks to Marshall – or, rather, no thanks to him – Helen was in the frame alone, set up as prime target, and it made her madder than hell. She was still seething when they left Prison Service HQ more than an hour later.

Marching across the street, with Marshall trotting behind, Helen stabbed off the car alarm when she was ten yards away. She yanked the door open and hurled her briefcase inside.

Marshall came panting up. 'You okay to drive?'

'I'm fine to drive but don't for a second think I'm okay.' Helen glared at him over the roof of the car.

'Oh, come on . . .'

'No – you come on.' It was the wrong place for this, in broad daylight in the street, but there was no stopping her. 'I didn't hear you coming to my defence, I didn't hear *you* admit we discussed which cell we'd place Anthony Kelly in.' Helen battered on, even though Marshall was glancing uncomfortably across Page Street at the row upon row of windows.

'And the Area Manager kept bloody quiet, didn't he? He knew about it. And Andrews was on the wing ten minutes before the hanging. I bet he won't be coming to court!' Helen smacked the flat of her hand on the car roof, making Marshall squirm. '*You* were on duty. How come it's all my responsibility?'

'Because you're the Governor!' Marshall shot back icily.

Helen climbed in and slammed the door. There was no answer to that and she knew it. When it came down to the bottom line, Marshall had to answer to her. Every single employee in Barfield was her responsibility, just as every inmate was, and it was only now really dawning just what that entailed – and it scared the pants off her.

They drove in silence for a long time. Marshall seemed deep in thought and she glanced sideways at him, asking casually, 'Thinking about Anthony Kelly?'

Marshall appeared confused. He frowned, hesitated, and then said, pointedly staring away from her through his window, 'No, no, I wasn't as a matter of fact. You want to talk about it?'

'No, not really.'

Marshall nodded and for the rest of the journey they discussed the building works and the progress of the new security system. Anthony Kelly was forgotten – for the rest of the journey at least.

*

Whatever shenanigans were going on at Prison Service HQ, the next morning it was business as usual for Helen.

The building work at Barfield was now well advanced. Externally, the five main accommodation wings were complete. The fire damage had been cleared away and new security roofing installed which made access virtually impossible. Aluminium-frame windows had been fitted in three of the wings with specially toughened titanium steel bars painted yellow. The cells were in the process of being refurbished so that eventually each would contain a toilet and washbasin, making slopping out a thing of the past.

Helen was slightly late in arriving, and Mavis, for once, was on the ball. The staff car park was full of contractors' lorries, and Helen had been held up at the main gate by some officious little turd of a foreman who wouldn't let the Jaguar through. She'd given him short shrift, and Jobsworth had jumped to it when she announced that she was, in fact, the Governor of this establishment.

'You got an eleven o'clock meeting with the POA, then one at twelve with HMS,' Mavis greeted Helen, waving a sheaf of papers. That was the Prison Officers Association and Head of Management Services. 'And these are the lists of interviews. I've spaced them, fifteen minutes each . . .'

She followed Helen through into her office, but stayed by the door, deciding that discretion was called for as first the raincoat was tossed aside and then the briefcase dropped.

'You wanted the applicants for the new educational department. They're in that file, so I've listed them as well,' Mavis said, pointing but not advancing. 'You've got a full afternoon.'

'When don't I have one, Mavis?'

'You also wanted to start checking the meals as the main kitchen is almost functional . . . I can put that back.'

'Nope,' Helen said decisively. 'I've had a lot of complaints about boiled potatoes, boiled potatoes and more boiled potatoes.' She went round the desk, rubbing her hands briskly. 'Right, Mavis, start them coming in.'

Mavis scuttled out and Helen picked through the phone messages, memos and yellow Post-it stickers festooning her desk. 'Are these in order?' she called out. '*Mavis?*' she yelled, looking to the door, and was rather abashed, taken off guard, by the appearance of a tall, good-looking black guy who reminded her a bit of the young Harry Belafonte. He wore a red polo-necked sweater, black velour sports jacket and neatly pressed cord trousers.

'Mr Udding, Governor,' Moira said, eyeing him up and down as she closed the door.

He was totally relaxed, smiling in a friendly way at Helen, while she was flustered, unable to find his CV amongst the applicants' files that Mavis had supposedly organized. Helen interrupted her sorting to wave her hand. 'Come in, please sit down. I'm sorry, I was late in this morning.'

'Well, I suppose with all the construction going on you have your hands full.' He sank down and crossed his legs, a glimmer of amusement in his eyes as he watched her rooting through the files, getting more and more frantic.

'Yes, it's double security, checking every man and moving round the inmates we have here as the work progresses.' She pounced on the CV. 'But it is progressing.' She flipped it open, swiftly taking in the relevant details, back on track.

'Right, it's John, and . . .' finger running down the sheet '. . . very impressive. Want to tell me why you're leaving your present job?'

'The Governor and I do not see eye to eye.'

That was bang up front, and Helen appreciated it. She was temperamentally impatient with wafflers of all descriptions, and John Udding seemed right on her wavelength. She encouraged him to continue.

'He seemed to think because I'm black I should be

concentrating on black prisoners, whereas I feel that whatever I am should not in any way differentiate me from the other officers.'

'And how do they, the inmates, react to you?'

John Udding's smile seemed to light up the room. 'Once they see the "brother" act doesn't work they are probably more antagonistic towards me than they are with the other officers.' He shrugged his broad shoulders. 'But I reckon you just have to give it time, no need going in heavy-handed.'

Helen was nodding. She liked the look of him, and she liked his laid-back approach as well. Men confined within four walls, often banged up for fourteen hours a day, were dangerously frustrated enough – 'headin' a shed', as they called it – without being riled by short-tempered prison staff. She said, 'And the other officers, how do they react?'

'Pretty much the same as the inmates,' John Udding said, and with the smile came a deep rumbling laugh from the chest.

The laugh as much as the CV impressed Helen, and she too was smiling as she ushered him through to Mavis's office. 'Thank you very much for coming in,' she said, shaking hands.

Moira was ready and waiting, smoothing her sweater down so that her bust stuck out. 'I'll walk you through to the gate guard, Mr Udding. This way.'

'Shall I bring in the next?' the hovering Mavis asked Helen, who had paused at the door to watch the pair going out together. 'Governor?'

'I would say that was the intention,' Helen said tartly.

Marshall appeared, back in his baggy suit mode. 'Anthony Kelly's counsel has complained about having to interview him in the closed visit room.'

Helen pursed her lips. 'Yes, I read her terse little memo.' She swept into her office. 'Next, Mavis.'

Marshall caught Mavis's elbow. 'Who was the black bloke?' he muttered.

'They all are,' Mavis told him, wide-eyed, with an emphatic nod of the head. 'Well, so far.'

Marshall followed her into the corridor. 'What?' he said, his face a picture of shock and consternation. 'Black?'

CHAPTER 23

GARY MARSHALL and Jumbo Jackson were going at a clip along the main tunnel, footsteps booming, heading for C Wing. Marshall had been filling in the big, bearded officer on the applicants Helen was interviewing.

'They're all there, linin' up for the new education department and prison officers' positions.' His gaze took in one of the closed-circuit TV cameras overhead. He spoke without moving his lips. 'They're all darkies!'

Turning a corner they came up to the two sets of barred gates through which a crocodile of prisoners was being escorted to the workshops by six officers.

'Norman Jones, cell forty-eight,' Jackson said in an undertone, gesturing ahead. 'We think he's gonna blow.'

'How you doin', John, okay?' Marshall was nodding to the men filing through. 'You're lookin' fit, Eric. Okay, Lennie? Donald . . .'

Marshall and Jackson passed onto the wing, to be met by Russell Morgan. The barrel-chested Scot was red in the face, perspiration shining through the sandy tufts of thinning hair. 'He scares the pants off me an' I don't mind admitting it.'

Marshall looked up to the landing. He buttoned his jacket, gave Jackson the nod. 'Right, let's sort the bastard.'

The bastard in question was sitting with his back towards the door, the whole set of his body tense, fists bunched in his lap. Marshall entered quietly, Jackson looming behind in the doorway like a man mountain.

'You want us to get nasty, is that what you're after?' Marshall's voice was soft, little more than a murmur.

'He won't talk, won't speak to anybody,' Morgan said from the landing.

Marshall stood with legs braced apart, hands by his sides. He didn't raise his voice. He was very quiet, very calm. 'Stand up.'

Norman Jones leaned forward and in slow motion rose to his feet. He turned with the same long-drawn-out deliberation until he was facing them. He was about three feet away from Marshall. He raised his hands to shoulder height and made claws of his fingers. From his throat came a low animal growl. Marshall didn't move a muscle. He said very quietly, without a tremor, 'Right, you want to play it that way? You got two seconds to straighten out.'

Jones growled again, way deep down. Jackson sidled in alongside Marshall. He slipped his hand into his pocket, worming his fingers through the leather thong of his baton. When Jones saw this he smiled.

Nodding encouragement, Jackson beckoned him forward with a curled finger the size of a Cumberland sausage. 'Come on . . . if you want.'

Helen was steaming through the job applicants at a rate of knots. As Marshall had observed, they were all black, and several were women. Zania Tullbrooke was an arts graduate in her late twenties with a BA in literature and drama, applying for one of the education officers' posts. Barely five minutes in, there was a phone call and Helen had to cut the interview short. She apologized to the applicant, made a note in the file ('Promising') and rushed down to the new, state-of-the-art main kitchen, recently completed, where the trolleys were being loaded and prepared for lunch.

Pale and paunchy, thinning reddish hair under a floppy

white cap, the head cook awaited her, impatient at the delay Helen's inspection was causing. He lifted the stainless-steel lids one by one to reveal the food heaped in deep square compartments, and rattled off: 'Vegetable soup and bread rolls as starter. Steak and kidney pie, boiled potatoes, peas and green beans, main course. Jam roly-poly, pudding.'

Helen tucked the clipboard under her arm and held out her hand. 'Could I have a plate? I've had a few complaints that the food isn't very hot when it's served. And how often have you served boiled potatoes?' she asked, peering at the stodgy white mound. 'Well, since I've been here?'

The cook dug in the ladle with a vengeance. 'That's not my fault. It's because of the rebuilding. Got to go down three corridors, outside, then through the main tunnel to the wings.'

A couple of Red Band orderlies lurked nearby with furtive grins. The kitchen employed a mixture of prison staff, civilians and orderlies, and they formed an appreciative audience as Helen sampled the various items. They were impressed that the Governor was taking a personal interest.

'Vegetables a bit overcooked, and the potatoes could do with a few more minutes.' She indicated the pudding. 'Is this served with custard?'

'Not today. Milk was late arriving.'

Helen tasted it while the cook stood by, arms tightly folded.

She looked round. 'Where are the specials? The diets and the allergy trays?'

'With the work goin' on I don't have the space to prepare the specials. I do the medical ones, but the diets' – he shrugged – 'they can just eat less.'

Helen's bleeper went. She switched it off and dropped it back in the pocket of her linen jacket. 'You were in the army, weren't you?' She searched round the spacious area with its huge ovens and free-standing preparation counters for a phone.

'Yes, ma'am, fifteen years.'

Helen's snide smile showed she had a nasty edge. 'Thought so,' she said, striding off. 'Thank you.'

There was a clatter as the cook slammed the lids back on. Grins intact, the audience melted away, having been thoroughly entertained by the performance.

Helen was rushing everywhere this morning. First to the kitchen, now to the hospital wing. Over the phone Dr Thomas had told her that Arnie Franks, who had Aids, had been admitted, and was in a bad way.

'I've segregated him in a cubicle. I think you'd better see him right away.'

There were five open beds on the wing, screened off by curtains, and four segregation cells with beds in them. These were for those patients in isolation like Arnie Franks, or for prisoners who had to be kept under secure conditions, ill or not. The hospital was a favourite staging-post for would-be E-men.

A face mask dangling by its ribbons on the collar of his white coat, Lorcan Thomas was stripping off skin-tight latex gloves. Two auxiliary nurses were dealing with minor injuries, and an inmate sat morosely hunched over, one hand cupped to his nose, blood seeping through his fingers.

'How is he?' Helen asked. She was faintly flushed and panting from having to run all over this damn place like a scalded hen.

'He's not very good. His breathing is erratic. It's liver failure, and because of his condition—' Dr Thomas broke off, his handsome features tightening in annoyance. From one of the segregation cells came a loud voice, grinding monotonously on. Jumbo Jackson stood outside the door, one hand under his armpit, studying his thumbnail with weary boredom.

'Recommendation ten from Judge Tumim's report, the abolition of excessive, unnecessary medication for prisoners,' chanted Norman Jones from behind the closed door. 'Recommendation seventeen: increased time out of cells for all prisoners to bring them in line with the private sector's jails which have contracts for a fourteen-hours-per-day out-of-cell period.'

Jackson raised his hand. 'Governor . . .'

'In a second.' Helen looked towards the open door of Franks's cell and then into the dark brown eyes of Lorcan Thomas. 'Is he dying?'

'Yes.'

'You goin' to see him, Doc?' Jackson interrupted again, nodding behind him to where the voice droned on without pause.

'Recommendation twenty: the abolition of the arbitrary use of segregation and hospitalization for prisoners deemed at risk or subversive . . .'

'Only I have to get back on the wing,' Jackson said.

Dr Thomas laid his hand on Helen's arm. She was acutely aware of the gentle pressure – ridiculously so when a man was dying of Aids not ten feet away and a psycho was drivelling on like a speak-your-weight machine.

Dr Thomas said, 'I think you should wear a surgical mask. He's had severe nosebleeds and—' A beady, irritated glance towards the closed cell with its non-stop drone. 'I've asked to re-examine prisoner Norman Jones.'

'I'll be right with you,' Helen said to Jackson. She donned the mask handed to her by one of the nurses and entered Franks's cell.

Dr Thomas checked the medical record and snapped the plastic folder shut. He moved purposefully towards the closed door, with a curt nod for Jackson to open up. 'Right, this one's trouble, isn't he?'

Arnie Franks reminded Helen of a phantom figure, pale and shrunken and insubstantial. But for his laboured ragged breathing he might have been a bloodless corpse. He lay perfectly still, his eyes closed, a drip attached to his arm and a tube feeding oxygen through his nose.

Helen sat by the bedside, wearing the mask. She wasn't

proud that she was glad the poor sod was unconscious, because God only knew what she could have found to say to him. Besides, she couldn't concentrate. Not with that bloody voice going on and on and on. Even here, through the wall – getting louder, it seemed – that never-changing mechanical voice grated on, making her want to scream and smash something.

'Recommendation twenty-seven: better-quality education for all inmates, in particular those inmates held in hospital . . .'

She was so wound up that she jumped when Lorcan Thomas came in, tying his mask. He checked the equipment, flicked the drip-feed with his fingernail, and sat down on the edge of the bed opposite her.

His eyes over the mask made her shiver. 'I've already been in touch with the medics at two of his previous prisons, and without medication he becomes excessively violent.' Dr Thomas inclined his head to the wall, where they could hear the chanting voice rising to screaming pitch.

A nurse was trying to reason sternly with him, which struck Helen as not only a thankless task, but a lost cause. 'Mr Jones! Mr Jones, we have on record from your previous doctors that you have in the past been agreeable to the—' In order to be heard, her voice rose to a shout. 'This is for your benefit. No one is forcing you to do anything against your will, only to do what is best for you!'

Helen squeezed her eyes shut. It was a madhouse. She could understand only too easily how people went off their heads. When she opened her eyes again Dr Thomas was leaning over the inert, laboriously breathing figure. He took the frail hand in his own ungloved hand.

'How you doin', my old mate? What you want? Eh?' He shook the limp hand tenderly. 'What is it, old fella?'

Franks's eyelids flickered. Dr Thomas leaned even closer, straining to hear above the ranting, chanting voice as the ashen lips trembled.

'Hold me hand, help me fight this, son . . .' Pathetic little tears dribbled out from beneath his eyelids. Dr Thomas placed his hand on Franks's forehead.

'Let go, Arnie,' he said, so gently that Helen wanted to weep. 'Everything is going to be just fine . . . There's a good lad.'

'Recommendation thirty-seven: life-sentence prisoners should come into line with Europe and Ireland and be given Christmas home leave after serving a fixed term. The mandatory life sentence to be abolished.'

Helen's nails were gouging her palms. Not just wrought up at the sight of Arnie Franks, she was plain fucking mad. Her eyes felt dry and hot as she gazed helplessly at the last feeble remnants of life leaving the wasted, shrivelled body.

'Is this all there is to it?' Franks wondered aloud. The eyelids slid open and the blank, sightless eyes stared into eternity.

Helen couldn't take it any more. She stood up, trembling all over with fury. She strode out, punched open the door of the next cell, marched in and stood there, eyes blazing.

Norman Jones was rocking to and fro on the bed, the veins on his neck standing out, screaming at the wall. His face was a mess, purple swellings on his jaw and both cheeks, one eye nearly closed.

'Those detained in prison establishments whose mental conditions fall within the provisions of the Mental Health Act should be accorded automatic access to the same quality of life as those detained in psychiatric hospitals.'

Two nurses and an officer watched over him from a safe distance, afraid to go anywhere near. But Helen was too angry to be afraid. Standing tall, shoulders back, she pointed straight at him.

'*Shut up!* YOU – SHUT – UP!'

Norman Jones jerked round, blinking rapidly with his one good eye. He was so astounded that a woman's voice could drown his own that he could only stare glassily at Helen, his mouth hanging open.

'A man is dying in there,' Helen said, bringing her voice down. Her chest rose and fell with a couple of steadying breaths. 'Thank you,' she said, icily controlled, and abruptly left the cell.

Lorcan Thomas was outside. He unfastened the tapes and removed his mask. 'He's dead.' It sounded matter-of-fact, though Helen knew that was only how it sounded. For a moment he just stood there, and then he sighed and went over to the medical supplies cupboard, fishing for his keys.

Helen moved thoughtfully towards him. 'You know, when the prison is full – for want of a better description – we will need a full-time doctor.'

Lorcan Thomas opened the cupboard door, his hand passing over the labelled bottles and cartons of drugs. 'Not my idea of heaven, sorry. I knew the previous doctor – that's why I stepped in after the riot. But as a full-time . . .' He glanced over his shoulder, shaking his head. 'No way.'

Helen gave a small shrug of disappointment.

'Some of your inmates, Miss Hewitt, scare me. Some of them repel me.' He was looking at the door of Jones's cell. 'There is so little kindness in here, and not everybody is able to deal with the dregs of humanity.'

Helen raised her chin. 'They're not all dregs, Doctor.'

The flash of quiet defiance in her eyes surprised him. 'Perhaps you have a vocation.'

'Maybe I have,' agreed Helen rather sadly.

Russell Morgan said wearily, 'All I can do is repeat what I was told. The education department should be ready next week.'

The three men went away grumbling. They were falling behind in their studies. Two of them were midway through Open University degrees, and one was doing an NVQ in computer design drawing. Aware that the workshops and classrooms were now fully refurbished, they were disgruntled that courses hadn't resumed.

As usual the TV was blaring away in the corner of the association area, with no one paying it any attention. Snooker and table tennis were in progress, and a pungent odour drifted from the tiny kitchen where a group of cons were cooking up a fierce curry.

Morgan wrinkled his nose at the smell. He was a steak and chips man himself. Alan Fisher diffidently raised a hand as the senior officer wandered by. 'Mr Morgan, I don't suppose you've any news for me, have you?'

'What about?'

'My probation officer. Before the riot he said that I was on the list for a weekend visit.' Fisher gazed at him hopefully through large rimless spectacles. Aged forty-seven, with dark brown hair and a rather shy, hesitant smile, he looked younger than his years. He didn't fraternize much, but was always pleasant in that withdrawn, softly spoken manner of his.

'I dunno, Alan, best to ask the Governor tomorrow on her rounds. I just work here, mate.'

Head hanging down, a very subdued Norman Jones was led through the gates by Jumbo Jackson and another officer. Morgan called to him. 'Hey, Jumbo, what's goin' on?'

'Waste of ruddy time,' Jackson groused, coming over. They watched Jones move to the trolley, like a man in a coma, and help himself to a cup of tea. Jackson muttered, 'Doc says he's got a screw loose. He should be on—'

'Mr Morgan, did you find out?' Brian Samora, the Scouser, stood there, holding up his tattered scrap of paper. 'My query?'

Morgan turned on him balefully. 'Brian, you been askin' the same question for months now. If you get twenty-one days on your original sentence it stands to reason the days will be attached to your release date.' He held up his finger. 'Now, I told you that, the Gov told you that, half the wing has told you that. Piss off, go on.'

'But I got some off for good behaviour!' Samora protested, staring forlornly after the two officers, who had moved away.

'Tell you who you should ask,' Walter Brinkley murmured helpfully, nudging Brian's elbow. His expression serious, he nodded towards the tea trolley. 'Norman over there, bloke in forty-eight. He'll put you straight, Brian, real friendly. Go on, ask him.'

Samora hesitated for a moment, then set off eagerly. 'Oh, great, thanks.'

Brinkley pinched his nose to stop himself from snorting with laughter.

At the stove in the kitchen alcove, Snoopy and three other inmates were busy. One large pan contained a bubbling curry, its eye-watering smell camouflaging a bubbling potion on the next gas-ring – an explosive mixture of fruit, brewer's yeast, aftershave and metal polish. The ageing process was dependent on willpower and any unexpected pad spins.

'Smells good,' Snoopy pronounced, keeping one eye on the screws and another on the hooch being poured into a flask, using a tea-towel as a strainer. He winked at the pourer. 'Nothin' like a vindaloo!'

Grinning, Brinkley was rolling a burn, tongue flicking out to lick the paper as he watched Samora approach Jones, who was staring into space sipping a cup of tea.

'I don't know what to do. What would you do?' Fisher's voice was soft, his eyes anxious. 'They said weekend, Walter, due for a weekend – you know, to start adjusting.'

Brinkley stuck the roll-up in the corner of his mouth, nodding. His eyes were on Brian, who was backing away from Jones, his face stricken with terror. Jones went past the Scouser without a look, carrying his tea in the palm of his hand.

'When was the last time you was out?' Brinkley asked Fisher, lighting up.

'Fifteenth of May nineteen eighty-one.'

'Christ!' The bell rang for the end of association. 'Well,

you'll need more than a weekend to adjust, mate. Been a lotta changes since eighty-one.' Brinkley raised his eyebrows, peering innocently over his specs at Samora, who was drifting back, his face ashen under its olive hue. 'All right? Explain it to you, did he?'

Samora fumbled for words. 'He . . . he . . . You know what he said? If I spoke to him again, he'd—' Samora gulped. 'He'd bite me tongue out of me 'ead.'

CHAPTER 24

MOIRA STOOD at Helen's desk, a sheaf of letters she'd just finished typing in one hand, her pad in the other. The job was varied and interesting, and it was important, Moira felt; certainly more so than her previous one with an estate agent, typing up fictitious descriptions and soft-soaping clients.

She got on reasonably well with Mavis, and she had tremendous admiration and respect for Helen. The woman was doing a difficult job in impossible circumstances, and if she got a bit short-tempered and snappy at times who wouldn't, for God's sake? This morning, though, she looked very tired, Moira thought. The Crown Court trial was starting tomorrow, which was an additional strain and burden on top of everything else.

'These just need your signature. Mr Smith, the new probation officer, is here, and a Mr Soames asked if you would call him. He's the prosecution barrister for the trial.'

'Thanks, I'll sign them and leave them in the out tray.'

Helen was signing the last one when Mavis brought in Malcolm Smith. He was still trying to get to grips with the job, and seemed both earnest and pedantic, where she would have preferred briskness and efficiency.

'Thanks for coming in.' Helen waved him to a chair. She had a lot on her plate, and was anxious to get this over with. 'It's about Alan Fisher.'

'I'm attempting to get all the records but it's a long

process. You know the entire department went up in smoke?'

Helen did, but the last thing she wanted was excuses. She waited impatiently while he opened his briefcase and rooted inside.

'According to his file he was put forward for a weekend visit,' Malcolm Smith said, handing it over. 'He's got a parole date in eighteen months . . . well, be half that now. It was suggested he be transferred to an open prison nearer his home.'

Helen skimmed through it. 'This is appalling,' she said, checking the dates. Fisher had been promised home leave months ago, which had been put back no less than four times.

'With the new Home Office ruling regarding home leave it's making a lot of extra paperwork.'

More excuses. What about some action? 'Well, we have to get the department organized – and fast,' Helen told him. She got up, a heavy hint that she'd like to see him on his way. 'Thank you very much for this.'

Moira buzzed through on the intercom. 'Call on line two. Mr Soames. Is it all right if I go off to lunch now?'

'Yes, thank you, Moira.' Helen flicked off and came round the desk. 'I'll contact you as soon as I've checked through this. Thank you.' Malcolm Smith was gone before he knew it. Helen laid the back of her hand to her forehead and picked up the phone. Her forehead felt hot. Was it flu or was she simply overworked and overwrought?

'Helen Hewitt. Ah, Mr Soames, I'm sorry, I meant to return your call . . .'

Well, she had and she hadn't, but it was too late now.

Gordon Soames had long flowing grey hair and an acerbic manner. His questions were not so much devious as positively Machiavellian. Helen didn't trust him an inch, even though he was supposed to be on her side. Technically on her side, she reminded herself. If blame was to be apportioned and heads were to roll, she would have to watch her rear.

There was a park fifteen minutes' drive away, and Helen agreed to give up her lunch hour to meet him there. A few mothers with toddlers were feeding the ducks as they strolled along the gravel paths under the trees and a windy sky that had flecks of rain in it. Soames wore a long black overcoat, a silk Paisley scarf bunched at his throat, and carried a fürled umbrella. A man for all seasons, prepared for all eventualities. He gave her a sly glance, staring ahead, his entire focus seemingly on the bird twittering on a branch of a leafless tree.

'One could say this chance meeting could be termed unethical.' He weighted the word 'chance', still not looking at her directly as he began to walk slowly, his eyes now travelling down to the highly polished caps of his handmade shoes. 'But a rather fortunate one. Ah!' He quickened his pace and she thought he was aiming for the edge of the duckpond when he turned abruptly. This time his entire attention was directed at Helen and he unnerved her.

'You must understand that I was not on duty,' Helen was at pains to explain. 'In fact, on the night it happened I was having dinner with Mr Andrews and my area manager, John Bunny.'

'Yes, I suppose after the riot at Barfield the prison must be in a very disorganized state,' Soames said, managing to sound icy cool with a hint of grudging sympathy.

'Not that disorganized, Mr Soames.' Helen bridled.

He smiled, and she thought he might have trapped her. 'Good, I was hoping you'd say that.' He had. He went smoothly on, 'I am very confident that the case will be concluded and dealt with in as short a time as possible. That said, there is one area that troubles me.' He gazed at the darkening sky, the sagging lines of his face dominated by the beaked nose with its wide nostrils. 'The defendant Anthony Kelly is pleading, as all four men are—'

'Not guilty, yes, I know.'

Soames nodded, digging the tip of his umbrella into the damp gravel. 'Have you met Miss Knatchbull?'

'No, but she's obviously had numerous meetings with Kelly over recent months, and she has also seen the cell and—' Helen stopped. 'Why did you ask if I knew her?'

'Miss Knatchbull is worried that her client can be' – Soames gave the slightest of shrugs – 'got at. This is obviously not meant to sound as if I am undermining Barfield's security, you understand.'

Helen wasn't fooled. Precisely what the devious bastard *was* intending to do. And he damn well knew it. She simmered in silence.

He went on smoothly, 'I believe if there was any possible inference that the present conditions at Barfield could be used in Anthony Kelly's defence, if any negligence could be directed—'

This was too bloody much. Helen swung round to face him. 'Anthony Kelly committed a crime. I didn't send him to Barfield. I didn't sentence him.'

Soames raised a plump hand, a small condescending smile playing on his lips. 'I am glad to hear you have a very positive attitude. Miss Knatchbull is a formidable lady.'

The spits of rain became a steady downpour. They returned to their cars, his olive green BMW parked alongside the Jaguar.

'I have no intention of calling you for the prosecution,' Soames revealed, unfurling his umbrella. 'And I presume as you have had no contact with Miss Knatchbull's solicitors you are not called for the defence.'

Since he wasn't offering any shelter from the rain, Helen got into the car and lowered the window. 'If I was it would be highly unethical for me to speak to her. But I am perfectly willing to be a witness.'

'Good, and I feel confident that you would be more than a match for the delectable Miss Knatchbull,' Soames said glibly, performing a half-bow under the spread umbrella.

'Do you think she will call me for the defence?' Helen asked.

'Not if I've got in first.' His sardonic smile was accompanied by a mocking salute as he moved off.

Through the rain-smeared window Helen watched him get into his car. Oddly enough, while she didn't particularly like the man, and definitely didn't trust him, there was something attractive in his blasé, buoyant self-confidence. Hellfire. Was she really that desperate?

Helen stood at the window of her office, checking her appearance in the small round mirror of her compact. She brushed a hair from the shoulder of her suit, then tilted her chin critically. If she could have swapped anything, it would have been her nose. Not for one of those pert button jobs, but for something perhaps more elegant and refined. Trouble was, Helen thought, she'd then need an elegant and refined personality to go with it.

'We still haven't found anyone to claim Arnie Franks's body,' Mavis said worriedly, appearing at the door.

Helen snapped her compact shut. 'Mavis, I can't deal with this right now. I'm due in court in . . .' She frowned at her watch. Time to get moving. She came round the desk. 'Ask the new probation officer attached to C Wing.'

'Mr Daily?'

Helen sighed. 'No, C Wing, Mavis, as in Crow. Tell him it's not approved yet but we can start the procedure for arranging a weekend leave for Alan Fisher, 214.'

'Fisher,' Mavis said, jotting it down. 'F for Fish.' Her eyes twinkled impishly from under her thick eyebrows, which made Helen chuckle.

'Yes!' She smoothed down the lapels of her smart black

jacket and wafted her arms aloft. 'Do you think the devious Mr Soames will approve?'

Marshall and Jimmy Malahide arrived at the courthouse together. Helen saw them climbing out of Marshall's Rover as she parked her car in one of the few vacant spaces. Malahide was neatly turned out, she was gratified to note, sharp creases in his trousers, buttons on his uniform brightly polished; in civvies, she reckoned, the hulking Yorkshire lad might have been taken for a nightclub bouncer.

As the two men walked up the steps to the main entrance they were joined by Dr Thomas. From this distance it seemed to Helen that he was possibly suffering from a hangover. He had that too wide-awake look about him, like someone who had emerged gasping and tingling from a purging cold shower. Helen wondered if there was another notch on his gunbelt from last night. Or was Moira Levitt the lucky recipient of his favours twice in a row?

The imposing granite façade of the Crown Court gave way to drab sixties utility inside. Corridors led off from an austere reception hall, gold-leaf lettering on varnished boards indicating the various courtrooms. As always there was the smell of polish, even though the floors looked scuffed and worn dull. Helen's heart always sank on entering such places. It was the endless waiting in draughty corridors, sitting on hard benches, staring for hours at blank pastel walls that sapped her morale.

There was a throng of people outside the courtroom. Marshall and Malahide were standing near the double doors, in a group with four other officers from Barfield. About to light up, Marshall was given a dig in the ribs, and stuffed the packet away with a long-suffering expression. Further along, DCI Dunes was sitting with two uniformed police officers. Standing apart from the others, Anthony

Kelly's parents, a nondescript middle-class working couple, clutched each other's hands. Nothing in their orderly life had given any indication that one day they would be called to a courtroom and that Anthony, their only child, would be charged with murder. The previous arrest and subsequent trial of their son had devastated both of them; now they were numb with shock and confusion, and unable to shed any more tears. There was no sign of Lorcan Thomas, so Helen assumed he was already inside.

Marshall nodded, and the prison officers stiffened self-consciously as Helen came up. She looked the men over. 'If it's not a rude question, who's sort of running my prison this morning?' Then her stern expression softened into a smile. 'It's not Walter Brinkley, is it?'

Almost visibly the tension eased, and even Gary Marshall found a lukewarm grin.

'Could I please check your names?' A female usher with a clipboard pushed her way through. 'Miss Hewitt, Mr Marshall, Mr Malahide . . .'

Helen caught her elbow. 'I was just wondering how long I'll have to wait.'

'I'm sorry, I really couldn't say.' She moved on briskly. 'DCI Dunes, Mr Clark, Mr Edwards . . .' She turned back, craning over heads, at the sound of burring from Helen's phone. Helen had taken it out and was extending the aerial. 'Excuse me, Miss Hewitt, no portable phones are allowed inside the courtroom.'

Helen acknowledged her. So if there was a mass breakout or Barfield burned to the ground while she was in court, Helen thought philosophically, she'd be none the wiser. But what was the betting they'd hold her accountable?

As the examining doctor, Lorcan Thomas was first in the witness stand. With four defendants standing trial, each with his own QC and their attendant junior counsels, solicitors and clerks, the court was full to capacity. Opposite them, on the other side of the courtroom, sat the jury of seven men and five women, who had been sworn in the day before. They had a clear view of the four defendants, all wearing suits and collars and ties, sitting in line abreast, a uniformed police officer behind each one.

Directly below the witness box, a clerk in a starched collar and black coat stood at a long table on which were placed the exhibits, each one tagged with a yellow label. This motley collection of odds and ends, like the remnants left behind at a car-boot sale, were of intense interest to the crowded court. They possessed the macabre fascination of ordinary objects given an entirely new significance by the part they had played in the final moments of Colin Foster.

A man was dead, no question of that. But had he been murdered?

'Death was caused by strangulation. The deceased had no other external injuries.' Dr Thomas had his notes to hand, but thus far had had no need to refer to them. 'On my examination the flex was still attached to the victim's neck but had been loosened as mouth-to-mouth resuscitation had been performed by two auxiliary nurses. Both noted the victim showed no sign of life on admittance to the hospital wing.'

Gordon Soames nodded. Under the grey wig, his face had a florid handsomeness, his beaked nose a positive advantage in that no one was in any doubt where his attention was focused.

'Dr Thomas, do you identify this – exhibit three – as the flex removed from the victim?'

The clerk passed it up.

'Yes, this is the flex I removed from the victim's neck.'

'I also ask you to identify the next exhibit, number four.' Soames nodded to the clerk, who passed it up. 'A grey sock.'

Lorcan Thomas turned it over several times in his hands. 'This item, or one similar, was removed from the victim's mouth. I did not remove it myself, but auxiliary nurse Jones did. The item . . .' He looked slightly at sea.

Soames pressed him. 'Do you know if that is the sock that was discovered in the victim's mouth, Dr Thomas?'

'I really couldn't say.' He dangled it between thumb and forefinger. 'One grey sock looks pretty much like another.'

This brought forth some mirth from the public gallery, which a single hawk-eyed glance from the judge was enough to silence.

Thomas shrugged. 'I'm sorry, but the said item was, I believe, placed into a plastic bag in the hospital wing and was removed by the police.'

Soames was happy with that. Evidently so were the four defence counsels, for no further questions were asked. The hard questions would come later.

Russell Morgan put his head round the door of the probation room attached to C Wing. 'I got Fisher for you, Mr Smith. He's got a visit this afternoon. We'll be serving lunch in ten minutes.'

The senior officer stood aside. Alan Fisher sidled into the cubbyhole of a room, sparsely furnished with a table and three chairs, a couple of NACRO posters and one for New Bridge voluntary visitors' scheme tacked to the walls.

Malcolm Smith said drily, 'Then it's lock-up – I do know the routine, Mr Morgan, thank you.' He pulled a chair away from the table. 'Come in, sit down.'

Morgan closed the door but lingered a moment, watching through the glass panel. Further along the corridor behind him the kitchen orderlies were wheeling the big trolleys through the gates into C Wing. He hoped the probation officer got the message. One man being late for meals was enough to disrupt the whole ruddy system. Threw everything behind.

Smith waited until Morgan had gone. 'First let me

apologize for not contacting you before now,' he said, flipping open the file.

'Yes, sir. Governor said there was delays.'

The temperature in the room was average, yet Fisher was sweating. He'd received a knockback so many times, and was desperately afraid that his precious home leave, so near and yet so far, would elude him once again.

'Made it very hard on all the inmates after the riot, including myself taking over.' Smith stroked his straggling moustache, the kind that seemed to come as part of the set for men with curly hair. He rubbed his thin, veined hands together. 'Well, I won't waste time. Miss Hewitt has—'

'She said she'd look into it for me.' Fisher's eyes blinked anxiously behind his glasses.

'She did, Alan, that's why we're here now.'

'Oh, my God . . . Does that mean I got to go all through the assessment again?' Fisher slumped back in his chair.

'No, no, not at all,' Smith was quick to assure him. Fisher closed his eyes in relief. 'I just need to check with you that nothing in the interim has changed.' He studied the file. 'Your wife . . .'

'June.' Fisher was nodding eagerly, sensing that he was in with a chance. This time it was really going to happen. 'She's coming in to see me this afternoon.'

'And June met with your previous probation officer, didn't she?'

Morgan was back again. He tapped on the glass panel and leaned in. 'It's eleven forty-five, Mr Smith. If Fisher wants lunch he's going to have to come on the landing now.' He closed the door and strolled a few paces, arms folded, swaying from side to side.

Fisher said quickly, 'I don't mind missing lunch, sir.' He leaned forward. 'June, she's got a room for . . . well, our room ready, and then the girls . . .'

'So there is no problem with your marriage?'

'No, none at all, sir. She's stood by me all these years.' It was touching, the pleading in his face, and Smith decided to put him out of his misery.

'Well, Alan, I don't see any problem.' He smiled. 'All I will say at this time is it's looking very positive.'

Alan Fisher nodded mutely, lips compressed. He was very close to tears. He got up as the door was tapped again, but it wasn't Morgan, it was Brian Samora, who entered with his hands clasped to his chest.

'Mr Smith, could I just speak to you a minute? It's deadly important.' He fumbled for his bit of paper.

'Oi!' Morgan was behind him, heavy hand on his shoulder. 'Come on, Brian, you've not booked to see Mr Smith now, have you? Get back on the wing. *Now.*'

A hurt Samora was shoved out, a softly smiling Fisher following him. Morgan glanced back briefly. 'Sorry about that but we've got to get lunch served.'

Many of the wives and girlfriends had made an effort, but June Fisher stood out from them. She was an attractive blonde, a couple of years younger than her husband. Under a double-breasted black blazer she wore a salmon blouse with a single gold top button and pleated black trousers, an outfit that showed off her trim figure.

Sitting across from her, Alan Fisher seemed in contrast to merge into the background, thin dark receding hair, anxious expression and prison pallor. 'He said it was on the cards, the new Governor's just got to approve it.' His quiet tones were difficult to hear above the hubbub from the other tables. Toddlers scampered at their mothers' feet, babies whimpered, and a woman's broken sobbing formed a continual nagging distraction.

June sighed wearily. 'You know, I've been waiting a long time, Alan. I've done what you told me. I've never brought the papers with me because they check everything at the gates.'

'I know, I know.' He held up a restraining hand and

sneaked a furtive look around as if someone might be listening. 'But one of the reasons they're gonna release me is they don't know anythin' about the divorce.'

'I can't keep on waiting.' She was trying to be kind, and fair to them both, but the delay was frustrating. 'You say I can't send them but you've also got to sign the deeds over to me.'

'They read the mail, June, they'd know. I'll sign them when I come out. You got my word, I'll sign. I promise you.'

June Fisher sighed again. This year, next year, some time never.

Snoopy's wife, Meryl, had chosen a table right in the middle of the visits' room, as far away from the screws as possible. They patrolled the aisles now and then, but usually kept watch from the sidelines. And there was plenty of activity going on to keep them occupied.

'Everything go okay at the gates?' Snoopy asked, leaning on his sharp elbows, head sunk between his angular shoulders. A curl of smoke drifted up from the hand-rolled cigarette stuck in the corner of his mouth.

'Yeah, they searched me bag, me coat, and—' Irritably, Meryl shifted the baby on her lap so she could crane over to peer down at the five-year-old crawling under the table. 'Arnold, I told you, play with your puzzle, sit. *Sit* on the floor near me.' She straightened up, shaking her head. 'He's gettin' to be such a handful, you know.'

'*Arnold!*' Snoopy looped a long arm below and hauled him out. 'Sit on the floor and stop messin' about, you hear me?' Under cover of dragging on the cigarette he said, 'You got it?'

Meryl gazed at him and closed one eye. Snoopy attracted the attention of an officer. 'Okay if I hold my kid?'

Getting the nod, Meryl handed over the eighteen-month-old baby. Wrapped in a knitted shawl, her chubby brown legs dangled from the padded Pampers and romper-suit bottoms.

'Who's beautiful? Who's a little beauty, eh?' Snoopy tickled the baby's chin. 'Yeah, come on, give us a smile, come on!' The baby gurgled. 'Where is it?' Snoopy muttered.

Meryl looked round. 'They checked out the nappies last time, so it's under her sweater.' She reached down. 'Gimme that, Arnold. *Don't* put it in your mouth!' She took the cigarette butt from him and tossed it into the ashtray.

Meanwhile Snoopy had palmed the package, about the size of a boiled sweet. It was fastened to a length of dental floss. Head bent as he nuzzled his daughter, he slipped the loop round a tooth and popped the tiny package in his mouth. His Adam's apple went up and down as he swallowed. If he could retrieve it without breaking the dental floss, well and good. If he couldn't, he'd have to wait until tomorrow morning.

CHAPTER 25

DCI DUNES had put on horn-rimmed glasses to read his notes. His hands rested on the wooden bar of the witness box, the typed sheets laid out on the varnished oak surround beneath it.

'Lastly, I questioned prisoner Anthony John Kelly. This was approximately two and a half hours after the incident had occurred. He was still in a very distressed state, but agreed to be interviewed. May I refer to my summary, my lord?'

The clerk passed up a copy of the interview to the judge. He studied it for a moment and then nodded. 'Yes, please continue.'

'Mr Kelly stated: "I was just leaving the cell when Victor" – that would be Victor Braithwaite, my lord – "walked in. I was very uneasy because I had been given a spliff."' Dunes looked up. 'A marijuana cigarette, my lord.' He carried on reading, '"I had never smoked one before and I was feeling sick and dizzy."'

A burnished gleam of silvery-blonde hair visible below her curled wig, Christina Knatchbull was listening intently, occasionally scribbling with a gold fountain pen on a yellow legal pad. Gordon Soames reclined on the bench seat in front of her, fingertips pressed together, exceedingly calm and just as confident.

The packed court was silent and attentive, just the odd cough and shuffle as Dunes went on with his evidence. He reached the part of Anthony Kelly's testimony which dealt with the details of Colin Foster's final few minutes.

'"He tied the end of the wire to the bottom of the metal frame of the window. It was too short so Steven, I think, drew up a chair for him to stand on. The noose was still around Colin's neck and he was lifted onto the chair. Then he went limp and we all started to panic. Someone pressed the alarm bell and the officers came into the cell. I did not know at the time Colin was dead, I was told later."'

The judge needed to clarify something. He pulled up the sleeve of his red robe and leaned on one elbow. 'Detective Chief Inspector Dunes, from Anthony Kelly's interview with you, he determined that all three were actually smoking, is that correct?'

'Yes, my lord. When I questioned Kelly regarding the smoking, he, er . . .' Dunes sorted through the pages, then glanced up.

'Continue.'

'He answered that Steven – Mr Wolton – was rolling them in the cell. I then asked the defendant how many he had smoked. He said two.'

The judge nodded, making a note. 'And all the three other defendants have denied partaking of this "spliff"? Joint?'

'Yes, my lord.'

Christina Knatchbull had a private little knowing smile on her face. She turned her head to look along the row of her fellow defence attorneys. Julian Booth acting for Victor Braithwaite. Tony Fielding acting for Steven Wolton. John Wilding acting for Harry Reynolds. It was three against one that her client was lying. Three testimonies to break down if Anthony was to be believed. The odds weren't daunting, not to her; she reckoned they were pretty good.

'Yes, you can tell Fisher,' Helen said into her mobile phone. She'd had time to think about it, more than enough time, hanging around all day, drinking machine coffee. She dropped the phone into her shoulder bag and rubbed the nape of her neck. This endless waiting really pissed her off when she had a million and one things to be getting on with.

DCI Dunes appeared at the open door of the waiting room. He looked in, belting up his raincoat. 'They've recessed until ten thirty tomorrow.'

'Shit!' Helen stamped her foot. 'I've been here all bloody day!' She went into the corridor. People were spilling out from the courtroom. Beyond them, at the far end, Dr Thomas was deep in conversation with a young female clerk. Quite clearly she was basking in the attentions of such a gorgeous hunk. If he wasn't careful, Helen thought, he'd wear it to a fine point before it dropped off.

Norman Jones was in the market for some good stuff, and the main man, of course, was Snoopy. The two of them were conferring during association, while Brian Samora stood nearby in a stupor, red-eyed from the single hit of crack slipped to him by Snoopy in exchange for two phonecards. The tall Rasta was doing brisk trade; he had a captive market.

'This is the best gear on the street but it's expensive.'

In the palm of his hand Snoopy held three tiny greyish-white rocks, wrapped in a clear plastic sachet. Smoked in a pipe or heated in tinfoil, the freebase cocaine acted almost instantaneously, the euphoric high lasting up to an hour. And Snoopy should know: he had a great rush going and didn't look like coming down before lights out.

'How much?' Jones asked.

Despite his state, Snoopy's reactions weren't slow. He turned away with a lithe swivel as Malahide and Malcolm Smith came onto the wing. The officer looked round, then led the way towards the TV alcove, calling out, 'Fisher? *Fisher!*'

Startled, Alan Fisher pushed through the group watching *The Bill*, a show the cons loved because it was so hilarious. Like a video promo for the Met.

Smith took him aside. 'You've got your weekend, Alan,' he said quietly.

Fisher's face lit up like a child's on Christmas morning. 'When? Is it this month?'

'Three weeks' time. I wanted you to know.'

Fisher grabbed his hand. 'Oh, thank you, thank you very much!'

Smith patted his shoulder and turned to leave. Samora stood in his path, swaying slightly, trying hard to focus.

'I got to ask you . . . er . . .'

'What is it, Brian?' The cogs in Samora's brain weren't meshing. He kept smiling, then looking lost because he didn't know why, then smiling again because it didn't matter why. 'You said it was important,' the probation officer prompted him.

'I've lost it . . .' Samora was searching his clothing. 'Lost me paper.'

Fisher skipped across to Snoopy's side. 'I'm going out,' he whispered excitedly. *'I'm going out!'*

Snoopy looked down at him, eyes wide and goggling. 'I already am,' he burbled. 'Totally out of it.'

Gary Marshall had nipped out for a quick drag and was pacing up and down outside the Crown Court when a breathless John Bunny arrived, taking the steps two at a time. 'Is Miss Hewitt in the witness box?'

The glass door was pulled open and Malahide stuck out his blond head. 'Prosecution counsel just called her.'

Marshall took a final lungful and ground the half-smoked cigarette underfoot before following them inside. The three men slipped quietly into their seats just as Helen was coming to the end of her prepared statement. Gordon Soames had instructed her to keep it short and sweet, and she'd done just that. The prosecution counsel was anxious not to provide any hostages to fortune.

'I am satisfied that no blame for the tragic outcome of these events could be levelled at the officers on duty that night,' Helen said, speaking without notes – again at Soames's suggestion. It would create a much better impression with judge and jury if her testimony appeared to be spontaneous rather than concocted and worked over by a barrister burning the midnight oil.

'I have no further questions, my lord.' Soames seated himself with a swirl of his gown.

The judge looked towards the four defence counsels. There was silence for a few moments, and then Christina Knatchbull rose slowly to her feet, her eyes lowered to the sheaf of notes in her hand.

'May I ask your age, Miss Hewitt?'

'I am thirty-three.'

'Could you explain to the court the different governor ranks?'

Christina was starting gently, as Soames had warned Helen she would. He had also expressed the view that Helen would be more than a match for the ice maiden. The cool blue gaze and the glacial beauty were weapons in her armoury, that was quite obvious; but Helen was confident enough in her own abilities not to feel cowed or intimidated. To the rest of the court it was a fascinating contest, these two attractive and intelligent women facing one another. The usual coughs and shuffles were absent. Sitting between Malahide and John Bunny, with four Barfield officers in the row behind, Marshall was as rapt as everyone else.

Helen explained, 'Governors are scaled in ranks from five upwards. Governor One being the highest rank.'

'Which rank from one to five are you, Miss Hewitt?'

'I am Governor Three rank.'

'And how long have you been Governor Three rank?'

'Nine months.'

'So you were a Governor Four until recently taking over Barfield Prison, a Category B, all-male prison?'

'Yes, that is correct.'

Christina put down her notes and leaned forward on her fingertips. 'And before taking over the running of Barfield Prison you were Deputy Governor at Cattering Hall, an all-female prison?'

'Yes, that is correct.'

'You took over Barfield Prison after the highly publicized riot?'

Soames got to his feet, wearing a slightly pained, indulgent expression. 'May I ask my honourable friend why she feels it necessary to give details of Miss Hewitt's career, and what bearing it could possibly have on the case?'

Christina's icy demeanour melted into a smile as she addressed the judge. 'My lord, the circumstances in Barfield Prison are very important to the defence of Anthony Kelly.'

The judge gave the briefest of nods. 'You may continue, Miss Knatchbull.'

'Thank you, my lord.' She half turned, to include both the judge and the jury. 'Perhaps I should clarify the reason behind my line of questioning. Mr Kelly was placed at risk the moment he was admitted to Barfield. As Miss Hewitt is a new and very young Governor . . .'

Soames was up again. 'My lord, Miss Hewitt's professional credibility is not in question at this trial.'

'I suggest my honourable friend should read the papers,' Christina responded crisply. 'Since Miss Hewitt took over Barfield two men have escaped in a heli—'

'Very well.' The judge shooed her along. 'You may continue.'

Soames was seeking to catch Helen's eye with a look of warning. She received the message. This wasn't the expected line of questioning, and he wasn't happy with it. Helen stayed calm and composed, hands folded together at her waist as she waited patiently for the defence counsel to finish glancing through her notes.

'Miss Hewitt, how long was Anthony Kelly held at Barfield?'

'Almost two days.'

'Did you interview him?'

'No, I did not.'

'So you didn't know him at all?' Christina's immaculately shaped eyebrows were raised, her head tilted to one side.

'I knew his age, plus information regarding his crime and his sentence,' Helen said.

'But you did not actually see him on his admission?'

Helen drew herself up a little. 'Until a prisoner has been seen by the probation department and the medical staff, until I receive a full and detailed report of his needs – be they medical, educational or domestic – I let the—'

Christina spread her arms and swayed forward. 'How long does that take?' she asked, brimming with bright-eyed interest.

Helen tightened her lips. She wasn't dim enough not to know when she was being patronized. 'In Anthony Kelly's situation, perhaps two days. I would like to point out – in case you are not aware of it – each wing has its own governor, plus a senior officer, and—'

Christina cut right across her. 'I'm sorry, Miss Hewitt, but who put Anthony Kelly, a young nineteen-year-old first-time offender into a cell with two prisoners both serving long sentences for violent crimes?'

This brought an immediate objection from the counsel representing Reynolds, who leapt to his feet. 'My lord! My client's previous record has no bearing on the present case.'

'Please rephrase the question, Miss Knatchbull,' requested the judge.

She had no need to rephrase it. The question had been asked; it might be expunged from the record, but not from the minds of the jury. She referred to her notes. 'Miss Hewitt, is cell twenty-nine, D Wing, designed for two occupants?'

'Yes, it is.'

'How many occupants were allocated to cell twenty-nine, D Wing, the night Colin Foster hanged?'

'Three.'

Christina carefully turned a page and looked up. 'We have heard in court today that it is against Barfield Prison regulations to allow men to associate in their cells. We have also heard that, on the night Colin Foster died, four men were in the cell.' She glanced towards the jury. 'The deceased makes five.'

'My lord.' Soames lumbered up, irritation breaking through. 'I cannot see why Miss Knatchbull feels it necessary to repeat what has already been proved without objection.'

'Please rephrase your question, Miss Knatchbull.'

Again no need. She was winning on points. She said, 'You stated that no officer was to be blamed for the tragic events, yet surely, Miss Hewitt, they were sadly lacking in their duty that evening,' her eyes glinted coldly, boring into Helen, 'to allow five men in cell twenty-nine.'

'I'm sorry,' Helen frowned, 'what exactly is your question?'

The counsel's tone sharpened. 'Do you admit, Miss Hewitt, that there was negligence on the part of the officers on duty that night? The night Colin Foster died?'

Soames held his breath as he waited for Helen to reply. It would be tempting, and understandable, for her to react angrily to this direct accusation. He let the breath go with relief as Helen, maintaining her poise, said in a firm, even voice, 'I am satisfied there was no negligence.'

'You are satisfied?' Looking round in astonishment and back again. 'That in this cramped cell, Anthony Kelly, a nineteen-year-old boy who had never been in prison before, and only arrived the day before—'

Soames had heard enough. 'My lord, Miss Knatchbull is goading the witness.' He sat down again, giving her a hard stare.

'Please make your questions more direct, Miss Knatchbull,' the judge said, the suspicion of a sigh withheld in the dry voice.

'Why was Anthony Kelly placed in cell twenty-nine, D Wing, Miss Hewitt?'

'I had no alternative, no other accommodation available,' Helen said, trying to get the point across without raising her voice.

'May I ask you, Miss Hewitt, if you had had an alternative, would you still have delegated Mr Kelly to cell twenty-nine?'

'Not necessarily.'

'Not necessarily?' Christina echoed, as if Helen had made some startling admission. She looked across the court to where Kelly was sitting alongside his fellow defendants. Naturally enough, the eyes of the jury followed hers.

'These three men then forced Anthony Kelly to take part in a sickening trial—'

At once there were objections from the three other defence counsels, to whom the word 'forced' was like a red rag to a bull. Ignoring their protests, she steam-rollered right over them.

'—accusing the deceased of being a nonce! A nonce!' Louder now, rapping out the words above the noisy disruption along the table from her: 'Anthony Kelly only twenty-four hours earlier had never even heard the expression!'

There were cries of 'My lord,' and then a babble of voices as all the defence counsels started speaking at once. During this, Tony Fielding, QC for Wolton, got to his feet.

'My lord, there has been no proof whatsoever that my client ever used force.'

The judge waved him to be seated. He waited for the court to settle, his eyes flicking everywhere. 'The jury will please ignore the implication that force was used by the defendants.'

Still on her feet, leaning over her papers, Christina cast a mischievous look at Soames, who was tightly shaking his head.

Soberly watching all this from the witness stand, Helen had retained her calm expression throughout. To Marshall, Bunny, and the Barfield officers, she presented a model of perfect composure and quiet dignity. In the face of such blatant provocation it was a bloody marvel. Inwardly, Helen was seething. She felt she had been manipulated, that her straightforward answers had been distorted. She swallowed her anger as Christina turned to her once more.

'May I ask you, Miss Hewitt, from a humanitarian aspect, do you believe any proportion of blame can be attached to Barfield Prison?'

Helen straightened her spine. 'Miss Knatchbull, I take full responsibility for the present running of Barfield. I am trying every means possible to curb the use of drugs—'

This was an issue Christina wasn't keen to have aired. She could put a stop to it, and did. 'Thank you very much for admitting responsibility,' she interrupted, with an airy wave of her hand. 'I have no further questions, my lord.' And with a bow to the bench she sat down, a small frozen smile of triumph on her face.

It was very neatly done. The Governor was personally responsible for Barfield Prison and everything that went on there – as she had just admitted. By implication, then, the Governor herself had shouldered the blame for what had taken place in cell 29.

'No questions?' The judge looked towards the other defence counsels. He tapped his papers into line. 'This will be a suitable time to adjourn.' He nodded to the clerk, who rose to his feet.

'This court stands adjourned until ten thirty tomorrow morning.'

*

At nine o'clock that evening, alone in her office, Helen was speaking on the phone. 'If necessary, move him. Mr Gordon, I don't want Anthony Kelly harassed in any way, is that clear? Thank you.'

She replaced the phone and sat for a moment in the quiet stillness. The desktop before her was covered with letters, documents and circulars from HQ, files stacked a dozen high. Right or wrong, good or bad, every decision was down to her. She could do nothing more but give of her best, and pray to God it was good enough.

The Governor of HMP Barfield put her head in her hands.

'I take full responsibility,' Helen heard herself mumbling through clenched teeth. She jerked up, eyes hot and blazing, and with a sweep of her arm sent the whole bloody lot flying. It didn't make her feel any better. She could not think of a time when she had felt less like handling this overriding 'responsibility', because deep down she knew it had not been her fault. She had gone by the rules, she had told Bunny, and she had discussed it with Gary Marshall – so why *should* she carry the entire blame? She had not, as had been implied, acted without due caution. It was not her fault. It was not, she repeated, her fault, and she was not prepared to take any blame.

CHAPTER 26

VICTOR BRAITHWAITE was the first of the defendants to take the stand. Along with the dark suit, the neat collar and tie, his appearance had undergone a dramatic transformation. Dental work had replaced the black gap with two gleaming new teeth. Whereas before his empty smile had been a threatening grimace, he now seemed a rather ordinary, sensible sort of chap who, to his utter bewilderment, had been caught up in a series of unfortunate incidents which ended in tragedy.

He played up to this new image for all it was worth. With his counsel Julian Booth gently leading him along, Braithwaite expertly turned on the appropriate emotions – downcast, puzzled, sad, respectful, even tearful – as and when called for.

'We was all messin' around and Colin, that's Colin Foster, he was sort of the main joker. I made some remark about him being a nonce.' Victor turned to the judge, at pains to assist his lordship. 'Sex offender, sir. Anyway, Colin takes this the wrong way, he gets a bit uptight, and he says, "If I'm a nonce, you prove it." We were still jokin' – I mean, it wasn't serious, even Colin was laughin'.' Victor bent his head. He sniffed loudly, and then the tears were forced out. 'It was just a joke . . .'

Helen and Marshall, sitting together, looked at one another. If this didn't get the top Oscar, it at least merited best supporting role.

Booth waited for his client to recover. 'Did you ever refer to yourself as "the hangman"?'

Braithwaite shook his head. 'No, I did not.'

'Did you give the titles "judge", "jury" and "solicitor" to any of the other members in cell twenty-nine?'

'No, no, I did not.'

'Did you tie the deceased Colin Foster's hands behind his back?'

'No, I did not.'

'Did you assist in hanging the deceased, Colin Foster, in any way?'

'No, I did not.' Braithwaite added quietly, 'He did it himself.'

Booth faced the bench. 'I have no further questions.'

Braithwaite tensed visibly as Christina Knatchbull stood up.

'Mr Braithwaite, may I ask you how long you are presently serving at Barfield Prison?'

Braithwaite looked to his counsel. But he had no option. 'Fourteen years.'

'Mr Braithwaite, were you, on the evening of Colin Foster's death, smoking illegal substances in cell twenty-nine?'

'No, I was not,' he insisted. 'I have never in my life smoked cannabis resin or marijuana because I'm asthmatic.'

Christina Knatchbull nodded to herself, apparently making a note of something. She glanced up quickly. 'Why were you in cell twenty-nine the night Colin Foster died?'

'Um, to get some tobacco,' Braithwaite answered, thinking fast.

'But you have just stated that you did not smoke because you have asthma,' Christina said lightly, and she even smiled, which was a wonderfully adroit touch.

Watching her closely, Helen was torn between personal animosity towards the woman and professional admiration. She respected people who were good at what they did, and

Christina Knatchbull, she had grudgingly to admit, was first-rate.

Braithwaite's place in the witness box was taken by Wolton. In all its essentials, he told the same story. But he lacked Braithwaite's assurance, and the nervous darting of his eyes in his cunning ratlike face didn't help. 'He got up on the chair, just foolin' like, and then . . .' he cleared his throat, '. . . oh, yeah, I think Officer Malahide it was walked past, or somebody did – said the prison authorities was inspecting, like, and . . . er, next second, he sort of fell over or the chair toppled . . .' Wolton shrugged, palms out. 'We thought he was kiddin', his body was limp, see. It was just a joke.'

'I have no further questions,' Tony Fielding said, sitting down, relieved to have got that over with.

Braithwaite sat alongside Anthony Kelly in the dock. Facing forward, he spoke out of the corner of his mouth. 'You hearing all this, Anthony? You getting it all, Anthony?'

On Kelly's other side, also facing forward, Reynolds muttered, 'You'd better be hearin' this good, Anthony, understand me?'

Kelly stared down at his shoes, fingers digging into his knees.

'You do the right thing, son,' he heard Braithwaite say soothingly. 'We all in the same place, right?'

He clamped his mouth shut when he realized that Christina Knatchbull was staring at the three of them. She made a note before rising and turning to the witness box.

'Could I ask how long you are serving for your present sentence, Mr Wolton?'

As with Braithwaite, she hadn't mentioned or referred to his actual crime – information she was not permitted to reveal – and thus, like Braithwaite, Wolton had no choice. Still he hesitated.

The judge regarded him sternly. 'Please answer the question, Mr Wolton.'

'Five years.'

'Thank you. I have no further questions.' Christina sat down.

Next it was Harry Reynolds's turn to give his version of events. His line was that of the innocent bystander, who just happened to be there when what started out as a harmless prank went tragically wrong.

'I didn't even take any notice, I was reading,' he told his counsel, John Wilding, in a tone of innocent surprise. 'They was just messin' around, so I kept reading. Next thing, Colin, he's on the floor, then the alarm went and Mr Malahide came runnin' in. Colin didn't make a sound or call out. They was laughing one second, and then' – he threw up his hands in total astonishment – 'I was told he was dead!'

'I have no further questions, my lord.'

'Mr Reynolds,' Christina said, rising, 'could I ask you how long you were acquainted with my client before this unfortunate and tragic incident took place?'

'No more than a day and a half.'

'Thank you, Mr Reynolds.' Reynolds turned, preparing to leave the stand, when she lifted her head, palms pressed together at her breast. 'There's just one more question. Could I ask you how long you are presently serving in Barfield Prison?'

'Eleven years,' Reynolds said, hardly moving his lips. His face was rigid, a muscle twitching in his cheek.

'No further questions, thank you, my lord.'

She inclined her head to the bench and sat down. But Reynolds wasn't off the hook. Soames was on his feet, holding his gold-rimmed spectacles to his eyes as he skimmed through his notes. He removed the spectacles with a flourish and gave Reynolds a fishy-eyed stare.

'You were reading a book, they were messing around, the deceased made no sound, he did not call out, is that correct, Mr Reynolds?'

Reynolds's nod was jerky. 'Yes, like they was crackin' jokes, know what I mean?'

'I am trying to know what you mean, Mr Reynolds,' Soames retorted drily. He indicated Christina, sitting directly behind him. 'I believe Miss Knatchbull would be close to the distance to the opposite wall of your cell, would you agree?'

'Maybe,' Reynolds conceded warily.

'Maybe. Well, we'll give a few inches, but the distance is not great. It is, by any estimation, very small and claustrophobic, is it not?'

Reynolds shrugged. 'I dunno.'

'And there were five men in this small space, including yourself, is that correct?'

'Yes. It's only a double cell but they moved an extra bunk in for Kelly.'

A subdued yet persistent murmuring spread through the court. From the prosecution counsel's graphic demonstration it was now apparent how tightly confined the five men had been while the 'accidental' hanging took place. And how ludicrous was Reynolds's claim not to have been aware of what was happening. Soames pursued it, hammering home every detail with a gently sardonic world-weariness.

'And in this small, constricting and confined space, you are asking the jury to believe that a man put a noose round his own neck, tied the other end to the window bars, fell from the chair breaking his neck, and you – you, Mr Reynolds – did not see anything because you were immersed in your book?'

This brought on head-shakings and muffled snorts of laughter. The court went quiet as the judge gazed swiftly around. Christina Knatchbull found nothing to amuse her. Leaning on one elbow, writing away, she glanced up at Reynolds, who was now gripping the rail, his face flushed with the indignity of being publicly mocked. He glared down at Soames.

'I had earplugs in!'

In the dock, sullenly facing forward, Braithwaite kept up the relentless pressure: 'See, Anthony, we're all backing each other.'

'We all do it,' Wolton whispered hoarse encouragement, 'none of us will go down for it.'

Kelly felt sick. He was trembling, flinching from Braithwaite's brawny tattooed shoulder under the tight, straining suit that was only inches away from his. He shut his eyes but he couldn't shut out the voice.

'Only needs one of us to screw it up, Anthony . . . so don't even think about it.'

Christina Knatchbull displayed her ID through the grille in the iron door and a police officer opened up. He led her along to the holding cell in the basement of the Crown Court, where Anthony Kelly sat on the bed, waiting to be ferried back to Barfield for the night.

She stood for a moment, holding her bulging briefcase. The last few days had been intense and she was feeling the strain. She was tired and ready for a drink.

'Do you mind if I sit down?'

'No.'

He wouldn't look at her, which was a bad sign. She thought he trusted her, that they had established a relationship, but now he stared away from her, morose and hunched over.

Christina sat down on a hard chair, hands folded in her lap. 'Anthony, you will be in the witness box tomorrow. I want you to be very positive, tell the court exactly what you have told me.'

'So much has happened since then.' She had to lean forward to catch the hesitant, mumbled words. 'I can't remember it all . . .'

Christina waited. She watched him closely, with concern, his lips tightly pursed as if he was scared to speak. At last he said huskily, 'Every time I think about it I feel the same way, all over again. They're all lying, we were all smoking, they're lying, Miss Knatchbull.'

'Yes, I know, but you tell the truth.'

'It'll go against me, though, won't it?' He stared into the far corner. 'That I was stoned?'

Christina said quietly, 'I will have to ask you why you didn't leave the cell, Anthony.'

His chin wobbled. He gulped and his face broke down completely. 'They wouldn't let me.'

Christina stood up. She really was tired, though to all appearances as much in control and immaculately groomed as at any time throughout the long day in court. She said, 'Just remember that, Anthony, because if they had, you wouldn't be on trial for murder.'

She left him then, staring blankly into the corner of his own private hell.

The cell door had been unlocked ten minutes earlier, in good time for breakfast at seven thirty. Russell Morgan pushed it open, peering inside. 'You not up for your breakfast then, Norman?'

He went in, and didn't at first see Jones, who was crouched down by the lavatory bowl, fingers laced across the top of his head. Morgan advanced cautiously.

'You sick?'

As he bent over, Norman Jones uncoiled and in three paces he was behind Morgan, between him and the door. He pushed the door shut and leaned his back against it. His face was pale, dark, greying hair hanging over his ears. It was his eyes that terrified Morgan. They were quite blank, quite mad.

'I'm not sick,' Jones said, shaking his head.

Morgan thought about rushing him, and then thought no more about it. The sad and the bad he could deal with; the mad scared the living shit out of him. He had his whistle and baton, but he was far from certain that Jones would give him time to use either. He didn't move forward, which might have been interpreted as a threat, simply held out his hands in a gesture of reason and mute appeal. But he had grave doubts that you could reason with a fucking madman.

Jones smiled. 'Ask me nicely.' His arm stretched out and he pointed at the floor. 'Go on, down on your knees.'

Morgan was shaking his head. 'Don't do this, Norman.'

Jones continued to smile his empty smile. 'I know what you're going to do, so I want a bit of respect.' The wide blank eyes were locked on Morgan's, the voice now with a rasping edge to it. 'Get down on your knees.'

Morgan's shirt was sticking to his back. Slowly he went down on one knee, and then the other, his belly hanging over his trousers. He wet his lips. 'Please let me out of your cell, Norman.'

'My lord, certain matters have now come to light,' Christina Knatchbull said. 'As a result I now ask your leave to call Anthony Kelly.'

Sitting with Malahide, Helen watched as the young man was brought forward and escorted into the witness box by a police officer. She had expected nothing from the other defendants, no help at all from three hardened cons – and that was precisely what she'd got. But she had hopes for Kelly. There was no way he could support or lend credence to the ridiculous fabrication presented thus far to the court.

Helen was settling herself when an usher entered through the double doors. He looked round and came over, leaning towards Malahide, who was the nearest to him.

Malahide turned to Helen, his face suddenly grim. 'That bastard Norman Jones has got Mr Morgan hostage.'

'What? *Jesus.*'

Helen shouldered her bag, already moving along the row, Malahide edging after her. They hurried out.

On the witness stand Anthony Kelly was an oddly subdued figure. He stood with his arms hanging limp at his sides, dark bags under his eyes from a night of broken sleep, or perhaps no sleep at all. Mrs Kelly was finding it difficult to bear. She was bowed forward, weeping into a tissue, the comforting arm of her husband, whose eyes were on his son, round her shoulders. As in the cell the night before Anthony Kelly avoided Christina Knatchbull's gaze, answering her questions in a low, drab voice that might have issued from a robot.

'Do you smoke, Mr Kelly?'

'No, I don't.'

'On the night of your first day at Barfield Prison, were you offered any substances to smoke?'

'No, I was not.'

Christina's head went back. She blinked several times, and then tried again. 'Mr Kelly, can I just clarify – when I asked you if you were smoking substances, I was not referring to an ordinary cigarette. Now I ask you again. On the night Colin Foster died in cell twenty-nine, D Wing, were you offered any substances to smoke?'

Kelly's eyes went slowly up to find three pairs of eyes watching him from the dock. Braithwaite's mouth was a thin, straight line, chin jutting out. Either side of him, Reynolds and Wolton waited without the tiniest flicker of expression.

'No, I was not.'

Christina drew a long, deep breath. 'So you were not under the influence of any narcotics during the so-called kangaroo court held in cell twenty-nine . . .'

'No, I was not.'

She was stunned. There was nowhere to go after that. No other line to pursue. He had backed his fellow defendants all the way, which left Christina Knatchbull impotent and angry, and the case she had carefully prepared in ruins.

She listened tensely as Soames got up to cross-examine, but nothing came of it; her client wouldn't be budged, responding in the same flat, robotic drone.

'Colin took some flex out of his own pocket. He said he wasn't a nonce and he would prove it by hanging himself.'

He'd had his chance, Christina thought, and he'd thrown it away. And she knew why. One thing she wasn't sure about, and that was who she was most angry with – Anthony Kelly, herself, or the Governor of Barfield Prison, Helen Hewitt.

It took five officers, Jumbo Jackson and Andy Gordon amongst them, to subdue Norman Jones. This entailed dragging him from the cell and running him along the landing in a screw lift: two officers either side, one in front gripping him by the hair and holding his head to the floor.

By the time Helen arrived he'd been taken off the wing and was down the Block. Stripped down to his shorts, he was thrown into a padded cell, arms strapped to his sides in a restraint harness.

Her immediate concern was for Morgan. He kept saying over and over again, 'I'm okay, I'm okay,' when clearly he wasn't. He was white to the lips, body shaking, tremors coursing through his hands. The fear that all prison officers had to live with, day after day, kept under iron control, had broken through his defences. Gary Marshall had an arm around his shoulders and was talking to him in a low, soothing voice, while Helen could only stand helplessly by, feeling excluded. She was one step removed from the direct physical contact and ugly confrontation they had to deal with, protected by the prison officers who formed a shield between her and the inmates. She felt this difference keenly now, unable to share the bond, an outsider.

Morgan was nodding, endlessly repeating, 'I'm okay, I'm okay,' while Marshall walked with him along the landing and down the spiral stairway.

Helen checked the cell. There was no damage, not even any sign of a struggle. She went down to the ground floor, where Marshall awaited her. He'd sent Morgan off to the officers' rest room for a cup of tea.

Helen said, 'I'll need a full report as to how Norman Jones was able to take Mr Morgan hostage.'

Marshall barely nodded. He was shaken too, and in a foul mood. 'What's the update on the trial?'

'I left just before Kelly went into the box,' Helen said. 'I think she might get him off.' Marshall gave her a stony stare, and she held up both hands. 'He's innocent, Gary. We all know it.'

Not the way Marshall saw it. 'Up to a point. Kelly put himself in that cell. He did it when he committed his first crime.'

Helen didn't want to argue with him. And, besides, he was right.

Although anxious to return to the court, first she wanted to see what state Norman Jones was in. She had some idea the moment she came into the punishment block, hearing his animal screams and yells, his raging curses as he kicked and head-butted the padded walls of his cell. Dr Thomas was peering in through the spy-hole. Next to him stood a heavily breathing Jumbo Jackson, and Andy Gordon, massaging his skinned knuckles.

Dr Thomas stepped back, shaking his head. He wasn't altogether happy to go in there, and Helen didn't blame him.

A minute later Marshall arrived, out of breath, his jowls quivering. 'Just got a call. Anthony Kelly denied everything, smoking dope, the lot. His counsel couldn't budge him.'

Helen felt she'd been hit by a truck. '*What?*'

'Well, they got to him, didn't they?' Marshall said, wearing a sick grin. 'Stupid little bugger lied.'

'Shit!' Helen hit the wall with her fist. It hurt like hell, but she was past caring. His one chance and he'd blown it. The stupid fucker had thrown his life in the trash can.

'I'm sorry, that's bad news,' Lorcan Thomas said. 'Well, for Kelly.' He nodded to Jackson, who looked as if he was ready to break somebody, anybody, in two with his bare hands. 'Let's have another look at Norman. I've been told he needs to be sedated.'

Hearing the metal flap sliding open, Jones whipped round. He staggered, almost losing his balance, constrained in the canvas and leather harness. He stuck his head forward, the arteries standing out in his neck like fat throbbing worms, bloodshot eyes bulging. White strings of saliva hung from his mouth, matted in his hairy chest. He looked like a freak in a sideshow.

'*You seen enough?* YOU WANT SOME MORE?'

Dr Thomas closed the flap, his expression pensive, and delivered a considered opinion. 'I think we should let him cool off, wait till he comes to his senses, or not. But I'm not going in there with him. And I want that belt off him.'

'You wanna do it?' Eyebrows raised, Jackson balanced on the balls of his feet. 'You know what?' He had a helpful suggestion. 'You can do it with one of them darts they use in the zoos to knock out a rhino.'

Lorcan Thomas started to smile, until he realized that Jackson wasn't joking.

'Anthony John Kelly in his interview to the police made it plain that drugs were being smoked, that his co-defendants tried and hanged the deceased, Colin Foster, in a "kangaroo" court. Before you today, he has denied that version of events and said that Colin Foster hanged himself.' The judge paused in his summing up. His gaze moved along the two rows of the jury, lingering momentarily on each face. 'It is for you to decide if his retraction of the statement taken by Chief Inspector Dunes is now the truth. If it is capable of being believed, then he is entitled to be acquitted.'

*

It took the jury a few minutes under two hours to reach a verdict.

Marshall came hurrying from the car park just as Helen and Malahide were leaving the court house. He pushed through the throng of people and met them on the steps with a look of inquiry.

'Harry Reynolds and Steve Wolton seven years, Victor Braithwaite eleven years,' Malahide said.

'Bloody hell. What about Kelly?'

Helen walked on to her car. Christina Knatchbull emerged from the court house and rushed down the steps to catch up with her. She strode up, eyes glittering in a face of ice, as Helen opened the door. 'He's all yours for the next six years, Miss Hewitt. I hope you can live with it.'

She waited for Helen to answer, but Helen averted her face. It made Christina even more infuriated. 'Anthony Kelly was innocent. You should have protected him.' Her voice was bitter with accusation and anger. She had lost her case and that was what made her so deeply angry. She was used to the wasted lives of unfortunate youngsters like Kelly but what she was not used to was losing. When she still got no response from Helen, she strode away to her immaculate black Saab convertible. The alarm bleeped as she hurled her briefcase and files onto the back seat.

Helen watched her drive out, still standing by her own car, and then, as the car park emptied, she saw the roof of the white prison van above the high brick car-park wall. She slammed her car door and walked to the side entrance where she could see the yard exit from the court house.

By the time she got there, the first three prisoners were aboard the van. Last came Anthony Kelly. He had lost so much weight in the lead-up to the hearing that his suit hung on him, the collar of his shirt was too large and his neatly knotted old school tie formed a poignant reminder of what he had been and where he had come from.

Kelly's right hand was cuffed to an officer and Helen heard the soft 'Mind your head, son,' as Kelly stepped up to get into the van and then, as if in slow motion, he turned his head, his frightened eyes staring helplessly towards Helen. His expression was not one of accusation, of anger even, more like that of a frightened child. Then he was gone, the van passing Helen as she remained standing, head slightly bowed.

She wasn't weeping, she made no sound, but tears trickled down her cheeks as she slowly raised her head, every muscle in her body tensed, her hands clenched into fists at her sides. This was the moment that she realized quite what a daunting task she had taken on. Helen knew now that she must never depend on anyone else's assumptions or judgements. She had to rely on herself, trust in her gut feeling, and if she was unsure about anything, no matter how small, she must at all costs double, treble check, because as the Governor she could not make mistakes. When it came down to it, just as Gary Marshall had said to her curtly that day in the car, 'You are the Governor.' Helen knew that then she had not truly been the Governor, and was ashamed of her stupidity and egocentricity.

'I've failed,' she murmured. And the knowledge and weight of what she faced alone made her legs shake.

Helen sat behind the wheel of her car for several minutes summoning up the tremendous resolve it required to reach out and start it. She would have liked to sit there even longer, the rest of the afternoon perhaps. Very tempting but impossible, of course, she thought, finally turning the key. She had a prison to run.

CHAPTER 27

THE NEW HMP Barfield was nearing completion. Several months' work and the better part of sixty million pounds had brought about a transformation. Teams of contractors were still busy in two of the five accommodation wings, finishing off plastering and painting; over half the classrooms and workshops were ready for use, and the refurbished gymnasium had been fitted with a sprung pine floor.

One building, however, was still under construction. Situated at a distance from the wings, behind the exercise yards, it resembled something from a science-fiction movie: an ominous grey block of smooth-sided concrete, austere and windowless, behind its own high wall. The SSU – Special Secure Unit – was gradually taking shape.

John Bunny had taken to paying regular visits to check on how the work was progressing. The area surrounding the SSU, masked off with tarpaulins, was a mire of muddy tyre-tracks, piles of sand and stone chippings. The sounds of hammering and drilling echoed from within the cavernous building; cranes swung overhead, lifting into place entire sections of the air-conditioning system, flexible metal ducting which resembled immense silver worms.

A yellow hard hat on his balding head, trousers stuffed into green wellingtons, the Area Manager picked his way across the site to where Helen stood, arms closely folded, feeling the chill through her Burberry raincoat on this damp, drizzly morning.

'Have they given you an exact date?' Helen asked.

'The Secure Unit will be completed on schedule.' It was a sensitive subject, and he wasn't keen to discuss it. With the long catalogue of Prison Service cock-ups over the past year and a half (Whitemoor and Parkhurst being the most notorious examples), the management structure was feeling the strain. It was under attack from all quarters, and any suggestion that Barfield wouldn't meet its completion deadline – after the vast amount spent on it – made John Bunny prickle with defensive irritation.

For once this wasn't Helen's problem. She had been busy with the organizational side of things, recruiting new officers and appointing heads of the various departments. All of which was nearly in place. The bricks and mortar, installing the new high-security systems, getting the plumbing to function – that was up to HQ and the likes of John Bunny.

They went towards the chain-link fencing sheeted over with tarpaulins. Bunny ploughed grimly through the mud in his wellingtons while Helen kept to the wooden planking, stepping carefully past the pools of stagnant water. Yells and shouts of 'Goal! Goal!' from a five-a-side football match floated over from the exercise yard of C Wing.

'Security still a hazard though, isn't it?' Helen said. 'So – any truth in the rumour we may be privatized?'

She couldn't resist teasing him, though Bunny failed to show even a glimmer of amusement at her mischievous suggestion.

'It's exactly that, Miss Hewitt, just a rumour. Barfield has cost the government too much money to let it go to private contractors.'

Smiling to herself, Helen led the way through the gate. A large sign, big as a billboard, had been erected on concrete posts:

WARNING – NO ENTRY

ALL PERSONNEL MUST
CARRY IDENTIFICATION
BEYOND THIS POINT

Helen said, 'I would have thought that was the reason to recoup the losses.' She marched on, giving him a parting shot over her shoulder. 'I'd keep the hard hat on, Mr Bunny – suits you!'

There was a hectic air about the prison today. A new batch of officers had arrived, along with some recently appointed educational and recreational staff. They assembled in the large committee room on the ground floor of the admin block for an introductory briefing: forty people altogether including the wing governors, chief officers, and the management team directly responsible to the Governor, Helen Hewitt. The model of the prison was in the middle of the table, with several piles of information packs in plastic covers.

Gary Marshall got the proceedings under way. 'Ladies and gentlemen, would the new personnel sit in the front seats.'

Zania Tullbrooke, the new education officer, and two other women, made their way forward. The door opened and the room went so quiet you could have heard a pin drop. With Helen leading the way, in trooped a dozen officers, immaculate in brand-new uniforms. All of them were young and well-built, over six feet tall, and all were black. While Helen took a seat next to Marshall, they filed into the front row and sat down. A low-pitched buzz swept the room.

Russell Morgan was standing in a group near the back. 'Bloody hell,' he murmured under his breath, giving a look at Jumbo Jackson and Andy Gordon. The Governor didn't believe in letting the grass grow under her feet. Changes were happening thick and fast.

With a nod from Helen, Marshall started by introducing himself. 'Deputy Governor Gary Marshall, HOC, Head of Custody.' The room quietened once more as he pointed to the model. 'These two wings, C and D, the Segregation Block and the VP Wing are now secure until this section wall is reopened to the new wings. Control unit here, and this is the new maximum secure unit . . .'

The old hands amongst them realized the significance of this. The SSU was purpose-built to house Category A prisoners – those who were 'highly dangerous to the public or police or the security of the State'. With the opening of the new unit, Barfield would never be the same again. Its status would be changed and category upgraded to deal with and securely contain the most powerful, daring and ruthless criminals in Britain.

Helen rose and surveyed the crowded room. 'As you must all be aware, the rebuilding has advanced somewhat in the past months, but until the new security system is fully operational we still have major "at risk" areas.' Reading from her notes she went on, 'We will also be expecting a new HHC – Head of Health Care – and a full-time doctor in residence.'

Helen looked up. A handsome, dark-haired woman in her early thirties, very poised and graceful, had just entered the room. Apparently oblivious to the stares her late arrival had caused, she sailed confidently forward.

'Ah,' Helen said, 'and Miss Collins will be the resident psychologist and drama coach.'

'The staff car park is a bit hazardous this morning.' Maureen Collins rather grandly extended her hand to shake Helen's. 'Sorry if I kept everyone waiting.'

Helen returned the handshake with a smile that was

polite rather than heartfelt. She said, 'You didn't, but I'm sure you'll catch up.'

With the transfer of Anthony Kelly from D to C Wing, a strange and rather sinister change had occurred. It was as if he had undergone a rite of passage. Jumbo Jackson noted it the moment the young man arrived on the wing, wearing a T-shirt, track-suit bottoms and black Puma trainers. There was definitely a bit of a swagger to him. And it wasn't a new phenomenon to Jackson: he'd seen it before – young, first-time offenders who once jumped at their own shadows gradually shedding their fear, growing an outer skin of surly insolence and aggression as the prison regime seeped into their pores. Kelly was infected by it, a prime candidate; Jackson could see the transformation taking place in front of his eyes.

'Should never have brought him back to Barfield,' he told Russell Morgan darkly, shaking his head. The men were lining up for lunch, holding their trays.

Morgan gave a so-what-else-is-new? shrug. 'Well, they did, and we got to deal with him.' As always, it was the prison officers who got the shitty end of the stick.

Kelly was laughing loudly, acting the goat. Norman Jones, back from the punishment block, was behind him, a glowering, taciturn presence until the next time the faulty circuit snapped in his brain and he blew a fuse.

'Come on, get moving, stop the nattering!' Jackson called out.

Kelly shot the big, bearded officer a sour look and held out his tray for a dollop of mashed potatoes. 'You got six for protectin' a nonce!' Jones sneered softly in his ear.

Kelly tried to act tough. 'I got six for doin' a nonce in!' he bragged, as if he'd been talking that way all his life.

Jones gave a hollow, mocking laugh. 'Oh, yeah! Big boy now, are you? And you didn't hear me right. Victor was the nonce, you protected a nonce. He's back on D Wing. You want some advice?'

They moved off with their trays. Kelly stayed with Jones, watching him closely, listening.

'You seem to be tryin' to get some credit. You have to deal with Victor.' Jones raised an eyebrow, nodding. 'He owes you . . .'

Alan Fisher came up to the trolley, smiling his thanks to the orderly who dished out his grub. Morgan raised a finger. 'Fisher, you got to report to the probation department this afternoon.'

'Eh!' Fisher's gentle smile turned into a huge beaming grin. 'You think I'd forgot?'

'It's finally come through,' Morgan said to Jackson.

'What?'

'He's got a home leave.'

Dr Thomas held up the hypodermic syringe. Five pairs of dulled eyes watched him. Every week he gave his lecture to a group of addicts in the medical room of the hospital wing. The men were all in their twenties, shaggy-haired and unshaven, habitual users of anything they could get their hands on or that phonecards could buy.

'So if you have to use it, sterilize it. Better still, don't bloody use it.' Dr Thomas looked round the five seated zombies. Was any of this penetrating, or was it solely to appease his own liberal conscience? With a sigh he placed the syringe in a metal tray. 'Okay, that's all for this morning.'

The men got lethargically to their feet. 'Come on, lads, move it.' An officer beckoned to them. 'Back to the wing.'

On the way out they passed Helen coming in, giving four of the new recruits a guided tour. Lorcan Thomas came forward as Helen brought them in.

'Dr Thomas, this is John Udding, he's been working in Liverpool. Mr Tucker, Mr Leonard, and Mr Brittain.'

They shook hands all round.

'Look at this.' Dr Thomas picked up the syringe with a sorrowful shake of the head. 'I don't know how they're going to sterilize it. The rubber at the end of the plunger has disintegrated completely through constant use.' He held it up for them to see. 'Instead of a rubber washer they're using a small strip of black polythene from a dustbin liner, wrapped and held in place by a piece of cotton thread.'

Sighing, he went to the sink to scrub his hands. Helen gathered them round. 'It's madness, isn't it? I'm not allowed to supply needles, so all we're trying to do is teach them to sterilize the ones they somehow bring in. I've had sniffer dogs, cell searches, and the stuff is still getting in.'

Dr Thomas dried his hands on a paper towel. 'I've got to get to my surgery.' He slipped out of his white coat and reached for his jacket.

John Udding had experience with drug users and had worked on rehabilitation programmes. 'Is crack here yet?' he asked, looking from Helen to Dr Thomas. 'That really causes problems.' He indicated his thumbnail. 'That amount can be cut as much as twenty, thirty times. The craving is virtually instantaneous and results in aggression and violence because it's so highly addictive.'

Lorcan Thomas looked at Helen, rolling his eyes. 'That's not coming in here as well, is it?'

The party passed through the gates into the corridor. One of the officers on duty in the observation booth came out and locked up behind them.

Moving ahead, Helen kept up a running commentary. 'HQ's new ruling is any inmate found taking drugs or having them in his possession gets an immediate twenty-one days added to his sentence. Some nicks are operating drug-free zones. When we are fully operational I would like to put them into practice here.'

'You mean the days of "Welcome to the Kasbah" finito, then?' Dr Thomas said with a grin.

They passed through another set of gates into the main

linking corridor. Coming towards them, Marshall was escorting another half dozen or so recruits, Zania Tullbrooke and Maureen Collins among them.

He signalled to Helen. 'Just taking my group over to the education section.'

Helen nodded, her attention distracted by Lorcan Thomas, who wasn't in such a flaming hurry to get to his surgery that he couldn't spare a few moments to chat to Zania Tullbrooke. Already the petite, exceedingly attractive girl was smiling, introducing him to the two female members of the education department.

Christ, did he never let up?

Helen and her group fell into step with the others. 'I'm catching up,' Maureen Collins said behind her, and when Helen turned the psychologist gave her a languid smile. 'Very impressive.'

Very impressive? Helen thought with a scowl, marching on. *Very impressive?* What was that, a pleasantry, a compliment, or a put-down?

Or just her jungle instinct that a rival female had appeared on the scene?

Malcolm Smith pushed the small stack of documentation across the table. Rail timetable, National Coach timetable, rail pass, bus pass, a warrant with HMP Barfield letterhead identifying the holder as Fisher, Alan, on home leave for a specified period. In addition there were release forms to be completed by the probation officer, countersigned by the Governor, and forms to be filled in and signed by Fisher.

Smith dropped a brown envelope on top of the pile. 'You also requested three months' pay, Alan.'

'Yes, sir, to buy my daughters and wife something.' He blinked behind his glasses, adding with quiet pride, 'I've been saving, kept only a pound for myself.'

'It's all there, Alan, but you can count it if you like.'

Nervously, Fisher laid the crisp new ten- and five-pound

notes on the table one by one. The sight of so much money thrilled him, filling him with wondrous visions of what it could buy. Prices had risen, he knew that, of course, so perhaps wise not to be too premature. After all, he hadn't been inside a shop in fourteen years.

The bright, airy corridor smelled of fresh paint and there was hardly a scuff mark on the dark green composition floor. Narrow slit windows, barred on the outside, let in beams of sunlight. The opposite wall consisted of large glass panels to waist height which would allow patrolling officers an open view of the classrooms. For the moment the classrooms were empty. Some contained desks, wall-length blackboards and cork boards for posters; others had rows of computer terminals and laser colour printers, all of it brand spanking new.

'Oh, this is fantastic!' Zania Tullbrooke enthused, peering in. 'Are the rooms soundproofed?'

'Yes.' The group pressed forward as Helen pointed out the features. 'Each section can accommodate fourteen, so classes can be conducted back to back without being disturbed. We have eight computers and word processors per wing.'

Marshall unlocked the big yellow-barred gates and waited for them to pass through. The new officers, Zania and the education staff, even Maureen Collins, were all nodding, quite clearly impressed. As for him, he didn't reckon much to their zeal and enthusiasm. This was a prison, not a bloody holiday camp. Next they'd be opening up saunas and massage rooms, booking the inmates in for jacuzzis and sunbeds.

'Art department, sewing section with four machines . . .' Helen gestured to the large empty rooms, freshly plastered and yet to be painted. Electrical wiring waiting to be connected trailed from the walls. Closed-circuit security cameras were installed high up in the corners.

'This is not finished, but it will be the music section. We'll have numerous instruments, and the area over there has been earmarked to build a recording studio.'

At the back of the group, Marshall was adding his own lugubrious footnotes to Helen's commentary. 'Only needs one of 'em to blow and there's a few hundred grand down the toilet.' He walked on, muttering to himself. 'They got one each – toilet – per cell!'

Helen ignored him. At the next set of gates the group clustered round as she explained the new high-tech security system. 'All corridors and main open areas are monitored' – she pointed out the cameras – 'plus a central locking system controlled from the MS2D operations room.' She unlocked the heavy gate and heaved it open. 'Still require keys, but they reckon the cameras will add to security.'

'My personal opinion,' Marshall chipped in, 'is when the inmates see them we'll get a few Des O'Connor impersonations and a lotta aggravation.'

'Miss Collins?' The psychologist was lingering behind, and with a tight smile and a sweep of the hand Helen ushered her through.

If the classrooms had brought appreciative nods, the vast gymnasium with its high ceiling and new pine floor would have made any Olympic athlete green with envy. Exercise cycles, rowing machines, step-up and electronic striders were ranged in rows, along with multi-exercise butterfly benches and barbells for full body workouts. There were benches with weighted pulleys for dips, squats and leg curls. Two cubicles equipped with padded couches, weighing machines and aerobic meters provided physiotherapy and fitness testing.

The group stood in the centre of the polished floor, gazing around, while Helen's voice echoed in the huge space.

'The gymnasium section is not in use yet but, as you can see, it's fully equipped, plus indoor squash courts, netball, and so on. The new outdoor astro-turf football pitch plus two larger exercise yards will not be in use until the prison is officially opened.'

Marshall waggled a thumb at the cubicles. 'If they twist a muscle they can put their name down for a physiotherapy session.' He gave them a heavy-lidded look. 'Remind you of a health farm yet?'

Maureen Collins pivoted on her heel, surveying the ranks of machines with a frown. 'Not in use yet? Bit of a waste, isn't it?' she objected. 'If it's finished, why not—'

'The security isn't, Miss Collins,' Helen said, with saccharine sweetness. She pointed to the far corner where two technicians on movable scaffolding were installing the closed-circuit cameras.

The psychologist gave them a passing glance and made no further comment. Which was just as well, because Helen didn't take kindly to being lectured, especially by her own staff.

CHAPTER 28

MARSHALL WASN'T small exactly, though he appeared so next to John Udding as they came onto C Wing. The new officer wasn't only tall, he had a pair of shoulders on him broad as a barn door. His uniform shirt emphasized his build, its crisp whiteness in startling contrast to his dark handsome face.

Marshall rapped on the window of the officers' station where Morgan was sipping a brew and Malahide had the *Sun* open at the sport pages. The two men stood up as Marshall entered.

'Mr Morgan and Mr Malahide, this is John Oooden.'

Udding corrected him with an easy smile. 'Yew-ding.'

'Mr *Yew-Ding* is with you, Russell,' Marshall said with exaggerated care. He turned to go.

'There was a call for you, Gary, hospital . . .' Malahide called after him.

'Somethin' up?'

'No, your wife.'

'Ah, gotcha.' Marshall clicked his fingers. 'Thanks.'

Morgan followed him to the gates. 'Wife all right, is she?'

'No.' Marshall twisted the key in the lock. Morgan didn't pursue it. Instead he nodded over his shoulder.

'Right now we're bloody overrun with officers.'

'If you think Oooden, Odden, *Yew-ding* is a big bloke, wait till you see the others,' he said, going off.

Malcolm Smith came down the stairway with Alan

Fisher, accompanied by an officer. The probation officer carried a thick wadge of files, which he handed over to Morgan, who stood aside to let them through. As they set off along the corridor Morgan gave a thumbs-up and shouted, 'You take care, Alan – and for God's sake don't miss the train back!'

Fisher ducked round with his shy grin and a little wave.

Morgan locked up and beckoned Udding to him for a walkabout. He wanted to check out the new fella for size – though the size of him, in the strict sense of the word, was all too apparent. With the men all banged up, the association area was empty. They strolled down the wing, Udding casting an eye over the cell cards in the slots beside each door.

'Any I should be extra wary of?' he asked, keeping his voice down. Sound travelled and ears were listening.

At least he knew that much, Morgan thought. They went onto the upper landing. 'Cell forty-seven, kid called Kelly, he got a six on top of his sentence.' He slid the flap aside.

Anthony Kelly looked up from the table where he was writing a letter, staring back at the eyes observing him through the spy-hole.

'I reckon he might want to hurt himself,' Morgan said, moving on, 'so we got him next to one we're very wary of – keep an eye on them both.'

After his recent experience Morgan had good reason to be wary of Norman Jones, who lowered the *Playboy* he was reading as Udding peered in. Casually he ran a hand through his hair, and even that simple action seemed insolent and threatening.

'Roddy Marsh,' Morgan said, gesturing to the cell at the end. 'He's always checked through the night.' He pulled a face. 'It's just started, self-mutilator, and a bad 'un.'

Udding nodded, making mental notes as they walked on.

'All in the wing report book,' Morgan said, leading the way down.

'You're going out on trust, Alan, and you know the rules. I'm sorry you had to wait so long, but the new Home Office ruling requires a lot of paperwork.' Until the next new Home Office ruling – and the one after that, Helen thought – which would require even more. They seemed to change their minds twice a week and change them back again the week after.

Fisher stood in front of the desk, nervously rubbing his hands. 'We will accept no excuses if you are not back at Barfield before ten o'clock Sunday evening,' Helen warned him sternly.

'I will be, Governor, I know how important it is. I'll lose my parole date and the possible transfer to an open prison nearer home.' He smiled anxiously, eager to demonstrate he was taking this very seriously. 'I wouldn't be stupid enough to foul it up.'

Helen's instinct told her she could trust him; she prayed she could trust her instinct too.

Paperwork finalized, interviews with the probation officer and the Governor over, one final stage remained in the long and complicated procedure leading up to an inmate's home leave: being processed through Reception.

Down to his boxer shorts and socks, Fisher stood at the counter while Andy Gordon brought his brown cardboard box from storage. The box was like a time capsule: the clothing it contained hadn't been in fashion since Margaret Thatcher became Prime Minister and beer was fifty pence a pint. When Gordon took the lid off there was a smell of mildew.

'Right, Fisher, grey suit, brown shoes, white shirt, tie.'

The officer laid them on the counter. The suit was cheap polyester with thin lapels and frayed cuffs, and the narrow trousers had deep turn-ups. The shoes were an awful pair of brown Hush Puppies, badly scuffed and shiny in patches. The tie was a wrinkled green strip, two inches wide, with orange ships' anchors on it.

'Looks a bit creased,' Gordon sniffed, holding it up critically. 'I dunno, goin' out to see the wife and kids lookin' like a dosser . . .'

Fisher's face fell. With his short back and sides plastered to his head and neatly parted, and his owlish spectacles, he looked like a timorous schoolboy He said glumly, 'How much would a new one set me back?'

'You mean like this?' From under the counter Gordon brought out a fancy floral tie in a Cellophane box. He removed the lid. 'Well, at least twenty quid, right?' He appealed to one of the other officers. 'Maybe more.'

'Twenty quid.' Fisher gazed at the tie and fingered it longingly. 'Hardly got more'n that for the whole weekend, mate.' He sighed, shaking his head. 'Twenty quid?'

Gordon's straight expression cracked in a smile. 'It's yours, you great clod! Go on, we had a whip round for you!'

Fisher's face was a picture of confusion. Blinking, he looked from the tie to Gordon and back again, and then round at the smiling officers.

'Not all screws are bastards, Fisher. Go on . . .' Gordon presented him with the box. Then he held up the old wrinkled tie between thumb and finger. 'And use this one to tie up your pants, you got no belt.'

By chance, Helen saw him leaving. She was up in the central control room with its large horseshoe-shaped desk and banks of monitor screens. Three technicians in white overalls were running a test on the new surveillance system, switching between cameras, and there he was, stepping through the door in the main gate, a slight and insubstantial figure in his pitifully shabby grey suit.

A bit lost and confused, he moved hesitantly from beneath the shadow of the high walls. After a few paces he turned to look back at them. His colourful floral tie blazed out like a beacon.

Helen smiled, pleased for him and charmed. 'Have a nice weekend, Mr Fisher.'

Morgan opened the door of the classroom and waved the eight prisoners forward. 'In you go, sit at the desks. No talking, just file in and sit down.'

John Udding brought up the rear. Standing at the door with Morgan, the two of them watched the men, silently awestruck, take in their surroundings. Everything gleamed, clean and new, not a speck of dust anywhere. Some of the computer consoles even had the manufacturer's label still stuck to them.

Not the only shock. Zania Tullbrooke's arrival caused more raised eyebrows and nudges. Wearing a tailored jacket and a pale yellow blouse that set off her smooth dark skin beautifully, her long hair swept back and held by a matching ribbon, she appeared as a vision with her bright vivacious smile and bouncy confidence.

'Hi, this the first section?' she greeted Udding.

'This is Senior Officer Russell Morgan,' Udding introduced them. 'Zania Tullbrooke, assistant in the education department.'

'You're their education officer?' Morgan was grinning fit to bust. 'Well, soon as the word gets out you'll have this place bulging at the seams. Zania, is it?' he asked, eyeing her up and down. 'You'll be assessed, all right.'

The heads of the men turned in unison as Zania moved to her desk at the front of the class. Brian the Scouser nudged the bloke next to him and made an I-couldn't-half-give-her-a-good-going-over gesture with a locked elbow, fist like a piston. Dumping her files down, Zania faced the ogling class. She wasn't stupid; she knew what they were all thinking – officers included. She glanced through the glass panels to the three of them on duty in the corridor, watching with interest and covert smirks, wondering how this petite, gorgeous young woman was going to handle such a horny bunch.

'Okay, first let me get to know who each of you are—'

'I'd like to know you, sweetheart,' Brian growled, flicking his tongue, getting a few cheap laughs.

They died instantly as Zania's cool gaze raked over them.

'And I want you all to know right from the start that I will take no sexist remarks, no racist remarks. You are here to be educated. If you want to waste your time and my time you will be out. Is that understood?'

The men sat still as rocks in dead silence.

'I know some of you are hoping to take Open University degrees, and that due to the closure of this department you are behind in your studies,' Zania said, sorting through her files. A mumble started at the back, and her pointing finger was like a poisoned dart.

'Will you stop talking? *You!*'

Malahide unlocked the upper-landing doors on D Wing, getting the inmates assembled for their exercise period. Two officers waited at the top of the caged spiral stairway, ready to escort them down.

'Come on, get a move on,' Malahide said impatiently. 'Stop rappin', Snoopy.'

The tall Rasta came boogying along the landing, dreadlocks swinging. 'I hear one of my brothers is on your team, boss. That true?'

Malahide turned on him. 'Get down to the association area and shut up.'

'Hey, man, what is it with you?' Snoopy protested, but all he got in return was a glare. He scuttled down.

On the lower landing, Zachary Tucker, one of the new recruits, was opening up and moving them out. Malahide came down the stairway, keys jangling, and stood watching as the men lined up. He beckoned Tucker over. 'The big guy up front, Victor Braithwaite, he's to be watched. He got an eleven on top of his life so he's not a happy man.'

Braithwaite noticed he was being talked about. He stared brazenly at Zach Tucker and yelled out, 'Oi, Malahide! They lettin' the coons in now, are they? Thought I could smell somethin' on the wing.'

Snoopy whirled round. 'You big bastard, Braithwaite.' He was seething. 'You'll get what you deserve.'

'I guess you're used to it,' Malahide said to Tucker.

'Guess I am. What you say his name was?'

'Victor Braithwaite.'

The two officers moved past the line of men. The new security system was now functioning, with two cameras trained on the entrance. As a double safeguard, the two sets of gates were operated both electronically from the control room and by an officer with keys.

'Four of them strung up an inmate – hanged him,' Malahide muttered, putting Tucker in the picture. 'Trial must have cost half a million quid. They got legal aid and my mother can't get it to take her bastard landlord to court.'

He looked up to the camera, pressed the gate release and stepped back. Nothing happened. The inmates were shuffling about, getting restless at the delay.

'What's the hold-up?' Tucker asked with a frown.

Malahide gave a weary shake of the head. The system was up but it wasn't damn well running. Just the kind of situation that had the potential for trouble, men milling around, edgy and impatient. He looked up to the camera. 'Delta Wing for exercise yard.'

Seconds went by, and finally there was a whirring and a clunk as the electronic bolts shot back.

''Bout bloody time,' Malahide grumbled, turning his key in the second lock. He pushed open the gate. 'Walk on, come on, keep moving.'

The men shuffled forward, Malahide counting them silently as they passed through.

Maureen Collins had a dual role, as psychologist and drama coach. She had strong opinions about both, and she wasn't backward in expressing them. Helen discovered this quickly as they sat in Helen's office, sifting through the lists of prisoners who had put their names down for counselling and therapy. This was a programme that covered every kind of personal and social problem, from drug misuse and sexual offending to relaxation sessions, anger management and other dysfunctional behaviour.

'I've usually worked with the probation department, as a lot of insight comes out of the improvisation sessions. There is one thing I think I should make clear from the outset. I like as little interference as possible. The group usually functions better if they feel they're not being monitored.'

Helen could live with that. She nodded, though she wasn't entirely sure what Maureen had in mind. Drama to Helen in this context meant role-playing, or one-act plays maybe. Improvising with this lot could end up with some of the head cases swinging bollock-naked from the helicopter wires. She said, 'I agree, but I suggest you also draw in some of the officers to interact in the improv— er, productions.'

'I'm not averse to that,' Maureen granted airily.

Helen's smile was brittle. 'I'm glad you're not. We've had a lot of new students sign on for the education department but I think that's because of the glamorous Zania Tullbrooke. Not too many signed up for your drama group.' She laughed suddenly, hand over her mouth. 'Sorry, that sounded awful. Right, anything else?'

'No, I think I've covered everything.' Maureen rose up and drifted rather than walked to the door. She had a dancer's grace and fluidity of movement, though it did seem a bit arch and self-admiring. 'Thank you,' she said, politely distant, and departed.

Helen stared at the closed door for a moment. Jury definitely still out on that one, she decided. She'd seen a bit of a mirror image of herself. Maureen was as confident as Helen had been. Perhaps that was the wrong word to use because Helen was still hanging on to that layer of self-confidence; if she lost it, then she might as well pack it all in. No, it was, she surmised, simply that perhaps Miss Collins had not had so many knocks or emotional setbacks as she had. Maybe she would also like Helen to take them on the chin and come back fighting – but, there again, maybe she would not. Only time would tell.

With all the inmates of D Wing in the exercise yard, it was a good opportunity for John Udding and Zach Tucker to check out who was who. They wandered off separately, keeping their eyes and ears open. One end of the yard had been screened off with large green tarpaulin sheets, and several men had clustered there, taking turns to peer curiously through a small gap.

Udding strolled over. Snoopy spotted him and his face lit up in a big beaming smile. 'Hey! Man, am I glad to see you! We need all the brothers we can get on our side in here. Put it there!' He jigged over, hand out flat, fingers splayed. 'Can you get me back on C Wing? Braithwaite – aggravation – know what I mean?'

'See what I can do.' Udding brought his palm down slap on Snoopy's, but then took Snoopy's hand in a fierce grip. 'Just one thing . . . I'm not your brother.'

'I'm with you, that's cool,' Snoopy said uncertainly, his hand still gripped. 'We got to maintain an advantage, we got to help each other.' Udding let go and Snoopy backed off, his smile faltering. 'Right on, chill out, huh?'

Brian Samora was bent over, squinting through the gap in the tarpaulin. 'It's a swimming pool, any money on it.

Hey, Walter, have a look at this, what you think it is out there?'

Brinkley took a sken. He hadn't a clue. Never seen a building like it before: ominous grey cube of a thing, smooth and featureless, with not a single window. It gave him a chill.

'I dunno, nuclear bunker, maybe . . .'

'What?' Samora exclaimed, stunned by the idea. 'What they want a nuclear bunker here for?' He elbowed somebody aside who was trying to push in. 'Gerroff, I was here first.' He put his eye to the gap and goggled. It was the first nuclear bunker he'd ever seen.

The simple act of boarding a bus threw Alan Fisher into his first panic. There was no conductor. Instead the driver was looking up at him expectantly as Fisher stood there, dithering.

'Where to?'

'Er . . . railway station.'

'Twenty-five pence.' Fisher stared at him stupidly. The driver pointed. 'Slot it in there.'

Fisher reached for the money and then remembered he had a bus pass. More fumbling, feeling himself going red, acutely conscious that the half-dozen or so passengers were watching him. He showed the pass and was startled when the ticket zipped out. Then he jumped as the doors hissed shut behind him with a thump. The bus moved off. Clutching his ticket, Fisher swayed down the aisle and sank gratefully into a seat, his heart hammering.

He'd dreamed of this day for a long, long time, but he'd never imagined it would be like this. He felt naked and vulnerable, as if he'd shed a skin: every sight, every sound, every sensation like a painful dart striking right to the sensitive core of him.

He sat huddled within himself, nervously fingering his tie, and stared wide-eyed out of the window at the fields and hedgerows. Because that was the most remarkable thing of all. The scenery was actually *moving*.

Waiting in the supper line-up on D Wing, Braithwaite leaned back to the man behind him, a big goofy grin on his face.

'I signed up for classes, half the wing has. You should see the notice board, it's like jammed with names!' He thrust out his lips and made a wanking gesture. 'Be a lot of that tonight.'

Further down the line, Lennie Allroyd had done some jostling to get in behind Snoopy. Allroyd was from Brixton, a small, wiry West Indian who always wore a brightly coloured woolly hat pulled low over his eyes.

'You got any more gear?'

'No, man, nothin' till next visit,' Snoopy mumbled, eyes dreamy and heavy-lidded.

Allroyd was suspicious. 'But you had one today – you said you was scorin' big, man.'

'Concentratin' on the liquor. It's comin' in twice a week.'

Allroyd didn't know whether or not to believe him. Then he decided for sure. The guy was always stoned out of his skull, and it wasn't just hooch that got him so high.

The orderly started dishing out their food as Braithwaite moved off with his tray. He looked back with a nasty grin, always the shit-stirrer. 'Hey, Rasta, I'm going to cut your dreadlocks.' He winked heavily. 'Enjoy your dinner . . .'

Snoopy stared after him. He looked down at the food on his tray. Even if there was nothing in it – no powdered glass or toenail clippings or turds – he couldn't eat with any real enjoyment any more. He moved away from the trolley, Allroyd by his side, watching the swaggering Braithwaite mount the spiral stairway.

'Kelly wants that bastard hit, ask around.' Snoopy was breathing hard, his hands tightly gripping the tray. 'Be cash and easy if he's pissed. It'll cost but be worth it.' He glanced down at Allroyd, eyes suddenly wide and alert. 'I need the whole wing legless, man. Victor's like an ox, know what I mean?'

John Udding came through the gates. He caught the eye of Zach Tucker, overseeing the supper line, and beckoned him over.

'Dreadlocks' cell. When was it last stripped?'

'I dunno, why?'

The two officers clammed up as Snoopy and Allroyd went past towards the stairway. Then Udding said quietly, 'Got a white slip, says your Rasta's dealin'. Tell your SO.'

Tucker nodded, but something was bothering him. The white slips were anonymous tip-offs from the inmates. Sometimes they were used maliciously to get at other cons or to even scores, but now and then they provided useful information. What bothered him was that Udding was not following the usual procedure: bringing the tip-off himself directly from C Wing to D Wing was bypassing his own senior officer. What was he after, brownie points?

Malahide and Udding hadn't exchanged more than a couple of words since the new officer arrived. But they got to the point of nearly swapping punches as well as words in the officers' rest room. It had blown up out of nothing – at least, nothing on the surface, but there was something so fundamentally different in temperament and approach within each man that it riled the other, brought out the two extremes in a bitter stand-off.

Malahide thought the new man was throwing his weight about, trying to prove that he knew best. Udding just thought that Malahide was a racist and a thick Yorkshireman, in that order.

'I got the wrong attitude?' Malahide said, incredulous and angry, hitting himself in the chest, when really he wanted to smack Udding one right in his handsome black chops.

'I reckon so.' Udding was playing it cool. Losing your

temper meant you were losing the argument. 'Works both ways, you prefer to do duty in one of the old run-down places, or, like here, we get to use the facilities as well. So everyone benefits, makes for a better atmosphere.'

'And you'd know all about that, would you?' Malahide was nodding and grinning, eyes cold and blue.

'I know a hell of a lot more than you,' Udding said calmly.

'You tip off that Rasta we were going to do a strip-search? Is that how you're working it?'

Now it was coming out. This big blond oaf was as subtle as a bag of cement. 'You want to make this personal?' Udding asked, even quieter. 'You saying I'm showing favours to blacks because I'm one? That what you're saying?'

'What I'm saying is there's a lot more of us—'

At that moment it didn't seem to be the case, because Zach Tucker and four other black officers walked in. Malahide's face tightened, but he refused to be intimidated. He jabbed his finger. '*You* got the wrong attitude, mate. You think the cons are sent here for a bloody holiday!'

Udding didn't react when he saw Helen, arms folded, leaning in the doorway. Malahide had his back to her. He was bristling with pent-up anger.

Udding went on, 'Their punishment, man, is being sent down, loss of freedom, full stop.' He was needling Malahide, but he also meant what he said.

'Oh, yeah? Your sister gets raped, how do you feel about him comin' in here – takin' friggin' music lessons – gettin' stoned from your Rasta pals?'

His fists were bunched, and he was ready to swing. He looked round sharply as Helen said, 'Is this a private bout or can anyone throw a punch?'

Malahide stared at her for a moment, biting his lip. 'It was private, Governor. Excuse me.' He went straight out, not looking at anyone.

Helen had a white slip in her hand. She raised her eyebrows. 'You wanted to see me about this?'

'Somebody on our wing gave the tip-off a Rasta was dealin' on D Wing, but . . .'

'But?'

'Could be a racial thing,' Udding said.

'Racial?' Helen looked towards the black officers who were helping themselves to coffee. 'The whole point of the white slip box is that the complainant can remain anonymous. So it could have been written by a black prisoner.'

Udding conceded the point. He turned to the board on which the photos and details of the inmates were posted, and tapped Snoopy's picture. 'Said he's dealing . . .'

'I'll look into it,' Helen promised him.

'I think you should look into Mr Malahide.'

Helen drew back. She said curtly, 'I did overhear your conversation, Mr Udding. I want no racial tension between my officers.' She hoped he got her meaning: racism was a two-way street. It wasn't only blacks who could be victimized. She went to the door, intending to leave it at that, but then had another thought.

'You said that the loss of freedom was the prisoners' punishment. I used to think like that but I've changed my mind. Loss of freedom is not enough.'

Udding had misread her, and the surprise showed in his face. The odd thing was that Helen had surprised herself too. Until this minute, articulating it, she hadn't realized that her attitude had changed. Six months ago she would have agreed with John Udding, but not any more. It shook her. Was she being sensible and realistic, at last seeing things as they were, or had the iron entered her soul? She gave him a soft smile, almost apologetic. 'Maybe that didn't quite come out the way I meant it to but, that said, I have changed many of my views on the prison system. They're not quite formed yet but I'm working on it. It all takes time. Nothing happens overnight.'

He nodded, unsure exactly what she was implying, but she seemed wrapped in her own thoughts as she gave another of her lovely smiles and walked out.

The iron was not in her soul, or in her heart. It never would be. What was creeping in was a firmer, stronger view of the interaction between herself and the inmates. She was moving through a new phase, capable of standing outside herself and watching, weighing up situations more dispassionately. She was, even if she herself hadn't noticed, becoming more centred. She rarely, if ever, blew her top as she used to, or swiped everything off her desk in a fit of temper. Helen Hewitt was growing up and she was also toughening up. She was beginning to become the Governor in reality. The massive ship still had no clear captain but she was on the bridge; she was getting there, and far from making her appear iron-like, she was softening outside as the inner core hardened. But it still had some way to go.

June Fisher had been expecting the call since teatime. Even though she was dreading it, it was a relief when it finally came, at a few minutes after nine o'clock.

Ron was sitting on the sofa watching TV, or pretending to, while she spoke on the phone. Sarah, her eldest daughter, wearing jeans and a tank-top, was sprawled in an armchair. She had inherited her mother's blonde hair and slim figure, but her pretty looks were spoiled by a scowl as she watched from under her fair eyelashes.

June hung up. She took a breath as if to steady herself, blinking rapidly. 'He's at the station.'

Sarah sat up abruptly. 'Well, I'm out of here. I'm not staying to see him, I've got nothing to say to him.'

'That's up to you, Sarah.' June picked up her car keys from the sideboard. 'I'll be all right on my own, Ron. I won't even get out of the car.'

Ron nodded, his smile tense. This was a bad time for all of them. Hopefully it would soon be over.

'He's got a bloody nerve even coming here,' Sarah said, glowering. 'Susan won't see him either, you know.'

'Like I said, it's up to you, both of you. If you don't

want to see him, you don't have to.' June touched Ron's shoulder, and he reached up and took her hand, looking up at her. 'We just want him to sign the deeds of the house over to us.'

'And the divorce papers,' Ron said, squeezing her hand.

June squeezed back. 'Then none of us need see him ever again.'

Even though it wasn't raining, Alan Fisher had put on his raincoat because the evening had turned cool. He walked up and down outside the station entrance with his canvas holdall, watching for the car. He didn't even know what make of car to watch out for. He couldn't keep his hand still, jingling the loose change in his pocket, fingering his floral tie, smoothing his hair. A car pulled in, but it wasn't her. He turned away and continued his pacing . . . jingling, fingering, smoothing, palpitating.

CHAPTER 29

IT WAS a big night on C Wing. One of the officers had taped the Liverpool versus West Ham match, and already the seats were filling up. Walter Brinkley was in the front row, giving somebody the elbow. 'These are reserved, mate. Move – c'mon, *move it!*' He stood up and waved. 'Oi! Anthony, got you a seat!'

Above the bustle in the association area, the snooker and ping-pong, the men in the kitchen annex cooking up a curry, the Tannoy boomed out: 'Anyone who wants to watch the football match go to association. The video will start in five minutes.'

Brian Samora hopped from foot to foot, waiting for the phone. 'Come on, mate, the match is gonna start. We're runnin' a book – no one knows the result.'

Over by the bulletin board, Jumbo Jackson was keeping an eye on the men signing up for classes and workshops. Some were serious about it, some were sniggering, and he was making sure that along with their names they weren't writing lewd suggestions addressed to Zania Tullbrooke. Bringing that woman in here was like dropping a firecracker into a barrel of gunpowder. At night it was a wonder the wing didn't rock on its foundations at the jerking off that went on.

'Hey!' Samora called out, still waiting his turn for the phone. 'Will you sign me up for the black chick with the legs?'

Jackson grinned derisively. 'What you want, Brian? Computer training? Accountancy? Economics?'

Samora gave him the finger. 'Sit on this!'

'If you can't read or write, Brian, what's the point?'

The Scouser turned his back, cursing under his breath. Russell Morgan clocked the exchange. He strolled over to the bulletin board, Anthony Kelly in the middle of the cluster of men scanning the lists.

'What's the drama thing about?' Kelly asked.

'Poofters,' somebody suggested.

'Well, son, if I was you I'd sign up for something,' Morgan advised Kelly. 'You got six years, you could qualify as a doctor in the time you got.'

Kelly's head snapped round. 'Piss off!'

Morgan laughed. 'Very cocky now, aren't you, Kelly?' But it was sad really. No longer the frightened kid. Trying to act tough now, play the hard man. Not only sad, pathetic. Morgan strolled on.

'A minute, Brian, come here.' He waited as Samora shuffled over. 'That true? You can't read or write?'

'Course I can, he was just being a bastard,' Samora muttered, eyes shifting about. He turned to go.

'Hang on, just listen, will you?' Morgan aimed his thumb at the board. 'There's beginners' classes for inmates with learning disabilities.'

No way would Samora admit to it. He couldn't read his bit of paper, everyone knew it, but still he wouldn't relent. He almost snarled, 'I ain't got no bleedin' disability. What you think I am – one of you lot?'

As per usual, fat Roddy Marsh was on his own. Sucking on a roll-up, right down to his fingernails, he mooched around, either shunned or made fun of as a 'div', the wing's resident simpleton. He couldn't play snooker or table tennis, had no interest in football, so there weren't many options open to him. He was leaning against the wall, staring blankly at nothing, when a shadow fell across him. Marsh looked up with fearful brown eyes.

Norman Jones leaned closer. He mouthed softly, 'Go an' tell 'em Liverpool won, son, one – nil.' The game had kicked off, the rows of men staring up at the screen, jumping up to cheer when the team they had backed was on the attack. Jones bared his teeth in a grin, his face only inches away from Marsh's. 'Go on, there's a good lad, tell 'em.'

Marsh backed away, then slunk off, eyes to the ground.

Jones cocked his head, listening to a message over the Tannoy. 'Would any prisoner willing to assist in the library put his name down. Any prisoner willing to assist the new library section please go to the bulletin board.'

Jumbo Jackson was still on the look-out for smut and sexual innuendo on the lists. Jones strolled over. He tapped some Golden Virginia into a paper and rolled it with one hand, running it over his tongue.

'If I do the library schlepp does that mean I don't have to go to the workshop? Only I done it at Wakefield and the Scrubs, the library . . .'

'Sure, you want me to check?'

Jones stuck the roll-up in the corner of his mouth and flicked his lighter. The flame danced between them. 'I'm not askin' for favours.' He inhaled deeply and went off in a cloud of smoke.

'What does Stormin' Norman want?' Morgan asked Jackson.

'Offered to work in the library.'

'Norman?' Morgan stared after him, deeply suspicious. 'Wants off the workshop, does he? Been complainin' about headaches, skivin' bastard.'

A storm of cheering went up and chants of '*Liverpool, Liverpool.*' Morgan looked over. Robbie Fowler was facing the Kop, his fist punching the air. Rush ran up and hugged him, and then the youngster was surrounded by red shirts. Morgan said, 'Nobody's been allowed to give 'em the result.' He turned his head away and put his mouth to Jackson's ear. 'Norman doesn't get any privileges, right? You got that?'

Marsh was watching the men leaping about round the TV set when a shadow passed over him. Jones didn't stop, didn't speak, one look was enough. Marsh stumbled forward. The men jumping up and down got him excited, and he started jumping up and down too, his pudgy fists paddling the air ecstatically.

'Liverpool won! Liverpool won, one – nil! *One – nil!*'

All hell broke loose. Most of it fell on Marsh. He went down under a torrent of blows and kicks. The TV set was pulled off its shelf and smashed. The VCR was ripped out and mangled. Then it turned into a free-for-all, fists flying, with everybody wading in. Whistles blew, boots pounded. Batons drawn, Morgan and Jackson charged across, as a four-strong back-up spilled out of the officers' station.

Another big night on C Wing was over.

'I know,' Helen said, 'but that's the third TV set in six months. They'll be lucky to get a black and white one this time.'

She banged the phone down, gnashing her teeth. If they ever got to hear of it the tabloids would love that. Prisoners smashing up colour TVs which were then replaced at the taxpayer's expense. She could write the headlines herself.

There was a tap at the door and Lorcan Thomas peered round. 'Morning!' he said breezily. 'I was just wondering if you were free tonight?'

It took an effort to stop her jaw dropping open. 'Yes, I am.'

'Good, there's a nice little Italian . . .' He waltzed a few steps. 'Bit of the old Español on a postage-sized dance floor.'

'Is it dressy?'

'No. Well, semi-upmarket, casual. About eight?'

'Fine, look forward to it.' She realized her smile was spreading and tried to curb it before she looked utterly gormless.

He turned to go, and then swung back on the door. 'You found my replacement yet?'

'Not yet, few weeks to go.'

'See you tonight.' A quick grin and he was gone, leaving Helen in a bit of a dither. She straightened up and ran a hand through her hair, letting the smile come, gormless or not. A date, and on a Saturday night as well. Things were looking up. She felt like a schoolgirl: it was so long since she had been held in someone's arms – so long since she had been to bed with a man it was embarrassing. She was racing ahead, already seeing herself in the candlelight. She could, if she closed her eyes, smell his aftershave – it could have been some kind of antiseptic but that was nice. He was always so clean and fresh. And she loved his hands: clean nails, long delicate fingers. If she'd been left to herself for much longer she would have let out an orgasmic moan but the telephone broke her romantic daydream. It was C Wing again: one of the prisoners was demanding they get a television immediately because he was missing one of the soaps. Helen sighed with irritation.

'They will get a television set when I have a moment to arrange it. I have better things to do than worry about a bloody television set. Talk to Maintenance but don't waste my time. As I said before, they smashed it, let them realize that having a set is not obligatory but a privilege.'

Helen replaced the receiver, pursing her lips. So much of prison life was taken by the inmates as 'their right' when it was the opposite. They were never made aware of how many privileges they had until they destroyed them. She frowned: this incidental irritating problem, if looked at coldly, was yet another indication that inmates believed they could demand whatever they wanted, showing over and over again that they ran the prison and not the officers. It was wrong. Yet again this was a change of attitude for Helen. Six, seven months ago, she had believed that they should be given everything possible to ensure their time in custody was productive and rehabilitating. Now she was changing her mind. The wheels never ceased to turn, as one after another of her radical beliefs on rehabilitation changed.

Fisher wasn't sure whose room he was in, Sarah's or Susan's. He sat on the edge of the bed in his striped pyjamas, a roll-up smouldering between his fingers, and looked slowly round. Illuminated by the bright shaft of sunshine, everything in the small back bedroom glowed pink and white. Everything matched too: duvet and pillow covered in tiny blue flowers, frilly cushion on the white-painted hardbacked chair, frills on the curtains and the embroidered cover on the oval-shaped dressing table.

A few stuffed toys, no longer played with, sat in a neat group in the corner. Posters covered the walls. Guns N' Roses. He'd heard of them, but not the heavy-metal bands: hairy-chested young men in leather pants with metal studs in their ears and noses, tattoos and long greasy hair. More likely to be sixteen-year-old Susan, Fisher decided, than Sarah, who was nearly nineteen. Then he noticed the make-up tubes and jars, the pots of cream on the dressing table, and he was confused again. Would Susan be wearing make-up at her age? What did he know? Bugger all.

The room was conspicuously neat and tidy, just a clean ashtray on the bedside cabinet. Feeling guilty, Alan stubbed out his cigarette in it. He could hear music and muffled voices from downstairs, and June's voice said, 'Will you call him? I'll start breakfast.'

Kneeling, Fisher slid open the small flat drawer in the bedside cabinet. Right on top, as if just slipped in there, was a framed photograph. It was of a birthday party, a big cake and candles, June holding the knife and smiling into the camera, with her two teenage daughters beside her. Fisher subsided onto the bed, clasping the photograph to his chest. He pulled the duvet over his head and brought his knees up. The soft, low, moaning sound seemed to escape from him rather than be vocally uttered, and it stilled suddenly when Ron rapped lightly on the door.

'Breakfast in a few minutes, Alan. Alan . . .?'

Wearing a cardigan over a knitted top, jeans and white plimsolls, June leaned against the kitchen counter, watching Ron finish his breakfast. It was a few minutes after ten o'clock. There was a phone-in on Radio 2 interspersed with pop songs, and the Monkees were singing 'I'm A Believer'.

Another song was running through June's head. It was the sight of Ron's hands that did it as he wiped the bread round his plate. Square dependable hands, thick at the wrists. How did the words go? *He may not be the man some . . . girls think of as handsome . . . but to my heart he carries the key.* That's what he was to her. Nothing out of the ordinary, nothing special to the rest of the world, and she was glad of that. A good steady, ordinary, dependable bloke, special to her and no one else. That's what she liked about him.

Ron drained his coffee and carried his dirty plate and mug to the sink.

June straightened up. 'You've no need to stay, honestly, I can handle it. You go. You don't want to lose Saturday morning business now, do you?'

'Well, you know where I am.' Ron put his big arms around her and hugged her. 'All you have to do is call.'

Fisher didn't mean to creep up on them, but in his stockinged feet and with the radio playing, they didn't hear him come in. He carried a small gift-wrapped package which, when he saw them embracing, he slipped behind his back. June kissed Ron's cheek, and then turned as Fisher coughed.

'Oh, you're up. Ron's just off to the garage.'

'Sleep all right, did you?' Ron asked.

'Fine, thanks.'

Ron pulled on a cracked and creased leather jacket and

went to the back door. 'See you later. Ta-ra, June.' With a final look back at Fisher he went out.

There was a moment's awkward silence. Fisher stood uncertainly, taking in the kitchen. He still wore the shirt he had travelled in, collar undone and shirtsleeves rolled up, the package concealed in his hand. 'It's different . . . table used to be against the wall, didn't it?'

'It's a different table, Alan,' June said, 'and it's been decorated twice, maybe more.' She pulled out a chair for him. 'Eggs and bacon?'

'Don't go to any trouble.' He sat down, fidgeting with the package under the table. 'I lied,' he said, looking up at her. 'Didn't sleep a wink, bed was too soft, not used to it.' He gave a quick, nervous smile. 'Could I have an omelette?'

June nodded and went to the fridge. He watched her carry the eggs to the worktop and take down a blue-striped bowl from the shelf and a metal whisk from a hook.

'You kept the house nice, June.' He remembered the package. 'I got this for you.'

June hesitated, and then took it from him. She turned it over in her fingers, chewing her lips, and then tore off the wrapping. It was a bottle of Yardley's toilet water.

'Your favourite, isn't it?'

June nodded and placed it to one side. The last time she'd worn Yardley's toilet water was when Sarah was starting primary school. She returned to the counter and broke the eggs in the bowl.

'Very smart,' Fisher said. He was nodding and gazing round at the pine units and shelving, the dishwasher and microwave, the extractor hood over the cooker.

'Yes, well, Ron's a great help. He's very handy with cupboards and carpentry and anything mechanical.'

'Surprised the social services haven't copped the fact he's been living here. Maybe they reckoned he was just the decorator.'

June glanced at him sharply. 'I needed every penny I

could get,' she said, 'and I don't get any subsistence now. Ron's got his own garage.'

'And I own this house,' Fisher said.

June didn't say anything. She was beating the hell out of the eggs, her knuckles white as she gripped the whisk. It took her a minute to get in control. She said, 'You want mushrooms and tomatoes in the omelette or straight?'

'Er . . . mushrooms, please.' Fisher fiddled with the knife and fork. He cleared his throat. 'The girls, will I be able to see the girls?'

'They'll be working. Sarah's got a job in a wine bar and Sue's part-time at a new boutique in the open-air market.'

'I know, but that's not what I asked.' He pressed down on the fork. 'I'd like to see them.'

'They don't want to see you.' It came out very harsh and unrelenting, and June checked herself. She looked at him over her shoulder. 'They're grown-up now, Alan, you probably wouldn't know them.'

'I sort of looked forward to seeing them, June.' He laid the fork down and clasped his hands together on the table. 'And I'll sign the house over, the divorce papers, just like we agreed.'

Moving to the fridge to get the mushrooms, June spun round, backing off, as Fisher stood up. He frowned at her, hands hanging limp at his sides. 'I was just going to put the toast on, June.'

She put one hand on her beating heart and held up the other. 'Just . . . just sit there, I'll do it for you.' Her eyes were wide, as if actually seeing him for the first time. 'Did you not bring a change of clothes?'

He pushed the chair back with his legs. June pressed against the counter, her throat dry. From the corner of her eye she could see the shiny whisk in the yellowy egg mix in the bowl, but that was no bloody good. Fisher moved out from the table. She couldn't see his eyes; they were masked by the bright window reflecting in his glasses.

'I need to go to the toilet.'

He went out, banging the door. June closed her eyes. Her shoulders slumped, and pain jabbed her neck muscles like a white-hot needle.

Upstairs in the green and white tiled bathroom with its matching bathmat and cut-out mat round the toilet, fluffy towels piled neatly in the bamboo rack, Fisher stared at himself in the small square mirror above the washbasin. He clamped his jaw tight but it did no good. His face was changing before his eyes. Tears welled up as his face slowly crumpled. And then he was weeping profusely and silently, huge drops dripping from his chin into the washbasin. He didn't know how long he cried, he wasn't aware of anything until June's voice seemed to float towards him from a great distance, even though she was standing right outside the door.

'Alan . . . *Alan?* What are you doing in there?'

He stepped back, wiping both hands across his cheeks. He sniffed and said hoarsely, 'Be all right if I have a bath?'

'Of course it is. Water's hot.'

He put the plug in and turned on both taps. In the bathroom cabinet he found the usual assortment of men's deodorants, a shaving brush and a can of Gillette foam. He took out the foam and shook it. On the narrow glass shelf next to where it had stood there was a razor, and next to that a packet of razor blades.

Maureen Collins stood amongst thirty large cardboard boxes filled with books. A light haze of dust floated in the sunbeams filtering through the high windows of the library. There was dust everywhere – the aftermath of the building work – on the racks of empty shelves, on the tables and chairs, heaped into the corners of the room. Three Red Band orderlies had made a start with brooms, dustpans and black plastic bags. But to get this lot sorted, Maureen sighed, looking at the mountain of boxes, she would need a small army.

She dumped the stack of books she was holding back into its box. 'Oh, great. None of these are in any kind of alphabetical order.'

John Udding came in and stood to one side. 'Miss Collins, we've got a couple of helpers for you.'

Norman Jones and Walter Brinkley entered, followed by another officer. She nodded to the two of them and smiled. 'I'm Maureen Collins.'

Brinkley was looking round in confusion, which swiftly turned to dismay. 'Oi!' he said to the officer. 'Where's that black chick? Isn't she in here?'

Apparently he had signed up on the wrong list. He jammed his taped-together glasses hard onto his nose, having serious second thoughts.

Jones was giving Maureen a real hard stare. She fronted him out, losing none of her poise and cool detachment while she did it. She looked to him expectantly.

'Prisoner 872, Norman Jones, C Wing, Miss.'

'Well, Norman, thanks for offering. If you could start on that box.' She turned to Brinkley. 'And you are?'

He clapped a hand to his forehead and staggered. 'I got a migraine. I gotta go back.'

Jones was already at work, humping the box across to the shelves. Brinkley was holding the sides of his head in both hands, moaning pitifully and looking near death. Hunched over, he was led out.

Maureen opened the lid of a box. She looked across and smiled. 'Well, it's just you and me, Norman.'

Jones paid no attention. Sleeves rolled up, revealing the tattoos on his bulging arms, he was already carrying another huge box over to the shelves. He worked that way all morning, sticking diligently to the task, and by midday had moved the entire lot. By then his blue workshirt was stained dark with sweat, his long hair, streaked with grey at the temples, hanging limply over his eyes.

Then working alongside her, he helped sort out the books and stack them on the shelves. The orderlies had cleaned the place and gone, leaving the two of them and a bored officer on duty.

'I think we should try and get the educational section at one end, the bodice rippers in another section . . .' Kneeling, Maureen indicated what she had in mind. 'And then the . . .'

'Classics?' Jones said, holding up a copy of *Bleak House*. 'Where you want the classics?'

She pointed. 'Centre back shelves, all along there.'

On his knees beside her, Jones delved into a box and lifted out a pile of books. He said, 'You know, they won't look for a book – prefer to order it from the local library, gives 'em something to do. Well, that's the way it was in the other nicks.' He dumped the books down and their shoulders almost touched. He jerked back a little. 'Sorry, I must stink like a polecat.' He lifted his arm and sniffed.

Maureen sat back on her haunches. 'What do you read, Norman?'

'Me?' He was checking titles, sliding them onto shelves. 'Bit like Mike Tyson,' he said, looking round at her with a grin. 'Well, according to the papers he's reading Tolstoy. I'm ahead of him.' He leaned nearer, with a confiding whisper, 'Man after my own heart is Genet!' He jumped up. 'Ah, refreshments!'

An officer had brought in a mug of tea and a glass of water. Jones took them from him, avoiding his eyes and not saying a word. He carried them back, handed the mug to her, and thirstily drank the water in one go. He wiped his mouth. Maureen sipped her tea, nodding her thanks to the officer.

Jones was studying a book intently. 'You're a psychoanalyst, aren't you, Miss Collins?'

'No, psychologist.'

'You reckon any of the men here will read this?' He held up the spine. 'Margaret, Duchess of Argyll's *Table Etiquette*?'

Maureen shook her head, laughing softly. 'We get what we're given, Norman.'

He looked at her, quiet and serious. 'Bit like life, isn't it?'

The big square shape of Malahide filled the doorway. He'd been there for a minute or so, watching Prisoner 872, C Wing, and Miss Maureen Collins. He lumbered over. 'I've come to take him back to the wing, Miss Collins.'

She nodded, and said to Jones, 'Thank you for your help. I'll be in Sunday. If you want to give me a hand I'd be grateful.'

Jones gave a shrug and a smile. He followed Malahide to the door, who gestured for him to lift his arms. He submitted to the rub-down, staring straight ahead, his nostrils flaring, physically recoiling from the officer's touch. Malahide waved him on. Jones went out, and it seemed as if a boiling cloud of rage had departed from the room.

June halted half-way down the staircase. 'His bus pass and maps and things are still in the room.'

Ron, in his garage overalls and heavy boots, awaited her in the hallway. By temperament placid and patient, even he had his limits. He said, 'But the bastard's still not signed, has he? Well, when he gets back I'll talk to him.' He looked up at her. 'One word from you or me and he's never going to get out.'

'He scares me, Ron,' June said. She jumped as the doorbell rang, and gripped the banister.

Ron opened the door. Fisher stood in the gabled porch, a plastic carrier-bag in one hand, a brown paper package under his arm.

'Hello, Ron. I just been round that new shopping mall – prices knocked me for six.' He stepped into the hallway. 'The wife in, is she? Only I saw the car in the drive. What is it?'

'It's a Mazda,' Ron said, shutting the door.

Fisher saw June and nodded to her. She came down and edged aside as he started up the stairs. Ron said, 'You want to go to see a film with us tonight?'

'No, thanks, Ron. I want to see my girls.' Fisher turned, hesitating for a second. 'And, Ron, I hope you don't mind, I borrowed your razor.' He gave a little twitchy smile and went up.

June waited, biting her lip. 'I said leave out the electric razor,' she whispered, knocking his arm. 'I *said*, Ron.'

Afraid of being overheard, she moved towards the kitchen. Ron cast a final look up the stairs and followed her. 'One foot out of line and I'll call the police . . .'

Directly above, Alan Fisher stood motionless on the landing. He waited for the kitchen door to close, and then went lightly into the small back bedroom.

Chapter 30

A TOWEL around his waist, Anthony Kelly was next in line for the shower. The cubicle door swung open and Norman Jones stepped out. In one movement he grabbed his towel from the rail and wrapped it round him. He didn't fraternize, especially with first-timers barely out of nappies, so he ignored Kelly's smile, already pushing past him, toilet bag in hand.

Officers stood watching, and there were lines of men waiting their turn, but with the hiss of water and billowing steam Kelly felt it was safe enough.

'How much should it cost for me to have Victor Braithwaite taken care of?'

Jones slowly turned his head. 'What you askin' me for?'

His stare was so intimidating that Kelly backed off. 'Just everyone respects you for knocking off a screw and . . .'

'The only thing I did was destroy my life an' I got eighteen years to think about it.' The voice was flat, stating facts. 'Now, if you think that deserves respect then you should start straightenin' out.'

He went off. Kelly said to Walter Brinkley behind him, 'It was him told me that Victor's a nonce.'

Without his glasses, Brinkley squinted after Jones. He turned back with a sarcastic grin. 'So, feel even more of a prick now, do you?'

*

Helen opened the front door, her heart pitter-pattering. She was wearing a calf-length dress in peach, V-necked with thin straps. Buttoned all the way down the front, it allowed the wearer to decide how much cleavage and leg to reveal. For the moment Helen had chosen to be discreet, but the night was young.

She had a smile ready. 'Right on time!'

'And may I say, Governor, you look ravishing.' Lorcan Thomas was nodding approvingly.

Helen laughed. 'Would you like a drink before we go?' She was feeling giddy and girlish.

'Better not, the others are waiting.' He nodded behind him to a black Mercedes. 'Might as well go straight there.'

Helen put on her coat and pulled the door shut. Holding her peach satin handbag, she followed him down the steps to the pavement. Moira waved to her from the back seat. In the driver's seat, Helen glimpsed a male profile.

'I own up!' Lorcan Thomas grinned, not in the least shamefaced. 'Bit of match-making!'

He opened the passenger door for Helen, who was making fast work of hiding her disappointment. She wasn't sure how successful she'd been, and was thankful that the darkened interior during the drive cloaked her expression.

Far from being as bad as she feared, the evening turned out to be even worse. She ate the food and drank the wine, both excellent, and tried to enjoy what would have been, had there been just the two of them, the romantic, intimate atmosphere. But there were four, and the atmosphere was spoiled. And her blind date, Dr William Hancock – 'Call me Bill' – was a depressing, overweight man in his early forties with a florid complexion. After the third bottle of Nebbiolo d'Alba he became maudlin about his failed marriage and even more bitter about his divorce.

In a world of their own, Lorcan Thomas and Moira sat opposite them with their heads close together, clinking wine glasses, him murmuring, her giggling. Helen watched them covertly as she tossed back her drink, hardly listening to the morose man droning on beside her.

'So we had a very one-sided amicable divorce, she got the house, the kids, the car, the savings. I got a bag of clubs and two suitcases, so she was very amicable.' He filled Helen's glass. 'What about yours?'

'My what?'

'You said you were divorced.'

'Very friendly and a long time ago,' Helen said, bored to tears. 'I got the cat.'

Moira's silver lamé top was gaping open, showing that her lift-and-separate bra was doing its job well. She was gazing from Thomas's eyes to his mouth, and back to his eyes again, as he went on, 'It's an emergency house call, my first, and I'm sweating because I can't find the farm. I drive up a lane and there he is, waving his arms around. Only drags me into the cowshed, shoves me towards this immense pregnant cow. I said, "I'm a doctor not a vet, Mr Jones," and he hands me a bucket . . .' Moira was biting her lip and shaking all over, her breasts jiggling about. 'And he says, "You can see the wife after if it makes you happy."'

Moira collapsed against him, nearly upsetting her wine.

'She left me for my partner.' Bill Hancock sighed, eyes on the tablecloth.

'I'm sorry,' Helen said mechanically. She swallowed a yawn.

'She accused me of always working. Too bloody right I was – standing in for him so he had a lot of time off for my wife. In the end, you know, it's that that gets you.'

He paused. Helen didn't realize it until she became aware that the droning in her ear had stopped. She said, 'I'm sorry? What gets you?'

'The betrayal,' Bill Hancock said bitterly. 'I think women are more deceitful than men.'

An Italian waiter in a natty red waistcoat and puffed

sleeves wheeled up a vast sweet trolley overloaded with goodies. He stood at Helen's shoulder, rubbing his hands.

'Nothing for me, thank you.'

Moira perked up. 'Ohhh . . . I'll have the trifle, please.'

The waiter wheeled the trolley round to serve her. Lorcan Thomas's attention drifted in Helen's direction. 'Not on a diet, are you?'

'No.' She leaned over the table. 'I'm afraid I have to go home.'

'The crème brûlée,' Bill said, pointing, 'and the strawberry tart,' obviously compensating for his ex-wife, ex-partner, failed marriage, acrimonious divorce, 'and some fresh cream, and chocolate sauce . . .'

'But you're not on duty tonight, are you?' Thomas said to Helen with an air of surprise. 'And I wanted you to talk to Bill.'

'I have been talking to him,' Helen said, getting her bag, 'or listening.' She stood up and made an impatient fluttering gesture, leaning over. 'Just make up some excuse.'

Seeing Helen move off, with Thomas going after her, Moira called out, 'Don't you want anything?'

'Just coffee,' he called back, and followed Helen through the tables. 'Have you got a headache or something?'

Helen stopped on the edge of the tiny dance floor and faced him. 'No, I haven't.' A trio was playing, not a very good one, and thus far no one had braved the floor. 'But if I have to listen to further details of your friend's divorce I'll have a full-blown migraine.'

He seemed less apologetic than disappointed. 'It's just that I know Barfield will be looking for a full-time doctor and—'

Helen gave it to him straight. 'I don't get much time off,' she said icily, 'and I didn't realize this evening was set up for me to interview your replacement.'

Behind his shoulder she could see Moira moving towards them. Helen thought she saw a glint of green in her eye.

Lorcan Thomas made a gesture that was meant to be

placatory and came out half-hearted. 'I suppose a dance is out of the question?'

'The ladies' is first on the right,' Moira said, coming up and slipping her arm through his.

Helen's brief smile cost her. 'Thank you, Moira. Goodnight.'

'Is she leaving?' Moira asked, resting her chin on his shoulder as Helen turned on her heel and marched from the room.

Lorcan Thomas kissed her neck. 'Ask Bill for his car keys.'

Moira watched with narrowed eyes as he went after her. Reluctantly she returned to the table. Bill Hancock's head was down, digging into a heaped plate of crème brûlée, strawberry tart, cream and chocolate sauce.

Fisher sat at one end of the long curved bar, a Coke in front of him. Ear-splitting disco music thumped from speakers above his head, sending shock-waves up from the floor and into his spine from the padded seat of the bar stool. The packed crowd of young kids jostled all around him, shouting at one another in what he supposed was meant to be conversation. He'd put on his new shirt with the floral tie, his old grey suit, and his new pair of trainers, the cheapest that Shoe Express had in stock.

He didn't know wine bars like this existed, never mind ever having been in one. The kids were drinking strange foreign beers straight from the bottle, and it surprised him how many had chunky metal rings and studs attached to various parts of their anatomy. Not just the blokes either. A laughing girl had a jewelled stud through her tongue. No wonder the country was going down the tubes.

Sarah was serving at the other end of the bar, her gossamer fair hair piled up on top, with long strands trailing over her ears. She wore a halter-dress with a skirt so short it was practically indecent. Fisher had been watching her for at least fifteen minutes. She hadn't seen him, or even if she had, he reflected, she probably wouldn't know who he was.

The young barman, ponytail and gold earring, moved along collecting empty bottles and glasses. 'You want another? Excuse me, you want anything else?'

'Ask the young lady to come and serve me, will you, son?'

The barman knew his type. Dirty old man. He said, 'She's busy right now.' He swept away the empty glass. 'Want another Coke?'

'At one-fifty, you must be jokin'.' Fisher gave him a stare. 'I'm her father, so don't mess around. Go and get her to speak to me. I seen you ring up wacky amounts, sonny, so just do it.'

The barman still wasn't sure but he went and did it anyway. Sarah looked along the bar, the laughter dying on her face. With a tight mouth and hard eyes she came up to him. 'I've got nothing to say to you, just go away.'

'I've been away, Sarah. I just . . . just wanted to see you.' He tried to smile. 'You've grown into a lovely girl—'

'No thanks to you.'

'You got every right to feel angry.'

'I also got every right to tell you I don't want to see you.'

'Couldn't we just talk?' Fisher pleaded.

He would have made more impression on a lump of granite. 'No, because I don't finish here until three and then my boyfriend takes me home.'

'I'll wait up,' Fisher said, 'meet him.'

'No, you won't.' Sarah cast her eyes around. 'I don't want any of my friends knowing about you.'

He tried to think of a way through, but there wasn't any. He shrugged in defeat. 'I'm sorry, you get back to work.'

Her father counted for so little that Sarah was already taking another order. She reached for two Budweisers from the cold cabinet, but somehow couldn't help glancing back at him. After all, he was the father she hadn't set eyes on in fourteen years. But it was too late, both for him and for her. The stool was empty.

June came into the kitchen to find Fisher sitting at the table, eating fish and chips out of newspaper. She pulled the dressing gown tighter, holding it to her throat.

'You had me worried sick, Alan. Where've you been?'

He picked out a chip and contemplated it sadly. 'Everything's changed, and these . . .' shaking his head in disbelief '. . . three quid, used to be ten bob.'

June waved her hand vaguely. 'Do you want salt, vinegar or anything?'

'No, they threw that in for nowt.' He popped the chip in his mouth and chewed ruminatively. 'We don't get chips often.' He glanced at his wife, and then quickly away again, as if the sight of her stabbed him to the heart. 'I don't belong here, I know that.' He tried to swallow and couldn't, his face twisting horribly. 'It's just . . . hard, and I got nobody to blame.'

Ron appeared in the doorway. June gave a small shake of the head. Fisher wasn't supposed to see it, but he did. He smiled.

'It's all right, Ron, come in and sit down. Have a chip!'

Ron edged in, but stayed by the door.

'You done well by my kids, I appreciate it.' Fisher was about to go on, and then changed his mind. He was finding it hard to speak. 'Don't suppose you got a beer in that fridge, have you?'

Ron shook his head. 'No, there's never any drink in the house.'

He exchanged a look with June, and they both waited and watched in silence as Fisher toyed with the chips, his head sunk over them.

'I won't be botherin' you again,' he said huskily. 'Be all over by tomorrow . . .'

The Mercedes pulled up outside Helen's front door. She released the seat belt and felt for her bag. 'There was no need for you to do this,' she said. 'I could have got a minicab.'

Lorcan Thomas reached for the door handle, but Helen stopped him. 'Please don't get out.'

As she stepped onto the pavement he leaned across the seat to look up at her. The lamplight made his face seem pallid. 'I'm really sorry about tonight.'

Helen looked down at him. 'So was I.' She slammed the door shut and walked up the steps, not looking back as the car drove away. So much for her schoolgirl crush. She felt humiliated and, slamming her front door closed, she hurled her coat and bag onto the sofa, then poured a large Scotch. She sat in front of a tedious travelogue film on the TV, then switched from channel to channel and, after glaring furiously at some programme that was supposed to be a sex guide, she flicked off the TV.

Helen drained her glass and, leaning forward, carefully placed it on her coffee table. There were quite a few rings from cups of coffee and late-night cocoa mugs and she wrinkled her nose; the whole flat needed a thorough clean and the ironing was stacking up, growing daily. She sighed. The evening had been a fiasco. She was irritated that young Moira considered herself an equal. She didn't like to admit it but that really annoyed her and, of course, that Moira was obviously getting her leg over Dr Thomas and Helen wasn't added salt to the wound. She had fancied him from the moment she first saw him, and now she knew he had absolutely no interest in her. Another drink was required as she stared at her own reflection. She began to inspect every inch of herself as she threw off each garment, carefully chosen for her so-called big date.

Naked, with her hands on her hips, she studied herself in her wardrobe mirror. 'You don't know what you're missing, Dr Thomas.'

Her body was firm, big-breasted, but her waist might do with perhaps an inch off. But she was, she determined, in good shape. It was just a pity that no one but herself was privy to that.

Bright and early Sunday morning Maureen Collins entered the library, and gazed round in surprise. 'Good heavens. This all your doing?'

Over three-quarters of the shelves were filled, empty cardboard boxes piled up near the librarian's desk. Norman Jones turned and looked towards her from half-way along the second aisle. He plonked a stack of books down, dusting his hands. 'Yep, brought me in after breakfast. I've got this bookcase and the one on the far side to finish. All in alphabetical order and . . .' he walked round and gestured casually, 'magazine rack sorted.'

Maureen didn't have to feign how impressed she was. She went over, smiling to herself, to where Jones was leafing through a magazine.

'Strange, isn't it? The reading matter they allow. Real-life detective and murder stories.' He held it up, meeting her eyes. 'You'd think it would be banned. Some of it's pretty horrific . . . rape and torture, mutilation, sexual deviations.' He dropped the magazine into the rack. 'But then, life is full of incongruities, isn't it?' he said, with a kind of lazy smile.

'Yes . . .' Maureen studied him with a frown. 'Have you done something different with your hair?'

'Nope, just had a shower.' He flicked a loose strand back from his forehead. His fingernails were clean, trimmed, cut square. He said, 'These drama classes you're starting, you play those head games?'

'Not sure what you mean.'

'Act out your mother, father, and yourself? That's what most of them do, isn't it? Lot of shouting and waiting for the primal scream?'

His face was sober and his eyes serious, but she felt that she was being teased. She moved to the bookcase, idly checking that the titles were in the correct category. They were. 'It can be therapeutic,' she said, 'and give an insight into the mind of—'

'Answer me this.' Jones wrapped one arm across his chest and held up a finger. 'Say you have a prisoner who during your drama class lets out he was an abused child, and that is the fundamental seed for all his criminal activities.' He shrugged one shoulder. 'You can't release him, you can do nothing. Damage has been done.'

'Well, I disagree.' She was having a discussion about psychotherapy with a con, Maureen realized. That's how clever and sharp he was. *Very* sharp. 'I can make him come to terms with the abuse, help him to be able to adjust.' Dammit, she was even defending herself.

'Adjust to what?' He wouldn't let her off the hook. 'Eight, ten more years?'

The door opened to admit Jumbo Jackson. He stood jingling his keychain. 'I have to take him back to the wing. Lunch.'

Maureen nodded, but her eyes were on Jones, who was watching his fingertips running along a row of books. 'What kind of man would, out of choice, choose to work in a prison?' he mused, loud enough to be heard by the officer. 'All day locked up. Even if they hold the keys they're still like us, behind bars.'

Jackson had been joined by Malahide. Both officers were listening.

Maureen leaned her elbow on the bookcase. 'Were you abused?'

Jones threw back his head and laughed. 'No, but I knew you'd ask me that. You haven't read up on me, Miss Collins?'

'No.'

'Time to go back on the wing, Norman,' Jackson called out.

Jones looked at the two officers, his expression deadpan. There was something in his stance, in the set of his shoulders, that had changed the moment they had entered. It was a subtle difference, but Maureen had noted it. She couldn't figure this man at all. Highly intelligent, perceptive, yet with a dark undercurrent of something barely held in check, as if the battle within himself never ceased.

'Where would you like the *Kama Sutra*?' he asked her, and again that teasing little grin.

Maureen smiled broadly, and then laughed aloud. Jackson was not so amused. In fact, he was plain pissed-off. 'Now, Norman, come on!'

Sauntering out, an officer either side of him, Jones looked back at her. 'You have a wonderful laugh,' he said from the door, 'it's like music in here,' and went out.

They took him down the stairs to the ground floor and through the big iron door opening onto the covered walkways. Church bells could be heard chiming faintly in the distance. Norman Jones walked between them past the exercise yards, and waited while Jumbo Jackson unlocked the main entry gate leading to the accommodation wings. Malahide pushed him forward, and it might have been this, or it might not, which dictated what happened next. Because as Jackson relocked the gate on his side, intending to return to the admin block, Jones went berserk. Without any signal or warning whatsoever, he threw his full fourteen-stone muscled body weight at Malahide, got him pinned against the wall, head-butted him in the face, bursting his nose, and kneed him in the groin.

Jackson blew a blast on his whistle, at the same time fumbling with his keychain to unlock the gate.

At the sound of the 'Officer Down' whistle, every officer

within hearing distance literally dropped what he was doing and ran like hell. Within seconds eleven of them converged on the incident to find a red-faced Jackson grappling with Jones. Malahide was out of it, a real mess. Slumped against the wall, glassy-eyed and suffering from concussion, his face and the front of his uniform were covered in blood. In itself this was nothing out of the ordinary. Just one more statistic to add to the 2,540 assaults on prison officers in the past year.

Chapter 31

THE BOUTIQUE where Susan Fisher worked had an open frontage onto the outdoor market. The fine weather this Sunday lunchtime had brought out crowds of people, including families, and there was a festive air amongst the stalls with their bright billowing canopies.

She was arranging Indian scarves on a rail when Fisher first glimpsed his daughter. Thinner than Sarah, though just as tall, she was wearing jeans and a colourful embroidered waistcoat over a sweater. Without make-up, her skin glowed with the bloom of youth. He observed her from a distance, and then drifted slowly nearer through the shoppers and browsers. She became aware that someone was standing nearby, and flicked a half-glance over her shoulder.

'Morning, these are all fifty per cent off,' she informed him, cheerful and friendly.

'It's me, Susie,' Fisher said. 'It's your dad.'

She carried on with her sorting. Standing there, Fisher felt a sharp pang of anguish that she was going to reject him without a look or a word. But then very slowly she turned to face him. She seemed suddenly pale.

'I wouldn't have known you.'

'I recognized you straight away,' he said. 'Just like your mother used to look.' He was smiling, or trying his best.

'I don't know what to say to you.'

'You don't have to say nothing. I was here, now I'm on my way.' He nodded over his shoulder, as if to indicate that was the way he was headed. He took a painful breath. 'I always loved you, Susie, I'll never stop . . . but I won't bother you. Just wanted one last look. No harm done, eh?'

She looked him straight in the eyes, and he barely caught the whispered, 'You did the harm . . .'

Fisher's head went down. 'I know,' he said abjectly, 'and I have to live with it for the rest of my life.'

He couldn't say any more, and she had nothing to say. She turned and went into the shop. Fisher watched her for a few moments, her back to him as she went mechanically through a rack of dresses. With that one last long look he left her, moving off until he was lost in the drifting Sunday crowd.

Susan's hands had stilled on the dress rack and her shoulders were shaking. Tears streaming down, she turned round and blindly searched the blurred anonymous faces in the sunshine outside.

The panic didn't set in right away. It took all of ten seconds.

Fisher stood at the ticket-office window, showing the clerk his rail pass and timetable. 'I can't have missed it. Look, I got the timetable here . . .'

'No, it's been changed. New timetable as from yesterday, so your next train is not for two hours.'

'Oh, my God!'

'You might be better off to try the coach station.'

He did try, and he wasn't. The coach station was fifteen minutes' walk away, and Fisher ran it in seven. He talked to a helpful driver who looked at his rail pass, shaking his head, and pulled out his own National fare tariff. 'That's no good on a bus, anyway. And by coach it'll cost you nearly thirty quid.' He checked the list. 'Twenty-seven pounds fifty pence.'

'*What?*' He had less than two pounds in his pocket. 'Oh,

Christ, I better go back to the station, I ain't got that much cash.'

'Like I said, faster by train.' The driver shrugged. 'Take a good four and a half hours by coach.'

Fisher was off and running.

'I honestly find this insulting,' Maureen Collins said, her eyes blazing. 'If you are to question my motives at this stage even before I have—'

Pacing the library floor, Helen swung round and let the woman have it. 'It is *my* job to question everything, Miss Collins. Now I don't know what the hell went on here . . .'

And that was the trouble. Nothing seemed to have happened to make Norman Jones suddenly blow a fuse. Helen had questioned Jumbo Jackson about Jones's behaviour in the library immediately prior to his attack on Malahide, and according to the officer Jones had said 'something about the *Kama Sutra* and she was laughing', which was a fat lot of help. Unless it meant that the connection was sexual somehow.

'Do you really think I would be stupid enough to jeopardize my job?' Maureen demanded. She swept out her hand to the shelves. 'The prisoner concerned worked exceptionally hard and was highly intelligent and methodical.'

'The prisoner, Miss Collins,' Helen said, her voice under tight control, 'has already cut the throat of one officer in his last prison. He held one hostage and he's just broken another one's nose now.'

Maureen came right back at her. 'Then who was it gave that prisoner permission to assist me in the library?' She nodded grimly, having scored a bull's eye. 'Miss Hewitt, before you start making any insinuations or accusations concerning my professional capabilities I would say someone else should be severely reprimanded for placing me at risk. Shouldn't they?'

Helen couldn't say much to that because the woman was right. Someone's balls would be in the grinder for this. She hoped to God they wouldn't be hers.

Jumbo Jackson was receiving some earache from an exasperated Governor Lyons on the same subject. Late Sunday afternoon was always a quiet time, and they were performing the usual recce on C Wing landing, peeping into the cells to make sure it stayed that way.

'Mr Morgan said he'd told you about Jones – he's a ruddy psychopath.' Lyons had a swift peek, slid the flap shut, and moved on.

'He was also the only volunteer,' Jackson pointed out, reasonably enough, 'and since he's been on his medication he seemed to be . . .'

He slid the flap back and took a gander. The cell appeared to be empty. He stuck his eye in the hole.

'Roddy? Show yourself, son. Roddy?' He stepped back sharply, nearly treading on Lyons's foot. 'Shit! Open up.'

Jackson had seen enough blood for one day, but the day wasn't over. Roddy Marsh was curled up in the corner next to the toilet bowl, both wrists slit open, leaking the stuff everywhere.

'. . . thirty-five minutes late due to a fault on the line. British Rail apologize for the delay.'

The fourth time that message had come over the speakers. It was damn well recorded, he knew it was.

Fisher pressed his face to the window and stared out at the empty platform. They'd been stuck here for at least twenty minutes, at this back-of-beyond little station somewhere between Warwick and Kenilworth. The panic was real now, and he couldn't quell it. He couldn't even see the station clock from here, and he didn't possess a watch.

The solitary figure of a ticket collector trudged along the platform under the dim lights. Fisher stuck his head out.

'Oi! What's the bleedin' hold-up? I got a connecting bus to catch.' He flopped down in his seat, holding his head. 'Oh my God. I don't believe this . . .'

Shaking his head, Gary Marshall gazed lugubriously at the bank of monitor screens in the central control room. He wasn't averse to modern technology, he just felt the money could have been better spent on basic security precautions. 'If we've got all this bloody equipment, why wasn't the library covered? How the hell did it happen?'

Seated in the swivel chair in the centre of the horseshoe-shaped desk, the duty officer shrugged. 'I wasn't told the library was open.'

'It isn't,' Helen said tersely, 'but that's no excuse.'

A red light flashed, and the circuit panel for C Wing lit up. The duty officer switched monitors. Helen leaned forward as the face of an officer appeared on the screen.

'Prisoner Roddy Marsh. Bad mutilation.'

Helen gripped the back of the chair. 'Shit!'

On another screen they could see Marsh, pale and shaking but on his feet, being led down the wing by two auxiliary nurses, both of them masked and gowned, wearing latex gloves.

'He's a champion mutilator.' Marshall sighed, nodding to the screen. 'Something must have provoked him, he doesn't usually do it on a weekend.'

Fisher jumped down from the haulage truck, giving the driver the thumbs-up. 'Thanks, mate.'

The truck revved and set off up the slip road, billowing blue smoke, leaving him on the hard shoulder of the motorway. He was somewhere north of Coventry, and still, by his rough reckoning, about forty miles from Barfield. The late arrival of the train meant he'd missed his bus connection, and he'd been lucky to have found a lift so quickly.

There wasn't much traffic at this hour. Headlights approached, and he stuck out his thumb hopefully. The car whipped by, and Fisher felt sick, knowing that his chances of somebody stopping were remote.

He looked back down the empty motorway. Only one thing for it, he thought, gritting his teeth. Lugging his canvas holdall, raincoat bundled up under his arm, he began to run along the hard shoulder. He was in pretty good shape, but he'd have to be a bleeding marathon man to make that ten o'clock deadline.

Dr Thomas had been called in, and he was waiting for Helen in the hospital wing. Roddy Marsh lay on a bed in one of the open cubicles, both wrists heavily bandaged, a nurse standing over him. He had to be watched every minute in case he tore off the bandages and tried to reopen the wounds.

'Your self-mutilator, classic,' Thomas told Helen. 'He'd somehow shoved a razor blade right up to here. The previous doctor must have stitched him up and not noticed it.'

He demonstrated with his own wrist how Marsh had managed this, a common trick used by self-mutilators. He had inserted a razor blade deep into an open wound and then been stitched up with the blade still inside. The doctor tapped his wrist, and added with a rueful grin, 'So he had it with him in case of an emergency, so to speak.'

Following hard on the Norman Jones incident, Helen didn't see the humour of this. She said snappily, 'What do you suggest I do? Run all the self-mutilators through a metal detector?'

'Maybe get this one over to a mental hospital,' was Dr

Thomas's not very serious solution. If that policy were applied to all the country's inmates in need of psychiatric treatment, fifty new mental hospitals would have to be built and the prisons would be half empty.

'Did you go over to the Block and check on Norman Jones?' Helen asked him.

Her edginess communicated itself, and he said testily, 'I've only just got here.'

'I thought he was on medication.'

'He is. Largactil, three tablets per day.'

Marshall came in, a pill-box full to the brim in his hand. 'Found these in Norman Jones's mattress. That's the good news. Bad news is it looks like Fisher's gone on extended home leave.'

It had been a pig of a day, and that was all Helen needed. She was just about ready to erupt.

Soaked through with sweat, Fisher ran flat out along the hard shoulder. Somewhere back there he'd dropped his raincoat, and by the time he realized it was gone it was too late. A car went by and he automatically thumbed it, in vain, not even breaking his stride. He blinked, peering up ahead. A car was parked on the hard shoulder, its hazard lights flashing. He sucked in a gulp of air and pounded on, hope rising within him.

The woman had nursed the car along until she came to an emergency telephone, and it took a few minutes to get through to the control centre. 'I think the engine overheated. I'm on the hard shoulder, just before junction sixteen . . .'

She turned to double-check the location, her eyes widening in shock at the sight of the figure stumbling towards her, gasping and frantically waving his arm.

'Oh, God, there's a man, he's running towards me, help me . . . *Please, he's coming towards me! Get the Police!*'

She left the phone dangling and dived back to the car,

scrambled inside and locked the doors. A moment later his face appeared in the rearview mirror, and she felt the car judder as Fisher, dead on his feet, collapsed against it. Crouched over, he slithered round to the passenger side, his hands squealing on the glass. His chest was heaving, his voice ragged. 'Please . . . please, you got to help me. I'm . . . I'm from . . .'

Petrified with fear, the woman cowered down in the seat. His head was sideways at an angle, mouth gaping, his breath misting the glass. He looked crazed. She screamed, '*Get away! Get away from me!*'

Her three-year-old was sleeping peacefully in his child seat in the back of the car. The toddler jerked awake and started screaming, infected by his mother's terror.

Fisher was shaking his head, trying to calm the woman, make her understand. 'I don't want to hurt you, I need to go . . . get to the . . .' He peered in through the windscreen, but that set her off again. 'The prison, can you hear?' He had to shout. '*I'm from the prison. Help me.*'

He spun round, startled, at the sound of a wailing siren. Doing ninety, a patrol car was racing down the motorway, blue lights flashing. He stumbled a couple of paces and then stopped, panicking, not knowing whether to make a run for it or stay. It was too late to decide. The patrol car screamed to a stop in front of the car, leaving a trail of burnt rubber. An AA van was also heading towards them along the hard shoulder, its yellow light revolving.

Two officers were already out of the car. One of them made a wide sweeping gesture. 'Away from there, come over here, hands on your head.' Fisher stood dithering. '*Put your hands on your head!*'

The other officer was leaning in at the woman's window. She wound it down and said in a weak, trembling voice, 'He's an escaped prisoner . . .'

Fisher turned to the first officer, his fists clenched in the air, and yelled, 'I've not fuckin' escaped, I'm trying to get back!'

The patrol car screeched up to the main gate of Barfield Prison. The rear door swung open and Fisher was out even before it had stopped.

'I dunno how to thank you fellas, but I owe you. God bless you!'

He ran to the gate and hammered to be let in. A bolt slid back in the small iron door and two burly security guards stood there with folded arms.

Fisher wiped his mouth with a trembling hand. 'Prisoner Alan Fisher . . . reporting back.'

The two guards looked at each other under the low peaks of their caps, and one of them tapped his watch. 'One minute after bleedin' ten, Fisher, that's what I call cuttin' it fine.'

Sitting at her desk in the lamplight, Helen said into the phone, 'Thank you very much, Mrs Fisher.'

Slowly she replaced the receiver and sat brooding, fingernails beating a staccato rhythm on the blotter. Gary Marshall came in with some good news.

'It's all right,' he said, smiling. 'Fisher's back.'

'No, it's not all right,' Helen snapped. 'Take him down to the Block.'

'Oh, come on,' Marshall appealed. 'He was only one minute late.'

'If he had killed his entire family, who do you think would take the responsibility for that?'

Marshall was astonished. Both at what she had said, and that the Governor was revealing herself in a totally new light. He had never before seen her so cold, so implacable, so unforgiving.

He said with a puzzled frown, 'Fisher? He's a harmless little bloke . . .'

Helen was staring in front of her. Something in the steady, calm gaze of her eyes chilled him. She said quietly, 'He is a liar.'

The next morning, Helen had Alan Fisher brought up to her office. Malcolm Smith, his probation officer, sat in on the interview. One look at Helen's face and Fisher knew he was in for a rough ride. He sat nervously on the edge of his chair, full of apologies.

'I'm really very sorry, Miss Hewitt, but the train timetable was out of date, and I tried—'

'Sorry isn't good enough, Mr Fisher.' Helen was in no mood for excuses. 'You lied. In fact, you've been spinning a load of bullshit for months. Your application for parole will be reviewed.'

Now he'd been rumbled he had nothing to gain, nothing to lose. 'So she told you, did she? June? My wife?' Fisher thrust his head forward. 'Well, let me tell you something. If I had told you about the divorce, told you that she only wanted me to sign over the house to her, that she's been claiming social security payments all these years, I'd never have got out. You know as well as I do how much importance they put on having a secure family.'

The mild, amiable façade was cracking as a deep torment rose to the surface; here was a man at war with himself. Hands clenched in his lap, his entire body was shuddering. It was a pitiful sight, but Helen stayed impassive. A few short months had made the difference. Living amongst them, day in and day out, had changed something fundamental inside her. On one level she felt sorry for Fisher, but all the same her attitude had hardened, become coldly pragmatic.

She watched him now, his body hunched over as if in pain, his face contorted.

'I served my time and I did it the hard way because I wanted to. I never wanted protection in the VP Wing. I had the shit in my food, I had the glass in me dinner, and I never complained because I deserved it . . .'

'I know, Alan, I know,' Smith said, trying to calm him.

'No, you don't know. You don't know 'cos it's written on a bit of paper. You think you understand?' He shook his head bitterly. 'It was me, me that made June not bring my daughters to visit. *Me!*'

Helen rose and went to the door. She indicated to Jumbo Jackson through the glass panel that she was ready to leave.

'I battered my own little boy to death, me,' Fisher said in a ghastly hoarse whisper. 'I broke his skull, his arms and twisted his legs, me. I don't know to this day why I did it. Being drunk was no excuse. I never thought I'd ever be released. I didn't even think I had the right to hope.' He looked up with haunted eyes to Helen standing by his chair. 'Truth is, Miss, I killed my son.'

Helen turned away. She picked up her briefcase and went to the door. 'Mr Fisher, you will lose all privileges and will be held in the punishment cells. Thank you, Mr Smith.' She gave a curt nod to him and went out.

Fisher's crime did not take her by surprise. She was fully aware of why he had been in Barfield for so many years. She felt no revulsion; it was a tragic, horrific crime and Fisher lived with it, bore the pain of it. But Helen would have been responsible if Fisher had committed another crime after she had allowed him out. Then she would have carried the blame because yet again it had been her decision, above the probation department, above everyone else's. As Governor she had the final say on the prisoners being given weekend home leave. She gritted her teeth: never go on trust, check, double check. And tomorrow Mr

Smith would receive a severe reprimand: he must at all costs contact the families, even meet them before a prisoner was released for a home visit.

Naked except for his underpants, Norman Jones sat on the spongy floor of a padded cell in the segregation wing, a blanket draped round his shoulders. The cell contained nothing else, unless you counted the toilet bowl. Like a furtive nocturnal animal, he cocked his head to listen. The wide corridor outside the cell door magnified every sound. Down the wing a key turned in a lock, shattering the silence. A gate slid open, and footsteps boomed and echoed, coming closer, closer. Two people, possibly three.

A cell door swung open, and he heard the sound of scuffling feet. Footsteps approached his cell and stopped outside. The flap rattled back and Helen's eyes appeared in the hole. She looked at him and he looked at her, neither with any expression. The flap slid shut.

Helen walked back to the cell two doors along where Alan Fisher stood, head bowed, holding his pillow, grey blanket, and a single sheet. The officer gestured him inside.

'Alan! Alan!' Faint cries from the exercise yard floated in through the high narrow window of the cell. 'Fisher!'

Hands cupped to his mouth, Walter Brinkley stood with Brian Samora next to the chain-link fence, yelling down to the small slatted windows of the punishment block situated in the basement of the prison.

'Hey, Alan, did you have a good weekend then? Alan? Alan, can you hear?'

'Hi, Alan, mate,' Brian joined in, 'have a great time, did ya? We was told you come back in a patrol car!'

A pair of white hands gripped the slatted grille. The top of Fisher's head hove into view, and then his face, ghostlike, spectacles glinting, pressed itself against the iron grille.

'Yeah – one minute after closing time. My daughters

give me a big party with a cake. Wife had banner out. "Welcome Home, Dad."'

Brinkley and Brian grinned, giving him the thumbs-up.

The flap in the cell door slid open. Helen stared in.

Fisher slowly turned to the cold blue eyes peering at him through the flap. He gave a small guilty shrug, a sad half-smile as if apologizing for being caught out in yet another lie. The flap snapped shut and he huddled on his bed. The sounds from the exercise yard drifted and echoed as he closed his eyes, then squeezed them tightly as if to try and block out the nightmare. He could not recall what had happened – he had been on a week-long binge, one of the times when days and nights merged into a dark blur. June had almost got to the point of a breakdown with his constant drinking, his disappearances, his attempts to straighten himself out, but he had been incapable of curbing his drinking. If it hadn't been for June making sure when his mother died that they bought the house they had been renting, he would probably have drunk all the money – that, or gambled it away. He had held a good steady job when they first married. They had been childhood sweethearts and innocent, sweet June had no idea that even at sixteen Alan had a drink problem. He had always managed to keep it under control, had a good job with reasonable pay and prospects. The intermittent drinking bouts were mostly at weekends so he was able to function. It only got out of control when he was promoted to sales manager. Then he felt he needed a few drinks at lunchtime and it spiralled from there. Two beautiful daughters and a new baby son, a good job, a lovely wife he adored, a consuming guilt after each drinking binge, but he couldn't stop it. Even when he got fired he lied and said he'd been made redundant. And then the drinking went into overdrive. Unemployed, his drinking became so bad that he began to lose days, sometimes weeks, and June put up with it and put up with him. But his guilt and remorse made him wretched, made him need to drink even more.

Fisher loved the boy, but when drunk he was sure June had been with somebody else and his rages and accusations made their life together impossible. He frightened his daughters, he scared June until she said he had to get help or they would be finished. He was sober, stone cold sober, and trying to remain so when June had taken the girls to see a film. He remembered that, even remembered thinking that she was probably going to dump the girls at her mother's and meet up with a man. He was sure she was seeing someone else, that the cinema was just an excuse.

He began drinking the moment the front door closed and he remembered the little one crying in his cot, and then nothing, as if a tight black clamp had inched over his brain. He remembered nothing.

The trial was a blur, questions, questions, and he could not look anyone in the face, could not meet anyone's eyes because of what they said he had done. Fisher hunched further against the wall, pressing his backbone against the cold wall until it hurt. He *wanted* to hurt because the agony inside him was like a burning, searing blaze. It ate into him until his body was drenched in sweat.

The voices from the exercise yard diminished as the men were led back to their cells. There was only the odd distant cry or disembodied shout but otherwise the eerie echo of prison silence, reminding him, as it did every night of his life, that he had silenced his own baby boy.

Part Four

The Governor

CHAPTER 32

RUSSELL MORGAN trudged up the spiral staircase behind Jim Malahide. The night before he'd been on pints of Old Peculier and whisky chasers. His head throbbed with each step, and his mouth tasted like the bottom of a parrot cage.

And Malahide wasn't the most considerate of companions at seven in the morning. More like a blundering rhinoceros. His method was to turn the key and send the door crashing back whilst calling in a loud voice, 'Come on, out yer cells!'

Morgan moved in the opposite direction along the landing, wincing each time Malahide turned the key, anticipating the *crash* of the door, hearing him shout, 'Get up, you lazy bugger, Brian, come on.'

Morgan unlocked a cell and gently pushed the door ajar. 'Come on, Walter, rise and shine, your favourite time of day.' Across the landing, through the half-open doors, yawning men in pyjamas were clambering out of their bunks. Morgan opened Alan Fisher's door. 'Morning, Fisher, your wake-up call.' With the thought of a pint mug of hot tea down in the officers' station on his mind, he didn't bother looking inside.

Malahide strode back along the landing, getting the laggards out. There was no movement from Fisher's cell, so he stuck his head inside, intending to tell the lazy bastard to get his arse in gear. Something about the stillness of the figure on the bed made him draw breath. Slowly he backed out. Morgan saw him, and he saw the look on his face. He pushed Malahide aside and went in. He knelt down and pulled the blanket away. A plastic carrier bag covered Fisher's head, fastened tightly with string around his neck. Morgan took the limp hand and felt for a pulse. He waited for over a minute, and then placed the hand back beneath the blanket.

For just a few seconds more he stayed kneeling, an expression of mingled pain and genuine sadness in his eyes. Poor miserable bastard. Ending up inside a Tesco bag like a frozen chicken. Morgan pushed the emotion down, buried it deep. He climbed heavily to his feet and turned away, hitching up his pants. 'One less for breakfast.'

Down to his underpants and socks, Snoopy stood outside his cell, his gear heaped beside him, while John Udding and Jumbo Jackson conducted a pad spin. An officer was going through each item of clothing, feeling along the seams, turning his socks inside out.

Snoopy couldn't figure it. No one else on the wing was being strip-searched. Why him? Why *only* him? He smelled a whopping great stinking rat.

'You'll be all right.' Victor Braithwaite leaned in his doorway, arms folded, loving it. 'You, Rasta face, I'm talkin' to you . . .'

Jackson heard him and came out. 'You wanna go back to punishment, Braithwaite?'

Braithwaite ignored him. 'Any time you want, Rasta, any time,' he said softly, nodding his head. 'Like workin' with blacks, do you, Jackson?' he called out, as the officer went back in.

Inside the cell Udding was down on his hands and knees. Wearing latex gloves, he was examining every inch of the floor. He'd done under the table and round the toilet, and was peering under the bed. Jackson was bored, and besides, he thought it a pure waste of time.

'Braithwaite's a pain in the arse and so are these tip-offs. It's probably him doin' it, anythin' for aggravation.'

'I wanna know when the gym's open,' the pain in the arse shouted from the landing. 'Hey, Jackson, I wanna work out – you hear me?'

'Hang on.' At full stretch under the bed, Udding brought out his gloved hand and held up a condom between finger and thumb. 'Get him in.'

'Can't smoke that, can you?' Jackson said with a sarcastic grin.

Of course you couldn't, but Udding found it hard to believe that an experienced officer like Jackson didn't know that condoms were used to store and carry hooch around. You could get two full pints in one, which was then concealed under an armpit and passed round during the exercise period or at association.

Udding stood up as Snoopy was brought in. 'See this? Found it under your bunk!'

Snoopy stared at it curiously, as if it was an artefact from Mars, and held out his thin pale palms. 'Could've fooled me, man, I not seen it before. What's with you, bro?'

Udding shot him an icy glance. 'I'm not your brother.'

Snoopy twitched a lazy shrug. 'Wanna bet?'

Helen was on the phone when Marshall put his head round the door. He was about to withdraw when she beckoned him in. She pushed a hand through her hair, blinking rapidly. 'All I'm saying, Mr Bunny, is that somebody should have given me prior warning.' She held the mouthpiece away and stuck a two-page Prison Service circular in Marshall's hand. 'You read that?' She frowned into the phone. 'Is that the official date? Well, when it's confirmed please let me know. Thank you.'

She hung up and leaned back in the chair, rubbing her hands distractedly as Marshall studied the document. '"Statement of next stage of market testing,"' he read out loud.

'"The Prison Service today issued to governors a preliminary list from which one or two prisons will be selected for . . ."' He paused and glanced at her. '"Privatization."'

Helen waved him to continue.

'"Prisons listed for possible privatization, Aylesbury, Coldingly . . ."' His eye took in all the names. 'We're not listed,' Marshall said, with evident relief.

Helen signalled to Maureen Collins, who had appeared from Mavis's office. 'Give me a minute, Maureen.' She took the circular from Marshall and flipped over. 'Next page, Gary.' She found the section and read: '"It has been decided that nine adult male prisons will be subjected to more detailed qualitative analysis. Barfield is first on the list. Already contracted out are Wolds, Blakenhurst, Doncaster."'

'Any word about changing the official category? I mean, is this an A or B nick?'

Helen tossed the circular down. 'We'll be assessed on performance to date. Home Office have requested details on escapes, assaults, prisoner activity.' She tightened her lips, her expression grim. 'No wonder we're on the list. Anything else?'

Marshall perched on the corner of the desk. 'Fisher topping himself wasn't perfect timing. He had high alcohol content in his blood.'

'I know. Anything come up from the strip-searches this morning?'

'We found a condom in Oswald Snooper's cell.'

'Well, what am I supposed to do about that?' Helen said acidly. 'Applaud?'

Maureen Collins was hovering at the door, impatiently checking her watch. 'I can come back if—'

'No, just give me a second.' Helen drummed her fingers on the circular. 'I just received this, and the date to open up to full capacity is still to be confirmed.' She looked up at him meaningfully. 'But we're instructed to stand by, so it's any day as from now, Gary.'

It was maddening and frustrating to have so many questions left unanswered, decisions not taken or delayed for no apparent reason. The lack of any clear direction from the top made everyone ratty and ill-at-ease. It was little wonder, Helen thought, that a recent survey had shown that a high proportion of prison governors had trouble sleeping and woke up exhausted. They were unable to absorb what was being read or found themselves unable to listen to what was being said – summed up in the telling phrase, 'My brain doesn't work.' They also complained of suffering from chest pains, cold sweats and panic attacks. All these stress-related symptoms were put down to the never-ending changes issuing from HQ, month after month, which had started with Lord Woolf's report on the 1990 riot at Strangeways.

Here at Barfield, as everywhere else it seemed, they were running around like headless chickens, totally in the dark about what would happen next. Would the prison's category be upgraded? Would it be privatized? Would a Governor 1 rank be required to run it? How many extra prisoners were they expected to take, and when? As if the job wasn't hard enough, this vacuum of a coherent and consistent policy directive made it bloody impossible.

Marshall got up to leave. 'Norman Jones is back on the wing, no place else to put him. He should be transferred to a psychiatric hospital.'

'I'm pushing for a bed in Broadmoor,' Helen said. She came round the desk, aware that Maureen Collins was still lurking. 'That it?'

'With their rate of suicides I'd say we might get lucky,' Marshall reckoned with a sour grin. He went to the door. 'If alcohol is on the wings, so far one condom's not much to go on.'

On his way out he nodded to Maureen, who bustled in. Helen was clearly about to leave on her rounds, and she was waiting rather impatiently.

'I just wanted to run a few more names by you. They're

prisoners who have asked to join the drama group.' She detached a sheet from her clipboard. 'Ellvison, C Wing. Pallaker, also C. Rugpera, Baranie, Norman Jones and Alan Fisher, C Wing.'

'He won't be joining,' Helen said.

'Oh. I thought he was out of punishment?'

'He is. But I wasn't referring to Norman Jones. Alan Fisher.' Helen's hand was out for the list. 'He's dead.'

'Oh.' Maureen blinked a couple of times. 'So I've got an extra place available?'

'Yes.'

Accompanied by Russell Morgan, Helen did a walkabout on C Wing. Afterwards they went down to the officers' station, where Jumbo Jackson, John Udding and Andy Gordon were sitting around with a brew. With his experience prior to Barfield of drugs seizures and rehabilitation programmes, Udding was keen as mustard to root out substance abuse on the wing; the other officers, Helen could tell, were unimpressed, or perhaps a trifle sceptical about his fiery zeal. Drugs and prisons went together like a horse and carriage.

'Last night I went over to the maintenance department,' Udding informed her, 'asked them to check all the garbage chucked from the cell windows. Found five more condoms.'

Jackson raised his eyes to the ceiling. Morgan stood impassively with his arms folded. Helen was a bit short on enthusiasm herself.

'We're up for an in-depth performance analysis, so possession of condoms isn't my main concern. Anything else?'

'Anthony Kelly's on heroin,' Udding said.

Helen was impressed. Clever the way he'd done that, saved the best till last. She looked to Morgan. 'I want to see him.'

He nodded and followed her out. There was something on his mind, and now was as good a time as any.

'Officer Malahide. I think he should be transferred.'

'Right now I have all my time cut out trying to find Norman Jones a place in a psychiatric hospital,' Helen said shortly.

Morgan scratched his neck. 'Just that young Malahide seems . . . Well, you got to admit he's an unlucky sod.' He ticked off his fingers. 'First he lets two go in a helicopter. He gets put on D Wing an' a bloke hangs. Then he gets his nose busted on C Wing. Then Alan Fisher tops himself . . .' He shrugged, 'nuff said.

'Unless Mr Malahide asks for a transfer, he's like Norman Jones,' Helen replied, already on the move. 'We're stuck with him.'

She gestured to Udding, and together they walked to the exit. Gordon came up to Morgan, who said behind his hand, 'If we're runnin' a quarter full now and we got trouble, God help us when the gates open.'

Brightly lit and freshly painted, with a shiny floor, the main tunnel giving access to all the wings stretched off into the distance. Helen and Udding approached a set of gates painted bright yellow, a camera lens pointing down at them. Helen pressed a button and stood waiting, keys at the ready, for the electronic release to be operated. Still waiting, she swung her keys. 'You know anything about these privately run prisons?'

'No. Only what I've read about them,' Udding said, nodding towards the camera. 'Lot of teething problems.'

The security officer in the control room was trying to handle simultaneous requests from all over the building. Each gate had to be electronically unlocked and then relocked, with time allowed for the officers to use their personal keys. Foreshortened by the angle, Udding's face was on one of the screens as he stared up at the camera.

'Bit slow off the mark, aren't they? If we got to wait at every gate this long . . .'

Helen jabbed the button again. 'Governor, Officer Udding, gate one. What's the delay?'

Finally it was their turn, and the bolt slid back. The security officer watched them pass through. This new system was great, he thought, perfect, if only he had fourteen pairs of hands.

Anthony Kelly showed Helen the insides of both his arms and rolled down his shirtsleeves, smiling all the while as he did so. Twice now his name had been mentioned in recent wing reports for disruptive behaviour which, along with Udding's assertion that he was on drugs, made Helen want to check him out for herself. Okay, so his arms were smooth and white without puncture marks, but she wasn't fooled. It was that soporific smile that did it. He wasn't actually here in the probation office of C Wing, sitting on a hard chair across the table from her. He was a zillion miles away somewhere on a soft rose-tinted cloud. It was her task to bring him down to earth with a bump.

'That's right, Mr Kelly, you keep on smiling. But I'm warning you, if you are found with drugs in your possession . . .'

'I know the new regulations, extra twenty-one days.' She hadn't even dented him; the smile stayed intact. 'You want a urine sample?'

Helen stared at him for a moment, remembering the distraught youngster in the courtroom of only a few months ago, scared half to death, his parents weeping in the public gallery. Now he was acting the tough guy, pretending to be streetwise, and stoned out of his tiny mind.

She said sadly, 'Why are you doing this to yourself?'

'If I can lose Monday and Tuesday, that's nice; Thursday, Friday, even better.' Smiling from ear to ear. 'What have I got to lose?'

'Your life.'

The smile turned icy. 'Who gives a shit if I lose that?'

'I do, Mr Kelly,' Helen said, a flash of coldness to match his, 'because while you're here you're my responsibility.'

Andy Gordon held up his watch to the door panel, and Helen nodded. She closed the file. Kelly got up, swaying, the sudden movement disorientating him. He blundered out in a purple haze, almost colliding with Gordon and obviously not giving a fuck. Helen picked up his file. She was sorely tempted for one wild second to tear it in half. She rammed it in her briefcase. Kelly might think he had become a hard man but he had a lot more to learn; building muscles did not necessarily make you tougher or harder. Anthony John Kelly was still a young man but he was one who would have to be watched, as he steadily became institutionalized, not through any form of education the authorities had to offer but by turning into a criminal, a drug addict of his own foolish volition. How to stop the downward spiral? Helen pursed her lips; she was beginning to know, and part of the knowledge was that she had to be far stronger, tougher on the unfortunate ones like Anthony John Kelly.

Gregory Colly, the Matchstick Man, was taking the air in the new sports field at the rear of the gymnasium. It was as smooth and green as a billiard table. Fresh white lines marked out a basketball area, and beyond that there was a full-sized football pitch with gleaming white goalposts and brand-new nets. No matches had been played on it yet, though eventually teams would come in from neighbouring towns and villages to give the cons a game. The old gag – too hoary to raise even a limp smile any more – was that Barfield played all its matches at home.

Humming to himself, smiling because he was out in the fresh air, Colly strolled round the perimeter, a lone figure watched over by two officers, Tommy Nelson and the new man, Zach Tucker. Occasionally he bent over, searching for matchsticks, but they were, quite literally, thin on the ground. He stopped next to the wire and stood on tiptoe, craning his neck.

'What's that? New building over on the right. Is it a greenhouse?'

'Nope. Helicopter terminal,' Nelson said.

'Yer kiddin'.' Colly looked at Tucker. 'Is he kiddin' me?'

'Yeah. Go on, get your exercise.'

Colly strolled on, humming. As he moved out from behind the gymnasium he came into view from the main wings, and at once, because he was alone and his bald head was so distinctive even at this distance, a chorus of yells and whistles and catcalls went up.

'Dirty bastard!'

'Nonce, nonce, nonce!'

'Piss on you, pervert!'

'You fuckin' sicko shit!'

'Dirty cunt, Colly!'

He didn't seem to hear, just kept on humming, smiling cheerfully. He pounced suddenly with a cry of delight. 'Found one!' He tucked it carefully away in his shirt breast pocket.

'We keep all our matches for him,' Nelson told Tucker.

Colly looked up, a big childish beam on his face as he spotted Helen striding along the pathway that separated the sports field from the exercise yards. He waved, waggling his fingers, a bit clownlike. Helen saw him, nodded briefly, and carried on. Colly's smile faded – he was hurt that she hadn't stopped. Then just as quickly he was grinning again as he walked jauntily over to the officers, not a care in the world.

'So how is it going for you? Get a lot of flak, I bet. You're the first darkie screw I've met. Mind you, I hear there's a lot of 'em doin' bird so it's only right.'

It was so innocent that Tucker didn't take offence. Jumbo Jackson came along the gravel path outside the wire. He beckoned Tucker over. 'Astro turf, one hundred and sixty grand's worth,' he said, surveying the immaculate playing area. He would be the first to use it. 'What you think of our Matchstick Man, then?'

'Harmless little bloke.'

'Tell that to the mothers of the little girls he raped and butchered.'

Tucker covered his shock. He turned to stare at Colly, who was meandering about, searching the ground for matchsticks.

'Union meetin' in the pub tonight,' Jackson said in his ear. 'Word is, Barfield might go private.'

Helen looked up at the camera, tapping her foot. They'd better get the security system sorted, and damn quick, before a situation developed. All this waiting around was bad for efficiency, even worse on the nerves.

At the far end of the main tunnel Malahide was also waiting, Victor Braithwaite beside him in a dark blue track-suit, carrying his gym kit in a plastic bag. Malahide's nose still looked puffy and tender, dark circles under his eyes from what had been two lovely shiners. By the time the security guard in the control room got round to them, Braithwaite was spitting feathers. As soon as the gate swung open he barged straight through, striding stiff-legged down the tunnel, leaving Malahide behind to lock up.

The electronic bolt in Helen's gate slid back and she passed through. She relocked, and it was only as she turned that she saw Braithwaite bearing down on her. He seemed to fill the space, a bundle of pent-up rage, face twisted, the veins standing out on his neck. A tremor of naked fear went right through her. She was trapped between a locked gate and this large, wild-eyed man, with Malahide still some distance away.

She stood her ground, showing nothing, as Braithwaite strode up. He looked straight ahead, not at her. He seemed about to blow. He reached out and gripped a bar of the gate, staring through. The moment passed, and then Malahide arrived, clearly on edge.

Jumbo Jackson had appeared on the other side of the gate. 'Bloody hell, be here all night,' he grumbled to the camera. 'Come on, we're losin' valuable drinking time.'

Helen took Malahide aside. 'You okay?'

'No, nor is that bastard,' he muttered. 'He's asking for extra gym time.'

Helen watched as the gate opened and Braithwaite stepped through.

'Stay with Mr Malahide,' she ordered Jackson. 'Jimmy! A word.' Malahide hung back. 'In future Victor Braithwaite *must* be accompanied by two officers.'

Malahide frowned down at her. 'I was okay.'

'Maybe *you* were,' Helen said, 'but I wasn't.'

The meeting chaired by a representative of the Prison Officers Association was being held in the upstairs room of a local pub, and Helen joined some of the officers in the lounge bar before it began. She bought a round of pints for them and a Bushmills and water for herself. It was one of the few opportunities she got to socialize with them. She would have liked to do it more often, because that way you picked up on grass-roots feeling, but the demands of her job, and the intense pressure she was under, gave little time for any kind of real life, social or otherwise.

And she wasn't the only one under pressure, Helen thought, watching Russell Morgan sink half his pint in one go. He belched softly behind his hand, giving her a look. 'Malahide's very keyed-up.'

'Aren't we all? Well, what do you suggest I do with him?'

'Get him away from prisoner Norman Jones.'

'And havin' Victor Braithwaite back on D Wing is

creatin' a lot of problems,' Jumbo Jackson chipped in from the corner seat.

The beer brought out Morgan's grousing streak. He was a good senior officer, but certainly no bleeding hearts liberal. 'Bend over backwards,' he said dourly, glancing round the circle, 'keep them occupied, keep them busy, like kids.'

'Lot of them are, unfortunately, very disturbed,' Helen said, 'and we don't have enough highly qualified officers to deal with them.' She felt the flicking glances and held up her glass. 'All those present excluded, of course.'

'He's very young too,' John Udding said. He looked towards Helen. 'Malahide.'

Helen took a sip of whiskey and stared into her glass. 'You know, I sometimes wonder what would happen if you paid every inmate the money it costs to keep them here.'

Morgan wagged a finger. 'Ah, but the public want punishment, Miss Hewitt, not rehabilitation.'

There was a general movement from the bar. The officers with Helen finished their pints, and she gathered her belongings together, preparing to leave.

Jackson stood up. 'We're goin' upstairs, meeting about . . .' He raised his bushy eyebrows at Morgan. 'You heard Barfield may be privatized?'

Everyone had. Another day, another rumour. They were dropping from the skies.

'Can I get you another?' Morgan asked Helen. She was mulling it over when Lorcan Thomas happened to walk in. He was not alone. One of the younger female officers was with him, head thrown back, roaring with laughter.

'Another time, thanks,' Helen said, grabbing her coat.

CHAPTER 33

'ANYWAY,' WALTER Brinkley said, 'we got these big long sticks and we stripped them down of all the bark, then we got some string and we bent safety-pins, fishing rods, you know . . .' He frowned into space. 'And there was this sort of floating, what you call it, er–'

'Turd?' Brian Samora said.

Maureen Collins pointed at him. 'Shut up. Go on, Walter. Was it like a dock for boats?'

Eight of them were sitting in a semi-circle in the chapel, facing Maureen, who held a clipboard on her crossed knee. Behind the group, Malahide leaned forward in his chair, listening intently, continually clasping and unclasping his big freckled hands. Snoopy, Samora and Lennie Allroyd sat together, bored already with the proceedings. Norman Jones wasn't paying any heed to Brinkley's rambling reminiscence. Hunched forward slightly, arms folded, his entire concentration was focused on Maureen, who now encouraged Brinkley to continue.

He pushed up his glasses, nodding. 'Yeh, that's right – but it was rotten, some of the planks like, know what I mean? Rotted. Water was all muddy.'

'Yes, go on.'

Allroyd was almost nodding off. Snoopy yawned hugely. He covered his mouth, leaning against Allroyd, keeping his eyes to the front. 'You get it?'

Together, the pair leaned forward as if Brinkley's story

had suddenly become the most engrossing they had ever heard. Smuggled under Allroyd's arm, the officer's cap found its way up Snoopy's sweatshirt. In exchange, Snoopy wormed a tightly folded packet from the side of his woolly hat and palmed it across. The two of them sat back, Snoopy's arms crossed over the bulge.

'It was hot, really sunny, and we'd got pop, you know, lemonade, and it was like a big adventure, and we made a raft . . .' Brinkley tugged at his collar and squirmed his neck as if it really was hot. But it wasn't the remembered heat that was bothering him. It was a deeper, buried memory. He pushed his glasses with a quick, jerky movement. 'That's it.'

In the control room, Helen stood watching the group on one of the screens. She could see their lips moving but couldn't hear anything. Two officers were operating the panel now, and one of them was trying to explain the delays.

'They're all on a queue system, right? So if a gate button is pressed to be opened in E corridor and you've got four more waiting at Charlie, Delta and Foxtrot wings—'

Helen chopped her hand down. 'I don't want excuses, I don't want delays, I don't want any officer to feel insecure.' She looked to the three screens showing the long main tunnel. 'I know how it feels. Punch up the sound, will you? Chapel.'

'Brian?' Maureen Collins was saying tartly. 'You're eager to interrupt. You want to tell us your memory?'

He gave a rapid shake of the head. 'No. Not got one. An' I don't see the point of this. I think I'd be better off in edee-cashun.'

Helen went to the door. 'There will be five hundred prisoners in Barfield any day now, so cut down the delays.'

On the screen Maureen said, 'How about you, Roddy?'

Marsh shrank down in his seat, his belly hanging on his knees. 'No, nothin'.'

They were all getting bored now, Malahide included,

everyone except Norman Jones. Maureen could feel his eyes upon her. She was expert in handling groups, but even she felt uncomfortable under his fixed, almost unblinking scrutiny.

She was glad when Eric Titchmarsh volunteered. No one else was. He was a round-shouldered little man – only an inch or so over five feet – with a completely bald head, who was always rabbiting on about his days in the RAF. Brinkley suspected that the nearest Titchmarsh had been to the RAF was sitting in the three-and-nines watching *Angels One Five*.

'That was the first time I flew solo,' Titchmarsh boasted, looking round confidently. 'I was in the RAF, followed in my dad's footsteps.'

'Did you look up to your father?' Maureen asked him.

'He's short enough to look up to anybody.' Brinkley guffawed.

Titchmarsh jumped up. 'You done service, have you? You scummy little git.'

Brinkley got to his feet, and Maureen said calmly, 'Sit down, Eric, and you, Walter.'

Jones yanked Titchmarsh's arm to pull him down. The little man fell against Allroyd, who gave him an elbow in the ribs. There was a brief scuffle during which Jones slapped Brinkley across the back of the head. Malahide moved forward but didn't interfere, as Maureen remained cool and in control. She waved them down.

'Norman, there was no need for you to do that. If Eric doesn't want to remain with the group it is his choice. However, if you touch another member of the group, *you* will be out. Is that understood?'

Looming behind Jones, Malahide was flexing his fist as if itching to have a crack at him. The least little excuse would be enough. Or no excuse at all. The room had gone very quiet, everyone waiting for some kind of explosion. Even Snoopy and Allroyd were attentive.

Slowly subsiding into his chair, Jones said softly, 'Yes, Miss Collins. Sorry.'

Malahide tapped his watch. 'Time to take them over to the workshop.'

Snoopy and Allroyd couldn't get out fast enough. They scrambled up, first in line at the door, the others herding behind them. Jones remained standing, watching Maureen fold the chairs.

'There will be another group this afternoon. Anyone wishing to attend . . .' she raised her voice as they skived off '. . . please inform your wing governor or SO.'

Jones looked back at her from the door. 'See you this afternoon,' he said with a lurking smile.

Ten of them in blue overalls were grouped round the instructor, Pete Walbrook, a rather scruffy young man with long hair and an untrimmed moustache. It was joinery at this end of the workshop, metalwork at the other, where three cons were operating lathes, wearing visors and gloves to protect them from the cascades of sparks. A partly assembled cabinet stood on the bench, along with sections of a drawer that Walbrook was fitting together to demonstrate its construction.

'These joints are known as mortise and tenon. You can see how they slot together to make a tight fit.' He turned the cabinet round. 'Sides are tongue-and-groove softwood, and the metal inlay will be fitted last for the glass top.'

Snoopy was on the edge of the group, keeping an eye on one of the men working the lathes. The man had switched off the machine and was busy with a metal cutter and file. Snoopy looked to Anthony Kelly and gave a quick wink.

'Now on this drawer, it has simply been nailed,' Walbrook said, showing it round. 'But with the method we've been working on today there's a craft and a genuine feel for the grain of the wood . . .'

A bell signalled the end of the workshop period. Russell Morgan came in. 'Please return to your benches. All tools returned to the duty officer. Please return to your benches, remove overalls.'

There was some horseplay and laughter as the group dispersed. The man from the metalwork section came over, his clenched hand close to his side. As he passed by, Snoopy took delivery, and kept on going, sliding the key under the gold wristband of his watch.

Morgan was growing impatient. 'Come on, you know the routine, stop nattering! Get your gear in the lockers.'

Side by side, Snoopy and Kelly stood in front of their lockers, removing their overalls. Snoopy sneaked a glance round before opening the door, then quickly stuffed the overalls on top of the peaked cap and officer's white shirt with black epaulettes.

'It's finished,' he told Kelly, meaning he had the key. 'You stocked up?'

'Yeah,' Kelly muttered back. 'Just hope it doesn't spring a leak or it'll look like I pissed meself. You?'

'If mine splits I'll look like Niagara.' Snoopy grinned. 'Back me up through the airport.'

Kelly was more nervous than he cared to admit. He licked his lips. 'What about Victor Braithwaite?'

Snoopy closed the locker and turned the key. He punched the metal door with his fist and growled, low and nasty, 'I'm havin' him done for *me*, man! All go down the same time. We sort out the kitchen and we're out.'

The more immediate problem was getting the key past the 'airport' – the metal detector at the door. Two officers patted the men down and sent them through, one at a time. Snoopy and Kelly were jostling each other, acting stupid and stoned. The other men in the line were getting pissed off with their antics, and so were the officers. Laughing like a high-pitched hyena, Snoopy boogied under the arched rail and when the machine beeped gave a display of gobsmacked astonishment.

Kelly made a grab at him, feigning annoyance. 'Get yer watch off, Snoopy, it does it every time.'

Snoopy wove about, rolling his hips, and started to slide off his watch. Fed up to the back teeth by now, the officer wafted him to keep moving and get out of his bloody sight. Snoopy grinned, flicking out his tongue in a sexual manner. 'Tongue and groooove, man!'

Kelly came through and dug him in the back. 'Don't overdo it!'

'Kelly! No talking!' Morgan warned him. He turned to the officer next to him. 'Gov's orders, keep an eye on Kelly.' He glared after snake-hips Snoopy, jiving into the corridor. 'And if that bastard's stoned again he shouldn't be doin' metalwork.'

The drama group was down to five for the afternoon session. As a professional skiver, Walter Brinkley preferred it to anything that might resemble work or require effort. Eric Titchmarsh was back, along with Roddy Marsh and Norman Jones, and a new member, a plump Indian who sat and dozed.

It was hard work getting anything sensible out of Marsh, though Maureen Collins was patiently coaxing him along. 'What did your father do?'

'Shafted me mother and pissed off.' Marsh beamed round at the laughter, pleased at being the centre of attention. 'I got more uncles than the Royal Family.'

Maureen folded her arms, waiting for the laughter to die down. Given any encouragement, this could turn into the Roddy Marsh Show. She looked at Jones, who hadn't laughed or even cracked a smile. His piercing eyes were like laser beams.

'The first time I had an out-of-body experience was experimenting with hallucinatory drugs. LSD.' The room went very quiet. Over by the window Malahide sat watching, hands tightly clasped in his lap. Jones went on in a soft mesmerized monotone: 'Most people don't understand what LSD actually does. It raises your level of vibrations and allows you to exist on another plane. There are lots of planes of existence of different realities . . .'

Marsh's mouth was hanging open. The rest of the group was just as baffled, frowning from one to the other.

'We all vibrate at a certain level, and when the level is raised everything . . .' his hand floated in the air '. . . all seems heightened. The physical body is only one plane of reality, we can leave that plane and then there is no need for the physical body. That's what happens after death.' His hand drifted downwards, though his piercing gaze never left Maureen, who was studying the floor with a slight frown. 'I understand death,' Norman Jones said.

Two Red Band orderlies were washing the dinner trays in the kitchen annex of D Wing, making one hell of a din. Snoopy leaned in the doorway, a cigarette drooping from his lips, tapping a tray against his knee.

'Have to be done down the main kitchens,' one of the orderlies said, squinting over his shoulder through the rising steam. 'We just wheel 'em onto the wings, we dunno which urn goes to which wing. Do one, gotta do them all to make sure.'

'You sort it with the others tomorrow night, then?' Snoopy asked, and received a nod. Snoopy casually passed over his tray, but first he made sure that no one was lurking nearby, watching or listening. He sauntered off along the landing. The orderly turned over the tray. There was folded money sellotaped underneath.

Snoopy was leaning against the guard rail when Jumbo Jackson came up onto the landing. He uncoiled slowly and raised his hand respectfully. 'Mr Jackson, sir, I want to be transferred off the wing. I'm gettin' a lot of aggravation from Braithwaite. You hear me, man? I mean, man, he's a racist.'

Jackson kept on going. 'I'll put it on report. Move along,

it's lock-up.' He raised his voice to the others dawdling outside their cells. 'Lock-up!'

Five minutes later Snoopy was behind his locked door. He stood listening to the sounds of receding footsteps and the murmur of voices as the wing settled down. Finally satisfied, he unzipped his flies and inserted his long fingers. The soft blobby shape was difficult to grasp, but after a moment's struggle he slowly and carefully eased out a bulging condom filled with vodka, tightly bound with a rubber band. He held it wobbling in his palm, grinning with delight, humming a reggae tune under his breath.

Kneeling at the toilet bowl, Snoopy started reeling up a piece of twine. Attached to it were four condoms, also filled with vodka. He fastened the new one and lowered the liquor stash back down.

Helen stood at her desk, phone tucked under her chin, and reached out to lift a slat in the blind. Mavis was covering her computer terminal, getting ready for home, talking to Marshall who was leaning against the desk. Helen tapped on the glass panel and beckoned frantically.

Her voice, however, showed no agitation, remaining calm and pleasant, as she said into the phone, 'So that's Mr Andrews, Mr Duncan, the Area Manager, two further Home Office officials . . .' She nodded. 'Yes, got that, yes, and—'

She covered the mouthpiece as Mavis entered. 'No, get Gary in here.' Mavis went to fetch him. 'Could you say that again? Yes, thank you. Goodbye.' Helen put the phone down and bent over the desk, adding another name to the list. 'Keller.'

Marshall came in with Mavis, who was carrying her coat.

'Mavis, arrange for security passes for . . .' She finished writing and laid her pen down, staring at the list. 'You know anyone called Gordon Keller?'

'Me?' Mavis said blankly.

'Not you – Gary. You know him?'

'Sorry?'

Helen handed the list of names to Mavis. She put her hands on her hips. 'We've got forty-eight hours,' she told them. 'Barfield is being checked out day after tomorrow, three p.m. That's the Home Office high ranks, plus all the top brass from HQ. All they forgot was Princess Anne.' She sighed, and ran her hands through her hair. 'Every cell is now allocated. We are, in case you were not aware of it,' she swept her arms wide, 'house full.'

Helen remained with her arms folded, deep in thought, and then she slowly raised her head. 'Well, if I'm to be shafted, I won't go quietly.' She sat at her desk, turned on her computer and began to make long lists of memos, checking which officer was on or off duty. She wanted every single man in Barfield when the big walkabout went down, every single new recruit, all the new or old officers returning from Detach Duty. She wanted a show of uniforms to bank her up, stand alongside her, because she was going to give a speech. And even if it meant risking everything, nothing on God's earth was going to stop her voicing what she now felt, how her feelings, her attitude towards running a prison the size of Barfield, had changed. She would go out with a bang, and not, in any way, a whimper.

Marshall looked fatigued, grey in the face. He said dully, 'We're in good shape for any analysis, anything HQ wants to throw at us. Er . . . you need me to stay on late?' He shuffled, glancing at his watch. 'Only . . .'

'No, no, goodnight.' Helen was too preoccupied with her own to spare a thought for Marshall's problems. He hesitated, and then went out, passing Mavis who was returning from her own office, leafing through a hefty dark blue Prison Service directory.

'Night, Gary.' Mavis turned a page and ran her finger down the entries. 'Keller, Gordon, he's Governor One rank overseeing the main dispersal prisons.' She moved nearer the desk, reading. 'Big union man apparently, has publicly spoken out against the Home Secretary's privatization announcements, and he's—'

Helen was nodding. 'He's after Barfield.' Her voice sank. 'In the end they did just use me as a bloody caretaker.' It was a body blow, but she didn't sound angry or bitter or resigned; it was more a wry, sad amusement, as if all along she had been fooling herself, trying to convince herself of something she knew not to be true.

Mavis stood there, holding the manual, not knowing what to say. Rumours had been flying around Barfield for months. But she hadn't expected the news to come down so hard or so fast. Secretly she was amazed. In Helen's place she would have blown her top, thrown something, made the air blue. All those months of work and strain, busting a gut to get the place up and running, and for what? She put the manual down on the desk, fingers trembling, feeling outrage on Helen's behalf.

'You've done a damned good job here.'

'Thank you, Mavis. Go on home. That husband of yours will be waiting.'

Mavis went into her office and put on her coat. Through the slatted blinds she could see Helen standing in shadow outside the circle of lamplight, her arms folded, looking down at the main yard of the prison. Her prison. Until the day after tomorrow.

CHAPTER 34

SNOOPY'S REQUEST had been approved. He was back on C Wing.

It was shortly after nine o'clock the next morning when he climbed to the upper landing. His possessions filled five cardboard boxes, two of which he carried under his arms. Anthony Kelly had another, as well as Snoopy's pillow, blanket and sheets, and two officers helped with the rest.

'Prisoners down for the drama group must have their names on the notice board.' From the officers' station, Morgan was speaking over the Tannoy. 'Education and workshop notices have been changed. Please read the bulletin boards for further details.'

Snoopy and Kelly walked side by side along the landing, the two escorting officers a few paces behind.

'Gymnasium is now open daily, computer instruction and engineering classes will commence as from today. Barfield Prison is now fully operational. Will all inmates please check the bulletin board. Barfield is now fully operational, so timetables will be changed.'

The booming voice served a good purpose, loud enough to cover Snoopy's as he put the final pieces in place.

'We got to get the gear to the kitchen by lunch. It'll be in the tea urns for tea break – it's the last chance. Word is, we got a full house. Gotta go for it tonight, you with me?'

'What about Braithwaite?'

They arrived at the cell, its door standing open. Snoopy shot Kelly a glance. His lips mouthed, 'Tonight,' and then he turned with a broad grin to the officers. 'Thanks a lot. I appreciate this, man.'

The group was examining and trying on some white papier-mâché face masks that Maureen Collins had laid out on a trestle table which had been set up on the small stage of the chapel. It was an idea she'd picked up from an article about releasing hidden neuroses and childhood traumas in *Psychology Today*. They were like excited kids, giggling and snorting, nudging one another, and she was starting to wonder if the idea was so brilliant after all.

'This morning we will begin to re-enact some of the subjects we discussed in the previous classes.' She rapped her knuckles on the table. 'Please leave the masks alone.'

Brian Samora had swivelled his mask to the back of his head, and was walking round the stage backwards.

'Brian, you asked to come back into the group. You mess around one more time and it will be the last time.' Maureen swivelled it round to cover his face.

'Me eye-holes are too small,' Samora complained, his whining voice muffled. 'I can't see.'

James Malahide and Zach Tucker were sitting down in the front row, not paying much attention. In Malahide's opinion the woman was barmy. And *she* was supposed to be helping *them*. 'Snoopy's been put on C Wing,' he was saying. 'Braithwaite's been gettin' at him. It took three officers to carry all his friggin' gear. Tapes, stereo, Gameboy, shavin' cream, hair tonics, aftershave . . .'

'Excuse me,' Maureen interrupted curtly. 'I'd appreciate it if you didn't whisper to each other, it's very distracting. But you are welcome to join the group and participate.'

Malahide goggled at her. He'd sooner participate in a witches' coven. Tucker shook his head and hunched deeper into his chair.

Maureen was anxious to get started. She clapped her hands. 'Okay, let's form our circle.'

The two officers watched the seven of them form a ragged circle, Maureen pushing Roddy Marsh into his place. She took her place between Eric Titchmarsh and Walter Brinkley and extended her arms.

'As we did yesterday, link arms. We must learn to trust each other . . . comfort each other.' The group moved closer together, arms interlinked. Malahide rolled his eyes to the ceiling. Tucker nudged him. Norman Jones had pulled Titchmarsh to his other side, swapping places to be next to Maureen.

'Close your eyes,' she said, setting an example.

The others closed their eyes but kept on peeping at one another and sniggering. Samora and Brinkley were arm-wrestling. Maureen was well into it, eyes shut tight, breathing deeply. Jones leaned towards her, his face almost touching hers. His hand moved down from her waist to slide over her bottom.

'I like your perfume.'

'I'm not wearing any.'

Jones breathed softly in her ear, 'I know . . .'

She opened her eyes to find his, unblinking, inches away.

Gary Marshall leaned his elbows on Mavis's desk, speaking into the phone. 'If there's any change you can call me on this extension.' He put the phone down and sat rubbing his chin. He hadn't shaved that morning, and the stubble emphasized his ghastly pallor.

Mavis came through from Helen's office. 'If you want me to have your kids until the worst is over . . .'

Marshall shook his head. 'Thanks, Mavis. I don't think it can get any worse.'

*

Wearing the white masks, they were re-enacting Walter Brinkley's fishing experience. They had constructed a raft using four folding chairs, and Brinkley, his two boyhood 'pals', Titchmarsh and Samora, were crouching down holding make-believe fishing rods. Roddy Marsh stood to one side biting his nails, his mask shoved up on top of his head. Norman Jones had turned a chair round and was leaning his elbows on the back of it, looking on with tolerant disdain. Below the stage area, Malahide and Tucker had risen to watch the proceedings.

At first it seemed good-natured, the three of them yelling and laughing as they pretended to hook a fish. Then for no apparent reason Brinkley suddenly snapped. He stood up straight, fists bunched at his sides, his voice muffled yet loud and uptight from behind the mask. 'This is bloody stupid. *It's stupid!*'

Titchmarsh and Samora shied away as he tore off the mask and flung it down. He looked oddly naked and vulnerable without his glasses, his chin quivering. He took a pace back, blinking myopically at Maureen Collins who slowly approached him, and picked up a chair in both hands.

Malahide moved forward, but Maureen signalled him to stay where he was. 'Put the chair down, Walter.' Her voice was low but imperative. *'Put – it – down.'*

His face twisted and he raised the chair as if he meant to throw it. Jones came up silently behind and in one swift movement took the chair away from him. Brinkley stood like a helpless child, emotions chasing themselves across his face.

Maureen reached out her hand, not quite touching him. 'Does it always hurt you to remember the fishing trip?' she asked gently.

Brinkley bowed his head and nodded. It took him a moment to find his voice. 'I tried to reach him. I caught his hand and . . . I had hold of him, but I got scared, he was pulling me in.' He gulped hard. 'I let go. *I let go*. He kept on shouting, saying he couldn't swim.'

Maureen slowly began to circle the make-believe raft. 'Could you swim, Walter?'

'*No, no!*' Brinkley flailed his arms. 'No, there wasn't a swimmin' baths near us.'

She continued to circle round, drawing Titchmarsh towards the raft and gesturing to Samora to move closer. 'Walter, reach out with both hands now. You'll feel Brian and Eric's hands. Hold on to them. They understand. You were just a little boy, Walter.'

Brinkley broke down, sobbing. Samora was hanging back, as if the sight distressed him. But then, overwhelmed by compassion, he came forward and put both his arms around the wretched man, nearly in tears himself.

'Aw, don't cry, Walter, I don't like it, you all upset. I'm 'ere, you hold on tight, mate.'

Maureen was nodding to herself, with a trace of a smile. It was working. The barriers were coming down. Malahide looked at Brinkley and then at her, shaking his head dubiously.

Helen was taking a break, making herself a cup of coffee. A buzz of conversation floated in from the new main lounge. With the influx of officers the rest room had been extended, and there was now an additional large area comfortably furnished with sofas and easy chairs, a TV with satellite channels, and tables where the officers could eat their meals. Russell Morgan and James Malahide were standing just inside the lounge entrance, their voices clearly carrying through.

'Maybe you're readin' more into it,' Morgan said.

'I am not. She's out of her depth, and if anything was to happen she'd not be able to control them.' Helen stopped stirring her coffee as Malahide went on, 'I put any money on it, she's never had any experience in a nick this tough.'

The cup went down, slopping coffee into the plastic tray. Blazing mad as she was, Helen took a moment to fight for control. She was in icy command when she marched through into the lounge. Her gaze raked over the twenty or more officers chatting and eating lunch as she gave it to them straight.

'I am sick to death of being run down by you – all of you. I've had it for almost eighteen months and right now I don't need it.' She glared from face to face: Morgan, Malahide, Jackson, Gordon, Udding, Tucker and the rest. 'When are you bastards going to back me up?'

Morgan had his hand up. 'Hang on a second, Miss Hewitt.'

'I wasn't talking about you, honestly,' Malahide said anxiously. 'It was that Miss Collins and her drama group.'

Helen felt herself turning pink. She wished the ground would open up. Her chin wobbled then as the farcical nature of it struck her, and the room was filled with her laughter. The men were grinning, enjoying it too, and liking her all the more because of her wonderful laugh and the fact that it was at her own expense. Attitudes were changing, perhaps had already changed. The battle wasn't over, but they were on her side.

Morgan gestured to the others and tried to explain. 'Lads seem to think she's gettin' too friendly with Norman Jones.'

Right on cue, the woman in question walked in, a perfect moment of bad timing. The room went dead quiet.

'Ah! Miss Collins,' Helen said, her eyes still moist.

'Have I interrupted something? I wanted to see you.'

Helen turned about, giving Morgan a wink. 'I'm just going to my office.'

'I need a quick word,' Morgan said, catching Helen on the way out. 'More white slips, still saying there's alcohol coming in, a lot of it.'

'Be a good idea to keep your eye on the complaints box. Whoever it is is using it often enough.' She lowered her voice. 'And no more drama classes for you-know-who, okay?'

Waiting in the kitchen annex, Maureen tapped her watch. 'Er, if it's not inconvenient . . .'

Helen nodded and followed her through into the corridor.

Some of the officers were discussing the white slip situation. 'Maybe ask Zania who on C Wing can spell a word of more than four letters,' Malahide proposed sarcastically.

'Some of 'em are taking A levels and Open University degrees,' John Udding replied, giving the Yorkshire lad a hard stare. 'You got one, have you?'

Marshall was leaning with his hands braced over the draining board in the kitchen annex. He looked to be in a bad way, as if he had just quit crying or was about to start. Morgan put his arm around his shoulder. 'You should take time off, mate, do yourself a favour.' He peered into Marshall's grey, haggard face. 'Listen to me, Gary, you maybe think you're able to handle it but—'

The officers were passing through into the corridor, and Marshall hunched further into the corner, not wishing to be seen in this state. His shoulders were heaving, and he was now crying openly but still trying his utmost to keep it in. Morgan tried to give what little comfort he could to a man suffering such agony.

Helen wasn't in the mood for Maureen Collins today. Maybe she was never in the mood, she thought. The woman had a self-righteous hectoring tone that grated. But Helen had no choice as they walked briskly along to her office.

'Walter is deeply disturbed by an incident in his childhood. Do you have anything on his records?'

From her desk Mavis waved a fax, catching Helen's eye through the open door. Helen went inside. 'He's been on report over two hundred and fifty times,' was her tart response.

'I suppose that's a no!' Maureen said, pursuing her. 'Typical. Norman Jones is part of the group and I . . .'

Reading the fax, Helen moved through into her office.

'. . . I know both his parents died when he was very young. His previous probation reports actually go back a long way, foster homes, lot of institutions.'

Helen moved round her desk, still reading the fax. She looked up. 'I'm sorry, are you talking about Walter Brinkley?'

'Norman Jones,' Maureen said, emphasizing each syllable.

A beady glint came into Helen's eye. 'Thirty-eight years old and twenty-two of those years locked up.' She folded her arms, still holding the fax. 'What exactly did you want to see me about, Miss Collins?'

'I don't think Mr Jones works well in a group session.'

'So what do you suggest?'

'Intensive one-to-one therapy and, as his case interests me, I am prepared—'

'No.'

Maureen visibly rocked back as if she'd walked into a glass door. 'I'm sorry?'

'I don't think it's advisable, Miss Collins.'

'You don't think it's advisable!' Another glass door she'd marched slap into.

Helen yelled for Mavis, and when no Mavis appeared she strode through into her office, rattling the sheet of paper. '*Mavis!*'

Maureen went after her, spots of anger burning in her cheeks. 'All I was suggesting is that I have closer access to him,' she insisted, as if Helen was being deliberately stupid and obtuse.

'I think you are already too close to him.' Helen picked up the phone on Mavis's desk and dialled an internal number.

'Has something been said?' Maureen leaned over, palms

flat down. 'I think you should tell me if it has, or if anything has been implied regarding my interaction with the prisoner.'

'Is Mr Marshall still in the club room?' Helen listened, nodding. 'Fine, I'll hold.'

'I don't know what your sexual preferences are, Miss Hewitt, but mine are not men. Perhaps I should have put it on my CV. I believe somewhere inside Norman Jones is a decent human being. You obviously don't.'

Helen had had quite enough hectoring for one day. She said coldly, 'Miss Collins, you have already complained to me about being put at risk. Your physical safety is my main concern, and as such—' She broke off. 'It's Helen. I've just got notification that there is a place for prisoner Norman Jones at Broadmoor.' She stared at Maureen, who had drawn back, lips tight as a trap. 'We are to arrange his transportation from this end and—' She covered the phone. 'Was there anything else, Miss Collins?'

On her way out Maureen passed Mavis coming in, carrying a huge flower arrangement wrapped in cellophane.

'From us for your office!'

'Thank you.' Helen smiled. She cradled the phone under her chin while she made a note on the fax. 'So if you'll get all his documents ready . . .'

The two kitchen orderlies, wearing white jackets and trousers, floppy white caps hanging over one ear, were keeping a sharp eye on the head cook and three officers, who were having a real chin-wag over by the menu board. Eight trolleys were lined up, each with two big urns for tea and cocoa. The urns were filled first before being designated to a particular wing so that the vulnerable prisoners' food and drink wouldn't be tampered with.

One of the orderlies lifted the lid of an urn and gave a nod. In went a bucketful of pure alcohol. The lid was clamped down.

'Bloody condom's gone in, mate!'

'So what? Get a move on.'

One bucket down, three to go. As each urn was filled, four orderlies started wheeling the trolleys forward to where Andy Gordon, James Malahide and Tommy Nelson stood chatting with the cook. The orderly from D Wing, Snoopy's man, came in. Nervous and sweating, he sidled past the trolleys. The two orderlies had returned with the four empty buckets and stashed them under the sink unit. They sauntered back to the end of the line. It happened quickly. The D Wing orderly got the nod and dipped his hand. Folded notes were passed over and slipped inside their caps. They strolled on, whistling.

The afternoon tea detail was so routine that none of the officers paid it any attention. There were more important things on their minds.

'Word is we could go private and then somebody said they'd heard Keller – used to be at Durham – was comin' round with the Home Office and HQ.' Gordon leaned confidentially into the group. 'I know we've given her a lot of flak but . . .' He glanced at each face. 'She's not scared, know what I mean? Lotta bottle, agree? But it looks like she's gonna get *phhhtt!*' He stuck his elbow out.

The D Wing orderly came up. 'Trolleys ready for association, sir.'

Nelson picked one at random. 'Okay, that one to VP Wing.'

The officers stood aside as the trolleys were wheeled through to the corridor. The lethal brew was on its way. Just under twenty-four hours before the big-wigs did a major tour of the fancy new prison, the inmates were going to have their own celebration, and one that would not be forgotten or missed. The brew was pure alcohol, over thirty per cent of the inmates had committed drug- and drink-related crimes . . . This would be one hell of a night.

*

The chiv was nearly ready. Lennie Allroyd had wrapped a thick layer of adhesive tape round the handle of the plastic knife to aid his grip. Now, woolly hat pushed back from his forehead, he worked patiently to finish it, using a piece of sandpaper smuggled from the carpentry workshop to shape the blade to a dagger-like point.

He looked round quickly as the Tannoy boomed outside, '*Tea up. Tea up.*'

The cells were being opened along the landing. Allroyd took his time. He rolled the sandpaper into a spiral and forced it down the spine of a book. His palms were damp, and he was aware of his breathing. He blew the plastic shavings from the newspaper into the toilet bowl and flushed them away.

'Lennie! Hey! *Lennie!*' Victor Braithwaite called to him from the cell next door. 'Your mate Snoopy went cryin' to C Wing,' he taunted with a cackling laugh. 'You're all the same, you darkies, pussy-whipped.'

Zach Tucker unlocked Allroyd's cell. 'Come on, association, tea's up.' He pushed the door open a few inches and carried on.

Allroyd eased the chiv to the bottom of his washbag and pulled the cord tight. His flask under his arm, he stepped outside and followed the swaggering Braithwaite along the landing and down the stairway.

CHAPTER 35

THE STEEL mirror fastened to the wall vibrated with the heavy thud of the reggae beat. Shoulders twitching, dreadlocks swirling, Snoopy jigged in the narrow space. He stopped in front of the mirror, staring into his own eyes. Then he picked up the razor blade from the table, took a dreadlock between his fingers, and sliced it off. He kissed the dreadlock and fastened it with a safety pin to his woollen hat. One by one he cut them off and pinned them to the hat.

What had to be done had to be done, man.

Five minutes later he was zipping up his tracksuit. Beneath it he wore the prison officer's shirt and tie. His hair cut short now, he put on the peaked cap, turned it back to front, slipped on his woolly hat with its circle of dreadlocks over the top, and pulled it down to his ears. He checked himself in the mirror and grinned at the ace effect.

The inmates on C Wing were drifting down to association. Snoopy went down to join them, fingers clicking, a big smile for everyone. Lines of men were forming at the trolley. Some were taking mugs of cocoa and having their flasks filled, but as Anthony Kelly moved amongst them, spreading the word, they dumped the cocoa and queued for the second urn, topping up their flasks. A single sip and their expressions flipped. Jesus. This wasn't home-made hooch. It was pure grain alcohol. With this stuff you could climb the walls and walk across the ceiling and down the other side.

There was an apt music video playing on the TV – Martha Reeves belting out 'Dancing In The Street' – and everyone was sliding, thank you very much, easily and comfortably into party mode.

Norman Jones was standing alone, making a roll-up. Kelly went over, jerking his thumb. 'If you got a flask it's free. Everyone on the wing's gettin' some, and it's not that home-brewed crap.' He threw a light punch. '*Celebrate*, the nick's gonna be full.'

Jones licked the paper, his eyes narrowed on Kelly, and rolled it one-handed. 'Victor getting it tonight, is he then?'

'Who?' Kelly made a show of frowning blankly. 'Hey, get moving, it'll be all gone.'

Jones sucked in smoke around a cryptic smile. 'I don't drink.'

Malahide was keeping tabs on Brian Samora and Walter Brinkley. They seemed to be arguing. He moved in slowly from a distance.

'Ah, come on, I'm the only one not gorra flask,' Samora whined, 'so you can get my share in yours and we split it.'

Sipping from his mug, Brinkley took the flask from under his arm. 'Get back to the tea urn then, go on. They're still dishin' it out.'

About to scurry off, Samora saw Malahide approaching and stuck the flask back under Brinkley's arm.

Brinkley stared at him. 'What you doin'?'

Malahide's six-feet-six shadow fell over them like a black raincloud. 'What you got there, Brian?'

'Er, nothin'.' Samora had an inspiration. 'Just me pen, like I need it fer the edee-cashun class.' He held up his felt-tip pen. 'It's just a pen, Mr Malahide, sir.'

'He's lyin',' Brinkley said promptly, and Samora nearly had a heart attack. Brinkley grinned. 'He's gonna ink up. Is it okay? Boss, sir, Your Majesty, if I give him me red felt-tip and he gives me his green? You won't put us on report for that, will you?'

'No. Go on.' With a bored wave of the hand Malahide went on his way. Behind his back, at the trolley, a chain had formed, flasks passing back and forth so fast they were practically a blur.

Kelly was getting anxious. His hard act and tough talk were wearing thin now that the time was near. He sought out Snoopy, who was faking his usual stoned self but was actually sharp as a tack and keyed-up, adrenalin pumping. 'Wait, just keep cool, stuff'll take hold soon . . .'

'You sure this is gonna work? I mean, all those monitors?' Kelly was worried about the security cameras at every gate.

'One black face same as another, man,' Snoopy assured him. 'Chill out, man. We're gonna make it.'

Martha was still dancing in the streets, and half a dozen inmates had decided to join her, jiving in front of the TV. Whoops and cries and slightly hysterical laughter came from various groups scattered about the association area. Norman Jones stood alone, smoking and looking on, laughing softly to himself.

At the door of the officers' station, Russell Morgan was putting on his officers'-issue black belted raincoat. He beckoned Malahide over.

'I'm going off now, gonna have a few jars with Gary. Relief is here.' He raised his head towards the TV. 'Gettin' a bit rowdy over there.'

He buttoned up and headed off to the pub.

Jumbo Jackson was having trouble getting them down to the showers on D Wing. Stupid bastards were acting like a bunch of giggling schoolgirls, only worse. Finally he got them rostered and heading towards the stairway, carrying their towels and washbags.

'Keep moving. Stop messin' about, Victor.'

Victor Braithwaite had lurched against the guard rail. He hung onto it and then stumbled downwards, gripping the barred cage of the stairway, a big vacant grin on his face. A burst of raucous laughter rang out as the men bumped and jostled one another.

Jackson did a check on the open cells, making sure nobody was lurking behind. He pushed open Braithwaite's door and looked in. There was an empty flask on the floor, its metal stopper and upturned plastic cup on the bed. Shaking his head, Jackson carried on down the landing.

The shower room was boisterous tonight, a lot of towel-flicking and shouted obscenities as the naked men waited in line. Some of them were in almost as bad a state as Braithwaite, who was staggering about, red-faced with laughing, grabbing at shoulders to prevent himself falling.

Near the front, Lennie Allroyd called back, 'This stall's empty, Vic.'

A gap opened up. Dodging the flicked towels, Braithwaite wove his way forward. Allroyd stood aside and gave him a small push towards the end stall. At the same moment an argument broke out. It was the bald, diminutive figure of Eric Titchmarsh who caused the diversion, making a sudden lunge at the prisoner in front of him.

'You nicked my shampoo, you little prick, that's mine.' He tried to snatch it from him. 'You thievin' bastard, I'll have you!'

The jostling men closed in around them like a rugby scrum, whooping encouragement. It wasn't a real scrap, just a bit of pushing and shoving, but it served its purpose in grabbing the attention of Jumbo Jackson and Zach Tucker and blocking their view of Allroyd, half crouching near the shower stalls, hand inside his washbag.

Braithwaite was leaning back against the tiled wall, hair plastered flat to his head by the jet of water. Through the rising steam two figures appeared, towels swathed around their heads, slits for eyes. Braithwaite didn't even see them, never knew what hit him as his legs were kicked from under him and he went down hard, his broad muscular frame thudding to the tiled floor. Two pairs of hands pinned his shoulders. Allroyd was in fast. He wrenched Braithwaite's head back by the hair, raised the pointed blade and drove it down at the exposed throat, deep into the jugular. The white plastic was engulfed in a bubbling red fountain, the spray from above swirling it over his hairy chest.

'This isn't shampoo, it's conditioner, look.' Jackson was holding Titchmarsh at arm's length. 'Look at the label! Can't you fuckin' read?'

'I can fuckin' read!' Titchmarsh snarled in a slurred voice. 'What you think I'm wearin' glasses for?'

'But you not got a hair on yer head, Eric,' Jackson said. 'Now tell me the truth, is it yours?'

'*Yes*! Just because I'm bald don't mean I don't have to condition me head!'

It was like bedlam in here tonight with this rowdy lot, and Jackson had had enough. He signalled wearily to Tucker, who shouldered through the swaying surge of men, most of them helpless with laughter.

'All right, come on, settle down,' Tucker said, hauling bodies. 'Start moving out.'

He pushed through and took a gander into the stalls, turning off the showers that had been left on. Allroyd was quietly on his way. Carrying his washbag, his other arm around Titchmarsh, he was covered by three or four prisoners as they headed for the exit.

Hearing the hiss of the shower, Tucker called out to the end stall, 'Come on, time's up!'

He moved towards it and then noticed that water was cascading into the drainage channel outside the door. The water was streaked with red. Tucker ran the last few paces and skidded on the wet tiles. He got a glimpse of the sprawled body before he slipped and went down himself. Jumbo Jackson whipped round to see Tucker scrambling up, watery red blood dripping from his hands, the front of his uniform shirt saturated in it. Thinking he'd been chivved, Jackson gave a blast on his whistle.

'For chrissakes, gimme a hand here!' Tucker yelled. 'Man

down, we got a man down.' He shook his head wildly as Jackson charged forward, arms out as if to support him. *'Not me, it's not me!'*

Jackson went down on his knees inside the stall. Braithwaite's head was jammed at an angle against the wall, the blade sticking out from his neck, blood pulsing in waves from the gaping wound. There wasn't a speck on his face, washed clean by the jetting shower, but the rest of him had a rose-tinted hue.

An alarm bell jangled in the corridor, and then the general alert siren started its monotonous wail.

'Open the bloody gate! It's the alarm, you bastards!'

Russell Morgan wrenched at his raincoat, nearly tearing off the buttons. He stared up at the camera and slammed the gate with his hand. 'Open the fucker!'

Jumbo Jackson panted up behind him, his hands and uniform smeared with blood. 'Check your wing. We got D Wing inmates pissed out of their heads.' The bolts slid back. Jackson yelled to the camera not to relock the gate, and ran after Morgan. Reinforcements were on their way, and the less delay the better.

Little Richard's 'You Keep On Knocking But You Can't Come In', blasting out from the TV, hit them like a tidal wave as they turned the corner to the gates of C Wing. Morgan had his key ready, gripping the bars impotently, while Jackson was shaking his fist at the camera. 'What the bloody hell are you waiting for? It's an alarm, open the gate!'

On the far side of the association area Malahide was wading through the jiving prisoners, trying to reach the TV set. 'Turn it down. *Turn it down!'*

Andy Gordon didn't have a clue what was going on. Men were slumped all over the place, pissed out of their skulls. One of the kitchen orderlies was down on all fours, throwing his guts up. Nearly drowned out by Little Richard, the general alert siren wailed, although Gordon couldn't figure out why, as the wing seemed to be secure. 'Is it security testing again?' He cupped his hands, shouting to Malahide through the din. 'Eh? Jimmy!'

Concealed in a corner of the kitchen annex, Snoopy unzipped his tracksuit and kicked his legs free. He peeled off his woolly hat and stuffed the hat and tracksuit into one of the ovens. He turned the peaked cap to the front, smoothed his shirt collar and pulled his tie straight. Then he pressed back, the sweat streaming down his face, as he spotted Morgan and Jackson coming onto the wing. They didn't relock, and the gate swinging open drew him like a magnet. But still he waited. Give it a minute, maybe two. Let the Scotch twat get into the fray first, then make his move. Don't wreck it by acting rash, man.

Morgan was standing, hands on hips, surveying the drunken turmoil all around him. '*Malahide!*' The veins bulged on his neck. '*Get over here!*'

Brian Samora came weaving by and peered groggily at Jackson's sodden uniform and bloody hands. 'Eh, is that tomato ketchup, Mr Jackson? Or you busted somebody's snozzer?' Samora danced round him, jabbing his fists. 'Ya keep'a knockin' but ya can't come in . . . Ya keep'a knockin' but ya can't come in . . . Ya keep'a knockin' . . .'

Jackson gripped Samora's face between his massive hands. 'You're pissed, Brian,' he said, pushing him away.

Morgan stripped off his raincoat and threw it over a chair. Still seething at the shambles on his wing, and at Malahide for letting it go this far, he didn't notice as the raincoat was whisked away, Snoopy buttoning it up and walking off.

Jackson was too busy hauling men to their feet. He dragged the groaning kitchen orderly up by the scruff of the neck and set him on a chair. 'Oi! Malahide, get 'em back to their cells.' He took out his whistle and blew a shrill blast, striding over to Malahide, who wasn't having much success with the dozen or so inmates bopping to Little

Richard. The men were simply ignoring him. For all his size and strength there was panic in his blue eyes. He was out of his depth.

'What's the matter with you? Look at 'em,' Jackson said, pointing to a couple of inmates slumped over the snooker table, 'they're all drunk out of their heads. *Get 'em back in their friggin' cells* . . .' He looked round for assistance. 'Oi, Udding, give us a hand.'

John Udding wasn't even on the wing. It was Snoopy. He was near the open gate, staging a struggle with Kelly, hissing in his ear, 'Wait, wait. I'll give the word.'

A roar went up as somebody put a snooker cue through the TV screen. A drunken brawl started, chairs flying about, though miraculously Little Richard kept right on rocking through it all. Holding Kelly's hands behind his back as if he were cuffed, Snoopy pushed his struggling 'prisoner' into the corridor. They turned the corner to the next set of gates. Hat pulled low, raincoat collar turned up, Snoopy pressed the button and fumbled for his key.

'Udding with prisoner Kelly. Open up, takin' him to the Block. Come on, man!'

The security guard in the control room checked the two figures on the screen and thumbed the release button. 'Udding, gate two. Entry.' Then his attention switched to the mayhem on the other screens. 'Christ, bloody get back-up for C Wing. C Wing!'

It was hopeless, and even with the arrival of Udding and Tucker, Morgan knew he was fighting a losing battle. 'For chrissakes get the Dep in, all hell's breaking loose!' He pulled two inmates apart, yelling over his shoulder, 'Somebody contact Mr Marshall, he's at the local!'

Jackson was already on the phone in the officers' station. Udding stood outside, staring down at a drunk lying sprawled across the doorway. 'Looks like the pub's opened up here. What's going on?'

Jackson slammed down the phone and marched out, kicking the drunk out of the way. 'They want back-up in the VP Wing. They're all pissed as well.' He gestured grimly, 'Get 'em banged up and start the count,' and glared ferociously as a chorus of drunken singing echoed throughout the wing.

Colly was singing along with Pat Boone. It was his all-time favourite, 'Red Sails In The Sunset'. They certainly didn't write them like that any more. He tipped the flask and licked the last few drops from the rim. The light from the Anglepoise lamp threw into splendid relief his matchstick models. All the years, the painstaking effort, the dedication that had gone into them. Incredible. He levered himself up, missed his footing, and stumbled against the windmill, almost dislodging it from the shelf. Colly slowly straightened up, swaying, staring befuddled at the windmill. Incredible, and for what? He gripped the flask, took a swing, and smashed the windmill to smithereens. He swung the flask and the galleon was reduced to matchwood. He swung the flask again and smashed down.

Somebody – Walter Brinkley wished he knew who the cunt was – had smacked him in the mouth, and he sat on the stairway, head bent forward, blood dripping into his hands.

Over half the wing was still out, but one by one they were rounding them up and banging them away. Brinkley was no danger, and Brian Samora was harmless enough, dancing with himself round the overturned snooker table.

Malahide and Udding had cornered Norman Jones, who was the only stone-cold-sober con on C Wing. He raised his hands, not aggressively or defensively, just saying, 'Back off, let me be.' Udding was prepared to give him the benefit of the doubt. Malahide wasn't. He hated Norman Jones so much he could taste it, and feared him in equal and exact measure. And he'd never get a better chance than this.

Easing the baton from his pocket, Malahide twined the leather thong around his fingers, and got a good one in across the side of his head. Jones fell back against the wall, taking the blow and shaking his head. Udding tried to restrain Malahide from going in again, but it was too late – for Malahide. Jones had snapped. He was off his tree and out of his trolley. He sprang forward, spitting and snarling and growling in his throat like a wild animal. He got Malahide's baton in his front teeth, snapping them clean off, and kept on coming. Russell Morgan had been half-way down the stairs when he saw Malahide take the first swipe. Now he charged straight in, baton flailing, and the two officers with him did likewise. Udding stood back, not taking part, but that still left four of them, batons out, beating Jones to the floor. He curled up, body hunched, protecting his head, as the batons and boots went in.

'*Fight, fight, fight.*' The chant went up all over the wing.

It took four officers, plus Morgan, to drag Norman Jones kicking and screaming back to his cell. When he came down again, having locked up, the senior officer was done in to the point of exhaustion. He pointed a trembling finger.

'I saw that, Malahide, and you . . .' He pointed to Udding. 'Pair of you, see me when they're all banged up for the night.'

Helen was on her way to C Wing to find out what the hell was going on down there. By all reports it sounded like the proverbial piss-up in a brewery. Accompanied by two officers she entered the accommodation wings, and after yet another frustrating delay with Security passed through the gate into the main tunnel.

A prisoner under escort was coming towards her, hands cuffed behind his back. From twenty yards away she recognized him as Anthony Kelly, and the officer looked like John Udding, though with the peak of his cap pulled low over his eyes and his raincoat collar turned up it was difficult to tell. Kelly was struggling, but the officer had him under control. As they hurried past, the officer said, 'Taking this one down the Block. Get to the wing, it's out of control.'

Helen nodded, glanced to the floor, and carried on. Quickening her pace, an officer either side of her, Helen said in a low voice, 'It's not Udding. Just keep walking. Let him get to the gate.'

Helen reached the next gate at the same time as the prisoner and his escort arrived at theirs. She pressed the button and gestured urgently to the camera, her key in the lock and ready to turn the moment the bolt slid back. She glanced behind her. The prisoner and his escort were looking up at the camera. Key in hand, the officer's finger was on the button. The electronic bolt opened, Helen and the two officers passed through, and Helen swiftly relocked and stood in full view of the camera.

'Get Security into this corridor now. *Do not open interlocking gate.* We have two prisoners attempting to escape. Prisoner Anthony Kelly and . . .' She looked through the bars along the tunnel. 'I don't know who the other one is but it's not Officer Udding. He's wearing track shoes!'

Hunched inside the raincoat, Snoopy repeatedly jabbed the button. He glanced over his shoulder towards Helen and then desperately up at the camera. 'Open the gate. Officer with prisoner. *Open the gate!*'

The corridor alarm went off. Snoopy wouldn't give up, punching the button and hitting out at the gate. Kelly turned round to face Helen, letting his arms fall by his sides. They'd been rumbled and he knew it. Both of them trapped like rats in a concrete pipe with no way out.

The three pints of Old Peculier he'd sunk with Marshall earlier that evening were fast being sweated out of Russell Morgan. It was pouring off him. Not only was he very tired, having been on duty since seven-thirty that morning, he was also very angry. And not just with Malahide and Udding, but with himself too. He had the pair of them on the carpet in the officers' station, laying down the law.

'You listen to me! I never want any aggravation going down between prison officers in front of the inmates again. You had no need to hit him, Malahide.'

'But *you* hit him,' Malahide pointed out indignantly.

'We all friggin' did. That lets you off the hook,' Morgan said with a glare at both of them.

Which made Udding blazing mad. 'I didn't! And if this is going down on report I'll bloody *say* I didn't.' He jerked his thumb at Malahide, his lips tightening. 'You should put on report that he's a liability.'

Morgan jabbed a finger, telling them to shut it as the Governor came onto the wing, a raincoat draped over her arm. She looked round despairingly at the shambles left behind by the revellers: the smashed television set and overturned snooker table, broken chairs, clothing scattered about, odd shoes, cups and mugs left where they'd been thrown, vomit on the stairway. Another job for the brown-overalled squad.

'Go on,' Morgan told the two men. 'Get Maintenance started and clear this mess.'

Helen could see how uptight they were as they strode off, and how knackered Morgan looked as she came through the door. 'This is yours, isn't it?'

'Aw, shit!' Morgan took the black raincoat from her. He hadn't even realized it was missing.

Helen said threateningly, 'And if this belongs to any officer . . .' From her pocket she took the key that had been found in Snoopy's possession. 'Any injuries? Apart from Victor Braithwaite?'

'Nope.' Morgan decided not to mention Norman Jones. 'We'll have a lot of hangovers by morning.'

'You know we've got HQ at three.' Helen nodded to the wrecked association area. 'So by morning, Russell, this had better be back to normal.'

'Thank God it happened tonight, then.' He grunted as he picked up an empty flask from the floor. 'Don't know about you but I could do with a snifter meself.'

Helen stared at the flask on the table. 'Where's Gary? It was his duty tonight.'

'Oh, he was here, Miss Hewitt,' Morgan blurted, rubbing his hands briskly. 'But he, er, went off to sort somethin'.'

Helen knew he was lying, and Morgan could tell that she knew. Both of them knew damn well Marshall was down the boozer. She was about to take him up on it, when Morgan, one of her best senior officers as far as she was concerned, a real mainstay, suddenly hunched away from her, pinching his nose. His hand was shaking. Every day was a strain, but today he'd taken a crock full.

Helen touched his shoulder. 'Go home, go on, it's all under control. Go home.'

Snoopy was being banged up by Officer Nelson in the punishment block.

'Nice try,' Nelson said. 'Feel a bit like Samson now, do you?' He grinned, looking at Snoopy's close-cropped hair.

'Lights out!' came over the Tannoy, and a moment later the wing was plunged into darkness, just a faint glow from the officers' station.

In his cell on C Wing, a still inebriated Brian Samora was standing on a chair, squinting at his bare arm in the mirror. Concentrating hard, he was jabbing the red felt-tip into the skin, engaged in his very own do-it-yourself tattoo.

'Lights out!'

The cell light went out.

'Awww, shit,' said Samora in the darkness.

A tinny transistor down the wing was playing 'Help Me Make It Through The Night'.

Wearing his day clothes, Norman Jones was lying on top of his blankets, staring up at the darkened ceiling. His face was covered in bruises, one eye nearly shut with an angry red swelling, and his mouth was bleeding from having his front teeth knocked out. His arms were folded protectively over his chest, nursing the pain of two fractured ribs.

The peep-hole slid open and Morgan's eye appeared.

'Any complaints, Norman? Norman? You don't want to file a complaint, do you?'

Jones slowly shook his head.

Morgan closed the peep-hole and made his way back down the wing, a single dim night light burning overhead. The brown-overalled clean-up team were hosing down the stairway and mopping the association area where somebody had pissed on the floor.

Morgan was about to get his raincoat and call it a day when Gary Marshall came through the gates, unsteady on his pins. He made a floppy gesture of the arm, and said unnecessarily, 'I was in the pub . . . then heard . . .'

'You look worse off than some we had on the wing,' Morgan greeted him. He wrapped his arm affectionately round his shoulder. 'All right, mate, are you?'

Marshall wobbled, and Morgan had to hold him up. He was past the weeping stage. The alcohol had numbed him into a state of stoic resignation. 'Nope, but it's almost over.'

It wasn't Marshall who crumpled, it was Morgan. Holding Marshall's face in his hands, he had to fight with all his might to keep it bottled inside. But he was losing the battle. He cleared his throat and said gruffly, 'I'm sorry, tired out.'

Marshall slapped him softly across the face. 'It's me that should be cryin', not you, you big soft bugger. Come here.'

Still wobbling, he put his arms around the stocky, exhausted Morgan and gave him a bear-hug.

CHAPTER 36

TODAY WAS the big day. The VIPs from the Home Office and senior people from Prison Service HQ were due to arrive soon after lunch, and there was a mountain of work to get through before then. Helen's first call was a visit to the hospital wing to check on the walking wounded from the previous night's drunken revels. Marshall went along with her, though judging by his rinsed-out eyes and pasty complexion he was himself a suitable case for treatment.

As for Helen, she had never looked better. Hair shining and make-up immaculate, wearing a superbly tailored dove-grey suit with wide lapels, she had decided on her highest heels which, with her shoulders thrown back, gave her a statuesque bearing.

Marshall unlocked the gate and followed her long stride into the hospital annex. 'Wings cleaned and back in order. Both escapees in the Block.' He was giving her an update digest from the sheaf of morning reports attached to his clipboard. 'I've arranged transport for Norman Jones. He got into a bad fight last night, we needed the doc to sedate him, but his gear is packed and ready.'

Helen paused in the doorway and gazed round. It definitely looked like a hospital today. All the beds were occupied, two extra cubicles had been set up, and the rows of chairs were filled with the sorriest-looking specimens Helen had seen since the last Tory Conference. Dr Thomas was attending to the pale, dazed Matchstick Man in a curtained cubicle, and three auxiliary nurses were flitting here, there and everywhere.

'We've got hangovers and belly-aches,' Marshall said, gesturing round. 'The bloody stuff was lethal. Pure alcohol.'

'It didn't come from here, did it?' Helen addressed the question to Dr Thomas, who was crossing to another patient.

'No, it did not,' he replied curtly. 'I'm afraid Colly is in a catatonic state. How in God's name did it get on every wing?' He went off, shaking his head.

Marshall spoke quietly in Helen's ear. 'I think we know who's been bringing it in.'

'You think?' Her voice was just as quiet, but deadly with it. 'You had better sort it, Gary, and before three o'clock.'

There was a hunted look on Marshall's face as he moved heavily to the door. Dr Thomas noted it, but if Helen did she gave no sign. She was the Iron Lady this morning. She called out to Dr Thomas, 'Get Norman Jones's medical records ready, will you?'

He nodded, watching her, and crossed to the desk.

'Oh, Gary . . .' Half-way through the door, Marshall turned, shoulders slumped, weighed down. 'Mavis has a list of every officer on duty today. Will you make sure all of them, and any staff not on the wings, are in the officers' section . . .' She held up her watch and tapped it with a fingernail. 'Two-thirty. That's all of them, Gary.'

He sighed, turned about, and trudged off.

'Have the mortuary removed prisoner Braithwaite yet?'

Dr Thomas stood in front of her, hands stuffed into the pockets of his white coat. He seemed edgy, though Helen couldn't think why. He said shortly, 'Coming for him any minute.' His lips had a curl to them. 'We'll be neat and tidy by three, Governor. Not a stiff in sight.'

Inside one of the cubicles, its curtain drawn back, Norman Jones was being helped into a wheelchair. He was wearing a prison-issue dressing gown over striped pyjamas, and slippers on his bare feet. His head was heavily bandaged, and one of his hands was bound in a stocking sling. He moved stiffly, in obvious pain, and had a vague, shell-shocked look, seeming not to know where he was or what was happening to him. It was rather sad and pitiful.

'You know how badly beaten he was? Or is?'

Helen widened her eyes. 'The entire wing was drunk and disorderly, Dr Thomas.'

The nurse placed a brown paper bag containing his toiletries and a few possessions in Jones's lap, along with a tattered paperback, the sum total of his worldly goods.

Jumbo Jackson appeared in the doorway. 'We're ready for prisoner Jones, van's outside. Hello, Norman!' he said, as the nurse wheeled him from the cubicle. 'Who's a lucky man then, eh? You heard all the stories about Broadmoor, have you?'

As he went by the paperback slipped from his knee to the floor. Helen bent to pick it up. Norman Jones was trying to turn his head, but couldn't because of the bandages, and gesticulating weakly.

'Wait a minute,' Dr Thomas called.

Helen was reading the flyleaf. 'No, let him go,' she said.

Dr Thomas stared after Jones as he was wheeled out, and then turned his stare on Helen. He was a man who rarely lost his temper, but this looked like being one of those rare occasions. His nostrils flared, as he tried to control his breathing.

'You mind if I say something to you? I mean, I've obviously heard all the rumours, that you may be out of Barfield—'

Helen slowly closed the book and placed her hand gently on the cover. She looked up at him. 'I'm sorry? What?'

Dr Thomas went over to his office and held open the door. Helen checked the time, still a million things to do, but went inside. He closed the door.

'This'll only take a minute, and what I am about to tell you may be unethical but—'

'I have the Home Office and HQ here this afternoon,'

Helen reminded him, still fidgeting with her watch. The tension was getting to her; she was only now beginning to realize how much.

'Yes, I know,' Dr Thomas said. 'But do you know that Gary Marshall's wife has terminal cancer?'

Helen looked at him blankly as the fact took its time to sink in.

'She might even be dead. Now if he hasn't chosen to tell you, that is his business, but at the same time you should have been the first person he told.'

Helen turned away from him, frowning slightly.

'Do you understand what I'm saying? If your officers can't talk to you, then you're not the right person for this job you're so obsessed with—'

Helen spun round. 'What?'

Dr Thomas put up his hand. 'No, let me finish. You may have a vocation but don't for one second think you're the only one here that has. You've got officers that care, Helen, and you've also got some that get away with beating up a mentally sick man like Norman Jones. As a doctor I am responsible for the inmates' well-being, and . . .' He hesitated, then looked at her straight. 'I've changed my mind. I want to stay on here.'

'Good.' Her tone was clipped, her nod brisk. 'I wish you'd been able to talk to me before now—'

Her bleeper went. She took it out and checked the message. 'Excuse me.' She went to the door.

'Helen, listen, if ever you need—'

'No, you listen.' Facing him, her look was as straight as his had been. 'Don't talk down to me. For eighteen months I've had no private life, just Barfield. You suddenly feel more than medically responsible for the inmates. I was responsible for you, for every prisoner and every member of staff. I needed you to confide in me. You might just be too late.'

'Then I apologize.' Dr Thomas moved towards her. He

took a breath and let it go abruptly. 'But I doubt if you would have listened.'

'I've made a lot of mistakes,' Helen admitted. 'I have only now truthfully really understood what it means to be Governor.'

Dr Thomas had looked at her often, but he was seeing her for the first time now. It had taken guts to say what she had. The woman had strength and honesty and, above all, complete, unflinching integrity.

He leaned forward and kissed her on the cheek. 'Good luck,' he said softly.

'Thank you.'

Helen opened the door and looked back at him. She was smiling. 'And having a schoolgirl crush on you wasn't always a great help.'

Standing in the doorway, Thomas watched her walk through the ward to the gates, speaking on her radio. Marshall's distorted voice crackled through.

'I'm going up to the control room.'

'I'll see you there, Gary,' Helen said, striding on.

Walter Brinkley stared down at the fried eggs and bacon, sausage and fried bread, swimming in grease, and pushed the tray back to the orderly. He turned away from the breakfast trolley, head throbbing, and gingerly touched the huge square of Elastoplast that entirely covered his nose.

Brian Samora went by at a snail's pace in a sagging T-shirt, sipping a mug of tea. 'I couldn't face eatin' either. I got a shockin' headache. I did me tat last night.'

A speck of consciousness swam up through Brinkley's hangover.

'What?'

'Me tat. I inked up, do you wanna see? Hold this.'

He handed Brinkley his mug and pulled his T-shirt over his head. He turned side on to show the top of his arm. It took Walter a minute to focus, and when he did he saw that it was a tattoo in red felt-tip. He squinted more closely. 'What does "nairB" mean?' Brinkley asked, puzzled. '"Nerd"?'

'No, you prick, it says Brian,' Samora told him scornfully.

Brinkley looked again. A big grin spread across his face, and then he was laughing soundlessly, shaking all over. 'Oh, you pillock, you done it by the mirror, didn't you?'

Samora grabbed his own shoulder and peered down at it with a frown.

'Hey!' Brinkley beckoned urgently to Eric Titchmarsh, passing by with his tray. 'He done his own ink! Got his name back to front, no kiddin'.' He doubled over, choking with laughter. '"nairB". "*nairB*" . . .'

Samora's shoulder became the prize exhibit, everyone wanted a look, and soon the entire wing was rocking with laughter, even the officers were creasing themselves.

Samora himself wasn't amused. Just very confused.

On her way to the control room, Helen made a quick detour to the chapel where she found Maureen Collins unpacking the white masks and drama props in preparation for the morning's session. She showed her the paperback that Norman Jones had dropped. Maureen was clearly touched when she read the inscription.

Helen felt something of the same emotion. She said hesitantly, 'I apologize for the way I spoke to you, Maureen.'

'Thank you,' Maureen said, handing back the book.

'I'll make sure you get this,' Helen said, slipping it into her pocket. Her radio crackled. It was Marshall, paging Helen's call sign, Victor 1. 'I'm on my way, Gary.'

He was waiting for her in the control room, the green glow from the screens emphasizing the lines of worry etched deeply into his face. Helen went straight to him, and put both hands on his arm, the contact firm, supportive.

'I'm very sorry about your wife. If you need any time off, if there's anything at all, please ask me . . .'

Marshall gave a small, tight shake of the head. 'There's nothing.'

The hard carapace of the Iron Lady fell away. 'You make me feel very inadequate,' Helen said wretchedly. 'I should have got to know you better. I apologize.'

'Thank you.' The emotion was all there, just beneath the surface, and he sublimated it, as he had every day over the past agonizing months, with business as usual. 'I got all the staff coming in, as you requested, and . . . what's this?'

He took the paperback book she proffered and stared at the cover. It was the collected plays of Jean Genet, the French novelist and playwright, who had spent many of his early years in prison.

'It belonged to Norman Jones. Look in the flyleaf.'

Marshall did so, and read out the inscription. '"For Maureen Collins, whose laugh was like music".'

'Norman Jones wrote all those notes in the complaints box, Gary.' Helen pointed to the flyleaf. 'It's the same handwriting.'

On the screens the civilian catering staff and workshop instructors were passing through Security in the gate-lodge. The scruffy joinery instructor with the drooping moustache, Pete Walbrook, came into view, carrying a large canvas bag of tools. 'Take a lot more than one of my hacksaws to saw through the bars you got up now,' he joked.

The gate guard pointed upwards. 'Smile, you're on camera, Pete!'

Walbrook glanced up with a broad grin.

Looking from the book in his hand to the screen, Marshall said, 'It could be him, according to Norman. He comes in on a regular basis for the workshops.'

He and Helen watched as the guards carried out a thorough search of the canvas bag, and then asked Walbrook to remove his overcoat, which was also closely examined. They handed them back to him.

'Norman was wrong,' Marshall said, shaking his head. 'They've not found anythin' – not so much as a condom.'

'I'll have that dressing table finished for you today,' Walbrook was cheerfully telling one of the guards, collecting his gear. 'This the new security measures, is it?'

Eyes narrowed, Helen watched the instructor moving past the barrier. Something that Marshall had just said was ringing in her head like an alarm bell. She jabbed the intercom button and leaned towards the mike. 'Please body-search Mr Walbrook! Take his trousers down if necessary.'

Plainly, Walbrook didn't like it, but he had little choice.

Reluctantly he unfastened his belt and lowered his trousers. Taped to his thighs and the insides of his calves were several bulging condoms, filled with vodka.

'My God,' Helen exclaimed, 'he's a walking distillery!'

Shirt-tail flapping, trousers around his ankles, Walbrook was a pathetic sight, and his whingeing whine was pathetic too. 'Aw, shit, look, I needed a few extra quid, no harm done, eh? Come on . . . I meant no harm, I was broke.'

Helen went to the door, her face a mask of suppressed fury. 'Alan Fisher had been drinking before he killed himself. No harm? Victor Braithwaite was drunk, according to Dr Thomas. No harm?' She pointed to the screen. 'I want him charged. *No harm*! Tell that to Gregory Colly.'

'I'll get the gate cleared,' said Marshall. 'We don't want the Home Office confronted by rows of condoms.'

Helen's big bellowing laugh floated back as she went out into the corridor and down the stairs. Marshall remained in the control room, anxiously awaiting the arrival of the visitors. Ten minutes later four black limousines drew up outside the gate-lodge. Amongst the dozen or so sober-suited figures who disembarked, which included Operational Director Royston Andrews and Sean Duncan of the Home Office, Marshall picked out Gordon Keller at once. Tall and austere, with a knife-edge parting in his iron-grey hair, he strutted towards the main gate with a kind of arrogant swagger.

Marshall touched the shoulder of the duty officer seated at the console. 'That's the wannabe Governor of Barfield.'

Marshall turned and his stocky figure hurried down the corridor. He called out after Helen and paused as she turned to face him.

'They're trying to trip us up. They're here early, just seen the lot arriving in the main drive.'

Helen frowned. 'Damn, I'm not ready.'

Marshall gave a shrug, digging his hands deep into his pockets. 'Yes, you are.'

She looked into his doleful face and realized what a compliment he was paying her. She accepted it. 'Thank you.'

'I'll get every one of the lads to back you to the hilt. I'd say you get the big 'uns to give you the walk down.'

She couldn't help but chuckle. He tucked his squat hand under her elbow. 'Nothing like a uniformed show of tough buggers, rest get sittin' in rows. You give that speech.'

'How do you know I'm giving a speech?'

Marshall grinned. 'Well, I was in your office, saw it on your computer. And, if you don't mind, I got a few details you just might like to add.'

This time she did laugh out loud, and she liked his hand cupped at her elbow. She just wished he'd been able to place it there before.

Sporting flashy new ID tags, the party was taken on a tour of the recently completed Special Secure Unit. John Bunny was giving the spiel, priding himself on his knowledge of the state-of-the-art technology incorporated in the grey, featureless cube, built at a cost of many millions to house fourteen maximum security prisoners.

Standing in the new red-paved yard inside the high fence, the party was enjoying a brief glimpse of watery sunshine when Marshall hurried up. He nodded to Andrews and Duncan, fidgeting with his tie as he waited for Keller to notice his presence. He deigned to after a moment, growing weary of John Bunny's monologue.

'Gary Marshall, Miss Hewitt's deputy, right? Gordon Keller.' Marshall shook the limp, cold hand. 'She not available?' Keller said. It wasn't so much a question as a veiled criticism. Damn bad form for the Governor not to be first to greet people of such importance.

'The air conditioners and filters are US imports,' Bunny burbled on, making the most of his captive audience. 'In fact a lot of the design for the SSU is based on the American penal system.'

He shooed them forward so he could point out more fascinating features. Marshall hung back, having spotted Helen heading their way from the main block. She was striding out confidently, hair bouncing on her shoulders, and looking, Marshall had to admit, bloody terrific.

'You all set and standing up?' he murmured to her as she joined the group. Helen nodded. 'I'll get them into the lecture hall soon as I can.' Marshall made the introductions. 'Mr Keller, this is Miss Hewitt.'

Keller swung round to find her already with a smile and her hand out.

'Helen, isn't it?' He offered his own hand but not a smile.

'Yes, Mr Keller, nice to meet you.'

'All the central heating and air conditioning is controlled from outside,' Bunny was saying. 'Again this is to ensure security. And the entire building is fire-proofed.'

As the party moved through the gate back into the main prison area, Marshall stood to one side, speaking into his radio. 'All personnel to lecture hall as arranged. We're on our way to exercise yard two. Will tour wings, canteen, kitchens, control room.'

He tagged on with Andrews, Duncan, Bunny and the rest while Helen walked in front with Keller.

'I hear you've been recruiting new officers,' Keller said. 'What about the ones that have been on Detach Duty?'

'Some will return but a number have decided against it.' Helen had made the decision not to mince words, and she didn't. 'If I am to remain here I'll obviously have a large ratio of locals. Unless you are taking over,' she said, giving him a frank look.

'Not really made my mind up,' Keller mused with a small sigh. 'And if it's to be privatized then . . .' He shrugged his narrow shoulders, glancing towards Royston Andrews. 'I wouldn't be interested.' He paused to sniff the air, jingling the coins in his pocket. 'Can't get the decent officers, big problem already at Doncaster.'

'That's why I hand-picked officers with experience, to back up the trainees,' Helen said.

Andrews, Duncan and the rest of the party moved closer, listening to the conversation.

'Not to back you up?' Keller said with a thin smile, aware that he had an audience. 'I don't think any young recruit is being thrown into the lion's den straight away, not like in the old days.' He gave her a sideways look, his eyes heavy-lidded. 'You wouldn't even remember those days, would you?'

'No. I'm not ready for my pension yet, Mr Keller.' Helen's smile flashed brightly. Marshall had to turn away, hiding a delighted smirk, at the expression on Keller's face. He looked as if someone had just trodden on his bunion.

Still smiling, Helen turned to Sean Duncan. 'The inmates will shortly be taking exercise, which will leave us time to tour the entire new prison facilities.'

With a sweep of her hand she moved on, leading the way.

The Operational Director sat in the middle of the front row of the lecture hall, Duncan and Keller beside him, the rest of the party ranged on either side.

They were becoming restive, waiting for the Governor to make her presentation. They had finished the grand tour, and were now impatient to hear Miss Hewitt's considered assessment of Barfield's refurbishment over the past eighteen months since the time of the riot. When she got here, that was. Andrews looked at his watch for the third time in as many minutes. The large hall was somewhat chilly, the platform in front deserted, the bank of empty seats rising behind. Where the devil was she?

With a sigh Keller took out his cigarettes, and was about to light up when Bunny leaned across with a warning frown. 'No smoking. Governor is also making the entire office section a No Smoking zone.'

'Really?' Keller rammed the packet back into his pocket. 'Staff must love her!'

Andrews looked at his watch yet again, and then glanced up with a frown at what seemed to be distant thunder. It was the sound of marching feet. The double doors swung open to reveal a long empty corridor. The tramp of feet got louder as Helen came into view, at the head of over sixty prison officers, four abreast, leading the ranks of smartly uniformed men into the lecture hall.

Four officers peeled away to mount the platform behind Helen, while the rest filed into the rows of seats. Following on came the wing governors, the managers of all the specialized units, the security guards from Reception, and Dr Thomas and his medical team. Mavis came in with Maureen Collins, Zania Tullbrooke and several members of the education department, who all took their places behind the rows of officers.

It was quite a sight, and couldn't have been more impressive if Helen had deliberately arranged it for theatrical effect. Which, of course, was precisely what she had done.

Russell Morgan slipped into his seat next to Gary Marshall, whose face bore an expression of dazed disbelief. He still couldn't believe Helen would have the nerve and the guts to carry this off, and then, all of a sudden, watching her eyes and the set of her jaw, he changed his mind. From the corner of his mouth he muttered almost inaudibly, 'She's going to go for it.'

Helen stood in front of the four seated officers, waiting for the hall to settle. She had no script or notes. What she had to say was impassioned and heartfelt, a simple, clear statement of belief.

'Barfield Prison has cost the British taxpayer sixty-nine million pounds. It has facilities that any school, college or university would get down on their knees and beg for.' She paused, raising her chin the tiniest fraction, getting ready. This was it coming up, the bit that was going to cause the ructions.

'I believed that the loss of freedom was the ultimate punishment, and that it was every inmate's right once inside prison to be given the opportunities we provided. I now believe it is *not* his right. He must be taught to earn every single privilege that in our modern prisons today are taken for granted.'

From the third row back, Marshall was staring up at Helen, slowly shaking his head in mute wonder. Christ, she really *was* going for it. The full works. No holds barred.

Royston Andrews had a pad on his knee, calmly taking notes. Sean Duncan had a furtive look, as if he wanted to stop the proceedings here and now, but lacked the balls. A perspiring John Bunny didn't know where to look or what to do. He kept glancing at his masters, Andrews and Duncan, for some kind of lead. Helen Hewitt was talking sacrilege here, going head-on against official policy. Were they going to let her get away with it? Apparently so.

Outwardly, Keller was his usual disdainful self. Barfield was his if he wanted it. But the worm of doubt was wriggling away inside, and he was no longer sure he did. Helen Hewitt had staked a claim. That's what she was doing right this minute. He was older, tireder, and he didn't know if he could summon up the energy to compete with, let alone match, her firebrand passion and commitment.

Keller knew that on paper he had the experience to beat her. But he wasn't a fool. In addition to passion and commitment, she had something he couldn't touch, couldn't even get within hailing distance of, and it was staring him in the face.

She had a vision of the future.

Helen Hewitt was the future.

'If any prisoner on release after serving a custodial sentence returns immediately to a life of crime, we have failed. If that man has gained criminal experience from inside the prison that held him, we have failed.'

Helen went on, calm and controlled, yet relentless.

'If any man raping a woman rapes again on his release, we have failed. If a man kills and murders again on his release, we have failed. If any man on parole, any man on home leave, commits a crime and does not return to his prison, we have failed.'

Helen looked down at the rows of faces before her. These were the men and women who would have the duty and responsibility of running the most modern maximum-security prison in the country. Over the weeks and months ahead prisoners would be arriving almost daily, wave upon wave of them, as Barfield gradually built up to its full complement of 540 inmates. In return for their dedication and loyalty, the prison staff and officers deserved and had a right to receive the fullest support from those at the top: Home Office, Prison Service, and not least the Governor. If chosen for the job, she would not be found wanting on that score; she would play her full part.

'At the same time we must never lose sight of the fact that no matter how hard it is to find, there is, inside every criminal, a decent but sometimes helpless, frightened human being. We must not fail him either, just as we must not fail the victim. The punishment *must* fit the crime.'

Helen's heart fluttered in her chest. By their rapt silence

she had hoped and believed she was getting through to them. Now she felt a deep sense of her own failure as somebody started a slow handclap. It was joined by another, and another, but this made her even more determined to have her say, come hell or high water, whether they cared to listen or not. She ploughed grimly on.

'Only by implementing a tougher, harsher regime can we hope to decriminalize the criminal, and truthfully begin his rehabilitation, whose aim is for him to take his place once more as a productive and law-abiding citizen of our society.'

It was then, right at the finish, that the shock hit her. These weren't slow handclaps at all. The officers were applauding her. Russell Morgan was up in his seat, applauding vigorously, as were Jumbo Jackson, Andy Gordon, John Udding, Zach Tucker, Tommy Nelson – all the officers in the hall were applauding because she was giving voice to what they too believed.

She realized something else. The applause wasn't just for her, for Helen Hewitt the woman, but for what she was. The Governor.

PRIME SUSPECT

For Jackie,
a guiding light

My thanks to

Elaine Causon, my researcher and assistant who deserves so much credit for *Prime Suspect.* To Jenny (Mealy Mouth) Sheridan who paid for the lunch at which *Prime Suspect* was conceived. My thanks to Sally Head, Don Leaver, Ken Morgan, Roy Stonehouse, Sheelagh Killeen, and to all the cast of *Prime Suspect*, and my admiration and sincere thanks to its director, Chris Menaul.

chapter one

Mrs Corrina Salbanna was woken from a deep sleep by the sound of the front door banging in the wind. She squinted at her bedside clock; it was almost two. Swearing in her native Spanish, she threw off the bedclothes and stuffed her plump feet into her slippers.

She shuffled up the steps into the hall and towards the still-open front door, wrapping her dressing-gown around her against the chill. The naked light bulb gave the seedy hallway a yellowish hue that did nothing to enhance the peeling wallpaper and brown, flaking paint. Pursing her lips, Mrs Salbanna slammed the door hard. There was no reason why anyone else in the house should be allowed to sleep if she couldn't.

As she turned again towards her warm bed, she noticed a light beneath Della Mornay's door on the first-floor landing. She put two and two together; it must be that little tart who had left the door open. Della owed three months' rent, and had been warned about bringing men back to her room. Now was the time to catch her red-handed. Moving as fast as she could, Mrs Salbanna returned to the basement and collected the master keys, then panted back up to the first floor.

'Della, I know you're in there, open the door!'

She waited, with her ear pressed to the door. Hearing nothing, she rattled the door-handle. 'Della?'

There was no response. Her face set, Mrs Salbanna inserted the key, unlocked the door and pushed it open.

The large room was as seedy as the rest of the run-down Victorian house, which had been divided into bedsits long before Mrs Salbanna and her husband had taken it over in the sixties, and many of the rooms still had the feel of the hippie years. Only the posters in this room had changed; Jimi Hendrix had given way to more modern rock and movie heroes. The first thing Mrs Salbanna saw was a large photograph of Madonna, lips pouting, which dominated the squalid, clothes-strewn room from above the head of the old-fashioned double bed. A red shawl had been draped over the bedside lamp; in its glow Mrs Salbanna could see that the pillows and red satin eiderdown had been dragged to the far side of the bed, revealing the stained ticking of the mattress.

There was no sign of Della. Shivering, Mrs Salbanna looked about her with distaste. She wouldn't put it past the little bitch to be hiding; she'd been devious enough about not paying her rent. She sniffed: stale body odour and cheap perfume. The smell was stronger when she peered into the mahogany wardrobe, but it contained only dresses and shoes.

The wardrobe door, off its hinges, was propped against the wall. Its full-length, fly-blown mirror was cracked and missing a corner, but reflected enough to show Mrs Salbanna a leg, protruding from beneath the bedclothes on the floor. She spun round.

'You little bitch! I knew you were in here!'

For all her weight, the landlady moved swiftly across the room and crouched down to grip Della's exposed ankle. With her other hand she threw the bedclothes aside. Her mouth opened to scream, but no sound came; she lost her balance and fell, landing on her backside. In a panic she crawled to the door, dragging herself up by the open drawer of a tallboy. Bottles and pots of make-up crashed to the floor as her scream finally surfaced. Mrs Salbanna screamed and screamed . . .

By the time Detective Chief Inspector John Shefford arrived the house in Milner Road, Gray's Inn, had been cordoned off. He was the last on the scene; two patrol cars were parked outside the house and uniformed officers were fending off the sightseers. An ambulance stood close by, its doors open, its crew sitting inside, drinking tea. The mortuary van was just drawing up and had to swerve out of the way as Shefford's car screeched to a halt just where its driver had intended to park. Shefford's door crashed open as he yanked on the handbrake. He was on the move, delving into his pocket for his ID as he stepped over the cordon. A young

PC, recognizing him, ushered him up the steps to the house.

Even at two-thirty on a wintry Sunday morning, word had got round that a murder had been committed. There were lights in many windows; people in dressing-gowns huddled on their front steps. A couple of kids had appeared and were vying with each other to see how close they could get to the police cordon without breaking through it. Five Rastafarians with a ghetto-blaster were laughing together on a nearby wall, calling out remarks and jokes, as if it was a street party.

Shefford, a bear of a man at six foot two, dwarfed those around him. He had been notorious on the rugby field in the late seventies, when he played for England. With his curly hair standing on end, his crumpled shirt and tie hanging loose he didn't look or feel in a fit state to start an investigation. He had been hauled out of the celebration bash at the end of a long and tedious murder case, and he was knackered. Now he was about to lead the investigation of another murder, but this one was different.

Many of the officers in the dark, crowded hallway he had worked with before. He scanned the faces as his eyes grew accustomed to the darkness. He never forgot a face, and he greeted each man he knew by name.

At the foot of the stairs he hesitated a moment, straightening his tie. It wasn't like him to shrink from an unpleasant duty, but he had to force himself to mount each step. He was sweating. Above the confusion of voices a high-pitched wailing could be heard. It seemed to be coming from the direction of the basement.

Hearing Shefford's voice, Detective Sergeant Bill Otley stopped pacing the landing and leaned over the banister. He gestured for his guv'nor to join him in the darkness at the far end of the landing. He kept his voice low and his eye on the men coming and going from the victim's room.

'It's Della Mornay, guv. I got the tip-off from Al Franks.'

He could smell the booze on Shefford's breath. Unwrapping a peppermint, he handed it over. The boss wasn't drunk; he probably had been, but he was straightening out fast. Then Otley shook out a pair of white overalls for each of them. While they struggled to put them on, their dark recess was lit at intervals by the powerful flash of a camera from the bedsit.

As Shefford dragged on a cigarette he became aware of a familiar low, gruff voice that had been droning on all the time he had been in the house. He moved towards the door and listened.

'. . . She's lying next to the double bed, on the side nearest the window and away from the door. She's half-hidden beneath a red silk eiderdown. The window is open, a chest of drawers in front of it. We have a sheet, a blanket, a copy of the *Sunday Times* dated December 1990 . . . Looks like it's been used to wrap something in. She's lying face down, hands tied behind her back. Wearing some kind of skinny-rib top, mini-skirt, no stockings. The right shoe is on the foot, the left one lying nearby . . . '

'She been raped?' Shefford asked Otley as he fastened his overall.

'I dunno, but it's a mess in there.'

Mrs Salbanna's hysterical screaming and sobbing was getting on Shefford's nerves. He leaned over the banister and had a clear view of DC Dave Jones on the basement stairs trying to calm the landlady. An ambulance attendant tried to help move her, but she turned on him with such a torrent of mingled Spanish and English with violent gestures that he retreated, fearing for his safety.

The pathologist was ready to talk, so Shefford and Otley were given the nod to enter the room. Shefford took a last pull at his cigarette, inhaled deeply and pinched it out, putting the stub in his pocket. Then he eased past the mess of broken bottles of make-up and perfume, careful where he put his size eleven feet, to stand a little distance from the bed. All he could see of Della was her left foot.

The brightly lit room was full of white-overalled men, all going about their business quickly and quietly. Flashlights still popped, but already items were being bagged and tagged for removal. The bulky figure of Felix Norman, the pathologist, crouched over the corpse, carefully slipping plastic bags over Della's hands. He was a rotund man, oddly pear-shaped with most of his weight in his backside, topped off with a shock of thick, grey hair and an unruly grey beard. Rumour had it that his half-moon spectacles had been held together by the same piece of sticking plaster since 1983, when a corpse he was dissecting suddenly reared up and thumped him. But it was just a rumour, started by Norman himself. It was his voice Shefford had heard muttering into a tape recorder.

He looked up and gave Shefford a small wave, but continued dictating. 'Obvious head injuries . . . possible penetrating wounds, through her clothes, her neck, upper shoulders . . . Lot of blood-staining, blood covering the left side of her head and face. Room's damned cold, about five degrees . . . ' Norman broke into a coughing fit, but he didn't bother turning the tape off. He bent over the lower end of the corpse, but Shefford could not see what he was doing. Then he glanced at his watch and continued, 'Say two to three degrees when she was found, the lights and everybody tramping around must have warmed the place.' He winked at Shefford, still talking. 'Window half-open, curtains part-drawn, no source of heat . . . Door to landing giving a strong draught, front door had been left open . . . ' He felt the corpse's arms and legs, examined the scalp, then began checking for a weapon or anything lodged in the clothing that might fall when the body was removed, without pausing for breath. 'Complete absence of rigor, no hypostasis visible . . . ' Again he bent over the body, then sat back, waving a thermometer. He squinted at it. 'Deep rectal temperature . . . Can't bloody read it for the life of me . . . Ah, time is two thirty-eight am, thirty-five point eight degrees, so assuming she started at thirty-seven that puts it back to . . . '

Shefford shifted his weight from foot to foot and swallowed hard. As Norman gently rolled the body over he could see the blood matted in the blonde hair, and he had to turn away. It wasn't the sight of the blood, he had seen enough of that in his time, but how small she seemed, small and broken.

Two white-clad men moved in to examine the carpet where the dead girl had been lying. Norman had another coughing fit and Shefford took the opportunity to ask how long she had been dead.

'Well, my old son, she would have cooled off pretty quickly in here, with that window open an' no heating on . . . Any time between midnight, maybe a little later, and . . . at a rough guess, twelve-thirty.'

'Was she raped, Felix?' Shefford asked, although he knew Norman wouldn't answer.

Norman just gave Shefford a foul look; he no longer bothered answering questions that presumed he was telepathic or had X-ray vision. He looked around the room and called to an assistant, 'Right, body-bag!'

Two men lifted the body into the black plastic bag. Shefford winced and averted his head, shocked at the disfiguration of her face. He had seen only her profile, which was hardly recognizable as human; her nose and cheek were a mass of clotted blood and the eye was completely gone.

'Not a pretty sight,' said Norman, without emotion.

Shefford nodded, but his voice was muffled as he replied, 'She was, though – pretty. Her name's Della Mornay. Booked her myself when I was on Vice.'

Norman sniffed. 'Yeah, well, let's get her out of here an' down to the mortuary. Quicker I get at her, faster you'll get results.'

Even though he had asked once, Shefford could not stop himself repeating the question, 'Was she raped?'

Norman pulled a face. 'Fuck off, I'll tell you everything you wanna know after the post-mortem.' He stared around the bedsit while the bag was closed and the body lifted onto a stretcher. 'They'll need a bloody pantechnicon to take this lot down to Forensic. You had breakfast? You'd better grab some before you schlepp over to me. Gimme a couple of hours.'

With a wave, Shefford shouldered his way to the landing. He paused and turned his back to the uniformed PC as he swiftly transferred a small object into Otley's hand. No one had seen him slip it from under the mattress. Otley quickly pocketed the little book.

It was not yet dawn, but the street was just as lively when Shefford left the house. The spectators watched avidly as the stretcher was carried to the waiting mortuary van and the police brought bag after bag of evidence from the house. Mrs Salbanna and Shefford himself had both identified the corpse.

The Scenes of Crime officers, or SOCOs, had started fingerprinting every possible surface, covering most of the room in a film of grey, shining dust. They were none too happy; many of the best spots had been carefully wiped.

After snatching a quick breakfast in the canteen and detailing Otley to make sure the Incident Room was being organized, Shefford was at the mortuary by nine o'clock. DI Frank Burkin and DC Dave Jones joined him there to discuss the day's itinerary. They sat in the anteroom of the main laboratory, all but Jones blatantly disregarding the large NO SMOKING notices.

While they waited, John Shefford used the payphone to call his home. It was his son's birthday the next day and Otley, the boy's godfather, wanted to know what to buy him. His wife, however, had more on her mind.

'Have you booked the clown for Tommy's party, John?' Sheila asked. 'I gave you the number last week, remember?'

Shefford was about to confess that he had forgotten all about it when he was saved by the bell; Felix Norman's assistant came to fetch him.

'I've got to go, love, they're ready for me. See you later!'

Gowned up, masked and wearing the regulation wellington boots, Shefford joined Norman.

*

Two bare, pale feet protruded from the end of the green sheet, a label bearing Della Mornay's name and a number tied to one ankle. Norman started talking before Shefford had even reached the trolley.

'Death, old mate, was around twelve-fifteen – it's a classic, her watch got broken and stopped. The gold winder, by the way, is missing, so they'll have to comb the carpet. The watch face is intact, but the rope that was used to tie her wrists must have twisted the winding pin off the watch. Now, you asked if she was raped; could be. Recent deposits of semen in the vagina and rectum, and in the mouth, extensive bruising to the genital area. I sent the swabs over to Willy at the lab . . . ' he checked his watch, 'five hours ago. Might get a blood type this afternoon. OK, the wounds . . . '

Norman threw the green sheet over the head to expose the torso, and pointed to the puncture marks. The body had been cleaned, and they showed up clearly.

'Upper right shoulder, right breast, lung punctured here, and here. Another laceration to the throat, sixth deep wound just above the navel. The wounds are neat, made with a small, rounded object, the point narrow, flat and sharp, like a sharpened screwdriver, perhaps. Not all the same depth – one three inches, one six inches, the one in the right breast is even deeper.'

Shefford examined the wounds and listened intently, nodding his head. Felix Norman was one of the best in his field, and Shefford had learned from experience to let him have his say before asking any questions.

Norman continued, 'OK, she also has a deep puncture to her left eye, probably what finished her off. A real mess, wanna see?'

'No, just carry on,' replied Shefford with distaste, running his hands through his hair.

Norman referred to his notes. 'Oh, yeah, this is interesting. Look at her hands. They seem to have been scrubbed, with a wire brush, by the look of them. But there's a nasty little nick here, and there's a smell of chlorine, some kind of household bleach. No doubt I'll find out the exact brand when I've been given the time a man of my calibre likes to have in order to do his job thoroughly! Anyway, it looks as if the scrubbing job on her hands has eliminated any possibility of blood or tissue fragments under the nails. She probably didn't put up much of a struggle, but then, her hands were tied . . . '

Shefford avoided looking at the naked torso as much as possible. 'Anything else?'

Norman sniffed. 'Yeah, something strange . . . ' Laying his clipboard aside, he picked up one of the corpse's arms. 'See, same on both sides? Deep welts and bruising to the upper arms. At this stage I can't say what caused it, but she might have been strung up. I'll have to do some more tests, but it looks like she was put in some kind of clamp. Interesting, huh?'

Shefford nodded. Somewhere at the back of his mind a bell rang, but he couldn't capture the memory . . . Norman covered the body again and continued, peering over his glasses, 'Right-handed killer, height difficult to estimate at this stage, especially if she was strung up, but four of the wounds entered the body on an upward slant and two are straight, so I reckon he's around five-ten. But don't quote me until I've . . . '

Shefford pulled a face. Norman, for all his bravado, went strictly by the rules and hated being pressed for results before he was one hundred per cent sure.

'Thanks mate. Get back to me as soon as you've got anything. When the report's ready, Bill can collect it personally. And, Felix – I really appreciate it!'

Norman snorted. He had worked fast, but then he and John Shefford were old friends. He watched as Shefford removed his surgical mask and began to untie his gown.

'You got anything, John?'

Shefford shook his head. 'Looks like one of her johns was into bondage and things got out of hand. See you . . . '

At the station, Della Mornay's effects were being sorted and examined. Her handbag had been found, but it contained no keys. They were able to dismiss robbery as a motive as her purse, containing fifteen pounds, was in the bag and a jewel box on her dressing-table, containing a few silver chains and a gold bangle or two, was undisturbed.

In King's Cross, Della Mornay's territory, fifteen of Shefford's men were interviewing every known prostitute and call girl. They were getting little assistance, but the feedback was that Della had not been seen for weeks. There was a suggestion that she might have gone to Leeds to visit a friend dying of Aids, but no name was mentioned.

The painstaking task of checking every forensic sample, the tapes of fibres, the fingerprints, was barely begun, and had brought no results so far. The entire area was combed for a murder weapon without success. In that neighbourhood no one ever volunteered information, especially to the police.

Shefford and Otley met up again at Milner Road and spent an hour or so interviewing and looking over the bedsit again, but they discovered nothing new. Mrs Salbanna, recovered from her shock, was already asking when she could let the room.

Shefford was hungry and very tired. He had a few pints and a pork pie in the local, then kipped down in his office while Otley went home to his flat to fetch his guv'nor a clean shirt. Shefford often stayed over at his place and left a few items of clothing there for emergencies.

Although he could have done with putting his head down for a few hours himself, Otley sprayed the shirt with starch and ironed it, paying special attention to the collar. Pleased with his handiwork, he slipped it onto a hanger and sat down for a cup of tea. He had a system for avoiding washing up; he simply used the same cup, plate and cutlery all the time. He ate all his main meals in the station canteen, and had even given up his morning cornflakes because they were a bugger to get off the bowl if you left them overnight.

The silver-framed photographs of his wife, his beloved

Ellen, needed a good polish, but he'd have to leave them until his next weekend off. They were the only personal items in the flat that he bothered with. Ellen had been the love of his life, his only love, since he was a teenager. Her death seven years ago, from cancer of the stomach, had left him bereft, and he mourned her now as deeply as the moment she had died. He had watched helplessly as she disintegrated before his eyes. She had become so weak, so skeletal, that he had prayed, anguished and alone, for her to die.

It had been obvious to everyone at work that Skipper Bill Otley had personal problems, but he confided in no one. His solitary drinking and his angry bitterness had caused many arguments, and his boys, as he called them, had at last left him to himself. In the end, John Shefford had taken him aside and demanded to know what was going on, earning his abusive response, 'Mind yer own fuckin' business, my personal life's me own affair.'

Shefford had snapped back angrily that when it affected his work it became the boss's business, and Otley would be out on his ear if he didn't come clean about what was tormenting him. He pushed Otley to the point where he finally cracked.

Once he understood, Shefford had been like a rock. He was at the hospital, waiting outside the ward, when Ellen died. He had organized the funeral, done everything he possibly could to help. He was always there, always available, like the sweet, beloved friend Otley had buried. When Shefford's son was born he asked Otley to be godfather; the bereaved man became part of the family, his presence demanded for lunch on Sundays, for outings and parties. He and Ellen had longed for children, in vain; now his off-duty time was filled with little Tom's laughter and nonsense. So Otley wouldn't just iron his guv'nor's shirt; he would wash it, and his socks for good measure. John Shefford meant more to him than he could ever put into words; he loved the man, admired him, and backed him to the hilt, convinced that he would make Commander one of these days. No one would be more proud of him then than Bill Otley.

With the clean shirt over his arm, Otley whistled on his way back to the station.

At eleven, Detective Chief Inspector Jane Tennison parked her Ford Fiesta and entered Southampton Row police station. It was a crisp, frosty day, and she was wrapped up well against the cold.

She was officially off-duty, but had come in to prepare some final papers for a session in court the next day.

None of the blood samples taken from the bedsitter had yielded a clue to the identity of Della Mornay's killer. Hers was a very common group and the only one found at the scene. But the DNA tests on the semen taken from her body was a different matter.

The new computerized DNA system was still at the experimental stage, but already the results of thousands of tests taken in the past two years had been entered on it. As a matter of routine, Willy Chang's forensic team ran the result from Della Mornay against the existing records and were astonished to find a match; a visual check on the negatives, using a light-box, confirmed it. The man Della Mornay had had sex with shortly before her murder had been convicted of attempted rape and aggravated robbery in 1988.

Willy Chang was jubilant; here was the lever they needed to press the government into releasing funds for a national DNA profiling system. He picked up the phone.

The message caught Shefford on Lambeth Bridge, on his way home for lunch and only a stone's throw from the Home Office labs. He hung up the handset, turned the car around immediately and punched Otley's arm.

'You're not gonna believe this, we got a friggin' suspect! He's got a rare blood group and it's on the ruddy computer!'

*

For the past three months DCI Tennison had been working on a tedious fraud case involving a tobacconist who was being sued for non-payment of VAT. The man's ferret of an accountant had more tricks up his sleeve than a conjuror, and a long series of medical certificates exempting him from court appearances. But tomorrow, at last, Judge George Philpott would complete his summing-up. Known as the legal equivalent of Cary Grant for his good looks and slow delivery, Philpott had already taken two days; Tennison hoped he would finish quickly for once so she would have time to check her desk before the end of the day.

Not that there would be anything of interest; in all her time on the special Area Major Incident Team, known as AMIT, there had been little but desk work. She had often wondered why she had bothered switching from the Flying Squad, where at least she had been busy. The set-up of five DCIs and their teams had appealed to her, and she had believed she would be able to use her skills to the full.

Sitting at her desk, Tennison heard a screech of brakes from the car park. She glanced out of the window in time to see Shefford racing into the building.

'What's DCI Shefford doing in today, Maureen?' she asked her assistant, WPC Havers. 'He's supposed to be on leave.'

'I think he's heading the investigation.'

'What investigation?'

'Prostitute found dead in her room in Milner Road.'

'They got a suspect?' Tennison snapped.

'Not yet, but they're getting all the Vice files on the victim's pals.'

Tennison bristled. 'How did Shefford get it? I was here until after ten last night!'

Maureen shrugged. 'I dunno, guv, I think it was a middle-of-the-night job. Probably hauled him out of the afters session in the pub.'

'But he's only just finished with that shooting in Kilburn – and there were the Iranian diplomats before that.'

Tennison clenched her fists and stormed out. Maureen winced at the banging of the door.

DCI Tennison paced up and down the corridor, trying to talk herself down. Eighteen months she'd been waiting for a decent case, dealing with more paperwork than in her entire time at the rape centre in Reading, and now the boss had gone out of his way to give DCI Shefford the case that should have been hers. She'd known when she applied for the transfer that she would be in for a tough time; had she stayed where she was she'd have been promoted to a desk job by now.

But five years with the Flying Squad had toughened her up. She went back to her room and put a call through to the Chief's office, determined to have it out with him, but he was in a meeting. She tried to work on her statements for the court hearing but her frustration wouldn't let her concentrate.

At midday Tennison was again disturbed by the racing of engines from the car park. Shefford was off again, and in a hell of a hurry. She gave up trying to work and packed her things; it was nearly lunch-time anyway.

Tennison missed the 'heat' as Shefford gathered his team together, his booming voice hurling insults as he fired orders at them. He was moving fast on the unbelievable stroke of luck that had given him his suspect on a plate.

George Arthur Marlow had been sentenced to three years for attempted rape and assault, but had served only eighteen months. He had still been protesting his innocence when he was led away from the dock.

The case had been a long-drawn-out affair as Marlow insisted he was innocent. At first he had denied even knowing the victim, referred to only as 'Miss X', but when faced with the evidence he told the police that he and 'Miss X' had been drinking together in a wine bar. He stated that she had blatantly encouraged his advances, but when it came to the crunch she refused him.

Marlow's blood tests at the time had shown him to have

an exceptionally rare blood group; he belonged to a small percentage of AB secreters, of whom there is only one in 2,500 head of population. He had been one of the first to be entered on the new computer, and when a lab assistant ran his details through the system she hit the jackpot.

The warrant was ready. Shefford, high on adrenalin, called his men together. Already he had dribbled coffee down his clean shirt, and he followed it now with cigarette ash. Otley brushed him down as he bellowed, 'DCI Donald Paxman holds the record in the Met, lads, for bringing in a suspect and charging him within twenty-four hours. Gimme me raincoat . . . Fags, who's got me fags?'

He shrugged into his coat with the effortless ability of the permanently crumpled man, lighting a cigarette at the same time and switching it from hand to hand as his big fists thrust down the sleeves. 'We smash that record, lads, and it's drinks all round, so let's go! Go, go!'

Jane Tennison let herself into her small service flat which she had shared for the last three months with her boyfriend, Peter Rawlins. Six feet tall, broad-chested, his sandy hair invariably flecked with paint, he was the first man she had lived with on a permanent basis.

Peter came out of the kitchen when he heard her key in the door and beamed at her. 'OK, we've got Chicken Kiev with brown rice, how does that suit?'

'Suits me fine!'

She dumped her briefcase on the hall table and he gave her a hug, then held her at arm's length and looked into her face. 'Bad day?'

She nodded and walked into the bedroom, tossing her coat on the bed. He lolled in the doorway. 'Want to talk about it?'

'When I've had a shower.'

They had spent a lot of time talking since they had met; Peter had been in the throes of divorce and Jane had provided a sympathetic ear. Marianne had left him for another man; it had hit him hard because it was not just any other man, but Peter's best friend and partner in his building firm, And she had taken with her the little son he adored, Joey.

Jane and Peter's relationship had begun casually enough; they had been teamed together in the squash club tournament and had since met on several occasions for the odd drink or cup of coffee after a game. Eventually he had asked her to see a film with him, and on that first real date she had listened to the details of his divorce. It was only after several films that he had even made an attempt to kiss her.

Jane had helped Peter to move into a temporary flat while his house was sold, and gradually their relationship had become closer. When he started looking for a permanent place to live she suggested he move in with her for a while. It wasn't very romantic, but as the weeks passed she found herself growing more and more fond of him. He was easy-going, caring and thoughtful. When he told her he loved her and suggested they look for a bigger place together, she agreed. It was a pleasant surprise to her how much she wanted to be with him.

When she had showered, Jane sat at the table in her dressing-gown and Peter presented his Chicken Kiev with a flourish. She was so grateful and happy that she had someone to share her life with that she forgot her problems for a moment.

As he opened a bottle of wine she cocked her head to one side and smiled. 'You know, I'm getting so used to you, I don't know what I'd do if you weren't around. I guess what I'm trying to say in my roundabout way is— '

'Cheers!' he said, lifting his glass.

'Yeah, to you, to me, to us . . . '

Marlow seemed dazed by the arrival of the police. He stood in the narrow hallway of his flat, holding a cup of coffee, apparently unable to comprehend what they wanted.

'George Arthur Marlow, I am arresting you on suspicion of murder . . . ' Otley had to repeat the caution, then remove the cup from Marlow's hand himself to put the handcuffs on him.

Moyra Henson, Marlow's girlfriend, appeared from the kitchen, followed by the smell of roasting lamb.

'What the hell's going on here? Oi, where are you taking him? He hasn't had his dinner . . . '

Ignoring her, they led Marlow out to the car as quickly as possible. In his bewilderment, he almost cracked his head on the roof of the patrol car as he was helped inside.

The uniformed officers went in to search the flat, while a WPC took Moyra into the kitchen and told her that Marlow had been arrested on suspicion of the murder of a prostitute. Moyra's eyes widened and she shook her head, disbelieving.

'There's been a terrible mistake, you can't do this to him, it's a mistake . . . ' She broke away from the WPC and ran to the front door. She shrieked like a banshee when she realized the police were taking out clear plastic bags of clothing at a rate of knots. Marlow's shoes, jackets, shirts, all listed and tagged, were shown to Moyra while she protested shrilly. But she didn't attempt to stop the officers, and they remained for hours, searching and removing items. When they had finished, Moyra was taken to the police station for questioning.

She was no longer irate, but coldly angry. She hated the pigs, hated them. They had already put George inside for a crime she knew he hadn't committed, and now she was sure they were about to frame him for murder. All the whodunnits she watched on video and the moral standpoints of *Dallas* and *EastEnders* had taught her her rights, and not to trust the bastards.

Jane lay curled in Peter's arms, telling him about Shefford and his attitude to her; not quite openly antagonistic but near enough. It was pretty much the same with all the men, but Shefford was so macho that he took pleasure in sending her up, albeit behind her back.

It was still a new thing for her to have someone to listen to her problems. She had been in such a foul mood when she had arrived home, making love to him had taken all the tension away. It was good to have Peter, to feel loved and wanted. She told him how the Chief had given her the usual speech about waiting, but she had to make a decision soon. The longer she waited and accepted the cases no one else wanted, the more she knew she would be put upon. If Kernan didn't give her a break she would quit. The men gave her no respect . . .

Peter laughed. 'They don't know you, do they?'

She grinned. 'No, I suppose they don't. I'll get a break one day, and by Christ they'll know what's hit them then.'

He bit her ear. 'Get them to play a game of squash with you, they'll soon take notice of that determined little face. First time I played against you I thought: Holy shit, this one's a maniac.'

She laughed her wonderful, deep, throaty laugh. When they made love it no longer mattered that her bosses had overlooked her; only Peter was important. She had said it to him that afternoon, and told him she loved him.

He cuddled her close. 'I'm glad we've got each other, because things are not going too well for me. We may have to stave off looking for a bigger place, the company's in bad shape and I'm having to spend capital until I get back on my feet.'

She murmured that it didn't matter, the place was big enough. She asked him then how it had felt, knowing his wife was having an affair with his best friend, a subject she had always steered clear of.

He sighed, stared up at the ceiling. 'Like my balls had been cut off. I couldn't believe it at first, it must have been going on for years behind my back. Then I felt like a bloody fool, you know, that I hadn't clocked it faster. He was always round the house, but we were partners and I just accepted that he was there to see me. And he was screwing my wife in my own bed!' He punched his palm, hard; it made a satisfying smack. He sighed again. 'I wanted to beat him up, have it out that way, but there was no point. I just walked away from it all. She's got half the money from the house and I bought him out of the company, that's one of the reasons why cash is so tight at the moment. I should have just told him to fuck off, but I'm not like that and there's Joey to consider. I reckoned that if I got nasty about the divorce she'd try to stop me seeing Joey. I love that kid, couldn't bear not to see him.'

Jane stroked his cheek gently. 'Any time you want him to stay he's welcome, you know that, don't you?'

He hugged her.'Yeah, I do, and I appreciate it. You're the best thing that's happened to me in years. I know things'll work out for you, just be patient.'

She smiled, without mentioning that it was exactly what her Chief's attitude had been. But she had no intention of being patient. Peter didn't really understand how important her work was to her, but he was to find out sooner than either of them anticipated.

George Marlow was quiet and co-operative. His fingerprints were taken and he was led to the cells. He stammered a little when he asked to phone his lawyer, seeming shaken, and gave the number. Although on the point of tears, he went out of his way to be helpful, but he still kept asking why he had been arrested.

Shefford had been on the go all day. Now he was preparing himself to question Marlow. His face was flushed and he was chain-smoking, cracking jokes; it was obvious that the adrenalin was still flowing.

The men on the team were clapping him on the back, calling him a lucky bastard, what a break! Several were laying bets on the outcome.

DI Burkin suddenly rememberd something. 'Hey, it's his kid's birthday tomorrow! While we've all got our hands in our pockets, we gonna chip in an' buy him something? You know Otley, he's so tight-fisted the kid won't even get an ice-cream cornet from him. What d'you say, fifty pence each?' In great humour, they all coughed up.

Before he went down to the interview room, Shefford called his home to tell Sheila, his wife, that he would be late and she shouldn't wait up. He was too keyed up to pay much attention to what she was saying.

'You didn't answer me this morning, John. Have you booked the clown for Tom's party?'

'Yeah, yeah, I'll get it sorted . . . ' He handed the phone to Bill Otley and whispered, 'Talk to the missus, mate, you're his bloody godfather, after all. I haven't got time . . . '

He lit another cigarette and turned to the files as Otley took the phone and promised faithfully that he would dress up as a clown himself if they couldn't get Biffo for the birthday party.

The lads had been wrong about their skipper; Otley had spent more time and money in Hamley's toy shop that weekend than they could credit. The train sets had cost an arm and a leg, but he was prepared to dip into his savings. He and Ellen had spent hours planning what they would spend it on when he retired; now his godson would be the one to benefit. It was making the decision that took the time, as well as wandering around enjoying himself in the store.

Otley replaced the receiver and turned to Shefford. 'OK, guv? Need anything else? Marlow's brief's on his way, be about an hour. Arnold Upcher, represented him on his last caper. Tough bastard, but he's fair. Doesn't scream a lot like some of the buggers.'

Shefford winked. 'I want a crack at 'im before Upcher gets here. Nice one for us, eh? What a stroke of fuckin' luck! See if we can't sew up Paxman's record. Get a bottle of fizz over to the Forensic lot, tell 'em I love 'em, and tell Willy to stand by for all the gear from Marlow's place. And, yeah, I'm ready, let's go for the bastard.'

George Marlow was sitting in the cell with his hands in his lap, head bowed. He was wearing a blue striped shirt with the white collar open at the neck; his tie had been taken away from him. His grey flannels were neatly pressed and his jacket hung over the back of his chair.

With his Mediterranean looks it was obvious that he

would have to shave twice a day, but as yet his chin was clean. He raised his head when a uniformed officer opened the door and asked him politely to accompany him to the interview room.

DCI Shefford had given instructions that Upcher was to be stalled if he arrived early. He wanted a chance to question Marlow without his lawyer present. He drew himself up to his full height, threw his massive shoulders back and strode down the corridor to Room 4C. He noticed the way Marlow actually jumped with shock when he kicked the door open.

With a gesture to Marlow to remain seated, he swung a hard wooden chair around with one hand, placing it exactly opposite the suspect, and sat down.

'George? I am Detective Chief Inspector John Shefford. This is Detective Sergeant Bill Otley, and that's DC Jones over by the door. Before we get involved with your lawyer – I mean, we might not even need him – I just want to ask you a few questions, OK?'

He drew the ashtray towards him, scraping it along the formica of the table until it squealed, then lit a cigarette. 'You smoke, George?'

'No, sir.'

'Good . . . Right then, George, can you tell us where you were on the night of the thirteenth of January? Take your time.'

Marlow kept his head down. 'January the thirteenth? Saturday? Well, that's easy. I was at home with my wife. We don't usually go out, we get a video and a takeaway . . . Yeah, I was with my wife.'

'Your wife? You mean Moyra Henson, the girl you're living with? She said she's not your wife, she's your girlfriend. Which is it, George? Come on, son, don't mess us about.'

'Well, she's my common-law wife, we're not actually married.'

Shefford's tongue felt and tasted like an old carpet. He searched his pockets and found a wrinkled piece of

Wrigley's chewing gum at the bottom. It must have been there for some time as it had lost its outer wrapper, and the silver paper was covered with fluff and ash from using the pocket as an ashtray. He picked the foil off, examined the grey gum, then popped it in his mouth and chewed furiously. Marlow watched his every move, as if transfixed.

Shefford folded the wrapper into a narrow strip, ran his fingernail down it, then tossed it aside and lit a cigarette. 'What were you doing, say around ten o'clock?' he asked casually.

'I'd be at home . . . Oh, hang on, earlier . . . I know what I did earlier.'

Shefford inhaled the last of his cigarette and let the smoke drift from his nostrils. 'Well, want to tell me?'

With a rueful smile, Marlow shrugged his shoulders slightly. 'I picked up a girl. She was on the game.'

'You knew the girl, did you?'

Marlow shook his head and glanced at Otley, who was sitting a few feet away taking notes. 'I'd never met her before, but I saw her outside the tube station, Ladbroke Grove. She was, you know, bending down, peering into cars as they went past . . . Ladbroke Grove tube station. I pulled up and asked her how much.'

'But you didn't know her?'

'No, I'd never met her before. I asked her first how much, and she said it depends. You know they like to hustle as much as they can out of you . . . '

'Oh, yeah? But you been done before, George. You don't like hassles. Della Mornay pisses you off, right? Right?'

Marlow frowned, then looked at Shefford. 'Della Mornay . . . ?'

Otley checked his watch and wondered how it was all going down in the interview room. It was past seven and Shefford had been at it since four-thirty, now with Arnold Upcher sitting in on the session. Otley strolled down to the basement corridor and peered through the glass panel; he could just see Marlow, sitting with his head in his hands.

'Has he confessed yet? Only it's drinking time!'

The PC on guard raised his eyebrows. 'Been a lot of shouting goin' on in there, and at the last count Shefford had consumed five beakers of coffee.'

'Ah, well, he would – this is pub hours, son!'

Otley turned away and went to the pub to join the others from Shefford's team. He ordered a round and sat down with his pint, telling them there was no news as yet.

'But he had his head in his hands, looked like the guv'nor's cracked him. Gonna break that bloody record . . . '

They set about betting on how long it would take Shefford to get a confession from Marlow and whether or not he would break Paxman's record. They might not have been so confident if they had been privy to the statement that was being taken from Marlow right then.

chapter two

Shefford was using the regulation tape recorder. Marlow craned his head forward and directed his speech at the built-in microphone.

'I dropped her off at the tube station, and paid her.'

'OK, so then what did you do?'

'I went to Kilburn to get a video, and I was home by . . . about ten-thirty.'

Marlow rubbed his chin. He needed a shave now, the stubble made him look darker, swarthier.

'Like I said, Inspector, I remember, when I looked back, she was peering into another car, a red . . . maybe a Scirocco, I dunno, but she was looking for the next customer. I just got the video and went home, got there at ten-thirtyish. I can't remember the exact time, you'll have to ask Moyra, she'll remember.'

'And you maintain that you did not know this girl you picked up? You had never met her or seen her before?'

'No, sir. Like I said, she just came over to my car.'

Shefford opened a file and held out a photograph of Della Mornay, taken from Vice records. 'Is this the girl you picked up?'

Marlow leaned forward, without actually touching the photo, then sat back in his chair. 'I'd never met her before, I didn't know her.'

He looked to his brief, then back to Shefford. 'I picked her up at about seven-thirty. It was dark, I don't remember her all that well . . . '

'You had sex with her, George! You tellin' me you didn't see her face? Come on, George . . . '

Marlow shifted his weight in his chair. 'It was in the back of the car!'

'Let's go again, George, an' I want all the details.'

Peter was stuffing his work clothes into the overflowing laundry basket when Jane woke up. He rammed the lid on the basket. 'We need a washing machine, you know.'

She yawned. 'Yeah, but the kitchen's too small. Besides, the launderette does it for me, they'll even do the ironing if you want, but it's fifty pence per article. I'll get Mrs Fry to take a load down in the morning.' She yawned again. 'What's the time?'

'It's nearly six. I've got some bad news.' He sat down beside her. 'Well, not bad news for me, but for you, maybe! It must be telepathy . . . You know, after you said Joey could stay, Marianne called. She's bringing him over to stay the night. I didn't even have to ask, she suggested it.'

'That's OK! What time's he coming?'

Peter shrugged. 'Oh, about seven-thirty. Look, you don't have to do anything.'

Jane freaked. 'Is she bringing him? I mean, will she come in?'

He shrugged again. 'Look, I can take him for a hamburger, he'll be no problem.'

'Bollocks! Go down to the corner Indian, they're still open, and get some fish fingers. Kids like fish fingers, and baked beans, and Mars Bars . . . No, tell you what, Smarties. I'll make up the spare bed while you're gone.'

'It's already done, and I've put that Anglepoise lamp by the bed, he sleeps with a light on.'

'OK, I'll wash my hair and get dolled up.'

'You don't have to, he's only six, for Chrissake! He won't care what you look like.'

'Ah, but Marianne will be looking me over, and I want to make an impression. After all, I'm the Other Woman!'

'Not quite!'

'Oh, go on, get going . . . '

Jane rolled up the newspaper he had left on the bed and whacked him on the head with it, then dashed to the bathroom. Joey would be arriving soon, and she wanted to be ready.

At Southampton Row, Moyra Henson had been interviewed over and over again. She gave Marlow a perfect alibi and wouldn't be budged; he was at home, she insisted, as he had said in his own statement. He had been at home watching television with her. Marlow had not left the flat all evening, and they had gone to bed together.

When she was finally let go, DI Burkin was ordered back to her flat to impound Marlow's car, a brown, automatic three-litre Mark III Rover. He took two officers with him and gave Moyra a lift home.

She kept up a constant stream of abuse all the way back in the patrol car, sitting between the two officers. They didn't say a word. Burkin, uncomfortable in the front seat with his long legs cramped against the glove compartment, was also silent, though Moyra's voice was beginning to grate on his nerves and he would be glad when they got shot of her.

There was no sign of the Rover; it was not in the parking bay or anywhere in the vicinity of the flats. Sullen and uncooperative, Moyra accused the police of stealing it themselves.

*

As she shampooed her hair under the hot water, all Jane could think of was how John Shefford had done her out of a murder case. She had to make an effort to shake herself out of it, she was becoming obsessed. Before she knew it, Peter was back from the shop.

He yelled that he'd got a few extras. He opened the bathroom door.

'I got a chocolate cake, that one you like. It needs defrosting so I've left it on the draining-board, OK?'

'Yep, just give me a few minutes to get my glad-rags on and I'll set the table.'

But by the time she had dressed and dried her hair, Peter had done it all. Jane shrieked that she had wanted the best china, and started collecting the plates. Peter caught hold of her.

'Hey, this is just fine! Don't put out the best stuff, he's liable to smash something.'

'Do I look OK?'

He held her at arm's length. 'Yeah, nice blouse, looks Victorian.'

'Well, it's not, it's cheap Laura Ashley, so I bought two, but they're my best!'

She was wearing a full skirt from Next and a pair of red suede shoes she had never worn before; every time she had put them on she had felt they were a bit too flash, so they were pristine, not a scuff in sight. It tickled Peter that she was making such an effort, even down to perfume.

When the doorbell rang Jane flushed, and he grinned. 'Just relax, she'll only stay a minute.'

Jane hovered near the kitchen while Peter opened the door. Joey flew into his arms, yelling, 'Dad! Dad!' Peter swung him up and kissed him, then put him down, but Joey hugged his dad's legs.

Jane peered at the door, expecting the ex-wife. First came a huge bag, large enough for Joey to stay two months, then a box of toys. Finally Marianne's back was visible.

She spoke to someone who was invisible to Jane. 'I won't be a sec, darling!'

Peter's face was like stone. He had not even acknowledged Marianne's new husband, his old friend.

Marianne was wearing a short, frilly evening dress. Her blonde, shoulder-length hair was the type that novelists describe as silky, a real shampoo advert. To Jane's surprise she seemed much younger than her thirty-eight years.

'Hi, Pete, I've brought everything he could possibly need, and a lot he might not . . . '

Peter turned to introduce Jane. 'Jane, this is Marianne.'

'Hi, nice to meet you, it's good of you to have Joey.'

'Oh, that's OK, nice to meet you.' She bent down to the little boy, who still clung to his father's legs. 'And you must be Joey? You know what we've got? Fish fingers, do you like fish fingers?'

'What else have you got?'

'Chocolate cake, you want some? Yes? Come on, then, let me show you the kitchen.'

She held out a hand to Joey, who shied away at first, but then he edged forward and gripped her hand tightly. 'I got a new Revenge of the Joker mask!' he confided.

'Have you? Is that from Batman, then?'

Joey nodded. Anxious to get away from Marianne's critical gaze, Jane smiled and said, 'Would you like a drink, Marianne?'

'No, Steve is waiting . . . '

Duty done, Jane and Joey scuttled into the kitchen, but Jane could hear every word through the thin door. She showed Joey the cake box, opened it and reached into the top cupboard for a plate.

Marianne smiled and tossed her streaked, blonde hair back. She leaned confidentially towards Pete.

'Pete, I'm pregnant.' She gave him a long, direct look.

Peter swallowed. 'It's not . . . ' He glanced nervously towards the kitchen.

'Who knows? Anyway, I really appreciate this. You know what I was like in the early stages with Joey, I'm so sick every morning, awful.'

He pulled himself together. 'You look OK!'

'Well, it's all show. Underneath this I'm white as a sheet and getting hideously fat.' She wasn't; as far as Peter could recall she hadn't even put on much weight with Joey. Marianne went on, 'She's not at all what I expected! Is it working out?'

He nodded, and glanced again towards the kitchen door. 'You'd better go, I don't want him getting upset.'

'Oh, he's fine, and I should say goodbye to . . . what's her name?'

'Jane.' Again Peter looked towards the kitchen door. 'Jane! Marianne's leaving!'

The partly defrosted cake was half-way to the plate when it slipped off the bread knife and back into the box, showering Jane in the process. Peter opened the door to see her covered in chocolate and cream, trying in vain to wipe it off with a tea towel.

'Bit of an accident! Good to meet you, Marianne, hope you have a nice dance.'

'Oh, it's not a dance, just a small dinner party.'

Jane covered her astonishment with a smile. If she had got herself done up in a dress as glitzy as that, it would have been for a ball at the very least.

Joey kissed his mother, apparently unperturbed at her leaving, then ran back to the kitchen to stick his fingers in the blobs of chocolate and lick them.

As the door closed behind Marianne, Jane cocked her head to one side. 'So I wasn't what she expected, huh? Next time I'll borrow a WPC's hat!'

There was a crash from the kitchen as the entire chocolate cake, box and all, fell to the floor. Joey looked crestfallen, expecting to be punished, but Jane just looked at the mess on the floor and handed Joey a spoon.

'OK, let's have tea!'

It was eleven-thirty when Shefford completed his interrogation of George Marlow. He discussed the results briefly with Arnold Upcher; he was sure he had enough evidence to charge Marlow. Upcher, tired himself, pursed his lips and gave a small shrug.

'Then if you feel you have the evidence, Inspector, there is little I can do. But he's been here since early afternoon, that means you've got twenty-four hours. You will, of course, inform me if you go for extra time?'

Shefford was confident that he could charge Marlow without having to present all his evidence to a magistrate and beg for the statutory three days' delay to consolidate his case, or 'three-day lay-down', as it was known. Exhausted though he was, and a little punchy, he was still going strong. His main concern was to get the statements transcribed from the tapes.

Upcher, needing time to review Marlow's situation, had said little as he took his leave of Shefford. He knew intuitively that something was wrong, but until he had time to digest the case he wouldn't even contemplate discussing it.

None of it made sense; Marlow was a handsome, attractive male, a man with a good, steady relationship at home. He was popular, he had a job that he thoroughly enjoyed and which brought him good money and his employers had even held it open for him when he was convicted of attempted rape. Upcher had succeeded in getting the burglary charge dropped, and in Marlow's defence at the trial he had played heavily upon the confusion about which party had made the initial approach, whether both of them had been drunk – they had been seen in the same bar, and Marlow's claim that she had led him on and subsequently refused him had rung true. In Upcher's opinion the victim was a very disturbed woman whose evidence was unreliable, and he had been shattered by the verdict. Not just from a professional point of view; his relationship with Marlow was good, he actually liked the man and believed him to be innocent.

Marlow had taken it well, although Upcher was surprised that he had requested his representation for this, a much more serious charge. He had borne Upcher no grudge about losing the case, and had even admitted that, drunk or sober, he should not have forced himself on the woman, even though he had truly believed it was what she wanted. He had said, with a rueful smile, 'I'll never drink more than my limit again, so I suppose some good'll come out of it. I didn't hurt her though, Arnold, she made that up, the cops got it wrong.'

Was Marlow a rapist and a murderer? Upcher thought not, and could not believe he had misjudged the man to such an extent. The question occupied his thoughts all the way back to his Queen's Gate flat.

The Arnold Upchers of this world are expensive, and anyone seeing the tall, angular man in the hand-tailored suit parking his dark green Jaguar in the residents' bay could have been forgiven for mistaking him for the famous conductor who had once lived in the elegant service block a stone's throw from Hyde Park. With the remote control he locked his car and set the alarm, allowing the chill night air to clear his head. By the time he reached his door, Upcher was convinced that the police had got it wrong again. Marlow was innocent, and he would prove it.

Jane crawled to bed at midnight. She had exhausted her stock of stories before Joey finally fell asleep, from the three little pigs to a strange mixture of Batman confronting the Ninja Turtles.

Peter was sitting up waiting for her. He flipped the bedclothes back and patted the mattress. 'Come in, my beauty! And tell me a story . . . '

She snuggled into bed and gave him a blow-by-blow description of the goings-on at the police station.

'They were like kids playing at cops and robbers! I don't know what they were up to, but they stopped me working. They've got a nice juicy murder that should have been my case, and you know what I've got instead? A dyspeptic accountant who's had his bloody case adjourned four times in a row! Last time I had to wait at court all morning like a prat until he sent in some fictitious doctor's note, and then I was told to go away. Next thing, the little sod'll up and leave the country – I would, in his position. He owes ten years' income tax and VAT. I've got to know the little pest so well over the past three months that I can tell you what he'll be eating for breakfast, and even when I suggested that another adjournment would be . . . . Am I boring you?'

Peter smiled. He had only been half-listening.

She closed her eyes. 'I don't think I could manage another sentence, I'm so tired . . . Oh, God, am I tired!'

Peter switched the bedside light off and reached for her, wanting to draw her close, but she muttered, 'I'm afraid I'm too knackered . . . anyway, haven't you had enough for one day? Book me in for tomorrow night, OK?' She was fast asleep as she finished speaking.

Peter lay awake for about ten minutes, then put the light back on to read his book. Jane started to snore and he gently eased her onto her side. She gave a little grunt and then a pathetic, 'Sorry . . . I'm sorry . . . '

John Shefford was dog-tired by the time he arrived home, but his brain was ticking like a bomb. The events of the day kept repeating themselves like a news reel in his head and he had to drink half a bottle of Scotch before he felt the dark clouds gathering to cushion him to sleep.

It seemed only a moment before the alarm woke him. His head throbbed and he took four aspirin before he could get out of bed, crunching them between his teeth and hoping that they'd reach the parts that screamed for numbness.

Sheila had his breakfast ready. As she dished it up she reminded him of his promise about the clown for Tom's party. She had wrapped the presents and heaped them on the breakfast table, where Tom had found them at the crack of dawn, and he was beside himself, in a fever of excitement. They had both been touched by the lads' whip-round for Tom, which they had presented in cash in a large Metropolitan Police envelope to be put into his Post Office savings account.

By seven, Shefford was none too happy. He tried

to show enthusiasm, but he was getting ratty trying to eat his breakfast with one hand and fend off his son's new boxing gloves with the other. His nagging headache wouldn't shift, and he had another three aspirin with his coffee. Sheila was still going on about the clown, and he gave his solemn oath that not only would there be a clown, but that he would perform magic acts that would silence even Tom.

The little lad had started boxing his sister, and her screams cut through Shefford's head like a knife. Sheila removed his half-eaten scrambled eggs.

'I'm not expecting you to be here, that's why the clown's important. God forbid I should ask you to do anything so normal as to be home at half-past five with Tom's godfather for his party, it'd be an act of madness on my part . . . '

'Look, sweetheart, maybe I will make it, if things go well. We had a hell of a breakthrough yesterday; we've got a suspect and I think we can charge him. If we can do it this afternoon I can get home, and Bill's promised to dress up, how's that?'

Sheila screwed up her face and snorted. 'Haw, haw, promises, promises! And would you take those gloves off him, and tell him they can only be worn under supervision. I never wanted him to have them in the first place . . . '

Shefford crooked his finger at Tom, who shadow-boxed up to him, ducking and diving as his father had taught him.

'OK, Tom, off with the gloves. The rule's been laid down by the boss, you only use them when I'm around, OK? So give me a quick jab-jab, and a left hook before I go.'

Tom was fast and managed to clip his father on the nose. Sheila laughed, but Shefford's eyes watered and he grabbed the gloves, pulling them off as the telephone began to ring.

'Daddy, it's for you!'

Shefford listened to Felix Norman with difficulty while his daughter wound the phone cord around her neck and

Tom raced up and down the hall with his rugger ball, weaving around the defence – his father – and scoring a try in the kitchen doorway.

It was Norman's habit to get to the lab at seven each morning to escape the rush hour, though rumour had it that he was more concerned about avoiding his wife, as he was invariably found there late each night.

'What in God's name's going on there?' he yelled.

Shefford glared at his son and pointed in the direction of the kitchen. This gesture was famous in the household and was always obeyed. His daughter jabbed her lethally sharp elbow in his balls as she untangled herself from the curly cord and he grimaced, giving her a good whack on the back of the head, which had no effect at all. She hurtled after her brother, whooping at the top of her voice.

'OK, sorry about that, Felix old mate, but it's Tom's birthday. No, he got the ball last year, this year it's boxing gloves . . . ' He reached automatically for his cigarettes.

'Noisy little sod's a real chip off the old block . . . Well, wish him happy birthday from me. How's your suspect measure up, by the way? Is he right-handed?'

Shefford sucked on his cigarette. 'Yep . . . How's this for size; he's five feet ten and a half, well-built, looks like he works out.'

On the other end of the line, Felix puffed at his cigar. When the two men were together in one room they created such a dense fog that they were known as the Danger Zone. 'I'd say, John boy, you're a lucky sod. By the way, I was talking to Willy last night. Did he mention to you that he reckons there's not enough blood in that room?'

'You mean she wasn't killed there?'

'It's his department, but I'd say he's probably right.'

The press release that morning said little, just that a known prostitute had been murdered. Della had no family and no one volunteered any information about her movements. It was the same story all round; none of Della's friends and associates the police had contacted so far had seen her for weeks. Of ten residents of the house who had given statements, not one could say when they last saw her. Mrs Salbanna had been staying at her daughter's to help with the children while her newest grandchild made an appearance, and had not been home much for several weeks. Anyway, Della had been avoiding her for months because of the rent she owed. It was as if she had never existed, and, sadly, no one seemed to care.

By eight-thirty Shefford was at his desk, going over the typed-up statements from the previous day. He also had the full details he'd requested on Marlow's previous conviction. As he sifted through the information an alarm bell rang in his head, the same as on the previous day. Something was trying to break through . . .

Sergeant Otley brought coffee and doughnuts on a tray.

'Otters, there's something niggling me about this guy. Can you check something out for me, but tiptoe it? A girl was murdered in Oldham when I was there; get me the information on her, but keep schtum.'

Otley licked sugar off his top lip and replied, 'Yeah, what you think, he maybe did others?'

Shefford nodded. 'Yeah. Watch out for me on this, I knew the one in Oldham too, know what I mean?'

Otley sucked jam and sugar off his fingers and carried his beaker of coffee to his own desk. He inched a drawer open and brought out Della Mornay's diary.

'What do you want done with this?' he asked.

Shefford bit into his second sugar-coated bun. 'Hang on to it, old son, I'll check it out later. I'm goin' down to the cells, then upstairs, give the boss everythin' we've got. I reckon he'll give us the go-ahead to charge the bastard. If we finish it, you gotta hire a fuckin' clown's outfit!'

Laughing, Otley replaced the diary in his desk drawer. He called out as Shefford left, 'Eh, Big John, there's two hundred quid riding on us from DCI Tibbs' bunch, says we can't beat Paxman's record!' Otley could hear Shefford's big, bellowing laugh all the way down the corridor.

*

Shefford was still laughing while he waited for the cell door to be opened. He wanted to have a look at Marlow; he always did this just before he charged a suspect. There was something in a murderer's eyes, he had never been wrong yet.

Freshly shaved and showered, the prisoner looked somehow different this morning. Shefford was slightly taken aback; there was an eagerness to Marlow, a light in his eyes when he saw who it was at the door.

'Can I go?' Marlow asked.

Without speaking, Shefford shook his head slowly.

Jane Tennison parked her car with difficulty. DCI Shefford's dented and filthy Granada was angled across his space and hers and she had a tight squeeze to get out of the driving seat. Her pleated tartan skirt brushed against the Granada and she dusted it off in disgust, hoping that this would be the last time she would have to wear her court outfit for a while, unless the nasty little accountant engineered yet another stay of execution.

In the female locker room, she hung her smart black blazer with the brass buttons in her locker, straightened her high-necked Victorian-style blouse, ran a comb through her short fair hair and slicked some gloss on her lips, all in a matter of moments. She rinsed her hands at the row of washbasins and thumped the soap dispenser, which was empty as usual. Her irritation deepened when she caught sight of Maureen Havers, wasting time tittering with someone at the open locker-room door and fiddling with the Alice band she often wore to keep her thick, red hair off her pretty face. As she talked she whisked it off, shook her hair and replaced it, still giggling, then shut the door.

Havers started to sing as she opened her locker, then stopped short.

'Mornin', guv, didn't realize you were here.'

Tennison dried her hands and stepped back from the mirror. 'D'you think this skirt could do with being shorter?' she asked.

Havers peered around her locker door. 'Looks OK to me. That shirt suits you.'

'I'm in court this morning, remember?'

'Ahhh, it's Cary Grant Philpott, is it? In that case you'd better take the skirt up about a foot, keep him awake!'

A short time later, Havers breezed into the office with the pile of photocopying Tennison had asked her to do.

'We'll have to wait, the machine's in use.'

Tennison exploded. 'Tell whoever's on the bloody thing to get off it, I must have the stuff before I go to court!'

Havers beamed good-naturedly. She was used to Tennison's outbursts and knew better than to answer back. She had once, and regretted it; Tennison had a very sharp tongue. A perfectionist herself, Tennison expected the same diligence and professionalism from everyone else. Her pinched, angry look warned Havers that she was brewing a real explosion.

'I'll nip down and see if it's free, boss, OK?'

'Like now, Maureen, would be a good idea!'

Havers couldn't resist a little dig. 'OK, boss, but DCI Shefford's team have sort of got priority. They arrested someone yesterday for the Della Mornay murder, so the Paxman record's being challenged again. DCI Shefford's lads have started the countdown.'

Tennison frowned. The name of the victim, Della Mornay, rang a bell, but before she could ask any questions Havers had ducked out of the door. She chewed her lips, drummed her fingers on the desk. 'Come on, why do I know that name . . . ?' She remembered, then; in the Flying Squad two years ago she had brought Della Mornay in for questioning, but for the life of her she couldn't remember what the case was. Something to do with a pimp who had beaten up one of his girls . . . Della was a tough little bitch, blonde and rather pretty. She had refused to give evidence against the man. The fact that she had once interviewed the victim made Tennison all the more angry that she had not been given a chance to handle the case. Mike Kernan, the Superintendent, was going to hear about this.

Tennison closed her office door and turned just as Sergeant Otley bumped into her.

'Oh, sorry, ma'am.'

'I hear you've got a suspect, that right?' She meant to sound just interested, but she could not disguise the sarcasm.

'Yep, brought him in yesterday lunchtime. Word's out that the ink won't be dry on the warrant before the boss charges him. The DNA result was bloody marvellous.'

'Yeah, and such good timing! I heard there wasn't much else happening.'

Otley shrugged. This was the one he didn't like, the know-all who had been prowling around for the past eighteen months. He had studiously avoided any contact with her, just in case he was roped in to work with her.

'I wouldn't say that, ma'am. The team's pretty tough, John Shefford drives us hard.'

She turned, without agreeing, and he watched her push through the swing doors in her neat jacket and skirt. As the doors slammed behind her, he gave her the finger.

Kernan toyed uneasily with a felt-tipped pen as he listened to Tennison's complaint. He had never liked her, had been against her joining AMIT from the word go, but she had been more or less forced on him. She had more experience than at least one of the other DCIs, who was already on his second case. He cleared his throat and replaced the cap carefully on the pen.

'You want a transfer, is that what this is about?'

'No, I want to be given a chance. I was available for the Mornay case, but DCI Shefford was called in from leave to take it over. I want to know why I have had not so much as a sniff of anything since I've been here.'

Kernan opened his desk diary and noted that he had a lunch appointment before replying, 'It was my decision.

Shefford knows the area and he once arrested the victim on a prostitution charge. She was also one of his informers . . . '

'I knew the victim too, sir. I've been checking my old records and I brought her in for questioning two years ago . . . '

'I'm sorry, I was unaware of that . . . '

'Are you saying I would have got the investigation if you had been aware of it, sir?'

'Look, I'll be honest. Shefford's one of my best men . . . '

'I know that, sir, but he's just finished that big case and he had been given two days' leave. It was a long and difficult case, he needed to rest. I could easily have attended the court session today and handled the investigation, but I was overlooked. All I want to know is, why, and is this going to continue?'

Kernan looked at his watch. 'As you said, you had to be in court. According to the roster you were not available, but when you are you will have your chance, along with the other four officers . . . '

'DCI McLear is on a murder case right now, sir. He has nowhere near my experience, he came here six months after me. I notice his desk isn't loaded with petty fraud and tax evasion cases. I have had nothing else since I arrived.'

'Look, Jane, if you want a transfer then put in for it through the right channels.'

She was spitting mad, but managed to control herself. 'I don't want a transfer, I want to do the work I have been trained for, and I want you to give me your word that I will not be overlooked again.'

Kernan gave her the same speech he had spouted at her the last time she had complained, and she sighed. She had the distinct feeling that he couldn't wait to get her out of the office. She looked down at her shoes and seethed as he continued, 'It takes time, Jane. If you are not prepared to wait then perhaps you should consider asking to be transferred. As I have said to you before, we all appreciate your record, and your obvious abilities . . . '

'But you are not prepared to let me put them into practice, right?'

'Wrong. Just bide your time, don't rush things.'

'Rush, sir? I've been here eighteen months.'

'I've said all I intend saying at this point. I am sorry you feel the way you do, but until a case comes up that I feel is right for you, then . . . '

'Then I carry on as before, is that what you were going to say, Mike? Oh, come on, don't fob me off again. You gave me the same speech last time. You know I've been treated unfairly; all I'm asking for is a chance to show you, show everyone here, what I'm capable of.'

'You'll get it, I give you my word.' Kernan looked pointedly at his watch. 'Now, I'm sorry, but I have to get on. Just be patient, I'm sorry I can't be more positive, and your turn will come.'

She walked to the door, depressed that she had failed yet again to convince him.

'Thank you for your time!'

As the door closed behind Tennison, Kernan leaned back in his chair. A few more months and she would leave of her own accord. He had never liked working with women and knew that his men felt the same way. All the same, he knew she was right. She was a highly qualified officer, it was just something about her, about all the high-ranking women he had come across. Maybe it was simply the fact that she was a woman.

Tennison had missed breakfast in the rush to get Joey ready, but her anger seemed to have sharpened her appetite. She decided to have a bite to eat in the canteen.

She ate alone, eavesdropping on the rowdy conversation from the next table. DI Burkin was cracking a joke about somebody being trapped on a mountain when the 'bing-bong' went. He and DI Haskons were wanted in Administration. They stood up, laughing. Young DC Dave Jones, newly transferred from Cardiff, turned from the counter with his loaded tray to see the two DIs heading towards the exit.

'You want me along?'

Burkin pointed a finger and Jones's eager face fell. 'You always interrupt my jokes, Daffy. Give yourself fifteen, then get down to the Incident Room.'

Tennison watched in amazement as Jones tackled the vast amount of food he had piled on his tray; sausages, eggs, chips, baked beans, a heap of toast and two puddings with custard.

'Brunch, is it?' she asked, pleasantly.

'No, ma'am, I missed my breakfast because I had to go over to the labs for the guv'nor.' He stuffed a huge forkful of food into his mouth.

'You're on Shefford's team, then?'

Unable to speak, Jones nodded vigorously.

'I hear he's going to charge the suspect this morning, is that right?'

Jones wiped his mouth on a paper serviette. 'Yes, ma'am, he and Sergeant Otley are with the Super now. It looks good, the Sarge said.'

Tennison sipped her coffee. 'Have they found the car? I hear your suspect says his car's been stolen?'

Jones had timed his eating badly; again, he could only nod. He was relieved when the 'bing-bong' went; this time it was for Tennison.

She drained her coffee cup and picked up her bag of groceries. Passing Jones, she smiled. 'See you.'

'Yes, ma'am.'

Several officers, some of them uniformed, acknowledged her as she made her way to the door. There was an air of embarrassment; no one seemed to like her, but her rank of DCI demanded respect.

Jones waited until she had left before he burped loudly, which was received with a smatter of applause, then he continued eating at a frightening rate. He didn't want to miss the big moment. The Sarge had told him it was a dead cert that they'd charge Marlow, and Paxman's record would be smashed.

It was Maureen Havers who had put out the call for Tennison, to tell her that the photocopier was now out of order, so she was still unable to do the stuff Tennison needed for court. She asked if she should take it to another station or wait until their own machine was repaired.

Tennison dropped her bag on the desk. 'I don't believe this place, can't they get a bloody mechanic to fix it? What the hell's wrong with it, anyway?'

'Someone used the wrong type of paper and it's all jammed inside. We're trying to find the guilty party, ma'am, but it's really fouled up this time.'

Tennison rolled up her shirt-sleeves. 'Right, I'll fix it myself, at least it'll keep me occupied for a while. We'll take all the copying, and that stuff on my desk is for the shredder, let's do something useful . . . '

With their arms full of paper, they passed the open door of the Incident Room. The men were standing around in groups, with DI Burkin in the centre telling another of his shaggy dog stories.

'I hear they're charging the suspect. You heard anything, Maureen?'

Havers had to jog to keep up with her. 'Yes, ma'am, they'll break the record. There's a booze-up in the pub, whole station'll be there. Kitty's over a hundred and fifty quid already.'

Tennison squatted to peer inside the photocopier. 'Fucking thing's jammed all right, look at the mess! How do you open it up?'

Havers knelt beside her to read the instructions on the side of the machine. 'It says here, lift lever A, release spring . . . '

Tennison pushed her aside. 'I'll do it, get out of my light . . . Now then, pull what where?'

She yanked the lever and the machine split itself in two. 'Oh, shit, now what?'

'How about waiting for the mechanic, ma'am?'

Tennison froze her with a look. 'I've started, so I'll continue . . . '

For what seemed an age, the only sounds in the office were the ticking of the clock and the flick as Kernan turned the pages of Marlow's file.

'Christ, what a stroke of luck, John, bloody marvellous. What about the blood on the jacket?' He looked from Shefford to Otley, approvingly.

Shefford grimaced. He had a weird tingling in his left arm, all the way to his fingertips. He flexed his hand, rubbed the wrist.

'Willy's working his butt off. Should . . . should come through any time now . . . ' The pain was shooting down his arm now, and his chest felt as if it was being crushed . . . 'It was the size of a pinprick, they're waiting for it to expand at the labs, then we can check . . . Oh, Jesus . . . '

The pain was so bad it made Shefford fight for air. Kernan looked up, concerned. 'Are you OK, John?'

'I dunno,' Shefford gasped, 'I've got . . . like a cramp in my arm . . . '

He went rigid as a new spasm of pain hit him. He snorted, and Kernan saw blood oozing from his nose. There was a terrible look of fear in his eyes.

The pain seemed to be blowing him apart, like the bomb he had felt ticking inside his head. It was blowing up, he was blowing up! Rubbing his arm frantically, he snorted again and the blood poured down his chin. Then he pitched forward, cracking his head on the edge of Kernan's desk.

The Super was already picking up the phone, shouting for a doctor, an ambulance, as Otley grabbed Shefford and tried to ease him back into his chair. But the man was so big that Otley staggered under his weight.

Shefford's body suddenly relaxed and his head lolled on Otley's shoulder. Otley cradled him in his arms, shouting hysterically for an ambulance . . . Kernan ran round the desk to help him lower Shefford to the floor. They loosened his tie, opened his shirt, and all the while Otley was saying over and over, 'S'all right, John, everything's OK, just stay calm . . . Don't move, guv, it's all being taken care of, ambulance is on its way . . . '

The photocopier throbbed into life and shot out three crumpled sheets of sooty paper. Tennison gave a satisfied sigh and stood up, brushing at the black specks on her hands.

'Right, Maureen, try it with a sheet we want to shred, just in case it eats it.'

It seemed that a herd of elephants suddenly charged down the corridor outside. Tennison opened the door and stepped back to avoid being trampled as the stretcher-bearers raced along. They passed too swiftly for Tennison to see who their patient was under the oxygen mask.

The corridor suddenly filled with people, propping doors open, running to follow the stretcher. Word went round like wildfire; John Shefford had collapsed.

Tennison hurried into her office to watch the ambulance in the street below, but found the window space already occupied by two WPCs. She slammed the door.

'Get away from the window, come on, move it!'

WPC Hull whipped round. 'Sorry, ma'am, but it's DCI Shefford . . . '

'Well, peering out of the window isn't going to help him! Come on, move over, lemme have a squint!'

Tennison could see the ambulance with its doors open, the stretcher being loaded. She turned back to the room.

'OK, back to work. The copier's been repaired, and we may not have a lot of work to do but we might as well clear the desk. You never know, I might be needed!'

She meant it as a joke, and it was taken as one, because they didn't know then that Shefford would never regain consciousness. He was dead on arrival at hospital.

When the panic had died down, Tennison sat alone in her office and pondered . . . She was sorry Shefford was ill, of course she was, but someone had to take over the investigation. This time Kernan had to give her the job; everyone else on the rota was busy.

Deeply shocked, Otley shut himself in the gents' toilets and wept. He couldn't face anyone, and was unable to carry the news back to the men waiting in the Incident Room. He had lost the best friend he had ever had, his only real friend.

When he was able to face the men he found them sitting in stunned silence. He tried to tell them more, but all he could say was, 'It's Tom's birthday today, it's his son's birthday . . . I bought him a magic set, and . . .' He wandered over to his desk. There at the side was the big package, the train set he had taken so long to choose. He stood staring down at it. The men, deeply shocked, didn't know what to say.

Otley's voice was barely audible. 'We were going to set it up, surprise Tom. It's from Hamley's . . .'

DI Burkin, head and shoulders taller than his skipper, slipped an arm around him. The big officer's tears were streaming down his face, but Otley had no more tears. He clenched his fists, shrugged Burkin away.

'Right, let's nail this bastard Marlow! We do it for our guv'nor, we break the fucking record, agreed?'

It was down to Superintendent Kernan to visit Sheila Shefford. Otley had agreed to accompany him, but Kernan didn't know if it was such a good idea, the man was so distressed. In the end he decided to take DI Burkin along. No matter which way you looked at it, it was tragic.

Anticipating a harrowing time with Sheila and her family, Kernan's mood was not receptive. When Jane Tennison asked for a few minutes with him his first reaction was to refuse, but she had insisted it was important.

When he realized what she wanted he stared at her in disbelief. He was still in shock himself and he turned on her, ordering her out of his office. But she stood her ground, fists clenched.

'Look, please, I'm sorry if I appear heartless, but

all I am doing is offering to finish the investigation. John was ready to charge the suspect and someone has to take over, he's not going to be well enough. We can't hold Marlow much longer, we'll have to apply for a three-day lay-down, but either way someone has to take . . . '

Kernan gripped her tightly by the elbow. 'The man's not even cold! For God's sake, I can't make any decisions now. When I do, you will be the first to hear. Now *get out of my office* . . . '

'Cold?' She stared at him. 'He's *dead*? But he can't be . . . '

'I didn't realize you hadn't been told. John was dead when he reached the hospital. Now will you get out?'

Appalled, she shook her head as if to clear it, drew a deep breath, then plunged on, 'But you will have to make a decision, sir, and I am offering to step in right now. I can familiarize myself with the case tonight, and if charges . . . '

'I said I would consider your offer, Jane.'

'No, sir, you said you couldn't make any decisions right now. I think, however, a decision has to be made, and fast. You can't back out of this one, you know I am here. I am available and I am qualified. Someone's got to prove that bloody survey's a load of bullshit. You pass me over on this one and I warn you . . . '

Kernan's face twisted with barely controlled anger. 'You don't warn me, Chief Inspector, is that clear? Now you and your feminist jargon can get out of my bloody office before I physically throw you out. A friend, a close friend and associate of mine died in this room this afternoon, and I am just on my way to tell his wife and children. Now is not the time . . . '

'When is the time, sir? Because we don't have any to spare – if Marlow's not charged very soon he will have to be released. I am deeply sorry for what happened to John, please don't insult me by thinking otherwise, but at the same time someone has to— '

'Please leave *now*. Don't tell me my job. I will not be

forced into making a decision I will regret at a later date. Please leave my office.'

Maureen Havers hiccuped through her tears and Tennison put an arm around her shoulders.

'Do you want to go home, Maureen love? You can if you like, there's not much to do.'

Havers wiped her eyes. 'I'm sorry, I'm sorry, but he was always so full of life, and only today I heard him laughing, you know that big laugh of his . . . He said . . . he said he'd beaten Paxman's record!'

Leaving it that Havers could go home if she felt like it, Tennison left for court.

Superintendent Kernan called a two o'clock meeting with Commander Geoff Trayner to discuss the situation, particularly Tennison's request to take over the Marlow case. Neither man liked the idea, even though the file on the desk proved she was fully qualified and her ex-boss in the Flying Squad had given her a glowing recommendation.

Tennison had been with the Flying Squad for five years, and had taken a lot of flak from the men. Unlike two of her female colleagues in a similar position she had stayed her course. Her report noted that she had been offered a position training female officers because of her previous experience working with rape victims and her instigation of many changes which had been adopted by rape centres all over the country. She had turned the offer down, not wishing to go back into uniform, and had subsequently been transferred to AMIT. She was, as they were well aware, the only female DCI attached to a murder squad; with someone of her record it would be very difficult to bring someone in from outside to take over.

Kernan drummed his fingers on the desk. 'The men won't like it, you know that, but as far as I can see we don't really have a choice. There's no one free on AMIT except her. I've checked locally, and of the usuals I know Finley's in Huddersfield, Smith and Kelvin are still tied up on that shooting last week in Shepherd's Bush . . . And she's got a mouth on her, I don't want her creating a stink. She as good as threatened to resign if she was overlooked again.'

'She's one of these bloody feminists, I don't want any flak from that angle. We'll give her a trial run, see what happens, but if she puts a foot out of line we'll have her transferred and get her out of our hair. Agreed?'

Kernan nodded and slapped Tennison's file closed. 'I'll get her in to see you, and I'll break it to the men.' He pressed a button on his intercom and requested Tennison's immediate presence.

'DCI Tennison's in court today, sir,' his secretary replied.

'Hell, I'd forgotten . . . Let everyone know I want her the moment she comes in.'

Jane Tennison was lucky for once. The jury was out by two-fifteen and she was away. Still upset by John Shefford's death, she drove straight to the building site where Peter was working.

Peter was in his hut, talking to one of his workmen. Jane held herself rigid and waited until the man was gone, then rushed to Peter and sobbed her heart out.

It was a while before she was calm enough to make much sense, but he eventually pieced the events of the day together. He put his arms around her; it felt so good to have him to come to that she started crying all over again.

'You know, from everything you've said, this Shefford was well-liked, it must be a shock to everyone. Perhaps you should have given it a few days.'

He bent to kiss her cheek, but she turned away. 'You don't understand,' she snapped, 'Marlow will be released tomorrow unless we charge him. If they want extra time they have to have someone to take it before the magistrate, someone who knows what's going on. If the magistrate doesn't think there's enough evidence to hold him, he'll refuse the three-day lay-down.'

Peter didn't really care if they released Yogi Bear, but

he made all the right noises. At last she blew her nose and stood up, hands on hips.

'If those bastards choose someone else to take over, you know what I'll do? I'll quit, I mean it! I'll throw in the towel, because if I don't get the case – I mean, with Shefford dead it leaves only four on the AMIT team, and I know the other three are working, so they'd have to bring in someone from outside. And if they do, I quit. Then I'll take them to a fucking tribunal and show them all up for the fucking chauvinist pigs they are! Bastard chauvinists, terrified of giving a woman a break because she might just prove better than any of them! I hate the fuckers . . . '

Tentatively, Peter suggested that they go home early, have a relaxing evening, but she shot back at him, 'No way, because if they should call me and I'm not hanging by that phone, then the buggers have an excuse.'

'Use your bleeper.'

She grinned at him, and suddenly she looked like a tousle-headed tomboy, 'You're not going to believe this, but I was so pissed off I left it at the station.' Then she tilted her head back and roared with laughter. It was a wonderful laugh, and it made him forget the way she had snapped at him.

That was the first time he became aware of the two separate sides of Jane Tennison; the one he knew at home, the other a DCI. Today he'd caught a glimpse of the policewoman, and he didn't particularly like her.

The moment Tennison reached her office the telephone rang. She pounced on it like a hawk. She replaced the receiver a moment later and gave it a satisfied pat. She took a small mirror from her desk drawer and checked her appearance. She suddenly realized that Maureen Havers was sitting quietly in the corner.

'Wish me luck!' she said, and gave Havers a wink as she opened the door.

Havers sat at her neatly organized desk and stared at the closed door. She'd seen Tennison's satisfaction and knew something was going down. *Wish me luck?* She put two and two together and knew that Tennison was going after John Shefford's job. She was disgusted at Tennison's lack of sensitivity; she seemed almost elated.

Havers picked up the phone and dialled her girlfriend in Records. 'Guess what, I think my boss is going after Shefford's job . . . Yeah, that's what I thought, real pushy bitch.'

chapter three

Otley was the last to arrive in the Incident Room. He apologized to the Super and received a sympathetic pat on the shoulder.

The room was filled with palpable depression; there was a heaviness to every man. Some of them couldn't meet Otley's eyes but stood with heads bent. Only yesterday they had been laughing and joking with their big, burly boss. Shefford had been loved by them all and they took his death hard.

Kernan cleared his throat. 'OK, I've gone over all the reports on the Marlow case and it looks in good shape. I think, when I've had time to assess it all, we can go ahead and charge him. But until that decision is made, and I know time is against us, I am bringing in another DCI to take over. You all know Detective Chief Inspector Tennison . . . '

A roar of shock and protest drowned his next words, and he put up a hand for silence. 'Now come on, take it easy, just hear me out. As it stands, I reckon we'll have to try for a three-day lay-down, so I want all of you to give Inspector Tennison every assistance possible. Let her familiarize herself with the case, and then we can charge Marlow . . . '

Otley stepped forward. 'I'm sorry, sir, but it isn't on. Bring in someone from outside, we don't want her. We've been working as a team for five years, bring in someone we know.'

Kernan's face tightened. 'Right now she is all I have

available, and she is taking over the case at her own request.'

'She moved bloody fast, didn't she, sir?' Otley's face twisted with anger and frustration, his hands clenched at his sides.

DI Haskons raised an eyebrow at Otley to warn him to keep quiet. 'I think, sir, we all feel the same way. As you said, time is against us.'

'She's on the case as from now,' Kernan said firmly, unwilling to show his own misgivings. 'I'm afraid I can't discuss this further. She will assess the charges; just give her all the help you can, and any problems report back to me. Thank you . . . ' He got out fast to avoid further argument, but he heard the uproar as he closed the door, heard Otley calling Tennison a two-faced bitch, a cow who couldn't wait to step into a dead man's shoes. Kernan paused outside the room, silently agreeing with him. But the investigation was at such an advanced stage, they wouldn't be stuck with Tennison for long.

The Commander's voice was gruff as he briefly outlined the procedure for Tennison to familiarize herself with the Marlow case and to do everything necessary to ensure that he was charged. He told her abruptly to take it easy with Shefford's team, who had been working together for so long that they would not welcome an outsider. He didn't actually say, 'especially a woman', but he hinted as much. 'The Superintendent will give you every assistance, so don't be afraid to use him. And . . . good luck!'

'It would help if he could handle the application for the three-day lay-down,' Tennison replied, and the Commander agreed.

They shook hands and Tennison said she would do everything within her power to bring the case successfully to court. It was not until she was back in her own office that she congratulated herself, grinning like the Cheshire Cat because, at last, she had done it. She, DCI Tennison, was heading a murder case.

*

Late that afternoon, still stunned by his guv'nor's death, Bill Otley was clearing Shefford's desk. He collected the family photographs and mementos together and packed them carefully into Shefford's tattered briefcase. Finally he picked up a photo of Tom, his little godson, and looked at it for a long moment before laying it carefully on top of the others.

He snapped the locks on the case, hardly able to believe that John wasn't going to walk in, roaring with laughter, and tell them it was all a joke. His grief consumed him, swamping him in a bitterness he directed towards DCI Tennison, as if she was in some way responsible. He had to blame someone for the hurting, for the loss. He hugged the briefcase to his chest, knowing he now had to face Sheila and the children, he couldn't put it off any longer. Maybe it would be best if he left it till the weekend, and in the meantime he'd keep John's briefcase at the flat along with his shirts and socks . . .

He was still sitting at his desk, holding the case, when DI Burkin looked in.

'She's checking over the evidence, you want to see her?'

Otley shook his head. 'I don't even want to be in the same room as that slit-arsed bitch!'

Tennison was ploughing methodically through all the evidence on the Marlow case. The ashtray was piled high and a constant stream of coffee was supplied by WPC Havers. She was just bringing a fresh beaker and a file.

'Deirdre, alias Della, Mornay's Vice record, ma'am. The reason they gave for not sending it before was that King's Cross Vice Squad's computer records are not compatible with Scotland Yard's, or some such excuse.'

Flicking through the file, Tennison took out a photograph of Della Mornay and laid it beside the photos of the corpse. She frowned.

'Maureen, get hold of Felix Norman for me and find out how long he'll be there. Then order me a car and tell DC Jones he's driving me. I want to see the body tonight, but

I need to interview the landlady first. And ask for another set of dabs from the victim, get them compared with the ones on Della Mornay's file.'

Leaving Havers scribbling furiously, she walked out.

All the items from Della Mornay's room that Forensic had finished with had been piled onto a long trestle table. It was a jumble of bags of clothes, bedding and shoes. There was also a handbag, which Tennison examined carefully. She made a note of some ticket stubs, replaced them, then pulled on a pair of rubber gloves and turned to the clothing taken from the victim's body. The bloodstains were caked hard and black. She checked sleeves, hems, seams and labels.

Engrossed in what she was doing, she hardly noticed WPC Havers enter.

'Ma'am? Ma'am, DC Jones is waiting in the car.'

Tennison turned her attention to the filthy bedclothes. The smell alone was distasteful, and she wrinkled her nose.

'Dirty little tart . . . Tell Jones I'll be with him in a few minutes. And tell all of Shefford's team that I want them in the Incident Room at nine sharp tomorrow morning – all of them, Maureen, understand?'

DC Jones sat in the driving seat of the plain police car. He had left the rear door open for DCI Tennison, but she climbed in beside him.

'Right, Milner Road first. What's your first name?'

'David, ma'am.'

'OK, Dave, put your foot down. I've got a hell of a schedule.'

Della's room was still roped off. Tennison looked around and noted the fine dusting left by the Scenes of Crime people, then used the end of her pencil to open the one wardrobe door that still clung to its hinges. She checked the few remaining items of clothing, then sat on the edge of the bed, opened her briefcase and thumbed through a file.

DC Jones watched as she closed the case and turned to him. 'Will you bring me two pairs of shoes . . . '

She spent a considerable time looking over the dressing-table, checking the make-up, opening the small drawers. By the time she seemed satisfied, Jones' stomach was complaining loudly. He suggested it was time to eat. Tennison paused on her way downstairs and looked back at him.

'I'm OK, but if you can't hold out, go and get yourself something while I interview the landlady.'

When Jones got back to the house he found Tennison sitting in the dirty, cluttered kitchen in the basement, listening to Mrs Salbanna moaning.

'The rents are my living, how long will you need the room for? I could let it right now, you know!'

Tennison replied calmly, 'Mrs Salbanna, I am investigating a murder. As soon as I am satisfied that we no longer need the bedsit, I will let you know. If you wish you can put in a claim for loss of earnings, I'll have the forms sent to you. Now, will you just repeat to me exactly what happened the night you found Della Mornay? You identified her, didn't you?'

'Yes, I've told you twice, yes.'

'How well did you know her?'

'How well? You're jokin', I didn't *know* her. I let a room to her, that's all.'

'How often did you see her?'

'As often as I could, to get the rent off her. God forgive me for talking ill of the dead, but that little bitch owed me months in rent. She was always late, and it gets so if you throw her out on the street you'll never get the money back, right? She kept on promising and promising . . . '

'So you saw her recently?'

'No, because she was in and out like a snake. I hadn't seen her for . . . at least a month, maybe longer.'

'But you are absolutely sure that it was Della Mornay's body?'

'Who else would it be? I told you all this, I told that big bloke too.'

'And that night you didn't hear anything unusual, or see anyone that didn't live here?'

'No, I didn't come home till after eight myself. Then, because I'd had such a time with my daughter – she's had a new baby, and she's already got two, so I've been looking after them . . . Well, by the time I got home I was so exhausted, I went straight to bed. Then I was woken up by the front door banging. I put notices up, but no one pays attention. It started banging, so I got up . . . '

'You didn't see anyone go out? Could someone have just left?'

'I don't know . . . See, it's got a bit of rubber tyre tacked on it to try and stop the noise, so if they didn't want to be heard . . . But it was just blowing around in the wind, it was a windy night . . . I told the other man all this.'

Tennison closed her notebook. 'Thank you for your time, Mrs Salbanna.'

Tennison stopped off at Forensic on her way to view the body, and sat in silence while Willy Chang explained the complex details of the DNA test that had resulted in George Marlow being picked up on suspicion of murder. She looked at the slides.

'There was a big rape and murder case up in Leicester. They did a mass screening, every man in the entire village, and they got him. The semen tests took weeks to match, but in the case of such a rare blood group it's much easier to define. He's an AB secreter and belongs to group two in the PGM tests, so it narrows the field dramatically. We've been doing test runs on a new computerized cross-matching system, just using the rarer blood groups, for experimental purposes. Your man was tested in 1988, and was actually on record.'

'So you got a match from the computer, out of the blue?'

'Yes. When we got the read-out it was mayhem in here, it was such a freak piece of luck.'

'So the computer is infallible, is it?'

'Not exactly, it'll give you the closest match it can find.

We have to confirm the results with our own visual tests on the light-box. Want to see it?'

Tennison was shown two sets of negatives that looked like supermarket bar codes, with certain lines darker than others. The black bands on each matched perfectly. She made some notes, then asked to use a telephone.

She placed a call to her old base at the rape centre in Reading and requested the records of all suspected rapists charged as a result of DNA testing. She wanted to see how the judges had reacted, if they had allowed the DNA results to be the mainstay of the evidence.

Felix Norman slammed the phone down as a corpse, covered by a green sheet, was wheeled into the lab. Five students, all masked, gowned and shod in white wellington boots, trailed in after the trolley.

He gestured for them to gather round, then lifted the sheet. 'Well, you're in luck, this is a nice fresh 'un. I'm gonna have to leave you for a few minutes, but you can start opening it up without me.'

He picked up a clipboard and strode out to where Tennison and Jones were waiting. Greeting them with nothing approaching civility, he led them to the mortuary. At the far end of the rows of drawers he stopped and pulled on a lever, releasing the hinge, and slid out the tray with 'D. Mornay' chalked on it.

Before removing the sheet from the body, Norman reeled off a list of injuries from the clipboard, including the number and depth of the stab wounds.

'I hear you had a lucky break with the forensic results. Your suspect has a very rare blood group?'

Tennison nodded, waiting for him to draw the sheet back. He did so slowly, looking at DC Jones' pale face.

The body had been cleaned, the blonde hair combed back from her face. The dark bruises remained and the gashes on the head were deep and clear. Tennison frowned, leaning forward.

'Pull her out further, will you?'

Norman drew the drawer out to its fullest extent.

Tennison walked around, peering at the dead girl's face, then turned to DC Jones.

'Shefford identified her, didn't he?'

'Yes, ma'am, and her landlady, Mrs Corinna Salbanna.'

Tennison made a note on her pad, walked back again, then leaned in even closer. She stared for a long time before she asked to see the wounds on the torso. Norman pointed out the incisions, then indicated the deep weals on the tops of the arms.

'These seem to indicate that she was strung up. We'll do some tests with weights . . . And here, on her wrists, you can see the marks of the ropes, tied so tightly they left imprints, the mark of her watch strap too, see . . . '

'Where's the cut? Small cut on her hand?'

'Here.' He showed Tennison the corpse's right wrist. 'Small, but quite deep. Would have bled a fair bit.' He continued reading from his notes. 'Extensive bruising all over the front of the body, plus a good deal around the genital and anal areas, but nothing on the back or buttocks.'

Tennison nodded and again peered closely at the victim's face, then turned to DC Jones.

'I asked for another set of prints, will you make sure they're on the way, and the set from Della Mornay's file.'

Jones shifted his weight and muttered that he'd check it out. 'We already have a set, ma'am.'

Tennison snapped back, 'I need another set, and fast.'

Norman looked at his watch. 'My students are waiting, Inspector.'

Tennison was frowning. She turned again to Jones. 'Go and check on those prints now, Jones.' Then she addressed Felix Norman. 'I've got a few more questions I can ask while you work, OK?'

Norman sighed, covered the corpse and closed the drawer while Tennison added to the notes she had made during her inspection, then he led her into the dissection room.

For the next few minutes, Tennison watched as Norman, with apparent relish, helped a student remove the specimen's heart.

'That's it, ease it out . . . '

Jones returned and stood at Tennison's side. 'Prints are organized, ma'am.'

She ignored him and continued scribbling in her notebook. Jones watched Norman and his students as they worked on. Blood dripped into buckets set at each end of the trolley, and the stains on their gowns and rubber gloves made them appear ghoulish. On one lens of Norman's half-moon spectacles there was a clear fingerprint in blood. DC Jones' stomach turned over.

Tennison seemed intent on her notes. She did not so much as glance at Jones, who hadn't spoken for some time.

'How soon can you do the weight tests? I need to know exactly how she was strung up.'

'My dear lady,' Felix replied, 'we'll do them as quickly as we can, and you'll be the first to hear, though I'd have thought you had enough on your suspect to bang him up for life.'

He turned to the student and gave a helping hand as he opened the heart.

'Look at this, Inspector. This poor bugger's veins were so clogged up it's a wonder he lived as long as he did. Classic English breakfast causes this; bacon, fat . . . You like a cooked breakfast, Inspector?'

Tennison glanced around the room; Jones had disappeared. She smiled to herself.

The students clustered around Norman and took notes as he went on, 'Liver very dodgy, see just by the size . . . I hear through the grapevine that those wankers over at the labs can't even find the winder from the victim's watch. They've got fifteen square yards of carpet, combing it inch by inch. Right, now let's have a look at his testicles . . . Hmmm, well-endowed gent.'

Tennison knew she had as much as she was going to get. 'Thank you for your time, Professor Norman. As soon as you can on the— '

'You'll have my report, Inspector, but you should give us the time to do our job properly. And next time, gown-up, you know the rules.'

He turned to pierce her with his gimlet eye, as though she were one of his students, but she was gone.

When the Western finished at midnight, Peter switched the television off, poured a fresh cup of black coffee and carried it to the dining area. As he set it down by Jane's elbow she looked up, her eyes red-rimmed with fatigue.

'Thanks, love. I just have to wade through this mound, then I'll come to bed . . . '

'Maybe you'd be better off having a sleep now and getting up early?'

'You must be joking, I'll have to get up at five as it is, to plough through that lot on the chair.'

Peter planted a kiss on the top of her head, went back to the bedroom and settled down to sleep. In the end, Jane didn't come to bed at all.

As Tennison entered the Incident Room at nine the next morning, the men fell silent. They watched her as she walked to the table and sat in the chair their guv'nor had occupied the day before. She could feel their hatred; it prickled her skin. She had not expected such open animosity and it threw her slightly.

She kept her eyes down, concentrating on her notepad, then took out her gold pen and carefully unscrewed the cap. She raised her head.

'By now you are all aware that I am taking over from DCI Shefford, and I would like to take this opportunity to say how saddened and deeply shocked I am by this tragedy. John Shefford was a well-liked and highly respected officer.' She met the gaze of each man in turn as she spoke; several of them couldn't hold her eyes, one or two others, notably Otley, glared back, challenging her silently.

'I am not attempting to step into his shoes; I am the only available DCI and as such I shall appreciate all the co-operation and assistance you can give to enable me to grasp all the details of the investigation and bring it to a successful conclusion. WPC Havers will be assisting me, and she will give you details of everything I need. I will work around the clock . . . You wanted to say something, Sergeant Otley?'

Otley was standing, rigid with anger, tight-lipped. 'Yes, ma'am, I know you asked for this case specifically . . . '

She lit a cigarette and gazed at him, coldly. 'If you don't like it, put in for a transfer, through the usual channels. That goes for the rest of you; anyone who wishes to move can put in a formal request. Until then, I'm afraid you're stuck with me.' A murmur of resentment went around the room, but she ignored it. 'I'm asking for some more manpower. We've got more officers joining the team today, including Maureen Havers and four WPCs to assist with the paperwork.'

She picked up some items from the desk and began pinning them on the big notice-board. There were two photographs and two sets of fingerprints, highlighted with red and green arrows. She pointed at them as she spoke.

'Now, here's the really bad news. The photo on the right is Deirdre 'Della' Mornay; on the left is the murder victim. Here are the prints taken from the corpse, and these are the ones from Della Mornay's Vice file. There are nothing like the sixteen points of similarity needed for a match. The victim's clothes are all from expensive designers such as Giorgio Armani, not Della's line at all. Della's shoes are all English size five; our victim took six and a half, from Bond Street.'

She looked around as they took in the implications of what she was saying. Otley was stunned; he was aware of just how well Shefford had been acquainted with Della.

Tennison went on, 'We have obviously wrongly identified the victim, which makes our suspect's statement, in which he names the girl he picked up as Della Mornay, inadmissible. If we went to court with this, the case would be thrown out. Someone's been bloody careless. The officer who interrogated Marlow . . . '

Recovering quickly,Otley went on the attack, interrupting her. 'You know it was John Shefford! Are you tryin' to destroy him before he's even buried?'

She stared him into silence. 'What I want to know is how come Marlow named the victim as *Della* when the warrant gave her proper name of Deirdre? I'm told you did not state her name at the time, you just arrested him on suspicion of murder. In the tapes of his first interrogation by Shefford, Marlow insists not just once but three times that he did not know the victim, but at the end of the second interview he refers to the victim as Della Mornay. In his written statement, made that night, he again denied knowing her. In his third statement he is calling the victim by name! This would be thrown out of court, especially as Marlow's lawyer was in the room and witnessed his denials. The cock-up is therefore down to us. DCI Shefford made a gross error in wrongly identifying our victim, just as he did in giving the name to George Marlow.'

Otley frowned but kept quiet as she continued, 'I want new statements all round, and we'll get it right this time! So get them all in again and find out where Della Mornay is now, and get the victim's clothes and shoes checked out. Our priorities are to find the real Della Mornay and to get an ID on the body.'

She paused, stubbed out her cigarette and lit another. She was wiping the floor with them, and they knew it, hated it. No one said a word as she took a sip of water, then went on.

'So we move like hell. We haven't a snowflake's chance of getting the three-day lay-down, so if we don't come up with something today, Marlow will have to be released.'

She waited, hands on hips, for the howl of protest to die down. 'I'm afraid it's a fact of life! OK, anyone have any queries? No? What about Marlow's car, the brown Rover? Anything on that yet? I want it found. Right, that's it for now.'

The room was eerily silent as she passed them on the way out, but the moment the door closed behind her there was an explosion of cat-calls and abuse.

Otley thumped the table she had recently vacated. 'Fucking tart! She was after this before he was out of the bloody station! She was in with the Super almost before he was dead, the bitch! I'll give her queries, the hard-faced tart!'

'What about Marlow's car, Bill?'

Otley turned on Burkin. 'You heard her, cow wants it traced, so we trace it! Christ, how much evidence does she bleeding want, for God's sake? We got him, he did it! An' she's runnin' around familiarizin' herself, the stupid cunt!'

In the corridor outside the Incident Room, Tennison leant against the wall, eyes closed, breathing deeply to calm herself. It had been a tremendous effort to keep her cool in front of the men.

Once she was in control again, she headed for the lift to the Super's office.

The men dispersed to their appointed tasks in dribs and drabs. DC Lillie said quietly to his partner, Rosper, 'If the car was nicked, we ain't gonna find it. It's been stripped down by now.'

Rosper's pug-nosed face broke into a grin. 'Eh, you ever see that advert wiv the monkeys? Bleedin' funny . . . '

Otley and Jones were left alone in the room. 'What do you think, Skipper?' Jones asked.

'That tart's gunning for John. Well, let her try it; she bad-mouths him and I'll see her knickers are screwed . . . '

The phone interrupted him. He grabbed it. 'No, she's not here. Yeah? Yeah! Right, I'll send someone over. Thanks!'

He hung up and gave his first smile of the morning. 'That was Forensic. The spot of blood we got off Marlow's shirt cuff, the one they've been growing, matches the victim's! We got the bastard now . . . '

'This is a right bloody mess,' said Superintendent Kernan.

Tennison ran her fingers through her hair and Kernan continued, 'For God's sake don't let the press get wind of it. Can you handle it? DCI Hicock, from Notting Hill, is available now.'

'I can handle it,' Tennison snapped. No way would she relinquish the case to Wild Bill, even if she had to hang on to it by her teeth. 'I need more men, preferably from outside. If we have to let Marlow go, we'll need someone with surveillance expertise.'

'I'll see what we can do. Are you going to see him now?'

'I want a little chat with Marlow, off the record . . . OK?'

'Watch yourself, Upcher's a tough bastard.'

Tennison shrugged. 'But I bet he's not down in the cells now, is he?'

Kernan shook his head. 'Seems to me that Marlow wouldn't have hired Upcher unless he was guilty. His type cost.'

'We still can't prove he was ever in the bedsit. It's strange that there's nothing, not a single shred of evidence . . . '

'Forensic's still working on it?'

'Yes,' she said, standing up. 'They are, at their own pace.'

As soon as she left, Kernan picked up the phone. 'Put me through to the Commander.'

Before seeing Marlow, Tennison listened again to a short stretch of tape from his interview with Shefford. Then she was ready to face the suspect for the first time.

Marlow had been left to kick his heels in an interview room for some time, sitting in silence, watched by a uniformed PC. DI Burkin was sitting in the corridor outside, reading the paper. He was a well-built man, a prized member of the police boxing team, and his slightly battered face showed traces of his career. He rose to his feet when DCI Tennison approached.

'Sorry to keep you waiting. It's Frank, isn't it?'

Burkin nodded and jerked his thumb towards the interview room. 'He's got coffee, and he doesn't smoke.'

Tennison was taken aback by Marlow's handsome looks; the photographs in his file had given her completely the wrong impression. He resembled an old-time movie star, not exactly Valentino, more Robert Taylor. His blue-black hair was combed back from his face, high cheekbones accentuated his jawline. His amber eyes and long, dark lashes beneath thickly arched brows would be the envy of any woman.

He glanced at the uniformed officer for permission to stand, then rose to his feet. His clothes were well-cut, rather formal; a blue and white striped shirt with a white collar highlighted his dark good looks. His suit jacket hung neatly on the back of his chair.

'Please stay seated, Mr Marlow. I am Detective Chief Inspector Jane Tennison, this is Detective Inspector Frank Burkin. I suppose you have been told that the DCI in charge of this investigation . . . '

Marlow interrupted her in a low, husky voice with a slight northern twang. 'Yes, I know. I'm very sorry, he was a nice man.' He glanced at Burkin, then back to Tennison, placed his hands together on the table and half-smiled; a dimple appeared in his right cheek.

Tennison returned his smile involuntarily. 'You have been very co-operative, Mr Marlow, and I'm sorry to have to question you all over again. But you must understand that in taking over the case I need to know everything . . . '

'Yes, I understand.'

Tennison was furious with herself because her hand was shaking as she placed Marlow's statement and her notebook on the table. 'Would you just tell me, in your own words, exactly what occurred on the night of Saturday the thirteenth of January?'

Marlow began quietly, explaining that he had drawn some money from a cash dispenser in Ladbroke Grove. He was about to return home when he saw her standing outside the tube station, obviously touting for business.

'I'm sorry to interrupt, but who was standing?'

'Della Mornay!'

'Oh, you knew her, did you?'

'No, I didn't know her name, never saw her before. He

told me, said it was a tart by the name of Della . . . He told me.'

'Who, exactly, told you the girl's name?'

'Inspector Shefford.'

'OK, George, go on. Tell me what happened next.'

'I got into my car and drove past her, slowly. She came to the window, asked me if I was looking for someone. All I said was maybe, it depended how much. She said it was twenty-five pounds for full sex. If I wanted . . . '

Looking up, Tennison caught his strange, beautiful eyes. He looked away, embarrassed.

'Go on, Mr Marlow. Twenty-five pounds for full sex . . . '

He cleared his throat and continued, 'Masturbation fifteen. I agreed to pay the twenty-five, and she directed me to some waste ground beside the . . . the Westway, I think it is. We got into the back seat. We . . . ' he coughed. 'We did it, then she asked me to drop her back to the Tube. Then, as she climbed over the seats into the front she caught her hand, her left hand, on my radio. It's got a sort of sharp edge, and it was only a little nick, but I wrapped my handkerchief around it . . . '

'Er, sorry, George, you just said, "She cut her hand on my radio"?'

'Yes.'

'Which hand?'

He frowned and raised his hands, looking from one to the other. 'Her right hand, yeah . . . It was her right hand, because my radio's between the seats. It's got a sharp edge.'

He indicated the spot on his own wrist – exactly where the small cut was on the wrist of the corpse. 'You can take the radio out, it's portable. They're always being nicked out of cars, round where I live.'

He paused for a second and sighed. 'You found my car yet?'

Tennison shook her head. 'Go on. She cut herself?'

'Yeah. I gave her my handkerchief, wrapped it round her wrist. It's got my initial on it, G . . . Then I paid her, drove her back to Ladbroke Grove station. When I dropped her off, the last I saw of her she was picking up another punter. It was a red car, I'm not sure which make, could have been a Scirocco. I didn't kill her, I swear before God that was the last I saw of her. Then I drove home, got back about half-past ten, maybe nearer eleven . . . '

Tennison had been reading his statement as he talked. It was not word for word, but slightly abbreviated, as if he was getting used to repeating only the pertinent facts. 'You saw a red car stop. Was it facing towards you or in the opposite direction?'

'Oh, it was coming towards me. I was going down Ladbroke Grove towards Notting Hill Gate.'

'So you would have dropped her on the pavement opposite the car? Or did you swerve across the road and deposit her on the other side?'

'Oh, I crossed the road. Then when she got out I drove straight down to the Bayswater Road.'

'You live on the Maida Vale/Kilburn border, wouldn't you have gone the other way? It's a quicker route, isn't it?'

'I suppose so. I never thought about it, really. I went straight along to Marble Arch, into Edgware Road and straight to Kilburn to get a video.'

'Have you picked up girls in that area before?'

Marlow shook his head and looked down at his hands. 'No, and I wish to God I hadn't picked this one up either, but . . . '

'But?'

He looked up, and again she was caught by the strange colour of his eyes. 'She was very attractive, and I thought, why not . . . '

'George, had you picked this particular girl up before?'

'No, and I must have been crazy, after what happened up north. But I paid for that. I was drunk, and I swear to you she came on to me, I swear I was innocent . . . I served eighteen months, and when they released me I swore I wouldn't mess around with other women.'

'Mess around? It was a little more than that two years

ago, wasn't it? You were also charged with aggravated burglary.'

'Like I said, I was drunk. I just snatched her handbag . . . It was a stupid thing to do, and I lived to regret it.'

'So you never knew this girl you picked up?'

There was a tap on the door and Sergeant Otley peered through the window. Irritated, Tennison went out to talk to him.

'The lab came through, that speck of blood on his jacket, it's the victim's. Thought you'd like to know. Oh, and the Super wants to see you.'

'That's it? Nothing else? They can't place him in the bedsit?'

Otley shook his head. Tennison said, very softly, 'Not enough . . . '

She turned and went back into the room, leaving Otley cursing to himself.

'How much more does she need, for Chrissake . . . '

Tennison spent another three-quarters of an hour with Marlow. At the end of that time she stacked her files and notebooks and thanked him for his co-operation. Seemingly intent on putting her things away, she asked, as if it was an afterthought, 'You drove home, Mr Marlow? Is that correct?'

'Yes.'

'Do you have a garage? Did you put the car in a garage?'

'No, I left it outside my flat. There's a parking bay, under cover, for residents. They say they can't find it, has it been stolen, do you think? Only, I should get on to my insurance broker if it's true.'

Without replying, Tennison turned to walk out. He stopped her.

'Excuse me, am I allowed to leave yet?'

'No, I'm sorry, Mr Marlow, you are not.'

Tennison was exhausted, but she hadn't finished yet by a long chalk.

*

Burkin had been falling asleep. He snapped to attention when Tennison knocked to be let out.

'Marlow can go back to his cell. Then I need a search warrant for his flat. We'll go together,' she told him.

'Right, ma'am . . . I'll get the warrant.'

'Meet me in the Incident Room ASAP.' Tennison went down the corridor almost at a run.

For once the Incident Room was fairly quiet. Otley was sitting staring into space when Burkin joined him.

'She interviewed Marlow, then she went to see the Super.'

Otley smirked. 'An' she'll be interviewing all afternoon, I got girls comin' in from all over town. Keep her out of our hair!'

He fell silent as Tennison walked in with a big, sandy-haired man and introduced him as DI Tony Muddyman. 'Tony will be with us as from tomorrow. I've given him the gist of the case, but you'll have to help fill in the details.'

Otley had met him before and wasn't too sure about him, but several of the others greeted him like a long-lost cousin.

'Anything on Marlow's car?' Tennison asked Otley.

'No, not yet. There's a roomful of girls waiting for you.'

'What?'

'All known associates of Della Mornay. You asked for them to be reinterviewed and they're comin' in by the car-load. There were seventeen at the last count . . . '

'I haven't got time to interview them! Why don't you take their statements and leave them on my desk?'

To cover his fury, Otley crossed the room to the notice-board and pinned up a large poster. It advertised a benefit night for DCI Shefford's family.

'Is this the list of girls reported missing?' Tennison had picked up a sheet of paper from his desk.

'Yeah, it's got "Missing Persons Report" on the top hasn't it?'

'Cut it out, Sergeant.'

'One in Cornwall Gardens, another in Brighton, one in Surrey looks promising . . . '

'Fine, I'll take them, shall I?'

'Why not, I've got seventeen slags to interview.'

'Should have staggered them!' Tennison retorted. She beckoned Jones to her side. 'Can you check if there's a handkerchief among Marlow's things. He said he bandaged the victim's hand with it, initial G on the corner.'

She reached for the phone as it rang. 'Tennison . . . ' Peter was calling her; she gave a quick look around the room. Only Jones was close by, thumbing through the log book and shaking his head.

'OK, put him through.'

She turned to face the wall while she spoke, unaware that Otley was mimicking her behind her back, to the amusement of the men.

'I'm sorry, I can't really talk now, is it important?'

Burkin was waiting for her at the door. Otley strolled over to him.

'What's goin' on, are we chargin' Marlow?'

'You're joking . . . ' Over Otley's head, Burkin called, 'Ma'am, we've got the search warrant!'

'What's this for?' asked Otley.

'Marlow's flat, now we're looking for a handkerchief!' replied Burkin contemptuously.

With a promise to call Peter later, Tennison put the phone down and joined Burkin. As they left, Otley was at it again.

'Yeah, a bloody handkerchief, for that snot-nosed cow! Doesn't she know we've only got ten hours before that bastard has to be released?'

As Tennison and Burkin mounted the steps towards flat 22, the curtains of number 21 twitched.

Burkin knocked on the door. They waited a considerable time before they heard a lock turn and the door was flung wide open.

Moyra Henson glared at them, then looked to Tennison, who was sizing her up fast. It was the first time she'd seen Marlow's common-law wife. She knew Moyra was thirty-eight years old, but she looked older. Her face had a coarse toughness, yet she was exceptionally well made-up. Her hair looked as if she'd just walked out of the salon, and her heavy perfume, 'Giorgio', was strong enough to knock a man over at ten yards.

'Yes?' Henson snapped rudely.

'I am Detective Chief Inspector Tennison . . . '

'So what?'

Tennison was noting the good jewellery Moyra was wearing; expensive gold bangles, lots of rings . . . Her nails were long and red. She replied, 'I have a warrant to search these premises. You are Miss Moyra Henson?'

'Yeah. Lemme see it. Your lot shell out these warrants like Smarties, invasion of privacy . . . '

She skimmed through the warrant. Tennison clocked her skirt, the high heels and fluffy angora sweater with the tiger motif. Miss Henson might come on as a sophisticated woman, but she was a poorer, taller version of Joan Collins, whom she obviously admired judging by the shoulder pads beneath the sweater.

'I would like to ask you a few questions while Detective Inspector Burkin takes a look around.'

Moyra stepped back, looking past Tennison to the broad-shouldered Burkin. 'I dunno why he doesn't move in, he spends enough time here.'

Tennison was growing impatient. 'Could we please come in?'

Moyra turned with a shrug and walked along the narrow hall. 'I don't have much option, do I? Shut the door after you.'

The flat was well decorated and exceptionally clean and tidy. The cosy sitting-room contained a three-piece suite which matched the curtains and a fitted carpet.

Tennison looked around. 'This is very nice!'

'What d'you expect, a dump? George works hard, he earns good money. Found his car yet, have you? It's down to you lot, you know. This estate stinks, somebody must have seen him being taken away and nicked it.'

'I'm sorry, I can't give you any information on that. Really, I'm just here to have a chat with you. You see, I'm taking over the investigation. The previous Inspector died, tragically.'

'Good! Less of you bastards the better. Oi, what's he up to? Hey, sonny! You can put that laundry back, that's my dirty knickers! Are you some perverted crotch sniffer?'

'How do you feel about your boyfriend picking up prostitutes?'

'Wonderful, it gives me a friggin' night off!'

'I admire you for standing by him while he was in jail.'

'That bitch asked for it! She was coming on to him, and he'd had too much to drink . . . '

'Was he drunk when he came home on Saturday night?'

'No he was not!'

'And he arrived home at what time?'

'Half-past ten. We watched a video, then we went to bed.'

Tennison took a photograph from her briefcase and laid it on the coffee table, facing Moyra. 'This is the girl he admitted to picking up, admitted having sex with in his car. Now look at her.'

'What am I supposed to do, have hysterics? I feel sorry for the girl, but he only fucked her! Half the bloody government's been caught messing around at some time or other, but their wives have stuck by them. Well, I'm doing the same. Now, if you've finished wrecking my flat, why don't you get out of here?'

'I haven't finished, Moyra. Just one more question; did you know Della Mornay?'

'No, never heard of her.'

'Never?'

'No.'

'And George didn't know her, you're sure of that?'

Moyra folded her arms. 'I have never heard of her.'

Tennison put her notebook into her briefcase. 'Thank you for your time, Miss Henson.'

*

While she waited for Burkin to finish, Tennison had a good look around the flat. There were no handkerchiefs with the intial 'G' on the corner, either in the bedroom drawers or the laundry basket. Enquiries at the laundry Moyra had told them she used came to nothing.

The flat was very much Moyra's and only her things were in evidence; pots of make-up, knick-knacks, magazines. Just one small corner of the dressing-table held a neat, old-fashioned set of bone-handled brushes with George's initials in silver. Moyra, who followed them from room to room, told them they had belonged to his father.

Tennison was struck by the neatness of Marlow's clothes in the wardrobe. They took up only a quarter of the space, the rest of which was crammed with Moyra's things. His suits were all expensive, in tweeds and greys, nothing bright, and the shirts were of good quality.

The small bookcase in the lounge contained paperbacks, mostly by Jackie Collins, Joan Collins and Barbara Taylor Bradford. It was as if Marlow didn't really live there. Tennison looked again; there were a few thrillers that were more likely to be his, such as James Elroy and Thomas Harris, plus a hardback edition of *Bonfire of the Vanities* that she guessed belonged to him.

Finding nothing of interest, Tennison and Burkin left to start checking on the missing girls. They headed for Cornwall Gardens to question a Mrs Florence Williams.

Sergeant Otley had a feeling this was a good one, which was why he and Jones were there instead of Tennison. The report had only been in a few hours, but the description matched their victim.

The basement area of the flat in Queen's Gate, Kensington, looked as if a cat-fight had taken place in the dustbins, spewing rubbish among the broken furniture and bicycles that cluttered the approach to the door.

Otley peered through the filthy window. 'Are you sure this is the right address, Daffy?'

'Yeah. Knock on the door, then.'

'Christ, place looks like a dossers' pad, you seen in here?'

Jones shaded his eyes and squinted through the iron grille over the sash window. 'I thought this was a high-class area?' he muttered.

'It is,' snapped Otley. 'And shut your mouth, someone's coming.'

The door was opened by a tall, exceptionally pretty girl with blonde hair hanging in a silky sheet to her waist. She was wearing pink suede boots, a tiny leather mini-skirt and a skimpy vest.

'Yes?'

'I am Detective Sergeant Otley, this is Detective Constable Jones. You made a missing persons report?'

'Oh, yeah, you'd better come in. It might all be a dreadful mistake, you never really know with Karen, it's just odd that Michael hasn't seen her either . . . '

Otley and Jones exchanged glances as they followed the leggy creature into the dark, shambolic hallway.

'Trudi! Miffy! There are two policemen . . . '

The blonde turned to them and pointed to an open door. 'If you want to go in there, I'll get them. They're in the bathroom.'

The room contained a large, unmade double bed with two cats fast asleep in the middle of the grubby sheets. The furniture was a mix of good antiques and fifties junk, but the room was as much a mess as the rest of the flat. On the fireplace wall a large, moth-eaten stag's head hung at a precarious angle, with door-knockers hanging from its antlers.

'Do you want coffee or tea?' The blonde hovered in the doorway.

'Cup of tea would be nice, thank you.'

'Indian, China or herbal?'

'Oh, just your straight, ordinary tea, love, thanks.'

Jones perched on a wicker chair until he noticed one of the legs was broken and it was propped on a stack of books. He moved a heap of clothes from a winged armchair and sat down.

Otley whispered, 'What a bloody dump! Place looks as if it's not been cleaned in years.'

Jones flipped open his notebook. 'The girl that came in to the station is Lady Antonia Sellingham . . . So if Trudi's in the bathroom with Miffi, unless that's another cat, the blonde's a titled aristo. Typical, isn't it?'

Cornwall Gardens was a total waste of time. Edie Williams, reported missing by her mother, Florence, was a thirty-five-year-old mental deficient with a passion for watching trains at Euston Station. She had returned home that morning.

Otley sipped from the cracked mug of terrible-tasting tea, prompting the three girls to remember exactly when they had last seen their flat-mate, Karen. It was quite normal for her to spend several days at a time with her boyfriend, Michael Hardy, but he had been away, skiing. Antonia at last decided she had not seen Karen since Friday – no, Saturday.

'Do you have a photograph of her?'

'Oh, yes, lots. There's her modelling portfolio, would you like to see that?'

Miffy, a short, plump girl with a wonderful, chortling laugh, bounced out of the room. Lady Antonia asked if the police were worried that something had happened to Karen. Otley didn't reply but made a note of Karen's boyfriend's name and phone number. He glanced at Jones, whose eyes constantly wandered back to Antonia's legs.

The doorbell rang and Antonia strolled out, pausing to ask if anyone would care for more tea. None of them showed fear for Karen; they did not really believe that anything could have happened to her, it was just a bit odd that no one had seen her around.

Miffy returned and shrugged her shoulders. 'Can't find it, but we have got some photos of when we were in St Moritz, they'd be the most recent. I'll see if I can find them.'

She went off again in search of them as the leggy Antonia returned with a large cardboard box. 'It's my new pet, a chinchilla. Would you like to see it? It's just adorable . . . '

Before Jones could take up the opportunity to get closer to Antonia, Miffy came back with a large, expensive-looking album. She flipped through the pages, then stopped.

'Oh, here's a goodie, this is Karen.'

Otley took the book, stared at the photograph, then silently passed it to Jones. The atmosphere in the room changed in an instant; the girls picked up on the glance between the two officers. Suddenly they were afraid.

'Is something wrong?' Has something happened?'

Otley sighed and passed Jones his notebook, in which he had jotted down Michael Hardy's details. 'Could DC Jones use your telephone? And I suggest you get your coats, ladies. We'll need you to accompany us to the station.'

The girls left the room. Jones hovered. 'Er . . . Who do I call, Skipper?'

Otley gave him an impatient stare. 'You call the boy-friend, and we pick him up on our way back to the station.'

'Oh, right! His number's in the book, is it?'

'In the book in your friggin' hand, you fruit!'

The house in Brighton was a late Victorian building with a fish and chip shop on the ground floor. Elaine Shawcross, daughter of the proprietors of the shop, had been missing for ten weeks. Her parents were upstairs in their flat; while Tennison went to see them, Burkin ordered fish and chips for them both.

As he carried them back to the car he was surprised to see Tennison leaving the house. She climbed into the car and slammed the door.

'I've salted and peppered them, ma'am, did you want vinegar?'

'Yeah, I'd like to smother that Otley's head in it, might make his hair grow. Either Detective Sergeant Otley needs his friggin' head seeing to, or he's deliberately sending me on a wild goose chase. Give us me chips, then!' She crammed chips in her mouth and continued, 'He's pissed off with me because he's back at the station interviewing hundreds of toms! Ha, ha, ha!'

As they drove back towards London, Tennison stared out of the window. 'That snide bugger Otley did it on purpose! Sending us all the way down here, he's just stirring it at every opportunity.'

Burkin did not respond, and she gave him a sidelong look. 'So, Frank, what do you think of Marlow?'

'I'm sorry, ma'am?'

'I said, what do you think of the prime suspect? George Marlow?'

Burkin shrugged. He stopped the car at a red light and she could almost see the brain cells working as he chewed his lips.

Well, spit it out! You do have some personal thought on the matter, don't you?'

'Yes, ma'am.'

'So, tell me . . . '

'Well, I think he did it. There's something about him, I don't know what, maybe just intuition. But I think he's our man.'

She lit a cigarette and Burkin opened his window. She felt the cold blast of wind, inhaled deeply and wound her own window down. Burkin promptly closed the one on his side.

Tennison gave him a sidelong look. 'Draught too much for you, is it?'

'No, ma'am, just thought it might be too much for you!'

She stared out of the window, talking more to herself than to him.

'You know, being a woman in my position is tough going. I mean, I have intuition, but it's probably very different from yours. As a man, you feel that Marlow did it. Are you saying that your intuition tells you that Marlow is a perverted sexual maniac? Because this girl was tortured, strung up, beaten and raped . . . And you just *feel* it's George Marlow?'

'It's more than that, ma'am. I mean, he had sex with her.'

'So? That doesn't make him the killer. You've got to find the gaps, the hidden areas. His common-law wife is his alibi; she stood by him before, when he was convicted of a serious sex assault. He snatched the woman's handbag, knocked her about a bit, then he freely allowed them to take samples for DNA testing to see if they could find anything else against him. They didn't, so it was his first offence. His girlfriend must have gone through hell over that. No matter how hard-faced she seems, she's still a woman! She was betrayed by him, but they both used the excuse of drink. He had been drinking, and a lot of men do things when drunk that they'd never consider doing when sober, right? But our killer is a cold-blooded, calculating man. He scrubs his victim's hands . . . '

'Well, I agree with what you're sayin', ma'am, but there is something about him . . . '

'You can't bloody charge a man because there's something about him! You can only do that with evidence, proof, and we have not got enough proof to hold George Marlow.'

The radio crackled and Tennison went to answer it, saying, 'Maybe this will be it, fingers crossed!'

Control patched through a call from Forensic. It was Willy Chang, though Tennison could hardly tell. His voice was breaking up over the air.

'Inspector? We've *crackle* the carpet, every inch of *crackle*, *crackle* . . . have nothing. There's not one shred of evidence to prove your man was ever there. We'll keep at it, but I'm not hopeful.'

Tennison leaned back in her seat. 'Well, that confirms it. As I was saying, we have nothing, not a hair, a fragment of material, to put Marlow in that bedsit. She was covered in blood, but we've got not so much as a pinhead on a pair of his shoes . . . How did he get her in there and walk away without so much as a single stain?'

'But there was one, ma'am, on his sleeve.'

'Ah, yes, but he has a plausible explanation for that. The only thing that might possibly finger him is his car. If he killed her in his car he has to have left something . . . And by the by, Burkin, would you stop calling me "ma'am", makes me feel like a ruddy queen. I like "boss" or "guv'nor", take your pick. Kingston Hill coming up on the right . . . '

Otley led the three bewildered girls and the handsome, tanned young man to the canteen, pushing the door open to allow them to pass in front of him. Michael Hardy paused politely, and Otley waved him on, taking a good look at the boy's high-heeled cowboy boots and heavily studded biker's jacket. But it was the ponytail that got him; his eyes gleamed.

'Take the ladies to a table, sir, at the far end out of everybody's way, and I'll arrange some refreshments.' He watched, shaking his head, as the four of them seated themselves, then turned to the counter.

The two canteen workers were about to haul the shutter down, but he scuttled over. 'Hang about, Rose! I want four coffees for this lot, on the house. I'll get you a docket later.'

The other woman walked off in a huff, not even attempting to serve him. The charming Rose muttered to herself as she turned to the steaming urn and drew four cups of pale brown liquid, banged them on the counter. Otley loaded them onto a tray. 'Thanks, darlin'!'

He plonked the tray on the table, slopping the contents of the cups, and told them they would have to wait for Inspector Tennison to return. Then with a brief apology he wandered off.

He passed Maureen Havers, who had stopped to chat to DC Lillie.

'Have you heard, they're bringing in Hicock to replace her?'

Otley's ears flapped. 'What was that? Hicock?'

'Yeah, I got it from the Super's secretary.'

Otley nearly danced for joy. 'Great! Now we need a get-together, get a report done . . . '

DI Muddyman joined them. 'What am I missing?'

'Word's out that they're bringing in Hicock, Tennison's gonna get the big E . . . ' Otley beamed. 'We better give them a little assistance, I'll get a vote of no confidence going. That'll teach the pushy bitch.'

He was almost rubbing his hands in glee as he headed out of the canteen. DC Lillie was more interested in the group of girls in the corner. He nudged Jones.

'Eh, I thought all the toms were downstairs? I wouldn't mind interviewing that lot. Who's the puff with the pony-tail?'

Jones prodded Lillie in the chest. 'They're the victim's flatmates, you prat!'

'What, you got an ID on her?'

'Not official, we gotta wait for the Queen Mother! Skipper's sortin' it out, sent her off to Brighton.'

The men laughed amongst themselves, while Karen's four friends waited and waited for someone to tell them why they had been brought in, tell them anything at all. Officers came and went, but no one approached them. Michael was growing impatient, but he realized the long wait meant something terrible had happened. No one answered his questions, no one would tell him if Karen had been found.

'Was it Coombe Lane, ma'am?'

'Yep, should be off to the left . . . Yes, this is it. Oh, yeah, very posh.'

Tennison licked her fingers, then sniffed them. They smelt of fish and chips. She took a perfume atomizer from her bag and sprayed herself quickly.

They cruised slowly along Coombe Lane and stopped at a barred gate with a sign, 'The Grange'. Tennison hopped out to open it. The tyres crunched on the gravel drive and they both looked around, impressed.

The Tudor-style house, all beams and trailing ivy, stood well back from the road. There was a golf course behind.

'Obviously loaded, and no doubt Otley has sent us on another wild goose chase,' commented Tennison. 'OK, we both go in – and straighten your tie, Burkin!'

Large stone eagles and huge urns of flowers and ivy flanked the heavy oak door. There was an old-fashioned bell-push and, next to it, a modern plastic bell.

The deep bellow of a large dog was the first response to Tennison's ring. She stepped back and waited, hearing footsteps on a stone-flagged floor. Then the door was opened wide.

'Major Howard? I am Detective Chief Inspector Tennison and this is Detective Inspector Burkin. Do you think we could ask you a few questions?'

With a slight frown he replied, 'Yes, of course. Do come in.'

They followed the major through the echoing hall into a vast drawing-room with french windows overlooking a rolling, immaculate lawn. There were oil paintings and ornate statues in abundance, elegant sofas and chairs covered in rose silks. Even Tennison could tell that the thick, sculptured Chinese carpet was worth several years' salary. The whole place smelt of money.

A little over-awed, Tennison watched the major closely as he apologized for his shirt-sleeves and put his jacket on over his dark green cords and checked shirt. Tall and well-built, he had obviously been a very handsome man in his youth. Now, with iron-grey hair and a back straight as a die, he still exuded the sort of easy charm that comes with total confidence.

He turned to DI Burkin. 'Sit down, Inspector. Now, what can I do for you? Is there something wrong?'

Tennison stepped forward. 'Thank you, sir, I'll stand. I am Detective Chief Inspector Tennison. I hope we will not take up too much of your time, but we are enquiring about your daughter. She has been reported missing?'

The major looked surprised. 'By whom?'

Tennison was annoyed at herself for having to check her notebook. 'A young man by the name of Michael Hardy. He gave this address.'

The major frowned. 'Well, I hope this isn't some practical joke, that's her boyfriend. My daughter Karen doesn't actually live with us, she shares a flat with some girls in Kensington. I'd better call my wife, see if she can get to the bottom of this. Reported missing? Are you sure? I haven't heard the first thing about it. To be honest, I thought it was about Karen's car. She got a new Mini for her birthday and her parking tickets are always being sent here. We've had some fair old arguments about that. But please, I won't be a moment, excuse me.'

As soon as he was out of the room, Tennison walked across to the grand piano on which stood a number of family photographs. One, in a particularly large frame, showed a girl holding the reins of a pony and smiling into camera. She would be about ten years old. The next photograph was of a family Christmas, with everyone in paper hats roaring with laughter. Tennison's heart started thumping and she moved along to the photo that had caught her eye.

The beautiful, sweet young face, the wondrous hair . . . She was the epitome of youth and health, a smiling, vibrant, free-spirited girl. Tennison turned slowly towards Burkin.

'We've found her . . . '

Mrs Felicity Howard handed Tennison two large, professional photographs of her daughter, taken in the past year. They confirmed Tennison's suspicion. The major, knowing without being told that something was dreadfully wrong, moved to his wife's side and held her gently.

Quietly, Tennison said, 'I'm sorry to have to tell you that I believe your daughter may be dead. It will be necessary for one of you to come with us to identify the body.'

The major sat without speaking throughout the journey. He sat stiffly, staring straight ahead. Tennison did not attempt to make conversation; when she had radioed in to say that she was bringing Major Howard to identify the victim, she lapsed into silence.

*

Otley, Jones and Muddyman spent the rest of the afternoon interviewing prostitutes and call girls for the second time. They were all unhelpful, uncooperative, and one or two even had the cheek to complain about loss of earnings.

None seemed able to recall when they had last seen Della Mornay. It seemed that she was reasonably well-liked, but no one admitted to mixing with her when not on the streets.

The story was the same from the pimps and the patrons of the clubs and cafés frequented by Della Mornay. By late afternoon there was no evidence of any recent sighting of Della; it appeared that no one had seen her for weeks. At last, one very young girl volunteered the information that a friend of Della's, known only as Ginger, had contracted Aids and returned to Manchester. Perhaps Della had gone to visit her.

A few girls hinted that Della had the odd S & M client, but when asked for names their faces went blank; the reaction was the same when Otley enquired if anyone else had ever been picked up by any of Della's special clients. No one was interested.

Otley was gasping for a cup of tea, or something stronger, but the canteen was closed. He jerked a thumb at Muddyman and winked. Muddyman followed him out.

'Let's take a little break. We can use the office, she won't be back yet.'

Two of the tarts he had interviewed passed him on their way out. They waved; he gave them the finger.

'You know,' he said viciously, 'when you start talkin' to them all it makes my skin creep. They're like an alien species, opening their legs for any bastard that'll pay up. I'd like to get a water cannon, wash the lot of them off the streets.'

Muddyman shrugged. 'Well, if the johns weren't there they wouldn't be on the streets in the first place. Hose them and you've gotta hose the guys doin' the kerb-crawling after their skinny, dirty little cunts.'

Otley opened the office door carefully and looked

around; it was empty. He closed the door softly behind them.

Tucked at the back of one of his desk drawers was a half-bottle of whisky. He unscrewed the cap and offered it to Muddyman.

'Fuckin' toms, I tell you, we had this Marlow done up, we'd have sent him down if it wasn't for that bitch Tennison. Now we got to crawl through the gutters, makes me puke.'

'Maybe the one we found wasn't a tom?'

'Bullshit! She was in Mornay's flat, why else was she there, you tell me that? Don't give me any crap because she was wearing designer knickers, I've had girls come in dripping with mink, wearing high-class gear, but they're all the same, open the legs, drop in yer money!'

Muddyman thought it best to keep quiet as Otley was really sounding off. His face was twisted with anger and pent-up frustration.

'My wife, the most decent woman you could ever wish to meet, never done a bad thing in all her life, died of cancer, screamin' in agony. She was goodness itself, and she was a bag of bones. These slags, tartin' around, passing on filthy diseases . . . Why my wife? That's what I ask myself over and over, why does a decent woman die like that and they get away with it?'

Wisely, Muddyman decided there was no answer to that. Instead, he enquired for the third time what they were going to do about the three girls and Michael Hardy.

'What d'you think, we keep them here until ma'am comes back. I get their statements, I can't whip 'em over to the morgue, she's got a family . . . We wait, but it'll be worth it, because it's all going down on my report sheet!'

'The canteen's closed, Skipper, they're in one of the interview rooms – not the one with the tarts. They've been here for hours, an' I think Lillie's taken a fancy to the tall blonde one!'

Muddyman was referring to the youngest member of the team, DC Lillie, nicknamed Flower. He took the brunt of their wisecracks when Jones wasn't around.

Otley sucked in his breath and prodded Muddyman's chest. 'I'm doin' the report, an' I know how long they've been here, OK? When the canteen reopens we'll wheel 'em back up, an' you tell Lillie no chattin' up the blonde Puss in Boots, savvy?'

Muddyman bristled. Sometimes Otley got right under his skin, seeming to forget who was the senior officer. But he replied, 'I savvy, Sarge!'

In the mortuary, the wait for the body to be brought out seemed interminable, yet it was no more than a few minutes. The major stood in the small waiting room, tense and unspeaking.

After putting out a DO NOT DISTURB sign, Felix Norman opened the door of the waiting room and gestured to Tennison that everything was ready. He held the door open as Tennison led the major out, followed by Burkin. They formed a small group around the open drawer where Karen lay covered with a green sheet. Tennison looked at the major.

'Are you ready?'

He nodded. His hands were clenched at his sides as the sheet was drawn back.

'Major Howard, is this your daughter, Karen Julia Howard?'

He stared as if transfixed, unable to raise his eyes. He did not attempt to touch the body. Tennison waited.

After a long, terrible pause, the major wrenched his eyes from the body.

'Yes, this is my daughter,' he whispered.

His work forgotten, Otley was still holding forth to Muddyman. The only way to get rid of Tennison, who he instinctively associated with the tarts, was a vote of no confidence. He had spread the word to any who would listen, and was sure the team would back him. Suddenly, he remembered that he had intended to see the Super to tell him they thought the victim had been identified.

*

Tennison had many questions she needed to ask the major, but before she could phrase the first one, he said bluntly, without looking at her, 'How did my daughter die? I want to know the facts. I want to know how long she has been dead, and why I have not been contacted before this. I want to know when I can have my daughter's body, to give her a decent funeral . . . And I want to know who is in charge of this investigation . . . '

Tennison interrupted. 'I am in charge of the investigation, sir.'

He stared at her, then looked at Burkin. 'I am a personal friend of Commander Trayner, I must insist on speaking to him. I do not . . . I will not have a woman on this case, is that clear? I want to speak to the Commander . . . '

Tennison sighed. 'I am in charge of this investigation, sir. If there is anything you wish to discuss with me, please feel free to do so. I assure you we will release your daughter's body as soon as it is feasible. The only problem is if you want to have her cremated . . . '

'Cremated? Good God, no, a Christian burial is what I want for my daughter . . . '

'Then the delay should be minimal, Major. I'll see to it personally,' Tennison promised. 'I think perhaps the questions I need to ask you can wait until you have had a chance to recover. I will arrange for a car to take you home . . . '

'I want to speak to Commander Trayner. If I didn't make myself clear in the first place, woman, then let me repeat to you, I refuse . . . I will not have . . . I will not have a female in charge of this case.'

Tennison was about to reply when Burkin caught her eye. He gripped her elbow and whispered, 'Leave the room, let him cry, leave him . . . '

She allowed herself to be steered from the room. She stood in the corridor, angry at first, then looked through the small glass panel in the door. She could see the major; he slammed his fist into the top of the bare table.

'I have many friends, I know many people who could

take over this investigation . . . ' Then he disintegrated like a helpless child, his body sagged and he held out his arms, in desperate need of comfort from anyone, a stranger, even the Detective Inspector . . .

Gently, Burkin held the heartbroken man as he sobbed his daughter's name over and over.

Tennison felt inadequate and ashamed of herself for being so eager to question the major. In his grief and rage he had turned to the young Inspector, not to her. For a long time he wept in Burkin's arms.

Listening to him, Tennison was flooded with sympathy.

Eventually the door opened and Burkin emerged.

'He's ready to go home now. I'm sorry, ma'am, if I was rude, but I could see the old boy was . . . '

'You were quite right, Frank. Don't worry about it.'

He started back into the room, then paused and turned. 'Oh, Sergeant Otley wants you at HQ.'

'Did he just call you?'

Burkin evaded her gaze. 'Came in while we were in Brighton. Karen's boyfriend and flatmates have been brought in for questioning. Sorry . . . '

'I see! In future, pass on any information immediately, no matter the circumstances. I'll go there now, you see to the major. Was there anything else?'

Burkin shook his head. She watched him closely as she said, 'Otley stirring it up, is he? Next thing, he'll be going for a vote of no confidence.'

His sudden flush was enough to tell her she'd hit the nail on the head.

Burkin had been greatly moved when the major, with a tremendous effort, had pulled himself together and said he was ready to go home, ready to tell his wife, and that he would be available the next morning to answer any questions. He had even asked Burkin to apologize to Inspector Tennison on his behalf for his rudeness.

As Burkin helped him out to the car the major's back was ramrod straight. He shook the younger man's hand and was gone to break the news to his wife.

chapter four

Otley was furious to discover that Tennison had beaten him to it; her report on the identification of the murdered girl was already on Superintendent Kernan's desk. He couldn't think for the life of him how she had managed it.

It was out of order for Otley to come direct to the Chief Super but, knowing how the Sergeant felt, Kernan said nothing. He waited; Otley was still hovering.

'Something else, Bill?'

After a moment's hesitation, Otley blurted out that the men felt that Tennison wasn't sufficiently experienced. 'It's out of control, guv! The big interview room's full of toms bein' questioned for the third time, and not one's seen hide nor hair of Della Mornay. The Incident Room's full of blokes sitting around waiting for her . . . '

'Is this a consensus?'

'We all feel it, guv. She's just not right, she's not handling the men at all well. She's smug, she doesn't fit in, we all feel it. We've only got a few hours left, and the way she's going we'll have to let him go!'

Kernan pursed his lips and nodded a fraction. 'It's not entirely up to her, the situation's under constant review. Leave it with me, Bill, OK?'

Arnold Upcher sorted through some documents, then pushed them across the desk to Chief Superintendent Kernan.

'I thought these might interest you. They're cases from the last three years where the evidence depended solely on DNA tests. You can see for yourself, in every instance the judge threw the case out. I think my client and I have been most patient; if you have any further incriminating evidence then we'll discuss it, but I am not prepared to let him stay here another night if you cannot substantiate your suspicion of murder. And that's all you're holding him on – suspicion. It's not on; he has a solid alibi, he has been co-operative and totally honest with you. Come on, Superintendent! You've got the wrong man.'

Convinced that the Super was going to take Tennison off the case, Otley watched with a gleam of triumph in his eye as she entered the Incident Room, obviously harassed and sweating, with Burkin at her heels.

'Anything on Marlow's car yet?' she demanded.

Ken Muddyman answered her from the far side of the room. 'Not yet, ma'am, but we've got you a slot on the Shaw Taylor programme!'

'That's a good idea!' She heard Lillie sniggering behind her but ignored him.

'I was joking, ma'am!'

'I'm not! Laugh away, DI Muddyman, but time's almost up and Marlow's lawyer's with the Super now. Get on to the Press Office . . . '

Muddyman couldn't work out if she was kidding or not. Lillie interrupted them.

'Ma'am, Records sent this in, about Moyra Henson. She was picked up for soliciting fifteen years ago. I dunno if it's of any interest, but she's been on the dole for four years.'

'You never know. Stick it on the file.'

Otley chipped in, 'We've got twenty-two statements from the toms, and there's more of 'em upstairs. Nothing worthwhile yet. Plus her boyfriend and flatmates are waiting to be interviewed. What's goin' on, are we gonna charge him?'

It was coming at her too fast; Tennison floundered for a moment.

'I'd better see the girls first. Keep the Super off my back for a while. And I want to see everyone in here when I'm finished.' She looked around the room to see who was there. 'Ken, you'd better organize a WPC for the girls . . . '

Otley perched on the edge of his desk, watching with delight while she tried to cope, and failed.

'There was something else . . . ' Tennison continued. 'Oh, the identification. Her name's Karen Julia Howard.'

'We know,' said Otley.

'Oh . . . yes, of course you do. Right, I'm off.'

Following her, Ken Muddyman minced from the room, camping it up and blowing Otley a kiss as he went. The hoot of laughter could be heard all the way down the corridor.

The three girls' vagueness about Karen was infuriating; Tennison terminated the session after half an hour. By that time she knew that Karen had often spent days, even weeks, at her boyfriend's flat, but the couple had recently had a disagreement and had not seen much of each other since. When Karen had not returned for a couple of nights they presumed she had made it up with him.

On the other hand, Miffy conjectured, Michael obviously didn't make contact because he thought Karen didn't want to see him, but eventually he had called round. Discovering that no one had seen Karen, and she wasn't with her parents or any other friends, Antonia had reported her missing.

The last time the girls had seen Karen she had driven off in her white Mini to Ladbroke Grove for a modelling job. It was a knitwear advert, she had told them. She had taken her large portfolio and her Filofax. Perhaps Karen's agent would know the name of the firm.

The girls constantly looked at each other as if to confirm every detail. A couple of times they broke into tears; Tennison was patient with them but she kept pushing for the information she needed.

'Was there any mention of a new man in her life?'

They could think of no one. Miffy, her eyes red from crying, believed that Karen had loved Michael more than she pretended, but got fed up because he was a bit possessive.

'So they used to argue about it, did they?'

'Just sometimes. You know, she wanted to let her hair down a bit, but they had been going out together for years . . . '

'Did she drink a lot?'

'Oh, no! She didn't drink at all, or smoke. She was a fitness freak, always dieting, and her room at the flat was a no-smoking zone.'

Tennison stubbed out her fifth cigarette of the session, not that she was counting. 'What about drugs?'

They shook their heads in unison, Tennison thought a little too eagerly.

'You mean never? Not just a little grass or speed?'

Lady Antonia twisted her hands in her lap. 'Karen didn't like drugs, hated any of us having stuff in the flat. She wouldn't touch anything like that.'

'Not even coke? Did she use cocaine?'

'No, honestly. We've known each other for years, since school, and she got quite uptight about that sort of thing.'

Tennison sighed. 'OK, so what about Michael, she was a virgin as well, I suppose?'

Lady Antonia crossed her long legs and fiddled with the top of her boot. 'That was her business, I have no idea what she did in private.'

'Now it's my business, love. Karen was found in a prostitute's room, and I have to find out how she got there. Come on, what do you take me for? Are you trying to tell me that four girls, living in the same flat, never even mentioned sex?'

Lady Antonia pursed her lips. 'I don't think you have any right to ask us that sort of question.'

Tennison was getting more irritated by the second. 'I have every right, as I said before. Anyway, that's it for now, but I might need to talk to you all again before you leave. This officer will show you the way back to the canteen, go and have some coffee.'

Lady Antonia faced Tennison. 'I am going to complain about the way we have been treated, as if we were criminals. And we don't want to go back to that awful canteen. Please would you call my father, if you need to speak to us we are perfectly willing, but we have been here for . . . we really . . . I would like to go home.'

Tennison never took her eyes off the girl's face. The bravado disappeared fast, and Antonia blinked back the tears. 'Please, let us go home. We've been here for hours.'

Tennison pursed her lips. 'Antonia, isn't it? Yes? Well, all I can do is apologize for keeping you here for so long. You are free to go at any time, but I need to question Michael Hardy. As you all came together, perhaps you'd like to leave together. I'll order you a car. Your girlfriend has been brutally murdered, we are just trying to find out how she came to be in that bedsit . . . OK? And any assistance you can give us, give me, is really appreciated. So have a cup of tea or coffee, anything, just for a while longer . . . '

She watched the round cheeks flush, and the girl blinked rapidly. Her whole face seemed to be moving, trying to say something, but unable to form the words. Then she burst out, 'She was always happy . . . '

Antonia left the room, and Tennison could hear her sobbing outside in the corridor. She felt dirty, her hands were grubby, and she sniffed her armpits then made a quick exit for the locker room. Next was Karen's boyfriend, Michael Hardy, and though she was sure he was innocent he had to be checked out, eliminated completely. To do that she was going to have to be tough.

The cold water felt good as she splashed it on her face. She washed her hands, scrubbed them, then stared into the soapy water. The killer had used a wire brush on the victim's hands, scratched them raw . . .

Michael, obviously distraught, was sitting with his elbows on the table and his head in his hands. His voice was muffled.

'I can't believe she's dead, I can't believe it . . . '

'You said the reason you hadn't seen Karen was because you'd had a row, is that right?' Tennison asked him.

'I agreed not to see so much of her . . . ' he stopped, too choked to continue.

'She was murdered, Michael, and we found her in a prostitute's bedsitting room. Now, take a look at this photograph and tell me if you've ever seen this man, ever seen Karen with him. Come on, Michael, look at the photograph.'

He raised his head and stared at the mug shot of George Marlow. 'No, I've never seen him.'

'OK, now what I need to know is when you last saw or spoke to Karen.'

He coughed and ran his hands over his ponytail. 'I, er, I phoned her, the day before I went to Switzerland. The fifth of January.'

'Did you call her from there? While you were away?'

'No . . . '

'And you came back when?'

'I came home on the thirteenth, a week early. There wasn't much snow about.'

Tennison sat slightly straighter in her chair. 'Did you see her when you got back?'

'No. I went round to her flat yesterday. Miffy said Karen wasn't at home, they'd presumed she was with me. Then I called her parents' house. The housekeeper told me Karen hadn't been home since Christmas, so I rang round a few other friends. When I ran out of places to look for her, I went to the local police station and told them.'

'When was that?'

'Er, first thing this morning. I just said no one had seen her lately.'

'Ah, so we got two separate reports . . . Now, Michael, her car, the Mini. Have you any idea where it might be?'

'No . . . ' he thought for a moment. 'It wasn't outside the flat.'

All through the interview, Tennison was aware of a lot of coming and going outside. Faces popped up in the small window, but no one knocked. One of them was the Super, but he waved at her not to bother. She found it all distracting, so it was almost a relief when Michael burst into tears and she was able to pace around the room for a few moments.

Eventually Michael blew his nose in his handkerchief. Tennison sat down again.

'So let's get back to this argument you had with Karen.'

'It wasn't really an argument, it was just . . . just that she decided we were getting too involved, she wanted more time to herself. I agreed, but we didn't argue.'

'But you didn't like it?'

'No, I wanted to marry her. But she was only . . . she . . . ' His eyes filled up and he turned away, shrugging his shoulders helplessly as his voice cracked, 'She was only twenty-two years old . . . '

'So, you agreed not to see so much of her. Did you find out if there was someone else?'

'No, she didn't have anyone else.'

'How can you be so sure?'

'Because I know . . . She would have told me if there was something . . . someone else. I'm sorry . . . '

'So you don't think she had other boyfriends?'

'She had a lot of acquaintances, men friends, but most of them I knew. She didn't have anyone else, wasn't seeing anyone else.'

'But you were in Switzerland, maybe she met someone else while you were away?'

He shook his head and looked at the table. Tears trickled down his face and Lillie felt even more sorry for him. The boy kept looking at Lillie as if he could stop Tennison's stream of questions.

'Did you and Karen have a good sexual relationship?'

Michael's voice was a whisper. 'Yes.'

'Did she like anything . . . unusual? Was she a bit kinky?'

'No.'

'Do you know if she took drugs?'

'She didn't drink and she didn't take drugs.'

'Do you?'

'Pardon?'

'I asked you if you take drugs, do you use hash or cocaine?'

'I have . . . but not recently.'

'Did you score it?'

'How do you mean?'

'Did you buy it for yourself? Go out and score from people?'

'No . . . when I say I've used . . . I was offered some cocaine once, and grass quite a few times, but I've never bought any. Do you mean do I go out to a dealer?'

'Yes?' He shook his head.

'Michael, are you sure? We found Karen in an area where a lot of drug dealers hang out. You sure she wasn't using anything, or maybe going to get some for you?'

'*No*!'

'Did she pick up men?'

'*No! No* . . . Karen would never . . . Karen . . . '

He started to sob, hunching his shoulders, and Tennison leaned closer.

'Tell me, Michael, come on. If she was scoring for you it would make sense of where we found her, why we found her!'

Michael stood up, shaking with anger and grief, his face red with frustration. '*No*! She was a sweet, innocent girl, and you're making her out to be something dirty, something sick! You disgust me . . . '

'Sit down, Michael, *sit down*! Come on, now. You said that on the night of the thirteenth of January you . . . '

He gritted his teeth. 'I was at my parents' house, I went straight from the airport. We had dinner and I stayed the night. I've told you this, I've told you this three times!'

Tennison closed her notebook. 'Yes, you have, and thank you for being so co-operative. If you'd like to have a wash there's a gents' just along the corridor, and then DC Lillie will take you up to the canteen.'

He was slumped in his chair, silent. He didn't look up. She walked to the door.

'You can go, Michael, and the girls are free to go with you. Thank you . . . '

Tennison leaned back and lit another cigarette as Michael followed Lillie along the corridor, standing aside to allow Superintendent Kernan to pass. The Super stopped at the door of the interview room.

'Anything?'

Tennison shook her head. 'No,' she replied wearily, 'her car might give us a clue, if we can find it. None of them know where it is.'

'Sergeant Otley reckons you've got enough to charge him.'

She stood up and faced him. 'Detective Sergeant Otley is wrong.'

Kernan shut the door. 'What do you want to do?'

She pushed her fingers through her hair. 'We have to release him, we can't hold him any longer. In my opinion we don't have enough to make it stick . . . Let him go!'

At six-fifteen, Chief Superintendent Kernan left the Commander's office and spoke briefly to Tennison. He had agreed to the release of George Marlow.

Reluctantly, Tennison went to the interview room and told the men the bad news.

'We will keep at it until we have the evidence to arrest him and keep hold of him.'

Otley, as tired as everyone else, shouted that it was lunacy, Marlow was guilty. Tennison didn't even attempt to argue, but when Otley stood up in front of everyone, jabbed an aggressive forefinger at her and told her that if Marlow killed again it would be down to her, she snapped, 'That's enough, Sergeant! I've taken a lot of flak from you, but I've had you right up to here! You start acting like bloody cowboys and this is what happens. This investigation has been a cock-up from the word go. If anyone should be yelling and pointing the finger, it should be me! You all fucked up, so now we take it, we eat it, and start again from scratch. I want us on that bastard night and day. We'll get him back and we'll keep him. Now, I don't know about anyone else, but I need some sleep, so let's take a break. Tomorrow we'll reassess everything we've got.'

She packed her briefcase and left. Only a few murmured 'goodnights' marked her departure, but she was too tired to care.

Burkin and Jones remained at their desks, but the atmosphere in the room was thick with fatigue. Everyone was knackered, but above all, they felt defeated. Marlow had beaten them.

Otley sat for a few moments, devastated. He had been so certain that they had Marlow.

When his phone rang it took him a second to recognize the sound. He answered automatically, then sat bolt upright.

'Yeah, I got that! Thanks, mate, I owe you one!'

He jumped up and ran from the building.

It was drizzling as Tennison unlocked her car. She chucked her case inside and sat for a moment, trying to raise the energy to drive home.

The rain increased to a downpour as she drove slowly out of the car park and past the main entrance to the police station. George Marlow stood there with Upcher, waiting for a taxi. A cab pulled up, and as they stepped from the doorway Marlow spotted Tennison. He ran in front of her car, then to her window. Upcher put out a hand as if to stop him, but he ignored it and tapped on the glass.

'Excuse me . . . Excuse me, miss!'

She did not want to face him, but there was no way out of it. She lowered the window.

'I'd just like to say thank you, I really appreciate it. I knew you'd help me.'

She looked once again into those wide, amber eyes.

She said nothing, just gave him a stiff nod of her head and raised the window again. She didn't see Otley run out of the station towards her until he shouted to her. Then he saw Marlow stepping into the waiting taxi and stopped dead. He stood in the rain as the taxi did a U-turn and slowly headed back towards him. As it passed he could see Marlow's face pressed against the window, smiling.

Otley tapped on the passenger window of Tennison's car, gestured for her to open the door. He climbed in and shook his head, showering her with water, and wiped his balding head with a crumpled handkerchief.

'Is this important, Sergeant?'

'Yes, ma'am. I just got a call from DS Eastel at Sunningdale. They've found another one, about two hours ago. He's given me the tip because her hands are tied behind her back and she's been stabbed and beaten. He reckons, from our description, that it's Della Mornay.'

By the time Tennison and Otley reached Sunningdale golf course it was after eight. They were directed away from the clubhouse towards a crescent of exclusive houses. There were many cars parked at one end, where a narrow, private gateway led directly onto a small wooded area at the perimeter of the golf course.

A uniformed officer in a shiny black cape dripped water over their identification as he checked it, then sent them towards arc lights which had been placed around a nearby bunker on which the silhouettes of a few men could be seen. As Tennison drew nearer she could see more men sheltering beneath the trees.

Otley strode ahead, his shoulders hunched against the downpour. The ground was a shifting mud bath and Tennison gave up picking her way among the puddles. Her shoes were already sodden. As she reached the group on the bunker she found Otley already deep in conversation with his friend, DS Eastel.

Eastel shook her hand, then turned to a man taking shelter beneath the trees. 'He was walking his dog. The rain must have washed some of the soil away, exposing her arm. The dog made a pretty good job of digging her up. You want to take a look?'

Tennison stared at the dog-owner, who was obviously agog at what was going on. His dog still strained on his lead, barking continuously.

Neither Eastel nor Otley assisted her up the muddy bank and she slithered the last two feet. She clutched Eastel's arm to stop herself falling.

Eastel handed her a long stick. 'Take a look, see if you can make out her features, but keep off the sheeting if you can. They're almost ready to lift her.'

Tennison craned forward and gently lifted the matted hair away from the girl's face. Everyone stopped what they were doing to watch as Tennison peered at the pitiful face of the victim. She crouched down, then knelt on the plastic sheeting for an even closer look. The stench of decomposed flesh made her nostrils burn, but she forced herself to study what she could see of the girl's profile, trying to match it with the photographs of Della Mornay.

Eventually she let the hair fall back into place and accepted help to rise to her feet. She slithered as she tried to climb the bank and Eastel gave her a hand.

'I can't be a hundred per cent sure, but I think you're right. It looks like Della Mornay.'

The body was eased onto the plastic sheeting and lifted onto a stretcher, face downwards. The rain still pelted down as four men carried the stretcher up the bank and passed directly in front of Tennison. She stepped back to let them by, then asked them to wait a moment; she could see the rope that bound the corpse's hands. She turned to Otley.

'Is it the same rope?'

'I don't know, ma'am, but I think if she is our girl we should have her sent to our patch, get Felix Norman on it.'

Tennison nodded. Despite the mud she could see marks on the victim's arms, deep weals that looked similar to those on Karen Howard.

'Yes, get Felix. I'll go back to the station and wait for him to contact me, but I want him out here tonight.'

Otley nodded agreement. He watched as they carried the body away. 'You should never have released Marlow. Any money on it, that bastard did this one as well.'

She bristled. 'I had no option but to release him. If he's guilty, I'll get him back.'

'There's no *if*, you know it, we all know it. Why d'you think my guv'nor was so desperate to book him? He *knew* . . . '

'Like I said, Sergeant, when I've got the evidence we'll make an arrest, and this time we'll go by the book. This time there'll be no cock-ups!'

'Yeah, you do that, love! Go by the book, and if he kills again you can say, "I hadda stick to the rules!" That bastard is guilty, and my guv'nor knew it!'

'If he knew so much why did he foul up the way he did? Don't give me that bullshit! Right now it's the last thing I need. And you tell me, if a male officer of my rank had taken over this team, would you call him "love"?'

'I'm sorry, ma'am, slip of the tongue. But if you blacken my guv'nor's name, you start raking up the dirt on him, then . . . '

'Then what?'

'If you were a man I'd punch that snotty look off your face, I'd do it and wouldn't give a shit about the consequences. Right now I'm off duty . . . '

Tennison wanted to shriek, but she controlled the impulse to land a punch on Otley's sharp nose. She snapped, 'I don't give a damn whether you are off or on duty, Sergeant Otley. If Shefford hadn't been so damned eager to try and beat that bloody stupid Paxman's record, then maybe he wouldn't have fucked up!'

Otley looked at her with loathing. 'There was never any such person as Paxman, ma'am, it was a joke. The guv'nor just made it up to gee the lads up a bit, there was no record. If you'd known him you would have sussed that out! Just as he sussed that George Marlow was our man.

He even reckoned Marlow'd done a girl up north . . . '

Tennison turned quickly to face Otley. 'What did you say?'

'The boss reckoned Marlow had done a girl up north, years ago. That's why he wanted him nailed, wanted him banged up. And if he bent a few rules, so fuckin' what? Because Marlow's gonna kill again . . . and when he does, it's down to you and your fuckin' rules and your precious book.'

She clenched her fists to control her fury. 'You're telling me that Shefford believed Marlow had killed before? And said nothing? Is that what you're saying?'

Otley backed off, shrugged his shoulders. 'I'm not saying anything. I got a lift back with Eastel, I'm on my way . . . '

Tennison followed him. 'If what you say is true, why isn't it in the records? Or in Shefford's memos? Why?'

'As I said, ma'am, it was just supposition. He died before he could take it any further, he died, ma'am, remember? That's how come you're here!'

'I want your report on my desk first thing in the morning. And Otley, I've told you before, if you don't like working for me, then you can put in for a transfer.'

He stared at her and she was taken aback by the loathing in his small, dark eyes. 'You mean like the rest of the lads? Fine, I'll think about it. Good night.'

As he stomped off, Tennison became aware that their conversation had been overheard. She gave Eastel a cursory nod of thanks, then turned back to repeat her thanks to the officers still searching the area. She was very close to the edge of the bunker; she teetered and lost her footing, landed on her backside in the mud. There were sniggers. Two uniformed men jumped to assist her and she gave a grin. It was all she could do under the circumstances.

'Ah, well, they say mud's good for the complexion!'

It was the wrong thing to say and she knew it as soon as it was out. No one laughed; they had all seen the body of the girl, stripped, tortured and covered in the filthy, slimy mud.

chapter five

At ten o'clock Peter put a pizza in the oven as it didn't look as though Jane would be home. While he was eating it she phoned to tell him not to wait up as she had to go over to the morgue. She sounded tired and depressed.

'Things bad, are they, love?'

'Yeah, you could say that. We found another girl tonight. I'll tell you all about it in the morning.'

He knew she must be exhausted, she couldn't have slept for more than thirty-six hours, but he couldn't help feeling slightly irritated as he put the phone down. He was having a tough time at work himself; things were going from bad to worse and he needed someone to sound off at. He had tendered for a major building project that would have put him back on his feet financially; had gone in as low as possible, but had been pipped at the post.

He sat down to finish his pizza, which he'd overcooked and was hard as a rock, but he ate it anyway. Then he ploughed through his accounts, getting more depressed by the minute.

He was on the edge of bankruptcy and there seemed no way out. His share of the proceeds from the house had virtually been swallowed up by maintenance payments and business debts. He slammed the books shut and opened a bottle of Scotch.

A few minutes later the phone rang again. It was his ex-wife, asking if Peter could have their son to stay for the weekend now that he was settled. The thought cheered him up; Marianne had never been keen to allow Joey to stay overnight. His few Saturdays with the boy had left him feeling low.

'If he could maybe stay next weekend? Would that be convenient?'

'Yeah, sure! I mean, I'll have to sort it out with Jane, she's very busy at the moment, but I'm sure it'll be OK.'

'How's it going with the new woman in your life, then?'

'Going fine, Marianne.'

'Good. Oh . . . Nearer the time for the baby, early days yet, but later on perhaps Joey could stay longer. It'd help me out, and it's good for Joey to get to know you.'

'Marianne . . . '

'Yeah?'

'Marianne . . . Look, were you trying to tell me something the other day?'

'When?'

'Come off it! When you told me you were pregnant . . . '

'Oh, that! No . . . why, what's the matter?'

'Nothing,' he replied shortly, 'OK, talk to you soon.' He wanted her off the phone, he wanted to think . . .

'All right, then, bye!'

He put the phone down, absently. He didn't like her saying that he should get to know his own son, but it was more than that. He was trying hard to remember the date, the time he had gone to the house to pick up some of his things. Yes, it must have been about the time he had moved into Jane's . . .

Then it all came back to him; Steve not being there, Marianne a little tipsy . . . He knew it was madness, but when she wrapped herself round him the way she used to, teasing him, there had been no stopping . . . It could be. He knew her so well, that look . . . Or was she just trying to wind him up for some obscure reason? Was she jealous of Jane, angry that he was getting himself together? Could she be that small-minded? He tried to dismiss it, but the thought kept returning.

There were always so many things he should have said, things that should have been said months ago, but he never had. He never mentioned her new husband, who had once been his friend; the pain and humiliation of that betrayal were still too fresh. He found himself wishing that Jane would come home, and wondered how to tell her that his son might be coming to stay, not just for the odd weekend, but perhaps for weeks at a time.

*

In the Incident Room, Tennison was munching on a sandwich as her tired eyes searched the notice-board. The tickets for Shefford's benefit night were selling well. Her eyes came to rest on Karen Howard's face.

She heard a door bang and jumped, then got up to see if Otley had come back after his drink with Eastel. It might be a good time to attempt to iron out the ill feeling between them and to question him further about the other murder, the one 'up north'. She went through to the room Otley shared with the two DIs, but there was only the night cleaner emptying the wastepaper baskets.

The only thing on Otley's desk was a framed photograph of a rather austere-looking woman standing by a cherry tree, a white Yorkshire terrier at her feet. Tennison wondered if Otley had, as he said, put in for a transfer. She wiped the remains of her sandwich from her fingers and opened the top drawer.

There were a few photos of Shefford and his family, which made her feel guilty for snooping, but she continued. In the third drawer was a familiar file; Della Mornay's Vice record . . . She knew her copy was on her desk; the cover was almost identical, but a bit more dog-eared and perhaps a shade darker.

As she pulled it out a paper-clip caught onto the sheet beneath it. She took the whole lot out and detached the clip; underneath was a small red 1989 diary with thin cardboard covers. It had been doodled on and covered with cartoon faces, but the remarkable thing about it was the name, ornately decorated in felt-tip pen: Della. She knew there was no record of a diary having been found at Della's bedsit.

Tennison carried her finds back to her own office and flipped through the little book, slowly. It contained misspelt notes, appointments for hospital checkups, lists of cash against rent and expenditure. One entry read 'New dress, new shoes, streaks'. There were a number of pages missing throughout the year; they had been roughly torn out, in some cases leaving chunks of paper behind.

Was there also a diary for 1990? Tennison went back

and searched Otley's desk again, but found nothing apart from a near-empty whisky bottle.

She left everything as she had found it, apart from the file and diary, collected her copy of the file from her desk and returned to the Incident Room. She laid the two files side by side on the desk and began to compare them, fighting to keep her eyes focusing.

The box room felt airless. Tennison tossed and turned, got up to open the window. She had decided to sleep there so as not to wake Peter.

She lay down again, but kept seeing Della Mornay's face and hearing Otley's voice as he told her that Shefford had believed there was another murder . . . Going over and over her conversation with Sergeant Otley she dozed off at last.

At five-thirty in the morning Peter shot out of bed. He could smell burning.

He rushed into the kitchen and checked that everything was off, then followed his nose along the hallway. On the radiator near the door was Jane's raincoat; the back was singed, leaving a large, dark brown stain.

He looked into the spare room. The window was wide open and Jane lay sprawled face down, arms spread wide. He felt as if he was intruding and he gently closed the door, afraid to wake her.

At six-thirty Peter brewed coffee. He was due on the building site by seven. He carried a cup into the spare room.

'Jane . . . Jane!'

'What . . . What? *What?*'

'Hey, it's OK, it's me. Brought you some coffee. There's more in the pot, but I've got to go.'

'Oh, shit, what time is it?'

'Just after six-thirty.'

'Oh, God, I've got to get cracking. I've got to . . . I've got . . . '

She flopped back on the pillow. 'I am knackered, completely and utterly knackered . . . '

'So's your raincoat. You left it on the radiator in the hall and it's singed. I'll have a look at the heating when I get home tonight, shouldn't get that hot.'

'Oh, I turned it up, my coat was sopping wet.'

'Well, it's dry now . . . What time will you be home tonight?'

'Oh God, don't ask me.'

'Well, I am. I've hardly seen you for three days. I was thinking you might like to have dinner somewhere.'

It was the last thing she could think of. Still half-asleep, she gulped her coffee and flopped back on the bed.

'Do you think it would be OK if Joey came over, stayed the weekend? Marianne phoned last night . . . '

'Yeah, sure. You don't have to ask me, and I promise I'll try and get back by, say, eight? Is that OK?'

He leaned over and kissed her. 'Tell you what, call me when you're awake, then if you know for sure you'll be free I'll book a table at Bianco's, OK?'

'Sounds good to me . . . '

Tennison was showered and dressed, her hair washed but not dried, and on her way to the station by seven-thirty. She thought her raincoat smelt a bit off, but hadn't noticed the dark stain on the back . . .

For once the Incident Room was empty, so Tennison spent some time in her own office, checking the work rota for the day. Then she skimmed through the surveillance report on Marlow. Each shift consisted of four men; two occupied an empty flat opposite Marlow's and the other two a plain car.

The team reported little movement; after work Marlow had visited a video club and then gone straight home, remaining there with Moyra for the rest of the evening. There were one or two photographs of him leaving the flat; Tennison stared at his handsome face and noted again how well dressed he was. There was still no trace of his car, the brown Rover.

It was eight-thirty; the men would start to arrive soon.

She fetched herself another mug of coffee and lit her fifth cigarette of the day. At eight-forty-five she gave up waiting and set off for the mortuary.

She was just getting into her car when she saw Jones arrive on his moped. She yelled across the car park, 'About time too, Jones! Come on, we're going to the mortuary!'

Mumbling about having had no breakfast, Jones climbed into her car, still wearing his crash helmet.

Felix Norman turned the sheet back carefully. 'She took one hell of a beating, poor little soul. Died about six weeks ago, so we won't get any results on vaginal swabs. Lots of blood, I've sent samples over to the forensic girls. She's got similar wounds to your first victim, made by a long, thin, rounded instrument with a razor-sharp point. All the wounds are clean, and hellish deep. Could be a screwdriver, but it's longer than the weapon used on the other victim.'

Tennison was wearing a mask, but the stench of the body combined with the disinfectant fumes made her sick to her stomach. 'Any hope of getting anything from beneath her nails? You said she put up a struggle?'

'Well, she did that all right, but she had false nails. A couple have snapped clean off, and three are missing altogether. She has deep scratches on her hands, similar to the other one – her hands were scrubbed.'

Tennison nodded. 'And what about the marks on her upper arms, are they the same?'

Norman nodded but, as always until he had made out his report, he would not commit himself. 'They're similar. I've not compared them as yet, so don't quote me. Maybe he strung her up to clean her, I won't know until I've made more tests. He seems to have gone to great lengths to remove any traces of himself.'

He drew the sheet back from the corpse's face, revealing the side Tennison had not seen before. She had to turn away.

'Cheek smashed, jaw dislocated . . . '

'Can you give me any indication of his size? I mean, is he a big man, or . . . '

'I'd say he was medium height, five ten, maybe a little more, but he's very strong. These lower wounds were inflicted with one direct lunge, those to the breasts and shoulders are on an upward slant, which again indicate that she was strung up . . . '

Tennison swallowed, trying to remove the taste of bile from her mouth. 'Off the record, then, and I won't quote you, you think we're looking for the same man?'

Norman chortled. 'Off the record, and I mean that because I've worked my butt off to give you this much, until bloody two o'clock this morning . . . Yeah, I think it might be the same man. But until I've had more time, you mustn't jump the gun. It was a different weapon, longer, but the same shape.'

Tennison patted his arm, then turned to the row of seats by the doors. DC Jones was sitting there, looking very pale. As she watched, he put his head between his knees. Norman suddenly snapped his fingers and dug a hand into his back pocket.

He brought out a screwed-up bundle of notes. 'Eh, Daffy, I've got to give you some money, boyo!'

Jones looked up. 'Don't mind if you do,' he managed to reply.

'For the benefit night, man. What was it, a pony?'

Jones looked completely blank.

'Sorry, forgot you're an ignorant Welsh git! Twenty-five quid, was it?'

Jones nodded, still confused and sick. Norman handed him the cash with a flourish.

Tennison said cheerfully, 'OK, if you're feeling better, DC Jones, you can drive me back to the station!.

'Yes, ma'am. Sorry about this, but I was up half the night. The wife cooked a curry, must have turned my stomach. Sorry!'

She smiled and winked at Norman as she removed her mask. 'You'll call me with anything I can quote? And . . . thanks for coming out to Sunningdale. Bye!'

*

Jones followed Tennison through the main doors into the station, on his way to Forensic, and noticed the stain on her raincoat. It was in a most unfortunate position, as if she'd sat in something nasty. Embarrassed, he would have let it go, but WPC Havers, coming out of the Ladies', spotted it.

'Oh, boss, just a minute . . . '

'Whatever you've got, it'll have to wait.'

Havers blushed. 'It's your coat, you've got a terrible stain on the back!'

Tennison pulled her coat round to look. 'Oh, bugger, it singed! I got soaked last night and left it on the radiator. Can you take it and sponge it down, see if you can do anything with it? It's a Jaeger, really expensive . . . '

While Havers inspected the coat, Tennison looked at Jones. 'It's in a pretty unfortunate position, wouldn't you say, Jonesey? What did you think it was, menstrual cycle? Or curry tummy?'

He flushed and replied, 'I didn't notice it, ma'am.'

Tennison snorted. 'Oh, yeah, pull the other one! Thanks, Maureen.'

At nine o'clock George Marlow, looking extremely smart, left his flat and made his way to the paint factory he worked for. His shadows kept watch on both entrances to the building.

The main part of the factory with the massive vats for mixing the colours was as big as an aircraft hangar. The narrow lanes between the vats stretched from one end of the building to the other. The offices were ranged along the far side and all the windows looked out over the factory floor.

There were some outrageous stories spread among the workers about some director or other who had been caught giving his secretary a seeing-to on the desk. The embarrassed man discovered, too late, that he had neglected to draw the blinds. The entire factory had viewed the deflowering of the poor woman, Norma Millbank, who was so mortified that everyone had seen her thrashing on the desk-top that she quit her job on the spot. Since then the workers had lived in hope, but the blinds were usually kept lowered. But the offices were known from then on as the 'Fish Tank'.

The office George Marlow used when he was in London was at the far end. He shared it with three other salesmen, one of them a fresh-faced boy called Nicky, who had only been with the firm for sixteen months. A huge chart nearly covered one wall, and the men vied with each other to plot their progress in brilliant colours, like bolts of lightning. The bulletins were a great encouragement and stirred up the competition, not just among the four men in Marlow's office but all the salesmen. Every month there was a bonus for the highest sales, and George Marlow won it as often as not. He was known as the champion.

Marlow prided himself on being number one, and yet he was a very generous man with his contacts. He had trained and helped young Nicky Lennon, giving him introductions and special hints. Nicky was working on his accounts when the word went round that George Marlow had been picked up and charged with murder, and that he was on the factory floor right now!

They all knew that he had been in prison for rape, and that his job had been held open for him. When he had returned to work he had thrown a big champagne party, inviting all of them to ask anything they wanted, to discuss it and get it out in the open. He talked of his trial, the prison, and still he claimed he was innocent.

It had taken him a few months and some obvious ill-feeling and embarrassment before he was again the champion, accepted and fighting to regain the best-salesman sash. Never mind the bonus, it was the sash he wanted, and he won it fair and square the year he returned. He also won the respect of his colleagues, and because he was such a good worker and always ready to give assistance to the others, no one ever mentioned his spot of trouble.

Marlow was a known collector of jokes, he could

out-joke the professionals and keep on going. He was the man who knew everyone by name, their wives and their sisters, their troubles. There was always a special joke, and one their mothers could be allowed to hear. The secretaries flirted with him, a few had even dated him, he was so attractive, but Moyra was a strong woman who made it known that he was her man.

The men loved Moyra, because she was as good as Marlow with the wisecracks, and they socialized quite a lot, although Marlow's frequent trips north meant that they had few close friends as a couple. There were occasional dinners and parties at the factory.

When Marlow crossed the factory floor, the cat-calls and shouts that usually filled the cavernous building were ominously missing. Secretaries appeared around the sides of the vats, then vanished. Marlow could see police everywhere he looked, talking to the paint mixers, the sales personnel, the accountants . . . He couldn't find a joke inside him even if he tried.

He kept his head down and hurried towards the Fish Tank. He was pink with embarrassment, hearing the whispers following his progress, and he was glad to make it to his office, especially when he found it empty. He peered through the blinds, wondering why they were doing this to him. Echoing footsteps hurried past his window, the distant giggles made him sweat. Was he dreaming it, or were they all watching him, whispering about him?

It was no figment of his imagination. As the morning wore on it grew worse, and no one came to his office. The worst moment was when he spotted young Nicky, who stared at him with unabashed distaste, so obvious that Marlow thought he was joking. When he approached the boy he turned his back and walked away. Not one person spoke to him or looked him in the face.

He sat in his office and typed out his own resignation, as the group's secretary insisted she was too busy. He licked the envelope and stuck the flap down, then went to see the manager. But Edward Harvey was in a meeting with all the salesmen. Marlow could see them through the window; as he walked in they fell silent. He went straight to Mr Harvey and handed him the envelope.

'It's just a conference about the new paint for European distribution, George, not your territory, but you can stay if you want.'

At least when Harvey spoke to him he looked him in the eye, even though he was lying. When Marlow walked out they started to talk again, a low hubbub at first, but it grew louder. The blinds were lifted a crack and they watched him, the champion fallen from grace. This time he had fallen too far to be picked up.

Marlow hurried among the paint vats, then turned towards the offices. He shouted, and his voice echoed around the factory floor.

'I didn't do it, you bastards!'

DC Rosper and WPC Southwood followed Marlow as he hurried from the factory. Southwood suddenly nudged her partner as she saw DI Muddyman waving to them from the main entrance.

'He's just quit his job,' Muddyman said as he came close. 'I was just interviewing that little cracker from their accounts department, and he handed in his notice. Instructions are to keep on him, OK?'

Rosper turned this way and that. Marlow was nowhere to be seen. 'Where the hell is he?'

Southwood pointed. Way up ahead, Marlow was just crossing the main road, heading for the tube station. Rosper and Southwood took off at a run.

When Jones returned from booking Della's clothing into Forensic, Otley took him aside. 'Look, my old son, she's tryin' to rake up the dirt on our old guv'nor, so stick with her. You're young an' a good-looking lad; try an' get into her good books. Anything you find out about the old slag, report back into my shell-likes.' He tapped his ear, and continued, 'We're lookin' for anything to needle her, know what I mean? We want her off this case . . . ' He clocked Tennison heading towards them and shut up.

Tennison was talking fast. 'She was naked, hands tied behind her back, dead approximately six weeks. Like Karen, she wasn't killed where she was found. You'll get all the info as soon as I do. The rope's not the same type, but the knot is! We're going to have to talk to all those toms all over again!'

The Incident Room door opened and Otley waltzed in, closely followed by the Super. All twelve people in the room turned their heads to look.

Kernan gestured to Tennison to continue, then found a chair at the back of the room.

'Right, what you got, Muddyman?' she asked.

'Marlow's made several visits to Chester Paints, the last one this morning while I was there. He's just quit his job.'

'What was he doing in the first week of December? Was he in the London area?'

'Yes, it's a pretty slack period in the paint trade, he didn't go on the road again until . . . ' He flicked through his notes, but Tennison was off on another track.

'So we've established that Marlow was in London for both murders. Is there anything on his car yet? No? What about his neighbours?'

'My lads have questioned most of the ones in the block. He seems to be pretty well-liked, uses the local pub regularly. Several people remembered the car, but couldn't say when they last saw it.'

'You'd better turn your attention to Sunningdale. I want the biggest team you can muster, do all the houses bordering the golf course. Someone must have seen him, or at least the car. It's a collector's item, and an unusual colour, so go out there and ask them.'

The meeting broke up. As the room emptied, Otley said to Tennison, 'Did you arrange for the release of Karen's body? The morgue said they were finished, everyone else has finished with her, Pathology and Forensic. It was all waiting on you, and her parents have asked God knows how many times . . . '

'I'm sorry, yes, I've finished with her. Will you arrange it?'

Otley pursed his lips. 'Not my job, but if that's what you want . . . ' Kernan came up behind Tennison. 'I'll see you in your office, OK?' Tennison didn't have time to reply. Otley and Kernan walked off together and she gazed after them. She was going to look for one of those gigantic wooden spoons, and present it to Otley.

George Marlow inserted his key in the front door and pushed. The door opened about two inches and stopped dead; the chain was on.

He rang the bell and waited; nothing happened. 'Moyra? Moyra! Let me in!' he called. He had to ring and shout again before the door eventually swung open.

As Marlow walked into the hall, Moyra stuck her head out of the door and looked around, saying loudly, 'That old cow next door is going to do herself a mischief one of these days, glued to that bloody door all day!'

Suddenly she looked across at the block of flats opposite, stared for a moment. Then she unbuttoned her blouse, crossed the walkway and opened it wide.

In the surveillance flat DI Haskons, bored rigid, had been chatting on the radio with the two officers in the unmarked car. He sat bolt upright.

'Well, chaps, I think she's spotted us – I don't suppose anyone got a shot of her titties?'

Tennison found the Super sitting at her desk. Otley was with him. She asked Kernan about the press release.

'So we're not mentioning the weals on the arms this time either?'

'No, I kept it to a minimum.' He flicked a glance at Otley. 'Your decision to release Marlow could backfire . . . '

Tennison was furious, but she kept her temper. 'My

decision? You backed me up, have you changed your mind?'

Kernan ran his fingers through his hair and said to Otley, 'You want to give us a minute?'

'No, I want him to stay . . . sir.'

'OK . . . The consensus seems to be that this case is getting a little heavy for you to handle.'

Tennison couldn't hold back. 'Bullshit! I can — '

'Just let me finish, will you?'

'I'm sorry, sir, but I want to ask the sergeant a question.' She turned to face Otley. 'How well did Detective Chief Inspector Shefford know Della Mornay?'

Otley replied with a shrug, 'He knew her, nobody ever denied that. She was an informer . . . '

'So you agree he knew her well?'

Otley flashed a puzzled look at Kernan and shook his head.

Tennison banged on, 'Why did DCI Shefford wrongly identify the first victim?'

'Because they bloody looked alike,' snapped Otley. 'Her face was beaten to a pulp!'

'You knew her too, didn't you? Then why wasn't it realized until after I took over the case that the body identified as Mornay was, in fact, Karen Howard?'

'What's this got to do with anything?' Kernan demanded impatiently.'

Tennison opened a drawer and slapped two files on the desk. She stood directly in front of Kernan.

'When I took over the case, I requested Della Mornay's file from Vice. I was told that the delay in sending it was due to the computer changeover, leading me to believe that DCI Shefford had not had access to the records. I was mistaken.' She slapped the file. 'He did have it, but it was not recorded in the case file.'

'This is a bloody waste of time!' Otley protested, uneasily.

'Is it? Here's the one I received from Vice. And here's the one Shefford received. Two supposedly identical files, but in mine there was no mention of Della Mornay being used as an informer, no record of the fact that DCI Shefford was her arresting officer when he was attached to Vice.'

Otley pointed to the files. 'I don't know anything about that, but I do know that you've got some personal grudge against a man that was admired — '

Tennison cut him short. 'Shefford was so damned eager, even desperate, to make an arrest, judging by this . . . ' She stopped, realizing her voice had climbed almost to a shriek. She went on more calmly, 'I still want to know, if both you and Shefford knew Della Mornay personally, how the body was wrongly identified.'

Otley stared at her with loathing, tried to face her down. But she had him backed into a corner; his eyes flicked from side to side as he said, 'Why don't you leave it alone! The man is dead!'

Tennison pointed to two photographs on the wall. 'So are they! Karen Howard and Della Mornay! So explain this, Sergeant . . . '

Opening her desk drawer again she produced Della Mornay's diary. 'It was in your desk along with the original Vice file.'

Otley had no reply to make. Kernan thumped the desk. 'What the hell is going on?'

'This, sir, is Della Mornay's diary, not tagged, not logged in. There are pages missing, obviously torn out.' She turned to Otley and asked icily, 'Do you know what happened to those pages?'

'I can explain about the diary. I gave it to John . . . er, DCI Shefford. I presumed he would have . . . ' He dropped his gaze to the floor. 'I found it when I was clearing out his desk. He must have removed the pages.'

Through gritted teeth, Kernan whispered, 'Jesus Christ!' He looked at Tennison. 'You realize what this means? You are accusing a senior officer of doctoring evidence.'

'Marlow made two statements. In the second one he stated that he picked up *Della* Mornay. He has to have got her name from Shefford. Yes, I know what I'm saying. If I discover any further irregularities . . . '

'Any so-called irregularities, Chief Inspector, you bring straight to me. I will decide if the matter is to be taken further.'

'Until I have verification that both women were murderd by the same man, I'd like to keep the discovery of Mornay's body under wraps.'

'Marlow still your main suspect?'

'Yes, sir. I want him kept under pressure, round-the-clock surveillance. I know it's expensive, but if he's killed twice . . . '

Kernan nodded, and she continued, 'I'd also like to handle the press releases myself from now on, sir – reporting to you, of course.'

She had won, and she knew it. She walked out and left them there, closing the door quietly behind her.

There was a moment's silence. Otley just stood there, still looking at the floor, waiting for the explosion.

'You bloody idiot! She's effing wiped the floor with the lot of you! You were lucky this time, *she* let you off the hook, not me!'

Otley dug into his pocket and brought out his wallet. 'It was just the days John went to see her, nothing to do with the case.'

His face set, Kernan held out his hand. Otley laid a few crumpled pieces of paper on his palm.

'He was fond of her . . . ' When he looked up, Kernan was gone. He turned to face the photograph of Della on the wall. 'He was very fond of her.'

George Marlow was looking at the TV guide in his *Evening Standard*. He paid no attention to the large photograph of Karen Howard on the front page.

'You're home early,' Moyra commented from the doorway.

'Did you get a video?' he asked.

'Yeah . . . The cops've been here again, they took the rest of your shoes. I said they'd better bring them quick or you'd be selling paint in your stockinged feet.'

'No I won't,' he answered, 'I quit today before they could sack me.'

Moyra walked to the window, the tears pricking her eyes. She moved the curtain slightly to look across at the dark windows of the surveillance flat.

'Bastards! You'd think we were the spies, the way they carry on. I'm keeping the chain on the door all the time now. They've had all our keys, and I don't trust them. They could have had them copied . . . '

He looked up. He couldn't say anything to comfort her, and she was trying hard not to cry as she said, 'It's getting me down, George, like we're prisoners . . . '

'I'm sorry . . . ' He put his hand out for her, but she held back, folding her arms.

'Moyra, don't you turn against me. No one said a single word to me in the factory, except Edward Harvey, and even he didn't want to look me in the eye . . . I love you, Moyra, but I don't know how much more of this I can take.'

'I have to take it too, George. With you not earning, what are we going to do?'

He stood there looking forlorn and his voice cracked as he said, 'I won't let them beat me, I'll find another job . . . ' He shook his fists in the air in frustration and yelled, 'I didn't do it, I didn't do it! So help me God, I didn't do it . . . '

The telephone rang and he nearly jumped out of his skin. He stared at it as it continued to shrill.

Moyra sighed. 'I'll get it. If it's another of those filthy bloody perverts . . . And those kids next door . . . '

She picked up the phone but said nothing for a second or two, then, 'Oh, hallo, Doris . . . Yes, just a minute.'

She turned to George. 'It's your mum, it's a payphone.'

He shook his head, unable to face speaking to her.

'You'll have to talk to her, come on, love.'

He pulled himself up and took the receiver. Moyra was astonished that he could sound so bright.

'Hallo, Mum! I'm fine, yeah. How's your hip? It

is?' He whispered to Moyra, 'She's only using one stick now!'

He listened a while, then answered, 'Thanks, Mum, I wish the cops felt the same way. You know what they're like . . . I'm sorry, they're talking to everyone I know.'

Moyra watched him closely until he put the phone down and stood there, dejected.

'You never even mentioned you've no job, you should have told her.'

'It wasn't necessary.'

'It will be when you can't pay for her "residential home".' Moyra couldn't keep the sarcasm out of her voice.

'I'll manage, man with my experience can always get work. Things'll be OK, I'll go and see her. Will you get me the perfume she likes?'

Moyra wanted to weep; his whole life was turned upside-down, and hers, and he was asking her to buy perfume.

'She must have a drawer full.'

'I like to take her something, you know that. I'm all she's got.'

'You're all I've got too, George!'

He gave her a sweet gentle smile, showing his perfect teeth, his slanting, wonderful eyes. She loved him to bursting sometimes.

'I'll get us a cup of tea.' She didn't mean to sound abrupt, it just came out that way.

When Jane arrived home that night, later than she had promised, she wanted nothing more than a hot bath and to crash out.

As she walked into the bedroom, Peter took one look at her face. 'I suppose you don't want to go out to eat? Want me to get a takeaway?'

'Oh, yeah, but first I want a shower.'

'I booked a court, didn't the message get to you?'

She looked at him and realized that he had been playing squash. 'I'm sorry, love, I've been in and out of the station. I meant to call, but I kept getting waylaid.'

'You gonna be waylaid over this dinner?'

'What? The takeaway?'

'No, I told you, I asked you for a date when I could invite Frank King and his wife, and Tom and Sheila, to dinner. I told you.'

'I know, and I haven't forgotten. I've even arranged for Pam to come over tomorrow to help me sort out the menu!'

'Well, there's no need to go mad!'

'With my culinary expertise, darlin', I doubt it, but I'll have a go.'

He tipped her chin up and kissed her, looking into her eyes. 'It's important to me. I lost out on a contract; if I pull off this deal with Frank King we'll set up a partnership. He's got a big yard, employs fifty guys, and then Tom supplies the paint. We cut costs all round. I don't know if they want me with them, but it'd be a big plus for me, so the dinner's important.'

'I know, it's no problem, but my hunger is! Lemme have a shower, you get the nosh.'

The hot water felt good. Wrapped in a big towelling dressing gown, Jane switched on the television and lay on the bed to watch it. She could have gone to sleep there and then, but Peter arrived with the Chinese takeaway. She could hear him banging around in the kitchen but didn't have the energy to get up and help him.

The telephone rang and Peter appeared at the door. 'If that's for you to go out, I quit! *I quit!*'

It was Jane's mother on the line to remind her of her father's birthday and to invite her to a small party. Jane covered the mouthpiece and called to Peter, 'Pete! Pete, it's Mum! Are you free next Monday? It's Dad's seventy-fifth and she's having a little do! Pete?'

Peter brought the tray with the cartons of food and a bottle of wine. 'Sounds OK,' he said.

Jane listened to her mother carrying on about her

sister Pam's pregnancy and pulled a face. 'Pam's got water retention!'

Already tucking in to the food, Peter gestured that it would get cold.

'Mum, I'll have to go, we're just having dinner. Yes! I'll be there, and Peter . . . OK . . . Give Pop my love!' She put the phone down. 'Dear God, don't let me forget Dad's birthday card, remind me to send it off.'

It was almost ten. They settled back to watch TV as they ate, but Jane had no sooner lifted the fork to her mouth than the phone rang again. She pushed the tray away.

'I'll get it.'

Peter continued eating. He could hear excitement in Jane's voice, then her laughter. At least it sounded like good news. She came back into the bedroom, beaming.

'Guess what, I'm going to be on TV!'

'What? I thought *Opportunity Knocks* was defunct?'

'Ho, ho! No, I'm going on *Crime Night*, the police programme, and I will be the first female murder officer they've ever had on!'

'Oh, great! Finish your dinner, the crab and noodle's good.'

Jane twirled around, suddenly no longer tired. 'I pulled every string I could muster. Mind you, the Chief's got to give the go-ahead, but he can't refuse. I mean, to date we've got bugger all, but I know this'll bring us something, I just know it. I'm gonna get that bastard . . .

'When is it?'

'The twenty-second, they need a while to organize the mock-up film, and I've got to put together all the evidence we can use . . . Oh, shit! It's Dad's birthday!'

'Well, maybe they can have it another day?'

'Don't be stupid, the programme goes out at the same time every week . . . '

Peter threw his fork down. 'I didn't mean the bloody TV programme, I meant your Mum could change the party night!'

'Oh, sorry. It'll be OK, I'll just have to make a late entrance.'

'I'm not that dumb. Do you want to finish your dinner or not?'

'No, I'm not hungry.'

'Fine, then I'll clear away.'

He snatched up the tray. As he passed her she put out a hand. 'I'm sorry, I guess I'm not hungry.'

'That's OK, suit yourself, you usually do!'

'What's that supposed to mean?'

'It's Saturday night, Jane. I thought that just for one night, just one, you wouldn't be on the bloody phone!'

She sighed and flopped back on the bed. She was so hyped up about the TV programme that she hadn't given Peter a thought. But by the time he came back into the room she was sitting cross-legged, with that tomboyish grin he liked so much. For a moment he thought it was for him, but then she clapped her hands.

'I am going to nail him, Pete, I know it!'

'I'm going to the pub, see you later.'

When Peter got home she was asleep. He stumbled around the bedroom in the dark, cursing as he stubbed his toe. Past caring if he woke her up, he threw himself into bed and thumped his pillow.

Half-asleep, she rolled towards him and muttered, 'I'm sorry, Pete, but I get so tired . . . '

He looked at her shadowy face, then drew her into his arms. 'You're gonna have to start making time for us, Jane, you hear me?'

'Mmmm, yeah, I know . . . and I will.'

'Is that a promise?'

'Yes. I love you, Pete.'

She was asleep again, her head resting on his shoulder. He eased her gently back to her side of the bed and then turned over. He was more than worried about his business, and he needed the deal with Frank King to come off. He knew he wouldn't be able to keep afloat for much longer, he'd be bankrupt.

*

Moyra eased the bedroom curtain aside. She could see the small red dot of a police officer's cigarette. There were two of them; bored with sitting in the car they were taking a breather, walking around the estate. She let the curtain fall back into place.

'There's two of them still prowling around outside, George!'

Marlow lay face down on the bed, his naked body draped in a sheet that just covered his buttocks. He was lean, taut, muscular.

He banged his pillow. 'Just ignore them.'

'It's tough, they're outside day and night, and I know there's another two in the flat opposite us. I've seen them, I know they're cops, and they've got a camera.'

'You'd think they'd have better things to do with ratepayers' money.'

'Yeah, but it makes my skin crawl. And her from next door is in and out, talking to everyone! I feel everybody looking at me when I go out. Bastards, this is harassment! I'd like to get them, the bastards. Why?'

'They've got nothing better to do. It's the way they work, look at the way they treated me over that other business. They stitched me up over that! I just hope to God they find some other sucker and lay off us.'

'You hope! Jesus Christ, am I going nuts?'

'Then come here . . . Take your dressing gown off and come to bed.'

Moyra slipped off her Marks and Sparks satin robe. It was sexy, like the old film stars used to wear. Beneath it was a matching nightdress with thin ribbon straps.

'You look good, Moyra. That colour suits you, and it looks expensive.'

'Yeah, well, it was cheap, like me!'

'Don't say that! Come here . . . '

She sighed and sat on the edge of the bed. She wanted to cry, she wanted to bang on the window and scream at the pigs. 'I don't feel like it, George.'

'Then just lie with me, let me hold you.'

He took her gently in his arms and rested his head

on her breast. She stroked his hair.

'Why, George, why did you pick that bloody girl up?'

'Because . . . because she was there, Moyra, and if you think I wouldn't give anything to turn the clock back . . . I wish to God I'd never picked her up.'

'But you did.'

He propped himself on his elbow and traced her cheek with his fingers. 'I know I did, and I know I have to make it up to you, but if I swore to you now I'd never have another woman you wouldn't believe me. I've always told you, I've never lied to you, Moyra, never! I don't cheat on you like some guys would. I don't screw your friends.'

'What friends? I don't see anyone, especially not now. They can't get away from me fast enough.'

'I'm sorry . . . '

'I know, love . . . '

'I love you, Moyra, and if you ever left me, and I know you have every right, but if you were to finish with me . . . '

'I'm here, aren't I? I'm not going any place.'

She turned to him then, and he kissed her, a sweet, loving kiss. His beautiful eyes were so close that she could feel the long lashes on her cheeks. He covered her face with childish kisses, her lips, her eyes . . . She tried not to cry, but her body trembled.

'Oh, no, please don't cry, Moyra! Please don't cry!'

'I love you, George, I love you, but sometimes I just can't cope, and I don't want to lose you . . . You'll have to promise me, no more girls, please . . . please!'

He rolled onto his back and stretched his arms above his head. 'OK.'

'Promise me?'

He smiled and turned to her, cupping his head in his hands. 'I promise, Moyra Henson! And after the trouble I'm in, do you really think I would? I'll tell you something, I don't think I could, and I'm not joking. It's made me impotent, I can't do a thing!'

She pushed his chest and giggled. 'Wanna bet?'

He caught her to him then, hugging her tight, with his wonderful, gurgling laugh. 'Oh, my darling, I am a lucky man!'

chapter six

Karen Howard's coffin was completely smothered beneath wreaths of flowers, many of them from sympathetic people who had never even met her.

The funeral drew considerable media attention. Television news cameras followed the grieving parents and friends as they left the church. Tennison held back from the crowd and gestured for Jones and Otley to join her as Major Howard turned towards her.

He thanked them courteously for coming, and suggested that they might like to join the family at their home after the burial. Tennison thanked him for the invitation but declined. He seemed not to hear her, being more intent on sheltering his wife from the prying eyes of the reporters as he helped her into their car. Felicity Howard wore a wide-brimmed hat which only partially concealed a face etched with grief.

All Tennison could think of was how did a respectable girl like Karen end up in a sleazy tart's hovel. There was no hint of her being addicted to drugs, the usual reason someone like Karen did a bit of ducking and diving.

She spoke quietly to the two officers. 'I'll have to make a move. You go to the graveside and then back to the station, OK?'

Jones nodded and gave her a quick grin. 'Break a leg!'

She gave a short laugh and eased herself away from the mourners towards her parked car. Otley watched her departure with a smirk; a moment later he was approached by a newscaster seeking further news of the murder investigation. He replied that there was none, and that they would be informed as soon as anything developed.

The media had still not linked the Karen Howard case with the murder of Della Mornay. The report of the discovery of the body of a prostitute on Sunningdale golf course had merited only half a column in the nationals, and Tennison wanted it to stay that way. The press release had simply identified the victim and included a routine appeal for information.

The make-up department at the television centre was a small room off the main studio floor. Tennison had spent a busy hour with the producer, discussing the questions she would be asked and running through the mock-up of Karen's last known movements; now that she was sitting in Carmen rollers and protective gown, with no one to talk to, she had time to worry. She began to sweat; it was six-thirty and the programme would go out live at eight-fifteen. Would she make a fool of herself? Would she stutter? The more she thought about it, the more nervous she became.

The PA to the floor manager came in to go over a few last-minute notes. He reminded her that she was to pause after the third question to allow for the footage of the funeral that had taken place that afternoon. Two officers from her team were already in the telephone control room, running through the hot-line procedure before relaxing for a while in the hospitality room. As the time drew closer, Tennison found herself longing to join them. Her mouth was dry and she kept clearing her throat, but she wouldn't accept anything alcoholic. She clutched a glass of water and went over and over the questions and answers, knowing how important it was to get it right. She was very conscious of being the first female officer in her position ever to appear on the programme, and she couldn't foul it up.

Jane's father was sitting right in the centre of the sofa opposite the television, his hand on the remote control. Her mother was settling her grandchildren for the night, or trying to. They were dashing up and down the hall of the flat, screaming their heads off. She was getting a headache.

Jane's sister, Pam, yelled at them to be quiet and go to bed, but they paid no attention to their mother. Their father, Tony, glared at her over the evening paper and she told him to go and see to them. Peter, sitting on the arm of the sofa, gave the harassed Tony a wink and opened a bottle of wine.

'Can I give you a refill, Mr Tennison?'

'Thanks . . . Everyone should get in here, it's going to start in a minute.'

Peter poured the wine. The birthday cake and champagne were all on hold for Jane's arrival. Mrs Tennison came rushing in with more plates of sandwiches.

'Peter, check he's got the right channel for the video, she wants us to record it.'

Her husband looked daggers at her. 'Just come in and sit down, she'll be on in a minute.'

Peter looked at the video machine. 'Are you on the right channel, Mr Tennison?'

The *Crime Night* theme started and everyone took their seats. Mr Tennison, ignoring Peter's question, turned up the volume on the TV and sat back. 'Right, no talking . . . '

All of John Shefford's team were gathered around the bar, off the main hall where the benefit dinner was to take place. The MC stood in the doorway, bellowing himself hoarse.

'Take your seats for dinner, gentlemen, please! Dinner is now being served, please take your seats for dinner . . . '

No one paid him the least attention, especially Sergeant Otley, who was leaning over the bar tugging at the sleeve of the harassed barman.

'Is the TV set up in the back? I want to see the start of the programme.'

Dave Jones nudged him. 'Come on, let's go and eat. Someone'll have taped it.'

Otley shrugged him away. 'Go on in, we're on the

centre table. I'll be a few seconds, go on . . . Oi, Felix! you want a quick one before we go in?'

Felix Norman had appeared in the doorway, still in his overcoat. 'I can't find a bloody parking space!' he yelled.

The MC had got hold of a microphone and his voice boomed, 'Please take your seats, gentlemen, dinner is now being served!' He was obviously under pressure from a row of aged waitresses who were giving him foul looks. 'Please go in to dinner!'

At last there was a slow surge into the main hall where the tables had been set up around a central boxing ring. Norman downed his double malt and grinned at DI Muddyman.

'How's our man? I hope he's not been in here; he can't box and drink. When I was the amateur middleweight champion of Oxford, did I tell you, I had ten bouts . . . '

Someone yelled, 'How many years ago was that now, Felix?' Everyone had heard of his boxing prowess, sadly cut short by a hand injury, and no one paid any further attention in the crush as they all tried to get into the main hall at once. Superintendent Kernan was laughing at some joke, the tears rolling down his cheeks, and Otley whistled to him, pointing towards the hall.

'We're on table six, Mike, right up against the ring!'

As the men sorted themselves out and filtered into the hall, Otley scuttled round the bar and headed for the back room, where there was a small portable TV set. A little unsteadily, Otley propped himself near the door, and was squashed against the wall as the barman came through with a crate of bottles.

Tennison was on screen. Otley squinted. 'That's her, she's on! What's she think she's come as, Maggie Thatcher?'

He inched further into the room to get a better view. As he had organized the benefit night he had been propping up the bar since six-thirty, and the small screen made his eyes water. He could see six of Tennison, six of the bitch! And one was bad enough.

Tennison paused on cue for the footage of Karen's funeral. She was in fact coping very well. She was now half-way through her discussion with Brian Hayes; she was clear, concise and very direct.

'We know Karen left the offices of the MacDonald Advertising Company soon after six-thirty on the evening of the thirteenth of January this year. She told the people she was working with that she was going home to her flat in Kensington. No one was seen to meet her. She turned left into Ladbroke Grove, towards the side street where she had parked her white Mini.'

The picture cut to Brian. 'Karen Howard never returned to her flat. Were you in Ladbroke Grove that night, Saturday the thirteenth of January, at around six-thirty? Did you see Karen?'

Again the picture cut. The screen showed WPC Barbara Morgan, dressed in the dead girl's clothes, walking away from the film company's offices.

As Jane was no longer the centre of attention, her mother got up from her seat to get a glass of wine. She was told to sit down again and not interrupt the programme. She gave Peter a look and pointed to the video machine, whispering, 'Is it on the right channel, Peter?'

Mr Tennison pounded on the arm of the sofa. 'Be quiet!'

'Jane's not on, and I was just asking if you'd checked it's on the right channel.'

'I *have*! Now be quiet!'

Mrs Tennison sighed. The recreation of the dead girl's movements meant nothing to her; she was a stranger.

Major and Mrs Howard were sitting in front of their television set, holding hands tightly. The major had not wanted his wife to see the programme, but she had quietly insisted. They had been told so little, they knew only the bare essentials about the death of their beloved daughter.

WPC Barbara Morgan was wearing a blonde, shoulder-length wig and a jacket similar to the one worn by the real Karen on the night she had been murdered. The jacket had never been traced. The WPC also wore sheer black stockings, a leather mini-skirt and identical black ballet pumps. She actually carried Karen's own portfolio containing her modelling pictures.

On screen, Barbara Morgan began acting out the last known movements of Karen Howard. Walking casually along Ladbroke Grove, she headed towards the Mini.

The major and his wife watched the last known movements of their daughter, the last hours of her life.

'She looks like her.' The major's voice was very low and he gripped his wife's hand more tightly.

'No,' Felicity said, 'Karen was prettier.'

The tears streamed down her cheeks as WPC Morgan turned a corner into a side street, stopped by a white Mini and unlocked it. After putting the portfolio in the back she sat in the driving seat and tried to start the car, but the engine would not turn over.

Brian Hayes's voice accompanied the film. 'Having arrived for work at the film studio early in the morning, Karen had left her car lights on, and the battery was flat. A man working on the building site opposite was backing his truck into the street while Karen was trying to start her car. He stated that it was almost six forty-five.'

On the screen, the driver hopped down from his cab and crossed the road to offer his assistance.

'Got a problem, have you love?'

'Yes, I think the battery's flat.'

'You need jump leads, love. Sorry I can't help, but hang on a mo.'

He called across to his mates, asking if they had any jump leads, and was told they had not. The driver suggested that he and his pals could give the car a push, but he had to return to his truck as he was blocking a van from leaving the building site.

'Thanks for your help, but I think I'd better call the AA.'

Brian Hayes's voice again took up the story. 'Karen locked her car and waved to the driver as he moved off. Then she walked back to the main road.'

*

George Marlow was standing directly in front of the television screen, his hands stuffed in his pockets, his face expressionless, as Moyra entered the room.

'Turn it off, George. What are you watching it for? Turn it off!'

She didn't wait for George, she turned it off herself. 'What are you watching it for?'

With a sigh, Marlow asked, 'Why do you think?'

'You tell me?'

'Because somebody out there might have the fucking evidence that'll get me off the hook, that's why. I didn't kill her, but somebody did, and they're trying to make out that it was me. I want to see if there's anything I can help them with. Now turn it back on!'

'No!'

'Jesus Christ, Moyra! You don't believe me, do you?'

'I just don't want to see her.'

'It isn't her, she's dead. That's a policewoman.'

'I know that,' Moyra snapped. 'Why don't you go out and bloody pick her up while you're at it?'

Marlow shook his head in disbelief. 'Look, how many more times? If I could turn the clock back, if there was any way I could . . . but I can't. I picked that girl up and now they're saying that I killed her. I swear before God that I didn't, and maybe, just maybe, there's something in that programme that'll make me remember more. Somebody killed her, Moyra, but not me!'

'I don't want to see it.'

'Then leave the room.'

He bent to switch the set on again but she broke down. 'Why? Why did you do it, George? Why?'

'You mean why did I pick her up? Why did I fuck her?'

'*Yes! Yes, tell me why!*'

'Because she was there, and I was there, and she . . . She gave me the come-on, and she was . . . I don't know why! If I was to say to you that I'd never have sex with another woman, you wouldn't believe me. She was a tart. I picked her up, we did the business, I paid her. It meant nothing, it never means anything. I don't cheat on you, Moyra, and I never have.'

'You don't what? You don't cheat on me? *Jesus Christ, what do you call it?*'

'*Wanking off! And no, I don't call that cheating!* It's fast, clean and finished, and I pay for it.'

'You can say that again . . . '

'Yeah, I'm paying for it, I'm paying, Moyra. All I want is for them to find out who did it, find him and let me off the hook.'

Moyra snapped the TV set on. 'You want him found, what d'you think I want?'

The telephone rang. Moyra turned and looked as if she would yank it from the wall and hurl it across the room. Marlow gripped his hands together, trying to concentrate on the television.

'Don't answer it, Moyra, just leave it.'

Moyra marched to the phone. 'If this is another crank bitch, then I'm ready for her. I'm bloody ready for anyone.'

She snatched up the phone but said nothing, just listened. Then she sighed and held the receiver out to Marlow.

'It's your mother. George, it's Doris.'

She handed the phone over, not even bothering to say hallo to Mrs Marlow. She stood with her hands on her hips, watching the way he swallowed, closed his eyes for a moment as if trying to calm himself, make himself sound relaxed.

He said brightly, 'Hallo, my old love? Mum? Eh, eh, now what's this? You crying, sweetheart?'

Moyra sighed and turned back to the TV set, arms folded, only half-listening to George's conversation.

'Yes . . . Yes, Mum, I'm watching. We've got it on. Yes, I know . . . Look, I don't want to talk about it, can I call you back? Because I want to see it! No, no . . . I was released, Mum, it was just . . . No, they don't want to see me again, no, they released me. It was a big mistake . . . '

Moyra turned the volume up and turned to George. 'Jesus Christ, they got a car identical to yours! Look,

look at the TV! They're giving out your number plate! George!'

Marlow dropped the phone back on the hook and stared in shock at the screen. Moyra shouted for him to get on to his lawyer, but he slumped in his chair, hands raised helplessly. 'How can they do this to me? Why . . . ? Why are they doing this to me?'

'Oi, Otley, what the fuck're you doin' in here? You've missed the soup and the chicken frisky . . . mind, I don't blame you, we'll all be salmonellaed by tomorrow!'

Otley ignored the well-flushed Jones as he chuntered on. The barman had started the glass-washing machine, and the din from the main hall was drowning out the TV programme.

'Come on, Burkin's on first! He's matched against the Raging Bull of Reading!'

Otley pointed drunkenly at the screen. 'Look at this bull dyke, Jesus, hate her guts . . . She's comin' on like bleedin' Esther Rantzen! Look, d'you believe it? And I'm tellin' you, she's really done herself in.'

Jones stared at the small screen. 'Shit, it's Marlow's car, isn't it? I mean, the make?'

'Yeah, an' if that's not an infringement of personal privacy, she's given out his fuckin' registration number!'

Otley chortled, choked and drained his glass. Tennison, on screen, was discussing the Rover with Brian Hayes, then the camera zoomed in on her face for a close-up.

'Did Karen have a handbag with her on the night she died? Her portfolio was found in her car, but no bag. There was also her Filofax; it could be that she carried it in a handbag, and it has not been found. The witness who saw her stop at a cardphone and directed her to a payphone on Ladbroke Grove couldn't tell us if she had a bag or not . . . '

Otley exploded. 'Oh, that's bloody marvellous! By tomorrow mornin' we'll have every soddin' lost bag in the London area . . . This bloody woman is a total fuckin' idiot . . . '

On screen, Tennison was still talking. '. . . Telecom tell us that the coinbox was out of order that night. The AA have no record of a call from Karen . . . '

The bellowing of the Master of Ceremonies cut through the singing and shouting from the main room. 'Gentlemen, in the red corner we have DI Burkin, weighing in at sixteen stone fifteen pounds, let's hear it for him . . . And in the blue corner, the Raging Bull of Reading!'

Boos and cat-calls drowned Brian Hayes and Tennison. DC Jones gave up on Otley and returned to the hall to watch the fight. This was his first benefit, being the fresh man on the team, and he was having the time of his life. He seemed unaware that the orange juice was well and truly laced with vodka, but he'd know by the end of the evening. He was well on his way to getting totally plastered for the first time in his life.

Otley did not join table six until Crime Night was over and the fight was in the fourth round. Burkin looked very much the worse for wear, his nose streaming blood and one eye nearly closed.

During the break, Felix Norman climbed into the red corner, screaming instructions as if he was Burkin's second. 'Keep your fists up! Up, man! You're flayin' around like a bloody oik! Hit him with a good body, then one, two, one, two . . . '

Felix was hauled out of the ring as the bell rang for the next round. Men were bellowing from the back of the room for Felix to sit down, they could not see through his bulk.

Otley cheered loudly as he poured himself a large Scotch from one of the many bottles in front of him. Kernan was whistling and thumping on the table; Otley leaned across to him.

''Ere, Tennison's done 'erself in tonight, guv! Wait till you see what she bloody went on about in the telly programme. How she wangled that I'd like to know!'

'Yeeessssss!' Kernan was on his feet, fists in the air, as Burkin landed a good uppercut to his opponent's chin. The entire room erupted and chants of 'Blood . . . blood . . . blood . . . ' mingled with a pitiful request over the public address system for whoever had parked in front of the fire escape to move his car. The chanting mounted in a crescendo as Burkin staggered as if he was going to keel over, but he planted his elbow in the Raging Bull's ribs, and a small but visible head butt gave an opening for his right hand. The cheers were deafening as Burkin was proclaimed the winner.

The tinny blast of a worn-out record of *The Eye of the Tiger* started playing for the next bout as the buckets for donations to Shefford's family were being passed around. Otley sat back in his chair with a grin like the Cheshire Cat; he knew Tennison was in the shit, knew it, because he also knew that Marlow's car had not been reported stolen. To give out his registration number on live national television was going to create a nasty scene with Marlow's legal adviser. Otley's hands itched for his wooden spoon . . .

DC Jones was propped against the table, insisting on singing a solo, demanding to be let into the ring. His young face was flushed an extraordinary red, his shirt was undone . . . Otley chuckled; they'd got the poor lad well and truly pissed. He stood up to give Jones a helping hand and slithered beneath the table, where he remained for the rest of the evening.

Jane drove straight from the television studios to her parents' flat. The follow-up would not go on air for another hour and a half, and she was not required to wait for the phone-in. The two officers left in charge had her number, and she was ready to act immediately on any information that came in.

Her family had waited long enough, so the champagne was open and the candles on her father's birthday cake were lit when she rang the bell, just in time to join the chorus of Happy Birthday. She had forgotten to post his card, but presented it with a flourish with the two bottles of champagne she had picked up on the way from the television centre.

Her father hugged her tightly, proud of her achievements, although he never said much about it. She kissed him while her mother looked on, surreptitiously removing the supermarket price labels from the champagne bottles, but not before she noticed they were bought locally. Jane couldn't even spare the time to buy her Dad a present!

'Well, was I OK? What do you think, did I look OK?'

She was asking generally, but her eye caught Peter's and he gave her the thumbs-up. 'Well, come on, put the video on, let me see meself!' She sat down with a glass of champagne.

Her father leaned against the back of the sofa. 'What's this Brian Hayes bloke like, then? I listen to him on the radio, you know.'

'Oh, he's great! Did you think I was OK, Dad?'

''Course you were, love. Do you want a sandwich?

'No, thanks, I just want to see what I looked like. The second part'll be on soon.'

Peter started the video and ice skaters zapped across the screen in fast forward. Then came a snatch of *Dallas*, then back to the skating.

'Is this the video? Peter? Is it on?'

Peter straightened and flashed a look at Jane's father. 'Sorry, love, I think we recorded the wrong channel . . . '

'What! Oh, shit, no, you haven't, have you?'

The ice spectacular continued. As Peter looked on, Jane threw a beaut of a tantrum, only interrupted by the ringing of the telephone.

The second part of the programme reviewed the number of calls that had been received and mentioned further evidence in the Karen Howard case.

There had actually been ten calls connected with the murder, but only one was to prove worthwhile. Once the cranks and hoaxers had been weeded out, one caller remained. Helen Masters, a social worker, had seen Karen in Ladbroke Grove on the night of the murder; she had seen a man picking her up, a man who, she was sure, knew the victim.

It was almost midnight when two officers arrived at Miss Masters' house in Clapham to take a statement. She had seen a man she was able to describe in detail, and was sure she would be able to recognize again. She described the man as five feet nine to ten, well dressed, rather handsome, with very dark hair; she described George Arthur Marlow.

Jane and Peter argued all the way home from her parents' flat. They were still rowing when they reached their door. Peter was furious at her behaviour; they had all been waiting for her to cut the birthday cake, but as soon as she had arrived she had caused a terrible argument over her father not recording the programme. Her tantrum, which was how he described her tirade against her father, was disgusting, especially when she knew that they had recorded it at home anyway.

Jane refused to back down, it was important to her and her father had known it.

'Do you think he did it on purpose, for God's sake?'

'That's not the point! They all knew how important it was to me, but they didn't give a fuck! The stupid old sod should have let someone else do it! He always gets it wrong!' She stormed into the bedroom.

'Of course they bloody cared!' Peter slammed the front door so hard that it sprang open again and hit him on the shoulder. 'You arrive late, scream about the bloody telly, then get on the phone for the rest of the night!' He strode into the bedroom, still yelling, 'I don't know why you bothered turning up, you're a selfish bloody cow! He'd been waiting to see you, he's proud as punch about you!'

'Oh, yeah? Well, I've never heard him say it. If you must know, Mother has never even approved of me being in the Force, when I was in uniform she used to make me take my bloody hat off so the neighbours would know it was me! But Pam, oh, Pam could never do anything wrong, all she's done is produce children at such a rate she looks ten years older than she should . . . '

Peter sighed and chucked his coat on the bed. Jane's followed, so hard that it flew across the room. She kicked off her shoes and sat down grumpily on the bed.

'Actually,' said Peter, 'it was quite funny, watching you and your dad, with Torville and whatsit whizzing round on the screen . . . '

Jane grinned like the sun coming out. 'He's never got the hang of that video recorder. He taped bits of a football match over Pam's wedding film . . . ' She giggled and hummed a snatch of *Here Comes the Bride*, then shrieked, 'Goal!'

She threw herself back on the bed, laughing hysterically, while Peter stood shaking his head in wonder at her sudden change of mood.

'I'm going to have a drink,' he said.

'Great, me too, and make it a large one!'

When Peter brought their drinks to the bedroom he found Jane glued to the TV screen as the opening theme of *Crime Night* faded into Brian Hayes's voice.

'I only want to see myself, I'm sure that make-up they put on me looked appalling.'

She wound the film forward and stopped it; Peter heard her recorded voice. At the same moment the phone rang in the hall. Jane jumped to her feet and hurried to answer it. Peter sat on the bed and sipped his Scotch, watching Jane on the programme sitting a little stiffly, but looking very calm and together. The screech that emanated from the hall could hardly be anything to do with that cool woman on screen . . .

She banged open the door, fist in the air. 'We've got a witness who called in after the programme. She says she saw Karen Howard picked up by a man. She says the man knew her, because she's sure he called her name . . . And, Pete, the description, she described bloody George Marlow!'

Her fist shot into the air again. 'We got him! We got him, Pete!'

Pete held up her drink. 'You wanted to see your performance? Well, you're missing it.'

'Sod that, I'm gonna pick him up tonight.'

Peter looked surprised and glanced at his watch. 'Tonight? Are you going to the station?'

'You're kidding, I'm on my way right now . . . '

It was a while before she did leave; there were hurried phone calls while she was changing her clothes. She wiped the make-up off and gave Peter a perfunctory kiss, then grabbed her bag and bleeper and was gone.

Peter continued to watch her on screen, until he grew bored and switched the video off. He lay back on the bed and sighed . . . Sometimes, more times than he cared to think about, she made him feel inadequate. But tonight he didn't just feel that way, he was also irritated by her, annoyed by her attitude, her temper, her ambition. He started counting all the emotions she aroused in him, and it was like counting sheep. There were too many, too many to remember. He fell asleep.

chapter seven

'I was outside Ladbroke Grove underground station,' Helen Masters was telling DCI Tennison, 'waiting to meet one of the girls from the Hammersmith half-way house, Susan Lyons. She'd absconded a few days earlier, then she called to ask me to meet her. But she was late.'

Tennison nodded. Helen Masters was a terrific witness, a social worker, calm and unruffled, with, most important of all, a retentive memory.

'Were you standing on the pavement, or in the entrance?' Tennison asked.

'Mostly in the ticket area, it was a pretty cold night, but I kept checking outside in case I'd missed her. That was when I saw them.'

'And who did you see?'

'The man, at first. I just watched him for something to do. There's a bank across the road, a few yards down, and he was standing near the cash dispenser. He had dark hair . . . Then I saw Karen, the girl who was murdered. I'd seen her photographs in the newspapers, but it didn't register until I saw them in colour, on the TV programme. For a second I thought it was Susan, she's blonde too. I stepped forward . . . '

'How close were you?'

'Oh, about five yards . . . ' She looked around and pointed to a WPC on the other side of the room. 'She was about there.'

'And then what?'

'The man over the road walked to the edge of the pavement and called to Karen.'

Tennison leaned forward and watched Helen closely as she asked her next question. 'You heard him clearly, calling her name?'

Helen nodded. 'There was quite a lot of traffic noise, but he definitely called out her name.'

Tennison relaxed a little. 'Can you tell me what he was wearing?'

'A brownish jacket, with a light shirt underneath.'

There was a brief knock on the door and a uniformed DI entered. He gave Tennison a nod. 'We're ready for you, Miss Masters,' he said.

DI Sleeth led Helen Masters to the observation room next door, explaining the procedure as he did so.

'You will be able to see them, but they can't see you, it's one-way glass. Anything you want them to do, tell me and I'll give the instructions over the address system. Take your time, and don't worry. Any questions?'

She shook her head. DCI Tennison had already told her that another officer had to accompany her for the identity parade, to avoid any suggestion of bias. Helen gave Sleeth a nervous smile and sat in the chair he indicated, facing the one-way glass and the twelve men in the line-up. Sleeth gave Helen a small wink as he tested the microphone that linked them to the identification room.

The twelve men stood in a row, facing the observation window. Each man held a number in front of him; George Marlow was number ten. They were all dark haired and more or less of a size with Marlow, and two, like him, had a deep six o'clock shadow.

'Would you all please turn to your right,' Sleeth said into the microphone.

Helen looked at each man in turn, frowning, then made another request. Sleeth announced it.

'When I call out your number, please take one pace forward and say the name "Karen" clearly. Number one, step forward please.'

Number one turned slowly and obeyed. 'Karen!'

Helen shook her head and Sleeth said, 'Thank you, number one, you may step back.' He consulted with Helen and continued, 'Number eight, please step forward and say the name "Karen".'

The eighth man's voice was indistinct. 'Louder, please, number eight,' said Sleeth.

'Karen!' shouted number eight.

In the corridor outside the observation room, Tennison and Otley waited nervously. She was pacing up and down, smoking. The door opened and DI Sleeth came out.

'She wants a closer look,' he told Tennison, and led Helen to the main room. Tennison made no attempt to speak to her.

Otley tapped Tennison on the arm and gestured towards the observation room. It was against the rules, but she couldn't resist. They scurried furtively inside to watch.

Helen was moving slowly down the line of men. She paused in front of number two, but only for a second. She stopped at number ten, George Marlow.

'Come on, Helen, that's the one!' Tennison almost shouted in her excitement. Sudden panic made her check the sound system; it was set to receive only. She sighed with relief and whispered through gritted teeth, 'Come on, number ten, number ten . . . '

George Marlow stepped out of the line, holding his card in front of him and staring straight ahead. Tennison's spine tingled; it was as if he knew he was looking directly into her eyes.

'Karen!' he called loudly.

Tennison dragged on her cigarette as the tension in the viewing room built up. Otley leaned forward, gritting his teeth. She was staring too long at Marlow, taking too long . . . He drummed his fingers on the table.

'Come on sweetheart, that's him, yes . . . You've got him!'

The reception area of Southampton Row nick was a hive of activity. A woman was in tears because her Saab Turbo had been either towed away or stolen, and she swore to the desk sergeant that it had been legally parked. Two punks, wearing torn jeans and leather jackets, were being released after a night in the cells. The mother of one of the boys, a Princess Anne lookalike in a camel coat and Hermes scarf, was berating him in a voice that could have shattered glass.

'How could you be so stupid? This will ruin your chances of university! How could you do it . . . Do you know how long I've been waiting?'

Three of the men from the identity parade were leaving, pocketing their eight quid expenses, and in the midst of it all DCI Tennison was thanking Helen Masters, thanking her when she could have screamed the place down with frustration.

Arnold Upcher was guiding George Marlow through the crowd, but suddenly Marlow turned back and pushed his way past the punks towards Tennison.

'Excuse me, Inspector,' he said softly, and touched her arm.

Refusing to look at him, Tennison moved quickly, through the door which led behind the reception desk, reappearing next to the desk sergeant. Marlow faced her across the broad counter.

'Inspector Tennison! You're making my life a misery! I was dragged out of bed at four o'clock this morning with no explanation. You've got people watching me night and day, tell me why? You know I'm innocent. If you've got something personal against me, tell me now, what did I ever do to you?'

Upcher, disapproving, grabbed his arm to drag him away. Tennison gave Marlow a long, hard stare, then turned her head to find two men taking great interest in the transaction.

'Inspector Tennison? *Daily Express*, can you spare us a few seconds?'

With a gesture to the desk sergeant, Tennison said, 'Get them out of here!' The reporter was moved on by a uniformed officer at the same time as George Marlow, protesting, was being manhandled out of the door by Upcher.

'She's got something personal against me! *I didn't do it! I didn't do it!*'

Scenting a story, the reporter turned his attention to Marlow.

Everywhere Tennison went that day she encountered men with sore heads and matching tempers. Burkin was the worst for wear; his triumph the night before had been paid with a cut eye and lip. Tennison found the resulting lisp irritating.

'Where the hell is Jones?' Tennison demanded. 'I need him with me.'

Otley's piggy eyes were bloodshot and seemed smaller than ever. 'Dunno, ma'am.' He was having difficulty looking his guv'nor in the face; he had just been telling everybody that their great witness had picked out a tax inspector who'd been hauled in off the street. They were all at it; every time she turned her back one of them would purse his lips and run his hands through his hair in imitation of Tennison on TV.

Three minutes later Jones arrived, belching from the Alka-Seltzer he'd just forced down himself. His head throbbed, his tongue felt like rubber and he looked very pale and shaky. Totally unsympathetic, Tennison told him not to bother sitting down, they were going out.

WPC Havers came rushing in. 'The Super wants to see you, ma'am, right away.'

'Tell him you can't find me.'

'Marlow's lawyer's with him, screaming about you giving details of the car last night. Marlow's never reported it stolen.'

'Shit! Well, someone had better get it sorted, and before I get back. We all know how careless filing clerks can be, don't we? The Vehicle Theft Report's probably just been misfiled, hasn't it, Burkin?'

The DI was standing in the centre of the room, yawning. 'We keeping you awake?' asked Tennison.

'Sorry, ma'am, got a bit of a headache.'

'I just hope you won.'

He started to nod but thought better of it. On top of his injuries, the bevvies he had consumed after the fight didn't help.

'It was in a good cause, ma'am. I got him in the last round – at least, I think I did. Old Felix was virtually in the ring with me, he used to box for . . . '

Otley smirked. 'Made a nice little packet for the Sheffords, at twenty-five quid a ticket.'

'Yes, I know. I bought four tickets myself, I'm just sorry I couldn't be there.'

She jerked her head to Jones to follow her as she walked out. Otley pursed his lips; nobody had told him that split-arse had chipped in!

'It was George's decision to give notice,' said Edward Harvey, George Marlow's boss at the paint factory he represented. 'He was getting a lot of stick from the others. I'd never have asked him to leave, he's too good at his job, been with us ten years apart from the time he was in jail.'

'He told you all about that, did he?'

'Yes, came straight out with it. I know he was found guilty, but . . . '

'But . . . ?'

'Well, he was always a bit of a lad, popular with the girls. He swears he's innocent, and I really can't see why such an attractive bloke would go and do a thing like that. He was very distressed about it.'

'You're entitled to your opinion, Mr Harvey. Now, could you show us around? If you have time.'

'My pleasure.'

Mr Harvey, a cocky little man in his fifties, showed them the well-equipped production line, stopping now and then for a word with the men on the floor.

'We employ three hundred salesmen up and down the country,' he told Tennison, while Jones all but disappeared head-first into one of the mixing vats. 'We guarantee to match any colour you want; the difficult shades are still mixed by hand.'

Tennison looked around with interest. 'George Marlow always worked from London?'

'He started with the firm in Manchester. We moved our headquarters down here in eighty-two, and George came with us, but he kept his old routes. Had all the contacts, you see, and of course they still had family and friends up north . . . '

'They? Did Marlow travel with someone else?'

'Moyra always went with him on his trips . . . '

'How far back do your staff records go?' asked Tennison.

'Since we moved here. We had a computer system installed, but we've got all the files . . . '

'Would they include the hotels your salesmen used, expenses and so on?'

'This company is run like clockwork,' said Harvey proudly. 'We like to know where our men are and what they're doing.'

'We will need to examine them,' Tennison said, clocking Jones' incredulous reaction. 'Just Marlow's, of course.'

Harvey looked puzzled, but said mildly, 'Just so long as we get them back.'

*

Tennison was starving when she arrived back at the station. She grabbed a sandwich and tried to eat it in her office, but she was interrupted by Maureen Havers, who had contacted the Rape Centre about Marlow's earlier victim and managed to find out who she was.

'She wanted her identity kept secret, but it's Miss Pauline Gilling, ma'am, from Rochdale. She's been having counselling after a nervous breakdown, and the people in Rochdale say it would only aggravate the situation if we started asking questions.'

Tennison spoke through a mouthful of sandwich. 'I could be in line for a breakdown myself . . . ' She took a sip of coffee. 'Get back on to them and don't take no for an answer.'

She finished the rest of her sandwich and started gathering items for the team meeting. 'Oh, and Maureen, you don't know where I am if the Super asks, OK?'

They were all there. Otley was pinning black-and-white photographs of Della Mornay's and Karen Howard's bodies on the notice board. There were also blow-ups of the marks on their arms. He turned to the waiting men.

'Right, you can see the similarities of these marks. We got a DNA match on George Marlow's sperm with the blood samples from when he went down for rape, but that's no help with Della. It also doesn't help that he admitted having sex with Karen, and gave a very plausible reason, which seems to check out, for the spot of Karen's blood on his sleeve. We're sure his car's the key; find that and I reckon we've got 'im. So keep at it.'

He moved on to the photos of the bodies. 'The clearest evidence linking the girls, apart from the marks on the arms, is the way their 'ands were tied. Not the rope itself, but the knots.'

'Ah, *knot* the rope, eh, Sarge?' Burkin put in, still lisping.

Otley gave him the finger and replied, 'Yeah, very funny . . . The knots are the same, but any boy scout could tie 'em. Now it's your turn, Inspector . . . '

Tennison entered the room, munching a packet of crisps. Burkin waited while she sat down, then picked up from Otley.

'The sack that covered Della Mornay's body was the usual type of hessian, no markings, but there were traces of sump oil on it. There was also sump oil found on Karen's skirt. It doesn't mean a lot, Karen could have got it off her own car.' He nodded to Tennison. 'All yours,' and sat down.

She crunched the last few crisps and screwed the bag up, tossing it at the waste-paper basket and missing. As she bent to retrieve it they all saw the edge of pink lace. Otley, who never missed a trick, pursed his lips and crossed his legs like an old queen.

'Karen didn't put up much of a struggle,' Tennison began, spitting a piece of crisp onto her jacket and brushing it off. 'Her nails were short, clean, no skin or blood beneath them, but her hands had been scrubbed with something similar to the kind of brush used on suede shoes. Gimme Della's . . . '

Otley passed her a blow-up of Della's hands and she put it up beside the others. 'I asked for this because you can see scratch marks on the backs of the hands and fingers. Now, Della did fight, and her nails, unlike Karen's, were long and false. She lost them from the thumb, index and little fingers of her right hand.'

Burkin asked, 'Did Marlow have any scratches on him when he was stripped?'

'No, he didn't. George Marlow is still the prime suspect, but we have no evidence to put him in that bedsit, no eye witnesses to link him with either Karen or Della, no mention of him in Della's diary. The list of what we don't have is endless. But if Marlow killed Della before he killed Karen, then he knew her room was empty. He might even have known that the landlady was away, probably hoped that Karen's body wouldn't be found for weeks. His mistake there was in leaving the light on. Mornay's handbag was in her room, but there were no keys.'

Always ready to needle her, Otley piped up, 'That reminds me, ma'am – handbags. We got a good selection an' they're still comin' in; blue ones, green ones, big 'uns an' little 'uns. What d'you want me to do with 'em?'

Tennison responded quite calmly, considering. 'Get one of her flatmates in, let her go over them to save time. Right, the good news is, I'm going home. Sergeant Otley will now tell you the bad news.'

As she left the room, she could hear the moan that went up in response to the bad news; all weekend leave was cancelled.

'All leave, that is, apart from 'er own. We got to check through all that gear from the bleedin' paint factory, an' there's a lot. It's a wonder they 'aven't computerized their salesmen's bowel movements . . . Get to it!'

When he went to Superintendent Kernan's office later that evening, Otley found him sitting at his desk, writing memos. Kernan pushed his work aside and poured Otley a large Scotch.

Otley sat down, took a swig and sighed. 'We're gettin' nowhere, guv, we've 'ad nothing for days now,' he said bitterly. 'It's demoralizing, an' it's takin' good men off the streets.'

'Most of them have been on the streets, and we've still got nowhere,' Kernan replied. 'But now she's digging up unsolved murder cases on Marlow's sales routes. He covered the Manchester area, Rochdale, Burnley, Oldham.'

Otley shook his head in disgust and opened his mouth to speak, but Kernan wouldn't let him.

'And I've OKed it, so cool off, Bill. I know what you're after, but unless there's good reason for kicking her off the case, she stays put.'

'It's because she's a woman, isn't it? If it'd been any of my lads that done that cock-up on telly, given out Marlow's registration number . . . You know he never reported it stolen! There's no report in the log, and I heard his brief was in here creating about it . . . '

Pissed off with Otley's attitude, Kernan cut him short.

'Records had the report all the time, Bill. It was misfiled. She's off the hook, and so am I.' He paused to let it sink in and wagged a warning finger. 'Bill, a word of advice. Make it your business to get on with her.'

Otley downed his whisky and stood up. 'That an order?' he asked through clenched teeth.

Kernan didn't reply and he walked to the door, stopped with his back to the Super. 'John Shefford was the best friend I ever 'ad. When my wife died, he pulled me through. I miss him.'

Kernan said gently, 'We all do, Bill.'

Otley's back was rigid as he replied, 'Good night, sir, an' thanks for the drink.'

Outside the office, Otley stopped and shook out his old mackintosh, folded it neatly over his arm. *Jesus Christ, Otley, where the fuck did you get that raincoat, when you were demobbed? I'll start a whip-round, get you a decent one, fancy one of those Aussie draped jobs?* He could hear Shefford's voice as if it was yesterday and he ached with grief. He missed his friend more than he could ever put into words, especially to men like Kernan.

Maureen Havers tumbled through the double doors carrying a vast stack of files and gave him a glum smile.

'You seen what's coming in? We need a new trestle table for this lot . . . I thought you were on nine to three, Skipper? Haven't you got a home to go to?'

After a moment's hesitation, he offered to give her a hand, and as they walked along the corridor he said casually, 'Do me a favour, would you, Maureen? If anything comes in from Oldham, let me have a shufti first, OK?'

'Sure! You got relatives up there? You know, I was almost transferred to Manchester, but I failed my driving test . . . '

They passed through the second set of swing doors and suddenly Otley felt better, because he had something to do. He was off-duty, but had nowhere to go, not now John Shefford was gone.

*

It was a struggle for Jane Tennison to open the front door. The files she carried were slipping out of her arms, and she dropped her briefcase to save them. When she finally made it into the hall she shut the door behind her and leaned against it, exhausted but glad to be home.

Joey's voice wailed from the spare bedroom, 'Nooo-o-o-o! Daddy, don't go!'

'OK, Joe, just one more story,' Peter replied patiently.

Grateful that the door was closed, Jane tip-toed past it and into her own bedroom. She was in bed before Peter had finished the last story.

'And then, what do you suppose he did then?'

Silence. Peter peered at his son in the dim light of the Anglepoise lamp; he was asleep at last. He tucked the duvet around Joey's shoulders and sat for a moment, staring at the gleam of his ash blonde hair and the long, blonde lashes lying on his pale cheeks. He loved the boy so much, if only Marianne . . . But he mustn't think like that, the past was done, buried.

Sitting in the semi-darkness, he was unable to stop himself going over and over it in his mind; the anger and hatred, the terrible things that were said, the dragging sense of loss . . . and the last time he had seen Marianne alone. She was so flippant, sometimes he could strangle her . . . He knew he could never let it rest until she told him the truth. She was pregnant again and, from Peter's calculations, he knew that he could be the baby's father.

Jane was asleep as soon as her head touched the pillow. When Peter came to bed, needing her, needing someone, he found her flat out, snoring lightly. Suddenly angry, he threw his dressing-gown off, climbed in beside her and thumped his pillow.

She shot up, blinking in panic, then collapsed with a moan. With her eyes still closed, she mumbled, 'Whassa-matter with you?'

'Every night's the same. You're exhausted, asleep before I've even cleaned my teeth . . . '

She rolled towards him and opened her eyes. 'I'm sorry, Pete.'

'You make me feel guilty if I so much as touch you. We haven't made love for . . . I dunno how long, I hardly see you. And when I do see you, you're always knackered. Our relationship stinks!'

Tentatively, Jane put out a hand and stroked his chest. 'I love you.'

'You do? But if this – ' he lifted her pillow and brought out her bleeper – 'if this goes off, I don't exist! You're always either giving someone a bollocking on the phone or buried in files.'

He switched off his bedside light, plunging them into darkness, and lay down, not touching her. Jane giggled, 'You're right! I'm sorry, I will make more time for us . . . .'

He felt her moving beside him. A moment later, her nightdress flew across the room.

'There! Just to prove I'm not a frigid old bag . . . '

Peter smiled and propped himself on one elbow, reached for her.

'Daddy?' said a little voice. Framed in the light from the hall, Joey peered into the room. 'Daddy . . . ?'

Pulling the duvet over her head, Jane cracked up, with laughter. 'Ignore him, he'll go away . . . Go back to bed, Joey!'

Thinking it was a game, Joey snorted with laughter and jumped on the bed, trying to pull the quilt away from her.

'Don't, Joey! Go back to bed! *Joey*!'

He tried to climb into the bed, but Jane hung on. 'Joey, will you pass me my nightdress?'

'Why?'

'Because I don't have any clothes on, that's why.'

Peter lifted the duvet on his side. 'Come on, get in . . . '

As he snuggled down, Joey demanded in his piped voice, 'Tell me a story, about bums and titties!'

'Where did you learn those words?' Peter tried to sound angry, but Jane's sniggers didn't help.

'At school. My mummy goes to bed without any clothes on, sometimes, but sometimes she . . . '

He fell asleep mid-sentence. Peter lifted him into his arms. 'I'll just carry him back to his own bed. Jane? Jane . . . ?'

All he could see was the top of her head, but he knew she was asleep. He sighed; the pair of them were out cold, but he was wide awake . . . Wide awake and thinking about Marianne, naked, in bed with his ex-best friend.

chapter eight

Maureen Havers was complaining bitterly to Sergeant Otley. It was the third Sunday she had worked in a row, and she didn't like it. She dumped a pile of boxes on the desk.

'These are unsolved murders from the entire Manchester area, every location visited by George Marlow since nineteen eighty-bloody-four!'

Otley was unravelling a huge computer print-out from the paint factory. Its end trailed in a heap on the floor.

'Ma'am needs her rest, Maureen! You got anythin' from Oldham?'

She pointed across the room. 'It's on your desk, Skipper. Want some coffee?'

Otley grinned. 'Do I! And keep it comin', it looks like we got a real workload.'

The rest of the team began to appear in dribs and drabs, looking pretty unenthusiastic about being there. Then Burkin came racing in, the only one who seemed to have any life in him. Grinning, he waved a copy of the *News of the World* under Otley's nose.

'Wait till you see this! All is avenged!'

*

The two sisters didn't resemble each other in any way. Jane, older by three years, was a nightmare in the kitchen. She had chosen woodwork at school instead of domestic science, and actually preferred M&S ready-to-serve dinners than anything she attempted herself.

Pam, on the other hand, loved cooking. She had done a brief stint behind the counter at Boots the Chemist, then married and produced two children. Her third baby was due within the month. She was easy-going, sweet-natured and boringly happy squashed into Jane's tiny kitchen. Sunday mornings in her household were reserved for preparing the big lunch, but she had managed to send Tony and the kids off to Hampstead Heath so she could come round and help. Yet it was Jane who was brewing the coffee, Jane who set out the cups and saucers, who had brought out the well-thumbed cookery books and was frantically searching for a suitable dish for Peter's big dinner party. Everything Pam had so far suggested had been greeted by groans from Jane; she couldn't attempt a roast, she'd never get the joint ready at the same time as all the vegetables, and she'd never made proper gravy in her life.

'For Chrissakes, Pam, just something simple that looks like it's not, easy to cook but doesn't look like it, know what I mean? I've got the starters organized, just avocados with some prawns bunged in, but it's the main course I'm worried about.'

'How many is it for?'

'There'll be six of us. It's got to be something simple, I haven't cooked for so long I don't think I could cope.'

'Tell you an easy one – fresh pasta, a little cream and seasoning, then strips of smoked salmon. Plenty of good crusty bread, and fruit and cheese to follow. Are any of them vegetarians?'

The front door banged open and Peter appeared, with the *News of the World* open at the centre pages.

'Are any of your friends vegetarian, Pete?'

Ignoring her, Peter read aloud from the paper: ' "George

Marlow opened his heart to our reporter. He wept, saying he was an innocent man, but the police are making his life a misery . . ." '

Jane tossed her head, thinking he was joking. 'Very funny!'

He laughed. 'I'm serious! They've got a terrible picture of you, like something out of a horror movie. Dragon Woman!' He dodged her as she grabbed for the paper, and continued reading in a Monty Python voice. ' "This is the woman detective in charge of the murder investigation. To date, her only words have been 'No comment'." Should be at home with me, mate!'

Jane's next attempt to get the paper from him succeeded, but she tore it in half in the process. 'Now look what you've done!' he teased.

But she wasn't listening. Her mouth hung open as she scanned the article. She screamed, 'My God, they've got pictures of my surveillance lads!'

Still laughing, Peter was reading over her shoulder. ' "Marlow states that he is being hounded by a woman with an obsession – to lock him up . . ." '

'It's not bloody funny! It's buggered everything! We can't have any more line-ups, with his face plastered all over the papers. Not to mention the boys; I'm going to have to pull them off him now their cover's blown!'

She stormed out to the telephone, leaving Pam and Peter staring at each other. Pam whispered, 'I think I'd better go.'

George Marlow walked quickly up the steps of a large, detached house in Brighton and through the open front doors. A pair of glass swing doors admitted him to the hallway.

Following the directions of the receptionist, Marlow entered a high-ceilinged, airy room with windows overlooking the sea. Several elderly people were quietly playing draughts or chess, while one or two just sat silently in armchairs, their eyes focused on a future that no one else could see.

He knew where he would find her; alone in her wheelchair by the window, gazing out towards France. He walked silently towards her, stopped two or three feet away.

In a low voice that could not be heard by the other residents, he began to sing, 'When you walk through a storm, hold your head up high . . . '

His mother turned in her chair, her face lit with joy. As her son kissed her gently on both cheeks, she picked up the refrain.

' . . . And don't be afraid of the dark; at the end of the storm there's a golden sky, and the sweet, silver song of a lark . . . '

Mrs Marlow, or Doris Kelly as she used to be known, had spent the entire morning getting ready for his visit. Her make-up was perfect, her lipstick and eye shadow perhaps a trifle overdone, but she was still a beauty, retaining a youthfulness in her face that was, sadly, not mirrored in her once-perfect body. She had grown heavy, and the scarves and beads, chosen carefully to disguise the fact, didn't help. Her tiny hands, perfectly manicured with shell-pink varnish, glittered with fake diamonds.

'Hallo, my darling!'

When he kissed the powdery cheek, he could feel the spikes of her mascaraed eyelashes. She smelt of sweet flowers. The big, china-blue eyes roamed the room as if acknowledging the other residents' prying eyes.

'Take me somewhere special for lunch, George, I'm ravenous, simply ravenous. How about the Grand Hotel? Or we can have morning coffee, I'd like that. They're so kind at the Grand.'

He gathered her things into a carrier bag and hung it on the back of her chair, then wheeled his mother out, pausing beside grey-haired, docile old women for Doris to smile and wave gaily, and elderly gentlemen who begged her to sing their favourite songs that evening.

'Oh, we'll have to see, Mr Donald . . . Goodbye, William, see you later, Frank . . . '

She loved the fact that even here she was a star.

On Sunday evenings they hired a pianist, and she would sing. 'The old fools love to be entertained, George, but the pianist has two left hands. Do you remember dear Mr McReady? What an ear he had, pick up any tune . . . But now, without sheet music, this young man can't play a note.'

She sang snatches of songs as George tucked her blanket around her swollen legs, and called and waved until they reached the end of the driveway. Then she fell silent.

'Shall we have our usual stroll along the front, work up an appetite, Ma?'

Doris nodded, drawing her blanket closer with delicate, pink-nailed fingers. George started singing again, 'When you walk through a storm . . . ' but Doris didn't join in.

'Come on, Ma, let's hear you!'

'No, darling, my voice isn't what it was.' She put a hand to her head. 'Did you bring me a scarf?'

It was high tide, and the spray was blowing onto the promenade. He parked the chair beside a bench and brought out a silk square. Folding it carefully, he handed it to her.

'Thank you, darling. I was asking Matron if we could get a better hairdresser, only I need a trim, but I don't like the young girl that comes in. Oh, she's very sweet, but she's an amateur . . . '

George watched her tie the square over her head, carefully tucking in the hair. 'You have to watch these girls, they cut off far too much . . . '

George could see the reflections of her past beauty as she tilted her head coquettishly. 'All ship-shape, am I, darling?'

He nodded, and gently pressed a stray curl into place. 'All ship-shape. Now, how about singing me "Once I had a secret love, that dwelt within the heart of me" . . . ?'

Sitting in her wheelchair, wrapped in her rug, she swayed to the rhythm, her hands in the air like an old trouper. Being together like this brought the memories flooding back to both of them, and they were laughing too much to finish the song.

'You always liked the old ones best. Remember that Elvis medley I used to do?' She sat up straight and played an imaginary piano as she sang, 'Love me tender, love me true, all my dreams fulfil; for, my darling, I love you, and I always will . . . That was your Dad's favourite. I don't know what he would think about this . . . What does that Moyra think of it all?'

George's face fell. 'Now, Mum, don't start. Moyra's a good woman, and she's stood by me.'

He took a newspaper from the carrier bag. It was folded so that the article about him was on the outside. Managing to grin at her, he asked, 'What did you give them this photo for? I hated that school.'

Mrs Marlow pulled a handkerchief from her sleeve. 'Your Dad would turn in his grave . . . '

'Don't cry, Mum, don't . . . I'm innocent, Mum, I had to do something to prove it. They'll lay off me now, and I got paid a fair bit. I'll get a new job – they gave me good references. Things'll turn out, don't you worry.'

He walked to the railings at the edge of the promenade and threw the paper into the sea. When he turned a moment later to face her, his hands were in his pockets.

'Which one's got a present in?' he demanded. 'I want a song, though, you must promise me a song.'

She made a great performance out of it, finally fooling him into giving her a clue to which pocket his gift was in. He presented the perfume with a flourish and she made him bend down for a kiss. Her warmth and her love for him shone out, despite her fears.

On the way back to the home they sang, 'Why am I always the bridesmaid, never the blushing bride?', vying with each other to sing the silly bits and breaking into giggles.

Moyra was doing the ironing. While George put the kettle on he was singing "Why Am I Always the Bridesmaid?'.

'Every time you go to see her you come back singing those stupid songs,' Moyra complained.

'That was by way of a proposal,' he said as he put

coffee in their mugs and poured the boiling water. 'I reckon it's time I made an honest woman of you.'

'Not if your mother has any say in the matter; I was never good enough for you in her eyes!' Moyra retorted. 'And I notice she gave the papers that photo of you in your posh school uniform . . . '

He handed her a mug of coffee. 'Did I ever tell you about— '

She interrupted him. 'How beautiful she looked at the school prize-giving? How all the lads said she looked like a movie star? Yes, you did!'

'But I've never told you about afterwards, after the prize-giving.'

'I dunno why you go on about it, you were only at the school two minutes.'

'I walked Mum and Dad to the gates. They were all hanging out of the dormitory windows, giving her wolf-whistles. Mum was being all coy, you know, waving to the boys. She didn't want them to know we didn't have a car, that they were going to catch the bus. And then, just as we got to the gates, the wind blew her wig off. They all saw it . . . '

Moyra spluttered through her mouthful of coffee. 'You're kidding me! Blew her wig off!' She laughed aloud.

Offended, he blinked. 'It wasn't funny, Moyra. My Dad ran down the road to get it back, and she just stood there, rooted to the spot . . . ' He raised his hands to his own hair. 'I didn't know her hair had fallen out. Dad helped her put the wig back on, but the parting was all crooked. Underneath all the glamour she was ugly; an ugly stranger.'

'And everybody saw it? Did she ever talk about it?'

'She never even mentioned it.'

'I always thought it was just old age, you know. I've never said anything to her, but it's so obvious. How long has she been bald, then?'

'I don't know. She still pretends it's her own hair, even to me, says it needs trimming and so on.'

'Well, what do you know! Underneath it all the Rita Hayworth of Warrington is really Yul Brynner in disguise!'

He looked at her for a moment, then laughed his lovely, warm, infectious laugh. He slipped his arms around her and kissed her on the neck.

'Did you mean it, George? About getting married?'

He lifted her in his arms and swung her around. 'I love you, Moyra – what do you say, will you marry me?'

'Will I? I've had the licence for two years, George, and you won't get out of it.'

He smiled at her. Sometimes his resemblance to his mother took her breath away. He was so good-looking, every feature neat and clean-cut. Doris had been a real looker, and George was the most handsome man Moyra had ever known. Held tight in the circle of his arms she looked up into his dark eyes, eyes a woman would pray for, with thick dark lashes. Innocent eyes . . .

'I love you, George, I love you.'

His kiss was gentle and loving. He drew her towards the bedroom.

'George! It's nearly dinner time!'

'It can wait . . . '

DCI Tennison stared at the headline, furious. Then she ripped it down from the Incident Room door. She took a deep breath, crumpled the paper into a ball and entered the room.

The men fell silent, watching her. She held the ball of paper up so they could all see, then tossed it accurately into a waste-paper basket.

'OK, we've all read it, so the least said about it the better. But it's not just me with egg on my face.'

She crossed to her desk and dumped her briefcase. 'It makes our surveillance operation look like a circus.'

'Any word on what their readers' survey came up with, ma'am?' asked Otley with a snide smile. 'For or against female officers on murder cases?'

She gave him an old-fashioned look. 'Oh, you're a

biased load of chauvinists, and there's thousands more like you!'

'Don't worry, ma'am,' chipped in Dave Jones, 'you could always get a job in panto!'

He was holding up the photograph of her from the paper, but it had been added to in felt-tip. She started laughing and clipped him one.

Maureen Havers walked in as he raised his hands to defend himself. She tapped Tennison on the back.

'Why me? I didn't draw all over it. It was him!' Jones pointed to Burkin, who hung his head, although he couldn't really give a fuck. When she'd gone, Jones would get a right clip round the earhole.

Tennison turned to Havers, who told her she was wanted on the top floor.

'Oh well, here it comes. See you all later.'

Otley claimed everybody's attention as soon as she had gone. 'Right, we've all had a jolly good laugh, now get yer pin-brains on this lot. We want all these unsolved murders on the computer, so we can cross-check them for any that occurred when Marlow was in the vicinity.'

As they went reluctantly to work, Maureen Havers had a word with Otley.

'You finished with the Oldham files? Only they haven't been put on the computer . . .'

'I'll sort 'em, love. Haven't had a chance to look through them yet.'

Havers began to distribute more files around the Incident Room, which was greeted with moans and groans. Otley rapped his desk.

'Come on you lot, settle down. Sooner you get this lot sorted, sooner we're in the pub. As an incentive, first round's on me!'

But a pint wouldn't compensate for the tedious slog of sifting through hundreds of unsolved murders. Otley opened the Oldham file he had already checked over; he knew there was a problem, and now he had to work out the best way to deal with it.

*

The bar was full of familiar faces. At one of the marble-topped tables several of the lads were discussing the unsolved murders.

'I've looked at twenty-three cases,' Muddyman said, 'all around Rochdale, Burnley, Southport; and I've got one possible but unlikely . . . '

Rosper cut in, 'There was a woman found in a chicken run in Sheffield. Reckon she'd been there for months. The chickens were knocking out record numbers of eggs!'

'You know they've been feeding the dead ones to the live ones, that's why we've had all this salmonella scare. Got into the eggs,' Lillie contributed.

'This woman was seventy-two, an old boiler!' Rosper chuckled.

They were suddenly all aware that Tennison had walked in. She looked around, located Jones and went to lean on the back of his chair.

'Next round's on me, give us your orders,' she told them. 'The bad news is: I'm asking for volunteers. They've withdrawn the official surveillance from Marlow, so I want four men to cover it.'

Lillie stood up. 'Excuse me . . . '

'Great, that leaves three . . . '

'I was just going for a slash . . . '

Rosper laughed and she nailed him. 'Two! Come on, undercover's a piece of cake. Two more . . . '

She handed Rosper a twenty and sent him to the bar. 'Let's get those drinks in. I'll have a large G and T.'

Lillie pulled out a chair for her. 'How did it go, boss?'

The others pretended not to listen. Tennison said quietly, 'If I don't pull something out of the bag very soon, I'm off the case.'

Her gin and tonic arrived. She thanked Rosper and he handed her back her money.

'What's this?'

Rosper shrugged. 'It's OK, Skipper coughed up.'

'Is this a truce? Ah well, cheers!' She raised her glass to them, but Muddyman and Rosper were looking towards Otley, who was sitting at the bar.

'Cheers, Skipper!' Muddyman called.

Otley turned and grinned, as if he had got one over on Tennison, even in the pub.

With a few drinks inside them they returned to the Incident Room to work. The stacks of paperwork did not seem to have diminished much, despite the busy atmosphere. The room was thick with tobacco smoke and littered with used plastic cups. Tennison, a cigarette dangling from her mouth, was double-checking and collating results.

At nine o'clock, Muddyman stood up and announced that he was going home. Many of the others started to make a move and Otley approached Tennison.

'We've got several cases that need looking into: one at Oldham, another at Southport, an' we're checking one in Warrington. Ma'am? . . . '

Tennison looked up. 'Sorry.'

'Who do you want checking these unsolved cases?'

'Oh, anyone who's been cooped up here all day, give them a break.'

'OK,' Otley muttered. He made a few notes on a pad. 'I'll do the Oldham . . . Muddyman, Rosper and Lillie are on Marlow, so that leaves . . . Can you take the Southport case?'

'OK, just pin it up for me.'

Otley put the list up on the notice-board and picked up his coat. As he left he passed WPC Havers.

'You'll be able to retire on your overtime, gel!'

''Night, Sarge!' she replied, as she passed some telephone messages to Tennison. 'Why don't you take a break, boss?'

'Because I've got more to lose, Maureen.' She rose and stretched, yawning, then went to examine the list on the notice-board. 'I've lost track,' she sighed.

Only three of the men were left working. 'Go on home, you lot,' she told them. 'Recharge your batteries.'

DC Caplan put his coat on and asked, 'Anyone for a drink?'

'I've had enough liquid for one day, mate,' replied Jones. I'll be bumping into the mother-in-law in the night, she spends more time in the lavvy than a plumber . . . '

There was a metamorphosis taking place right in front of them, not that anyone noticed. DC Jones, of the polished shoes and old school tie, had taken to wearing striped shirts with white collars and rather flashy ties, similar to those favoured by DI Burkin. He was also knocking back the pints, was even the first in the bar at opening time. It was taking time, but he was at last becoming one of the lads.

As they left, still joking, Havers asked Tennison casually, 'What's with Oldham, then? He got relatives there or something?'

'What?'

'Skipper asked for anything from Oldham. I wondered what the attraction was . . . Mind if I push off?'

It slowly dawned on Tennison what she was talking about. 'He's doing it to me again!' She shook her head in disbelief and muttered a vague goodnight to Maureen, intent on getting to the bottom of it. Maureen saw her uncover one of the computers and start tapping the keyboard as she closed the door.

Tennison muttered to herself, 'Right, Otley, let's find out just what your game is! Jeannie Sharpe . . . March nineteen eighty-four . . . ' She moved the cursor down the screen, read some more, then picked up the phone to make an internal call. There was no reply; she put the receiver down and went across to the large table in the centre of the room where all the files were stacked in alphabetical order. Whistling softly, she selected the Oldham file and flipped through it, then carried it back to the computer.

'Ah . . . Jeannie Sharpe, aged twenty-one, prostitute . . . ' She compared the entry on the computer with the notes in the file. 'Head of investigation, DCI F. G. Neal . . . Detective Inspector Morrell and . . . DI John Shefford!'

She pushed her chair back, staring at the computer screen. Why was Otley so intent on taking the Oldham case? It had to be something to do with Shefford; it was too much of a coincidence. He had put her down for Southport with DC Jones; she snatched the list down from the notice-board. By the time she had retyped it she was seeing spots before her eyes. It was time to call it quits; but she, not Otley, was now down for Oldham.

'My car'll be here any minute! I was too tired to drive last night.' Dressed and ready for work, Jane was rushing around the kitchen. Peter, still half-asleep, stumbled in.

''Morning!'

'I got in a bit late, so I slept in the spare room. Feel this – d'you think it'll soften up by tonight?' She handed him an avocado.

'It's fine.' He stood in the middle of the kitchen and stretched. The avocado slipped from his grasp and Jane caught it deftly.

'I'll be back early to get everything ready for tonight. I'm doing what Pam suggested: pasta and smoked salmon. Prawns and mayonnaise in the avocados . . . Ah!' She whipped round and jotted 'Mayonnaise' on her notepad. The doorbell rang. 'And cream. Give us a kiss. I'll see you about seven. If anyone calls for me, I'll be in Oldham.'

She left Peter standing in the kitchen. 'Oldham, right . . . ' He woke up suddenly. 'Oldham?' But he was talking to himself.

Tennison and Jones followed the uniformed Sergeant Tomlins through a makeshift door in a corrugated iron fence. Tomlins was still trying to make up for his error at Manchester Piccadilly station, where he had assumed Jones to be the Chief Inspector.

'In nineteen eighty-four all this part was still running,' he said as he led them into the cavernous, empty warehouse. 'It was shut down soon afterwards, and hasn't been occupied since. The only people that came here were the tarts with their customers, and I think some still do.'

'We got the call at four in the morning, from a dosser

who'd come in for the night.' He pointed to an old cupboard against a wall, minus its doors. 'He found her in there.'

Tennison inspected the cupboard. 'Actually inside?'

'Yes. The doors were still on then, but not quite closed. She was lying face down, her head that way . . . This shed was used for dipping parts; the vats used to fill the place.' He spread his arms to indicate the whole area. 'They all went for scrap, I suppose. They lowered the stuff on pulleys – you can still see the hooks – then raised them again to dry.'

Dozens of rusty hooks still hung from the ceiling. Tennison looked around and asked, 'Hands tied behind her back, right?'

'Yes. Savage beating, left half-naked. Her face was a mess. Her shift was found outside, and her coat over there.'

They started to leave but Tennison turned back to stare at the spot where Jeannie Sharpe was found.

'Nasty place to end up, huh?'

'Well, these tarts bloody ask for it.'

She snapped at him, 'She was twenty-one years old, Sergeant!' but he was moving ahead, heaving the rubbish aside. He waited for them at the door.

'You wanted to have a word with her friends? Slags isn't the word for it . . . ' He pushed the corrugated iron aside for Tennison to pass. 'We clean up the streets and back they come, like rodents.'

She let the door slam back in his face. 'Sorry!' she said.

The flat was damp, with peeling wallpaper, but an attempt had been made to render it habitable. The furniture was cheap: a single bed, a cot, a painted wardrobe and a few armchairs, and it was fairly tidy, apart from the children's toys scattered everywhere.

Tennison was sitting in an old wing-chair beside a low table on which were two overflowing ashtrays, a teapot and a lot of biscuit crumbs. She was totally at ease, smoking and sipping a mug of tea.

Carol, a drably dressed but attractive blonde woman in her early thirties, was telling her about the last time she had seen her friend Jeannie alive.

'We were all together, just coming out of the pub, our local, y'know. We'd had a few . . . '

Linda, plump and cheerful with dark hair, interrupted her. 'I hadn't! I was on antibiotics, can't drink with them.'

'His car was parked, er . . . You know where the pub is?' Tennison shook her head. 'Well, it's right on a corner, y'know, so there's a side street . . . '

Finishing her tea, Tennison suggested they go and look.

The three women stood on the corner outside the pub. It wasn't easy to tell by looking at them which were the prostitutes and which the senior policewoman.

'See, there's the side street. He was parked just there. You could only see a bit of the car,' Carol was saying.

Tennison offered her cigarettes round. 'You couldn't tell me the make of it? The colour?'

'It was dark, I reckon the car was dark, but it had a lot of shiny chrome at the front, y'know, an' like a bar stuck all over with badges an' stuff. He called out to Jeannie . . . '

Tennison grabbed the remark. 'He called out? You mean he knew her name?'

'I don't think it was her name. It was, y'know, "How much, slag?" I said to her, hadn't she had enough for one night . . . '

Carol put in: 'Ah, but she was savin' up, wanted to emigrate to Australia if she could get enough.'

'So Jeannie crossed the road? Did you see her get into the car?'

Linda replied, 'She went round to the passenger side.'

'I looked over, y'know, to see, but he was turning like this . . . ' Carol demonstrated. 'I only saw the back of his head.'

Tennison stepped to the kerb and peered around the corner as Linda said, 'We never saw her again. She had no one to even bury 'er, but we had a whip-round.'

'Fancy a drink?' asked Tennison.

They piled into the pub and found an empty booth. Carol went to the bar while the locals sized up Tennison. They were mostly labourers in overalls.

Linda had produced a photograph of herself and Jeannie. 'Lovely lookin', she was. That's me – I was thinner then, and blonde. Cost a fortune to keep it lookin' good, so I've gone back to the natural colour. Set me back twenty-five quid for streaks! We used to get cut-price, mind, at the local salon, but they've gone all unisex, y'know. I hate having me 'air done with a man sitting next to me, don't you?'

Tennison opened her briefcase to take out her copy of the *News of the World*, but was interrupted by a man in dirty, paint-splashed overalls who strolled across from the juke-box. He put a hand on Tennison's shoulder and leaned down to whisper, 'I've got fifteen minutes, the van's outside . . . '

Turning slowly, she removed his hand from her shoulder. 'I'm busy right now.' He made no move to go, so she looked him in the eye. 'Sod off!'

He looked in surprise at Linda, who mouthed 'Cop!' and shot out before anyone could draw breath. Tennison carried on as though nothing had happened.

Carol returned with the drinks as Tennison placed the newspaper on the table.

'The barman says you just missed the London Express, but there's a train at four minutes past five.'

'I'll be cutting it fine . . . ' Tennison checked her watch and smiled. 'Dinner party! Is this like him?' She pointed to the newspaper photo of Marlow and took a sip of her drink.

'He's a bit tasty, isn't he?' Carol commented, and glanced at Linda. 'He was dark-haired . . . '

'You thought he had a beard, didn't you?' Linda said.

'Beard? You never mentioned that in your statement.'

'She couldn't get out of the nick fast enough, they're bastards,' Carol informed her. 'An' I'll tell you something for nothing – they never gave a shit about Jeannie. We're rubbish, until they want a jerk-off! Four kids we got between us, and no one's interested in them. An' that inspector geezer, y'know, him . . . ' She nudged Linda. 'I'm not sayin' any names, but . . . '

'I will,' said Linda. 'It was that big bloke, John Shefford. They got rid of him faster than a fart.'

Tennison asked, deadpan, 'What do you mean?'

'I reckon they found out about him an' Jeannie,' Carol told her confidentially. 'Next thing we knew, he was on his bike, gone to London. He was as big a bastard as any of 'em – bigger. Jeannie never had a chance: her step-dad was screwin' her from the time she was seven. She was on the streets at fourteen, an' that Shefford used to tell her he'd take care of her. Well, he never found out who killed her; they never even tried.'

'Poor kid, strung up like that, like a bit of meat on a hook!' Linda said. 'You have to be really sick . . . '

Tennison jumped on her. 'What? What did you say?'

'The dosser who found her, he told me.'

'You know this man? He got a name?'

'Oh, he's dead, years back, but he told me all about it. Hanging by her arms from a hook in the ceiling.'

It was getting late. Peter checked his watch anxiously and started to lay the dining-table. Where the hell was she?

The front door crashed open and Jane rushed in, yelling, 'Don't say a word, I've got it timed to the second. Don't panic!'

True to her word, everything was just about ready by eight o'clock, and she had put on a nice dress, though her hair was still damp. She ran quickly around the table, distributing place mats.

'Water's on, what else can I do?' Peter asked.

She stood back to look at the table. 'Right, glasses for red, glasses for white, starter plates, teaspoons . . . Napkins! Shit, hang on . . . '

She shot out to the kitchen, returning to fling a packet of paper napkins at him, then disappeared again, shouting, 'Bread, bread!'

The doorbell rang as she came back with the basket of rolls. She gave Peter the thumbs-up.

'All set! Let them in!'

Peter grabbed her and kissed her cheek, then they both headed for the hall.

When they had finished eating, Jane cleared the table and went to make the coffee, taking her glass of wine with her. The kitchen was a disaster area with hardly a square foot of clear work surface. She tidied up a little while she waited for the percolator.

Peter rushed in, obviously panicking. 'You're taking your time! Where are the liqueur glasses?'

'We haven't got any! You'll have to use those little coloured ones Mum gave me.' She drained her glass of wine. 'How's it going?'

He relaxed a little. 'Just getting down to business. Can you keep the women occupied? I'll take the tray.'

As he hurried back to his guests, Jane yawned and pressed the plunger on the percolator. The hot coffee shot from the spout, all over her dress. 'Shit!' Then she shrugged, wiped herself down as best she could, fixed a smile on her face and marched out with the coffee pot.

Frank King was obviously the dominant male, the one with the money and the big ideas. He had spread some plans on the table and was explaining them to Peter and Tom.

Frank's wife, Lisa, and Tom's wife, Sue, were sitting in the armchairs at the other end of the room, drinking apricot brandy from tacky little blue and green glasses. They were both dressed to the nines, perfectly coiffed and lip-glossed, but Lisa was the one with the really good jewellery. Jane poured them coffee.

'It's nice, isn't it? I like sweet liqueurs,' Lisa was saying to Sue. 'We spent three months in Spain last year; the drinks are so cheap, wine's a quarter of the price you pay here. Oh, thanks, Jane. Mind you, the price of clothes

– all the decent ones are imported, that's what makes them so expensive.'

Jane moved on to the men. Neither Tom nor Frank thanked her for the coffee and Peter, intent on what Frank was saying, refused it.

'Like I said, no problem. Get the bulldozers in and they're gone before anyone's woken up. Don't know why they make such a fuss about a few trees anyway. So, we clear this area completely, but leave the pool, which goes with this house here. The other we build at an angle, the two of them have to go up in less than three-quarters of an acre . . . '

'What sort of price are we looking at?' Tom wanted to know.

'The one with the pool, four ninety-five. The one without we ask three fifty. That's low for an exclusive close . . . '

Leaving them to it, Jane found a small glass that Peter had poured for her on the dresser. She carried it over to the women and sat down.

She took a sip from the glass. 'Christ, it's that terrible sweet muck!' Up again, Jane fetched a wine glass and went looking for the brandy. It was on the table beside Frank's elbow, and she helped herself to a generous measure. She had been drinking since lunchtime: gins in the pub, on the train, wine throughout dinner. She was tying one on, but it didn't show, yet. She captured a bowl of peanuts and sat down again. It seemed as though Lisa hadn't stopped talking.

'She goes on and on, she wants a pony. I said to Frank, there's no point getting her one if she's going to be the same as she was over the hamster. The poor thing's still somewhere under the floorboards . . . '

Sue took advantage of the pause to speak to Jane. 'Tom was telling me you have Joey at weekends.'

Jane was searching for her cigarettes. She nodded and opened her mouth to speak, but Lisa got in first.

'What I wouldn't give to have mine just for weekends! Au pairs have been the bane of my life . . . '

'Oh, I've never had any troub— '

Lisa steamed on regardless. 'I've had German, Spanish, French and a Swedish girl. I was going out one day, got as far as the end of the drive and realized I'd forgotten something, so I went back. She was in the jacuzzi, stark naked! If Frank had walked in . . . '

'Probably would have jumped on her!' At last Tennison had got a word in edgeways. She grinned.

Sue nearly laughed, but remembered in time that she wanted to stay in Lisa's good books. She changed the subject.

'You're with the Metropolitan Police, Jane? Peter was telling . . . '

Lisa broke in: 'Well, I'd better tell Frank to ease up on the brandy, can't have you arresting him . . . '

'That's traffic, not my department,' Jane replied, knocking back her brandy.

'Oh, so what do you do? Secretary? I was Frank's before we got married.'

'No, I'm not a secretary.' The day was beginning to catch up on Jane, or rather the tragic little Jeannie. *There was no one to bury her, so we had a whip-round* . . .

If Lisa had heard Jane's reply she paid no attention. Her peanut-sized brain was now fixed on wallpaper, and she was holding forth about which was best, flock or fabric. In her opinion, fabric held its colour better . . .

The three men were still sitting around the table, hogging the brandy bottle. As Jane helped herself to another large one, Frank pushed his glass forward without pausing for breath.

'I put my men on the main house, Pete's men on the second, and the two of them go up neck and neck. I'm looking for a quick turnover, so we do a big colour brochure with artist's impressions and start selling them while we dig the foundations. Tom does the interiors, and we split the profits . . . '

Jane was unused to being ignored. She downed the brandy and poured another to carry back to her perch on the arm of the only really comfortable chair which, oddly enough, no one had sat in. She knocked over the bowl of peanuts into the chair and spent a few minutes eating the spilt ones from the seat, then slowly slid into it herself.

Lisa had not drawn breath, but Jane's accident with the peanuts finally brought her verbal assault course on wallpaper to a grinding halt. There was one of those classic silences among the women, during which Frank's voice could still be heard.

Lisa turned her full attention on Jane. 'I hear you were on the *Crime Night* programme?'

'That's right, I was answering the telephones, I was the one passing the blank sheet of paper backwards and forwards.'

Missing the sarcasm in Jane's voice, Lisa ploughed on, 'I *am* impressed! I never watch it, it scares me, but I'm paranoid about locking the house. And if a man comes near me when I'm walking Rambo . . . ' She laughed. 'That's our red setter, I'm not talking about Frank!'

Jane switched off for a moment, gazing into the bottom of her empty glass. When she snapped to again she realized that Lisa hadn't paused once.

'But don't you think, honestly, that a lot of them ask for it?'

'What, ask to be raped?' Jane shook her head and her voice grew loud, 'How can anyone *ask* to be raped?'

She jumped to her feet, swaying slightly and glaring as if interrogating Lisa, who shrank back in her seat. 'Where do you walk your dog?'

'Well, on Barnes Common . . . '

'Barnes Common is notorious, women have been attacked on Barnes Common!'

Lisa rallied a little. 'Yes, I know, but I wouldn't go there late at night!'

'There are bushes, gullies, hidden areas. You could have a knife at your throat, your knickers torn off you, and bang! You're dead. But you weren't asking for it!'

'I . . . I was really talking about prostitutes . . . '

'What about them? Do you know any? Does Sue know any?' She turned to the men, she had their attention now.

'How about you? Can you three tell me, hands on hearts, that you've never been with a tom?'

Lisa whispered to Sue, 'What's a tom?'

Tennison snapped, 'A tart!'

In the ensuing silence, the telephone rang. Peter said, 'It'll be for you, Jane.'

She weaved her way to the door, but turned back, blazing, when she heard Peter say, 'I'm sorry about that!'

'Don't you ever make apologies for me! We were just having a consev . . . a conservation!' She slammed the door.

'Keep her off the building site, Pete,' Frank said in a low voice.

'Actually, I'd like an answer to her question,' said Lisa.

'I think that went off all right, didn't it?' Jane, creaming her face, was talking to Peter.

'You asking me?'

'No, I was talking to the pot of cold cream! You're going to do the deal, aren't you?'

'Yeah . . . Did you have to bring up all that about tarts?'

'Put a bit of spark into the evening.'

'It wasn't your bloody evening!'

'Oh, thanks! I broke my bloody neck to get that dinner on the table!'

'It's always you, Jane! You, you, you! You don't give a sod about anyone else!'

'That's not true!'

'You care about the blokes on your team, your victims, your rapists, your "toms" as you call them, you give all your time to them.'

'That's my job!'

'Tonight was for my job, Jane. But no, you've got to put your ten cents' worth in!'

'OK, I'm sorry . . . sorry if I spoilt the evening!'

The tiredness swept over her like a tidal wave. She had no energy to argue, and went for the easy way out, giving him a smile. 'OK? I apologize, but I think I had too much to drink, and they were so boring . . .'

He stared at her, infuriated. Her comment really got to him. 'This is business, Jane, do you ever think how boring all your fucking talk is? Ever think about that, ever think how many conversations we've had about this guy George Marlow? You ever consider how fucking boring you get? Do you? I don't know him, I don't want to know about him, but Christ Almighty I hear his name . . .'

'Pete, I've said I'm sorry, OK? Just let it drop.'

He was unwilling to let it go, but he shrugged. Jane put her head in her hands and sighed. 'Pete, I'm tired out. I'm sorry tonight didn't go as well as you'd planned, but you've got the contract, so why don't we just go to bed?'

The memories of the day swamped her: the smell of the factory, the smell of the two tarts' flat, her feelings, the smells, all muddled and out of control . . . She couldn't stop the tears, she just sat hunched in front of the mirror, crying, crying for the waste, the little tart who had been raped by her stepfather when she was seven, little Jeannie with no one to bury her, who Jane didn't even know, yet she was crying for her and all the other Jeannies who lived and died like that and nobody gave a shit for . . .

Peter squatted down and brushed her hair from her face. 'It's all right, love. Like you said, I got the contract. Maybe *I* had a few too many . . . Come on, let's get you to bed.'

Jane went to bed, but she didn't sleep for a long time. When she woke she found the kitchen full of the debris of dinner; not a single dish had been washed. She put her coat on, ready to leave for work, and took two aspirin with her coffee.

Peter, his hair standing on end, joined her.

'Pete, I've been thinking over everything. Last night . . .'

With a grin he reached for her, tried to kiss her. She stepped back. 'I love you, Pete, I really do, but you're right. It doesn't work, does it? I do put my work first. I don't think I can change, because I'm doing what

I always wanted, and to succeed I have to put everything into it. I have to prove myself every day, to every man on that force – and to myself . . . '

She was telling him that they could never lead the sort of life he wanted. It hurt a lot, and he wanted to gather her in his arms, make it all right. But the doorbell rang. They just looked at each other, with so much more to say and no time to say it in.

Peter said quickly, 'Don't say anything more now, let's talk it over tonight. Maybe I haven't been easy to live with, maybe if I was more secure . . . '

The doorbell rang again. 'You'd better go, Jane.'

'I don't know what time I'll be back.'

Peter stood for a moment after she'd left, surveying the kitchen, then he lashed out at the stack of dishes on the draining-board, sending them crashing into the sink.

Tennison sat silently beside Jones as he drove. It unnerved him. Eventually he said, just to break the silence, 'Still no trace of Marlow's car.' She didn't react. 'Are you OK?' he asked.

'I want that bloody car found!' she snapped.

'Trouble at home? I got all your shopping OK, didn't I?'

'Yeah!'

'I got an earful when I got home. My dinner had set like cement.'

'The difference is that you get your dinner cooked for you. At my place, I'm the one who's supposed to cook it.' She thought a moment. 'Shit's gonna hit the fan this morning, though. You got an aspirin?'

Chief Superintendent Kernan had come in early to review the Marlow case, and for once Tennison had got her oar in first. Now he listened in growing anger as Tennison and Otley raged at each other, but he let them get on with it.

'George Marlow was questioned in nineteen eighty-four about the murder of a prostitute, Jeannie Sharpe. John Shefford, then a DI, was on the investigating team. He was transferred to London because it was discovered that he'd been having a relationship with the murdered girl!' Tennison stormed. 'None of this is in the records. We now know that he was having a sexual relationship with Della Mornay; he must have known he'd identified the wrong girl, but he was prepared to cover that up as well!'

Otley was seething. 'Everything you're saying is a pack of lies, and if John Shefford was alive . . . '

'But he's not, he's dead, and you're still covering up for him. *You* requested the Oldham case, *you* wanted to go up there because you knew Shefford was involved . . . '

'That's not true! Della Mornay was a police informer . . . '

'She was also a prostitute, picked up and charged by John Shefford when he was attached to Vice – and what a perfect job for him!'

Tennison's last remark brought Kernan to his feet. 'That's enough! Just calm down!'

'Sir, I have been working against time ever since I took over this investigation, at first because of George Marlow's release, now because I'm going to be pulled off it. George Marlow is my only suspect, still my suspect for both murders, and now very possibly a third: Jeannie Sharpe.'

'I don't know anything about any previous case up north,' Otley insisted. 'I know some of the men fraternize with the girls on our patch . . . '

'Fraternize! Christ!'

Kernan thumped his desk, really pissed off. He pointed to Otley.

'Come on now, did Shefford think there was a connection between the first murder and the one in, er . . . Oldham?'

'I dunno, but I wanted to check it out. There was no ulterior motive.'

'So you knew John Shefford had worked in Oldham? Knew he'd been on this— ' Kernan thumbed through the file ' —this Jeannie Sharpe case?'

Otley was falling apart. He shook his head. 'No! I didn't know anything, but when I read the report and saw John's name down . . . Look, I know you knew, we all knew, he was a bit of a lad, so I just reckoned maybe I should check it out. That's all there was to it, nothin' more. If, as ma'am says, he was having a relationship with this tart, I knew nothin' about it.'

Tennison couldn't keep quiet. 'Just as you knew nothing about his relationship with Della Mornay? Bullshit! You knew, and you've been covering up for him . . . '

Kernan gave her the eye to shut up and keep it shut. 'Did you get anything from your trip to Southport, Bill?'

Otley shook his head. 'We're still checking, but no.'

Kernan nodded, then gave him a hard look. 'Well, keep at it. You can go.'

Otley hesitated. It was obvious that Kernan wanted him out of the office and wanted Tennison to stay. With an embarrassed cough, he turned to her.

'Maybe we got off to a bad start,' he said quietly. 'Should have taken a few weeks off after John . . . '

She gave him a rueful nod. 'I'll be in the Incident Room,' he said, and opened the door.

They waited until he had gone, then Kernan turned to Tennison and asked, 'What do you want to do?'

She looked him straight in the eye. 'I worked with a good bloke, in Hornchurch. Detective Sergeant Amson.'

Finally Kernan nodded. 'That's the deal, is it?'

'He's available, could be here in an hour or so. I'm going to drive up to Rochdale to see the woman Marlow attacked there. It would be a good opportunity to fill him in on the investigation.'

Kernan nodded again. Knowing she had won, Tennison went on, 'Marlow served eighteen months. All the cases were either before or after he was in jail. I want the surveillance put back on him.'

'OK. I'll do my best to hold Hicock off.'

'Thank you, sir. Detective Sergeant Amson.'

'I got it the first time.'

At ten Tennison was in the car park, getting some things from her boot, when Otley came up beside her.

'I reckon we got off on the wrong foot. I was just going back to the pub, wondered if you wanted a drink?'

'Has the Super not spoken to you?'

'No, I went and put a couple under my belt. I didn't know about John's spot of trouble in Oldham . . . '

Tennison said quietly, 'Yes, you did. You're off the case, Bill. I'm sorry, you've already been replaced.'

Otley seemed to shrink before her eyes. He turned to go and she said to his back, 'I want the names of every officer on my team who's taking sexual favours from prostitutes.'

He faced her again, but he had no anger left in him. She gave him a small nod and walked towards a car that had just drawn in to the car park. It was driven by the burly new sergeant, Terry Amson. He got out and opened the passenger door for her.

'I owe you a big one. My arse was dropping off in Hornchurch, I was sitting on it so much. How are you doing?'

She beamed and punched his arm as she climbed in. 'I think I'm doing OK.'

As he returned to the driving seat he gave Otley a small wave of acknowledgement. It wasn't returned. Otley's dejected figure was still standing there when they drove away.

chapter nine

Terry Amson drove fast and well up the motorway while Tennison put him in the picture on the murders.

'So we have three girls, Della Mornay, Karen Howard and Jeannie Sharpe, who were all strung up, with these clamp marks on their arms. The first two are different, but it's quite a coincidence.'

'Maybe he just perfected his technique! Have you tried talking to any of the guys he was banged up with? He's talkative, isn't he?'

'You could dig around while I'm with Miss Gilling, see if you can set something up for when we get back. And have a look at Marlow's statements, you never know what a fresh eye will come up with.'

The little terraced cottage that Pauline Gilling shared with her father had a neat, well-cared for garden. The inside was daintily decorated with Laura Ashley paper and a large collection of little glass animals, giving it a fragile feel which was echoed in Miss Gilling herself.

In her late thirties, she appeared older, with a pleasant but worried face. It took a while for her to unlock the front door, which was festooned with chains and bolts.

She sat on the edge of her chair and recounted the events of that day in a soft voice. It was as though she had learned it by heart; her eyes glazed slightly and she focused somewhere beyond the wall.

'It was the seventh of November, nineteen eighty-eight. At four-thirty in the afternoon . . . '

Tennison prepared herself to work this lady over. Without taking her eyes from Gilling, she settled herself on the sofa and took out a cigarette, nodding encouragingly.

'I was working in a florist's, and it was half-day closing. I don't work there any more.' She was wringing her hands unconsciously. 'The shop is called Delphinia's, and the owner's name is Florence Herriot. November the seventh is her birthday. She asked if I would go to the pub with her at lunchtime, for a sherry. I had an appointment at the hairdresser's, so I did not arrive until . . . ' She gave a strangled little cough, as if her throat was too tight, and continued, 'I arrived at two-thirty-five. I had a glass of sherry and stayed for approximately half an hour. I always come home to get father's lunch, but on early closing day I have my hair set, so I leave a tray for him.'

There was that strange little cough again. She was really tense now; her hands continually smoothed her skirt over her knees, which were pressed tightly together. Tennison said nothing, just waited for her to go on.

Her body went totally rigid and she had to force

herself to speak. 'I . . . I went up the path, I had my key out. I'd opened the door a few inches when . . . he called my name. "Pauline! Hallo, Pauline!" I turned round, but I didn't recognize him. He was smiling, and . . . he walked up the path towards me, and he said, "Aren't you going to invite me in for a cup of tea, Pauline?" '

She froze, like a rabbit caught in car headlights. Her mouth was open, but she made no sound. Deliberately, Tennison coughed, and she shook her head as if awakening, then started gabbling. 'I said I was sorry, I thought there was some mistake, I didn't know him. He came very close, pushed me into the hallway, got me by the throat, kept pushing me backwards . . . I was so terrified I couldn't scream, I was afraid for my father. I tried to defend myself with my handbag, but he grabbed it and hit me with it. The clasp cut my cheek open and broke my front teeth . . . '

After a decent interval, Tennison prompted gently, 'And then your father came in?'

'Yes. He was upstairs, I was lying on the floor, and he kept kicking me, then Daddy called out and he ran away. My father is blind, he couldn't see him, couldn't be called to identify him . . . ' She was going to cry.

'But you were able to pick George Marlow out of the line-up?'

Gilling swallowed, held back her tears. 'Oh, yes. He was clever, though; he had a beard when he attacked me, but he shaved it off before the identity parade. I still recognized him. It was his eyes, I will never forget his eyes . . . I know, if it hadn't been for my father, George Marlow would have killed me.'

Tennison crossed the room and squatted beside Gilling's chair. 'Thank you, you did very well, and I'm sorry to have made you go through it all again.'

Gilling shrank from her, fearing to be touched, and stood up. Her nervousness was beginning to grate on Tennison.

'I go through it all the time, every time the doorbell rings, every strange sound at night . . . I see his face, keep expecting him to come back, to finish . . . I had to leave my job, I can't sleep. He should have been put away for years, but they let him go after eighteen months. I live in terror of him coming back, because he said he would, he said he'd come back!'

Tennison climbed into the patrol car and breathed a sigh of relief. Beside her, Amson was immersed in a file.

'Marlow had a beard at the time of the rape, shaved it off for the line-up! That matches with what the toms said in Oldham, they thought the guy had a beard.'

He looked up. 'D'you think there's any truth in the story that she gave Marlow the come-on? She's, what, thirty-eight now, and a spinster . . . '

Tennison bridled. 'So am I, it doesn't mean I want myself raped, and my front teeth kicked in!'

'Take it easy, it's just that from the description she's a bit of a dog. Marlow, on the other hand, is a good-looking bloke, like myself.'

She replied with a laugh, 'Be very careful, Sergeant, or you'll be back rotting in Hornchurch!'

Two men were painting the row of garages on Marlow's council estate. They were making quite a good job of it, considering neither of them had done much in that line before. A few yards away George Marlow was standing, hands in pockets, watching them.

One of the men went to his nearby van for a new tin of paint. He opened it and stirred it with a screwdriver, then wiped the blade on his already paint-covered overalls.

'Excuse me, are you going to be painting the whole block, or just the garages?' Marlow asked.

'Just this lot, far as we know, mate,' DC Lillie replied.

'They aren't for residents, you know. Council rents them out to anyone who can afford them. The tenants have to park in the bay over there, known as Radio One . . . ' He flashed a grin at Lillie. 'Means you had one when you parked it!'

He waited for a response, which didn't come, so he went on, 'I had one, but it was nicked.'

'What, a radio?'

'My car. Rover Mark III, three-litre automatic. More'n twenty years old, collector's item, you know.' He stared down into the tin of paint, then up at the garages.

Rosper joined in. 'You leave it out? Bodywork must 'ave rusted up?'

Marlow touched the paint on the nearest garage door, then peered closer. 'Had a bit of filler here and there. Suppose some kids nicked it for a joyride, be stripped down by now. Had all my emblems and badges on the front, RAC and AA, owner's club . . . all on a chrome bar at the front.' He examined the paint again. 'I'm in the paint business, typical of the council . . . ' He put a hand out towards Rosper. 'Can I just borrow your brush? Like to see how this goes on . . . '

He dipped the brush in the paint and applied a stroke as Rosper and Lillie exchanged glances behind his back. Totally unaware, he said, 'You work out, do you?' He glanced round at Rosper. 'You look as if you do. What gym do you use?'

He chatted on, painting the door, while they stood and watched.

Late in the afternoon, Tennison and Amson arrived at Brixton Prison to interview convict 56774, Reginald McKinney. While they waited for him to be brought to them, Amson explained that McKinney had shared a cell with Marlow in Durham and had been picked up again a few weeks ago for breaking and entering.

The warder who brought McKinney told them there was a call from the station for them. Tennison asked Amson to take it, then offered the tall, skeletal prisoner a seat.

He was suffering from a migraine, and had come from the hospital ward. One of his eyes watered and his face was twisted in pain. 'We'll try and keep this short, Reg. Now, you shared a cell with George Marlow in Durham, that right?'

'That is correct.'

His eyes were crossing, it was like putting questions to a demented squirrel. 'You told your probation officer that you had met Marlow after your release.'

'That is correct.'

'And you were living in a half-way hostel in Camberwell then, yes? So where did you meet?'

McKinney looked up as Amson returned. He kept his back to McKinney and leaned over to whisper to Tennison.

'There's a buzz on, looks like another one in Warrington. They'll get back to me when they've finished checking.'

Feeling a bit perkier, Tennison turned back to Reg. He said, 'I've forgotten what you asked me . . . I've got a migraine.'

'Where did you and Marlow meet?'

'Oh, yeah . . . Kilburn. We went for a curry, then he drove me back to my place. Bit of a schlepp, an' I offered to get the tube, but he said it was OK. He wanted to do some work on his motor, in his lock-up.'

Tennison was careful not to show the excitement she was feeling. 'Lock-up – you mean a garage?'

'I dunno . . . ' He stopped a moment and rubbed his head, in obvious agony. 'The car was, like, an obsession with 'im.'

'He never mentioned where this lock-up was?'

'No . . . I got a terrible headache.'

A prison warder put his head round the door. 'Urgent call for DCI Tennison.'

Tennison took the call. The team were doing a good job; the Warrington murder had checked out, plus another one, in Southport. Both victims had identical marks on their arms.

George Marlow hung around the garages chatting and joking with Rosper and Lillie until dark. They got on well together, and had done a fair bit of painting, but the two DCs were beginning to wonder when he was going to go home – they couldn't paint all night. The floodlights had come on around the estate and were just enough to work by, but it wasn't easy.

'Bit late to be painting, isn't it?' Marlow enquired.

'We're on bonus, mate,' Rosper told him. 'Never know what's gonna happen with all this council privatization, so we gotta make the cash while we can.'

Marlow sympathized with them, then launched into a story about a bet he'd had with someone at the gym where he worked out when they heard sirens coming close.

All three turned to watch the cars drive onto the estate. In the first one were DI Muddyman with DC Jones, behind them Tennison and Amson. They had barely come to a halt when Tennison leaped out and ran to catch up with Muddyman.

As they hurried towards Marlow's flat she gasped, 'He's got a lock-up, some kind of garage where he stashes his car. Look for a set of keys, anything that might fit that kind of place. Get the bloody floorboards up if necessary.'

'I don't believe this,' Marlow was saying with exasperation to Lillie and Rosper as he wiped his hands on a rag. He stood and watched Tennison, Amson and Jones legging it up towards his flat.

'What are they after?' Lillie asked, watching him carefully.

'Me! I'd better get up there, the old lady next door'll have heart failure . . . ' He laughed. 'Not because of them, but because she's out playing bingo. Means she'll miss all the drama. Ta-ra!'

Moyra was at the door, looking at the search warrant. From the bottom of the steps Marlow called, 'Hi, you want me?'

Moyra was very near to tears as she stood in the hall and surveyed the wreckage of her home. The carpets had been rolled back, all loose floorboards had been prised up, the hardboarding around the bath had been removed, the toilet had been taken apart, even the U-bends of the handbasin and the kitchen sink had been disconnected. Every video had been taken out of its jacket, every book taken down from the shelves and shaken, every crevice in every piece of furniture delved into. Tennison and Amson had every key in the place laid out in the lounge and were examining them minutely.

Moyra's self-pity turned to rage, and she screamed, 'I don't believe this! I want everything put back as it was, and what you've done to the plumbing I want repaired professionally! You've had all our bloody keys down the nick before, why don't you tell me what you're looking for?'

Tennison gestured to Amson to close the door on Moyra, then turned to Marlow, who was standing in front of the fireplace, hands on his hips. 'Why don't you tell us, George? You know what we're looking for.'

'I know you've been asking the neighbours. I park my car outside, I don't have a garage.'

'But your car isn't always parked outside, George. We know you've got a lock-up.'

'When it's not parked here it's because I'm away on business. I drive – correction, I drove – for a living. Instead of all this, why don't you just try and find my car?'

There were thuds and hammering noises from the kitchen, and the sound of crockery being moved. Moyra's screaming voice could be heard telling Muddyman and Jones that the bottom of the percolator didn't come off. She started yelling for George.

Tennison turned to Amson. 'Tell them to keep it down out there. George, you've got a lock-up, we know it.'

'A lock-up? How many more times do I have to tell you? I park my car at the back of the flats!'

'We have a witness . . . '

'Not that old bat from next door!'

'No, a friend of yours.'

'What friend? I don't have one left because of your crowd. Mates I worked with for years turned their backs on me! You got a friend? Great, introduce me!'

'We have a witness who stated that you told him you had a . . . '

'Him? Was it someone I was inside with? Yes? Don't tell me, let me guess. It was Reg McKinney, wasn't it?' He shook his head, laughing. 'You must be desperate. Reg McKinney? He's no friend of mine. Stung me for fifty quid when we got out. He's a known nutter. Look at his record, in and out of institutions since he was a kid. He's no friend of mine, I told him to take a hike.'

There was a tap on the door and Amson opened up.

'Nothin',' said Muddyman with a shrug, 'but we need a plumber.'

In a low voice, Marlow told Tennison earnestly, 'I don't have a lock-up, I don't have a garage. If I had, maybe my motor wouldn't have been nicked. It's the truth!'

Suddenly anxious to get home to Peter, Tennison decided not to go back to the station to pick up her car, so Terry Amson gave her a lift home. She was very aware of the difference having a genuinely friendly face on her team made to her job. She knew she could talk to Terry and it wouldn't go any further.

Amson was saying, 'If he's got his car stashed somewhere between Camberwell and Kilburn, we'll find it.'

'If!' She looked at him sideways. 'Terry, now you've met him, what do you think?'

'For real? If he's lying, he's one of the best I've ever come across.'

'Yeah,' she said with a sigh. 'Tonight, for the first time, I had doubts.' She pointed ahead. 'It's the second house along.'

When he had stopped the car she turned to him. 'What do you think about John Shefford?'

'As a suspect? He was a crack officer, you know.'

She said sadly, 'He was also in the vicinity when Karen, Della and Jeannie Sharpe were killed. We're going to have to check him out on the two that just came in.'

'You know I'm with you on this, Jane, but there's only so far I'm prepared to go. I've got a wife and four kids to support, remember.'

'I don't like it any more than you.' She put her hand out

to open the door. 'Just keep it under your hat, but we've got to check it out. So you pull Shefford's record sheets, first thing in the morning, OK? You want to come in for a drink?'

Amson shook his head and Tennison climbed out. 'G'night!' she said, as he started the engine.

Jane felt for the hall light switch, pressed it down. The flat was quiet; she dumped her briefcase and took off her coat, shouting, 'Pete! Pete?'

There was no answer. She opened the kitchen door to find it clean and tidy, nothing out of place. She tried the bedroom; it was just the same.

Sighing, she unbuttoned her shirt and opened the wardrobe. One half of it was empty. She checked the chest-of-drawers – all Peter's were empty! Turning away, she unzipped her skirt and let it slide to the floor, stepped out of it and walked towards the bathroom.

As she opened the door the phone rang. She let it ring, looking around to see only one toothbrush, one set of towels. The answering machine clicked into action and she waited, listening.

'Jane, it's your mother . . . ' Jane saw the white envelope propped against the phone and reached for it. 'Didn't you get my message this morning about Pam? Well, in case you didn't, she's had a girl, eight pounds seven ounces, and she's beautiful! She was rushed into St Stephen's Hospital last night, I'm calling from her room . . . '

Jane picked up the phone as she ripped the envelope open. 'Hallo, Mum! I just got home.'

Jane drove to the hospital and parked, with the unopened letter from Peter on the seat beside her. She turned the lights off and reached for the white manila envelope with her name hastily scrawled on it.

It contained one sheet of her own notepaper. *Sweetheart,* she read, *I took on board everything you said this morning. I can't quite deal with you, or the pressures of your work, and at the same time get myself sorted out. I am sorry to do it this way, but I think in the long run it will be for the best, for both of us. I still care for you, but I can't see any future in our relationship. Maybe when we've had a few weeks apart we can meet and have a talk. Until then, take care of yourself.*

It was signed simply, *Peter*. She laid it face down on the seat and sighed, then realized that there was a postscript on the back.

I'm staying with one of my builders. When I get an address I'll let you know where I am, but if you need me you can reach me at the yard. Then he had put in brackets: *(Not Scotland Yard!)*.

Jane opened the door slowly, but remained sitting. Was it always going to be like this? Peter wasn't the first, she'd never been able to keep a relationship going for more than a few months. She flicked her compact open and delved into her bag for a comb, stared at her reflection in the oval mirror for a long time. She looked a wreck, her hair needed washing and the make-up she had dashed on in a hurry that morning had long since disappeared. She studied the lines around her eyes and from her nose to her lips, the deep frown lines between her brows. She fished in her bag and brought out her lipstick, closed the mirror and ran the lipstick around her mouth without looking at it. She was so used to freshening up in a hurry that she didn't need a mirror.

Locking the car, she walked briskly towards the bright hospital entrance. An anxious-looking woman in a wheelchair was holding an unlit cigarette. Jane smiled at her and she gave a conspiratorial grin.

'I don't suppose you've got a match, have you?'

'Yes, love.' Jane took a half-used book of matches from her pocket. 'You keep them, and mind you don't get cold. It's freezing out.'

As Jane headed for the night nurse at reception, she thought to herself, 'So what if you're going home to an empty flat? You've done that most of your adult life.' By the time she reached the desk she had persuaded herself that she preferred it that way.

She gave the nurse a cheerful smile. 'I've come to see my sister. I know it's late . . . '

After signing the visitors' book she headed towards the lifts, as directed. The woman in the wheelchair called out, 'Thanks for the matches!'

'That's all right, love. Good night, now!'

The corridor was deserted. Jane checked each room, peering through the little windows, until she found the right one. She could see Pam through the glass, holding the new baby, Tony's arm resting lightly around her shoulders. Although it was way past their bedtime her two little boys were there too, spick and span, swarming over the bed and admiring their new little sister.

Watching them, Jane's hand tightened on the door handle, but she found she couldn't turn it. They formed a picture of a family in which she had no place. She turned away and walked slowly back down the corridor.

She headed automatically towards the river, needing quiet, space to think. It was an ordeal to cross the King's Road; she found herself shrinking from the traffic, from the faces passing her in their shiny cars; happy faces, drunken faces, all going somewhere, all with a purpose, with someone . . .

She found herself in Cheyne Walk, beside the water. Tonight the Thames looked like a river of oil, sluggish and smooth, and she could not shake off the feeling that dead and rotting bodies floated just beneath the surface. She had come here to celebrate a new life, but all she could see was death, and pain.

By the time she returned to the hospital, visiting hours were officially over, but she slipped along to the private section without being stopped.

The room was decked with flowers and bowls of fruit, and the baby lay asleep in her cot, but Pam's bed was empty. This time she didn't hesitate, she walked into the room and gazed down at the baby girl, moved the blanket gently away from her face.

Soft footsteps behind her announced Pam's return. Jane looked up, smiling, back in control.

'Hi! Just checking she has all her fingers and toes! She's OK? Bit of a dent in her head, though . . . '

Pam climbed cautiously into bed. 'Her skull is still soft, it'll go. If you'd been here earlier you'd have seen Tony and the boys. Mum's staying until I go home.'

'I feel a bit cheap – no flowers, no fruit. But I'd just got in from work.'

Pam was still in pain. She shifted uncomfortably in the bed.

'Could you just plump up my pillows?' she lowered her voice. 'You know we got this on Tony's firm? It's a new scheme, a private patients' plan. We can all get private medical attention now . . . '

Jane rearranged her sister's pillows and straightened the sheets, then kissed her sister's cheek. 'Well, congratulations! What are you going to call her, Fergie? Eugenie? Beatrice? I mean, now it's all private . . . '

Pam pulled a face. 'Well, Mum's actually hinted . . . '

'What? No, you *can't* call her *Edna*!'

They were interrupted by a nurse, who gave Jane a pleasant smile that none the less indicated that she shouldn't be there. 'It's time for her feed, I'm afraid. Beautiful, isn't she?'

She disappeared with the baby, and Jane prepared herself to leave.

'You can tell this is private: no bells and everybody out!' She kissed Pam's cheek and smiled. 'I gotta go, anyway.'

'Thanks for coming. Give my love to Peter.'

'If I see him I will . . . ' She hesitated at the door. 'It's all off.'

Pam was instantly concerned. 'Oh, no! Why?'

Jane shrugged. 'You know me.'

'Is there someone else? I mean, are you OK?'

'No, there's no one else. I'm . . . It was a mutual decision.'

'Well, you know what you're doing. Is the case we saw on television over?'

Jane paused before she answered. Her family's total lack of understanding when it came to her work, to herself, on top of Peter leaving, swamped her, but she managed to keep her smile in place.

'No, I haven't got him – yet!' She gave her sister a little wave. 'G'night, God bless the baby.'

As she closed the door behind her, only the expression in her eyes betrayed Jane's loneliness. She had made a tremendous effort, forcing herself to come here. Having done her duty, at last she could go home and cry.

chapter ten

'What in Christ's name do you think you're playing at?' Kernan demanded.

'We had good reason to search Marlow's flat,' she protested. 'Bloke he was in jail with said he had a lock-up . . . '

'I'm not talking about Marlow! You've had Sergeant Amson going over Shefford's record sheets.'

How the hell had he found out so quickly? She opened her mouth to speak, but Kernan ploughed on, 'If you want information regarding one of my ex-officers, then you know bloody well you should have come to me!'

'I think we've got our wires crossed here.'

'Don't bullshit me, Jane! Are you so desperate? It's pretty low, just because you can't prove your case, to try shifting the blame to John Shefford!'

'I first mentioned my suspicions to Sergeant Amson last night, and until I have more evidence . . . '

'I'm telling you, back off! If there was one viable piece of evidence against DCI Shefford, you should have brought it to me. And don't harp back to the diary, that's sorted, and Otley's paid for it. Don't try to do my job, Inspector.'

She tried again. 'We've got two unsolved cases, one in Warrington and one in Southport, both with similar bruising to their upper arms, hands tied with the same sort of knots. George Marlow was in the vicinity when both . . .'

'Are you telling me Shefford was also in the vicinity? Have you got the evidence to start an internal investigation?'

'I don't know if Shefford was ever attached to . . .'

He wouldn't let her finish. 'I'm telling you he wasn't, because I've checked!'

'I apologize, but under the circumstances . . .'

'Under the circumstances I am bringing in DCI Hicock! Don't you know what you've done, Jane? You've been running around the country trying to rake up dirt on one of the best officers I ever had! It stinks, and I won't take any more of it.'

'Shefford falsified evidence, and is known to have been on close terms with two murdered girls, both prostitutes – Della Mornay and Jeannie Sharpe. Of the two other cases we have uncovered, one was a prostitute . . .'

Kernan strode to the door. 'The man is in the graveyard.'

'So are they, sir. Re-opening cases as far back as nineteen eighty-four is a slow procedure.'

'I've nothing more to say, I'm bringing Hicock in as soon as he can get here. You concentrate on the investigation you were assigned to for as long as you remain on it, is that clear? And if you want some advice, put in for a transfer. I want you off the Marlow case, and I want your report on everything that went down yesterday on my desk by lunchtime, is that clear?

'Yes, sir!' said Tennison.

Amson came racing up the corridor as she left Kernan's office, waving a sheet of paper.

'We've got another one! Blackburn, 'eighty-seven!'

Tennison hurried to meet him and grabbed the paper, but Amson wouldn't let it go until he'd finished. 'It's about one a year, apart from the time Marlow was in jail! Caplan and Haskons are still watching him, and everyone else is mustered in the Incident Room – apart from these three.'

Tennison looked puzzled, and he finally handed over the note. 'Otley coughed up the names of the blokes who were fooling around with the toms! They're waiting for the Super to call them in now.'

'What about Shefford?' she asked urgently.

'He's in the clear, on all the new cases. He may have done a surface job on the Jeannie Sharpe murder, but then he wasn't the DCI on the case, so you can't put it all down to him. And he wasn't around when the others were killed.'

'I'm glad,' Tennison said. He gave her a disbelieving look and she protested, 'I am! Even if it dropped me right in the shit!'

Amson looked around and lowered his voice. 'As a matter of interest, did you know that the Chief and Shefford were' – he crossed his fingers – 'like that? They played golf every weekend – not at Sunningdale! Chief was Shefford's guv'nor when he was on Vice.'

Tennison shook her head and raised her eyes to heaven. 'I think I'll leave that one well and truly alone!' she said.

At least thirty people were crammed into the Incident Room. The air was thick with smoke. Every chair was taken, and the latecomers were sitting on desks or propped against the walls. While they waited some drank coffee and ate sandwiches, but most of them just talked. The din was deafening.

Sergeant Terry Amson was setting up a projector in the centre of the room. Tennison was thumbing through her notes while she waited.

She looked up when the door opened. It was DI Burkin and two others, returning from the Super's office. They all looked rather sheepish.

'Sorry, guv, we've been upstairs.'

Tennison nodded, well aware that these were the men who had been a bit too familiar with the local prostitutes. She gave them a moment to disperse amongst the others.

Burkin had found a place next to Muddyman, who asked him what was going on.

'Got our knuckles rapped for off-duty leg-overs. She's got eyes in the back of her head, that one! Just a warning this time, so maybe she's not all bad, but rumour has it that Hicock's definitely taking over, no kidding. He's in, she's out.'

Tennison stood up. 'OK, can I have a bit of hush?'

She waited for the room to grow quiet. Slowly they sorted themselves out, and she was able to start the meeting. She played it to the gallery.

'Right. I've been told that unless we get results very quickly indeed, I'm on traffic . . . Joke! I don't think it's quite that bad, but there will be some changes around here if we don't pull something out of the hat. In case I don't get another opportunity, I'll say now that I appreciate your back-up, and all the hard work . . . '

There were moans and unprintable comments as the word went round. Tennison yelled, 'Come on, settle down! Maybe there's something we've missed, something that, if we all think about it, will whack us right between the eyes. OK, Sergeant . . . '

The lights went off, the blinds went down, and Amson ran the mock-up of Karen Howard's last night. They watched her stand-in talking to the builder who had tried to help her, then crossing the road and walking up Ladbroke Grove.

'Oh, boy, we gonna watch you again, guv?' Tennison recognized the voice from the darkness as Rosper's.

Amson summarized all the evidence as they watched. 'Karen Howard, our first victim. Her body discovered in Della Mornay's bedsit and mistaken for her.'

The film ended, followed by close-up stills of Karen's badly beaten body, then her various appalling injuries. The last frame was of the bruising on her arms.

'OK, take a good look at these marks. Now we have the other victim, Della Mornay, who was killed approximately six weeks before Karen . . . '

The shot of the decomposed body was sickening. The close-ups showed her upper arms and what appeared to be bite marks.

'The foxes had a go at her, and the dog belonging to the man who found her. But look at the arms again: the same marks, almost identical to those found on Karen.'

Another body was flashed up on the screen. 'Jeannie Sharpe, killed in Oldham in nineteen eighty-four. Again, note the bruising and welts on the upper arms. Fourth victim . . . '

Amson pointed to DI Muddyman and whispered, 'You ready?' Muddyman climbed to his feet.

'Another video now, this time of Angela Simpson, whose family sent it to us. She was knifed to death in a public park in nineteen eighty-five. She was a hair-dresser, well-liked kid, about to get married. This is her engagement party.'

The sweet face of Angela Simpson smiled into camera, showing off her engagement ring, then self-consciously kissing the young man beside her. Her smiling fiancé gave a thumbs-up sign, and Angela turned to the camera, laughing, and put her hands over the lens. Then she loomed very close and kissed the camera.

'During the house-to-house enquiries, George Marlow was interviewed. He had been staying in a bed and break-fast only fifty yards from the gates of the park where she was found. There were no marks on her upper arms, but look at this . . . '

There was a shot of Angela, lying face down, legs apart. Her hands were tied behind her back.

'The rope, the way the hands were tied, were just the same as in victims one and two.'

There was a slight commotion as a WPC entered and tried to find Tennison in the dark. She delivered a brief message and departed, clocked by the men. Frank Burkin stood up to take DI Muddyman's place.

'The fifth girl' – Burkin waited for the shot to appear on screen – 'was Sharon Reid. She was sixteen, still at school, and worked part-time in a local beauty salon . . . '

When he had finished they broke for lunch, and the discussion was continued less formally in the canteen. Reading the menu, DC Lillie was reminded about the old woman, the one found in the chicken run. She had had similar marks on her arms to the others. He asked Sergeant Amson, who was in the queue behind him.

'Marlow was in the vicinity, that's good enough for me to try and pin it on him.' He looked around Lillie to see what the hold-up was. 'Come on, Burkin!' he yelled.

Lillie persisted. 'But they didn't all have clamp marks . . . Oh, not ruddy Chicken Kiev again! The garlic's a killer!'

Burkin, his plate full, moved away from the counter, and joined Muddyman, who was holding forth about Marlow.

'I've been watching him for weeks now, he's a real friendly bloke, right? He chats to the lads every day. Just because he was in the area, it doesn't mean he's guilty.'

Burkin picked up the lurid plastic tomato from the table and squeezed ketchup all over his plate, then stuffed a huge forkful of chips in his mouth. Bits of potato flew everywhere while he talked.

'There must be hundreds of salesmen workin' that area, you could take your pick. You ask me, all that film was about this morning was that we've got more bloody tarts being bumped off' – he paused to burp – 'an' no bloody suspects.'

The 'bing-bong' sounded and a voice requested the presence of DCI Tennison in Administration. The men ignored it and carried on talking about Marlow; everyone who had had contact with him seemed to be convinced that he was a good bloke and therefore not a murderer. Terry Amson arrived and picked up on the conversation.

'He lied about the lock-up, we know that.'

'We've only got the word of an old lag on that, it's not proof,' Burkin retorted. There was another call over the PA system for Tennison. 'Looks like the boss is gonna get the big boys pullin' the rug on her . . . Coffee all round?' He looked at Lillie. 'Your turn.'

Maureen Havers found Tennison hiding in the locker room, eating a large hamburger.

'Is DCI Hicock a big, red-haired bloke? He's in with the Commander and the Super's there too. You're being paged all over the station.'

'Am I?' Tennison asked innocently. 'Well, they'll just have to find me.'

Having successfully evaded her bosses, Tennison returned to the Incident Room to continue the briefing. She pinned photographs of all six of the victims on the notice-board while she waited for everyone to settle down.

'Right! Six victims, no set pattern. They did not, as far as we can ascertain, know each other. They didn't look alike, they belonged to different age groups, different professions. Apart from certain minor similarities they were not all killed in the same manner. The only link between them all is that Marlow was in the area when they were murdered. Did he kill all six? Is there something we've overlooked, another link?'

Muddyman was slumped right down in his chair, totally relaxed. He waved a hand to attract Tennison's attention.

'In the case of Karen, a witness stated that she heard a man call out her name. It was the same with Jeannie. But what about Angela, the little blonde one? She was killed in the shrubbery in broad daylight, a good distance from the path, which was her usual route home. So how did she get there? If someone had called out to her . . . And the one who was raped, Gilling, she said he called her name . . . '

'Point taken,' said Amson, 'but you've got two toms, one hairdresser, a schoolgirl . . . How did he get to know their names, if he knew them?'

Havers had made her way to the front, using her elbows, and was standing by the photographs. She raised her hand, about to say something, but lowered it, not sure of her ground. She moved closer to Tennison and touched her arm.

'Boss, I think . . . It may be off the wall . . . '

'Anything, my love, I'm right up against it. What you got?'

'I did a bit of checking, but it all falls down with

Gilling. She was a florist, but there's one link with the others. It was mentioned once . . . '

'To Marlow?'

'No, not him – Moyra Henson.'

Tennison could barely hear her against the growing racket in the room. 'Come on, lads, keep it down a bit!' she yelled, then turned back to Havers.

'Go on.'

'When she was brought in for questioning I typed her statement. She put herself down as unemployed . . . '

'Yeah . . . Quiet! Quieten down!'

The noise slowly subsided. Some of the men closed in on Tennison and Havers, realizing something was going on.

Havers coughed nervously. 'She was picked up for prostitution, fifteen years ago, according to her record. But on that charge-sheet she's down as a freelance beautician. If she worked when she was travelling around with Marlow, he could have met the girls that way. But Gilling doesn't fit in . . . '

'Good on ya, Maureen!' Tennison gave her a quick hug. 'We'll check it out.'

Unaware of the tension, Jones walked in carrying an MSS internal fax sheet. 'This might be useful, ma'am,' he said to Tennison. 'I've checked back on Marlow's past addresses. They've been in Maida Vale for three years, and before that they were in Somerstown, not far from St Pancras. He's had the Rover for twelve years, so what if he had a lock-up close to his previous flat?'

Rosper had a sudden thought. 'Yeah! Those garages we've been painting, Marlow told us he tried to rent one, but the council leases 'em out to the highest bidder. Maybe he kept his old garage because he couldn't get one near by . . . '

The phone rang and DI Muddyman answered it, then covered the mouthpiece. 'Guv? You're wanted upstairs, you here or not?'

'No, I'm not! Go and bring that hard-nosed cow in!'

*

Moyra wasn't happy at being taken down to the station, and she made sure the whole estate knew about it.

'Had a good eyeful?' she screeched at her next-door neighbour as she was led out to the car. 'I tell you, they get more mileage out of you lot than a ruddy video . . . *Don't push me!*'

Marlow trailed behind them. 'I don't understand, do you want me as well?'

Tennison emerged from the car and held the back door open for Moyra. 'Not this time, George.'

They left him standing there, still trying to work out what was going on.

Tennison had a quick wash and checked that the Super had left for the day before she emerged with Maureen Havers from the locker room, ready to interview Moyra.

Amson was pacing up and down the corridor outside. 'Mrs Howard is sending some of Karen's latest model photos by courier, shouldn't be long. You all set? Got plenty of cigarettes?'

She took a deep breath and nodded, then followed Amson and Havers along the corridor to room 4-C.

Havers went in first, followed by Amson, who held the door open for Tennison. After a beat, Tennison followed, like a prize-fighter.

'I am Detective Chief Inspector Jane Tennison, this is WPC Maureen Havers, and Detective Sergeant Amson. Thank you for agreeing to answer our questions . . . '

'I had an option, did I?' Moyra interrupted.

Amson placed a thick file on the bare table in front of Tennison. She opened it and extracted a statement.

'You were brought into the station on the sixteenth of January this year, is that correct?'

'If you say so!'

'Is this the statement you made on that occasion?' Tennison laid it in front of her.

Moyra glared at it. 'Yesss . . . '

'And is this your signature?'

'Of course it bloody is!'

'Thank you. I would like to draw your attention to the front page – here. It states that you are unemployed, is that correct?'

'It says so, doesn't it?'

'So you are unemployed.'

'Yes, I'm on the bloody dole. What's that got to do with anything?'

Tennison extracted another document from the file and put it in front of her. 'We have this previous statement from you, dating back to nineteen seventy-five. You were charged with soliciting, and stated your profession as beautician.'

'Is there a law against it?'

'Did your training include a hairdressing course?'

Moyra was getting rattled. She answered abruptly, 'No!'

'So you are not a hairdresser?'

'No, but I once had a Siamese cat.'

'So you are a freelance beautician?'

'Yeah, you know, manicures, hands, facials.' She peered at Tennison across the table. 'You could do with a facial, smoking's very bad for your skin.'

'Do you work as a beautician?'

'What do you want to know all this for? You think George is a transvestite now, do you?'

'George Marlow, your common-law husband, is still under suspicion of murder. I need the answers to my questions to help us eliminate him from our enquiries.'

'Pull the other one, you're just interested in incriminating him.'

'I'd like you to tell me where you were on these dates: March the fifteenth, nineteen eighty-four . . . '

'No ruddy idea, darlin'. Ask me another.'

'The second of November nineteen eighty-five. Twenty-third of July, nineteen eighty-six. Ninth of April nineteen eighty-seven.'

'I dunno, I'd have to look in me diaries, not that I've got them that far back.' She bent down and started fiddling with her shoe.

'They were dates when your common-law husband

was travelling in Warrington, Oldham, Burnley, Rochdale . . .'

Moyra looked up. 'Oh, in that case I was with him. I always travel with him.'

'So on the dates that I have mentioned, you are pretty sure that you were with George, yes?'

'I travel with him, I stay with him.'

'Doing freelance work as a beautician?'

'Well, yeah. I do a bit.'

'In salons?'

'Yeah, no law against that.'

'There is if you've been claiming unemployment benefit and not declaring income, or paying tax on it. There's a law against that.'

Moyra actually shrank back in her chair, though her answer was bold enough. 'It's nothing, just a bit of cash, you know, pin money.'

'How long do you think it would take for me to check out just how much you've been earning?'

'You bastards never give anyone a break.'

'I'll give you a break, Moyra. No charges if – *if* – you give us a detailed list of the salons you've worked in, the names of your clients . . .'

As Tennison placed a pen and a sheet of paper in front of Moyra, Amson leaned over and whispered to her. With a nod to Havers, she followed him from the room.

'If this pins any of those cases on Marlow, she's virtually making herself an accessory!'

'What are you suggesting?' Tennison snapped. 'Get her lawyer in just when she's co-operating?'

'You're jumping the gun. What we need is a lever, something to push Marlow with. She's his alibi, and so far she's not backed down on that.'

Tennison banged the coffee machine with the flat of her hand. 'Christ, you're right! An' we need a fucking lever to make this machine work . . .' She looked at her watch. 'OK, leave it with me. I'll have one more go.' She smiled. 'But gently does it!'

*

Moyra was beginning to look tired. She leaned her head in her hand.

'I've listed the salons, but that doesn't mean to say that I work there regular. Sometimes they don't have any customers for me, and it's mostly manicures.'

'What's this Noo-Nail?' Tennison asked, looking over the paper.

'It's American, paint-on nails; your own grow underneath.' She held out a hand for Tennison to inspect. 'See, they look real, don't they? But that part's false.'

Havers, trying to look interested, stifled a yawn. Amson was half-asleep.

'Aah, I see!' Tennison nodded, then asked nonchalantly, 'Did you do Miss Pauline Gilling's nails?'

Without a flicker, Moyra replied, 'Look, love, I do so many, I don't know all their names.'

'Surely you'd remember Pauline Gilling? George was sent down for attacking her . . . ' She pushed a photograph across the table.

Moyra refused to look at the photo and snapped, 'No, no! An' she lied, she came on to George! She'd been in the pub, she lied . . . '

'What about Della Mornay? Did you do her nails?' She put another photograph on the table.

'No!'

'Take a look, Moyra. Della Mornay.'

'I don't know her!'

'No? You stated that George returned home on the night of the thirteenth of January this year at ten-thirty . . . '

Under pressure again, Moyra fought back. 'Yes! Look, I know my rights, this isn't on! I've been here for hours, I've answered your questions, now I want a lawyer.'

'George's car, the brown Rover, where is it? We know he has a lock-up, Moyra, and we'll find it, it's just a question of time. I'll need to talk to you again.' She stood up. 'OK, you can go, thank you.'

'Is that it? I can go home?'

Tennison nodded and walked to the door, leaving Moyra nonplussed.

*

It was light before Moyra got home. George made her a cup of coffee and brought it to her in the lounge.

'Bastards are going to get me for fiddling the dole and tax evasion. They know I've been working.'

'They kept you all night just for that?'

'There were a few other things.'

'What? What did she want to know? Ask about me, did she?'

Moyra stood up and started unbuttoning her blouse. 'What do you think?'

She walked out of the room and, after a moment's hesitation, Marlow followed her to the bedroom. She tossed her blouse aside and unzipped her skirt, leaving it where it fell. He picked them up and folded them while she went into the adjoining bathroom and turned on the bath taps.

'What are you following me around for?'

'I just want to know what went on!'

She turned on him, snapping. 'They wanted to know about the bloody florist! Kept asking me about her. I've stood by you, George, but so help me if I find you've been lying to me I'll . . . '

She turned and walked out. 'Put some Badedas in for me . . . '

He picked up the big yellow bottle and squirted some of the contents into the water, then stood in the doorway, watching her cream her face.

'I've never lied to you, Moyra, you know that.' He reached out to touch her but she slapped his hand away, finished wiping her face with a tissue.

'Where's the car, George?'

'It was stolen, I don't know where it is.'

She picked up her hairbrush. 'It wasn't here, George. You came home that night without it. I remember because your hair was wet, you said it was raining.' She turned to him while she brushed her hair, slowly. 'Is it in the lock-up? They're going to get you because of that bloody car . . . They can plant evidence, you know, and they're out to get you.'

'What did they say?'

'The bath'll run over.'

'What did they say?'

'Maybe they've already found it, I dunno. I've got my own problems. They'll get me just for doing a few manicures.' She threw the brush down on the dressing-table and stormed into the bathroom. Marlow picked up the brush and began to run it through his hair.

Peter looked around the bedsit. It was clean and close to the building yard. The best thing was the rent, a hundred a week. He had paid the landlady up front for a month. Dumping his suitcase without bothering to unpack, he went straight out again, arriving outside Marianne's just after breakfast. He watched from a distance until Marianne's husband had taken Joey to school, then rang the bell.

Marianne offered her cheek, which he kissed, and coffee, which he accepted. She tidied the breakfast dishes into the dishwasher and sat opposite him at the kitchen table.

'I've moved, so if you need me, here's my new address,' he told her.

'Oh, so it didn't work out with the policewoman?'

'No, it didn't.'

'I'm sorry.'

'Really? Because I won't be able to have Joey to stay? Well, wrong, because he can stay with me for as long as need be.'

Marianne unfolded the small note of his address and got up to pin it on the notice-board. He sipped his lukewarm coffee and asked, 'How are you?'

'I'm fine. Do you want toast?'

'No. I want to know if this new baby's mine. Is it?'

'What?'

'Come on, don't mess me around. I got the sort of nudge, nudge when you came round, so tell me the truth. Is it mine?'

'Well, of course not, don't be ridiculous!'

'That afternoon, it could have been mine, couldn't it?'

'No, I'm too far gone. I must have been pregnant, or just . . . Look, Pete, that was a stupid mistake, and I don't know why I let it happen. I'm sorry if by going to bed with you that one time I let you think . . . '

'Wait, wait! I don't think anything, I just wanted to know for sure, and now I do, I'll go.'

She caught his arm. 'I'm sorry, Pete, I know how much I've hurt you, and I'm truly sorry. But it was just something that happened.'

'Just something?'

Peter walked to the front door. He felt helpless, inadequate, there was so much more to say but he didn't know how to begin. The sweet smell of her in her dressing-gown, her softness, got in the way of his anger. It always had.

His hand was on the door, about to open it, when he turned back. 'I want Joey, every other weekend. I'll start paying maintenance as soon as my business is on its feet.'

Marianne nodded, but before she could say anything he had the door open. 'Goodbye, then,' she said at last.

Peter didn't reply. All the way down the neat gravel path, across the street to his truck, he couldn't even think straight. How had it happened? One day, a wife he adored, a son he doted on, a secure business, a house – albeit with a mortgage . . . He had had so much, and now it was gone. Marianne had a bigger house, a new husband, another baby on the way, and all Peter had was a rented bedsit and a suitcase. Even his business was in bad shape. In fact, no matter how he viewed his life, he was on a downward spiral. He just couldn't understand how it had happened that his best friend, a man he had been at school with, trusted and liked, had taken everything from him.

As he drove off, Marianne watched from an upstairs window. She felt wretched, part morning sickness and part guilt. She was genuinely sorry for him, sorry for leaving him, sorry for everything that had happened. He was such a kind, gentle man. She had never set out to fall in love with someone else, it was just one of those things.

It upset her that he had believed the new baby was his, but she hadn't lied.

She patted the curtains back into place and ran herself a bath. While she waited she started making out a list of groceries and Peter was forgotten.

Peter unpacked his belongings and went to a café for a bacon sandwich and a cup of tea. He arrived at work much later than usual and one of his chippies asked if everything was OK.

'Yeah, everything's fine.'

'How's the Inspector?'

'That's all in the past.'

'Can't say I blame you. That one looked as if she'd nick you if you laid a finger on her!'

Peter laughed loudly, and the chippie pushed the day's mail across the untidy desk. 'Looks like a lot of bills to me, guv'nor. Be out back if you need me.'

Peter had hardly given Jane a thought since he left. She had been important to him for the time he had been with her, but he knew he wouldn't see her again. There really wasn't any point. If the truth was on the line, there was a side to her that he hated, that masculine, pushy side. She had never been his kind of woman, and he doubted if any man could cope with a woman who loved her career more than anything else. At least he wouldn't have to listen to all the ramifications of who had done what, how and to whom, and what she was going to do about it. He wouldn't have to hear about her 'toms', her 'lads', or that bloody George Marlow. The next girl would be young, pretty and without prospects, and he'd make sure she could cook, didn't mind ironing shirts and liked kids.

'Boss! Karen's photographs have arrived.'

Tennison turned from the washbasin where she was brushing her hair. 'Be right with you.'

'Everybody's waiting in the Incident Room, and . . . the Super's in there.'

Tennison was suddenly not so cheerful. 'Shit! OK, I'll be there.'

A few moments later she found Superintendent Kernan standing in he middle of the Incident Room among a general hubbub. The moment she entered the room, silence fell.

'Sorry, guv, you wanted to see me?' She felt a flush creeping up her face.

'Just a few moments.' He gestured to the door, then said to Amson, 'Carry on.'

Tennison waited for him at the door and followed him out, hearing Terry Amson saying, 'Right, I want everybody to have a look at these new photographs of Karen Howard . . . ' She closed the door behind her and faced Kernan.

'This was on my desk when I came in.' He handed her a sheet of paper. 'They backed you one hundred per cent, refused to have Hicock take over. Did you know about it?'

Every single man had signed the petition. Tennison's eyes brimmed with tears. 'No . . . No, I didn't.'

'Things have taken a big turn, eh? You're lucky.'

'Luck had nothing to do with it, sir. We've worked our butts off.'

'Let me have all the new information as soon as possible, and' – he smiled – 'good luck!'

He strode away and she opened the door. All the men in the room had their backs to her; they were watching Maureen Havers.

'These shots were taken on the day Karen died,' said Havers, pointing to a group of photos on the notice-board. 'You can see quite clearly that her nails were short. But these' – she pointed to another group – 'these were taken a week before. Look at her hands.'

In the second batch Karen's nails were long and red. Sergeant Amson turned to Jones. 'Get on it, check with her flatmates, see where she got them done!'

While Jones looked up the number, the others crowded

around the photos. Still not one man had turned towards Tennison. Jones picked up the phone and started dialling.

Highly embarrassed, Tennison walked to the centre of the room. 'I won't harp on, but I want all of you to know that I appreciate you backing me up . . . '

Muddyman hurtled in, shouting, 'Suspect's on the move, guv'nor, with his girlfriend! The lads reckon something's going down!'

Jones was through to the flat. 'Lady Antonia? This is DC Jones from Southampton Row police station. We need to know if Karen used a beauty parlour or hair salon, and if so do you know if she had . . . excuse me . . . ' He beckoned frantically to Havers. 'What do you call them?'

'Nail extensions.'

Excited, Tennison was getting into top gear. 'Right, I reckon this is it, we've got him on the run . . . '

Jones slammed the phone down. 'Yes! She went to a place in Floral Street, Covent Garden; had an account there!'

Amson, already on the move, pointed at Jones. 'Check it out, Daffy! Take Rosper with you, and keep in radio contact!'

Tennison was champing at the bit. 'Let's go! Terry, you're with me!'

She ran out, Amson on her heels. DC Jones grabbed his jacket, a rather smart double-breasted job, and bellowed to Rosper, 'Let's go!' But he paused a moment beside Maureen Havers and winked. 'Good on ya, Maureen! See ya in the bar tonight.'

She watched him leave. 'What a bloody prat! Since he got those suede shoes he thinks he's Don Johnson . . . '

It was suddenly quiet, as it always was before the scream went up. Havers looked at the photographs Karen Howard's mother had sent, glossy six-by-ten modelling shots. They had only been interested in her nails, but now she looked at the girl's lovely face. Karen had been a beautiful girl with a freshness to her skin that shone out from the photographs. Her hair was silky, her eyes bright. It was obvious that she had still been an amateur, the poses weren't quite right, but maybe that was what gave her an air of innocence, of childlike vulnerability.

Havers was not the only police officer, male or female, who felt protective towards such victims, as if it was their responsibility to ensure that they could rest in peace. She brushed her hand across the photograph.

'I think we've got him, Karen, love,' she whispered. The dead girls stared sightlessly into the empty room: Karen, Della, Jeannie, Angela, Sharon, Ellen, as if they too were waiting to rest.

chapter eleven

As her patrol car raced through the heavy traffic, Tennison sat next to the driver, listening in on the open channel. Amson was sitting on the edge of the back seat, trying to see where they were going.

DC Oakhill was reporting George Marlow and Moyra Henson's every move direct to them.

'Suspect leaving taxi now, with Henson. Entering Great Portland Street station. They've split up, she's gone down to the trains and he's coming out on the north side, over.'

DI Haskons cut in. 'I got him! I'm on foot, heading down the Euston Road, outside Capital Radio, repeat, I'm on foot. He's hailed another bloody taxi, over.'

'I'll take the woman . . . ' Oakhill's voice faded out.

'We'll go straight to Euston, see if we can head him off at the pass,' said Tennison.

George Marlow leaned in at the taxi window to speak to the driver, and pointed towards Euston. Then he hopped in the back, but the taxi made a left turn towards Camden Town.

A plain car, driven by DC Caplan, slotted into the traffic behind the cab. His passenger, DI Muddyman, reported, 'OK, we're there. Suspect in black cab, heading for Camden Town. No, right, he's turned right, towards Euston again. We've got him, we've got him now, turning right again, back towards the Euston Road, over.'

DC Jones rushed out of the Floral Street beauty salon and stuck his head through the car window to talk to DI Burkin.

'They had her down for a full day on the second of January, the day before that modelling job where she had the long nails. But she didn't book a manicure, and they don't do these nails, whatever they're called. One of the assistants, a Dutch chick, says she recommended a woman in the market.'

'Shit,' Burkin said. 'We can't get the car in there. You leg it, and I'll meet you in Southampton Street.'

The black taxi weaved its way down a side street and reached the corner of Euston Road. There were two vehicles now between it and Muddyman's unmarked car.

The cab edged into the solid traffic on the Euston Road. Marlow was out of the door on the far side and had disappeared into a junk furniture store before any of them could blink.

'Shit! This is Muddyman. Marlow's out of the cab, taxi is empty, repeat, Marlow again on foot. Biker, come in, biker . . . '

Outside the junk shop the cyclist in the skin-tight Lycra pedal-pushers slowed down and bent to fiddle with his toe-clips. He spoke softly into his radio.

'He's out, heading along the Euston Road again, on foot, over.'

On the opposite corner, Muddyman was out of the car and following, keeping a good distance from Marlow.

Oakhill came close to losing Moyra Henson in the crowded complex of tunnels and staircases at Baker Street, and had to force the doors open to board the south-bound Jubilee line train.

He threaded his way through the carriage to stand by the

next set of doors. Henson was staring into space; then she turned and studied her reflection in the dark window, and fished in her handbag for a square, double-sided mirror. She licked her lips and threaded her fingers through the front of her hair and shook it out, then folded the mirror and zipped it back into her bag.

She was totally unaware of Oakhill watching her, strap-hanging only a few feet away.

Amson was leaning between the front seats with a map in his hand. 'He's here, could be heading for Euston or King's Cross, but he's ducking and diving . . . '

'Hold it, Control's coming through.' She raised a hand to the earpiece on which she was picking up relayed messages. 'He's jumped on a number seventy-three bus. No, he's off it, he's turned in the direction of Battle Bridge Road, behind King's Cross station . . . '

Amson pointed it out on the map. 'That's here. Doesn't look like he's going for a train, but there are lock-ups in the railway arches all along here . . . '

'Come on, you bugger, go for the car, get your bloody car!'

A voice said in her ear, 'You're out of luck, car five-four-seven. Your man's just gone into a café, he's sitting talking to the owner. It's the taxi stopover . . . '

Tennison pursed her lips and tapped her foot regularly against the transmission tunnel of the car. Her ear was aching because she was so uptight at the possibility of missing a radio call that she kept pressing the earpiece harder into her ear.

'What the fuck d'you think he's doing?'

Amson shrugged. 'Could do with a cup of coffee myself.' His fingers drummed against the back of her seat. He was shrugging it off, but like everyone else he was right on the edge, waiting, waiting . . .

Among the crowded little stalls selling jeans and T-shirts, DC Jones found a tiny booth containing only a small, white-covered table and two chairs. A sign nailed to the top of the wooden frame announced: 'Noo-Nails by Experienced and Qualified Beautician'.

Annette Frisby, the proprietress, was bending over a client's hand, carefully painting her new nails a violent pink. Jones squashed himself in beside them and showed Annette his identification and a photograph of Karen Howard.

'Have you ever done this girl's nails?'

She squinted at the photo. 'I couldn't tell you, I do as many as eight a day . . . '

'Look at her again.' He tried to squat down to her level and pointed at the beautiful young face. 'She was found murdered, on the fourteenth of January last. Look again, did she ever come to this stall?'

'January? I wouldn't have been here anyway. My friend takes over when I can't do it.'

Jones ground his teeth in frustration. 'Have you got her name and address?'

The café was too small to contain more than a long bar and a few stools. George Marlow was sitting at the far end, drinking cappuccino.

The only other customer got up and left. Marlow approached the man behind the bar.

'Can I have the keys, Stav?'

Stavros pulled a cardboard box from beneath the bar. 'Been away, have you, John? Haven't seen you for a long time.'

'Yeah. Mum was taken bad.' Marlow held his hand out for the keys. 'What's the damage?'

From across the street it wasn't possible to see the object that had been passed to George Marlow, but when he opened his wallet Muddyman could see him counting out ten-pound notes.

Moyra Henson had changed tubes twice, doubling back on herself, then she hurried onto a Central line train. Oakhill was certain that she had no idea he was tailing her.

He was four or five bodies behind her as she went up the escalator and emerged at Oxford Circus. Keeping well back, he radioed in for back-up, fast; Oxford Street was packed with shoppers and Moyra was moving like the clappers. He stayed on her tail in and out of Richard Shops, then across the road to Saxone, back again to another shoe shop, then on up the street to Next.

His back-up arrived; a plain-clothes WPC to take over the close tail, plus a patrol car. The WPC followed Moyra in and out of shops as far as Wardour Street, where she entered a shopping mall. The driver of the patrol car and the uniformed officer took up their positions near the exits. Oakhill kept about fifty yards back from Henson, while the WPC peered into windows and watched Moyra try on shoes from a few feet away.

The patrol car was parked a good distance from the café and Muddyman, directly across the road, kept the radio contact going, informing Tennison that it looked as though the suspect was on the move again.

'Yeah, he's buttoning up his raincoat. Shit! He's sat down again. He's having another bloody coffee!'

Tennison's foot was still tapping and she was chain-smoking, building up a real fug in the car.

A message started coming through from Jones. 'Would you believe Moyra Henson sometimes works from this booth in Covent Garden, and she was working here in January. An assistant at the Floral Street Health Club told me she directed Karen here. The woman who runs it can't say if Karen had had her nails done here or not, but she says that when Henson was working here Marlow used to pick her up! Moyra could have done Karen's nails, and if he saw her, knew her name . . . '

DC Jones was standing in the middle of a breakdancing troupe, battling to make himself heard. The steel girders above the stalls distorted the radio waves.

'How long does this Noo-Nail treatment take?' Tennison's voice asked.

'The woman said she can do eight a day, so it must take a while.'

'You hear all that?' Tennison asked Amson. He nodded. 'That's how he could have known their names! If the treatment takes a while and he was hanging around . . .

Tennison stubbed out her cigarette. They were both beginning to sweat; it was coming down, they could feel it.

'It's the two of them, then!'

'Looks like it,' Tennison replied. 'Let's pick Moyra up now, and see if the lads back at base have come up with anything from the cross-check. Della and Moyra both came from Manchester originally, it's just their ages, Della was a lot younger. Car five-four-seven to base . . . '

'Looks like she's been lying from day one!'

While Tennison gave the go-ahead for Moyra Henson to be picked up, Muddyman radioed in that Marlow was on the move. Then there was silence, but the crackle of the open channel added to the tension. Everyone was waiting . . .

'He's moving fast now, turning left out of the café, crossing the road. He's stopped, he's on to me, looking over . . . '

Another voice cut in. 'I've got him! He's just passed me, walking briskly, crossing the road again. He's heading for the lock-ups, he's walking right along Battle Bridge Road to the lock-ups . . . '

The radio controllers nearly deafened Tennison with their cheering, as if Arsenal had scored a winning goal in the Cup Final. Like the men in the street, they were feeding Marlow's every move to the cars and to the rapidly closing ring of officers in the area. Now they passed on the instructions for the lads to take up their positions . . .

'Yes!' Tennison yelled, and punched Amson's arm. 'He's going for the goddamned lock-ups, I knew it, I knew it!'

Amson tapped the driver on the shoulder to warn him to be ready. He started the engine.

Tennison was gabbling. 'Everyone keep back, just hold your positions, don't frighten him off . . . Stay put until we get the go . . . Over . . . '

They could only listen, they couldn't move out, couldn't see, in case they tipped Marlow off, as the team moved in. some were dressed as mechanics, bending over broken-down cars, another pedalled past with a ladder, someone else drove a grocery van, but they were moving in, surrounding Marlow. The tension was explosive . . .

George Marlow strolled casually along the street. He passed two open lock-ups where mechanics were at work. Cars in various stages of repair littered the street.

He reached the corner where a road ran at right angles under the railway lines. He paused, looked around, checking carefully to see if he was being followed.

'Hold your positions, no one move,' Tennison instructed. 'Let him open up and get inside before you grab him.'

Apparently satisfied that he was in the clear, Marlow walked unhurriedly, swinging the keys around his finger as he went. He approached a lock-up that looked as though it hadn't been occupied in years. A small access door was set into one of the huge main doors.

Tennison's tense voice broadcast softly, 'I want him to use the keys, everybody wait . . . wait . . . '

After another long look around, Marlow stepped up to the small door and selected a key from the ring.

Muddyman's voice was low, breathy. 'Shit, I think this is it, he's going for it. Stand by, suspect has his key in the lock. He's opening up! He's opening up!'

The small door swung open and Marlow raised one leg to step over the high sill as Tennison shrieked, 'Go! Go! Go! Go!'

The cars converged into the street, sirens wailing, but before they could get to Marlow the lads emerged from their positions like greyhounds after a hare: Rosper, Caplan, Lillie and Muddyman. They charged across the street and before Marlow could step right inside they had him. Rosper, the first there, grabbed Marlow by the scruff of his neck, almost tearing the raincoat off him as he dragged him from the doorway. Marlow stumbled as his foot caught on the sill, and the next moment his head was cracked back on the edge of the door. They all wanted a go at him – it was part tension, part adrenalin – and they handled him roughly, pinching the skin on his wrists as they handcuffed him.

Muddyman was shouting the caution as Tennison's car screamed up. She was about to get out when she hesitated, to give the boys a chance to spot her and ease up on Marlow. It was in that moment, no more than a few seconds, that she saw another side to her suspect.

He seemed completely unconcerned at being knocked around, arrested. In fact he was unnaturally calm. He looked up with a puzzled frown, first at Rosper, then Lillie. Tennison did not hear what he said, but she could see the expression on his face as if he was angry with himself.

But the lads heard him: 'Ahhh . . . the painters.' He seemed satisfied that he had recognized them, but there was still a look of irritation on his face. He hadn't suspected them, in fact he had trusted them. He had been foolish, made a mistake. They were not painters.

Moyra Henson emerged from a boutique with a large carrier bag and strolled along the mall, stopping beside the plain-clothes WPC, who was loaded with bags, to look in the next window. Their elbows nearly touched.

She was so intent on the goods in the shop that for a moment she didn't clock the reflection of the uniformed officer speaking into his radio a few feet away. Oakhill moved in and the WPC right next to Moyra dropped her bags and held out her ID.

'Moyra Henson, I am WPC Southill. We would like you to accompany us to the Southampton Row— '

Moyra swung her boutique bag to slap Southill in the face, then went for her, kicking and spitting, screaming that she wanted to be left alone. Her screeching drew everyone's attention: shop assistants rushed out to see what was going on, customers rammed into each other on the escalators, as Moyra's screams echoed throughout the mall. Her face was puce with hysteria.

She seemed to cave in suddenly, her back pressed against the window, hands up.

'I just want to be left alone, ahhhh, please, please leave me alone! Don't touch me! I'll come with you, just don't touch me!'

She started to retrieve her fallen purchases and stuff them into the torn boutique bag. She had hurled her handbag to the floor, spilling cosmetics, wallet, mirror all over the marble floor, and she insisted on picking everything up herself. She was crying now, her mascara running down her face, her hysteria over.

She allowed herself to be led to the waiting patrol car where she sat, sniffing noisily, her nose all red, and stared out of the window. As the car moved off and the siren started up, she seemed to gather her senses, taking a hankie from her bag and blowing her nose. WPC Southill watched closely as she pulled out a perfume atomizer and gave Oakhill the nod to check it.

'It's perfume, Chanel, and it's very expensive. Cost over thirty quid, and I only use it sparingly – I mean, too much and you overdo it. So if you don't mind giving it back? What'd you think I was gonna do, spray it in the driver's eyes and make my escape? Screw you, screw the lot of you, you're all wankers!'

She spent the rest of the journey to the station checking her wallet, counting her money and repacking everything in orderly fashion. But she didn't say anything else; she felt there wasn't any point.

The lock-up was cavernous. Water dripped constantly, forming pools on the floor, and the shape of it amplified the eerie sounds of the trains overhead. The place stank of damp, ancient oil and many other things.

The far end was pitch dark. Near the centre of the empty space Tennison could just make out a large, shrouded shape in the gloom. She chose to ignore the little scuttling, splashing noises of the rats.

'Everybody watch where you stand,' Tennison ordered, her voice echoing. 'Lights, are there any lights?'

Fluorescent lights blinked on slowly, casting a cold, blueish light which reflected in the puddles. Tennison advanced, picking her way slowly and carefully until she reached the middle. She lifted the old tarpaulin by one corner, exposing gleaming chrome and gold-brown paintwork.

'Well, we've got the car!' she called briskly, peering inside it. There was no radio between the seats. 'I want the Forensic crowd down here ASAP. The less we move or touch, the better.'

DS Amson was tiptoeing through the pools of water towards her. She stepped back, knocking into him, and turned to give him an earful when she saw his smile freeze. He was looking past her to the far end of the lock-up. Tennison followed his eyes.

'Oh, my God,' she whispered, and pointed. 'This is where he did it.'

Arrayed on the wall like an exhibit in a black museum were chains, shackles and a hideous collection of sharpened tools.

'How are you going to play it?' Kernan asked Tennison.

She was tense, champing anxiously at the bit. 'Henson first, break the alibi. Marlow's brief's on his way in.'

'Right, Jane, and . . . well done!'

'Not done yet,' she replied, flexing her fingers. 'Not yet.'

Flanked by Amson and Muddyman, with Havers in her wake, Tennison swept along the corridor to the interview room. Muddyman and Amson entered first, going to opposite sides of the room. Tennison walked straight to the table where Moyra Henson sat smoking, her solicitor beside her. Tennison could feel the change in her; she was afraid.

She addressed the solicitor. 'Mr Shrapnel? This is

Detective Inspector Muddyman, Sergeant Amson and WPC Havers.' With a nod to Havers to close the door, she sat down and placed some files on the table. 'You have been made aware that your client has not been arrested at this stage, but is here of her own free will to answer questions and assist in the investigation into the murders of Karen Howard and Della Mornay.'

'Yes, I am aware of the situation, and my client is prepared to assist in any way that will not incriminate her or instigate criminal proceedings against her,' the small, grey-suited man replied.

For the first time since entering the room, Tennison looked directly at Moyra.

'At twelve forty-five today we gained access to George Arthur Marlow's rented lock-up garage in King's Cross. A brown Rover car, registration number SLB 23L, was discovered on the premises, together with certain incriminating evidence. In your recent statement you claimed that you had no knowledge of the whereabouts of this car, is that true?'

There was no bravado left in her. 'I didn't know anything about it, I thought it had been stolen.'

'In the same statement you gave George Arthur Marlow an alibi, stating that he returned to the flat you share on the night of the thirteenth of January, nineteen-ninety, at ten-thirty. Is that correct?'

Moyra glanced at her solicitor, then back to Tennison and gave a nod.

'When I interviewed you on that occasion, you were shown pictures of murder victims, do you remember? You stated that you had never met any of the women in the photographs.'

Again Moyra nodded and looked to Mr Shrapnel. Tennison opened one of her files and brought out two photographs.

'On the sixteenth of May, nineteen seventy-one, you and Deirdre Mornay were on trial at Manchester Juvenile court.' She laid the photograph of Della on the table. Moyra did not react. 'In early January of this year, Karen

Howard was a customer at the booth in Covent Garden that you took over from Annette Frisby.' Karen's photo was put in front of Moyra. Again she did not react.

Two more photographs; this time of the bodies of the murdered girls.

'Moyra, you are not looking at the photographs. If you don't want to look at Della, then look at Karen. George called out to her, offered her a lift, then took her to King's Cross and tortured her, mutilated her. But first, he hung her on the wall in chains and raped her. Look at it, Moyra, see her hands tied behind her back, the marks on her body . . . *Look at her, Moyra!*'

Shrapnel raised his hands as if to say, 'That's enough!'

'Your client, Mr Shrapnel, stands to be accused as an accessory to murder. Don't you think she should know what that crime involved?'

'My client has co-operated fully— '

Slowly, Moyra put out a hand and picked up the photos.

'Your client, Mr Shrapnel, has systematically lied to us. Now she has a chance to— ' Tennison stopped and watched Moyra's reaction to the photographs; she stared at each one, then covered the one of Karen's body with her hands and closed her eyes.

Shrapnel was saying, 'Moyra is George Marlow's common-law wife . . . '

Tennison raised a hand to quieten him as Moyra started to speak to her.

'Would you get the men to leave, just the women stay . . . I won't talk in front of them.'

Amson gripped Shrapnel by the elbow and hurried out, followed by Muddyman. In the silence, Moyra sat with her hands over the picture of Karen, looking at Tennison with dead, unemotional eyes.

'I didn't know Della, I didn't even remember her. She was just a kid. But I did her nails, she used to bite them and . . . I didn't know her, it was just that she used to come and have the odd nail replaced, you know, if she'd broken one.'

Tennison nodded without speaking. Moyra didn't really

want to talk about Della, this was not why she had wanted the men out of the room, there was something else. Moyra tugged at her skirt, darting glances at Tennison, her whole body twisting and turning, her hands picking at her own false nails. She looked at Havers, chewing at her lip, then back to Tennison. Then she leaned forward, her chin in her hand, as if she didn't want anyone else to hear.

'He . . . he did it to me once,' she whispered. Tennison leaned closer, but Moyra immediately sat back, coughed and stared at Havers. Tennison waited patiently while Moyra straightened her skirt yet again, twisted her hair. Then she released a deep sigh.

This time she didn't whisper. She faced the wall. 'He made this thing, with straps, for here.' She touched her arm. 'He said it made . . . it made the vagina tight, you know, stretched out, but it hurt me. I didn't like it, I wouldn't do it.'

She hung her head, as if the horror was slowly seeping into her brain. She still couldn't face Tennison; her head sank lower and lower until it was nearly resting on her knees.

'I didn't know, I didn't know . . . Oh, God forgive me, I didn't know . . . '

Moyra buried her face in her arms and began to sob.

Amson, Muddyman and Shrapnel were all leaning against the wall of the corridor when Tennison's face appeared in the glass panel. She opened the door.

'George Marlow *was* home by ten-thirty that night, but he went out again at a quarter to eleven. She doesn't know what time he returned.'

She stood very erect, head up, eyes glowing. 'We've got him,' she said quietly.

George Marlow lay in his cell, staring at the ceiling. A uniformed officer outside kept a constant watch through the spyhole.

The key turned in the lock, and Marlow sat up,

swinging his feet to the floor as his solicitor, Arnold Upcher, stepped in.

With a glance at his watch, Upcher said, 'Five minutes!' to the officer, who remained in the open doorway. Upcher put his briefcase down on the bunk and faced Marlow.

'They are charging you on six counts of murder, George.'

Marlow shook his head, sighed, and looked up. 'I don't know what's going on, Arnold. On my mother's life, I haven't done anything.'

Arc-lights had been brought into the King's Cross lock-up to improve the illumination. White-suited Scenes of Crime men were moving in to start photographing and fingerprinting. The place was strangely quiet; only the constant rumble of the trains and the distant sound of a chained dog barking disturbed the silence.

The Rover had been surrounded by plastic sheeting. One man was kneeling on the plastic, leaning in through the open door, combing the fitted carpets with great care, passing anything he found to an assistant beside him.

DI Burkin and DC Jones were examining a row of old metal lockers.

'Oh, look at this!' exclaimed Burkin, holding up a hideous mask with cut-out eyeholes by his fingertips. He dropped it into a plastic bag.

In the next locker, Jones had found suits, shirts, ties, shoes, all covered in plastic dry-cleaner's bags.

'Even his sneakers, look . . . Neat bastard.'

Burkin sniffed. 'Jesus, this place smells like an abattoir.' He turned to stare at the wall where Marlow's chains and torture instruments hung, his nose wrinkling in disgust.

Two men were crouched near the wall, prodding at a small drain with sticks. Above the drain, where a single tap was fitted, a makeshift shower had been rigged up, with a plastic shampoo spray and a plastic curtain, spotted with black mould and streaked with blood. Beside it a dish contained soap, wire brushes and a plastic nail brush.

'This is caked in blood, we'll need swabs of it all,' one of the men was saying. 'Ugh, the drain's clogged with it, and this looks like skin . . . ' He covered his face. 'Jesus, the stench!' he mumbled, retching.

Burkin had found a handbag. He handled it carefully, wearing disposable plastic gloves. Inside was a wallet; he flipped it open.

'It's Karen Howard's!'

More arc-lights came on, bathing the Rover in a bright pool of light. The SOCO was holding a pair of tweezers up and peering at the tiny item they held.

'The carpet's been scrubbed, smells of cleaning fluid, and it's damp. What's this? Looks like a tiny gold screw.' He dropped it into the bag his assistant held open for him and something else caught his attention. 'Was your girl blonde?' he called over to Burkin and Jones as he carefully stashed a single blonde hair into a bag.

Burkin was examining a jacket, peering at it through the plastic bag. 'I got one of these jackets from his flat, he must have two sets of clothes . . . See his shoes, did you take his shoes from the flat?'

DC Jones wasn't ready for it, couldn't understand how it happened, but one moment he was doing his job, sorting through the gear, and the next he burst into tears. He stood there, unable to control his sobs, almost in surprise.

Burkin put an arm around his shoulder. 'Go an' grab a coffee, a few of the others might feel like one, OK?'

'I'm sorry, I'm sorry, I dunno what made me get like this . . . '

Peering into the cabinet again, Burkin replied, 'We all go through it, Dave. I think it's just natural, a release. . . . Mine's black, no sugar.'

Jones threaded his way across the duckboards, mindful of the plastic sheeting. He had to turn back because he couldn't remember if it was four black and six white or the other way round.

The silent shadows of the men loomed on the walls where hideous splashes of blood, and worse, had dried. The greenish glow of the fluorescent lights and the brightness of the arc-lights did nothing to lift the dank darkness, the stench, the horror. This was where that sweet girl was brought; he could only imagine her terror, only imagine it.

DI Burkin had pulled out a thick black wardrobe bag, the kind used by the uppercrust type of dry cleaners. It was strong, would have fitted a full-length evening gown, and it had a zip from one end to the other. It was slightly open at one end and he could see a tangle of blonde hair jammed in the teeth. They knew Marlow was strong – this had to be how he had carried his victims undetected, zipped up in the wardrobe bag, hung over his arm . . .

It was not for Burkin to find out, that was down to Forensic, but he wondered. He placed it into a see-through evidence bag, tagged it, then bent to check over Marlow's shoes. They were all neatly wrapped in clingfilm, ready to slip on and walk out, or walk into Della Mornay's bedsit. No wonder they had been unable to find a single item, a single fibre, in her room.

The tape recorder emitted a high-pitched bleep, and Tennison started talking.

'This is a recorded interview. I am Detective Chief Inspector Jane Tennison. Also present are Detective Sergeant Terence Amson and Mr Arnold Upcher. We are situated in room 5-C at Southampton Row Metropolitan Police Station. The date is Thursday the first of February, nineteen-ninety. The time is four forty-five pm.'

Tennison nodded to Marlow. 'Would you please state your full name, address and date of birth?'

He leaned forward and directed his voice towards the built-in microphone. 'George Arthur Marlow, twenty-one High Grove Estate, Maida Vale. Born in Warrington, eleventh September, nineteen fifty-one.'

'Do you understand why you have been arrested?'

He gave a half-shrug. 'I guess so.'

'It is my duty formally to caution you, and warn you that anything you say may be used in evidence. You have been arrested on suspicion of the murders of Karen Howard and Deirdre Mornay. Do you understand?'

'I am not guilty.' Marlow turned and looked at Upcher.

'Would you please describe to me the meeting that took place between yourself and Karen Howard on the night of January the thirteenth, nineteen-ninety.'

'I didn't know her name, I was told her name later,' Marlow began. 'She approached me. I asked how much she wanted. I drove her to some waste ground and had sex with her. I paid her for sex. I didn't know her, I had never seen or met her before. Then after I dropped her off at the tube station . . . '

'What about the cut on her hand? In a previous statement you said that she, Karen, cut her hand on the car radio which was between the seats.' Tennison held up the statement for Upcher to see.

'Yes, that's right.'

'The statement was taken on the fifteenth of January, nineteen-ninety. We have since discovered that there is no radio between the front seats of your car.'

He didn't seem to register what she had said. He began, 'I was at home at ten-thirty . . . '

'So, you arrived home at ten-thirty that night. Could you tell us what time you next left the flat?'

'I didn't, I watched television with my wife.'

'You are referring to your common-law wife, Miss Moyra Henson, is that correct?'

'Yes.'

'Miss Henson made a statement at three forty-five this afternoon. She states that you actually left the flat again at fifteen minutes to eleven. She cannot recall exactly when you returned, but you returned without your car. She says that your car was not stolen from outside your block of flats.'

'She's wrong! My car was nicked, I never went out again.'

'You have denied having any previous contact with Karen Howard.'

'Yeah, never met her before the night she picked me up . . . '

'Miss Henson has, on occasion, worked at a booth in Covent Garden. She has admitted that she met Karen, and that she gave her a nail treatment. You were there at the time and you spoke to Karen. Is that true?'

'No.' Marlow shook his head.

'You have also denied knowing the other victim, Deirdre Mornay, also known as Della. Miss Henson agrees, however, that contrary to her first statement, in which she too denied knowing Miss Mornay, she was in fact lying. I suggest that you are also lying and that you did know Della Mornay.'

Marlow sat back in his chair, folded his arms. 'I don't believe you play these games. Moyra is scared to death that you are going to arrest her for tax evasion and claiming unemployment benefit. She's terrified of the police since she was picked up on a false charge of prostitution. Well, you don't scare me, I'm innocent.' He spoke to Upcher. 'I don't have to answer any more questions, do I?'

The team were kicking their heels in the Incident Room. Jones asked generally, 'How's the guv'nor? She must be knackered.'

Burkin shook his head. 'Taking a long time. After what we found in the lock-up, I don't think he'd admit to knowing his own mother right now.'

Slumped in chairs, perched on desks, propped against walls, they waited.

Marlow was looking tired. 'How many more times do I have to tell you?'

Tennison pressed on. 'This morning?' she prompted.

'I told you, I got an anonymous call, I dunno who it was. He says to me that he knows where my car is, he's seen it on the TV programme, right? It's been reported stolen, right?'

'What time was the call?'

'Oh, about ten . . . Anyway, he says he knows where the car is, at King's Cross.'

'He told you that your car was in a lock-up at King's Cross, yes? Did he give you the keys?' Marlow shrugged, and she went on, 'Mr Marlow, you were seen unlocking the door.'

He answered angrily, 'Because he said I could get them from a Greek guy in a coffee bar. So I picked up the keys, but I didn't find my car because just as I opened the door the police jumped on me! I don't know why I have to keep repeating myself,' he said to Upcher. 'I've told them all this a dozen times . . . '

Tennison showed no sign of fatigue or impatience as she asked, 'What was the Greek man's name?'

'I dunno, the tip-off just gave me the address of the café.' He sighed.

Arnold Upcher shifted his position, checked his watch and glanced at Tennison. He was getting fed up. He looked around; Amson had sat down in the corner.

'Stavros Hulanikis has sub-let the lock-up to a man he knows as John Smith for eight years. After you collected the keys from him this morning, an officer, Detective Inspector Burkin, took a statement from him. Your Greek friend also does certain items of dry-cleaning and laundry for you, doesn't he?'

Marlow shook his head in disbelief, not bothering to answer. Tennison continued, 'Come on, George, how did you get Karen into the bedsit? Where are Della's keys? You knew the place was empty, didn't you? You knew, because Della Mornay was already dead.'

Marlow leaned towards her. 'You are trying to put words into my mouth,' he said emphatically. 'Well that's it, I'm not saying another thing.' He appealed to Upcher: 'Tell her that's enough! I agreed to this interview, I've done nothing but assist them from the word go! I want to go home.'

Upcher replied quietly, 'That won't be possible, George,' then turned to Tennison. 'It's almost ten.'

Marlow was getting really uptight. He shouted, 'I wanna go to the toilet, I wanna have a piss, all right? I have to call my mother, I don't want her reading in the papers that you arrested me again! I want to be the one to tell her— '

'I agree to a fifteen-minute break,' Tennison told Upcher. To Marlow she said, 'You will not be allowed to see Miss Henson, or make any phone calls until this interview is terminated. I will arrange for Miss Henson to phone your mother . . . '

Marlow pushed his chair back as if to stand up. Amson moved towards him.

'No! They don't get on. I don't want Moyra calling my mother.' He sighed with irritation and stood up with his hands on his hips, facing Tennison. 'This is a mess, isn't it? Oh, all right, I did it.'

Upcher jumped to his feet. Tennison just sat and stared at Marlow, then managed to pull her wits together.

'Could you repeat that? You are still under caution.'

Marlow closed his eyes. She could see his long lashes, every line of his handsome face. He licked his top lip, then he opened his eyes. The colour seemed even more startling, the pupils were like pin-points. As if watching in slow motion, Tennison felt every tiny movement recorded in her mind.

He tilted his head to the right, then to the left, and smiled. No one in the room moved; they all focused on Marlow, on his strange, eerie smile.

'I said I did it.'

There seemed to be nothing else to say. Everyone in the room except George Marlow held their breath, ready to explode, but he seemed totally relaxed. Eventually Tennison breathed out and said, 'Please sit down, George.'

He slumped into his seat. She watched him closely as she asked, 'What exactly did you do?'

He checked them off on his fingers. 'Karen, Della, Angela, Sharon, Ellen and . . . ' He screwed up his eyes, trying to remember, then snapped his fingers. 'That's right, Jeannie . . . '

Only Tennison's eyes reflected the impact of his words. George Arthur Marlow had just casually admitted to killing all six victims.

chapter twelve

When George Marlow had been led back to his cell, DCI Tennison lit a cigarette and inhaled deeply. The welter of emotions inside her was under rigid control, and she showed none of it to the others in the room.

She had just caught the man she had devoted every ounce of her energy to catching, a man who had caused her the loss of the only lover she had ever really cared about, had deprived her of sleep for days on end, had nearly lost her her job and her self-respect. She sat quietly and smoked her cigarette down to the filter, then stubbed it out.

DC Jones, his face flushed, raced into the bar of the local pub. Pushing the other regulars aside, he stopped in the middle of the floor, raised his hands in triumph and yelled, 'He's bloody admitted it! All six of them, he's admitted doing the lot!'

The team rose to their feet as a man, although one of them was Maureen Havers. The cheer went up; Jones grabbed Havers and danced her around the floor as everyone congratulated everyone else.

A group of DIs from another team looked on the feverish celebration with interest. When Havers finally sat down again, one of them came over to her, carrying his pint.

'What gives?'

Beaming, Havers replied, 'Our guv'nor's just got a suspect to admit to six charges of murder! Biggest case this station's ever had . . . '

DI Caldicott returned to his own table and spoke to his mates. The racket in the bar was so great that no one else could hear what he was saying, but they all turned to stare at Tennison's team and raised their glasses in salute.

DCI Tennison was facing the Superintendent across his desk. He poured her a large whisky and said, as he handed it to her, 'Well, congratulations! The trial'll be a long process, but you go home now and get some sleep, you deserve it.'

'Yeah, I need it. It was a long night.' She looked and sounded exhausted. Downing the whisky in one, she stood up and made for the door.

The phone rang and the Super picked it up. 'Kernan . . . Yes, just a moment.' He covered the mouthpiece and spoke to Tennison. 'You were right to stick to your guns. Six counts of murder! And the beautician link . . . It was a woman's case, after all!' .

He put the phone to his ear again, dismissively, and swivelled round in his chair; it's business as usual. 'I'm putting Caldicott on it,' he said into the phone. 'They're bringing the son in for questioning.'

Tennison rose to the bait. 'Fifty per cent of murder victims are women, so it looks as if I might have my hands full!' she retorted.

The door slammed behind her before Kernan could swivel round to reply.

'Woman's case, my arse!' Tennison muttered to herself, still seething about Kernan's comment. She spotted Maureen Havers peering at her from the double doors further down the corridor.

'Maureen, any of the lads about?'

Havers replied casually, 'Oh, I don't think so, we were all on two till ten. Oh, DCI Jenkins wants the Incident Room cleared, could you pop along before you leave?'

Pursing her lips, Tennison pushed through the other side of the doors and marched towards the Incident Room. Havers hung back and watched her go.

The Incident Room was crammed to bursting, but surprisingly quiet. Every single member of Tennison's team was there. Someone called, 'Here she is!' and they all watched expectantly as the door-handle turned.

Tennison walked in to cheers, whistles and the sound of popping corks. A huge bunch of flowers was pressed into her hand and Burkin started singing, the others quickly joining in: 'Why was she born so beautiful, why was she born at all? She's no bloody use to anyone, she's no bloody good at all!'

'Three cheers for our guv'nor, hip-hip . . . '

'*Hooray . . . !*'

Tennison nearly choked on her champagne, her back was slapped so hard. 'You bastards!' she spluttered. 'I thought you'd all pissed off! Cheers!'

She bit her lip, but the tears brimmed over. Then out came her great, bellowing laugh and she punched the air. 'We did it! We got him!'

Many months later, George Marlow stood in the dock to answer the charges against him. The Clerk of the Court read them out:

'George Arthur Marlow, you stand before this court accused of six indictments of murder. That on the fourteenth of January, nineteen ninety, you did murder Karen Howard, contrary to common law . . . '

Major and Mrs Howard were holding hands, staring straight ahead, unable to look at George Marlow, to turn their heads just a fraction to see him. He had taken their beloved daughter, he had raped her and mutilated her, and waiting for them to catch him had been the longest time they had ever lived through, a lifetime, Karen's lifetime. There would always be pain, that would never go away, and the confusion. Marlow had destroyed not just their daughter's life, but theirs.

' . . . That on the third of December, nineteen eighty-nine you unlawfully took the life of Deirdre Margaret Mornay . . . '

Two prostitutes, friends of Della, leaned forward for a glimpse of her murderer. One of them sat back, afraid of her own feelings. Looking at him, with his handsome face, his fresh, immaculate white shirt, if he was to pick her up she wouldn't be likely to refuse him. They nudged each other and stared at DCI Tennison, who was sitting with the prosecution counsel. Her face was impassive. She gave them an almost imperceptible nod.

'You are also charged that on the fifteenth of March, nineteen eighty-four, you murdered Jeannie Avril Sharpe, that in January nineteen eighty-five you murdered Ellen Harding . . . '

Carol and Linda had travelled down from Oldham. They were sitting in the gallery. Linda leaned forward on her elbows but could only just see the crown of his curly head. Jeannie had wanted to emigrate to Australia, she had wanted . . . But she had never got anything, anyone to help her, love her. Now, maybe, she could rest in peace. Maybe.

Carol twisted a paper hankie in her hands. She could hear him as clear as anything, calling to Jeannie, calling her to come to his car.

In her wheelchair at the end of a row of spectators, Mrs Marlow sat, as well-groomed as ever. She held her head high, making no effort to wipe away the tears that trickled down her face. Her pale blue eye shadow, her carefully outlined lips and powdery cheeks framed in false, chestnut curls, seemed to crumble before George Marlow's eyes. He couldn't look at her, couldn't bear it; she was dying in front of him.

A young man sitting near her was leaning forward in his seat, staring intently at Marlow.

' . . . That in July nineteen eighty-six you murdered Angela Simpson . . . '

The young man's face crumpled when he heard Angela's name, and he cried. He tried hard to control himself, but the years between Angela's murder and the arrest of George Marlow had been a nightmare. Five years, five long years of his life under suspicion, always wondering if somehow he could have saved her. Five years of nightmares, but above all the loss of his childhood sweetheart, the only girl he had ever loved.

When George Marlow's eyes flickered towards him he had never known such hatred. He had never believed himself capable of killing, but he could have killed Marlow with his bare hands; kill him, hurt him, make him feel the pain he had inflicted on Angela.

'. . . And in October, nineteen eighty-seven you murdered Sharon Felicity Read . . . '

Sharon's father sat stiffly at the back of the gallery in his best suit, starched shirt and bowling club tie. Sharon's mother had died, a year after they received the news; he had lost his wife and daughter because of the same man. Not a day passed without this quiet, respectable man remembering his daughter, his sweetheart, his own darlin' . . .

He wept because she had only just begun to grow into a woman, and he wept because he was haunted by his wife's face when he had told her that their daughter had been found. The arrogance of Marlow didn't anger him, didn't inspire him to revenge; it just left him with an overwhelming sadness, because nothing mended his heart.

Tennison kept her eyes averted from Marlow, her head bowed, but he seemed to draw her attention as if willing her to look at him. She stared suddenly as a door opened, throwing a wedge of light on to a dark figure, hunched at the back of the court. It was Moyra, and she had aged twenty years.

'George Arthur Marlow, having heard the charges against you, how do you plead?'

Tennison looked up at him. He was astonishingly handsome; his dark eyes, high cheekbones and glossy hair oozed vitality. She drew a sharp breath because he was looking at her. As their eyes met he seemed to smile, yet his lips did not move. It was just a lightness in his eyes . . . there was no anger, no malice.

'Not guilty, sir,' he replied.